CONVOLUTED

THE 1972
DURHAM FAMILY
TRIPLE HOMICIDE

CONVOLUTED

THE 1972
DURHAM FAMILY
TRIPLE HOMICIDE

Terry L. Harmon

ISBN: 9798326519740

This book is dedicated to the memories of Bryce, Virginia, and Bobby Durham,
and to all who have devoted time to investigating their murders.

TABLE OF CONTENTS

FOREWORD

On Friday, February 4, 1972, having recently been named by North Carolina's Sam J. Ervin, Jr. as the Chief Counsel and Staff Director of his Senate Subcommittee on Separation of Powers, I was sitting at my desk on Capitol Hill at the United States Senate. My secretary informed me I had an urgent phone call from my hometown of Boone, North Carolina. At the other end was a long-time family friend. Knowing I would want to be informed, he told me in grisly detail about an atrocious and horrific triple homicide that had been committed the previous cold and snowy night on the town's outskirts. He related that a local businessman, Bryce Durham, his wife Virginia, and their eighteen-year-old son Bobby had been brutally murdered. I was shocked and dumbfounded that such a terrible deed had been committed there. Although neither I nor my family back home had prior knowledge of the Durhams, the case drew national attention and gripped the citizens of Boone and Watauga County.

For the remainder of 1972 and most of 1973, as the Watergate scandal broke on the scene and I served as Deputy Chief Counsel of the Senate Watergate Committee in Washington, DC, I had little time to think upon that dreadful night in Boone or its lingering aftermath. Still, out of curiosity, I kept up with the investigation, the gruesome crime scene, and the characters surrounding this mountain mystery through conversations with Watauga County Sheriff Ward Carroll and Boone Chief of Police Clyde Tester.

During the summer of 1973, the Senate Watergate hearings took over regular TV programming, consuming the American public with the high-drama spectacle of a national "whodunit." After its conclusion in 1974, I decided to return to North Carolina and become a candidate for State Attorney General. During the latter part of my campaign, the Durham murder case was personally revived for me, when, as I greeted voters at a rally in Wilkes County, I was approached by an elderly couple who introduced themselves as Mr. and Mrs. Coy Durham. Mrs. Durham, with her gray, swept-back-in-a-bun hair and beautiful blue eyes filled with tears, said, "I've been praying to meet you." I was somewhat taken aback because I immediately sensed her tears were not tears of joy but of profound sadness. While Mr. Durham remained stoically silent, Mrs. Durham proclaimed she and her husband were the parents of Bryce Durham and the grandparents of Bobby Durham. With the fervor only a mother and grandmother can possess, she said she had a vision I would be elected Attorney General and asked me to pledge that, when I was elected, I would do everything within my powers to see the perpetrators of the murders brought to justice. I made that pledge to both myself and the Durhams.

Mrs. Durham must have intervened with the Good Lord, and I was elected Attorney General in November of 1974. One of my first jobs was to form an "unsolved murder squad" within the State Bureau of Investigation to work with local law enforcement to solve some of the state's age-old cold cases. Of course, the Durham murder case, which I refer to as "the murders on the hill," was at the top of my list. After all, I had made a promise to Mrs. Durham. I immediately assigned SBI Special Agent Charles Whitman to devote the overwhelming majority of his time helping solve Watauga County's mystery of the century.

Throughout my ten-year career as Attorney General, I never forgot the Durham Case, mainly because anytime I was within a fifty-mile radius of Wilkes County, Mr. and Mrs. Durham were there to greet me and ask that my office never give up on solving the case. Over the years, I have been interviewed dozens of times by radio and TV correspondents and newspaper reporters, most of whom have asked me the same question: "Who killed the Durham family?"

Finally, a fantastic book – *CONVOLUTED: The 1972 Durham Family Triple Homicide* – has been written about this case by author and wordsmith Terry Harmon, a fellow Boone native. I am in awe of Terry's grasp of the complexities and the twists and turns of this case and of his devotion to "getting it right." He takes us from the long winter night in February 1972 to Watauga County Sheriff Len Hagaman's press conference fifty years later in February 2022 – and beyond – revealing long-held secrets that leave you wanting more. Terry meticulously crafts a thrilling story, including how everybody and his brother either had or has a theory about why the Durhams were murdered and by whom – some ludicrous, some probable – but all demonstrating how curious the human mind can be. This notable work, consisting of diligent research and lively writing, is one I cherish, and I predict you will not be able to put it down.

Rufus Edmisten
North Carolina Attorney General 1974-1984
North Carolina Secretary of State 1989-1996

PREFACE

On Tuesday, February 8, 2022, exactly fifty years and four days after Rufus Edmisten received the call from his friend announcing the murders of Bryce, Virginia, and Bobby Durham, I was likewise contacted by a friend, whose text message informed me the Watauga County Sheriff's Office had announced the Durham Case was finally closed.[1] For half a century, the case had been the epitome of a murder mystery. I, like many others, had become doubtful it would ever be solved, so when the surprising announcement was made, it was welcomed, but it raised additional questions. Three days later, I attended Watauga County Sheriff Len Hagaman's follow-up press conference concerning this announcement. At its conclusion, I felt unsettled and unfulfilled, in part because I wanted more information. Within hours, I resolved to write a book about the murders and the decades of investigation that followed.

In February 1972, I was a child living with my parents and older brother and sister a scant two miles from the Durhams. My parents kept a few newspaper articles detailing that terrible winter night, and I periodically revisited those throughout my youth and adolescence. As time marched on, what befell the Durhams increasingly faded into the past, becoming more historical than a fresh reality, but while the case often laid dormant in my subconscious, it was never too far beneath the surface. The frequency with which I passed by the Durhams' former home during the course of my everyday traversing reminded me of it time and again.

While my six-year-old self never dreamed I would one day write a book about the murders, the 2022 developments ignited my determination to tell the story in more depth, detail, accuracy, and objectivity than it had ever previously been told. I began writing that very Friday night following the press conference and continued nonstop into the wee hours of the next morning. Throughout the years, I had collected information about the case, but after assembling it into my initial draft, along with the developments that had been made public just days earlier, I wondered if I would ever have enough material to warrant a book worth reading. As I began digging into newspaper archives and court documents, and as I pursued conversations and interviews with various individuals, my draft began taking better shape in terms of content and volume. Over the next two years, I invested hour upon hour into documenting the case and trying to condense a plethora of details from hundreds of resources into one comprehensive account.

Researching and writing this story became my intense focus and undertaking; it was a thrilling process, introducing me to interesting people, places, and pieces of information. At times, I was surprised by my good fortune in gaining access to certain materials and having particular people speak with me. Although I was investigating and writing about a fifty-year-old crime, I soon learned that, despite the passage of time, it remained a raw subject for some who asked me not to quote them as sources. A few felt strongly about their anonymity, sharing with me their concerns about retaliation or even being killed. I was told on more than one occasion to exercise caution with my investigation and with what I published. There are people, I was warned, who do not want this case delved into, including powerful people who perhaps played a role in the murders and could be implicated or who have gone to great lengths to keep it unsolved for so many years. All of this took me by surprise, and when I told one interviewee that perhaps I was naïve, he assured me I was. "I'd be careful," he said. "I really would be careful. I wouldn't make light of it."

Certainly, this project has been an education, including my exposure to dark things – things that, in my ordinary, everyday life, I had no prior knowledge of or experience with. I never imagined I would be familiarizing myself with topics ranging from odometer rollbacks and drug trafficking to hitmen and the physiology of strangulation, or that I would be visiting jails, examining investigative files and crime scene photos, and communicating with convicted felons and murderers. Writing about unpleasant and controversial subject matter is not for the fainthearted, and while I was initially a bit reluctant to embark on such an endeavor, I quickly gained a bold confidence that enabled me to forge ahead.

I also learned if I was going to go where this project led me, I needed to develop a thick skin. Soon enough, it became evident I would not please everyone, and there would be moments when my line of questioning would be off-putting, prompting occasional ire to be directed toward me. Not everyone wanted to speak with me, and not everyone granted me access to materials I wanted. I initially felt deflated when rejected or declined, but I learned not to let those roadblocks deter me. I honed my investigative skills and taught myself to keep looking for alternative means to the same end, to keep knocking, to keep asking, even if it was a longshot. I never knew when someone would tell me something jaw-dropping or provide the key to some hidden thing, and sometimes they did.

My borderline obsession with the case meshed well with my passion for history and my devotion to the pursuit of truth. As it concerned the Durham murders, I also yearned for justice. I fantasized this book would debunk falsities and shine light on all things hidden. My interest in genetic genealogy imagined some untested DNA sample might be run through continuously advancing scientific processes, and all conspirators and perpetrators would finally receive their just due. I hoped against hope that I might fully achieve the complete uncovering and making total sense of things that decades of investigation had been unable to.

My quest for ultimate truth and justice, while lofty, was nonetheless sincere, and that sincerity unexpectedly deepened upon my examination of post-mortem photographs of Bobby Durham. The only photo I had previously seen of his face had accompanied news articles about the murders and portrayed him as a handsome, confident-looking *man*, but in death, he seemed a vulnerable *boy*. Of course, it is hard to imagine anything engendering vulnerability more so than being at the mercy of one's killer(s). Bobby's victimization had been captured in 8 x 10 black and white glossies, and while the plight of his parents had likewise been documented and was equally deplorable, there was something about Bobby that especially resonated. Whatever else was going on behind the scenes, and whatever the motivation for the abuse inflicted on this family, I believe Bobby, who has been universally described as shy, kind, and likeable, had a particular innocence and was caught up in something not directly concerning him that resulted in his being collateral damage. All three of the murders were tragic, unnecessary, and unconscionable, but the cutting short of Bobby's young life and the photos of his corpse struck a particularly sympathetic chord within me, juxtaposed with indignation.

The life-extinguishing acts perpetrated upon the Durhams can easily be described with any number of adjectives, including brutal and deeply disturbing, but words to communicate the circumstances behind their deaths – the why and the how – come less readily. This is a labyrinthine tale, involving intricate and complex twists and turns that can be difficult to navigate. Add to that numerous sidebars which, while perhaps not directly tied to the killings, are oddly associated in a "six degrees of separation" fashion. As I wondered if I could piece the story together and convey it coherently, the summarizing and apt descriptor that repeatedly entered my mind and that I often muttered to myself following some odd discovery or encounter is the one I ultimately chose as the main title of the book – "CONVOLUTED."

Time on earth ceased for Bryce, Virginia, and Bobby Durham on February 3, 1972, and they seem frozen in that moment. When we think of them, Bryce is still fifty-one years old, Virginia forty-four, and Bobby eighteen. It is sobering to realize I am now older than all of them at the time of their deaths. Had they lived to their birthdays in 2024, Bryce would be one-hundred and four, Virginia ninety-seven, and Bobby seventy-one. How I wish they could have celebrated those birthdays, and how I wish I could turn back time, knowing now what lay ahead of them more than fifty years ago, and warn them of the impending danger. But time moves unhaltingly forward, so perhaps the best I can do for the Durhams is attempt to inform and educate inquiring audiences and to keep this most interesting case in the forefront of public consciousness, serving as a catalyst for ongoing discussion and investigation in hopes that ultimate resolution will one day be achieved. This is my fervent desire.

ACKNOWLEDGEMENTS

I owe a debt of gratitude to many people who have assisted me with the researching and compiling of this book, but I must offer special thanks to certain individuals:

First and foremost, I thank my retired attorney uncle, Jack Henson, who long ago helped foster my interest in all things historical and who shares my deep interest in the Durham Case. Throughout this project, he has been my fellow researcher, my sounding board, my advisor, my proofreader, my critic, and my encourager, and he has helped make this work the best it could be.

I thank my brother, Todd Harmon, for accompanying me on my trips to Georgia, for being a beta reader of my book draft, and for his helpful critiques.

I thank Watauga County, North Carolina Sheriff Len Hagaman, who I have known since he was my university instructor for a state and local government class, and whose physician father delivered my mother, and whose son is my work colleague. I thank him for allowing me to interview and e-mail him on numerous occasions, for his kind and patient responses to my multiple inquiries, and for providing me access to files that contributed key and revelatory insights into this case.

I thank former North Carolina Attorney General and Secretary of State Rufus Edmisten, who devoted many years to the Durham Case, for allowing me to interview and communicate with him and especially for writing the forward for this book.

I thank Ted Brown, with whom I have had dozens of interchanges. Ted's lengthy political career includes having served as Special Assistant to the Lieutenant Governor of North Carolina, Aide to U. S. Senator Lauch Faircloth, and Senior Policy Advisor and Deputy Commissioner to the North Carolina Commissioner of Insurance. In the early stages of this project, various individuals, including Rufus Edmisten (with whom Ted has had a long-standing friendship and a shared interest in the Durham Case), pointed me to Ted as a resource. Ted's assistance, particularly as it relates to the inner workings, culture, and people of his native Wilkes County, North Carolina, provided me with valuable insights.

I thank Stoney Birt, Shane Birt, Bob Ingram, Sean Kipe, Phil Hudgins, and C. A. O'Driscoll for opportunities to interact with them and for providing me with information pertinent to the alleged involvement of Georgia's Dixie Mafia in the Durham Case.

I thank the following additional individuals who granted me the opportunity to speak or otherwise communicate with them:

Richard Aldridge, Jane Allen, Patrick Anderson, Loy Ballard, Dwight Bearden, Bruce Bowers, Johnny Carroll, Sean Chandler, Monica Church, Karen Coffey, Jenny Cole, Wade Colvard, Jerry Combs, Donna Cook, Tommy Cornell, George C. Danner III, Kweta Danner, Dr. Clayton Dean, Tim Dowell, Gary Edmisten, Harold Edmisten, Diana Edwards, Anita Combs Eldreth, Tom Eller, Robert Ferm, Arthur Flowers, Ed Furr, Carroll Garland, Sonya Garland, Phil Ginn, Calvin Greene, Marsha Greene, Evelyn Greer, Frank Guy, David Hagaman, Barney Hampton, Billy Harmon, Jerry

Harmon, Tim Harmon, Luther Harrison, Patrick Hayes, Charles Heatherly, Garry Henson, Wayne Henson, Mozella Jackson, Roberta Jackson, T. J. Jackson, Carolynn Johnson, Frank Jolley, Edward Lankford, Chris Laws, Cyndi Silvey Lynch, Janis Mangum, Allison Faw Marcotte, Zoobie Martin, Paula May, Michelle Minton, Keith Norris, Lottie Oliver, Charlie Overcash, John Parker, Bill Pearce, Sam Pennica, Dustin Petrey, Brad Poe, Lester Reece, Sherry Reese, Lisa Roark, Darlene Roberson, Jeff Rucker, Jennifer Bradley Rudy, Shannon Russing, Arvil Sale, Sheila Shealy, Mark Shook, R. Rucker Smith, Ron Stock, Gail Storie, Steven Rambam, Dee Dee Rominger, Jimmy Terrell, Johnny Tester, Daren Thomas, Gina Thomas, Mike Townsend, James Trivette, Glenda Vance, Jerry Vaughn, Jackie Vines, Larry Wagner, Richard Walter, Carolyn Warren, Pat Whitman, Sarah Wilcox, Mike Wilson, Pat Wilson, Steve Wilson, Debbie York, Lewis Young, and anonymous others.

I thank Tim Opelt for his excellent work in producing the maps and drawings for this book,[2] Mike England for putting his professional touches on my cover design, and Gray Wilson for his legal review of my manuscript and his editorial recommendations.

I thank all those individuals within various law enforcement and governmental agencies, courthouses, libraries, universities, etc. who provided information or enabled me to access it.

Finally, I thank you, the readers, for your interest in this subject and for joining me on this journey.

INTRODUCTION

"I think they're dead."

Such a simple, straightforward statement, but one that would lead to more than fifty years of complexity and confusion.

Shortly before imparting these four words to a police dispatcher, twenty-year-old Troy Hall – accompanied by his pistol-wielding, private detective neighbor – had cautiously entered the home of his in-laws. While the family den bore evidence of recent activity – the TV playing, and food and beverages partially consumed – it was curiously abandoned. Advancing further in search of the home's occupants, one of the men unwittingly tracking blood from the den's carpet, they discovered the lifeless bodies of Bryce, Virginia, and Bobby Durham draped across the edge of a water-filled bathtub. The hair on their submerged heads ebbed and flowed in response to the force of the still-running spigot. A rope, fashioned in the form of a noose, loosely encompassed Bryce's neck. Their home had been ransacked, their vehicle stolen. According to Hall, he had been drawn to the scene by a whispered but frantic phone call from Virginia.

Twenty-one-year-old Johnny Tester was nearing the end of his shift at the local police station when he received Hall's late-night call. In the absence of a job following his recent college graduation, Tester's police chief father had offered him an interim opportunity to dispatch.[3] Never aspiring to a law enforcement career, he unexpectedly found himself on the receiving end of news regarding what was arguably the most heinous murder case in his county's history. The call understandably unnerved him. Things began moving fast, and he wondered to himself, "What is going on in Boone, North Carolina?"[4]

While the next few hours would summon no less than four law enforcement agencies and two emergency response units to the crime scene – blue and red lights illuminating the crest of the hill where the Durham family home sat on the outskirts of the town – the ensuing decades would involve dozens more people, from private investigators and theorists to forensic psychologists and psychics. Accusations regarding various suspects would generate controversy and debate.

The preceding decade had yielded only a handful of murders in Watauga County, and although local citizens could not believe what happened to the Durhams was possible there, the last murder, which occurred three years earlier in 1969 (and less than two weeks after Bryce Durham had purchased a Boone car dealership), was similarly gruesome, the victim being a widowed hospital nurse whose neighbor stabbed her, slit her throat, and dumped her body into a coal bin beside her house.[5] Still, people were baffled by the Durham murders, stating they did not think the family was "likely to have enemies – especially the kind who would kill them."[6] Because the details of the case were so unique – particularly being a triple homicide (the first ever mass slaying in the area[7]) and so cold-blooded and cruel – when they were called to the public's attention the morning after, shockwaves were felt in the neighborhood which quickly rippled out to the town, the surrounding communities, the county, the region, and the state. The case even received national and international attention. Within three days, the murders were reported in a Sydney, Australia newspaper.[8]

Beaten And Strangled
Three Members Of Boone Family Are Found Slain

3 in Family Killed, Left In Bathtub

Killings Of 'Friendly' Boone Family Baffle Town

"The [local] community…was shaken at its roots,"[9] and news reporters quickly learned of the acute fear and anxiety among the Durhams' neighbors. Next-door neighbor Clinard Wilson stated, "We're all shook up. I've got two guns and I aim to protect myself." Another next-door neighbor, Dean Combs, had learned some safety precautions when he previously lived north, and when he returned to his native Watauga County, he continued locking his doors and sleeping with a gun for easy access.[10] Another neighbor stated, "You read about that sort of thing, but it's a terrible shock when it happens next door."[11] Yet another neighbor recalled that, after the Durhams were killed, "There were some sleepless nights in the neighborhood for a while."[12] One neighbor vowed he and his wife would move away until the killers were caught.[13] Another individual living in a nearby apartment with two sons also moved away, and quickly.[14] In a house across the way and within a direct line of sight of the Durham house, Lois Thomas kept her hallway light burning nightly after the killings and did so for the next almost four decades.[15]

While most Wataugans never knew the Durhams, their deaths nonetheless felt very personal. Unspoken questions permeated many minds: "Is a stranger lurking in the shadows of my neighborhood? Will I be next?" According to Rufus Edmisten, "[It was] a horrible thing for the community, [which was]…scared to death that there was a bunch…just wanting to…kill people for the fun of it."[16] Blindsided by the unanticipated murders, residents also became more observant and vigilant.[17] Local sales of door locks[18] accelerated, and more burglar alarms were installed. The number of permits issued for the purchase of pistols doubled, and local gun dealers noted an increase in the sale of "short guns."[19] Some stores nearly sold out of ammunition.[20] A local banker reportedly began sleeping with a gun under his pillow,[21] and a Mount Airy, North Carolina attorney who came to Boone to handle the Durham estates purchased his first handgun for protection.[22] An eight-year-old boy, having heard talk of the murders, slept with his new Cub Scout knife.[23] Some tempered the fright, including a local hardware owner who admitted "there was a certain amount of fear for a while…[but]…it wasn't like everyone was shaking in his boots."[24] Two and a half months after the murders, however, it was reported that the "look of fear" remained in many local eyes and that "a stranger still [had] a slim chance of setting his foot inside a Boone household."[25]

The murders "terrorized the community for weeks and perpetrated one of the longest mysteries in the history of North Carolina."[26] Its impact would reverberate for generations to come, and a degree of innocence was forever lost, but the greatest losses by far were the lives of Bryce, Virginia, and Bobby Durham. And while the mention of their names would, regrettably and almost without fail, bring to mind what happened to them in the winter of 1972, they had a story beyond that of victims. And to a point, the story had been good.

PART I:

THE LIVES AND DEMISE OF THE DURHAMS

CHAPTER 1

THE GOOD LIFE

Although Bryce and Virginia Church Durham and their children, Ginny and Bobby, adopted Watauga County, North Carolina as their new home, they did not come far in terms of distance from their native Wilkes County.[a]

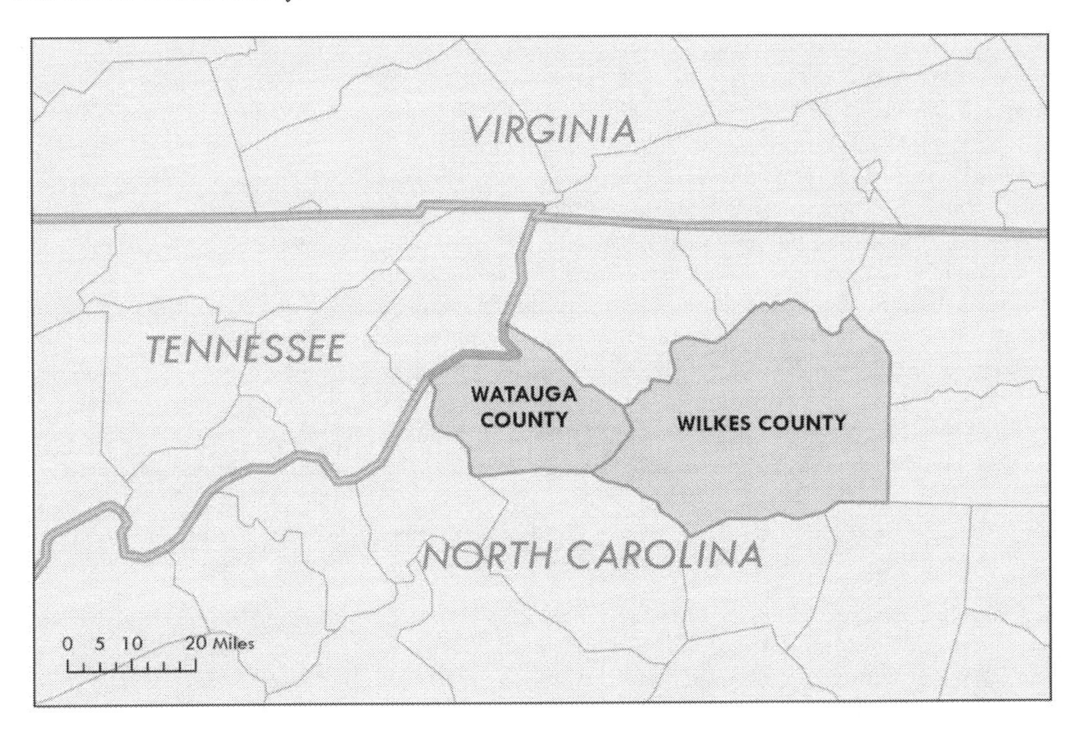

Baxter Bryce Durham was born in 1920,[27] one of four children of Coy and Collie Crabb Durham. His brother Ralph was three years his senior, while brother Bill and sister Gayle were, respectively, eleven and thirteen years younger.[28] The close-knit Durhams made their home in the small community of Lomax in Wilkes County, where they farmed and attended Pleasant Home Baptist

[a] In his research for this book, the author (a native of Watauga County) discovered he is a distant cousin of Virginia, Ginny, and Bobby Durham through their shared Wilkes County, NC ancestry.

Church. For almost fifty years, Coy was a Bible teacher, schoolteacher, and principal. Collie also taught school, and she and Coy tended the Lomax Post Office for more than three decades.[29] The three Durham boys enjoyed outdoor recreational activities including hunting.[30]

Bryce Durham at Appalachian State Teachers College - 1939, 1940, 1942 (Source: The Rhododendron, University Archives and Records, Special Collections, Appalachian State University, Boone, NC)

After graduating from Ronda High School in Wilkes County,[31] Bryce enrolled at Appalachian State Teachers College in Boone (the seat of Watauga County) in the fall of 1938 to pursue a degree in history and physical education.[32] While a student there, he became involved in football and traveled with the school's team until World War II interrupted his junior year.[33] In December 1941, three weeks after the United States' entrance into the war, Bryce traveled to Durham, North Carolina to enroll in defense courses at the National Youth Administration Camp.[34] Having no industrial experience, he participated in a sheet metal project, and in February 1942, after officials had conducted a city-wide survey, they recognized him as the camp's "youth worker most valuable to war production."[35] That same month, while still at the camp, Bryce registered for the draft.[36] He subsequently went to the San Francisco Bay area, joining thousands of others in search of defense positions resulting from "the wartime economic boom, fueled by federal investment in shipbuilding and repair." Bryce found work at the Hunters Point Naval Shipyard, "which operated as a ship repair facility throughout the war." In August 1944, he sailed from San Francisco to Honolulu as part of "Hunters Point Group 99,"[37] and he helped repair damaged ships at Pearl Harbor.[38] In September 1945, upon completion of thirty-seven months of service, a portion of which he spent in the Philippine Islands, Bryce was discharged.[39] He returned home to Wilkes County and accepted a teaching position at Mount Pleasant High School,[40] where he met his future bride.[41]

Virginia Dare Church was born in 1927,[42] the youngest of nine children of Calvin and Jennie Eller Church.[43] Calvin, who farmed[44] and also worked as a fireman on a steam shovel,[45] died three months prior to Virginia's birth, succumbing at the age of forty-six to lobar pneumonia after having contracted typhoid fever.[46] This left Jennie a widowed mother of seven daughters and one son – Winnie, Dovie, Gladys, Wayne, Faye, Sally, Mozelle, and Virginia.[47] Another daughter, Doshia,[48] had tragically burned to death in 1913 at age three when her clothing accidentally caught fire.[49]

Virginia Church

Although Virginia, as the youngest child in her family, was reportedly "spoiled rotten,"[50] she remained down to earth and could be a "barrel of laughs."[51]

By 1930, the Church family moved from their farm at Lewis Fork in Wilkes County to a rental house in Lenoir in neighboring Caldwell County. Daughters Dovie and Gladys helped support the family by working in a cotton mill.[52] In 1933, Jennie Church took on the added responsibility of raising a granddaughter, Gearldeane "Jerri" Bumgarner. As the youngest children in the household, Virginia and Jerri grew very close – more like sisters than aunt and niece. Described as "two peas in a pod," the blue-eyed blondes even resembled one another physically.[53]

In 1940, Jennie was back in Lewis Fork living on her own farm in a home she owned and working as a lunchroom supervisor.[54] Despite her family's circumstantial setbacks, Virginia graduated from Mount Pleasant High School in Wilkes County and from Bowling Green Business College in Kentucky. Returning home, she secured a position with Wilkes Auto Sales, Inc. in North Wilkesboro.[55]

Virginia Church Durham (Source: The Wilkes Record)

By 1945, the Church family was residing in the Purlear community of Wilkes County, and that was the year Bryce Durham met the tall, fair-skinned, attractive, and pleasant Virginia Church.[56] Their engagement was announced in February 1946,[57] and less than one month later, on a Saturday morning in March, they were wed "before an improvised altar of white flowers and greenery" in Virginia's sister Winnie's home near North Wilkesboro. Dressed in a long-sleeved, white satin and marquisette wedding gown and a veil held in place with pearls, Virginia "carried a bouquet of white gardenias and lilies." Her sister Sally served as her matron of honor, while Bryce's brother Ralph was his best man.[58]

Bryce & Virginia Durham

The couple made their home near North Wilkesboro, and after a year, Bryce left teaching for a more lucrative career,[59] following the footsteps of his older brother Ralph.[60] Early on, Bryce was employed by a Kaiser-Frazer car dealership in Elkin, North Carolina and was transferred to Wilmington, North Carolina. Forest Church, a fellow Wilkes County native, subsequently got Bryce into the auto loan business,[61] and Bryce gained employment as an auto finance credit manager in the Raleigh-Durham area of the state.[62] Changing jobs in 1950, he was appointed manager of the Blue Ridge Finance company office in Galax, Virginia.[63] Although Bryce and Virginia lived in Galax and purchased a farm there,[64] their children were born in Wilkes County two weeks shy of a year apart – Ginny Sue in May 1952 and Bobby Joe in May 1953.[65] By 1952, Bryce was the Galax branch manager for the Home Finance Group, Inc., an automobile financing company headquartered in Charlotte, North Carolina. Outside of work, both he and Virginia held offices in Galax civic organizations.[66]

Virginia Church Durham (Source: Wilkes Journal-Patriot)

Virginia Church Durham

By July 1961, Bryce became manager of the Home Finance Company's branch in Florence, South Carolina,[67] and a few months later, he was inducted into Florence's Rotary Club.[68] Those who knew the Durhams in Florence thought highly of them. Polly Howle worked for Bryce and described him as quiet and conservative and one of the greatest bosses she ever had. She recalled Virginia as "a very nice, well reserved, quiet woman. A Pat Nixon type." She also remembered Ginny and Bobby: "They sometimes would come to the office to wait on their mother to pick them up…. They were quiet and well behaved." Grover McQueen ran a rental car agency at the airport, and Bryce financed cars for him. McQueen only knew Virginia and the children casually, but he knew Bryce "fairly well" and described him as "very nice, pleasant, and nice looking…the kind of fellow you would want to do business with." Stafford Preston, who financed cars with Bryce and drank coffee with him "every couple of days," stated, "He was an extremely nice fellow, very well versed in auto loans. He was an expert in his field. A very high type fellow."[69]

Bryce Durham (Image courtesy of the Paul Armfield Coffey Collection, Digital Watauga Project)

Virginia & Bryce Durham

Bryce worked thirteen years for the Home Finance Group[70] and progressively became a successful, self-made businessman.[71] In 1963,[72b] the family relocated to Mount Airy in Surry County, North Carolina, where they initially rented an "old, dumpy house" from Bryce's attorney while their own home was being built.[73] Bryce was named manager and secretary-treasurer of the Mount Airy Auto Loan and Sales Finance Company, which was established by a group of local citizens. He worked there six years, and Virginia served as receptionist and bookkeeper.[74] Friends in Mount Airy described Bryce as "well thought of"[75] and as "a very fine man, active in church work and community affairs."[76] Even after the Durhams left South Carolina, they exchanged Christmas cards with Polly Howle for a time. She recalled Bryce phoning her from Mount Airy around 1967: "He seemed very well and very happy then. He always seemed happy, even when things weren't going well. He was a very Christian man." Dallas Coe, the chief jailer in Surry County, worked for Bryce for two years and stated he was a "prince of a fellow…one of the best men I ever worked for."[77] The family's Mount

[b] Once source says the family moved to Mount Airy in 1964. [Source: "Florentines Who Knew N. C. Murder Victims 'Shocked,'" *Florence Morning News*, Florence, SC, February 8, 1972, p. 2.]

Airy-based attorney and friend, John C. W. Gardner, Sr. described the Durhams as "young, vigorous, and attractive people." Harris Greene, of Greene Finance Corporation in Mount Airy and an associate of Bryce, recalled that Bryce "was very well-liked here, and I know that when he went to Boone, he was well-liked in the community there. I never heard anything derogatory said about him.... There were no nicer people than the Durhams."[78] Durham relatives recalled Bryce as intelligent, hard-working, kindhearted, decent, easy-going, and mild-mannered – a good businessman [who] did well for himself and who loved his family tremendously. "Bryce was a good Christian. He had a good Christian family."[79] Conservative in their faith[80] – reported by one source as "strict Baptists"[81] – the Durhams attended Bannertown Baptist Church.

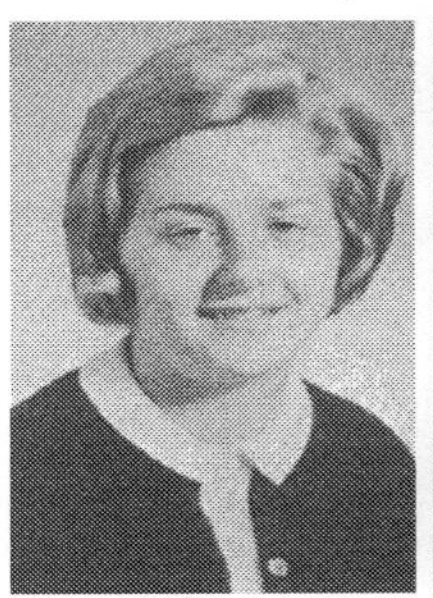

Ginny and Bobby Durham as high school students (Source: 1969 Mount Airy High School yearbook)

"Ginny Sue" and "Bobby Joe" (as they were known by some) attended Mount Airy High School. During her junior year, Ginny was a member of the dramatics club and of a girls' organization upholding Christian character and helping "create a more Christian atmosphere" throughout the school by sponsoring dances, Christmas programs, and talent shows, selling concessions during basketball season, and helping needy families.[82]

Meanwhile, Bobby was active in the Fellowship of Christian Athletes,[83] and within the Boy Scouts of America, he attained the highest rank of Eagle Scout. A fellow scout recalled him as being "as nice a guy as you'd ever wish to meet – reserved but not stand-offish," and a former teacher remembered him as a devoted member of the school's "Granite Bears" football team.[84] In 1968, Bobby played on the junior varsity team[85] and subsequently as a defensive guard on the varsity team[86] under Coach Jerry Hollingsworth. An acquaintance recalled, "To begin practice each day Coach Hollingsworth would have the team run around the field. Bobby was always first. I remember several players trying to slow him down each day by surrounding him to keep him contained." Another who knew Bobby said he was always leading his teammates during practices, and, in turn, earned their respect.[87]

Bobby Durham, Junior Varsity Football Team (Source: 1969 Mount Airy High School yearbook)

According to Ginny, due to their parent's strict conservatism, she was not allowed hobbies, and aside from Bobby's involvement in scouting and football, they were not permitted to do anything with friends, although she did date a boy during her junior year of high school.[88]

By the late 1960s and early 1970s – the era during which the Durhams came to town – Boone and its surrounding area were "galloping"[89] with economic, industrial, and educational opportunities.[90] Never before had there been such prospects of prosperity,[91] and in 1969, the year Bryce Durham purchased the Buick-Pontiac dealership, it was predicted "more will happen here in the next decade than anywhere else in North Carolina.... Things are moving in a fashion that wasn't apparent to most of us a few months ago...the progress and the activity can no longer be contained...the future looks good."[92] The following year, as Bryce's family joined him in Boone, the local newspaper declared, "A new decade enters.... And what tremendous opportunities ride in on the wings of 1970!"[93]

Founded in 1872, named for frontiersman Daniel Boone, and tucked into the northwestern corner of the state's Blue Ridge Mountains, Boone and its host county of Watauga had been decades-long victims of remoteness and isolation, and they lagged behind other portions of the state, due, in part, to a lack of roadways and transportation options.[94] A railway finally made it to Boone in 1919, its trestles signifying progress. In addition to bringing much needed opportunities for travel and growth, it commercially enabled the export of lumber and agricultural products and the import of building materials that accelerated the development of the town. The devastating washouts of a 1940 flood sounded the death knell for the railroad in Watauga County, and it was never resuscitated. Despite this loss, traditional subsistence farming continued, and livelihoods thrived for a time in such forms as cheesemaking, dairying, and truck farming. Over a course of decades, burley tobacco developed into a cash crop,[95] and the county was once the state's number one cabbage producer.[96] Eventually, a few industrial plants, producing electronic components,[97] lingerie,[98] and shoes,[99] were established. Between 1964 and 1969, more than eighty new businesses were established,[100] and by 1970, the southeastward expansion of the town was well underway. Farmland was gradually transformed for modern commercial, medical, and recreational use, and roads leading to Watauga County were improved.[101] This era also hailed the arrivals of a twelve-acre shopping center,[102] a new hospital, a new high school, a new courthouse, and even a new, modern mortuary.[103] Development was the talk of the day and would continue to be for the foreseeable future.

In 1967, the teacher's college Bryce Durham had attended in Boone in the late 1930s and early 1940s became Appalachian State University where Ginny and Bobby followed in his academic footsteps. Contributing to the university's "'bursting-at-the-seams' growth rate,"[104] were four new high-rise residence halls, a new library, a new administration building, a new science building,[105] and construction of a continuing education and conference center.[106] In 1969, college students had numbered 6,800;[107] by 1972, enrollment exceeded 7,600,[108] and the university's long-range growth plan aimed for 10,000.[109]

While the town's smattering of industries and the university became the county's leading employers, tourism as commerce was reaching a crescendo. The nearby town of Blowing Rock had, for some years, preceded Boone as a tourist haven. Flatlanders made annual pilgrimages there to enjoy the higher elevation with its cool mountain breezes and vistas.[110] Boone, seeing how Blowing Rock had benefitted and profited from tourism, began considering how it might also tap into and capitalize upon it, and this train of thought endured over subsequent decades. As a local promoter stated, "This area is one of the most desirable in the world.... We will sell ourselves short if we do not take advantage of the unlimited opportunities available to us."[111] An eventual goal of developers was to extend tourism and local employment opportunities beyond the fair-weather months into the winter season, and the construction of ski resorts changed that, making the area into a "year-round vacationland."[112] Northerners were being drawn southward, and that changed "the economic outlook for Watauga County," particularly as people acquired more money and more leisure time and were "looking for ways to spend both." As one local developer quipped, "Nothing makes a Southerner itch like newly arrived Yankees with fresh money."[113] Tourism became big business,[114] accounting for nearly $8 million in income in 1970.[115] The mountains were "becoming a weekend home and a vacation home to perhaps more than twice the permanent population. "Within the past six to seven years...a great change [had] come to Watauga County...."[116]

The Durhams had also come to Watauga County, and their move from Mount Airy to Boone may have been precipitated, in part, by the latter's rapidly rising economy, garnering Bryce's attention as a promisingly lucrative place to embark upon a new venture. On November 18, 1969, his ownership of the Buick-Pontiac dealership at 1115 East King Street in Boone became effective.[117] The sale of the agency seemed to happen quietly and suddenly.[118] Although Bryce had explored possible partnerships with family members and friends, those had fallen through. An acquaintance named Dick Patterson went to Boone with Bryce, but after thirty days, he changed his mind about investing and subsequently established his own car dealership in Mount Airy, leaving Bryce as the sole proprietor. Utilizing a bank loan,[119] Bryce purchased the business from George C. "G. C." Greene, Jr. and changed its name from Greene Buick-Pontiac, Inc. to Modern Buick-Pontiac Company. For a period of time following the sale, Greene maintained his association with the dealership as he continued to own the stock of used cars as well as the building and land.[120] The transition was not exactly smooth, and there was a high rate of employee turnover during the first year of Bryce's ownership.[121] The dealership had also been fledgling under Greene,[122] and although it made some gains with Bryce at the helm, working six days a week to make it profitable and carefully watching the money, it continued to struggle.

Virginia, a smart and competent businesswoman, was directly and enthusiastically involved in the enterprise, providing daily clerical and bookkeeping help and serving as the cashier.[123] Ginny and Bobby were in and out of the dealership on a regular basis[124] and were also involved in the business. Bryce occasionally had them go to Charlotte, North Carolina and drive cars back to Boone for him.[125] Two months into the dealership's reorganization, Ginny's name was even incorporated into a clever newspaper advertisement for its GMC "Jimmy."[126]

(As published in the Watauga Democrat, 1/22/70)

Bryce Durham pictured with employees Kelly Surratt, Gail Storie, and Lee Roche
(As published in the Watauga Democrat)

Although Bryce bought the dealership in late 1969, Modern Buick-Pontiac Company's two-day grand opening, replete with free refreshments and live music, was delayed until August 1970. By this time, "the entire operation" had been updated and the parking areas newly paved, making it "one of the most modern, best equipped, and up-to-date dealerships to be found anywhere."[127]

(As published in the Watauga Democrat)

Modern Buick-Pontiac (Source: Front Page Detective)

Bryce eventually added new employees, one of whom was Lester Reece, a mechanic with automobile dealership experience, who Bryce hired on the spot. Reece liked Bryce and found him to be "an awful nice man" to work for, describing him as a straight, smart, hardworking businessman who would help a person any way he could, no matter when or what, and who he never heard anything bad about. According to Reece, Bryce was typically all business with low tolerance for nonsense, but he did not stand on formality and would sometimes "shoot the breeze" with the guys in the shop. Reece also found Bryce to be an honest man who was upfront in his dealings with both employees and customers, and a family man, whose children were well behaved. Reece thought the entire family were nice, decent people who were respected by all.[128]

But other employees had difficulty getting along with the Durhams, finding them and their way of thinking hard to understand and being frustrated by never knowing what to expect from them. They also felt the Durhams were very critical of everyone at the dealership. Virginia, in particular, seemed to complain a lot about the employees, sometimes falsely accusing them of things and unduly influencing Bryce to accept those accusations as truth.[129] "A take charge kind of person,"[130] Virginia was the dominant figure in her family who typically had things her way.[131] Described as feisty[132] and self-assured, she was a no-nonsense, headstrong lady who could hold her own and, at times, be a little overbearing,"[133] According to Ginny, while her father was the peacemaker, her mother was difficult to get along with and was "awful" to the staff and had "blow ups" with them.[134] At times, Bryce and Virginia were even at odds with one another and "had some pretty good fusses."[135] According to salesman J. B. Webb, "Virginia seemed to run things,"[136] and on at least one occasion, she fired one of their workers.[137] In contrast to Bryce, who was "not a 'hard-nosed' businessman whose methods would offend anyone, but…'easy-going and even tempered,'"[138] Virginia was less constrained and, on one occasion, expressed ill will toward a customer following a vehicle dispute.[139] According to Ginny, Virginia was the boss and no one crossed her, including Bryce, who did whatever Virginia said.[140] While some of the employees felt that to be true,[141] others believed Bryce could draw a line when needed.[142] In one instance, he was unsympathetic toward a customer whose vehicle was being repossessed and seemed unphased that the young man had his pocketknife out, flipping the blade open and closed.[143] Although Bryce was not perceived to be as demanding as Virginia, he still wanted his own way, and due to these frictions, some of the employees wanted no dealings or friendship with the Durhams outside their work relationship.[144]

By early 1970, Bryce claimed the service department was losing money, and this became a point of contention between him and service manager David Hagaman, who believed the problem stemmed from the department's monetary intake being counted against used cars rather than departmental revenue. The tension heightened when Bryce requested salaried service department employees to work longer than their contracted forty-hour week. Employee Dave Miller reportedly placed a call to the labor relations board, upsetting the Durhams.[145]

Employees (L-R) Ray Brendell, Dave Miller, Lewis Ray, David Hagaman, & Lester Reece
(As published in the Watauga Democrat)

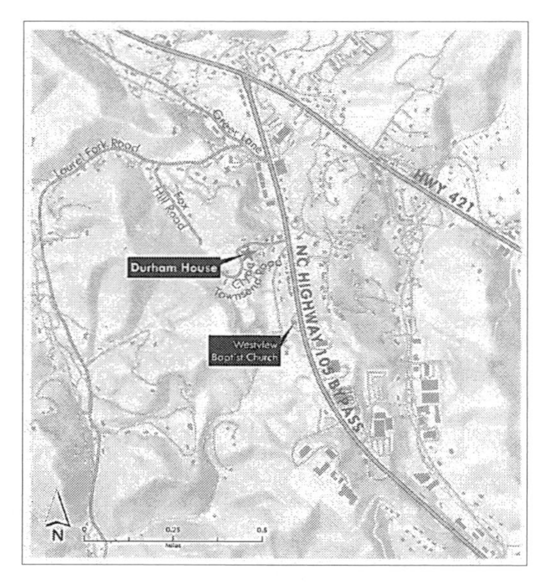

While Bryce had initially gotten his newly acquired dealership up and running, Virginia and their children had remained in Mount Airy so Ginny could finish school there.[146] In the interim, Bryce rented a motel room in Boone and returned to Mount Airy on weekends. Immediately following her 1970 high school graduation, Ginny enrolled in Appalachian State University's summer quarter.[147] Bryce reportedly "was eager to stay close to his daughter,"[148] and the family officially moved to Boone in September 1970 after a nine-month search to find a home.[149] Although Bryce had explored building a house,[150] he and Virginia ultimately purchased one that local builder Clyde Townsend had constructed in 1967 near the Highway 105 Bypass, just outside the Boone town limits. Townsend and his family had lived in the house until he sold it and its one-acre lot in 1969 to "Butch" and Sarah Wilcox,[151] from whom Bryce and Virginia subsequently purchased it.[152] The Wilcoxes had not been looking to sell the house, but Bryce had seen and liked it and approached Mr. Wilcox about purchasing it.[153]

Durham home in Boone, NC (Image courtesy of Watauga County Sheriff's Office)

During his junior year, Bobby Durham transferred from Mount Airy High School to Watauga High School, where he continued to play football,[154] and he began practice with his new teammates in early August 1970. The following year, he was one of nine seniors on the Pioneer's varsity team.[155] Although he was not first string[156] and never a star player, he took the game seriously and worked hard. Not physically the largest or strongest, he was a decent and fit player – described as "husky" – who could hold his own.[157]

Bobby Durham school picture (Source: Wilkes Journal-Patriot) and as a Watauga High School football player, Letterman, and Latin Club member (Source: 1971 Watauga High School yearbook)

Bobby Durham

Bobby continued his scouting participation, meeting weekly with Troop 109 at Boone United Methodist Church. As an Eagle Scout, he ultimately held fifty-two merit badges and became an assistant[158] to Scoutmaster Arvil Sale, who knew Bobby from scout camp even before the Durhams' move to Boone and found him to be a likeable kid.[159] Bobby also belonged to the First Baptist Church youth group in Boone.[160] He enjoyed golfing and skiing, was passionate about music,[161] and would occasionally play ball with younger boys in his neighborhood.[162] He became friends with high school classmates Gary Edmisten and Edwin Lawrence, and the three would occasionally camp in the western section of the county. During one such outing, Bobby taught Edmisten to drive a stick shift.[163] Bobby enjoyed cars, and while his father drove a late 1960s model Buick Electra 225 – known on the street as a "deuce and a quarter"[164] – Bobby drove a gold, two-door 1972 Buick Skylark with a vinyl roof, and he took fastidious care of it.[165] Bobby dressed well[166] and always had money to do things, which, along with his father's car dealership, gave some the impression the Durhams were wealthier than they actually were.[167c]

In June 1971, Bobby was among the 260 young men and women who graduated in the Watauga High School gymnasium,[168] and he subsequently enrolled at Appalachian State University. Like his sister a year earlier, Bobby began his college coursework the summer quarter after high school. He was considering a major in either economics or business,[169] perhaps intending to follow his father's footsteps in the automobile dealership.[170] He hoped to complete his degree within three years and, toward that goal, "he carried a heavy academic load – one hour below the maximum allowed…. He [did] well in all of his courses."[171] Although he had not been an honor roll student at Watauga High

[c] Years later, Ginny Durham would state there was a perception and assumption her parents, due to their involvement in auto finance, had money. [Source: Mackie, Ginny Durham. Interview with Carolynn Johnson & Wade Colvard. December 7, 2020.]

School,[172] "Eloise Melton, Bobby's [college] history professor for the fall and winter quarters" found him to be "an above average student" – well read, studious, and always prepared for class.[173]

Bobby Durham (Source: 1971 Watauga High School yearbook)

During the 1971-72 winter quarter, Bobby's high school friendship with classmate Phil Ginn was further solidified when they were enrolled in the same biology class and became lab partners. The two sometimes shared meals at one of the food venues on campus. They also belonged to a small circle of a half dozen or so friends with whom they occasionally went on social outings, including grabbing a bite at a local burger or pizza joint and attending high school and university sporting events.[174] During his first year of college, Bobby, not known for having had previous dating relationships, briefly courted Jacquelyn "Jackie" Vines, a niece of Boone Police Chief Clyde Tester. Bobby and Jackie had initially met at Watauga High School when he was a senior and a football player, and she was a freshman and a cheerleader.[175]

Despite Bobby's social activities, he was primarily a homebody, living a somewhat sheltered life under the auspices of his parents, who kept a tight rein and close tabs on him. He had a very slight speech impediment, and, according to Ginny, when he was a young child, it was made worse whenever Virginia (who Ginny recalls as very abusive) was mean to him. Virginia had high standards and expectations of Bobby, at times so unreasonable that he had difficulty meeting them. While proud of him, she occasionally criticized him in front of his friends, and this embarrassed him. Nevertheless, he respectfully strove to obey his parents. Bobby was close to Ginny, and he confided in her and found solace in their relationship. The two consistently "saved" one another, and Bobby depended on Ginny to be his relief. Ginny, whose days were filled with schoolwork, cooking and cleaning for her family, and helping at the dealership, eventually moved out, and Bobby told her he was hurt and could not understand why she left him alone with their parents. Thoughts of leaving him with their mother, in particular, made Ginny cry.[176]

Friends unanimously described Bobby as a good guy, quiet, unassuming, reserved, and passive. Although some perceived him as a bit of a loner,[177] he was simply not the initiator and was friendly and responsive to those who were, always willing to greet and chat with others. His shyness may have partially stemmed from his speech impediment,[178] which some noticed, and others did not. Although not a jokester, Bobby was quick with a smile or a laugh and had a good, dry sense of humor. Always a gentleman, he never used coarse language or spoke badly of others. Further described as nice, kind, polite, sweet, and loving – "a gentle soul" – he treated others well.[179] He was not highly opinionated[180] nor overly talkative and did not make himself the center of attention or bring drama to his friendships. He was steady and dependable, had a good business sense, was not afraid of work, and always carried his load.[181] According to an employee at the family's dealership, Bobby was "a number one kid."[182] In Phil Ginn's estimation, "He was a good-hearted fellow, and a straight-up kind of guy,"[183] the kind of friend anyone would have wanted.[184]

In October 1971, Wilkes Countian Ike Eller became the sales manager at Modern Buick-Pontiac Company,[185] and around December that same year, Dean Combs, who ended up being a next-door neighbor of the Durhams, began working as the dealership's service manager.[186] A native of Watauga County, Combs had been living in Ohio, but he had suffered a major heart attack and wanted to return home.[187] When Bryce learned Combs had worked as a mechanic and service manager at a Pontiac dealership in Cincinnati and had overseen twenty-two mechanics in the shop there, he pursued him on the phone. The service department at Bryce's dealership had been operating in the red, due in part to no repair orders being written on the work being done. A recent General Motors strike had also taken its toll on the dealership, making the ordering of parts difficult and causing labor concerns. Bryce wanted Combs to take charge, and Combs spent about half a day talking with him about the position and the dealership's less than favorable monthly figures. Within Combs's first month of employment, those figures were back in the black.[188] Although the business had previously been in trouble, things improved, and the Durhams were happy with the turnaround.[189]

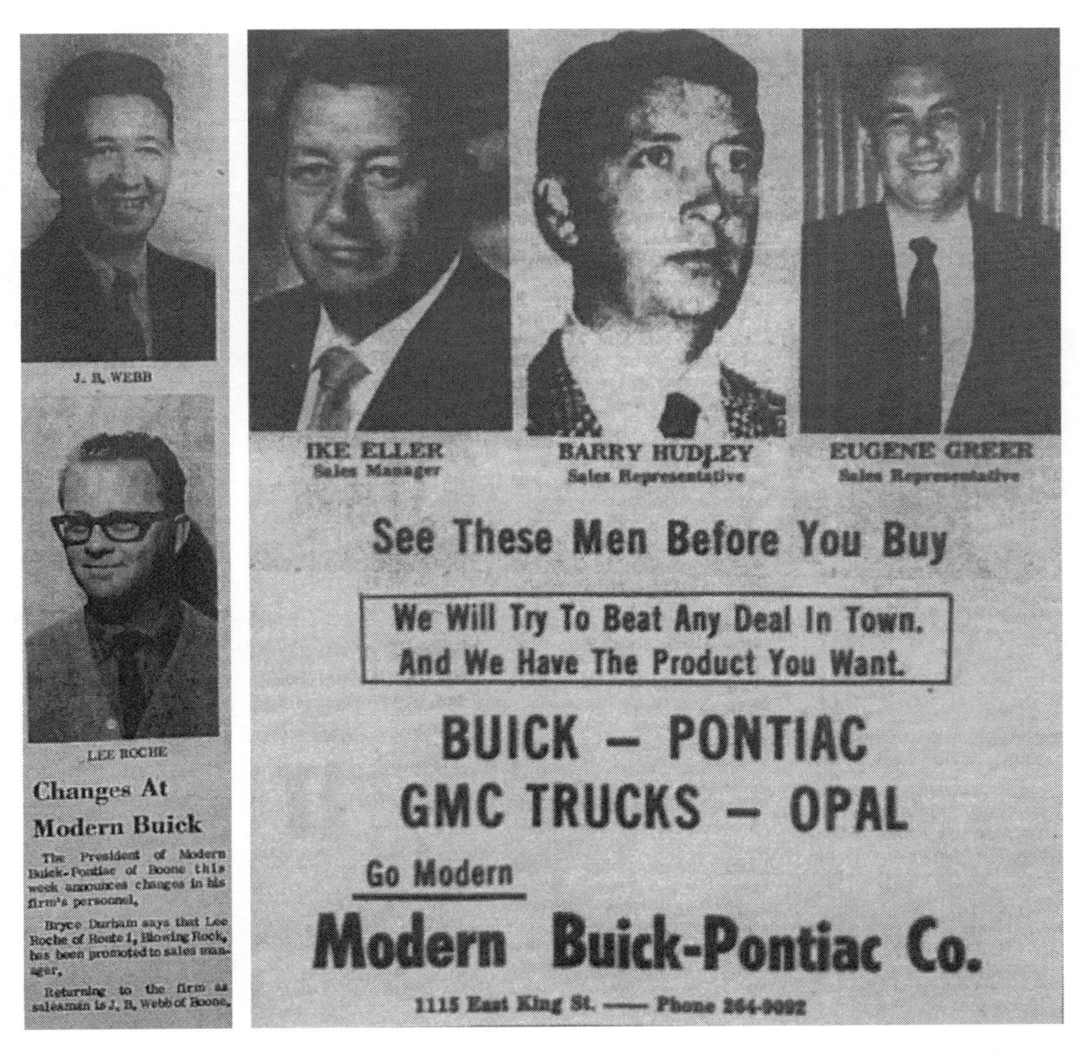

J. B. WEBB

LEE ROCHE

Changes At Modern Buick

The President of Modern Buick-Pontiac of Boone this week announces changes in his firm's personnel.

Bryce Durham says that Lee Roche of Route 1, Blowing Rock, has been promoted to sales manager.

Returning to the firm as salesman is J. B. Webb of Boone.

(As published in the Watauga Democrat; note Barry Hudler's surname is misspelled as Hudley)

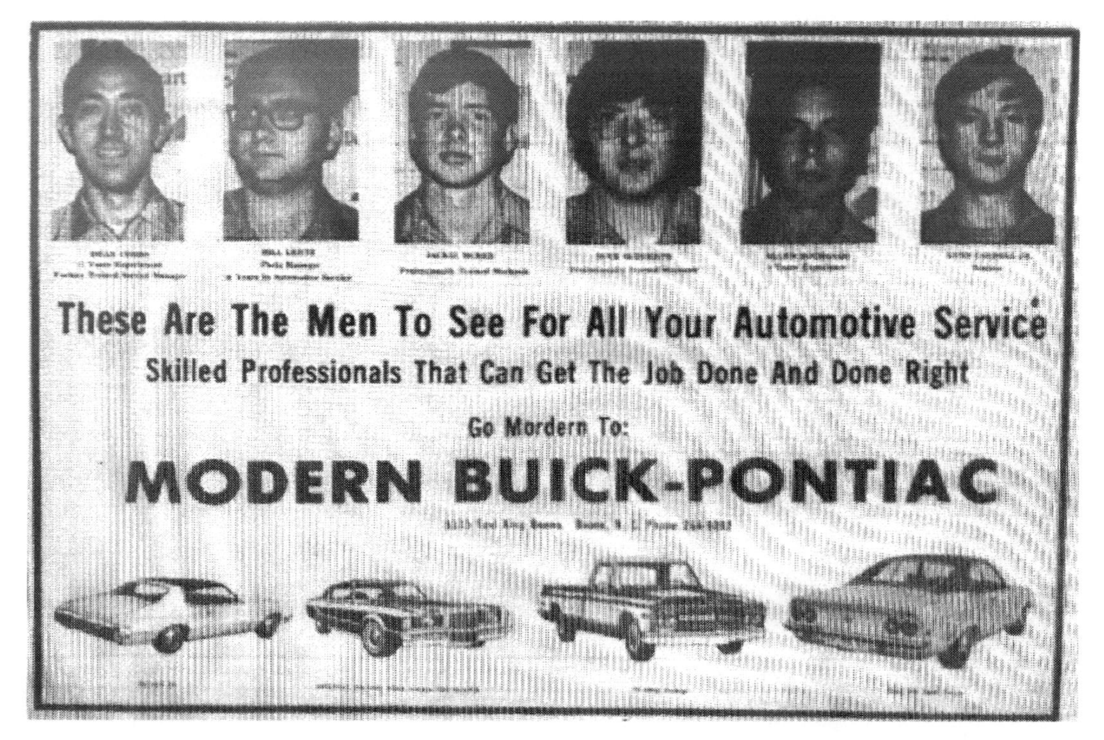

Employees (L-R) Dean Combs, Bill Lentz, Jackie McKee, Buck Sudderth, Allen Buchanan, & Lynn Carroll, Jr. (As published in the Watauga Democrat)

By this point in time, employee relationships with the Durhams seemed improved and favorable overall. Ike Eller liked Bryce and described him as "one of the best…you couldn't ask for a better man."[190] The two got along well, and Eller was about the happiest he had been in a long time.[191] Dean Combs thought the Durhams were nice, honest people, who treated him fairly:[192] "They all thought the world of Bryce. A man that couldn't get along with him, from what dealings I had with him, couldn't get along with himself 'cause he was soft-spoken, and yet he spoke with authority…on the business end of it. But he wasn't one of these screamers, you know, or nothing like that. Bryce seemed like an awful fine fellow. He had a fantastic personality." Combs never got to know Virginia very well because he had fewer dealings with her; she only occasionally called with a question about a repair order or a bill, but Combs felt she treated him well and was always nice to him.[193]

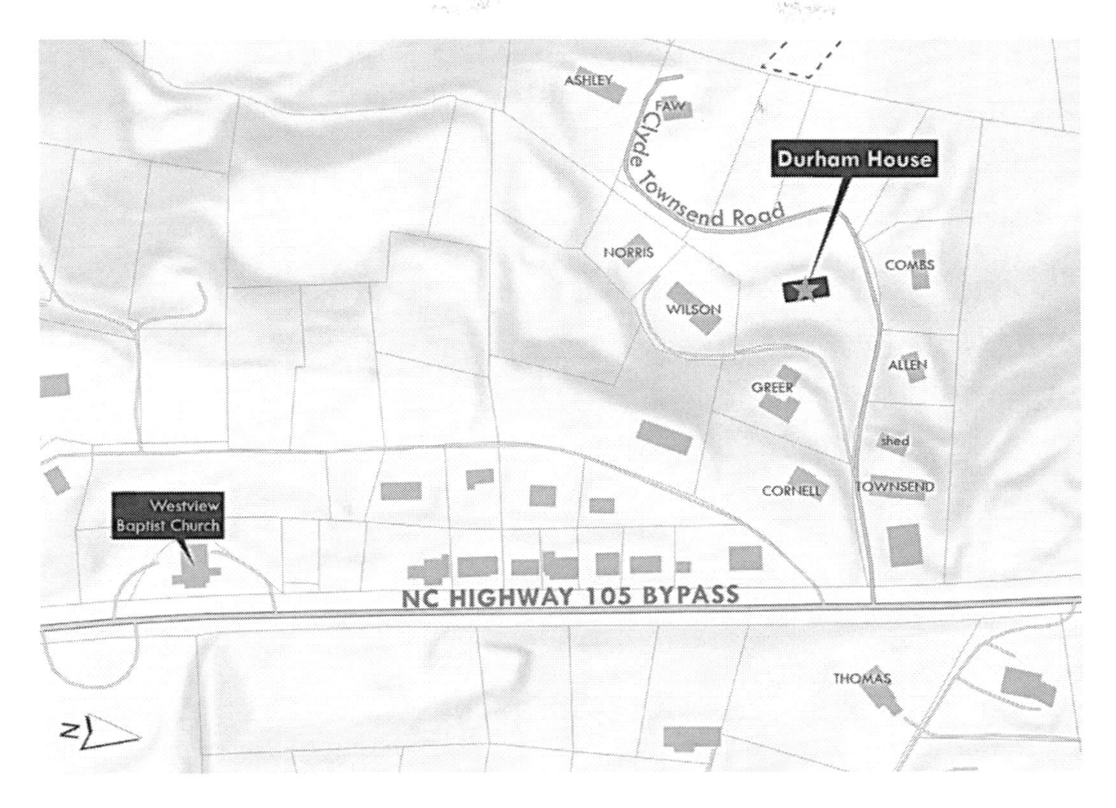

Meanwhile, the area around the Durhams' home was developing, and by February 1972, eight single family dwellings (including the Durhams') and two apartment buildings shared access to what would later be named Clyde Townsend Road.[d] As one faced the Durham residence, to the left and on the same hilltop were the homes of Clinard and Clara Wilson and Bill and Betty Norris. To the right of the Durhams were the homes of Dean and Opal Combs and Paul and Jane Allen. In a dead-end valley behind the Durhams were the adjacent homes of Bobby and Sheila Ashley and Bruce and Priscilla Faw. In front of and immediately below the Durhams was the home of Larry and Evelyn Greer, who had moved into their house in the summer of 1971.[194] Also, in front of and below the Durham house was the Clyde Townsend apartment complex, consisting of two buildings built between 1969 and 1970. The slightly older of the two sat along the 105 Bypass and contained eight apartments (numbers 1-8), "Snowflake" beauty shop (which belonged to Townsend's wife Snow), and Burkett & Stern, a surveying firm. The newer building sat behind the older and was comprised of four apartments (numbers 9-12) on the lower level, while two small apartments (numbers 13-14) and the more spacious residence of Clyde and Snow Townsend occupied the upper level.[195] Another home that also sat below the Durhams and along present-day Hodges Valley Road near its convergence with Clyde Townsend Road, was occupied by Jerry and Jeannie Cornell. Directly across the bypass, within clear view of the Durham residence, was the home of Lawrence and Lois Thomas. Many other homes were nearby, including those sitting along the 105 Bypass between Westview Baptist Church and Clyde Townsend Road.

---

[d] All mentions of "Clyde Townsend Road" between 1969 until circa 1997 are for points of reference only. The road was not officially named until the latter date when the 911 emergency system went into effect.

Clyde Townsend Road Households – February 1972

DURHAM: Bryce (51), Virginia (44), Bobby (18)

WILSON: Clinard (57), Clara (46)

NORRIS: Bill, Jr. (26), Betty (24), David (7)

ASHLEY: Bobby (26), Sheila (25), Scott (4)

FAW: Bruce, Sr. (28), Priscilla (29), Bruce, Jr. (8)

COMBS: Dean (35), Opal (33), Anita (11)

ALLEN: Paul, Jr. (27), Jane (23), Paul III (born Feb. 1)

GREER: Larry (23), Evelyn[e] (29)

TOWNSEND: Clyde (49), Snow (44), Mike (10)

Other Neighbors – February 1972

CORNELL: Jerry (29), Jeannie (26), Tommy (8), David "Beaver" (6), Jackie (1)

THOMAS: Lawrence (33), Lois (32), Daren (5), Paula (2), Denise (8 months)

Discounting the renters of Clyde Townsend's apartments,[f] each of these households, with the exception of the Wilsons and Greers, included children, who, in February 1972, collectively ranged in age from newborn to eighteen, Bobby Durham being the only teenager and the eldest of them all by at least seven years. The heads of these neighboring households – both husbands and wives – were in their twenties and thirties, the only exceptions being the Wilsons, the Townsends, and the Durhams. Clinard and Clara Wilson, aged 57 and 46, and Clyde and Snow Townsend, aged 49 and 44, were nearest in age to Bryce and Virginia Durham, 51 and 44.[196]

Of these neighbors, Clinard Wilson was a retired sheriff's deputy; Bill Norris, Jr. worked at his parents' restaurant in Boone; Larry Greer was an electrician; Jerry Cornell was a painter for the university;[197] and Clyde Townsend was a builder, real estate developer, and reserve sheriff's deputy.[198] By February 1972, Dean Combs worked at the Durhams' car dealership, while Paul Allen was employed as an accountant for a Boone insurance agency.[199] Bobby Ashley and Bruce Faw,

[e] Of all the individuals who lived in the Clyde Townsend Road neighborhood at the time of the 1972 murders, as of this writing, Evelyn Greer is the only remaining, original resident.

[f] The names of the occupants of Clyde Townsend's fourteen apartments have been forgotten with the exception of his son-in-law and daughter, Gary and Donna Townsend Cook (both age 22) and their children Gina (age 2) and Aaron (age 3 months), and the occupants of Apartment #9 – bachelor roommates Ricky Phillips (age 19), Lynn Greene (age 25), and Edward Lowrance (age 30).

who, like the Durhams, were natives of Wilkes County, were employed as the manager and meat manager, respectively, at the same grocery store.[200]

Among the neighborhood wives, Betty Norris worked as a secretary;[201] Clara Wilson was employed at Watauga House of Lighting;[202] Evelyn Greer was a nurse;[203] Opal Combs was employed by a women's garment manufacturer;[204] Jeannie Cornell worked for a local shoe factory;[205] and Snow Townsend ran her beauty shop. Stay-at-home moms Sheila Ashley and Priscilla Faw each had a young son and was expecting her next child;[206] and Jane Allen, a former schoolteacher, was the mother of a newborn.[207]

Durham home at top center. Clinard & Clara Wilson home at top left. Larry & Evelyn Greer home at center left. Jerry & Jeannie Cornell home at bottom left. Clyde Townsend apartments at right (Clyde Townsend & family occupied most of the upper level; Ricky Phillips, Lynn Greene, & Edward Lowrance lived in Apartment #9, visible at lower left of building. Image courtesy of Watauga County Sheriff's Office)

Durham home at left; Dean & Opal Combs home in background.
(Image courtesy of Watauga County Sheriff's Office)

Durham home in foreground; Lawrence & Lois Thomas home at far left in distance.
(Image courtesy of Watauga County Sheriff's Office)

Although Boone was on a progressive trajectory, it remained, in many ways, Small Town, USA. The *Watauga Democrat*, as any bucolic news publication was apt to do, covered citizens' life events from cradle to grave and all the community's activities and minutiae in between, from ballgames to beauty pageants, weather forecasts to women's fashion, and court proceedings to clearance sales. Just shy of over-the-fence or party line gossip, it heralded "personal mentions" of who was home for the holidays, who had visited whom, and who was in the hospital. But knowing one's neighbor as well as his business was oddly comforting and part of what made the place feel like home for its approximately 9,000 town citizens and 24,000 county residents.[208]

By the newspaper's estimation, no community had friendlier people than Wataugans, who would "speak to you on the street and accept you for face value."[209] But the Durhams were a bit reserved, and no one knew much about them.[210] Outside of their extended family, they did not visit others' homes, and no one came to theirs. According to Ginny Durham, her parents had no friends, no social life, "no nothing."[211] Despite the fact that, over a couple of years, the Durhams had gotten their dealership up and running and Bryce had joined the local chapter of the Rotary Club, where he was known "as a good, friendly Rotarian,"[212] opinions of the Durhams were mixed. The most commonly voiced descriptor was that they were "nice," but the family seemed not to have "establish[ed] a larger network of friends who really knew them as neighbors and business contacts." Local car dealer Lee Barnett, who was Bryce's fellow Rotarian and fellow church parishioner,[213] said Bryce was "a little quiet, but he was liked and looked up to."[214] Neighbors stated the Durhams to be "methodical, efficient, and systematic people who lived modestly and kept pretty much to themselves."[215] Bryce was not necessarily perceived as a people person or a great communicator.[216] Clyde Townsend, who lived less than a hundred yards away,[217] stated Bryce "was kind of distant [and] he liked to be left alone and to leave people alone."[218] He added that the Durhams "just kind of hung to themselves. They'd speak to you and talk with you, but they didn't socialize much."[219] Townsend's impression was echoed by neighbor Bill Norris, Jr., who found the Durhams friendly but, again, reluctant to mingle. In Norris's opinion, the Durhams were busy with their own lives but willing to wave and exchange greetings.[220] Eleven-year-old neighbor Anita Combs would wave at Bryce and Virginia, but she especially took every opportunity to wave at Bobby, who she had a crush on and who her father, Dean, occasionally gave a ride to the university. "All the little girls around there thought Bobby was just it; he was a good guy."[221] Neighbor Sheila Ashley observed the Durhams to be very quiet people, who were frequently gone from home.[222] Neighbors Bruce and Priscilla Faw never saw or spoke to the Durhams.[223] Neighbor Jane Allen did not know or recall speaking to them but recognized them as they came in and out of the neighborhood.[224]

When a local drycleaner stopped by the Durham home to inquire if the family would like to be added to his pickup route, he was told to go away and never come back.[225] But other Boone residents described Bryce and Virginia as approachable[226] and as good neighbors, quiet and hardworking.[227] While they put in long hours at the dealership, when warm weather and extended daylight allowed, they "puttered in the yard until dark,"[228] and Virginia kept their shrubbery in a neat row in front of their house.[229] As next-door neighbors whose lawns melded, the Durhams and Clinard and Clara Wilson "would visit back and forth from time to time," and according to the Wilsons, theirs "was one of the closest friendships the Durhams had made among their neighbors."[230] According to Mrs. Wilson, "Virginia and Bryce Durham, together with the rest of their family, were marvelous people. I don't think we ever had such neighbors who could compare with them."[231] Mr. Wilson added, "You wouldn't want to live next to any nicer people. They were good people. I'd say the best."[232] On the whole, "Bryce and Virginia were well-liked and respected."[233]

Foibles and flaws aside, the clean-cut, conservative, civic-minded, churchgoing Durhams seemed, in most ways, the epitome of the all-American family, and as far as anyone looking in from the outside could determine, life was good.

Meanwhile, "Boone Town" was becoming a boomtown, and it grew so rapidly that Southern Bell ran out of new telephone numbers to issue.[234] But too rapid a growth was warned against. A report compiled for the Watauga County Board of Commissioners and the Watauga County Planning Board, stated "the 'good life of plenty' which most Wataugans enjoy today did not exist a few short years ago. The 'good life' will not exist just a few short years hence unless programs are planned and initiated to direct and control the growth which will, from all present indications, continue over the next several years…. The county has seen during the last decade an abundance of growth, growth that is somewhat shocking…."[235]

Growth also brought an upward trend in crime and violence. The *Watauga Democrat* noted, "Criminals still constitute a very small percentage of the overall population, but we are reminded that the chances are growing from month to month and year to year that your time will come, and your person or property will fall prey to the criminal who respects neither. In Boone and Blowing Rock and the county at large we have been relatively free from the principal crimes of violence, but burglary has become common, larceny is commonplace and property rights are not secure like they used to be. However, we have fared relatively well, due to the basic quality of our citizenship and to generally active law enforcement efforts. But even the extent of crime locally, barring murder, rape and arson is high and may be expected to rise with the tide of growth…. So, our crime rate has become a matter of concern."[236]

One night in 1970, the Durhams experienced this firsthand when someone attempted to break into their home.[237] That same year, upon receiving news of a Watauga County native being found murdered near Gastonia, North Carolina, the *Watauga Democrat* wrote, "Those of us who've lived so long in this generally peaceful valley are inclined to reason that sinister things can't happen here: things like killing people who are going about their business in orderly fashion…. This sort of thing has become commonplace in other parts of the country but the full impact of the criminality raging over the land is felt only when one of our citizens is the victim…. Let us remember things like this can actually happen right here in Boone."[238] Indeed they could, and indeed they would, even threefold.

By the time the Durham family pulled into town, exciting things were happening on all fronts in Boone, North Carolina, but in sharp contrast to its progress and the upbeat demeanor of its hopeful citizens with their eyes cast toward the future was a darkly regressive moment in early 1972 that would, for a time, eclipse the community's bright outlook. In that particular moment, Boone, its tourist-attracting charm aside, became the repulsive setting for the grisly and heart-wrenching murders of Bryce, Virginia, and Bobby Durham. What the 1969 study on growth had predicted – that the "good life" here would "not exist just a few short years hence" – became a solemn reality for this family, but for far different and more awful reasons. The year that celebrated the 100th anniversary of the birth of Boone also mourned the deaths of the Durhams.

A little more than a century earlier, Charles Dickens had penned, "It was the best of times…it was the epoch of light…it was the spring of hope…" – words that could fairly describe the era of growth and prosperity that Boone was experiencing. But what happened to the Durhams could likewise be described by the contrasting words of Dickens: “It was the worst of times…it was the season of darkness…it was the winter of despair.”[239]

CHAPTER 2

STORM WARNING

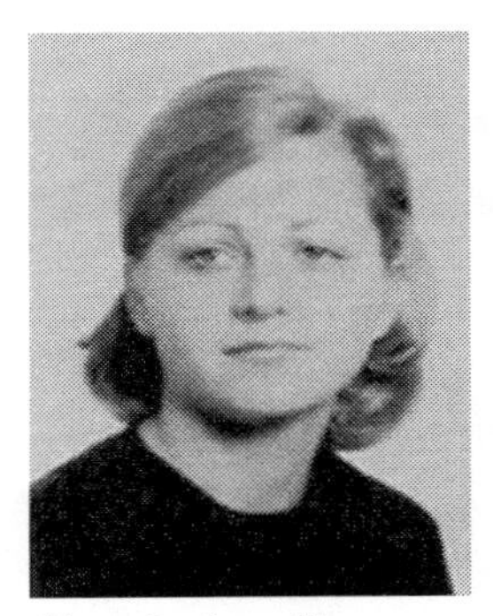

Ginny Durham (Source: 1971 Rhododendron, University Archives and Records, Special Collections, Appalachian State University, Boone, NC)

By the spring of 1971, nineteen-year-old Ginny Durham, while continuing her studies at Appalachian State University, had begun dating another nineteen-year-old student, Troy Hall, who had entered ASU in the fall quarter of 1969.[240] Troy's brother, Claude Hall, had a house trailer, and as early as 1970, Troy had sought to move it into the Greenway Trailer Park on the southeastern side of Boone. Troy and another brother, Ray Hall, were in the trailer moving business, and they left cards in the mailboxes of the trailer park's residents, one of whom was Cecil Small, the park's past middle-age and disabled co-manager. Small was a private detective and former security guard who lived in a corner lot trailer with his wife Mildred. Once Small let Troy know he had found a trailer space for him – two doors behind his own trailer – the Halls moved theirs in, and Troy occupied it.[241] One of Troy's roommates was fellow freshman Charlie Overcash. They had met in class and agreed to share the trailer their sophomore year.[242] Others who periodically inhabited the trailer were Ray Hall and Troy's friend and fellow ASU student, Billy "Babes" Lowe, whose family founded and owned Lowe's Foods and Lowe's Hardware in North Wilkesboro, North Carolina.[243]

Troy Hall (high school photo)

Despite the Durham family's move to Boone, Bryce, Virginia, Ginny, and Bobby maintained a close relationship with Bryce's extended family in Wilkes County and tried to visit them every Sunday, but the visits were soon affected by Ginny's relationship with Troy, who Bryce and Virginia knew next to nothing about. During a May 1971 visit at Bryce's parents' house, Bryce's sister, Gayle Mauldin, asked where Ginny was. Virginia said Ginny was dating a Hall boy and asked Gayle if she knew any Halls from North Wilkesboro, adding that Troy lived there with his Grandfather Hall in the Finley Park community (where "high rollers" and upper class "movers and shakers" lived in "beautiful and equally expensive homes"). When Virginia and Gayle failed to find any Finley Park Halls in the phone book, Virginia wondered if Troy lived with his maternal relatives instead. Virginia had further understood Troy's parents were deceased, and his late father's name was

Harold, but on a separate occasion, when Bryce's mother asked Ginny what Troy's father's name was, Ginny replied that she did not know and had never asked him.[244]

Despite this ambiguity, Ginny and Troy forged ahead in their relationship and, two weeks later, announced they had married in York, South Carolina.[245][g] Bryce and Virginia reportedly detested Troy from the start,[246] and they were initially convinced Ginny was pregnant. Once it was clear she had not "shamed the family," their attitude toward her and Troy improved for a while.[247] Meanwhile, Ginny informed her grandmother and other Durham relatives about the nuptials via telephone. A day or two later, Bryce's mother and sister traveled from Wilkes County to Boone to meet Ginny's new husband. Bryce forewarned his mother. "Why," she asked. "Is he a hippy?" Bryce contemptibly replied, "Hippy? He's worse than a hippy."[248] Bryce told his mother to hold her tongue and said they were going to try to make the best of it.[249]

When Troy met Ginny's family, he arrogantly believed he could talk them into liking him,[250] and he shared with Gayle Mauldin that all his family resided in Florida, explaining that, since they were unable to attend the wedding, he and Ginny had not invited her relatives.[251] Troy went on to say his parents (alive after all) were divorced, and his father, a wealthy Miami stockbroker, owned a private Learjet. Troy added if anyone wanted a free hop to California or elsewhere, just to let him know. Not wanting to rely on his father's wealth, Troy said he wanted to prove to him he could make it on his own. He already owned four trailers – three he was renting to fellow college students and the one he and Ginny were living in. Troy also said that, although he had been educated at a military school, he knew a lot of people in Wilkes County where he frequently visited his grandfather in Finley Park.[252]

Bryce and Virginia wanted the best for their children, and despite Troy's fanciful tales of grandeur, he was not their first choice for Ginny.[h] By summertime, family tensions had grown as a result of Ginny's relationship with Troy, who she defended during vehement arguments with her parents. Despite the strain, there were conciliatory moments such as when Bryce had an air conditioner installed in Troy's and Ginny's trailer,[253] and when he bought a raincoat for Ginny.[254] Shortly after her marriage, Bryce also gave Ginny use of one of the dealership's cars. She and Troy subsequently attended a Saturday night party, where Troy overindulged in cheese and vomited all over the car's interior. Bobby cleaned up the mess, and Bryce, no longer intending the car to benefit Troy, reallocated it to Bobby, a move that upset Ginny.[255]

Soon, the family's Sunday visits with Bryce's parents in Wilkes County no longer included Ginny, and Collie Durham attributed this to Ginny running off and marrying Troy.[256] Ginny said her father, in particular, opposed her marriage to Troy;[257] according to Bryce's mother, Bryce "was dead set against" it.[258] Despite Troy's statement that the Durhams had not been invited to the wedding, Ginny claimed they had refused to attend.[259] At the end of August 1971, however, it came to light

[g] Although no marriage license was issued for Troy Hall and Ginny Durham by York County officials, it is possible they were married there pursuant to a marriage license having been issued by some other South Carolina county or jurisdiction. [Source: York County, South Carolina Probate Court. Phone conversations with author. June 15 & 16, 2022.]

[h] Ironically, Ginny would state years later that she believed Troy to be exactly like her mother. [Source: Mackie, Ginny Durham. Interview with Carolynn Johnson & Wade Colvard. December 7, 2020.]

Ginny and Troy had not been married in May in South Carolina as they had claimed but had merely been living together. They subsequently revealed they were married in late August.[260i]

During Troy's and Ginny's co-occupancy of Troy's trailer, neighbors observed a lot of foot traffic there, and among their visitors were other trailer park neighbors, college friends, and Troy's brothers Ray and John.[261] Other frequent visitors were various young men, who neighbor Cecil Small believed to be homosexuals based on phone conversations he overheard. Oddly, Small and his wife Mildred had inside their trailer an extension to Troy's and Ginny's phone. Because Troy and his brother Ray did not want to miss any calls pertaining to their trailer-moving business, they asked the Smalls if they could have an extension installed in their home. The Smalls agreed, and the Hall brothers paid the Smalls' phone bill. From that point onward, the Smalls had two separate phones in their den – one for their own line and one for Troy's and Ginny's.[262] If no one in the Hall home answered by the fifth ring, the Smalls would answer the extension and take a message.[263]

On one occasion at the Halls' trailer, Troy showed Cecil Small and a propane truck driver several photographs of nude men and women engaged in sexual activity, including homosexual acts. Some of the photos had been taken by Troy, and others were taken by an acquaintance in a downtown Boone apartment. Among those depicted were individuals close to Troy, including a male friend who was a former Greenway Trailer Park neighbor and fellow university student. Other individuals associated with the propane company likewise confirmed seeing these or similar photos. When the company's manager, Joe Shuford, went to the Halls' trailer to deliver propane and discuss a past due bill, he saw on a wall pictures of nude people involved in all kinds of acts. Troy also pulled out a large stack of other photos of nude subjects and showed them to Shuford and two of Shuford's co-workers. One of them later described the photos as "rough," and Shuford declared them to be the worst he had ever seen.[264] In addition to showing these photographs to Small, Troy told him if he knew anyone from out of town looking for a good time to have them contact Troy and he, implying cash for sex, would make sure Small got a share of the money.[265]

In addition to being involved in these sexually oriented activities, "Troy was strongly rumored to be involved with drugs and drug trafficking."[266] A basketball buddy and visitor to the Hall trailer knew Troy smoked marijuana,[267] and drugs were reportedly being transported from Wilkes County to Troy's home.[268] According to Ginny, Troy was into Quaaludes.[269] Originally prescribed as a sedative to treat anxiety and insomnia, those who abused the drug could experience a euphoric effect – a "really powerful high" – as well as a level of relaxation that enabled "freer sex."[270] There were also rumors that Troy may have been involved in Satanic cult activities, and he reportedly checked out as many books as possible from the Appalachian State University library on the subject of devil worship.[271]

---

[i] Troy's and Ginny's marriage date is erroneously stated to be May 1971 in Ron Alridge's "Unlikely Victims: Killings of 'Friendly' Boone Family Baffle Town," *The Charlotte Observer*, Charlotte, NC, February 6, 1972, p. 1C. Within court documents pertaining to their separation and divorce, Ginny and Troy agreed in one instance that they were married in Caldwell County, NC and in another instance that they were married in McDowell County, NC, but there is no record of their marriage in either location. Another source erroneously states they were married at the Watauga County Courthouse in Boone. [Sources: Divorce decree, The General Court of Justice, Yadkin Co., NC, District Court Division File & Docket No. 76 CVD 185; Confession of Judgment, The General Court of Justice, Superior Court Division, Wilkes County, NC, Ginny Durham Hall (Plaintiff) vs. Troy Hall, Individually, Carolina Construction Company of North Wilkesboro, Inc., Troy Hall, Incorporator (Defendants), February 27, 1976; McDowell County, NC Register of Deeds Office phone conversation with author, May 19, 2022; Caldwell County, NC Register of Deeds Office phone conversation with author, September 16, 2022; York, Debbie. "Cold Weather-Cold Hearts," 2012, unpublished.]

While the era of the late 1960s and early 1970s encapsulated a counterculture characterized by "free love" and drug experimentation, Troy and those in his circle were pushing boundaries, and uncomfortably so for the conservative Durhams. Ginny's parents were distressed by their belief that Troy, who was considered "trouble"[272] and was described as both a "thug"[273] and a "mean person,"[274] was having a negative influence on her. Dark clouds were beginning to encompass the once close-knit family, and stormier days were fast approaching. By the fall of 1971, family relationships were in turmoil, and things were going from bad to worse between Troy and his in-laws.[275] He referred to Bryce as his "old rich dad-in-law"[276] and to Virginia as a "fester-minded bitch."[277] According to sales manager Ike Eller, the Durhams, Troy, and Ginny were "always into it over something."[278]

In November 1971, Gayle Mauldin gave birth to her second child, and Ginny and Troy went to the hospital in Wilkes County to visit Gayle and see the new baby. When Gayle inquired if Bryce and Virginia were coming, Ginny replied, "I don't know. We don't speak." When conversing later with her brother, Gayle asked Bryce about this, and he explained Ginny and Troy were angry because they believed Bryce should give them a new car. Troy had told Bryce he owed it to them, that it was due them. Bryce refused, telling Troy, "When you get a new Buick, you'll buy it." Later on, feeling sympathetic toward Ginny, Bryce gave her a car she could drive to her classes, but Troy drove it out of town, putting more than 5,000 miles on it in a week's time and burning out the motor. The car had to be pulled into the garage by a wrecker. Bryce suspected this was a drug trip, and when he asked what happened, Troy refused to explain. When Bryce berated him, Troy threw the keys at Virginia and left. On a similar occasion, the Durhams discovered that a car from the dealership Ginny had been driving had been taken on a 2,500-mile trip, and they suspected Troy had used it to make a drug run to Mexico.[279]

Even Troy's presence at the dealership became problematic.[280] There were rumors he "was running some stuff out of Florida in some of the demo cars,"[281] and on a few occasions, while cars were being loaded at the dealership to take to auction, Bryce observed Troy on the top rack of the car hauler, putting something inside the cars' glove boxes. Rather than confront him, Bryce waited until Troy was off premises, and, upon checking the glove boxes, found marijuana and some other drug he was unfamiliar with.[j] According to Cecil Small, until around the first of December 1971, Troy consistently brought home new vehicles from the lot, including several four-wheel drives, and showed them off to Small.[282] But after Bryce learned Troy was dealing in stolen goods and witnessed him making a drug deal in the late fall of 1971, he took the cars away.[283] Having become aware Troy was "messing in dope," Bobby Durham confronted Troy and Ginny about it at the dealership, telling them Bryce no longer wanted Troy hanging around there as he was trying to run a respectable business and did not want Troy ruining it.[284] Troy's friend "Babes" Lowe was a known drug addict and small-time drug dealer,[k] and another of Troy's acquaintances was twenty-seven-year-old Alfred Conrad "A. C." Greene, Jr., a native of Watauga County, who lived in Wilkesboro. Troy and A. C. were sometimes seen together at the dealership and reportedly had dope on the car

---

[j] Virginia Durham confided this to her niece Jerri and to her [Virginia's] sister Sally. [Source: Edwards, Diana (Virginia Durham's great-niece). Phone interview with author. October 14, 2023.]

[k] When Lowe was interviewed by Watauga County Sheriff Red Lyons concerning Troy Hall in 1994, he was a resident of a drug rehabilitation center, but his habit eventually overcame him. [Sources: Ted Brown. Phone conversation with author. May 20, 2022; William Asa Lowe, interview with James C. Lyons, June 27, 1994, Watauga County Sheriff's Office investigation file 118-H-1/2/3.]

lot. Bryce ran them off,[285] and when Troy kept returning and hanging out, Bryce repeatedly banished him.[286]

Mechanic Lester Reece witnessed a heated disagreement between Troy and Bryce,[287] and service manager Dean Combs similarly witnessed the family fighting heavily and loudly among themselves at the dealership.[288] Bryce and Virginia did not want Troy to be part of their lives or business,[289] and according to Combs, by the time he [Combs] started his employment at the dealership in December, "They had done put the skids in under [Troy's] feet," and Troy was not around the agency much afterwards.[290] Soon after, Troy called Bryce and told him neither he nor Ginny would be back, he didn't need Bryce's help, and he didn't "want a damn thing he had." Bryce told Troy that was fine and asked him, "How about returning my TV and other things?" Bryce then sent a truck to retrieve the television from their trailer. Meanwhile, some items from the Durham home had gone missing, including an $1,800 savings account book, and Bryce decided to change the locks on the house[291] and the dealership.[292] The house locks were reportedly changed three times,[293] and service manager Ike Eller changed those at the dealership.[294]

Realizing Ginny needed money, and rather than just giving it to her, Bryce offered her an opportunity to work in the dealership's office. By this time, however, Troy had become increasingly controlling of her, and whenever Ginny went into her father's office, Troy followed. Virginia felt Troy would not allow Ginny to work unless he stood over her to ensure she did not talk to her parents. Virginia told Ginny she could come to work in the office if she wanted to, but to "be sure she left 'that thing' [i.e., Troy] somewhere else."[295] Ginny did work at the dealership, including the parts department, until her relationship with her mother became unbearable.[296]

When Bryce's brother Bill saw him at their parents' home in Wilkes County at Thanksgiving in 1971, he thought Bryce was very quiet and not himself.[297] While Bryce and Virginia still occasionally visited Ginny and Troy, a big wedge remained between them. By December, Bryce stopped going inside their trailer and sat on the front porch or stayed inside the car reading a newspaper while Virginia entered.[298] Troy had apparently made some effort to take over the dealership, and around early December 1971, Bryce confided to a friend that he feared Troy and was worried Troy was going to kill him.[299] Likewise, Virginia was afraid Troy would kill her and Ginny[300] or perhaps set fire to the Durham home since Troy had previously threatened his in-laws, saying, "I will take care of you all,"[301] and had constantly "talk[ed] about how he would get money someday and [return] to Wilkes County and show these people."[302]

Bobby worried about Ginny.[303] They had remained close and kept in contact,[304] and on occasions when Troy was gone several nights, Bobby stayed with her.[305] Because of the strain between Ginny and their parents, they kept Bobby's visits from their father.[306] Ginny never complained about Troy and never explained his whereabouts. When Gayle Mauldin asked Virginia if Troy ever beat Ginny, Virginia stated she had told him "if she ever saw a mark that he put on Ginny Sue, she would kill him." She added, "I'd kill that bastard if it's the last thing I ever did." Even mild-mannered Bobby had been driven to threaten Troy with bodily harm. Bobby and Troy had begrudgingly put up with one another and generally stayed away from each other, but Bobby, tired of Troy mocking him, told him if the abuse continued, he would beat him up.[307] At some point, even Troy's friend "Babes" Lowe grew tired of him and no longer cared to be around him because he was scared of him and some of the things he was involved in.[308]

While returning to Boone from a trip to Mount Airy to visit old friends, Bobby stopped to see Durham relatives in Wilkes County and told them Troy was part of a theft ring, either helping steal or handling stolen property for someone else. He said Troy's trailer was full of items such as radios, cameras, and cassette recorders, but on subsequent visits, those items would be gone or replaced by others.[309] Bobby stated that, although he and his parents weren't sure, they thought Troy was "involved with a bunch from Asheville," North Carolina, and Bryce was going to find out.[310]

Despite the family's estrangement and the Durhams feeling threatened by Troy, there seemingly was a sort of holiday truce, with Bryce even buying a shirt as a Christmas present for Troy. Aware it was too large, Bryce gave it to him anyway, perhaps a gift symbolically "wrapped" with underlying disregard. The family ate what must have been an awkward dinner at the Durham home on Christmas Eve. Although Troy would later claim he and Ginny spent the night, implying a more congenial relationship with his in-laws, a neighbor stated the couple left the Durham home long before dark. Bryce's sister and mother frequently teased Bryce about the television program *All in the Family*, which had premiered that year. Comparing character Archie Bunker's son-in-law, Mike "Meathead" Stivic, to Troy, they told Bryce all he needed was for Ginny and Troy to move in with him. This upset Bryce, and he said, "Let me tell you one thing. Troy Hall has never spent one night in my house, and he never will as long as I live."[311][i]

At one point, Bryce learned via a letter from Charlotte, North Carolina that Troy had attempted to borrow money and stated he was a salaried employee at Modern Buick-Pontiac. Bryce informed the potential lender Troy was not an employee of the firm and never would be.[312] Around January 1972, Bryce and Dick Patterson, with whom Bryce had previously conducted business and had almost partnered with in Bryce's Boone dealership, reportedly "had bad trouble" as well as a heated discussion, which was believed to be about Troy, who somehow was connected to Patterson, although the exact circumstances were not revealed.[313]

January 1972 was also full of family developments. That month, Bobby paid what would be his last visit to his Durham grandparents in Wilkes County. When his grandmother asked him what he knew about Ginny Sue and Troy, he said he knew plenty and had something really important to tell her, but he would wait until his next visit.[314] In mid-to late January, on a date with Jackie Vines, Bobby confided to her about his family and their troubles with his sister, stemming from her involvement with Troy. As the couple passed the Durham home en route to Jackie's, Bobby pointed out where he and his parents lived and stated, "We can't stand Troy Hall." When Jackie asked what was wrong, Bobby said it was so bad they couldn't talk about it. However, just prior to arriving at Jackie's home, he pulled into the parking lot of a nearby business and shared that, although the family loved Ginny, she was estranged from them and had been completely cut off by their parents, who indicated to her that, as long as she was with Troy, she would remain apart from them.[315] Another friend remembered Bobby sharing some of these same family dynamics but did not recall Bobby saying anything derogatory about his brother-in-law.[316]

That same month, Bryce and Virginia learned the truth about Troy's origins – that he was not from a wealthy family and his parents did not live in Florida. In fact, sales manager Ike Eller knew Troy's

---

[i] Bryce's brother, Bill Durham, was under the impression that Troy and Ginny, for a time within the several month period they claimed to be married but were not, lived with Bryce, Virginia, and Bobby. According to Ginny, Troy visited her parents' home perhaps six times, including Christmas and other holidays. [Sources: Durham, Bill. Interview with Len Hagaman, Kelly Redmon, Carolynn Johnson, Wade Colvard, Larry Wagner, & Rufus Edmisten. August 6, 2019; Mackie, Ginny Durham. Interview with Carolynn Johnson & Wade Colvard. December 7, 2020.]

entire family in Wilkes County and told Virginia about them. She and Bryce subsequently investigated, and Virginia told her sister-in-law Gayle where each one of Troy's family members lived, adding that they were "trash."[317]

Troy Hall was born in 1951 in North Wilkesboro, and he and his twin brother Roy were the two youngest of eight children born to Robert "Rob" and Carrie Waddell Hall.[318] At the age of not quite four months, Roy died of acute enterocolitis. An older sister, Ruth, had similarly died of colitis at the age of not quite five months in 1939. Other siblings were Claude (1932), Lois (1934), Dorothy (1936), John (1941), and Ray (1943).[319] At the time of Troy's birth, the Halls resided in Wilkesboro[320] and later lived in the basement of a store they operated near the North Wilkesboro city limits.[321] Over time, Troy's father farmed and worked for the Work Projects Administration (WPA) and as a furniture factory laborer.[322] An alcoholic, Rob Hall disciplined Troy by smacking him across the face or hitting his legs with a switch, in a manner which Troy later described as "heavy." While Troy denied any other forms of abuse and never acquired scars from his punishments or had to be taken to a hospital, he admitted having "a difficult childhood." Although Troy claimed he had no childhood health problems,[323] a fourth-grade classmate recalled Troy telling him he had stomach ulcers, which was the reason Troy was served milk and crackers at school throughout the day.[324] According to Troy, he never missed developmental milestones and had no learning disabilities, although he did suffer two concussions around the age of eleven or twelve. When he was twelve, his parents separated but were reconciled. At age fourteen, he left home to live with one of his brothers.[325]

Rather than attending military school as he had told the Durhams, Troy attended part of his grade school years at Fairplains Elementary School before transferring to North Wilkesboro Elementary School. Described as very bright and mature for his age, he was reportedly able to skip some grade levels by way of early promotion,[326] although he was part of Wilkes Central High School's Class of 1969[327] at the age of eighteen, a normal age for someone completing secondary school. While in high school, he took advanced classes and earned As and Bs.[328]

The Hall family was close knit – some said clannish[329] – and Troy and his brother Ray were inseparable. They were also very close with John Frazier,[330] who was in the same high school class as Ray.[331] The Halls and Frazier aspired to be like the affluent young men who resided in the monied and upscale Finley Park community of North Wilkesboro, including Billy "Babes" Lowe and his brother Jimmy (heirs to the Lowe's Hardware and Lowe's Foods fortune), Tom Eller (son of Ike Eller), Tom Ingle (whose family owned an oil company and who later played professional football for the Chicago Bears), Ed Finley (future Chairman of the North Carolina Utilities Commission), John Swofford (future athletic director at the University of North Carolina at Chapel Hill and later commissioner of the Atlantic Coast Conference),[332] and Swofford's older brother, William Oliver Swofford (who became an American pop singer by the singular name of "Oliver").[333]

The W. Kerr Scott Dam and Reservoir, a manmade lake, was completed in Wilkesboro in 1962,[334] when many of these young men were teenagers, and some of them eventually acquired boats. Troy and Ray Hall spent a lot of time together at the lake,[335] and John Frazier's father owned the Trading Post, a store that sold boats among other things. While Frazier and the Halls were friendly with some of these wealthier young men, they were more like hangers-on and wannabes. This seemed especially true of Troy and his relationship with "Babes" Lowe, Troy being mostly interested in what he could gain from their friendship and what "Babes" could do for him. While Tom Eller was acquainted with the Halls, he thought them to be very sketchy and tried to keep them at arm's length.

Eller believed Troy helped supply "Babes" with drugs, and he thought Troy to be a weaselly huckster who could weave a big tale.[336]

With newly acquired knowledge of Troy's familial background, and considering that things had deteriorated so badly, Bryce and Virginia decided to contact their attorney to revise their wills. "They had had all of Troy Hall they could stand." Virginia believed him to be the biggest liar she had ever encountered, and Bryce wanted him out of his business, and Ginny too, as long as she remained with Troy.[337] One particular Wednesday around mid-January 1972, which coincided with a local newspaper article about the importance of making a will to satisfactorily handle one's estate and to decide how it would be distributed after one's death,[338] Bryce and Virginia left Ike Eller in charge of the dealership while they conducted some personal business. Upon their return, Virginia waved a document in her hand. It was their new will *(presumably a copy of either Bryce's or Virginia's as they each would have had their own)*, and she let Eller read it. Bryce subsequently invited Eller into his office and told him to spread word about the new will in Wilkes County so Troy's friends and relatives would hear about it. In Eller's words, Bryce "wanted to make sure that all those damn Halls knew about the will and exactly what was in it." And what was in it was the provision of a $1 inheritance for Ginny, with the remainder of their estates going to Bobby. When Eller informed "Babes" Lowe of the new will, Lowe, in turn, shared the news with Troy, who reportedly hung his head and walked away.[339]

The newly revised will became a hot topic of conversation among the dealership's employees, who referred to it as "the dollar will." Soon after, Virginia informed Bryce's family their new wills were in place and "no matter what happens to us, Troy Hall won't get one penny." She further shared she had informed Troy of the same, shaking her finger in his face and telling him, "You'll never get a damn thing we've worked for." Virginia laughed in the retelling of it, saying, "Boy, that made me feel good." According to Bryce's sister Gayle, when Bobby told his Grandmother Durham his parents' new will left everything to him, Mrs. Durham told Bryce he couldn't do that. "Bryce, you know you love Ginny Sue." But Bryce, disappointed in Ginny's behavior, replied, "I don't intend to do anything for her except see that she gets medicine if she's sick and see that she has something to eat."[340]

To cap it off, in late January Bobby returned home from school one day to discover Troy in the otherwise unoccupied Durham home "looking for things."[341] According to Cecil Small, Troy believed Virginia had found and confiscated the nude photos in his and Ginny's trailer, and he may have been in the house hoping to recover them[342] or possibly the new will. Two months earlier, while checking the heat in the Halls' trailer, Small had looked for the photos that Troy previously showed him, but they were gone.[343] According to Small, Troy believed Virginia's knowledge of the photos was the basis of his [Troy's] banishment from the dealership as well as Virginia's threats to get Ginny fired from her job at the university laundry.[344] Aware of this possibility, Ginny asked her supervisor around the second week of January if her mother called and told things about her, could she be fired. Her supervisor told her as long as she did her job, she had nothing to worry about. Ginny also confided that her parents told her she could no longer enter their home; they had changed the locks, and her key would no longer work. She added that Bryce and Virginia gave her dog to Bobby. The supervisor had never seen anyone as bitter toward their parents.[345] *[Ginny later denied she ever had these conversations with her laundry co-worker.[346]]*

Virginia believed something funny was going on as she learned Troy had never told anyone in North Wilkesboro he was married, and suddenly his siblings Ray, John, and Lois Hall Sebastian, were in

Boone all the last week of January and were in and out of the dealership with Troy and Ginny. In particular, Virginia commented numerous times to Bryce's family about Ray Hall, who was the only one of Troy's siblings she met. She was disturbed that he had been coming into the agency and looking around, staying a little while and then leaving. She was mistrustful of him and did not like him to look at her. At night, while the Hall siblings were together in Boone, they went out to undisclosed locations, and Lois left her children with Ginny, who babysat them at the trailer even though she had been sick. This angered Virginia, and she vowed she would get to the bottom of it.[347]

During the last week of January, Cecil Small witnessed Troy, with a bag or pouch hanging from his shoulder, pacing back and forth in his [Troy's] driveway until a red, white-topped Volkswagen Squareback with wide rear wheels arrived to pick him up. Small was familiar with the vehicle, having seen it at Troy's on prior occasions during which young men (characterized by Small's wife Mildred as "a bunch of weird hoodlums") would enter the Hall trailer while Ginny waited outside, sitting in the car until they left. The driver was a large man, approximately thirty years old, and another passenger or two were inside. Troy entered the back seat of the car, and they left, returning a short time later. The Smalls believed Troy was dealing dope.[348]

On Sunday, January 30, 1971, Bryce and Virginia and Bryce's parents paid a visit to Gayle Mauldin's home. Bobby had stayed in Boone to study for exams, and Virginia shared that he had been very nervous lately. Gayle inquired about Ginny, and Virginia said she had not seen her since the previous Wednesday and that Ginny had been sick and out of school again all week, so she and Bryce had taken some food by her trailer. Collie Durham asked if Bryce went inside, and Virginia responded, "God, no," and said she just sat the food inside the door. *[Ginny would later contradict this, testifying she and Troy ate supper with her parents on Saturday, January 29.]*[349]

The family then walked over to see Gayle's and her husband Charles's new house, and Bryce and Virginia expressed their concerns about Ginny's school performance and Troy's influence on her. Virginia said Troy was such a liar, that she and Bryce were living for the day Ginny left him, and that Ginny would surely come to her senses soon. They had promised to help her all they could, even sending her to any college in the world she wanted to attend, on the condition she leave Troy. As Bryce stood on the top deck of the new house with his hands in his pockets, looking out at the mountains, Gayle thought he looked quite sad. He was pale and stressed and seemed to have something heavy on his mind. She asked Bryce if the things weighing on him were making an old man out of him. He replied, "No, I think they're trying to make a dead man out of me."[350]

CHAPTER 3

THE LONG WINTER'S NIGHT

Snow began falling around 3:00 PM on Thursday, February 3, 1972,[351] four days after Bryce Durham's somber, premonitory statement to his sister. Troy Hall did not attend his university classes that day due to illness.[352] He was home, supposedly recovering from the flu, and considering the weather, Ginny felt it best he stay in.[353] Ginny had also been sick[354] and out of work the preceding week, and this was her first day back at her university laundry job.[355] Reportedly upset and crying, Ginny told a co-worker she was worried about paying her tuition, and she and Troy were planning to go to her parents' house that night to discuss it.[356] Late that afternoon, at the end of her shift, despite the ongoing embroilment with her parents over Troy, she reportedly phoned her father, requesting a ride back to her home. Although there is no indication how she got to work, perhaps Troy had taken her and returned home. If so, he did not remain there. About the same time the snow began, as he had previously done, he paced the road near his trailer awaiting pickup by "four hippies" in the same Volkswagen Squareback that had been there on several prior occasions.[357] Later that day, Bryce saw Troy and some men in a car at a service station.[358]

Bryce picked Ginny up within a half hour of her call, driving a new automatic, four-wheel drive, green and white GMC "Jimmy," one of four that had just arrived at his dealership. A "sure-footed" Quadratrack vehicle, the "Jimmy" was advertised as "an all-purpose 4-wheel drive run about" perfect for navigating winter weather.[359] According to Ginny, on the drive to her home, she and her father "had a serious talk," and he persuaded her to resume her studies. In a later assessment of their conversation, Ginny felt things were improving and said her parents had softened their attitude and recently suggested talking with her about possibly paying her tuition.[m]

At 4:30 PM, Troy's and Ginny's neighbor, Mildred Small, left her workplace less than half a mile from her residence and returned home. After checking the mail at her husband Cecil's request, she "stirred up a cake of cornbread for supper." Cecil had not been out of their trailer all day. He had returned home from a detectives' meeting in Raleigh, North Carolina late the previous night and slept in as Mildred left for work that morning.[360] By 5:00 PM, there was up to four inches of snow on the ground with wind gusts up to forty miles per hour[361] and temperatures ranging 15-20 degrees.[362]

[m] Contrary to accounts of Bryce and Virginia Durham being displeased with Ginny for dropping out of school, she was consistently enrolled from the summer quarter of 1970 through the winter quarter of December 1, 1971-February 29, 1972. It could be she was merely considering ceasing her studies, perhaps for financial reasons. [Source: Pitts, Grace (Appalachian State University Registrar's Office). E-mail to author. March 23, 2022.]

Between 5:00 and 6:00 PM, Ginny went to the grocery store in Troy's old white Ford Thunderbird.[363] Possibly due to a busted muffler, the car typically sounded so loud that neighbors knew whose car it was without looking.[364] She returned home just before dark[n] and carried a bag into their trailer.[o] Mildred Small, who was then sitting in a nearby car with Retha Coffey Campbell[p] and Campbell's children, witnessed Ginny's return. Campbell's husband Jim had stopped by the Small trailer to inquire if Cecil would sell him a welding torch. Retha was invited inside, but the Campbells were short on time and heading down the mountain to their home in Kannapolis, North Carolina. Because it was so cold and their infant daughter[365] was sleeping, Mrs. Campbell did not want to take the baby out of the car, so Mildred got inside to visit while their husbands talked.[366] Shortly after Ginny's arrival home from the grocery store, and despite his alleged recent bout with the flu and Ginny's concerns about him being exposed to the weather, Troy left to go study at the university library,[367][q] but not before having dinner in Boone with one of his brothers,[r] possibly at the nearby Town House Restaurant.[368]

Meanwhile, Bobby Durham was enrolled for the winter quarter and had been attending his university classes, including biology lab with his friend Phil Ginn.[369] He completed his last class at 5:20 PM,[370] and as was often his habit once his classes were done, he went to the dealership to study in the salesroom[371] and do odd jobs. Intending to leave his car at the dealership due to the weather, he planned to ride home with his parents.[372][s]

Bryce returned to the dealership and came inside only long enough to get warm. He told part-time salesman Earl Petrey that he [Petrey] would never make it home in his own car and, at 5:45 PM, with snow coming down hard, he gave Petrey a ride to his house on Spruce Street, less than a mile from the dealership, in the same vehicle he had used to transport Ginny. Bryce likely arrived back at the dealership shortly before 6:00 PM.[373] By that time, "virtually all community activity had ceased due to the snowstorm."[374] At some point, Bryce instructed his service manager Dean Combs to prepare everyone a four-wheel drive vehicle so they could get home that night and back to work the following day and to bring the "Jimmy" in and get the snow and ice off of it. When Combs shut down the service department, he and his fellow employees went home, leaving only Bryce, Virginia, and Bobby at the dealership.[375]

---

[n] The sun set that evening at 5:55 PM. [Source: https://www.almanac.com/astronomy/sun-rise-and-set/zipcode/28607/1972-02-03.]

[o] Ginny would later testify both she and Troy bought groceries that afternoon. [Source: Troy Houser, "Two Suspects Bound In Durham Case, Two Released In Triple-Murder Hearing," *Watauga Democrat*, Boone, NC, June 19, 1972, p. 2.]

[p] Retha Coffey Campbell is the aunt of Karen Coffey, present owner and resident of the former Durham home where the murders occurred. [Source: Genealogical research by author.]

[q] Ginny would later testify Troy had studied at the library for about three hours; since he would arrive home around 10:00 PM, that would put his departure from home to go to the library around 7:00 PM. [Source: Troy Houser, "Two Suspects Bound In Durham Case, Two Released In Triple-Murder Hearing," *Watauga Democrat*, Boone, NC, June 19, 1972, p. 2.]

[r] According to former SBI Agent Larry Wagner, Troy told investigators he ate dinner with his brother in Boone earlier that evening before he went to the library, but Wagner does not recall which brother. [Sources: Wagner, Larry. Interview with Charles Heatherly. December 18, 1987; Wagner, Larry. E-mail to author. May 8, 2024.]

[s] Bobby's car was left at the dealership that night. Bryce and Virginia's own passenger car was also left there. When investigators later looked beneath both vehicles, Bryce's and Virginia's car had no snow underneath, indicating it had not been moved since they arrived at the dealership the morning of February 3; Bobby's car had some snow under it, indicating he had arrived there later in the day. [Source: Bullard, Tim, *The Durham Murders*, Kindle Edition, 2012, p. 241.]

Ordinarily, the family would have gone home as well, but because Bryce intended to go to his Rotary Club meeting near Blowing Rock, there was not sufficient time, particularly with bad road conditions, to drive home first, especially since their house was about five miles in the opposite direction.[376] Phil Vance, a fellow Rotarian and local tire dealer, lived on Farthing Street (about a half mile from the dealership) and saw Bryce leaving the dealership alone at 6:00 PM. Vance followed directly behind him the entire ten-mile distance to Appalachian Ski Mountain.[377] It was a treacherous trek, and Vance was thankful Bryce's four-wheel drive vehicle was "sort of plowing a path up the highway" in advance of him.[378]

Since mid-January, Green Berets had been traveling from Fort Bragg, North Carolina to Appalachian Ski Mountain for a training operation, dubbed "Orbit Shot II," which entailed skiing eight hours a day, with the exception of one snowless week during which the soldiers climbed mountains and performed other tactical exercises.[379] Part of this Fifth Special Forces Group was scheduled to give a skiing demonstration to the Rotary Club, but due to the weather, only a dozen Rotarians showed up,[380t] and the demonstration was cancelled.[381] The club's dinner consisted of MREs (meals ready to eat),[u] likely intended as part of a military-themed evening.

While Bryce attended his meeting, it is believed Virginia remained at the dealership, continuing to work. Ginny said her mother often worked late at the end of a month,[382] and Virginia may have been closing out January's books and preparing for tax season. In a 6:00 PM phone call with a lawyer regarding a tax matter, Virginia stated, "I've got fourteen hours of work staring me in the face."[383]

Bobby and his friends, including Phil Ginn, had loosely made plans for supper on the university campus and to attend the 8:00 PM basketball game.[384] When Bobby did not show, Ginn assumed it was due to the bad weather.[385] Bobby and his friend Gary Edmisten had talked earlier in the week about going to a movie,[v] but when Edmisten called on February 3 to follow up, Bobby said he would just stay home with his parents. When Edmisten asked about coming to hang out at their house, Bobby told him not to get out in the bad weather.[w] Bobby possibly left the dealership at some point and went to the Roses store in the new Watauga Village Shopping Center, not far from Ginny's and Troy's home. A friend stated she talked to him (likely at Roses) around 7:30 PM and was "reasonably sure that he had just come in because the snow in his hair had not melted."[386] Virginia and Bobby may have eaten dinner together at the Roses cafeteria.[387]

Back on the university campus, Troy Hall stepped outside of the library around 8:00 PM to take a break and had a short conversation with a friend.[388] Around this same time, Troy's brother, Ray

---

[t] Among those in attendance at the February 3, 1972 meeting other than Bryce Durham and Phil Vance were local dentist Dr. Jim Graham, Sr., car dealers Glenn Andrews, Sr. and Lee Barnett (Rotary Club president), and Appalachian State University professor Eric DeGroat (Rotary Club secretary as well as director of safety and skiing at Appalachian Ski Mountain). [Sources: "Rotary Governor Speaks On Future Activities," *Watauga Democrat*, Boone, NC, August 26, 1971, p. 5A; "DeGroat Named Head Ski School," *Watauga Democrat*, Boone, NC, December 25, 1969. P. 8; "ROTC Cadets Get Training On Skis," *Watauga Democrat*, Boone, NC, January 27, 1972, p. 12B.]

[u] The MREs were specifically noted to be K-rations. [Source: Watauga County Sheriff's Office investigation file 118-H-1/2/3.]

[v] The 9:00 PM movie at the Appalachian Theatre on February 3, 1972 was a reshowing of the 1970 disaster drama *Airplane*. [Sources: Boye, Gary R. Facebook message to author. June 19, 2022.]

[w] Edmisten stated he called Bobby at home and Virginia answered and summoned Bobby to the phone. The timeline for a call to the Durham house, however, is difficult to reconcile since it is believed Bobby was at the dealership from approximately 5:30 PM to approximately 8:40 PM and arrived home with his parents around 9:00 PM, which would have been too late for Edmisten to have called regarding going to a 9:00 PM movie. [Source: Edmisten, Gary. Phone conversation with author. June 18, 2022.]

Hall, phoned his wife Kay to tell her his car had broken down, and he was at a service station in Lenoir, North Carolina, approximately twenty-eight miles southeast of Boone. Kay knew the call was long distance but, noting there were no sounds of tools or gas service bells in the background, she did not know for sure where he was calling from. Ray had left their home in Wilkes County early that morning and told Kay he would be home early that night.[389]

At the conclusion of the Rotary meeting around 8:15 PM,[390] Phil Vance was about one or two cars behind Bryce as they returned to Boone, and around 8:30 PM,[391] he saw Bryce turn into the parking lot of his dealership.[392] One route the Durhams could have subsequently taken home was by traveling north from the dealership on King Street/Highway 421 to the intersection with the Highway 105 Bypass, onto which they would turn left – about a four-mile trip. Alternatively, just a short distance north from the dealership, they could have turned left onto the 105 Extension, continued straight onto Highway 105 and traveled to its intersection with the 105 Bypass, at which point they would turn right – about a six-mile trip. Either way, in normal conditions, the drive might have taken twelve to fifteen minutes, but more time may have been required due to the weather.[393]

Around 8:45 PM, local resident Lester Johnson, who had been out working on furnaces that night with his father Don, came onto Highway 105 and saw a 1965-66 white four-door Ford with a 1971 North Carolina license plate following a green four-wheel-drive Jeep.[394x] Johnson then stopped to call home from a phone booth at the Union 76 station[y] near the corner of Highway 105 and the 105 Bypass and observed the two vehicles turn right onto the bypass. Johnson's call did not go through due to the phone being out of order *[whether the phone being used or the phone being called was not indicated]*, and he and his father proceeded onto the bypass where they saw both vehicles again, this time pulling out of the Westview Baptist Church parking lot onto the bypass in front of them. Johnson believed he saw one man, possibly more, inside the Ford, but he was unable to see the Jeep's occupants because its windows were fogged. The Jeep turned left onto Clyde Townsend Road, and the Ford pulled off on the right shoulder of the bypass. As Johnson approached the bypass's intersection with Highway 421, he looked back and saw the Ford still there.[395]

Around 5:30 PM, the Durhams' service manager and neighbor, Dean Combs, had driven up Clyde Townsend Road in a four-wheel drive vehicle borrowed from work. He noticed lights on inside the Durham residence and thought it odd as he knew the family was still at the dealership. Seeing no vehicles in their driveway, he thought perhaps the lights had been left on by mistake.[396] Once home, Combs ate supper and afterwards sat down in a chair near his front door to watch a television movie. He had seen a couple of vehicles fail in their attempts to climb the steep hill, and a while later he heard something spinning. His wife and daughter looked out their picture window, and he, looking out his door, believed it to be the Durhams coming in. The snow was blowing so hard he could

[x] A 1972 GMC "Jimmy" looked very similar to a 1972 Chevrolet K5 Blazer and somewhat similar to a 1972 Jeep Wagoneer, so perhaps this was the Durhams' vehicle, and the Durhams were taking the Highway 105 route home. The white Ford, as described by Johnson, did not match the car Troy Hall reportedly drove, which was an older model, two-door Ford Thunderbird, but the only four-door Thunderbirds were manufactured between 1967 and 1971, which was later than Johnson's 1965-66 estimation of the vehicle he saw. [Source: https://macsmotorcitygarage.com/the-more-door-thunderbirds-1967-71/.]

[y] The Union 76 station was also known as Dan'l Boone Union 76 and stood at the present location of the Circle K/Mobil station and The Pedalin' Pig restaurant. It was also sometimes referred to as the Pure Oil station; they were one and the same. "By 1970, the Pure Oil brand was phased out, and remaining service stations and auto/truck stops were rebranded as Union 76." [Sources: Watauga County Sheriff's Office investigation file 118-H- 1/2/3; Personal knowledge of author; https://en.wikipedia.org/wiki/Pure_Oil; Bullard, Tim, *The Durham Murders*, Kindle Edition, 2012, p. 373.]

barely see them pull into their driveway and up to the garage doors in a Blazer or the "Jimmy."[z] When he saw the vehicle's interior light come on, he resumed watching TV.[397]

"Several neighbors saw the [Durhams'] vehicle go up the hill. One *[perhaps Dean Combs]* noted it was about 9:00 PM because the 9 o'clock movie was coming on."[398] One news outlet reported neighbor Clyde Townsend saying "he heard the Durhams drive home from a Rotary Club meeting about 8 p.m.... After that he heard nothing."[399] *[Perhaps the reporter misunderstood Townsend, who may have meant he had heard from someone that Bryce left the Rotary meeting at 8:00 PM, and not that he personally heard the car arrive home at that time.]* Another news outlet stated Townsend (who was watching television with his family[400]) said he saw their vehicle go up the hill at 8:45 PM.[401] Townsend's ten-year-old son, Mike, kept watch out of a picture window on the backside of their family's upstairs apartment, informing his father of the ability of vehicles to ascend the steep hill toward the Durham house, and he saw the "Jimmy" succeed.[402] Another neighbor stated the family arrived home around 8:30 PM.[403] Some have suggested Bobby arrived home a half hour after his parents,[404aa] but there seems to be no evidence of that being accurate. Next-door neighbors Clinard and Clara Wilson were watching *The Flip Wilson Show* between 8:00 and 9:00 PM in their living room and neither observed nor heard anything unusual. Perhaps just after 9:00 PM, Mrs. Wilson went to wash dishes. The window at her kitchen sink faced the Durhams' home – a distance of approximately 117 feet. On most any evening, when the Wilsons saw a light in the Durhams' dining room window, they figured the family was home. On this particular night, Mrs. Wilson said she could see a blonde-headed woman, who she assumed to be Virginia Durham,[405] although a crime scene photo of the Durhams' dining area reveals sheer curtains drawn over their dining room window.

Likely between 9:00 and 9:30 PM *[and potentially as late as 10:00 PM]*, twenty-six-year-old Reed Trivette and his first cousin, Bernard "Bern" Harmon (age thirty-nine), turned onto the 105 Bypass. The pair was in Harmon's four-wheel drive Jeep, returning home to western Watauga County from Blowing Rock, where they had gone around 3:00 PM to drink beer at Holley's Tavern. Between 8:00 and 9:00 PM, the owner of the establishment informed them he needed to close early because of the bad weather. The men finished their drinks and bought a twelve-pack of beer to take home. According to Trivette, he and Harmon "were not drunk by any means," claiming they had only consumed about three beers each. Almost no one was on the roads due to the heavy, blowing snowfall that, by Trivette's estimation, was about a foot deep at that time. After turning right onto the bypass from Highway 105, they met no cars and saw no car tracks but witnessed a green Blazer with possibly a white or silver mid-body pulled off the road about twenty-five feet into an Oakwood

[z] It seems curious Combs would refer to the vehicle as possibly being a Blazer when he knew Bryce Durham had been utilizing a "Jimmy" throughout the day and had asked Combs to de-ice it for him before Combs left the dealership. A Blazer and a "Jimmy" look quite similar, but Combs, as a service manager, would have surely known the difference. It was already dark by this time, and Combs stated visibility was impaired by the blowing snow, so maybe it was hard for him to say with confidence exactly what type of vehicle he saw. Also, perhaps he was not completely sure this was the Durhams arriving home, or perhaps there was a Blazer at the dealership that Combs surmised the Durhams may have elected to bring home in lieu of the "Jimmy." Knowing after the murders that the vehicle taken from the Durham home was a "Jimmy," if Combs truly did see a Blazer rather than a "Jimmy," then he witnessed someone other than the Durhams pulling into their driveway.

[aa] Cecil Small once stated that Bobby's high school football coach, Bob Poe, who lived on Poplar Grove Road in Boone, drove Bobby home that night, and "Mrs. Henson" (likely Willa Jean Gragg Henson, aunt of Poe's wife, and also a resident of Poplar Grove Road), saw them. Small was likely conflating this with Poe driving his sons on Poplar Grove Road and finding the abandoned "Jimmy" *(see p. 80)*. [Source: Cecil Small, interview with Arlie Isaacs, September 6, 1974, Watauga County Sheriff's Office investigation file 118-H-1/2/3.]

Mobile Homes sales lot.[406bb] The Blazer's headlights and taillights were lit, but Trivette could not distinguish if it was running. He believed a door may have been open, and he saw three white men, all very large and more than two-hundred pounds, standing and talking. Two wore really long, army-style overcoats and toboggans, while the third wore a short, waist-length coat and a hat. The three men looked at Harmon and Trivette as they drove by. Harmon wondered if they needed pulling out and if they should stop. Starting to pull into the lot, Trivette told him, "No, go on. They're in a four-wheel drive." When Trivette and Harmon reached Clyde Townsend Road, they stopped on the bypass and looked toward the apartment of their friends Lynn Greene and Ricky Phillips and contemplated spending the night there. They then spotted a light blue or possibly mint green 1966-1968 Pontiac Bonneville *[Trivette knew because he had owned a 1966 model]*, with its lights on, coming down the Durhams' driveway and Clyde Townsend Road toward the apartment buildings. Trivette told Harmon he believed the vehicle would get stuck because it was bottoming out. As it neared them, Trivette spotted three of the car's passengers – a male driver, a male next to the passenger door, and a woman in between with either blonde hair or a light-colored scarf – although there may have been as many as four or five passengers. Contrary to Trivette's prediction, the car made it onto the bypass, turning right. Trivette commented to Harmon that perhaps they could follow them and have the opportunity to pull them out somewhere, but Harmon said, "No, as many people as they are in that [car], they could carry it out." Because no lights were on in their friends' apartment *[Greene and Phillips would later report they were asleep at the time of the murders]*, the cousins decided to proceed homeward, but Trivette looked back and saw the Pontiac heading in the opposite direction before slowing and stopping where the Blazer was parked.[407cc]

[bb] The lot sat where present-day Cash Custom Homes is currently located, near Westview Baptist Church.

[cc] Looking in one's rear-view mirror (equivalent to Trivette turning to look out the back window) while traveling on the Highway 105 Bypass toward Highway 421, visibility of the mobile home lot where Trivette said the Blazer was parked and where the Pontiac stopped is lost immediately after passing Clyde Townsend Road – a distance of approximately four tenths of a mile beyond the mobile home lot. Trivette related most of these details to the Watauga County Sheriff's Office during a circa 1989 interview, a 1992 phone call, and again in 2000. Many, but not all, of the details were consistently reiterated. In 1992 and 2000, Trivette mentioned the Blazer and three large men, but he made no mention of them in the circa 1989 interview. In fact, during the latter, when he was asked if he and Harmon saw any other vehicle, he said no. Trivette's description of exactly when he and Harmon encountered the Pontiac also differs within two of the accounts. In the earlier account, he said that, from a distance before coming to Clyde Townsend Road, they could see the Pontiac coming out of what they later learned was the Durhams' driveway, and after the Pontiac pulled onto the 105 Bypass, they passed one another about forty or fifty feet before Trivette and Harmon came to Clyde Townsend Road, and the Pontiac was traveling in the opposite direction about two miles per hour. During the 1992 phone call, Trivette stated the Blazer was possibly dark in color, and that the Pontiac was green, but not light green. In all accounts, Trivette described the Pontiac stopping near Westview Baptist Church, adding in an earlier account that the car may have either pulled over or gotten stuck. In the circa 1989 interview, Trivette stated that, a month or two after the murders, while discussing them with his friend Ricky Phillips, who lived in the Clyde Townsend Apartments, he told Phillips about the light green Pontiac he had seen exiting Clyde Townsend Road that night. Phillips responded that the Pontiac belonged to Troy Hall and reportedly said to Trivette, "Hell, he [Troy] must have been the one that done it, 'cause he must have been up there." In 2000, Trivette told Watauga County Sheriff's Captain Paula May he did not learn of the murders until about a week after they occurred. (Contrary to this, in the earlier, circa 1989 interview with officers from the Watauga County Sheriff's Department, Trivette had stated he was pretty sure he learned of the murders the following day.) After having knowledge of them, Trivette stated he and his wife went to the A&P grocery store near the Greenway Trailer Park in Boone, and Trivette saw the same green Pontiac parked beside the first trailer next to the road in the middle of the trailer park. He said the trailer was small, about eight or ten feet wide and about forty feet long, and Cecil Small's name was on the mailbox there. Later, when Trivette and his cousin and fellow witness, Bernard Harmon, discussed the murders, Harmon believed they had encountered the killers, who he surmised had stolen the Blazer (i.e., the GMC "Jimmy"), and that the driver of the Pontiac had a part in the murders, which explained why it stopped beside the Blazer near Westview Baptist Church. Trivette had first reported this to a detective at the Watauga County Sheriff's Department in 1972, but he was disbelieved because he and Harmon had been drinking that night. Harmon died several months after the murders from acute alcohol

Bruce and Priscilla Faw, who lived in the dead-end hollow behind the Durhams, were visiting Bruce's parents in Wilkes County. It had begun to snow there, so Bruce suggested they leave because the road to their Boone home could be hard to ascend. They departed Wilkes County at 8:25 PM and encountered a snowstorm at the top of the mountain where the Blue Ridge Parkway intersects with Highway 421. Eventually, after traveling through downtown Boone, they turned left onto the 105 Bypass around 10:00 PM and saw a fast-moving, small, blue or black car, possibly an Opel, with four or five people inside. The Faws spotted the car between the 105 Bypass/421 intersection and Clyde Townsend Road (a half mile distance), but exactly what direction it was traveling was not noted. Bruce said to his wife, "Look at those fools flying on this slick road." The Faws managed to get up a portion of Clyde Townsend Road until their car got stuck at the Durham driveway. *[This may have been the white Plymouth that investigators later found belonged to "a person in the area," and were satisfied had no involvement in the murders.[408]]* While Bruce walked the remaining distance to get their Jeep to pull the car, Priscilla remained inside, holding the brakes. As she waited for her husband's return, she looked around the neighborhood to see who was up, but the only light she saw was an outside light at the Durhams' home. She saw no vehicles or people around.[409] When Bruce returned, they managed to get their Jeep and car the rest of the way home.[410] *[This account of the Faws' activities the night of the murders differs in one major way from the account told to their daughter, Allison Faw Marcotte. Marcotte was born after the Durham murders, and her parents rarely spoke of that night and what her mother referred to as "the Boone murders," but based on what her father's sister, Rachel Faw Wiles, told her years later, after the Faws got stuck, Bruce told Priscilla he would go to the nearby Durham house for assistance. He knocked on the door, and although he could see and hear people inside, no one answered, which upset him. There was no indication as to who he saw or heard, but the Faws' arrival to Clyde Townsend Road around 10:00 PM would likely have coincided with the timeframe the killers were inside the Durham home.[411] If this account is accurate, it could be the Faws were fearful and reluctant to share it with authorities.]*

Also, around 10:00 PM, seventeen-year-old Richard Aldridge[dd] was braving the snowy conditions and driving along the 105 Bypass, making his way from his job at Kentucky Fried Chicken in Boone to his home on Greer Lane, which was just beyond Clyde Townsend Road. The only odd thing he noticed was a man walking the same stretch of road, coming from the vicinity of Clyde Townsend Road toward Greer Lane. This turned out to be a nearby resident who was later cleared of any involvement in the murders.[412] In a similar incident, Boone resident Jack Norris was out after dark looking for his missing horse (which had disappeared from the vicinity of Winkler's Creek Road, which intersects with Greenway Road) when he encountered a man along Greenway Road. The man's car would not start, and Norris gave him a ride to Clyde Townsend Road. *[Norris would*

---

poisoning, and Trivette, who quit drinking in 1990, told Paula May he would like to help and was willing to submit to a polygraph test or to hypnosis if it would help him remember more. [Sources: Trivette, Reed. Interview with Del Williams & Chuck Henson. Circa 1989, Watauga County Sheriff's Office investigation file 118-H-1/2/3; Trivette, Reed. Phone call to Boone Area Crimestoppers. February 5, 1992, Watauga County Sheriff's Office investigation file 118-H-1/2/3; Trivette, Reed. Interview with Paula May. February 1, 2000, Watauga County Sheriff's Office investigation file 118-H-1/2/3; May, Paula. Phone interview with author. March 27, 2022. May, Paula. Facebook message to author. April 14, 2022.]

[dd] In subsequent years, Aldridge became the son-in-law of Boone Police Chief Clyde Tester, served as a Boone policeman, and eventually had a career as a North Carolina Highway Patrolman. [Source: Personal knowledge of author.]

later wonder if the man was involved with the Durham murders, although his passenger could have simply been someone who lived in the Clyde Townsend Road neighborhood, including the apartment building there.][413ee]

By around 9:30 PM, Troy Hall had left the university library[414] arriving home around 9:55 or 10:00 PM.[415] He and Ginny settled on the couch to watch a recap of the IX Olympic Winter Games opening ceremonies, which aired between 10:00 and 11:00 PM.[416] Ten or fifteen minutes later, their television stopped working, and they either put a record on the stereo[417] or recorded music on the playback. Ginny began getting ready for bed. Sometime after 10:00 PM,[ff] an alarm clock went off and then their phone rang. Their phone had been out of order all day, which was not unusual in bad weather,[gg] and Troy had been working on it. The extension to Troy's and Ginny's phone that Cecil and Mildred Small had in their home also rang. Based on the understanding the Smalls would only answer the extension after five rings and, based on the fact Troy quickly answered the phone, the Smalls apparently did not pick up. By this time, Ginny had returned to their den, and, although she normally answered the phone, Troy turned off the alarm clock and leapt over her, almost throwing her in the floor to get to the phone, and he answered it after only one ring.[418hh]

According to Troy, he took a whispered but frantic and terrifying phone call [419] from someone requesting help. He did not initially recognize the barely audible voice,[420] and the loud music playing in the trailer made hearing more difficult.[421] Troy thought it was a practical joke, asking, "Virginia, is that you?"[422] Although accounts vary as to what Virginia is alleged to have said, the possibilities reported include Virginia asking for help and stating Bryce and Bobby were being held in a back room by "some men," "three men," "three blacks," "niggers," or "three niggers."[423] *[It was later reported Troy did not remember exactly what Virginia said*[424] *or if she indicated how many intruders there were.*[425] *A separate news report stated Troy said Virginia indicated there was*

[ee] A variation of this story is told by retired Boone Police Sergeant Jeff Rucker, who says Norris told him he encountered the Durhams' GMC "Jimmy" on Poplar Grove Road the night of the murders. At that time, Norris had property and a barn on Homespun Hills Road (the next road past Poplar Grove Road as one travels north on Highway 105). According to Rucker, Norris said he was out looking for his lost horse near that location when, from a hilltop, he saw the headlights of a vehicle on Poplar Grove Road. Norris approached what he later identified as the "Jimmy" to see if he could offer assistance. A man exited the driver's side and told Norris someone was on the way to pick "them" up. Norris did not know the man and was unable to identify him because of the blowing snow. If this version is correct, it would mean Norris likely encountered the killer(s), and based on other known time intervals, this would have been around 10:35 PM, which would have placed the killer(s) exiting the "Jimmy" and getting into the getaway car around 10:40 PM. [Source: Rucker, Jeff. Phone interview with author. October 4, 2023.]

[ff] A narrative on Bobby Durham's death certificate states the phone rang around 10:00 PM; some accounts say a little after 10:00 PM; one states about 10:10 PM; others report 10:15 PM and 10:30 PM; Troy would later testify it rang between 10:10 and 10:30 PM. [Sources: Henderson, Leonard. *Rub-Out, Rub-Out, Rub-Out: Three Bodies in a Tub.* Startling Detective, September 1972, p. 62; Robert B. Cullen, "Boone Stranglings Still A Mystery To SBI, Sheriffs," *Durham Morning Herald*, Durham, NC, July 2, 1973, p. 1B; Bullard, Tim, *The Durham Murders*, Kindle Edition, 2012, p. 258; "Slayings in Boone Revealed," *Statesville Record and Landmark*, Statesville, NC, February 4, 1972, p. 1. "Murder Reward Increased," *Asheville Citizen-Times*, Asheville, NC, February 12, 1972, p. 11; Troy Houser, "Two Suspects Bound In Durham Case, Two Released In Triple-Murder Hearing," *Watauga Democrat*, Boone, NC, June 19, 1972, p. 2.]

[gg] The local newspaper noted about a month prior to the murders that residents weren't always satisfied with their phone service, but Southern Bell was attempting to bring "better service to our fast-growing town," and had established new quarters in Boone. Its new equipment was to be activated and tentatively completed in August 1972, promising better service as a result. [Source: "Telephones Essential," *Watauga Democrat*, Boone, NC, December 20, 1971, p. 1.]

[hh] Because Ginny knew Troy had been unfaithful to her, his urgency to get to the phone caused her to think it might be another woman calling him. [Source: Mackie, Ginny Durham. Interview with Carolynn Johnson & Wade Colvard. December 7, 2020.]

more than one intruder, and during a probable cause hearing, Troy testified "he thought at the time that the caller said black people had Bryce and Bobby."[426]]

Moments later, the phone went dead. Troy turned off the music and informed Ginny of the call, telling her he thought it was her mother who had phoned, but also wondering aloud if the call had been a prank. Ginny had Troy try to call back several times, but he only got a busy signal.[427] Not thinking her mother "would play such a joke," she told Troy they needed to go to her parents' home right away. *[Ginny would later recount it was Troy who told her they needed to go.[428]]* They quickly dressed and went out to their car. New snow had drifted as high as the hubcaps. The motor turned over a few times, followed by a clicking sound. *[Ginny would later say "it just clicked," a common indicator of a dead battery.[429]]* The headlights dimmed and faded to dark.[430] This was approximately 10:10 to10:15 PM as attested to by the Halls' next-door neighbors, Chester and Minnie Nelson. *[If this timeframe is correct, the alleged phone call from Virginia Durham would have been received closer to 10:00 PM and could not have occurred as late as 10:30 PM.]* Mrs. Nelson worked at the Watauga County Hospital, and an hour before her shift was to end at 11:00 PM, she became ill with a headache. Her husband drove from the trailer park to the hospital – about a five- to seven-minute drive – and they returned home. When they arrived back at the trailer park, they saw Troy and Ginny sitting in their car, which was not running, and "Troy threw up his hand." Because the wind was blowing so badly, the Nelsons thought perhaps it had shaken the Halls' trailer, and they had gone to their car because they were afraid.[431] Unable to start their car, Troy and Ginny decided to enlist the help of their neighbor Cecil Small,[432] whose "car [a white Chevy with a 409 engine[433] – likely a 1961-1965 Chevy Impala[434]] was equipped with an engine-block heater, which was kept plugged into an outside receptacle."[435]

Cecil Small

Cecil Small's wife Mildred was watching a Burt Reynolds movie, *Hunters are for Killing*,[ii] and during a television commercial break had gone to the bathroom to sponge off and change into her pajamas.[436] Mildred asked her husband what time it was; he looked at a clock, and it was exactly 10:30 PM.[437] Cecil, not having been out of their home all day was barefoot and undressed,[438] and moments after Mildred left the living room, he heard a knock at their front door.[439] He could not see who was knocking but observed Ginny outside, her hair blowing with the snow.[440] Cecil opened the door and discovered the caller was Troy,[441] who had reportedly often sought Cecil out "for fatherly advisory conferences."[442] Troy and Ginny had frequently visited and spoken with the Smalls and "were forever…borrow[ing] a hammer or a saw."[443] Troy, "huddled against the wind and the snow," told Cecil he was really sorry to disturb him, but his car would not start, and he asked Cecil if he could drive him to his in-laws' home.[444] Cecil told Troy he was not sure his car would start either as he had not tried it all day.[445] Ginny was pacing the sidewalk nearby, and Cecil invited them both in[446] as Mildred finished buttoning up her pajamas and quickly grabbed her housecoat. Ginny had no head covering, and the wind split her hair in the middle and blew it around her face. Mildred had never seen Ginny wearing glasses, and she thought they magnified her eyes, giving her a horrified appearance.[447] Cecil could see Ginny was upset,[448] and Troy further explained that "Babe" [referring to Ginny] had gotten a call from her mother,[449] who sounded hysterical, stating someone was beating her husband and son.[450] Ginny added in a trembling voice, "Mother

[ii] Mildred Small would later erroneously recall the movie's title as "Searching for a Killer." [Source: Cecil & Mildred Small, interview with Caroline Walker (*Watauga* Democrat Staff Writer), February 23, 1989, Watauga County Sheriff's Office investigation file 118-H-1/2/3.]

said that someone had forced daddy and my brother into the back room and was beating them."[451] Cecil later recalled Troy telling him that Virginia had phoned to say "three colored people" were attempting to break in on them.[452]

As Cecil began putting on his cap and overcoat, Mildred returned to the living room and heard Ginny say, "My family isn't wealthy, but they do have some money!" indicating that the people attacking her family might be attempting to rob them. Troy asked Cecil three times if he had a gun and, although Cecil never answered, he [Cecil] went to the closet, took out his loaded revolver, and put it in his coat pocket. Troy stated, "I'm afraid there's something bad wrong. *Bad* wrong!"[453]

Meanwhile, also around 10:30 PM, as Jerry Harrison was traveling south along Highway 105 from his home in Boone, he passed by the Union 76 Station and saw a four-wheel-drive, green GMC there, like the one later described as belonging to the Durhams. He also saw a blonde-headed woman in a straddle-length brown coat using the phone booth there – the same phone booth Lester Johnson had used about an hour and a half earlier. *[In 1989, Harrison initially stated the woman he saw to be Ginny Durham because he had seen Ginny wearing that coat at a hearing at the courthouse in Boone, but he later acknowledged that, because he had not seen her face that night, he could not definitively say it was her at the phone booth. Ginny also wore a straddle-length, brown suede coat to her parents' and brother's funeral. The timing of Harrison's sighting of the woman at the phone booth, however, corresponds with the timeframe Ginny was known to be at Cecil and Mildred Small's home, meaning the woman at the phone booth could not have been Ginny.]*[454]

Additionally, at the same Union 76 Station on that same night, although no specific time was indicated, John Cashion,[jj] who managed the station, saw four or five big men hanging around. They kept going back and forth "between the pay phone and the store [within the station[455]]" and even picked up their cigarette butts and possibly wiped off the telephone.[kk]

[jj] John Cashion, a native of Wilkes County, was a brother to Paul Cashion of Cashion Oil Company in Wilkes County, and Paul (maternal grandfather of actor/comedian Zach Galifiankis) was the owner of the Union 76 station in Boone. In 1979, John Cashion was kidnapped, robbed, and murdered. He had been shot in the head and chest and was dumped, partially clothed, in a ditch near Grandfather Mountain and the Blue Ridge Parkway in Avery County, North Carolina. At the time of his death, he owned an auto rustproofing shop in Boone, and he was a prominent member of the Watauga County Democratic Party. His trailer was ransacked. The SBI investigated his murder, and William Jackson "Jackie" Wilson, an employee who Cashion had fired following a dispute, was charged. Those charges were dismissed, however, for a lack of evidence. James Cecil Berry was later charged and tried but found not guilty by a Watauga Superior Court jury that disbelieved Wilson's testimony in Berry's trial. Both Wilson's and Berry's fingerprints would be compared to the prints lifted in the Durham Case. Cashion's murder remains unsolved. [Sources: Hagaman, David. Phone interview with author. November 5, 2022; "Harry Galifianakis of Wilkesboro dies on Sunday," *Wilkes Journal-Patriot*, North Wilkesboro, NC, July 19, 2018 (online; https://journalpatriot.com/obituaries/harry-galifianakis-of-wilkesboro-dies-on-sunday/article_e5c0ae48-8b6f-11e8-bbd2-c74af19b510d.html); https://findagrave.com/memorial/24226700/john-archie-cashion?_gl=1*tahldp*_ga*MTMyOTE3MzExLjE1MzYyNjY4NTg.*_ga_4QT8FMEX30*MTY1NDl3NDE1OS4zNi4XLjE2NTQyNzQyODEuMA; "N. C. Democratic official is slain," *The Charlotte News*, Charlotte, NC, December 26, 1979, p. 1; "Bond Denied For Man Held In Cashion Death," *The Durham Sun*, Durham, NC, December 27, 1979, p. 9-C; "Boone Jury Acquits Man in Murder Case," *The Charlotte Observer*, Charlotte, NC, May 30, 1981, p. 2B; "Charges are dismissed in Dem leader's death," *The Charlotte News*, Charlotte, NC, April 25, 1980, p. 3A; "Boone Jury Acquits Man in Murder Case," *The Charlotte Observer*, Charlotte, NC, May 30, 1981, p. 2B; Watauga County Sheriff's Office investigation file 118-H-1/2/3.]

[kk] An anonymous caller to Boone Crimestoppers said this was told by Glenn Anderson, who worked for Cashion, and who Cashion had told. The caller stated Anderson was willing to speak with law enforcement. [Source: Anonymous caller, September 25, 1989, Watauga County Sheriff's Office investigation file 118-H-1/2/3.]

Back at Cecil Small's, Troy and Ginny "stood outside [Cecil's] car and waited while [Cecil] tried to crank it." When it started, they jumped in without speaking – [Ginny] in the middle and Troy following her.[456] The three left Cecil's trailer about 10:33 PM and drove[457] the four miles to Clyde Townsend Road. Once on the 105 Bypass (approximately three miles into the journey), Ginny reiterated that her mother said men were beating her father and brother in a back room. This was the last statement exchanged between the passengers until they arrived[458] around 10:45 PM.[ll] Their trip, which under normal conditions would have taken less than ten minutes, took longer and was reportedly "agonizingly slow because the roads were completely iced over, and wind-swept snow cut visibility to a few feet."[459]

Because Cecil did not know where the Durhams lived, he paused his vehicle beside Clyde Townsend's apartments, and Troy told him the house was "up yonder on the hill"[460]*[some 390 feet ahead].* They saw several lights[461] were on in the house. *[This is in contrast to neighbor Priscilla Faw seeing only the outside light of the house on shortly after 10:00 PM.[462]]* Clyde Townsend Road was clear on the lower half but snow-covered on the upper portion.[463] As Cecil's car ascended, it was only able to climb the steep road halfway, losing traction and starting to slide backward[464][mm] about a hundred yards from the house.[465] Cecil set the emergency brake and told the couple they would have to walk the rest of the way.[466] "You stay here, babe,"[467] Troy told Ginny, assuring her he would see if anything was wrong with her folks.[468] Young Mike Townsend, still keeping periodic watch on the traffic in and out of the road beside his family's apartment, had seen the Durhams' "Jimmy" descending the road only a short time before he witnessed the failure of Cecil's car to ascend the same road, and he reported to his father that people had exited the car and were walking up the hill.[469]

Front door of Durham home (Image courtesy of Watauga County Sheriff's Office)

As Troy and Cecil walked up the remaining portion of the road, they fell three or four times on the slick pavement[470] and had to move into the grass on either side[471] before coming to a point where the ground leveled off.[472] Reaching the house, Troy "ran to the front door," hammered on it and rang the bell, but no one answered. Attempting to open the door, he rattled the doorknob, but found it locked.[473] Having no key,[474] and with Cecil by his side, they peered into the large picture window to the left of the front door but saw nothing.[475] They then walked to the left around the house to the rear and pounded on the back door. Again, there was no response,"[476] and that door was locked as well.[477] They checked each window but never saw the Durhams.[478] Troy tried unsuccessfully to open one of the windows.[479] Because the kitchen window was too high to peer into, Cecil "cupped his hands together to make a stirrup and boosted [Troy]

[ll] A UPI report the day after the murders erroneously stated Troy Hall arrived around 11:30 PM. [Sources: "Prominent Boone Family Is Found Dead," *The News and Observer*, Raleigh, NC, February 5, 1972, p. 3. Bullard, Tim, *The Durham Murders*, Kindle Edition, 2012, pp. 584 & 592.]

[mm] According to Mildred Small, if her husband had been able to keep up his speed from the bottom of the hill instead of having to pause beside the apartments while asking Troy about the location of the Durham home, "he could have went plumb to the house." [Source: Cecil & Mildred Small, interview with Caroline Walker (*Watauga Democrat* Staff Writer), February 23, 1989, Watauga County Sheriff's Office investigation file 118-H-1/2/3.]

up." Troy could see the kitchen in disorder.[480] Cecil noticed a cut a couple of inches long on one of the back window screens, but because it did not look to be a new cut, he did not mention it and was not sure if Troy noticed it. As they came around the other end of the house, Cecil bumped his knee on an outdoor metal glider sofa that sat against the exterior brick wall, and he cursed in pain.[481] Continuing back around to the front of the house, they saw the garage door on the left was open about eighteen inches due to a faulty spring.[482][nn] Cecil asked if they could get into the house that way, and Troy lifted the garage door[483] enough for them to slide or crawl under it.[484][oo] A door inside the garage led directly into the wood-paneled den,[485] and when Troy reached the door and put his hand on it, he hesitated. He could see the room was ransacked, and "he jumped back as if he had [seen] someone inside." In response, Cecil, with gun drawn and cocked,[pp] asked, "What is it?" "Nothing," Troy replied. "Well, hell, go ahead," Cecil prompted. "I got you covered. Go on."[486] Cecil then followed Troy into the house.

From the den, one could turn left toward the front of the house and go into a small passageway connecting Bobby's bedroom, a bathroom, and the foyer before leading to the living room[487] or turn right and go through a small laundry area by the back door that led into the kitchen, beyond which was a dining area that connected with the living room.[488] The main floorplan flowed in a roundabout fashion, one room leading consecutively to the next, regardless of the direction taken. Due to the house being split-level, the living room, dining area, and kitchen were two steps higher than the other areas.[489] Three bedrooms were upstairs, including the master bedroom with an en suite bathroom utilized by Bryce and Virginia, another bedroom formerly occupied by Ginny, and the smallest of the three bedrooms, which the Durhams made into a sewing room. Another upstairs bathroom was entered from the hallway.[490]

The men entered the den, sometimes referred to as the "television room." Although one source stated the TV was still on with canned laughter, Cecil said there was no sound, which caused him to later surmise the killer(s) may have turned down the volume. In the den, they saw splotches of congealing blood on the carpet,[491] although Cecil had been initially oblivious to it and had stepped in it.[492] From the den, Troy went to the right toward the laundry area and kitchen, while Cecil cautiously proceeded to the left[493] toward a noise he heard coming from somewhere in the house. As he walked, he tracked blood all the way to the nearby bathroom.[494]

[nn] Another account states the door was only open about six to eight inches. According to Ginny Durham, her family left the garage door open about a foot so a cat could enter. This cat had just shown up and was a successor to their previous cat that had been shot by a neighbor. [Sources: Troy Houser, "Two Suspects Bound In Durham Case, Two Released In Triple-Murder Hearing," *Watauga Democrat*, Boone, NC, June 19, 1972, p. 2; Mackie, Ginny Durham. Interview with Carolynn Johnson & Wade Colvard. December 7, 2020.]

[oo] One report says Troy swiftly swung the door open; Cecil Small later stated they opened the door together. [Sources: Henderson, Leonard. Rub-Out, Rub-Out, Rub-Out: Three Bodies in a Tub. Startling Detective, September 1972, p. 61; Cecil & Mildred Small, interview with Caroline Walker (Watauga Democrat Staff Writer), February 23, 1989, Watauga County Sheriff's Office investigation file 118-H-1/2/3.

[pp] One sources says Cecil drew his gun en route to the bathroom, fearing killers might still be in the house, possibly in the darkened upstairs. [Source: "Killers Almost Spotted In Boone Triple Murder," *The Robesonian*, Lumberton, NC, February 6, 1972, p. 2A.]

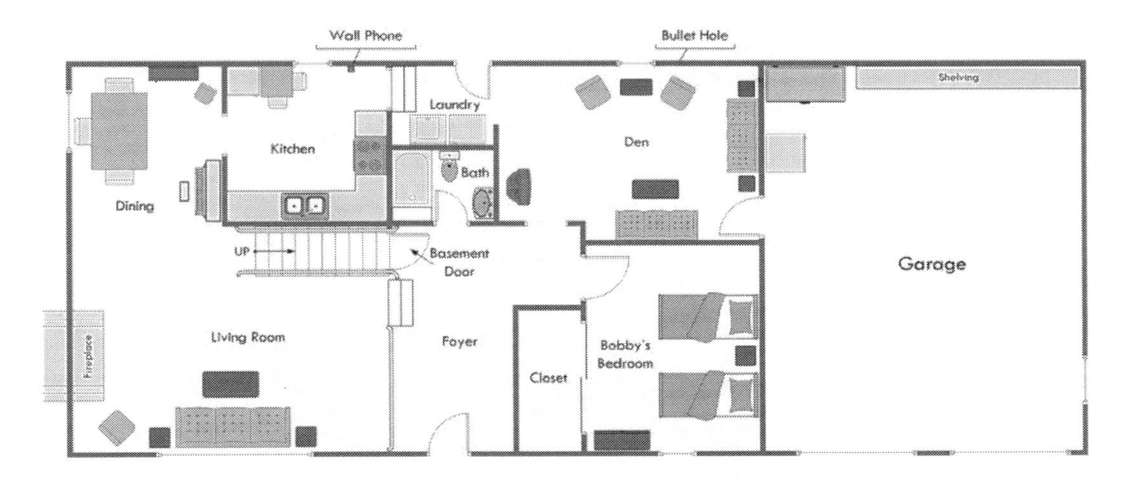

First level floorplan of Durham home

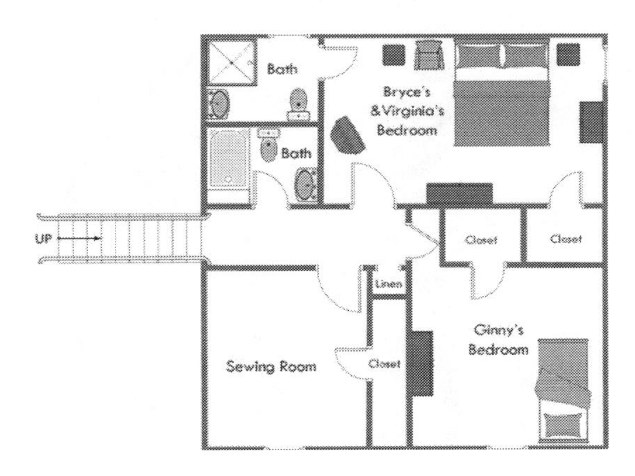

Second level floorplan of Durham home

One report states that, upon hearing dripping water and believing the sink to be running over, both men ran to the bathroom,[495] but this deviates from Cecil's firsthand account: "So, we entered the door in the den, and I seen the television a-playin'[496] [a girl was singing[497]]. There was no sound, but the picture was moving. And then I heard a noise, and I started to the noise, and I got in front of the bathroom door, and there they laid."[498] It was not the sound of water that drew Cecil in that direction, but a metallic bang. *[Even years later, Cecil would say, "I heard a noise, and I ain't ever figured that out."[499]]* As he went to investigate, he stepped on a pair of glasses that had been broken in the middle. Approaching the bathroom, he noticed the nearby bedroom (Bobby's room) had been ransacked – "drawers pulled out and dumped." Believing at least one killer to be in the darkened bedroom, he said, "You son-of-a-bitch. You're over behind that bed, I guess." But since Cecil had his gun, he thought to himself, "as long as he [the perpetrator] didn't come at me, why good enough." *[Cecil would later recall, "I'm standing there in that bathroom looking at them people, and whatever is back in there [the bedroom], I ain't bothering with them unless they jump me."[500]]*

Cecil discovered the Durhams' bodies side by side – first Bobby, then Bryce, and finally Virginia. Draped over the edge of the water-filled bathtub, their heads were submerged. The faucet was running full force, and the water was approximately one to four inches from overflowing the edge of the tub.[501qq]

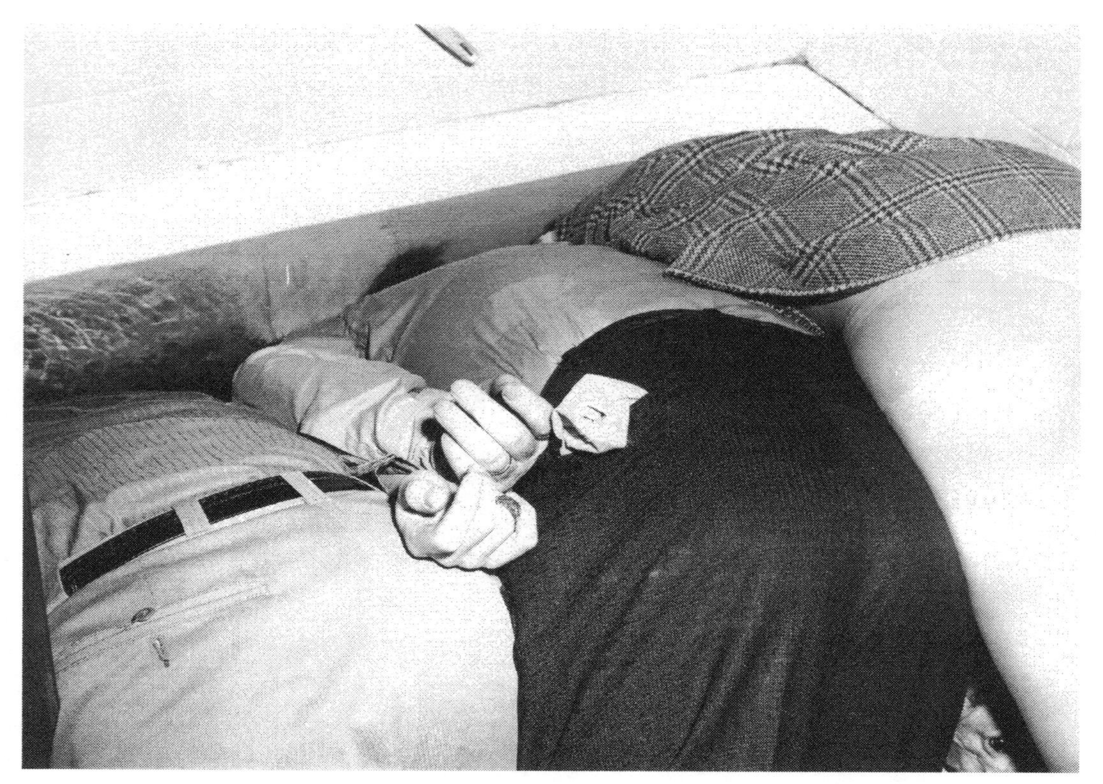

(L-R) Bobby, Bryce, & Virginia Durham
(Image courtesy of Watauga County Sheriff's Office)

Troy, in another part of the house, was hollering, "Is anybody home? Is anybody home?" Cecil called to him, "Here they are Troy. Come here." When Troy arrived at the bathroom and saw the gruesome scene, he seemed very upset and threw up his hands, exclaiming, "Oh my God!" He started toward the bodies, specifically toward Bobby, but Cecil grabbed his arm and said, "Don't touch 'em. Let's go. Let's get the hell outta here."[502] *[It was later reported that Troy testified Cecil advised him "to leave everything as was and get the authorities to the scene."[503]]*

[qq] One source erroneously stated the bodies "were found in the tub of an *upstairs* bathroom." [Source: "4th Suspect In 3 Deaths Is Released," *The Charlotte Observer*, Charlotte, NC, January 24, 1974, p. B1.] Although there were two bathrooms upstairs, one of which had a tub and was identical to the downstairs bathroom, the bodies were found in the *downstairs* bathroom. At least one newspaper erroneously reported Troy and Ginny Hall discovered the bodies. [Sources: "Durham Case Reward Upped; $5,000 Offered For Information," *The Journal-Patriot*, North Wilkesboro, NC, February 10, 1972, p. 1.]

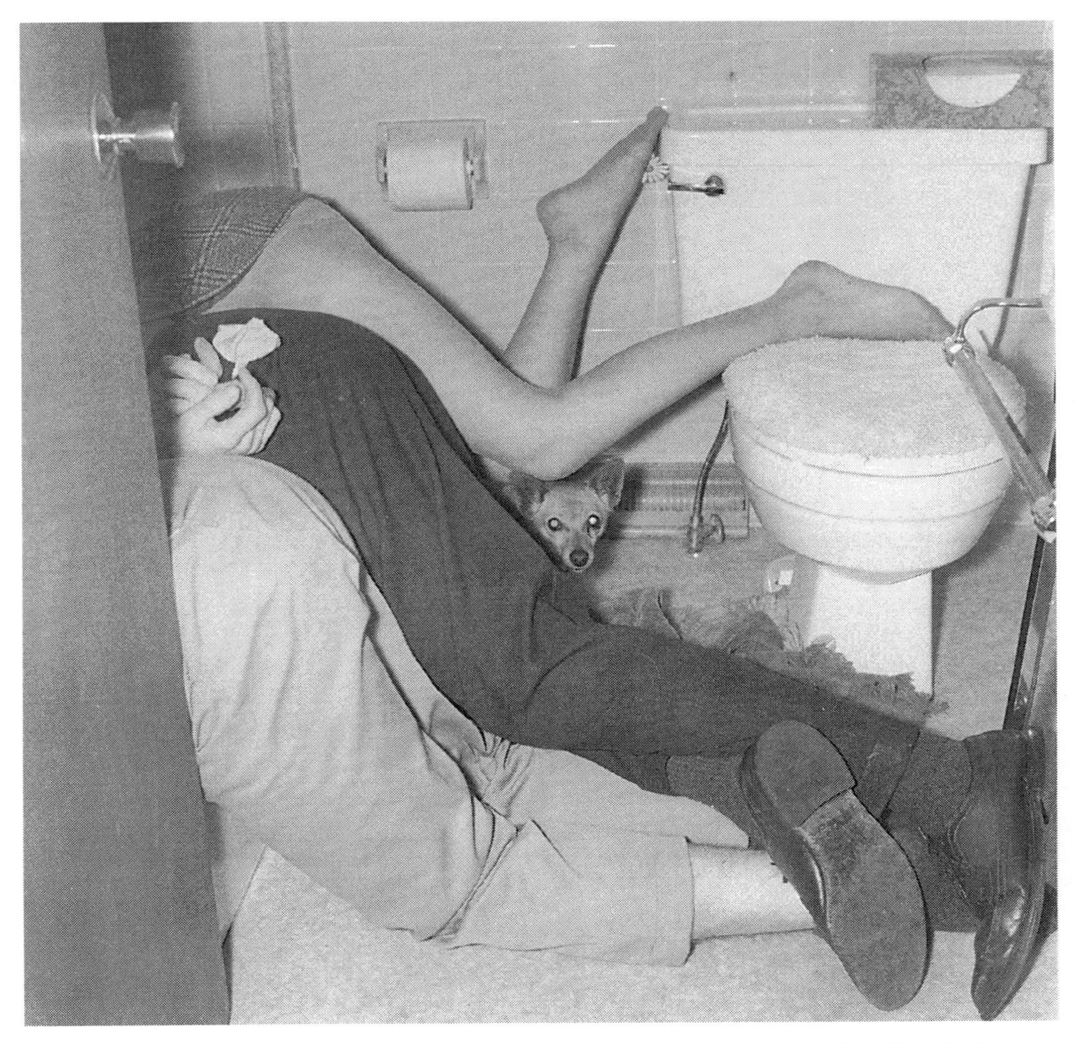

(L-R) Bobby, Bryce, & Virginia Durham (Image courtesy of Watauga County Sheriff's Office)

The two men quickly left the house,[504] Cecil backing all the way out the den door and the garage door[505] and making several observations about the condition of the rooms.[506] Once outside the front of the house, he put his gun in his pocket.[507] "Oh my God!" Troy again exclaimed, wringing his hands. "What are we gonna tell [Ginny]?" Cecil advised Troy not to get excited or she would start screaming. "Don't tell her anything. Don't tell her that we even seen anything. Tell her that they must be out over at the neighbor's somewhere."[508] The pair then half-slid back down the driveway, Troy arriving first and telling Ginny no one was home. Once the men were back in the vehicle with Ginny, Troy told her "they needed to make a phone call quickly," and Cecil attempted to back down to the bottom of the hill and onto the bypass. He had difficulty seeing, and Troy, seemingly no longer shaken by what he had just witnessed inside the house, opened his door to look out and help navigate. Seeing Cecil was about to hit a utility trailer on the side of the road, he told him to move over. In doing so, Cecil braked and lost control on some solid ice, and the car slid off the road[509] and down an embankment about 35-40 feet from the bypass.[510] *[When Boone Police Chief Clyde*

Tester later asked Cecil where he was going, Cecil said he didn't know,[511] and when State Bureau of Investigation Agent Charlie Whitman asked Cecil what he had been planning to do, Cecil replied, "I was just going to get away from there."[512] Years later, he stated it was his intention to leave the scene and drive to the police station.[513]]

With the car steeply leaning and on the verge of overturning, Troy and Ginny somehow managed to exit the passenger side while Cecil remained inside.[514] Cecil instructed Troy to go to one of the nearby apartment buildings and call the police as well as a wrecker from Boone.[515] Ginny accompanied Troy[516] while Cecil, having eventually exited the car, walked down to the bypass "to flag someone down for help [and stand] guard, more or less…seeing that nobody come [sic] in or out."[517] While standing there, he saw Boone Policeman Zane Tester driving his personal Plymouth car along the bypass, and although Cecil attempted to flag him down, Tester continued on, "right down there at the bottom [and] turned in."[518] *[This may be a reference to Tester passing by Clyde Townsend Road, and continuing to the next road below – Greer Lane – which was where Tester resided.]*

Troy knocked loudly on the door of Apartment #9, which was shared by bachelors Ricky Phillips, Lynn Greene, and Edward Lowrance.[519] *[According to another account, Phillips, Greene, and Lowrance went outside to offer their assistance to the stranded vehicle and its passengers and subsequently offered their phone.[520]]* It is unclear exactly when Troy told Ginny about discovering her family,[521] but it was likely as they entered the apartment as Mike Townsend recalls hearing her scream from his family's apartment directly above.[522] Troy called the Boone Police Department and reached dispatcher Johnny Tester, son of Boone Police Chief Clyde Tester and brother of Boone Policeman Zane Tester. Johnny Tester's shift was almost over when he received and logged Troy's call at 10:50 PM.[523][rr] *[While it is believed Cecil, Troy, and Ginny arrived on Clyde Townsend Road at approximately 10:45 PM, the coroner's summary stated they discovered the bodies at approximately 10:30 PM, but it also erroneously stated the discovery was made on February 4 rather than February 3.[524] At least one newspaper stated the bodies were found shortly after 10:30 PM,[525] which is the time Cecil said the Halls arrived at his trailer. Another report states the bodies were discovered at 10:50 PM, which is incorrect as that is the time the Boone Police Department was phoned.[526] One source states it took Cecil, Troy, and Ginny about twenty minutes to drive from Cecil's house to Clyde Townsend Road.[527] If that is true and they really did leave Cecil's house at 10:33 PM, they would have arrived around 10:53 PM, but that also cannot be true based on the 10:50 PM logging of the call to the Boone Police Department. One source says the call to the police department was received at 10:40 PM,[528] another 10:47 PM,[529] and others 10:49 PM.[530]]*

[rr] In October 1971, four months before the murders, a new $69,000 communications control center had been installed in the police station in downtown Boone and tied in all of the county's law enforcement agencies, including the Boone and Blowing Rock Police Departments, the Appalachian State University campus security police, the Watauga County Sheriff's Department, and the North Carolina State Highway Patrol. A relay station extended the broadcast equipment's coverage area to 100+ miles and enabled officers to call surrounding counties from their patrol cars. Officers were also supplied with devices similar to walkie-talkies that allowed them to be "in constant contact with the base station and all cars." The new equipment additionally included a "Dictaphone Recorder capable of recording every radio conversation…every telephone call received, and time, place and details…." According to Chief Clyde Tester, this recorder was of great value as it eliminated the need for someone to make a handmade log and allowed officers to recheck details via an adjacent playback machine. [Sources: "Law Enforcing Network Set Up," *Watauga Democrat*, Boone, NC, October 7, 1971, pp. 1 & 2; "Police," *Watauga Democrat*, Boone, NC, January 10, 1972, p. 2A; "$425,000 Jail Will Be Built On Water St.," *Watauga Democrat*, Boone, NC, October 23, 1972, p. 1.]

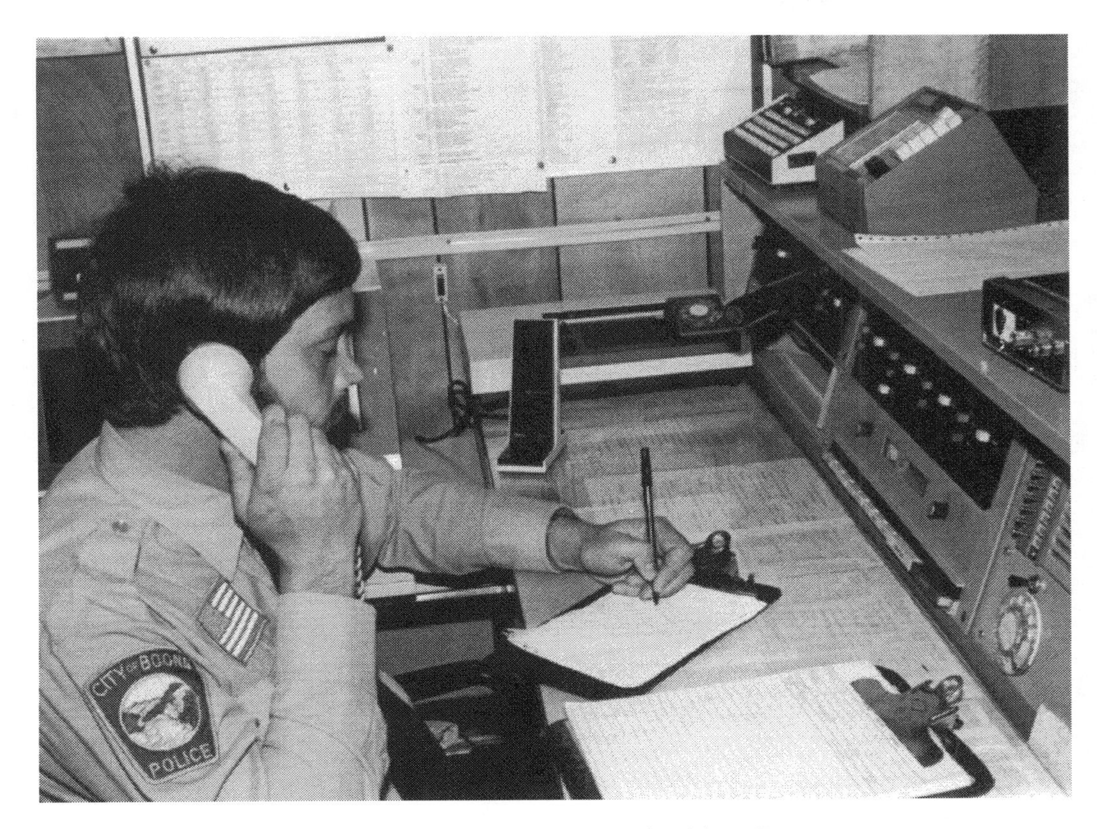

Boone Police Department Dispatcher Johnny Tester
(Image Courtesy of the George Flowers Collection, Digital Watauga Project)

A partial transcript,[ss] taken from a recording of the actual call is as follows:

TESTER: "An ambulance is on its way. Now, just hold it and settle down now."

HALL: "Wait a minute, I think they're out here. Listen, I'm gonna hang up. Are they out there?"

TESTER: "Uh, the ambulances will be there shortly."

HALL: "Yeah."

TESTER: "Okay, now is, uh, you say there was a robbery."

[ss] The reel-to-reel tapes used in the Boone Police Department's communications center were often taped over and reused, although there is no knowledge whether that occurred with this specific reel of tape. It had not been taped over as late as 1978, when a portion of the call was used in a WBTV News Report. Copies could have been made from the reel-to-reel tape, but there seems to be no recording still in existence of the full conversation nor a transcript of it. The Boone Police Department, the Watauga County Sheriff's Office, and the North Carolina State Bureau of Investigation have all stated that their agencies do not have this. [Sources: Tester, Johnny. Phone conversation with author. October 16, 2022; Main, Stephanie (Records Unit, Boone Police Department). Phone conversation with author. October 17, 2022. Grube, Angie (Public Information Director, N. C. State Bureau of Investigation). E-mail to author. November 1, 2022. Anderson, Patrick (Watauga County Sheriff's Office Deputy, Evidence and Property). E-mail to author. November 3, 2022.]

HALL: "I don't know. It's just the house was all messed up, and everything was thrown everywhere. I don't know what happened."

TESTER: "Okay, now who is the fellow, you know?"

HALL: "It's Mr. Bryce Durham, his wife, and his son Bobby. They're [sic] my father-in-law."

TESTER: "Are all of 'em hurt?"

HALL: "I think they're dead."

TESTER: "Oh."[531]

According to Johnny Tester, "The caller seemed to be mighty shook up,"[532] and "he almost couldn't decipher Troy's frantic plea for help." It was difficult for Tester to get enough out of Troy to know what had happened.[533] Troy did not want to provide the phone number he was calling from, but after Tester's insistence that protocol required it, he complied.[534]

Although the Durham residence was outside the Boone town limits, the Boone Police Department was the only law enforcement agency that had officers patrolling that night;[535] sheriff's deputies were off the roads due to the weather.[tt] Also, the police department was the county's sole dispatcher for their own officers, the Watauga County Sheriff's Department, and rescue personnel.[536]

After alerting his police chief father about the call, Tester contacted Watauga County Sheriff Ward Carroll, who said he would get dressed and be on his way.[537] *[Carroll, who had no previous law enforcement experience when he was elected sheriff in 1966, had been reelected in 1970.]*[538]

Left: Watauga County Sheriff Ward Carroll (as published in the Watauga Democrat). Middle: Boone Police Chief Clyde Tester (Courtesy of Janie Tester Aldridge). Right: NC Highway Patrolman George E. Baker (Courtesy of the Baker family).

Johnny Tester also notified the North Carolina State Highway Patrol station in Newton, and they dispatched Patrolman George E. Baker. Although one news outlet reported Baker was inside the

[tt] At this time, the sheriff's office only had a handful of deputies who were stretched thin and wore many hats, and one of them – Johnny Carroll, son of Sheriff Ward Carroll – had been a deputy since 1968 and was just recovering from the flu. His first day back at work was the day following the murders. [Source: Carroll, Johnny. Phone interview with author. June 29, 2022.]

Boone Police Department Communications Center when Troy's call came in,[539] he was actually on patrol in the area[540] and was the first to arrive on the scene.[541] Tester returned a call to the number Troy had provided. Troy answered, and Tester informed him officers were on the way.[542]

By the time Patrolman Baker arrived, Durham neighbor Paul Allen was returning home from the Watauga County Hospital where he had been visiting his wife and two-day-old son, but his Volkswagen failed to scale the steep road to his house. Because the crime scene was under the jurisdiction of the sheriff's office, and because Clyde Townsend was both a Durham neighbor and a reserve sheriff's deputy, Baker asked him to accompany him to the Durham house, and they took Allen and Troy Hall with them. As Troy had already done, Baker, Townsend, and Allen witnessed the Durhams' bodies in the bathtub.[543] Additional officers waited at the bottom of Clyde Townsend Road until the arrivals of Sheriff Carroll and some of his deputies.[544] *[Carroll lived some ten miles east of the Durham home, and driving in inclement weather would have taken around thirty minutes, which probably placed him at the scene around 11:30 PM, although testimony from others present that night indicate Carroll was already on the scene just after 11:00 PM.]* The blue light of Baker's patrol car ascending the hill drew the attention of neighbors, some of whom walked up to find out was happening.[545][uu]

Meanwhile, Ginny, following instruction from the State Highway Patrol,[546] stayed inside the apartment from which Troy had placed the call to the police, and she remained there until early the following morning.[vv] When Cecil Small saw her, she was sitting beside another woman, and she never came outside.[547] "In a conversation marked by periods of high emotion, [Ginny], more talkative than her husband...discussed a number of things," including the rift with her parents over her marriage to Troy, but how their relationship was showing promise of improvement.[548] According to Cecil, who was not aware when or if Ginny had been told about her family, she "wasn't crying or hollering or nothing like that."[549]

Troy had been unable to reach the wrecker service, so Cecil called again.[550] The owner's wife stated he was not there, but she would send him as soon as he returned. While he waited for the wrecker's arrival, Cecil walked back up the hill to the Durham house, and Sheriff Carroll and local newspaper editor and photographer Bev Ballard[ww] arrived. As Carroll entered the house, Cecil remained outside with a crowd of onlookers who had gathered in the Durham yard.[551]

[uu] Neighbors Jerry Cornell and Larry Greer, along with Greer's brother Gary, and Stewart Simmons (who lived on the 105 Bypass) were playing Rook at the Greer residence, which sat immediately below the Durham home. Larry's wife Evelyn and Jerry's wife Jeannie were also present. None of them were aware of what had transpired until they saw the emergency lights, after which the men went outside to see if they could determine anything. [Sources: Cornell, Tommy. In-person conversation with author. February 5, 2023; Greer, Evelyn. Phone interview with author. April 3, 2023.]

[vv] A newspaper article states the Halls left the apartment at 3:00 AM, but this contradicts the recollection of Johnny Tester, who believes that time to be closer to 12:30 or 1:00 AM. [Sources: Ron Alridge, "Unlikely Victims: Killings of 'Friendly' Boone Family Baffle Town," *The Charlotte Observer*, Charlotte, NC, February 6, 1972, p. 1C; Tester, Johnny. Facebook message to author. October 17, 2023.]

[ww] Ballard moved to Boone in 1971 to assume editorship of the *Watauga Democrat*. He was often called upon to photograph scenes such as automobile accidents, and his son Loy remembers his father describing some of what he had seen at the Durham home to his mother the morning after the murders. [Sources: "Ballard Is New Editor Democrat," *Watauga Democrat*, Boone, NC, June 17, 1971, p. 1; "Deaths And Funerals: L. Beverly Ballard, 54, Minister, Former Newsman," *The State*, Columbia, SC, October 2, 1981, p. 6-C; Ballard, Loy. Phone interview with author. January 26, 2023.]

Shortly before 11:00 PM, the Watauga Rescue Squad was notified of a need, and Captain Oscar Danner, Jr. and his crew were on call. Danner phoned fellow squad member Cecil Harmon and told him something had happened around the Hilltop area (a reference to the Hilltop Drive-In, just under a mile from the Durham residence). Danner stated he did not know what had happened, but it might be a shooting. Since Harmon and Roy Moretz (stepfather of Bobby Durham's friend Deryl Danner[552]) lived closer to the squad house, Captain Danner asked if they could respond, and they agreed. Turning onto Clyde Townsend Road just after 11:00 PM, they saw Cecil Small's car down the embankment. With chains on the tires of their 1967 Ford station wagon, they were able to completely ascend the Durhams' driveway. Upon arrival, they found Edsel Jackson of the Watauga County Ambulance Service was present as well as Sheriff Ward Carroll. Carroll initially denied the responders entrance into the home, saying the victims were presumed to be dead. Jackson asked, "Well, Mr. Carroll, how do you know they're dead? Have you examined them?" Carroll said he had not, and Jackson asked, "Well, will you please just let us and the rescue squad boys and an officer…in there and just check for a pulse?" Carroll relented but told them not to touch anything. The men proceeded into the garage and then the den, which Harmon recalled as being one of the least destructed rooms on the main floor in terms of ransacking. There they saw drops of dried or absorbed blood on the carpet and noticed drinking glasses and plates with mostly eaten food. A telephone was reportedly located against the wall directly opposite the door that led between the den and the garage. *[This may refer to the wall phone in the kitchen that could be seen from a certain vantage point in the den, or it may refer to another phone in the den itself. As of this writing, a phone jack is on the baseboard along the wall immediately to the perpendicular left of this door, and it may have been there at the time of the murders and may have had a phone connected to it.[553]]* The station on the television was signing off and the volume was up just enough for them to hear the national anthem.[xx] Proceeding onward, they exited the den into the small hallway where they passed by the open door of Bobby's bedroom. According to Harmon, "It was a mess [and] looked like somebody had been in a fight. They's stuff all over the room, all over the bed, and just tore up good." According to Harmon, in the nearby living room, lamps had been overturned and curtains pulled down.[554][yy]

When the responders came to the bathroom, water was continuing to run into the tub. The Durhams' bodies, still draped over the tub, were submerged in the water to just above their nipple lines. Harmon noticed Bryce had bruises on his face, as if he had been struck with a fist, and he appeared to have been hit pretty hard several times in the head with something like a pipe, leaving a big cut. He also had a rope burn around his neck, and his face was bleeding, although the water in the tub did not appear to be very bloody. Jackson checked for pulses and confirmed all the victims were deceased, which dashed the hope that at least one of the Durhams would be alive to help identify their assailants. The responders then exited the house through the front door. By that time, Sheriff Carroll was still awaiting the arrival of the State Bureau of Investigation. Wondering if they were having difficulty locating the house despite all the red and blue emergency lights flashing at the top of the hill and believing he had just seen them pass by, he decided to go back down Clyde Townsend

---

[xx] In that day and time, the playing of the national anthem usually took place around midnight and signaled the end of TV stations' daily broadcasts. If Cecil Small was correct in stating the TV volume was all the way down when he first entered the Durham home, that means someone turned the volume up at some point afterwards. This seems rather insignificant other than perhaps being an indicator the crime scene was not completely secured, and individuals were touching and handling things within the home.

[yy] Cecil Harmon's recollection of the condition of the living room is contradicted by a crime scene photo, which shows the living room in good order. [Source: Watauga County Sheriff's Office investigation file 118-H-1/2/3.]

Road to the 105 Bypass and escort them up to the house. Leaving the scene with the home's doors open and no other officer in charge, he designated Cecil Harmon and Edsel Jackson to stand watch and to prevent anyone from entering the house unless they were with the SBI. The men agreed, and shortly after Carroll's departure, they were approached by a "large-boned fellow" who had been standing outside in the small group of community onlookers gathering in the yard. Dressed in dark green or gray pants, perhaps a plaid shirt, and a work coat, he began to enter the house. Neither Harmon nor Jackson knew him and said simultaneously, "Hey sir, where are you going?" The man replied, "I'm going in the house." Harmon and Jackson told him he could not enter unless he was with the SBI. Pushing them aside, the man declared in a hateful tone, "I *am* the SBI!" and proceeded to enter, staying inside the house alone for ten to fifteen minutes. When Carroll returned, he asked Harmon and Jackson if anyone had been in the house, and they said yes, the SBI. Carroll asked what they were talking about, and they told him about the man. Later, when Harmon and Jackson asked someone about the man, they were informed he was Cecil Small. Cecil remained in the house until Carroll returned with the actual SBI.[555] *[Edsel Jackson's wife, Mozella, states her husband knew Cecil Small, even before the murders, and would not have let him in the Durham house: "Everybody knowed Cecil.... Cecil was no stranger to none of them up there. Everybody up there would have known him."*[556]*]*

After viewing the murder scene, Sheriff Carroll went outside and took Cecil Small into the front seat of George Baker's patrol car to obtain a statement from him. Troy Hall was standing nearby, and Cecil hollered from the patrol car for him to come so that Carroll could talk to him as well. Troy got into the back seat and leaned over the front seat to converse with Carroll.[557] Troy "recounted the incidents of the previous 2 ½ hours." In response to Carroll's questions, he said he was at a loss as to why anyone would want to kill his in-laws, but he did recall Bryce had been having some sort of labor dispute at the dealership resulting in "hard feelings on the part of several men in the set-up."[558] *[Ginny would also later recall her father being upset in this instance.*[559]*]* Carroll asked Troy what kind of car the Durhams had, and Troy stated they had a Buick, making no mention of the four-wheel drive "Jimmy." Troy said he did not know what they had driven home, and it was liable to be anything. Troy also told Carroll about the phone call and Virginia mentioning three "colored people." After they had given Carroll their statements, Carroll, Cecil, and Troy went back into the Durham house where they joined Patrolman George Baker, Bev Ballard, and Boone Policeman Fred "Shorty" Smith.[560]

Neighbors, including men from the nearby apartment building had come into the yard and were entering the house one or two at a time, viewing the bodies, and exiting. At one point Cecil Small walked "across the street" to ask a neighbor lady if she had seen anything, but she said she was not going to get involved and closed the door.[561][zz]

Meanwhile, around 11:00 PM, Kay Hall received a phone call at her Wilkes County home from Ginny, who asked to speak with Troy's brother Ray but did not mention the murders. Kay informed her Ray was not home.[562] Around this same time, Ginny phoned her uncle, Bill Durham, at his home in Greensboro, North Carolina to inform him of the murders. "Oh, Bill," she said, "I'm afraid they're

---

[zz] Small said the lady's husband was an ex-deputy, which means she would have been next-door neighbor Clara Wilson, but he also stated he believed her last name was Combs, which would have indicated next-door neighbor Opal Combs, who lived on the other side of the Durhams. Perhaps Small visited both homes in his quest for information. [Source: Cecil & Mildred Small, interview with Caroline Walker (*Watauga Democrat* Staff Writer), February 23, 1989, Watauga County Sheriff's Office investigation file 118-H-1/2/3.]

all dead." Within five minutes of that call, Bill was on the phone with the Boone Police Department, where an officer informed him the deaths were not confirmed but to expect the worst. About twenty minutes later, the police called Bill to verify some details, and the deaths were confirmed to him at that time. Bill then phoned his brother Ralph and subsequently went to his home, also in Greensboro, arriving there around 12:00 AM. The brothers called their sister Gayle a little later and asked her to await their arrival in Wilkes County so they could inform their parents together.[563] Upon learning about the murders of her brother, sister-in-law, and nephew, Gayle informed her husband Charles Mauldin. "Someone's killed Bryce," she said. Charles's immediate response was, "Troy."[564]

Officers from multiple agencies arrived on the scene shortly after 11:00 PM.[565] In addition to Patrolman Baker, Sheriff Carroll, and Police Chief Clyde Tester, others there reportedly included two county medical examiners.[566] In fact, there was only one medical examiner on the scene – Dr. Clayton Dean. Three local physicians took monthly turns as the on-call medical examiner, and the one on call that night was Dean's medical practice associate, Dr. Lowell Furman. It so happened Furman was hosting a poker game at his house that night, and Dean was in attendance. When the summons to the Durham home came from the Boone Police Department, rather than force his host into the cold, snowy night, Dean offered to go in his stead. As he would later recall, "I was not assigned the job, but I took his place and walked into that mess." Dean had been told three people were dead, but he had no idea what he was about to encounter; he imagined the deaths being asphyxia-related due to a gas stove. It was the first homicide he had ever been called to.[567]

George Flowers, an award-winning UPI photographer, television news correspondent, and retail merchant who owned a photo shop in Boone[568] was also dispatched to take crime scene photos. Flowers had a radio equivalent to those in law enforcement vehicles and had been designated as a special deputy for Watauga County. His photography skills were frequently called upon by law enforcement, and he had helped organize the Watauga County Rescue Squad. Following an assignment, Flowers personally processed his black and white film and then selected photos to share with news outlets via a UPI transmitter, which was also in his possession.[569] Flowers had previously worked for the Durhams, taking photographs of new cars at the dealership for advertisement purposes, and he spoke highly of them.[570] Among the images he captured at the scene were ones of the victims as they were found in the bathroom. Although the photos were black and white, the in-color reality of the cheery, lavender bathroom tile[571] belied the gruesomeness of what had been committed. Frosted glass shower doors, with depictions of swimming swans, had presumably been removed from the tub by the killers and were placed upright in the foyer outside the bathroom. The Durhams were draped over the shower door track on the edge of the tub.[572] Bobby's body was nearest the bathroom door and to the tub's faucet and drain.[573] Because Bryce's body slightly overlapped Bobby's, and Virginia's body slightly overlapped her husband's, investigators concluded they had been placed in the tub in that order.[574]

Those on the scene were followed by SBI agents,[575] including Boone-based Wallace "Wally" Hardwick, Jr, "a comparatively new and inexperienced agent,"[576] who called his headquarters in Asheville, North Carolina and alerted Jesse Newton "Red" Minter, Jr.,[577] supervisor of "the SBI's operations in the twenty-one-county Western District."[578] Minter subsequently assigned SBI Agents Charles "Charlie" Chambers and Charles "Charlie" Whitman to assist.[579] Chambers was the supervisor for the SBI's Northwestern District,[580] and Whitman was the assistant district supervisor and was living in Lenoir, North Carolina at the time. Whitman had been in bed about five minutes when he received the phone call from Hardwick shortly before 11:00 PM, and he arrived at the scene around midnight.[581] Because Hardwick was a rookie and overwhelmed, Whitman more or less took the lead.[582]

Even after Johnny Tester completed his dispatching shift and was relieved by communications officer Gray Isaacs, he remained at the police department for a while to assist Isaacs with the influx of telephone calls and radio traffic. Their telecommunications had a double console which enabled them to work in tandem. When the SBI photographer arrived asking for someone to take him to the Durham home, Tester obliged. Arriving around 12:00 AM, they, like several before them, entered the den via the garage.[583]

Also, around 12:00 AM, Sheriff Ward Carroll advised the rescue and ambulance personnel to go to Clyde Townsend's apartment and wait there until they were needed again. As they waited, everyone discussed the awful events and expressed disbelief that this had happened in Boone.[584] Carroll, reflecting on his six years in office, stated, "This is the worst crime that I can recall here.[585] We've had some bad ones, but I've never seen anything like this.[586] Not this bad."[587] He said it was one of "the most brutal" slayings he could remember,[588] and according to the SBI, "the triple slaying was one of only three on record in North Carolina."[589]

When found in the bathtub, Bobby and Virginia had no shoes on; Bobby's lace-up Oxfords and Virginia's zip-up knee-high or "fashion" boots were neatly sitting by the front door, which Agent Whitman interpreted to mean they had removed their snowy shoes upon arriving home. He examined all the soles and found them to still be wet. Bobby and Virginia also doffed their hats at the door. Whitman checked them at midnight and found them to still be damp.[590] Bryce was still wearing his Oxfords, but the rubber pull-on boots he had worn over them were found in the upstairs master bedroom along with his overcoat, which had been hung on the edge of the closet door. In his coat pocket was a military can opener for opening the MREs, which corresponded with the dinner served to the Rotarians that evening. A ration package was found just inside the front door, to the right, and included an open tin of cookies and a tin of pineapple chunks.[591] Presumably, Bryce had brought these home from his meeting, carried them from the "Jimmy" into the house, and immediately set them down. According to Whitman, the fact that Bryce's rubber boots and overcoat were in the bedroom was indicative he went upstairs after arriving home, and one "would have to assume that he got back downstairs. It would be a guess as to whether he was forced downstairs or if things had not started to happen when he came back downstairs."[592]

Interior stairs of Durham home (Image courtesy of Watauga County Sheriff's Office)

Bryce & Virginia Durham's upstairs bedroom. Note Bryce's overcoat on the edge of closet door. (Image courtesy of Watauga County Sheriff's Office)

Authorities believed the family had settled down to have refreshments and watch television[aaa] when they were surprised by intruders.[593] A partially eaten barbequed chicken purchased the previous day was on the kitchen table,[594] alongside a large butcher knife and Virginia's purse. Some of the purse's contents were strewn about the floor, but her wallet remained inside. Sweet potatoes were on the stove.[595] When Cecil Small had been in the home after the murders, he noticed in the den three glasses containing something which was later determined to be soft drinks.[596] The fact that three glasses (two filled and one partially filled) were present[597] indicated to investigators all three Durhams were together after arriving home. Ginny stated her parents were "big Coke drinkers" and did not consume alcohol.[598] One of the glasses, along with a plate of partially eaten chicken, sweet potatoes, and a pineapple chunk, and a deck of cards was on the padded coffee table, which had been pushed against the leather-covered couch, although some of the cards, along with bits of

[aaa] Assuming the Durhams only received the three major networks, as was common for most households in the area at that time, they likely would have been watching the CBS movie *Hunters Are For Killing*, ABC's *Longstreet: Anatomy of a Mayday*, or NBC's *Ironside: Bubble, Bubble, Toil and Murder*, all of which aired at 9:00 PM. All ended at 10:00 PM, except for the movie, which ended at 11:00 PM. Other shows began at 10:00 PM on ABC and NBC, including the Winter Olympics, but by that time, the Durhams were likely either being attacked or already dead. [Source: https://www.ultimate70s.com/seventies_history/19720203/television.]

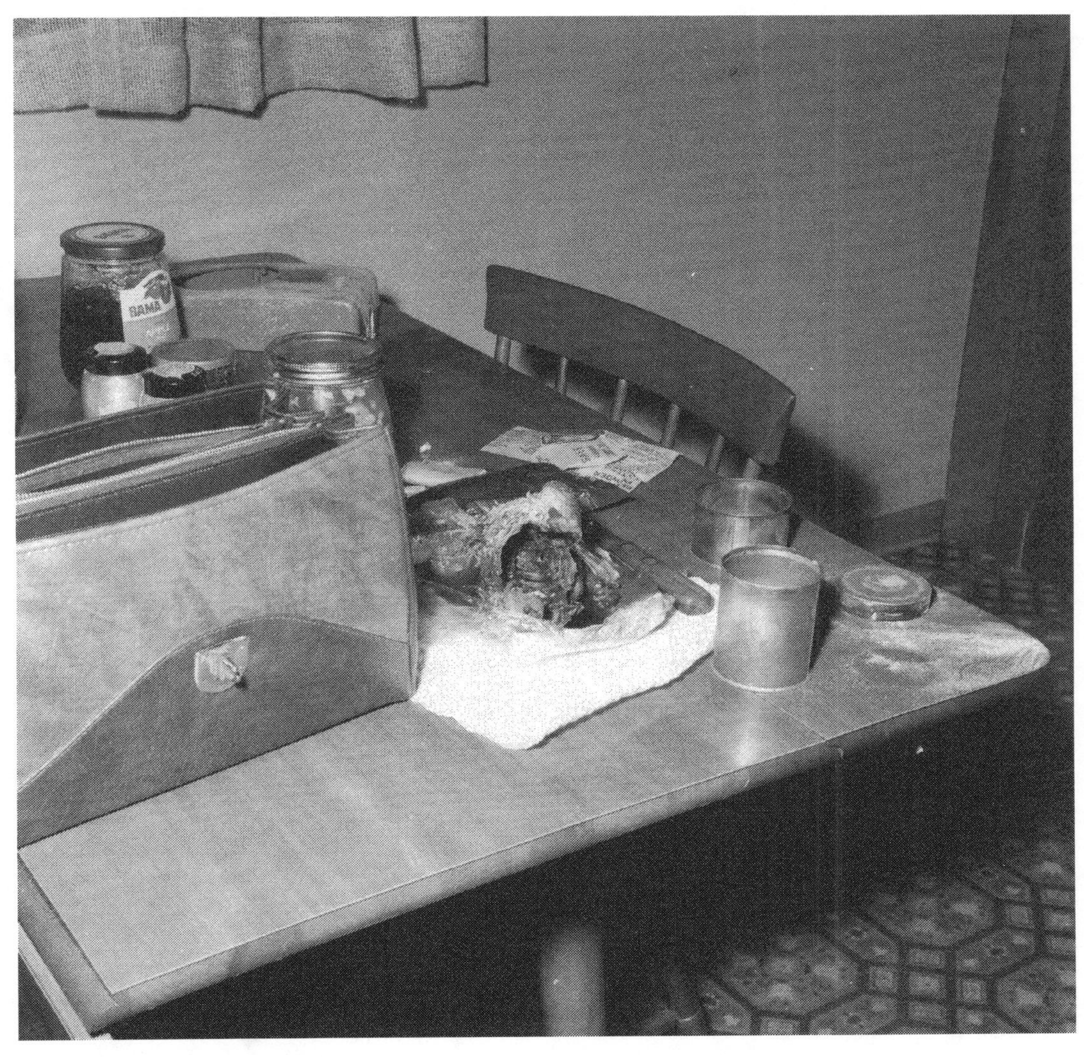

Durham kitchen. Note Virginia Durham's purse, a partially eaten chicken, and the wall phone cover sitting on table. (Image courtesy of Watauga County Sheriff's Office)

Durham kitchen. Note partially eaten chicken on table and items strewn on floor.
(Images courtesy of Watauga County Sheriff's Office)

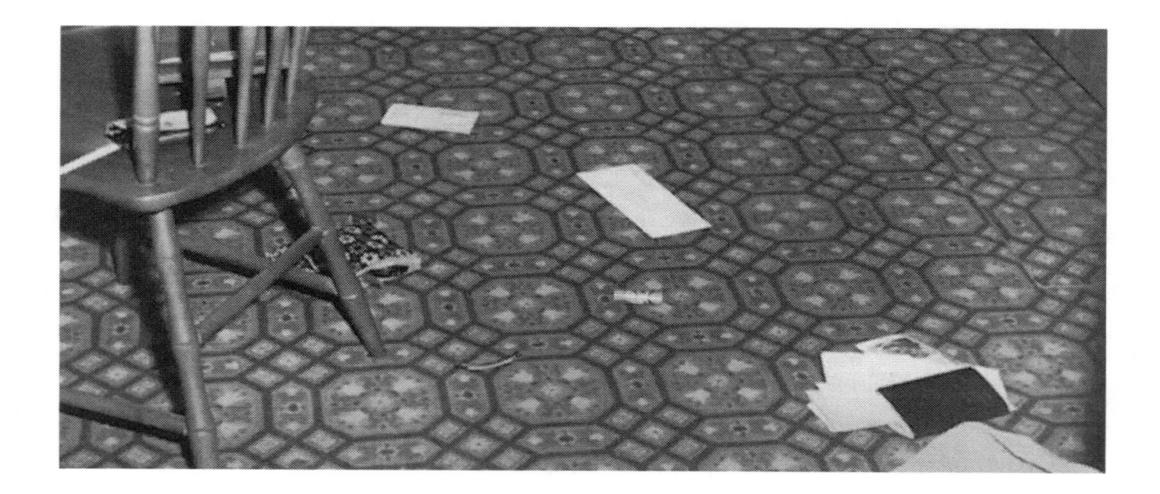

chicken, were scattered on the floor. Familiar with her family's habits, Ginny believed Bobby, who had recently determined to "beat Solitaire," was probably seated there, having been served food first,[599] while her parents were sitting in chairs. Mysteriously, two footstools and some pictures from the living room [sic; should be den] wall had been piled on the couch, some of them being in the spot where Bobby was presumed to have been sitting.[bbb] Investigators believed they had been placed there by the intruders and the pictures may have been removed as they searched for a strongbox[600] or "a wall safe or some other hiding place for cash and valuables."[601]

Den where Bobby Durham was believed to have been sitting on this couch eating and playing Solitaire. (Image courtesy of Watauga County Sheriff's Office)

Throughout the house, drawers had been pulled out of bureaus and dumped on the floor,[602] their contents strewn about.[603] In Bryce's and Virginia's bedroom, a picture was taken off the wall and set in a chair, drawers had been dumped, and a drawer was placed on the bed.[604] Virginia's sewing room was not badly disturbed. Ginny's former bedroom had drawers removed and dumped. A locker containing Bryce's gun collection was behind the door of this bedroom and bore a shiny padlock; it was untouched. *[One source stated Bryce "was known to have owned a valuable collection of guns" but erroneously indicated none of them could be located.[605]]* The contents of the upstairs linen closet were dumped, but another second floor storage area – a crawl space entered near the top of the stairs and extending over the living room and dining area – was unbothered.[606] Every closet had been opened[607] and rummaged. Bedding was reportedly stripped and piled in the floor,[608] although crime

[bbb] Crime scene photos depict the two footstools but not the pictures that were alleged to be piled on the couch. The room where the Durhams had been sitting was officially the den, which one report denoted as the TV room. The living room was a separate and more formal room on the other end of the house, at the front. Reports and observers sometimes erroneously referred to the den as the living room.

Durham den. Note section of paneling removed by investigators above chair at center, just past curtain, representing the location of a bullet hole. (Image courtesy of Watauga County Sheriff's Office)

scene photos reveal most bedding intact. Back downstairs, Virginia's London Fog overcoat lay crumpled beside the piano at the doorway between the living room and kitchen. Despite one of the emergency responder's recollection of overturned lamps and curtains being pulled down, crime scene photos depict the living room as virtually untouched.[609]

The basement had also been ransacked,[610] although some of the crime scene photos reveal parts of the basement in about the same general condition any common basement might be found. The ransacking initially gave the appearance of a burglary, but after further consideration, experienced investigators concluded it had been staged.[611]

Doorway between Durham dining room and kitchen. Note Virginia Durham's coat on floor and purse on kitchen table. (Image courtesy of Watauga County Sheriff's Office)

View from laundry area adjacent to back door looking into den (above) and kitchen (below)
(Images courtesy of Watauga County Sheriff's Office)

Bobby Durham's downstairs bedroom (Image courtesy of Watauga County Sheriff's Office)

Bobby Durham's downstairs bedroom (Top image courtesy of the George Flowers Collection, Digital Watauga Project; bottom image courtesy of Watauga County Sheriff's Office)

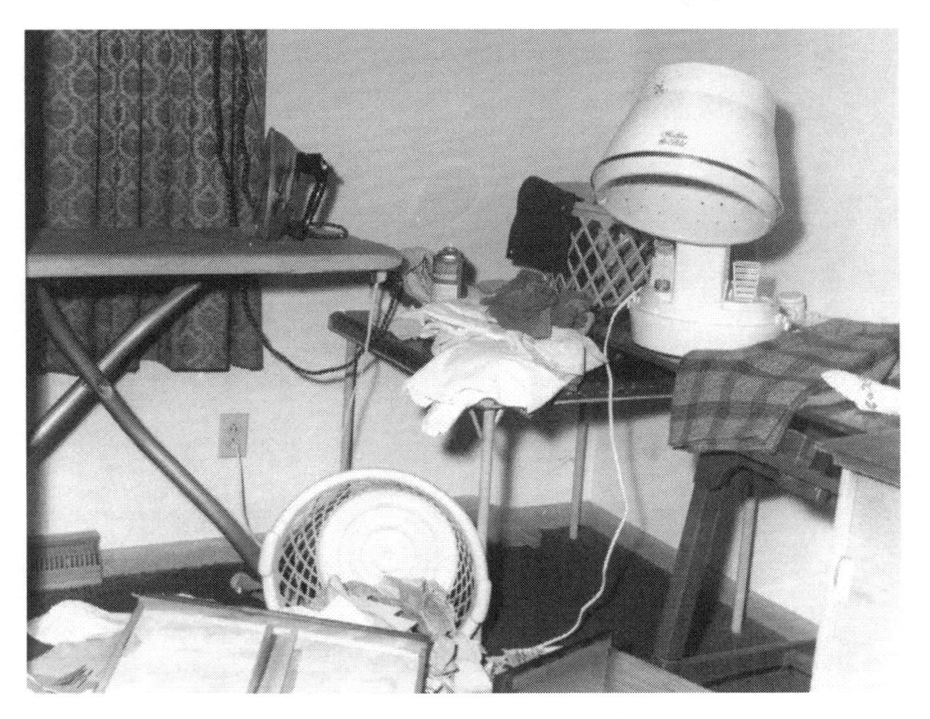

Sewing room and hallway with linens in floor (both located upstairs)
(Images courtesy of Watauga County Sheriff's Office)

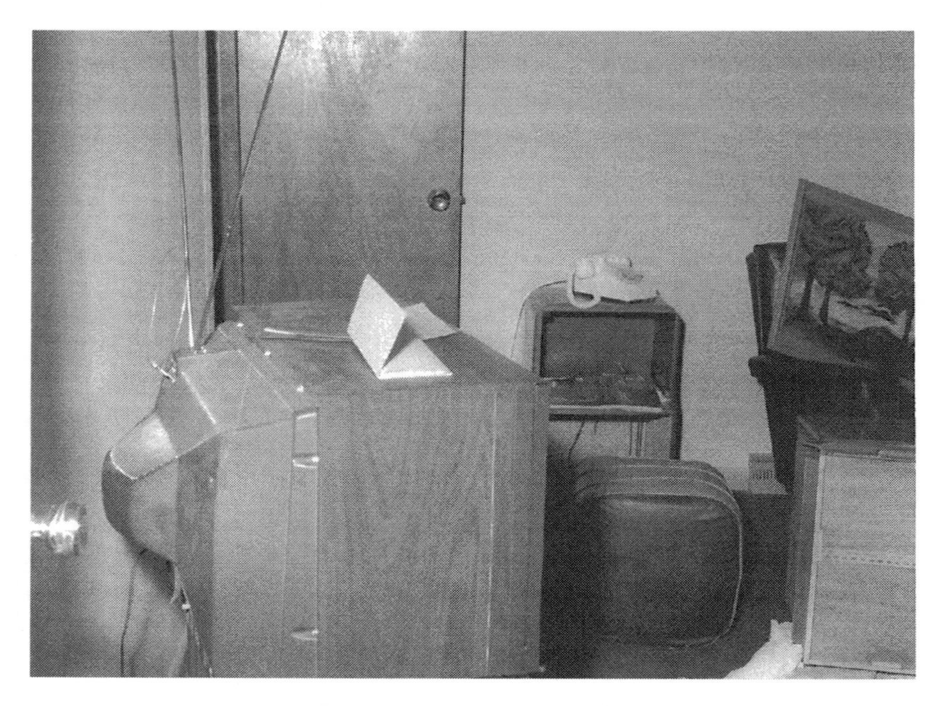

Bryce & Virginia Durham's upstairs bedroom
(Images courtesy of Watauga County Sheriff's Office)

Ginny Durham's former upstairs bedroom. Note that the images were taken at different times. (Top image courtesy of Watauga County Sheriff's Office; bottom image courtesy of the George Flowers Collection, Digital Watauga Project)

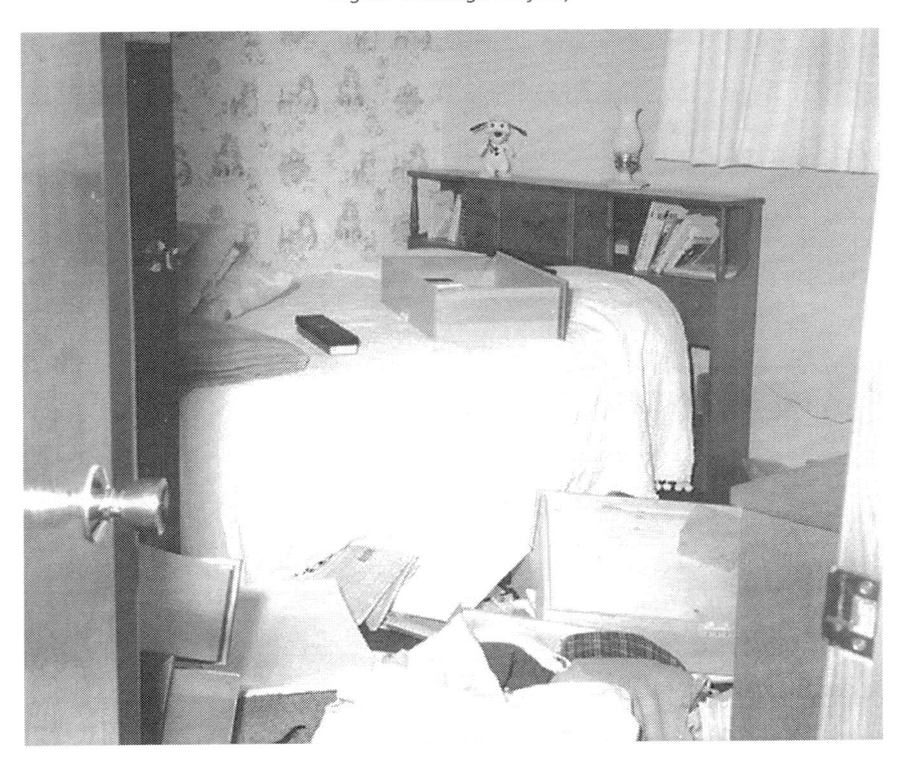

Durham dining area (above) and living room
(Images courtesy of Watauga County Sheriff's Office)

Durham basement (Top image courtesy of Watauga County Sheriff's Office; bottom image courtesy of the George Flowers Collection, Digital Watauga Project)

Durham basement (Image courtesy of the George Flowers Collection, Digital Watauga Project)

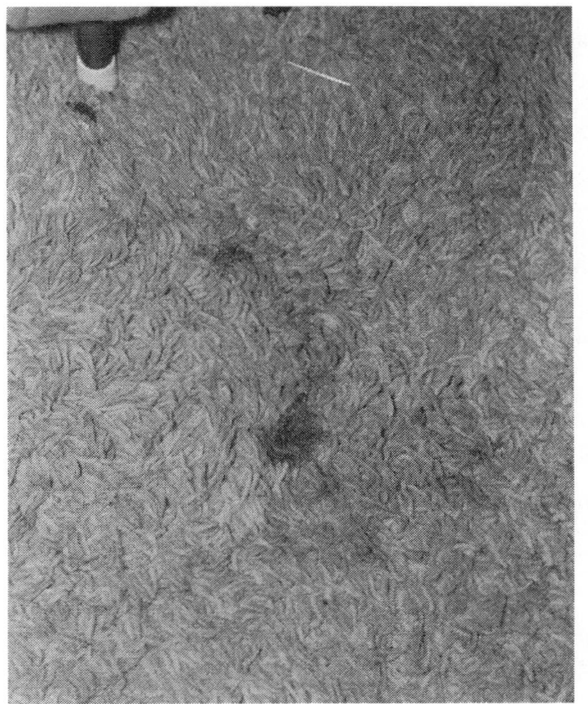

Blood stain on shag carpet in den
(Image courtesy of Watauga County Sheriff's Office)

Blood was on the shag carpet in the den, and a small pattern of blood gave the appearance of someone having stepped in a larger splotch[612] *[likely indicating where Cecil Small had stepped in and tracked the blood]*. Some blood spatter was on the walls.[613] Each of the victims had type O blood,[614] but the blood was somehow determined to be Virginia's.[615]

According to SBI Agent Charlie Whitman, "There [was] a telephone in the kitchen. It had been jerked out of the wall. It [had] a cradle and an earpiece and a coiled cord. It had been jerked out where the cord goes into the base.... This is why when they [Troy/Ginny] tried to call back they got a busy signal, allegedly."[616] In another interview, Whitman stated that a cord had been jerked from the wall telephone in the kitchen and was laying on the floor.[617] Cecil Small reportedly noticed a "telephone box" on the kitchen wall without a receiver. "Only the ragged ends of wires were present indicating that the instrument had been forcibly ripped away."[618] Crime scene photos depict the wall phone in the kitchen devoid of its outer casing, which was lying on the kitchen table, yet with the receiver, cord intact, sitting in the cradle because, upon entering the house that night, a law enforcement officer, fearing he would trip over the cord and receiver lying on the floor, picked it up and hung it back in place.[619] One source states the wall phone was found disconnected and confirms the receiver was lying on the floor.[620] Another states, "A telephone in the downstairs section was torn from the wall,"[621] and yet another states, "One telephone in the corridor literally had been ripped from the wall. Another was inoperable."[622] At least one phone appeared to remain intact on a bedside table in Bryce's and Virginia's upstairs bedroom,[623] but the fact that one or more telephones had been rendered useless caused authorities, based on Troy's telling them he had taken a call from Virginia, to surmise the intruders caught her "talking on the phone and yanked it out."[624]

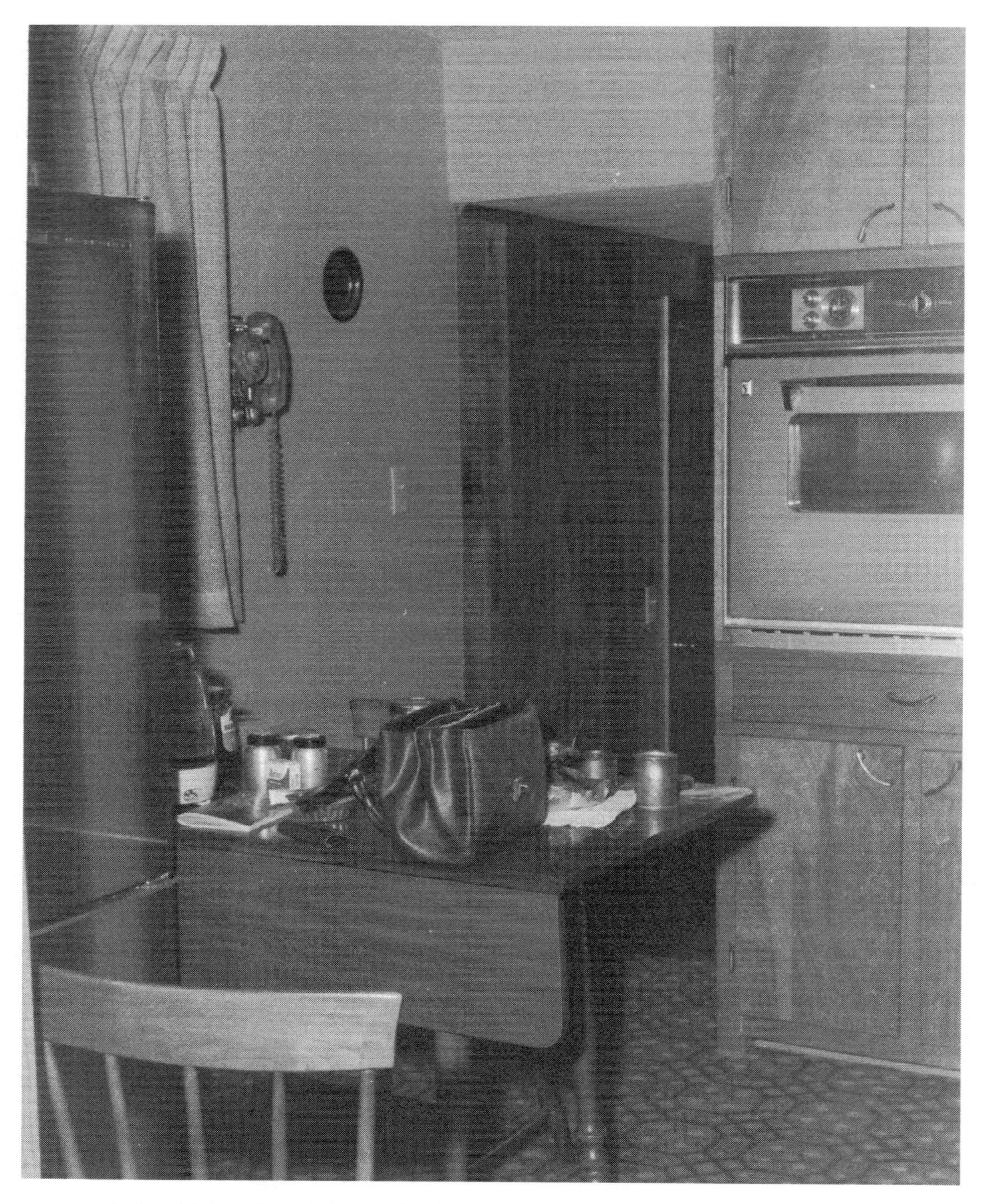

Durham kitchen. Note Virginia Durham's purse on table and wall phone missing its cover.
(Image courtesy of Watauga County Sheriff's Office)

Durham garage (Image courtesy of Watauga County Sheriff's Office)

Durham garage. Bottom photo shows door leading from the garage to the den.
(Images courtesy of Watauga County Sheriff's Office)

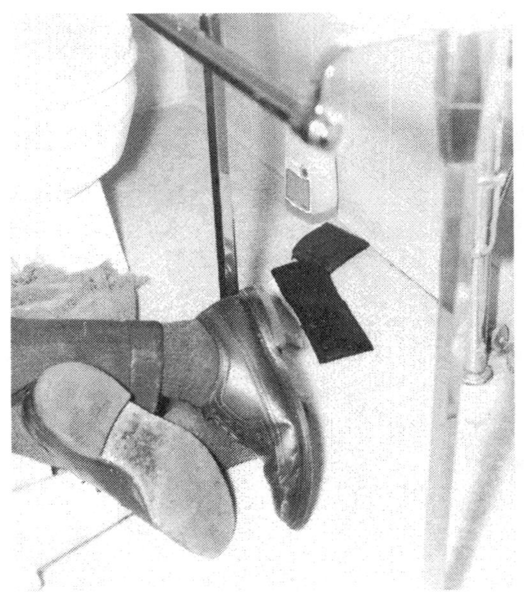

Bryce & Bobby Durhams' wallets lying beside their overlapped feet (Image courtesy of Watauga County Sheriff's Office)

According to one source, "Sheriff [Ward] Carroll and his colleagues realized that a considerable amount of loot had been taken from the home,"[625] while a contradictory source stated, "Several valuable items…were not touched."[626] There was speculation from day one that the Durhams may have had a large sum of money in the house, perhaps stashed in a shoebox, but never confirmed.[627] Bryce's and Bobby's wallets, found near their bodies, had been rifled and presumably emptied.[628] Some claimed a safe was in the basement, perhaps underneath the stairs, but that was also unconfirmed. Others said a footlocker was located there.[629] One source claims the family's safe had been opened and its contents spread across the den floor.[630] An empty breadbox was found in the basement and caused officers to wonder if it had contained something valuable.[631] Virginia's niece, Jerri Bumgarner Waddell, believed the breadbox contained Bryce's and Virginia's revised wills.[632] Perhaps the breadbox, rather than a shoebox, also held a large sum of money.

No vehicle belonging to or driven by the Durhams was found in the two-car garage or the driveway, which indicated the vehicle they had driven home had been taken.[633] Authorities speculated "the killers perhaps had driven to the Durham home in another vehicle thinking they could rely on [the Durhams' vehicle] for their getaway if their own car got stuck in the snow."[634] Although Troy Hall had told Sheriff Carroll his in-laws might have driven any number of vehicles home from the dealership, it was reported Troy and Ginny "were certain that Bryce…must have used" the GMC "Jimmy" that Ginny reportedly rode in with her father earlier that day, and a full description of it was subsequently communicated to law enforcement agents. Meanwhile, officers began canvassing homes along the 105 Bypass and rural roads on both sides of it. Neighbors told officers their dogs had started furiously barking around 10:20 PM; perhaps this was because strangers had approached the house.[635]

SBI Agent Wally Hardwick, Jr.

Between 10:30 and 10:50 PM (10:45 PM per Charlie Whitman[636]), SBI Agent Wally Hardwick, Jr., accompanied by his friend, Appalachian State University Director of Security and Communication and former North Carolina Highway Patrolman Gary Morgan,[637] had "almost met the killers face to face." While Hardwick and Morgan were en route to or from Morgan's home, they discovered the "Jimmy" on Poplar Grove Road but did not know at that time who it belonged to. Stopping to offer help, they exited their own vehicle and approached the abandoned "Jimmy." The engine was running, and they saw silver pieces inside. Moments later, at 10:52 PM,[638] Hardwick was called to the murder scene, still unaware of the vehicle's connection to the victims. Hardwick later recounted that, had he only found the vehicle a bit sooner, he might have seen and been able to identify the killers.[639]

Front of Durhams' abandoned GMC "Jimmy" on Poplar Grove Road in Boone, NC (Image courtesy of Watauga County Sheriff's Office)

Around 10:50 PM,[640] the same time Johnny Tester logged Troy Hall's call, Bob Poe, Bobby Durham's high school football coach and the recently appointed athletic director at Watauga High School,[641] in the company of his six-year-old son Brad, left their home at 1142 Poplar Grove Road, 2.6 miles from the Durham home and saw the "Jimmy" in a ditch on that same road, approximately 2.3 miles from the Durham home.[642] The headlights were on, and the motor and windshield wipers were running.[643] Poe was certain about the time because 11:00 PM was when he had to pick up his other son, fourteen-year-old Stephen, who was returning from a high school wrestling team trip.[644] When Poe and his sons drove back past the vehicle on their return home, he stopped and looked in the interior, thinking perhaps the driver was hurt and still inside.[645] Finding it abandoned and not encountering anyone on the road or seeing any footprints, he proceeded home and contacted the police. *[One article states Poe had heard a late radio news flash about the killings, but he had no police radio, and it seems highly unlikely any mainstream radio station would have had knowledge of the murders as early as 10:50 -11:00 PM.]*[646]

Rear of Durhams' abandoned GMC "Jimmy" on Poplar Grove Road in Boone, NC (Image courtesy of the George Flowers Collection, Digital Watauga Project)

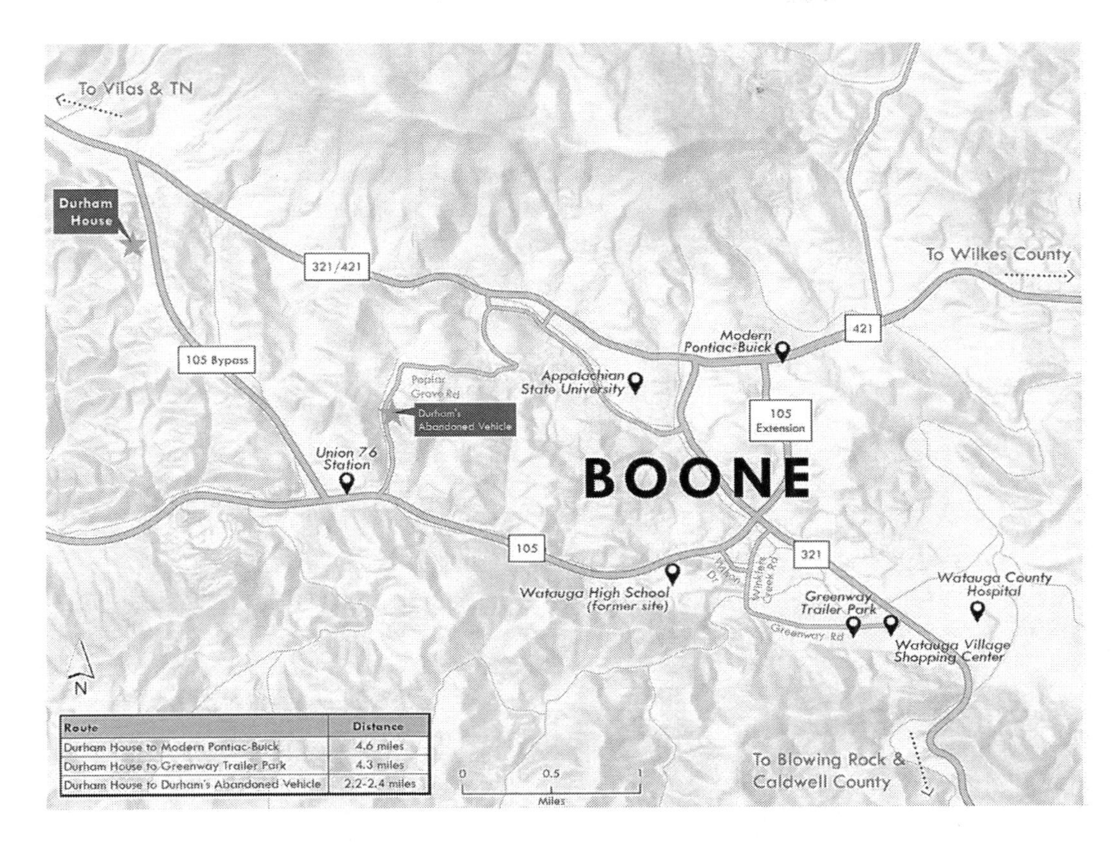

Route	Distance
Durham House to Modern Pontiac-Buick	4.6 miles
Durham House to Greenway Trailer Park	4.3 miles
Durham House to Durham's Abandoned Vehicle	2.2-2.4 miles

Between 11:00 PM on February 3 and 12:00 AM on February 4, Johnny Tester phoned Mildred Small to check on her well-being. She had been home alone ever since her husband left the trailer park with Troy and Ginny, and she had no clue what was happening. She had finished watching the TV movie, gone to bed, and tried unsuccessfully to sleep. She told Tester she was alright and asked why he was calling. Tester explained that Cecil and Troy had gone to the Durham house and "found three people dead and the house torn to shambles" and she might be next. Tester told her he had already dispatched a car to her home, and while they were speaking, someone knocked. Tester said the car had probably arrived, but he would hold the line until she saw who it was. He instructed her to open the door carefully. Armed with a gun, Mildred opened it and saw Boone police officers Bill Ehlers, Jr. and Tester's brother, Zane Tester. She told Zane to hold on while she told his brother they had arrived. Upon entering the home, Zane walked over and looked out a window and then asked Mildred what kind of case Cecil was working on for the Durhams. She replied, "Well, Zane, I don't know. Cecil's a private detective. He keeps his business strictly confidential, and he don't discuss his cases with me." She added that, to her knowledge, he was not working on a case for the Durhams. Zane told her Cecil had called in and said he was on a case for the Durhams, and that he [Zane] and Ehlers would sit across the street in their car until Cecil arrived home. Mildred then took a seat at a table near the window, and Ehlers returned with a gun and said, "Mrs. Small, we'd just rather you get out of that window. Somebody's liable to come along and shoot you." Mildred inquired, "What have I done? Why does anybody want to shoot me for?" Ehlers told her someone might mistake her for Ginny Hall and try to kill her – perhaps an affirmation that law enforcement considered the entire Bryce Durham family to be targets. Mildred would recount she and Ginny

were both small framed and had similar hair color, although she wore hers long and Ginny's was short. Mildred told Ehlers she would move to a rocking chair and watch television but turn the lights off, and he said that would be okay and returned to the car. At some point, a black car, possibly a Dodge, came down the street with no headlights, and the engine sounded like it was drowning out as if it was not receiving enough gas. It stopped in front of the Smalls' trailer, but the officers did not exit their car to investigate. Eventually, the driver got the car started and sped down the street, still without headlights. Around 1:00 AM, Mildred went to bed. Ehlers and Zane stayed on site until Cecil returned home around 3:00 AM.[647]

According to his wife Kay, Ray Hall returned to their Wilkes County home just before 12:00 AM, and although he had phoned her earlier to say his car had broken down and he was at a service station in Lenoir, he now told her that, if the law inquired where he had been that night, she should tell them he had been at his mother's working on a furnace. She told him the best thing to do would be to get a copy of the ticket for the work done on his car; however, he could not tell her what service station he had been at. Moments later, Ray and Kay started to Boone.[648] *[The purpose of their trip to Boone and their specific destination were not stated in the Watauga County Sheriff's Office investigation file.]*

Around 12:30 AM, once their interviews had been completed, Troy and Ginny asked officers for a ride home. Boone Policeman "Shorty" Smith agreed to drive them, and dispatcher Johnny Tester, who was off duty by that time, accompanied them. En route, Tester overheard the couple in the backseat, laughing about something, and he was baffled as to how they managed to find humor in anything considering their circumstances.[649][ccc]

Tester believes that, after the Halls were dropped off, Smith received a call in his patrol car regarding the "Jimmy" being seen on Poplar Grove Road. This alert may have been the result of citizen Bob Poe's reporting the vehicle to the police. Smith and Tester proceeded to the site, arriving there by 1:00 AM, looked the vehicle over, and notified Sheriff Ward Carroll and Patrolman George Baker that the "Jimmy," bearing dealer plates, had been located. Smith and Tester waited at the scene until Carroll and Baker, "accompanied by deputies and photographers" arrived.[650][ddd] There were "several lines of crisp tire-tread marks behind the "Jimmy" [indicating] that a second vehicle had been

---

[ccc] The behaviors exhibited by Ginny Hall, particularly in the days immediately following the murders, were scrutinized and judged, and perhaps unfairly. While some deemed moments of laughter and an absence of tears as unusual, if not inappropriate, individuals' emotional responses to grief are often varied. For example, not crying can be reflective of the numbing shock of a sudden or traumatic loss, and "grieving people often struggle to cry after a significant loss because they feel overwhelmed by so many emotions." Also, studies show that laughter can be a normal reaction to traumatic loss, serving as both a defense mechanism and a coping tool. Laughter in such circumstances does not necessarily denote happiness; rather, nervous laughter can be "an instinctual response to a situation that seems stressful or painful" even when it may be interpreted by others as "absurdly maniacal behavior." [Sources: "Why Can't I Cry When Someone Dies?" Renaissance Funeral Home (online) https://rfhr.com/why-cant-i-cry-when-someone-dies/; Eleanor Hailey, "The Utility of Laughter in Times of Grief," December 11, 2014, (online) https://whatsyourgrief.com/laughter-in-times-of-grief/.]

[ddd] A 1972 magazine article states that Carroll and Baker were notified about the vehicle just before 12:00 AM, and a 1972 newspaper article states they arrived at the scene around 12:30 AM, but Johnny Tester believes these times to be inaccurate and too early. [Sources: Henderson, Leonard. *Rub-Out, Rub-Out, Rub-Out: Three Bodies in a Tub.* Startling Detective, September 1972, p. 62; Bev Ballard, "In Durham Family Slaying: 3 Murder Suspects Jailed," *Watauga Democrat*, Boone, NC, April 27, 1972, p. 1A; Tester, Johnny. Facebook message to author. October 17, 2023.]

following.... Protecting these tracks with pieces of cardboard, Carroll had them photographed as well as moulaged with casting compound, hoping they might provide a lead to the killers."[651]

On the console of the vehicle's back seat, stuffed into a pillowcase, were five silver plates, one silver bowl, one silver platter, and one silver brush and mirror set,[652] along with other undescribed stolen valuables,[653] part of which, it was determined, had been taken from a storage cabinet in the Durham home.[654] Authorities dusted the vehicle for fingerprints and questioned several neighbors and residents in the community where the vehicle was discovered.[655] Prior to traveling to the site where the "Jimmy" had been abandoned, Carroll and Baker requested tracking dogs be brought "from the regional prison farm." The dogs showed no interest in the woods at the side of the road, and no footprints were found in the fields and woods on either side of the vehicle.[656]

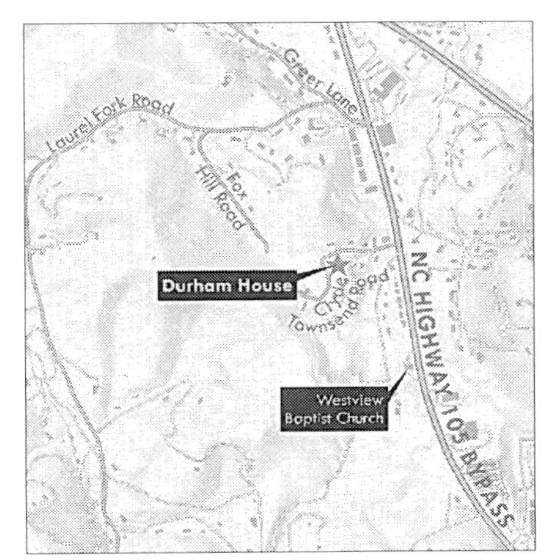

The tracking dogs also circled the "wide hollow behind the Durham home," leading "their handlers to a dead-end road *[unnamed at the time but presently Fox Hill Road]* where there were additional tire treads which were identical [to] those observed behind the GMC" on Poplar Grove Road. It was believed the intruders arrived "in a car which they parked out of sight down [this] dead-end road."[657] Although Clyde Townsend Road looped behind the Durham house and eventually dead-ended, Fox Hill Road branched off of nearby Laurel Fork Road and terminated near the dead-end of Clyde Townsend Road, the two more or less separated by an open field. From there, the killers may have crossed a pasture and a fence[658] (which may have been cut),[659] but from that point, "it would have been easy for the criminals to have gained access to the terrain just behind" the Durham home,[660] and "climb [up the slope] to the [rear of the] Durham residence, unseen by any of the other hilltop dwellers."[661][eee] Two footprints were reportedly found across the fence.[662]

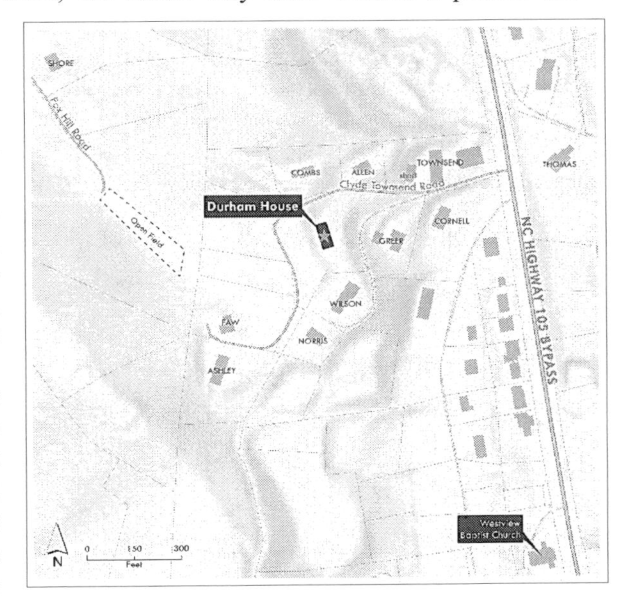

Northa Walker Shore,[663] a housewife from this valley behind the Durham house, who lived with her children at what was then the end of present Fox Hill Road, stated that, sometime between 9:30 and 10:00 PM, during the height of the storm on the night of the murders, "a car

[eee] As the crow flies, the distance from where the open field began (next to present-day Fox Hill Road) to the back of the Durham home was approximately 575 feet – a little more than one and a half football fields (540 feet), and equivalent to about a tenth of a mile.

had driven into the dead-end road near her house." She was unable to provide a description of the vehicle.[664]

[Shore's daughter, Lisa Roark, recalls seeing a Volkswagen bug with three passengers coming in and out of the road several afternoons prior to the murders but cannot recall what type of car her mother saw the night of the murders. It was unusual to see a car on their road as no outsiders typically drove it, and following the murders, law enforcement officers had the Shore family leave their home for a few days because footprints were found leading to one of their bedroom windows.[665] A note within the Watauga County Sheriff's Office Durham Case file states, "Neighbors that moved away were threatened because of VW that was seen by them the morning of murder – at fence behind the house." It is unclear who these neighbors were, or which house was being referred to, although perhaps it was the Durham house. Another note in the file credits Bryce Durham's sister, Gayle Mauldin, as the source regarding a black car going up the back side (presumably of the Durham home) off of Laurel Fork Road,[666] but without indication as to how she came by this information. Although it is a good possibility the killers were dropped off in this location, it is not known for sure. Another less likely theory is that they may have been dropped off at nearby Westview Baptist Church. To walk from the church along the 105 Bypass and up Clyde Townsend Road to the Durham home is 0.3 miles, and under normal conditions would take about six minutes. Walking along the bypass, however, might have exposed them to being seen by residents of any number of houses that also sit along that stretch of road or by motorists driving on the bypass. Alternatively, they could have cut across the valley behind the church to the house. It is also uncertain where the getaway car driver parked while awaiting his or her accomplices to finish their awful acts. Unnamed witnesses had reportedly seen a suspicious Cadillac-style car backed in and parked at a store on Highway 105, and they had wondered what a large vehicle like that was doing out on such a wintery night. This store was likely a reference to the store at the Union 76 station and near the phone booth at the corner of Highway 105 and the 105 Bypass. It was the only store in that vicinity in 1972.[667][fff]]

It was believed when the intruders left the crime scene they took the "Jimmy" and "doubled back to where they left their own car" or otherwise reconnected with the vehicle they had arrived in and then "traveled in tandem to Poplar Grove Road,"[668] where the "Jimmy" was abandoned moments later. The car following the "Jimmy" may have been immediately behind or could have lagged for some moments. The latter scenario may be supported by the fact that, between around 10:15 PM (per neighbor Clyde Townsend[669]) and shortly after 10:30 PM, a GMC "Jimmy" was seen coming out of the Clyde Townsend Road neighborhood (one source says it was specifically seen leaving the Durham residence[670]) and, without stopping,[671] it pulled onto the 105 Bypass and almost collided with perhaps two other vehicles, including an eighteen-wheeler that almost rear-ended the "Jimmy"[672] and a small black car that the "Jimmy" almost ran off the road.[673] The small black car's driver followed the "Jimmy" to the intersection of the 105 Bypass and Highway 105,[674] where the driver noticed another black car at the phone booth on the corner.[675] The driver then turned right toward Linville, while the "Jimmy" turned left toward Boone. This was presumably the Durhams'

[fff] Some have mistakenly believed there was another store directly across Highway 105 from the Union 76 station, which was true a decade later, but not in 1972. [Sources: Henson, Garry. Phone interview with author. October 11, 2023; Dotson, Tommy. Via e-mail from Katrina Hicks (Dotson's daughter) to author. October 11, 2023. Tax Record Parcel (ID 290024295800 Henson, Harold) sent to author via Facebook Messenger by Jonathan Miller, October 11, 2023.]

The open field, taken from the vantage point behind and below the Durham residence looking toward present-day Fox Hill Road. (Photo by author, 2022)

vehicle. The individual who followed the "Jimmy" is said to have arrived home (wherever home was) at 10:30 PM,[676] so he or she must have first encountered the "Jimmy" just prior to 10:30 PM and must have lived in close proximity to the 105 Bypass and Highway 105 intersection in order to have arrived home that quickly. *[Could the black car spotted at the phone booth have been the black car that reportedly went up the back side of Laurel Fork Road, possibly toward the open field behind the Durham home? And could it have been the small, blue or black car that Bruce and Priscilla Faw saw traveling at a high rate of speed on the Highway 105 Bypass around 10:00 PM on the night of the murders? And could it also have been the black car without headlights that stalled in front of Cecil and Mildred Small's trailer – near Troy and Ginny Hall's home – on Greenway Road later that same night?]*

Around 1:00 or 1:30 AM, telephone operator Barbara Woodruff received an emergency phone call from a man at a pay phone and put the call through from a "264" (Boone area) number to a "267" (west of Boone area) number. The male caller said, "It's done. We did it." He also said he would be on, and the people on the receiving end of the call, who seemed to Woodruff to be people in their twenties, sounded jubilant in the background.[677] Similarly, on the night of the murders (time undetermined), Boone resident Ina Eggers Wilson,[ggg] a sixty-four-year old widow, received an obviously misdialed call at her home, and the unidentified caller said, "Get over here! All hell has broke loose!"[678] Although curious, it is unknown if either of these calls were related to the Durham murders.

Also, in the wee hours of Friday morning, Watauga County Sheriff's Deputy Arvell Perry knocked on Clinard and Clara Wilson's door to make sure they were okay. This was the Wilsons' first knowledge of what had happened to their neighbors. In light of it all, Mrs. Wilson later recounted that, on Thursday morning, (the morning of the murders) around 11:00 AM, while her husband went to the Vilas Grocery, she went to take a bath. While in the bathtub, she had the radio playing, but she heard an unfamiliar voice in another room say, "We're in the wrong house." It was normal for the Wilsons to have their doors unlocked, and whoever entered their house left peacefully.[679][hhh] *[Based on a note in the Watauga County Sheriff's Office Durham Case file regarding a Volkswagen being seen on the morning of the murders at a fence behind a house, this could be an indication that occupants of a Volkswagen drove to the fence at the open field near the dead end of present-day Fox Hill Road, scaled the hill behind the Durham house, and mistakenly entered the Wilson home.]*

Around 2:00 AM, a law officer also knocked on the doors of neighbors Bruce and Priscilla Faw and Bobby and Sheila Ashley to check on the well-being of their families. Like the Wilsons, this was their first knowledge of the murders. *[When Bruce Faw was awakened, the officer allegedly mentioned Faw's footprints being found in the snow leading to the Durhams' front door,[680] which would align with him going to their house for assistance, as one version claimed, but considering the snow and wind and other foot traffic, including the later steps of Troy Hall and Cecil Small, it*

[ggg] Ina Eggers Wilson was the mother-in-law of Jerry Harrison, who had spotted a vehicle similar to the Durhams' at the Union 76 station, along with a blonde-headed woman using the pay phone there *(see p. 46)*. Mrs. Wilson's grandson, Luther Harrison, was a future officer with both the Boone Police Department and the Watauga County Sheriff's Office. [Source: Personal knowledge of author.]

[hhh] Mike Wilson (son of Clinard & Clara Wilson) says he is familiar with this story attributed to his mother but is uncertain if it actually happened. Wilson says his mother wondered if she and her husband had been the intended victims, and if the killers had entered the wrong house when they went to the Durham home. Mrs. Wilson also wondered if the killers were individuals who bore some grudge against her husband in his former capacity as a Watauga County Deputy Sheriff. [Source: Wilson, Mike. In-person conversation with author. August 6, 2023.]

seems unlikely Faw's footprints could specifically be identified or that officers could have known they were his footprints without first examining the soles of the shoes he wore that night.] The evening prior, Mrs. Ashley had been awaiting the arrival of her husband from his grocery store job. She and their four-year-old son Scott kept looking out the window, but the badly blowing snow limited their visibility to about six inches. Based on the estimated timeframe of the murders, the Ashleys surmised Mr. Ashley may have been driving up Clyde Townsend Road around that same time. Although it had been snowing terribly, Mrs. Ashley worried the killers may have seen her and her son looking out the window that night. The morning after, the Ashleys drove down the mountain from Boone to their native North Wilkesboro because Mrs. Ashley was frightened and did not want to stay at their home. Similarly, but in even greater measure, Priscilla Faw was so shaken by the murders that she left the house without packing any clothes. She refused to remain in North Carolina, and their family moved that same month to Mrs. Faw's native New Hampshire.[681] Other Durham neighbors, Bill and Betty Norris, upon being made aware of the murders, were questioned extensively by authorities. The couple had not seen or heard anything as they watched television in their home.[682]

Also, around 2:00 AM, the Durhams' sales manager, Ike Eller, said he learned of the murders when service manager Dean Combs called him, saying, "Troy Hall has killed Bryce and his whole family."[683] *[Combs refuted this, saying he never had or wanted Eller's phone number, and he did not know where Eller lived. Later, Eller would reiterate it was Combs who contacted him. According to one source, however, Combs did not learn of the murders until around 3:00 AM, an hour after Eller claimed Combs called him.]* Eller was devastated by the news,[684] and once he was more fully awake, he said he would start toward the dealership.[685]

At 2:00 AM, Gayle Mauldin phoned her niece Ginny to inquire about her well-being and to tell her she was coming to Boone. Ginny told her aunt she was doing alright but not to come as it was still snowing hard, and she would not make it. Gayle assured her she would come as soon as she could, and Ginny asked her to promise not to bring her [Ginny's paternal] grandparents. Gayle told her she would try but was not sure what they would do. When Gayle asked Ginny how she found out about the murders, Ginny stated she and Troy had been home when they occurred, and erroneously added that a State Highway Patrolman had come by to inform them something was wrong at her parents' home, after which she and Troy went there. In addition to the murders themselves, and equally sobering for Gayle to contemplate was that her ten-year-old son, Jeff, had planned to spend that night with his cousin Bobby, but the family decided against it when the snow began falling heavily. The winter weather had likely saved Jeff's life. Ginny told Gayle to get hold of herself; there was nothing she could do, and everything was alright and under control.[686]

Between 2:45 and 3:15 AM, rescue squad and ambulance personnel, who had been waiting at Clyde Townsend's apartment about three hours, were called back to the Durham house in the still blowing snow and asked to remove the bodies from the bathtub. As each body was retrieved, it sounded similar to a wet mop being lifted from a bucket, the water running off each victim and particularly from Virginia's shoulder length hair. According to responder Cecil Harmon, the bodies were removed so they could be photographed, and medical examiner Dr. Clayton Dean could examine them.[687] Crime scene photographs include ones of the bodies after they were removed from the bathtub,[688] but Dean states this alleged examination by him to be "absolutely false;" he had already left the scene before the bodies were removed from the tub and photographed, and he never touched nor examined them. "They were dead and leaning over a bathtub full of water when I saw them. Nobody touched them, and I didn't touch them either.... That's the way I left them to be taken by ambulance to Chapel Hill. They were still in the tub when I left." According to Dean, all he did was confirm the Durhams were dead by merely seeing their bodies in the tub – something not requiring an actual medical examination. "It was the middle of the night, and I was going home as quick as I could."[689]

Bobby was brought out first and laid in the hallway. After his body was photographed, it was carried out the front door to the ambulance. This process was repeated next with Bryce and then with Virginia.[690] Each time the back door of the ambulance was opened to receive another body, the blankets or sheets covering the previous one(s) would be caught and swept up by the wind.[691]

Bobby was dressed in a brown, long-sleeved, collared, button-up shirt, a white t-shirt, khaki trousers with a black belt, white underpants, and brown socks. He wore a class ring with a blue stone on his right hand and a wristwatch on his left wrist, indicating the current date and time. Crime scene photographs show Bobby was wearing the ring at the time his body was discovered in the bathtub, although it had slidden down to the middle joint of his right ring finger. When his body was photographed after being removed from the tub, the ring was missing, perhaps either having fallen off or been removed. With Bobby's body was an unopened brown envelope containing an undisclosed amount of money.[692]

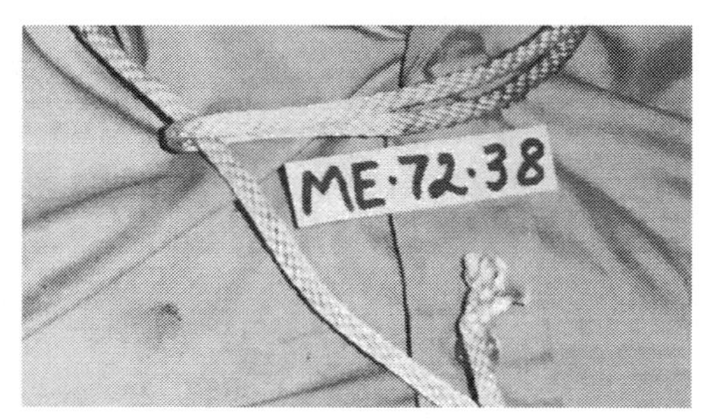

Rope found around Bryce Durham's neck. (Image courtesy of Watauga County Sheriff's Office)

Bryce was clothed in a blue, long-sleeved, collared, button-up shirt, an undershirt, dark plaid, cuffed pants, underpants, dark socks, and Oxford, lace-up dress shoes, the left one tied, the right one untied. He carried a pocketknife, a handkerchief, and a change purse and was wearing a watch and a wedding ring on his left wrist and hand. Some of his pants pockets were turned out.[693] His eyeglasses (which Cecil Small had stepped on) were broken across the bridge and found on the floor of the hallway outside of Bobby's bedroom.[694] A rope or nylon cord (later stated to be a woven cotton sash rope or a common rope) 58" long and ¼" in diameter, fashioned into a noose knot or slip knot (as opposed to a hangman's knot), was around his neck.[695] No other ropes or ties were found on the victims or in the house.[696]

Virginia wore a plaid jumper dress, a white, long-sleeved blouse with a collar and eyelet designs down the length of each sleeve, and pantyhose. A watch and ring were on her left wrist and hand.[697]

The only survivor of that night's terror was the family's pampered two-year-old Manchester dog "Tiny." Discovered "whining pitifully…the grieving pup could not be coaxed away from his dead mistress [and] had to be forcibly removed." Protective of his owners, the dog would have successfully bitten Agent Charlie Whitman's ankles had it not been for the boots Whitman was wearing. The dog whimpered as the bodies were taken by ambulance.[698] *[Although the dog may have been in the bathroom when Cecil Small found the bodies, he did not see it. As he later told a reporter, "I didn't go in there to sleep!"[699]]*

The deceased Durhams were transported to the Watauga County Hospital, arriving there around 3:40 AM. There they were reexamined, including having their temperatures checked, and then they were placed in the morgue.[700] Within an hour after the preliminary post-mortem examinations, Dr.

Dean made arrangements to send the bodies to Chapel Hill[701] so autopsies could be performed by University of North Carolina medical faculty.[702]

SBI Agent Bill Pearce received a call at his home in Raleigh, North Carolina and was directed to go to the crime scene. He arrived there while it was still dark and after the Durhams' bodies had been removed from the home. As part of the Trace Evidence Section, Pearce specifically focused on the sediment that had settled in the bottom of the bathtub. After draining the tub, he collected, dried, and weighed the sediment, which primarily consisted of silt from the well,[703] perhaps intermingled with a small amount of diluted blood that had emerged from the victims. Barely visible beneath the residue were flower-shaped, non-slip stickers, an odd and disturbing contrast between the whimsical and macabre.[704] Pearce then ran fresh water into the tub until the sediment was replicated. After collecting, drying, and weighing the new sample and comparing it to the previous one, he was able to reach a conclusion about how long the water had been running in connection to the timeline of the murders. *[When interviewed in 2023, more than fifty years after his analysis, Pearce could not recall what the conclusion was, but it is likely indicated within the SBI's case files.]* Another Pearce – SBI Agent E. B. "Chic" Pearce, as Director of Ballistics and Toolmark, was assigned to examine the bullet found in the wood paneling of the Durhams' den.[705][iii]

Durham bathtub following removal of bodies. (Image courtesy of Watauga County Sheriff's Office)

Bullet hole in paneling of Durham den (Image courtesy of Watauga County Sheriff's Office)

Within a few hours of returning home, Troy Hall phoned his brother John, telling him Ginny's family had been killed and asking him to come to Boone as he needed help.[706] John lived in Lenoir, North Carolina, approximately twenty-eight miles from Boone. He apparently received a subsequent emergency call from an operator regarding Troy, but the call was

[iii] In 2002, the SBI Crime Laboratory in Raleigh, North Carolina returned a piece of evidence to the Watauga County Sheriff's Office in care of Sheriff Red Lyons. This was a fragment of a copper-coated base, apparently of a bullet fired by a .22-caliber gun and likely pertained to the bullet found in the paneled wall of the Durhams' den. The evidence was noted to be in several small fragments and too fragmented. It had been held in an Open Case File in the SBI's Firearm and Tool Mark Section. "Due to advances in technology," the SBI no longer maintained the Open Case File, and therefore returned the evidence to the sheriff. [Source: Douglas M. Branch, Special Agent in Charge, Firearm and Tool Mark Section, NCSBI Crime Lab, letter to Sheriff James C. Lyons, April 15, 2002, Watauga County Sheriff's Office investigation file 118-H-1/2/3.

disconnected, and John utilized an operator to phone Troy's home between 3:00 and 4:30 AM. When Mildred Small answered the call on Troy's extension inside her home, the operator inquired as to her identity. Once that was established, John said he would talk to her. He asked what was taking place up there, and Mildred said she did not really know. A short time later, John arrived at Troy's and Ginny's trailer.[707] *[John told investigators he arrived around 3:00 AM, but that does not align with the recollections of Cecil and Mildred Small, who believed it was later.]*[708] Based on the forty-five minutes or so that passed between John's conversation with Mildred and his arrival, the Smalls wondered if he had called from a location closer to Boone than Lenoir; otherwise, he would have had to travel very quickly up the mountain, especially in that kind of weather. When John arrived, he knocked on the door of Troy's and Ginny's trailer. Finding no one at home, he got back in his car and left.[709]

Around 3:00 AM,[710] after most of the traffic up and down Clyde Townsend Road had ceased, service manager Dean Combs was awakened[711] to the lights of the Durham home and law enforcement vehicles[712] by friend and neighbor Clara Wilson calling to let him know what had happened.[713] Sometime around 3:00 or 4:00 AM, law enforcement officers pounded on the door of the Combs residence and came inside to speak with Combs and his wife.[714] At one point, Combs reportedly walked to the Durham house to see what was going on.[715] Because some of Combs's service department employees had no phones and would be heading to work that morning without any knowledge of the murders, he knew he had to be at the dealership to meet and inform them.[716]

Between 4:30 and 5:00 AM, sales manager Ike Eller and his wife Frances arrived at Modern Buick-Pontiac in Boone in anticipation of law enforcement officers speaking with employees who would be arriving later. Troy Hall and his brother John were either waiting at the door or arrived around 5:30 AM.[717] *[Ike Eller stated Troy and John came to the dealership between 4:30 AM and 5:00 AM,*[718] *and John Hall stated he and Troy arrived around 10:30 AM.*[719] *Ike Eller's son Tom recalls his father was summoned to the dealership by law officers and thinks it very unlikely Troy would have called him to come there.*[720]*]* Despite the snowy cold, John wore a short-sleeved shirt with no jacket and shoes without socks. Troy introduced John to Frances Eller, and when John extended his right hand, Mrs. Eller was chillingly surprised to see it was missing its thumb and every finger except for its pinky.[721][jjj]

Ike unlocked the door, and upon entering the dealership, Troy and John immediately began searching everything. When Virginia's locked desk posed an obstacle for Troy, he opened it with a file and went through her papers. "I know there's a copy of that damn thing here somewhere," he said. *[Ike Eller later recounted Troy saying, "The damn thing has got to be here somewhere."*[722]*]* Angry that he did not find what he was looking for, Troy kicked Virginia's high-heeled shoes from beneath her desk all the way across the showroom.[723]

Ike had left his coat hanging behind the door in Bryce's office, and oddly, Troy entered the office, took down the coat, felt of it, and then nodded to Ike, acknowledging that Ike's gun was in the coat pocket.[724] *[Ike would later confirm he had a gun in his pocket,*[725] *but it is unclear why Troy would have known about Ike's coat or gun or exactly what Troy's nod to Ike acknowledged or implied. Ike's son Tom states his father did not typically carry a gun, but he believes that, in light of the murders and the fear people were experiencing in the aftermath, his father may have taken a gun to*

[jjj] John Hall's missing fingers may have been a birth defect. [Source: Anonymous source. In-person interview with author. August 14, 2023.]

Boone that day for protection, and perhaps Troy suspected and discovered it, giving Ike a knowing nod to indicate he knew Ike had brought a weapon. Tom Eller was surprised to learn his mother had accompanied his father to Boone, but again, in light of the terrible crime that had been committed, perhaps neither Ike nor his wife thought it prudent for him to travel to Boone alone.[726]*]*

Troy asked for all the keys in Ike's possession, and Ike, believing Troy was now the rightful owner of the dealership in light of his in-laws' deaths, complied. The only key he held back was the one to Bobby's car because he "knew how much Bobby hated [Troy]."[727] Ike remained at the dealership until almost daylight.[728]

According to John Hall, the purpose of his and Troy's early morning appearance at the dealership was to collect employees' keys for Ginny and to search a file cabinet for a tag or keys to a vehicle. They also went that day to the Durham home to retrieve a pet. Although John could not recall in 1975 if this was a cat or dog,[729] it was likely the small Manchester dog, "Tiny," that had sat whining in the bathroom at the feet of the deceased Durhams. *[Cecil Small would recall that, after the dog came to live with Troy and Ginny, he (Cecil) visited their trailer. The dog sniffed of Cecil's shoes and, presumably detecting scent from the Durham home and perhaps from the blood Cecil had stepped in the night of the murders, it ran to the back of the trailer and, despite Troy's coaxing, would have nothing to do with Cecil.*[730]*]*

Having driven in the middle of the night from Greensboro, Ralph and Bill Durham, and Bill's wife Marie arrived at the brothers' parents' home in Wilkes County. Coy Durham had just begun stirring about in the house and was in the kitchen when they arrived around 5:00 AM; Collie Durham was still in bed. The brothers informed their father first, and he almost collapsed. While Ralph remained with him in the kitchen, Bill went into the bedroom to tell their mother the horrific news; he was not sure she would survive it. About an hour later, Bryce's sister Gayle and her husband, Charles Mauldin, joined them at the family home.[731]

Timeline Recap

Thursday, February 3

Unstated AM hour – A Volkswagen is seen near a fence behind a house, possibly meaning the fence at the open field below and behind the Durham house toward present-day Fox Hill Road.

11:00 AM – While bathing, Durham neighbor Clara Wilson allegedly hears an unfamiliar voice in her home saying, "We're in the wrong house."

3:00 PM – Snow begins to fall.

Between 4:00 & 4:45 PM (?) – Ginny Hall calls her father for a ride home from the university, and Bryce Durham transports her in a new green and white four-wheel-drive GMC "Jimmy."

4:30 PM – Mildred Small finishes work and returns to her nearby home.

5:00 PM – Up to four inches of snow is on the ground, and temperatures are dropping.

5:00 – 6:00 PM – Ginny goes grocery shopping and returns home; Troy Hall goes to dinner with a brother and then to the university library; Bobby Durham finishes his last class for the day (5:20 PM) and goes to the dealership.

5:45 PM – Bryce arrives back at the dealership after taking Ginny home, warms himself, and immediately takes Earl Petrey to his home.

Shortly before 6:00 PM – Bryce again returns to the dealership.

6:00 PM – Bryce departs the dealership to go to his Rotary Club meeting, and Virginia Durham has a phone conversation with an attorney regarding a tax matter.

Around 7:30 PM – One of Bobby's friends sees him, possibly at the Roses store, and possibly having just arrived there.

Around 8:00 PM – One of Troy's friends sees him outside the university library and converses briefly with him. Ray Hall calls his wife Kay to say his car has broken down in Lenoir, North Carolina. She does not know for sure that is where he really is – only that he is calling long distance.

Around 8:15 PM – The Rotary Club meeting concludes.

8:30 PM – Bryce arrives back at the dealership from his Rotary Club meeting.

8:45 PM – Furnace repairman Lester Johnson sees a 1965-66 white four-door Ford with a 1971 North Carolina license plate following a green four-wheel drive Jeep. The two vehicles turn right from Highway 105 onto the 105 Bypass. Moments later, Johnson sees both vehicles pulling out of the Westview Baptist Church parking lot onto the bypass. Johnson believes he sees one man in the Ford, but there may be more. He is unable to see who is in the Jeep because the windows are fogged up. The Jeep turns left onto Clyde Townsend Road, and the Ford pulls off on the right shoulder of the bypass. As Johnson approaches the bypass's intersection with Highway 421, he looks back and sees the Ford still there.

8:45 – 9:00 PM – Neighbors spot the Durhams arriving home.

9:00 – 9:30 PM (perhaps as late as 10:00 PM) – Reed Trivette and Bernard Harmon turn onto the 105 Bypass from Highway 105 and see a green Blazer with possibly white or silver in the middle of the body, pulled off the road about twenty-five feet into a mobile home sales lot just before Westview Baptist Church. The headlights and taillights are lit, but Trivette cannot distinguish if the vehicle is running. He believes one of the doors may be open, and he sees three white men, all very large and more than two-hundred pounds, standing and talking. Two wear really long, army-style overcoats and toboggans, while the third wears a short, waist-length coat and a hat. Moments later, Trivette and Harmon see a light blue or possibly mint green 1966-1968 Pontiac Bonneville with its lights on, coming down the Durhams' driveway and Clyde Townsend Road and turning right onto the 105 Bypass. Trivette spots three of the car's passengers – a male driver, a male next to the passenger door, and a woman in the middle with either blonde hair or a light-colored scarf – although there may be as many as four or five passengers. When Trivette looks back at the Pontiac, which heads in the opposite direction, he sees it slow and stop where the Blazer is parked.

Around 9:30 PM – Troy leaves the ASU library.

9:30 – 10:00 PM – Northa Walker Shore, a housewife living in the valley behind the Durham's home on present-day Fox Hill Road, sees a car drive onto the dead-end there during the height of the snowstorm.

9:45 – 10:15 PM – The Durhams are most likely attacked and murdered. Although 10:00 PM is the time of death indicated on all three victims' death certificates and would split the difference between 9:45 PM and 10:15 PM, the coroner's report was more liberal, stating their deaths occurred between 9:00 PM and 11:00 PM. This two-hour timeframe, however, is further narrowed by other events in this timeline.

Around 9:55 – 10:00 PM – Troy returns to his home.

10:00 PM – Durham neighbors Bruce and Priscilla Faw turn onto the 105 Bypass from Highway 421 and see a fast-moving, small, blue or black car, possibly an Opel, with four or five people inside.

Approximately 10:10 – 10:15 PM – At his and Ginny's home, Troy answers a phone call, allegedly from Virginia, stating Bryce and Bobby are being beaten. Meanwhile, in the Clyde Townsend Road neighborhood, after getting stuck at the Durhams' driveway, Bruce Faw, by one account, goes to the Durham home for assistance, and despite seeing and hearing people inside the house, the door goes unanswered. By another account, as Faw goes for assistance, his wife Priscilla remains in their car, looks around the neighborhood, and sees only an outside light burning at the Durham residence. She sees no people or vehicles. Hall neighbors Chester and Minnie Nelson see Troy and Ginny sitting in their non-running white Thunderbird in front of the Halls' trailer.

10:15 – 10:30 PM – Durham neighbors' dogs begin barking furiously (10:20 PM). Neighbor Mike Townsend witnesses the Durhams' "Jimmy" descending Clyde Townsend Road. Entering the 105 Bypass, the "Jimmy" is almost rear-ended by an eighteen-wheeler, and the "Jimmy" almost simultaneously runs a black car off the road. The driver of the black car follows and sees the "Jimmy" turn left onto Highway 105 and also sees another black car at the phone booth near the corner of Highway 105 and the 105 Bypass. Troy and Ginny go (10:30 PM) to Cecil Small's home to enlist his help.

Around 10:30 PM – Jerry Harrison sees a four-wheel-drive GMC and a blonde-haired lady at the phone booth at the Union 76 Station at the corner of Highway 105 and the 105 Bypass. Although no time was indicated, John Cashion, who worked at the station had seen, that same night, four or five big men hanging around, who kept going back and forth between the pay phone and the store and even picked up their cigarette butts and possibly wiped off the telephone.

Around 10:33 PM – Troy, Ginny, and Cecil depart the Small home. In their journey to the Durham home, they drive some of that time on the same portions of Highway 105 and the 105 Bypass that the drivers of the "Jimmy" would have taken (in the opposite direction) to get to Poplar Grove Road, but "Small said they saw no cars on the one-mile stretch of icy road as they rushed to the house. Since it had been only about twenty minutes since Virginia Durham allegedly called, he [believed] he just missed seeing the killers."[732] *[The "one-mile stretch" likely refers to the last mile of their journey, from the intersection of Highway 105 and the 105 Bypass to Clyde Townsend Road, which really is a distance of one mile. The distance from that same intersection to the intersection of Highway 105 and Poplar Grove Road is only about 0.2 miles, and that is the only other portion of roadway on which Cecil and the Halls might have passed the "Jimmy" before it turned onto Poplar Grove Road. It is a distance that only requires a matter of seconds to drive, even in inclement weather, and would have been their first chance to encounter the "Jimmy," and the subsequent one-mile stretch would have been their last opportunity.]*

10:45 PM – SBI Agent Wally Hardwick, Jr. and Gary Morgan find the abandoned "Jimmy" on Poplar Grove Road but are not yet aware of the murders. Cecil, Troy, and Ginny arrive at Clyde Townsend Road. Durham neighbor Mike Townsend witnesses the inability of Cecil's car to ascend the road and sees people exiting the car and walking uphill.

Around 10:47 PM – Cecil, Troy, and Ginny begin backing down Clyde Townsend Road and Cecil's vehicle gets stuck. One source states that from the time the trio left Cecil's home (around 10:33 PM) until they backed down the road from the crime scene (around 10:47 PM) took no longer than fourteen minutes.[733]

10:50 PM – Troy's call to the Boone Police Department is logged.

[The seventeen-minute timeframe between 10:33 PM, when Cecil and the Halls reportedly left Cecil's trailer and 10:50 PM, when Troy's phone call to the police department was logged, is very narrow and, if true, had to be jam packed with activity. The trio reportedly arrived on Clyde Townsend Road at 10:45 PM, which means twelve of those seventeen minutes were utilized for driving. That leaves five minutes for Cecil and Troy to walk up to the Durham house, walk around it, enter the home, discover the bodies, exit the home, back down the driveway, run off the bank of Clyde Townsend Road, exit the car, and go to the nearby apartments to call for help. Knowing for certain that the logging of the call to police occurred no later than 10:50 PM, then any adjustments for preceding events, if needed to make the sequence of events more plausible, would need to be made going backward in time. The need for adjustments depends on whether one believes all those movements could have occurred within five minutes. If the trio really did arrive at Clyde Townsend Road at 10:45 PM and started backing down the road at 10:47 PM, that means Cecil's and Troy's walk up the driveway, their examination of the Durham home, their discovery of the bodies, and their return to Cecil's car all transpired within two minutes, which seems unlikely.]

Around 10:50 PM – Bob Poe departs his home on Poplar Grove Road and encounters the abandoned "Jimmy."

10:52 PM – Agent Hardwick is called to come to the crime scene.

Just before 11:00 PM – The Watauga Rescue Squad is called to come to the crime scene. SBI Agent Charlie Whitman is summoned via phone by Agent Hardwick to come to Boone.

Around 11:00 PM – Ginny phones her brother-in-law Ray Hall at his Wilkes County home, but Ray's wife Kay informs her he is not home. Around this same time, Ginny places a call to her uncle Bill Durham to inform him of the murders, and Bryce's other two siblings receive the news soon after.

Shortly after 11:00 PM – Officers from multiple agencies begin arriving at the crime scene.

Perhaps 11:15 PM – 11:30 PM – Bob Poe reencounters the "Jimmy," still abandoned, on his return home and reports it to authorities shortly afterward.

Between 11:00 PM – 12:00 AM – Dispatcher Johnny Tester calls Mildred Small to inquire about her welfare. Zane Tester and Bill Ehlers, Jr. arrive at Mildred's trailer and begin a three-hour vigil, during which time a black car with no headlights comes down Greenway Road and stalls in front of the Small home, then restarts and speeds on down the road, still without headlights.

Just before 12:00 AM – Ray Hall arrives home in Wilkes County and instructs his wife Kay what to say about his whereabouts that night in the event that law officers inquire.

Friday, February 4

Around 12:00 AM – Dispatcher Johnny Tester arrives at the crime scene with the SBI photographer. Sheriff Ward Carroll instructs rescue squad and ambulance personnel to depart the crime scene and wait at the nearby Townsend Apartments.

12:30 – 1:00 AM – Boone Policeman "Shorty" Smith and dispatcher Johnny Tester take Troy and Ginny Hall home. Smith subsequently receives a call about the "Jimmy," and he and Tester proceed to it on Poplar Grove Road. Sheriff Carroll and Patrolman Baker, having been notified by Smith and Tester, arrive at the scene shortly after in the company of deputies and photographers.

Around 1:00 AM – Mildred Small goes to bed.

1:00 – 1:30 AM – Telephone operator Barbara Woodruff hears a man tell a jubilant group of young people, "It's done. We did it." *[Since he arrived home between 12:30 and 1:00 AM, did Troy Hall place this call?]*

2:00 AM – The Durhams' sales manager Ike Eller receives a call at his Wilkes County home informing him of the murders. Gayle Mauldin, having already learned of the murders, phones Ginny to inquire about her welfare and to say she is headed to Boone, although Ginny advises her to wait.

2:30 – 3:00 AM – Troy phones his brother John Hall to tell him the Durhams have been murdered and to request that he come to Boone and offer Troy assistance.

2:45 – 3:15 AM – Rescue squad and ambulance personnel are summoned back to the crime scene to remove the bodies from the bathtub so they can be examined and photographed.

Around 3:00 AM – Cecil Small returns home, and Zane Tester and Bill Ehlers, Jr. depart their stakeout at Small's home.

Around 3:40 AM – The Durhams' bodies arrive at the Watauga County Hospital.

3:00 – 4:30 AM – John Hall calls Troy but reaches Mildred Small instead. John arrives at Troy's and Ginny's trailer a short time afterward. Finding no one home, he leaves.

4:30 – 5:00 AM – Ike and Frances Eller arrive at the dealership in Boone, where they encounter Troy and John Hall. They all enter, and Troy and John subsequently search the premises. Before daybreak, approximately seven hours after the murders, Troy Hall has the keys to the Durhams' dealership in his hands.

CHAPTER 4

COME DAYBREAK

The sun rose in Boone at 7:25 AM on Friday, February 4,[734] and Bryce Durham's brothers, Ralph and Bill, Bill's wife Marie, and their brother-in-law, Charles Mauldin, were already at the Boone Police Department to put officers onto Troy Hall's trail. Bill spoke with Chief Clyde Tester. When Troy and Ginny Hall arrived there around 8:00 AM, Mauldin asked Troy if the house had been ransacked, and Troy began recounting the previous night's events of listening to music (his record player being on one side of his chair and the telephone on the other), receiving the phone call from a low-voiced person saying "three niggers" were beating Bryce and Bobby in a back room, and thinking some friends were playing a joke on him. He then told inconsistencies about going to the Durham house with Cecil Small and how they entered the *front* door. He stated Small had a gun, so *Small* went first and he followed, and the only room he saw was Bobby's and it had been ransacked. Troy shared that Small went into the bathroom and then pushed him out of the house, saying Troy didn't want to see that; it was too horrible. When Mauldin asked Troy if he had seen the bodies, Troy told him he *had not. [A note in the Watauga County Sheriff's Office investigative file indicates that, at some point, Troy stated he found the bodies and then informed Cecil Small, which is also inaccurate.]* Ginny, perhaps unaware Troy had already obtained the keys to the dealership from Ike Eller, asked SBI Agent Charlie Whitman when they could have the keys, fearing they would lose the franchise if they did not open it within three days. Later, when Bill Durham and Charles Mauldin were at Troy's and Ginny's trailer, Mauldin heard Ginny tell her uncle Bill at the door, "They just wouldn't accept Troy."[735] Meanwhile, the same morning around 8:00 AM in Wilkes County, Ray Hall's wife Kay witnessed him burning something unknown to her at their garage.[736]

News of the tragedy began to spread. Bobby Durham's friend Phil Ginn started that Friday as most other weekdays, going to the Boone Post Office for the early morning shift of his part-time job there. Finishing around 8:30 or 9:00 AM, he went to a doughnut shop, where he encountered somber individuals conversing about some murders that had occurred. He soon pieced together that Bobby and his parents were the victims.[737] As Ginn recalled, this news about his friend "was a gut-punch."[738]

Bobby's friend Gary Edmisten lived at the Oakwood Motel in Boone, which was owned and operated by his parents. As his mother prepared his breakfast that morning, she tuned into the local WATA radio station. Hearing news of the murders, Edmisten could think of nothing else the remainder of the day. Even for decades, he would be disturbed by the knowledge that, had Bobby gone to the movie with him that night, he might still be alive…or had Edmisten alternatively gone to the Durham home to hang out with Bobby, he may have been a fourth victim.[739]

That same morning, Jack Henson drove from his home in western Watauga County to Boone to attend classes at Appalachian State University. Like Edmisten, he heard news of the murders on the radio, so when he spotted TV stations' media vans in town, he already knew why they were there. Henson was a year ahead of Bobby in school. He had known of him at Watauga High School and now attended a college economics course with him. Similar to Ginn's experience, there was a pall over the classroom as the murders were revealed and discussed. Bobby's desk sat empty. The professor entered the room and sat silently at his own desk. A few moments passed before he said to his students he was sure they had heard what had happened, and he dismissed the class.[740]

Durham neighbor Jane Allen, who was still in the hospital in Boone with her newborn son, heard the shocking news from her husband the morning after the murders. The Allens had only moved into their home on Clyde Townsend Road a mere six weeks earlier, and although Mrs. Allen was initially apprehensive about returning to their home, she concluded that she had never heard of killers returning to the same location and murdering neighbors of their original victims.[741]

Virginia Durham's fifteen-year-old great-niece, Diana Waddell, was ill and out of school. Alone at her Greensboro, North Carolina home, she heard her relatives' names announced via radio news as murder victims. She and her family were bewildered, wondering why anyone would have harmed their loved ones. As she recalled, "It was so traumatic for the family. It really was."[742]

When Bryce Durham's mother, Collie Durham, received the news, it was devastating. "I first thought that they'd all been killed in a car wreck," she said. "I thought, well, if they got killed in a car wreck, there's nothing I could do about it, but Lord have mercy, when they told me what had happened, I just thought I was gonna die."[743]

Mike Wilson, son of Durham neighbors Clinard and Clara Wilson, along with his wife Cathy, had been at his parents' home the evening of the murders, having dinner and doing laundry, and they had left around 7:00 PM. On the job the following morning, his coworker commented it was bad about Bryce Durham. Wilson asked what he meant, and he stated Bryce and his wife and son had been killed. Just as Collie Durham had initially thought, Wilson asked if it was a car wreck, and the co-worker further explained someone had entered the Durhams' home and murdered them. Wilson immediately left for his parents' house, finding them sitting in their living room. His mother appeared as if she had been crying all night, and his father held a pistol and was trembling. Frightened and bewildered, they were trying to comprehend what had befallen their neighbors.[744]

While the entire Durham family was in the midst of distress,[745] the extended Hall family met inside an old bus[kkk] at the Wilkes County home of Troy's oldest brother, Claude, up Highway 18 out of North Wilkesboro and expressed worry that Troy may have committed the murders. "The old man Hall and Mrs. Hall" (likely a reference to Troy's parents) remarked, "If he did this, the law will catch him." They also shared their concern about Troy moving his trailer near them, which implied Troy had perhaps already been planning to leave Boone and return to Wilkes County. Among those present at this family pow-wow was Ray Hall's wife Kay, and mention was made that Ray's whereabouts the previous night was unknown. Claude Hall was home at the time of the murders,

[kkk] This was likely the 1955 Ford bus that Claude Hall owned. [Source: Watauga County Sheriff's Office investigation file 118-H-1/2/3.]

and his mother-in-law, Harriet Garris Harrold, was staying there.[lll] After the murders, she phoned Collie Durham and told her she needed "to have someone check out that old redhead," referring to Ray Hall. Mrs. Harrold told Mrs. Durham Ray had been out all night.[746]

Word also spread to other places in Wilkes County that morning, including a Wilkesboro pool hall, where Kent "Pig" Rhodes[mmm] entered, asking the occupants if they had heard about the murders and proclaiming to know who committed them. A renowned local athlete and bookie, Rhodes encouraged everyone to write on a piece of paper who they thought killed the Durhams and to place a wager. No one's guess matched the name of the close relative of Troy Hall's that Rhodes had written down.[747]

Although no connection ever seemed to be made to the murders, a car parked at Troy's and Ginny's trailer the next morning was curiously found to be registered to Pauline Durham Newman,[748] from Wilkes County.[749] Newman was a second cousin once removed to Bryce Durham.[750] She and her boyfriend, Jimmie Green Haynes,[751] also from Wilkes County,[752] ran a pizza parlor in Sparta, North Carolina, and Haynes reportedly had a used car lot at the same time Bryce Durham was in the auto loan business. It was believed Haynes may have been involved in auto thefts.[753] In 1980, he would be sentenced to four years in federal prison and fined $10,000 after he pleaded guilty to conspiring to sell narcotics and "use of the telephone and interstate travel in the aid of racketeering and extortion." At that time Haynes owned a daycare center, body shop, discount tire store,[754] and a seafood restaurant. He was reportedly acquainted with Ike Eller.[755] Haynes's fingerprints, as well as those of Pauline Newman's son, Ricky Newman, would eventually be compared to the latent prints from the Durham Case,[756] but to no avail.

At another point in the day, Troy returned to the dealership, this time with Ginny. Coming into the front office, Troy told the employees, "Okay, boys, we're going to get this thing together. You boys know what all happened, and I'm gonna put this dealership on the road." Service manager Dean Combs could not believe what he was seeing and hearing. He stated that Ginny made several trips in and out of the parts department, and he described her interactions with the mechanics as flirtatious. Combs thought the Halls seemed very "sassy" considering the events of the preceding night. He closely observed Troy and Ginny, stating Ginny's eyes looked like they were sunk back in her head. Combs believed both of them were under the influence of medication, drugs, or alcohol.[757]

At a poker game prior to the murders, Troy had declared he would own Bryce's dealership one day and was now, albeit unsuccessfully, trying to have it transferred to his name and carry on with the running of it.[758] Despite this, within a few days after the murders, local attorney John Bingham phoned Dean Combs and told him another local car dealer, Mack Brown, Sr.,[nnn] was looking into

---

[lll] Another individual present at the time of this Hall family gathering was Mrs. Louise Smith, who was working in the Claude Hall home the morning of February 4, 1972 and overheard these conversations. [Source: Louise Smith, interview with Arlie Isaacs, November 26, 1974, Watauga County Sheriff's Office investigation file 118-H-1/2/3.]

[mmm] Kent "Pig" Rhodes was a brother of Mickey Rhodes *(see footnote on p. 173)*, for whom Troy Hall served as a character witness during Mickey's federal trial for drug trafficking. [Source: Obituary for Kent Rhodes, *Winston-Salem Journal*, Winston-Salem, NC, August 18, 2010, p. A11.]

[nnn] Mack Brown, Sr. had served as the Watauga County Area Chairman for the North Carolina Automobile Dealers Association (NCADA), acting as a liaison between new car and truck dealers in the area and the NCADA and the National Automobile Dealers Association. [Sources: "Mack Brown Is Head Of Auto Dealer Group," *Watauga Democrat*, Boone, NC, July 24, 1969, p. 3; "Mack Brown Is Named County Auto Chairman," *Watauga Democrat*, Boone, NC, July 16, 1970, p. 1.]

purchasing the Durhams' dealership. Both Bingham and Brown advised Combs and his crew not to look for other employment as Brown wanted to keep them on.[759]

According to Cecil Small, throughout the day following the murders, Troy made several trips to his [Cecil's] trailer to ask if "they" (presumably law enforcement) had found anything out yet; likewise, Ray Hall came by several times to ask Cecil what he saw at the Durham home the previous night.[760]

Meanwhile, Dan Klutz[ooo] of Reins-Sturdivant Funeral Home in Boone had escorted the Durhams' bodies from the Watauga County Hospital to the University of North Carolina at Chapel Hill,[761] where their autopsies commenced.[ppp] The examiners determined Virginia (5'8" with blue eyes and blonde hair; no weight indicated)[762] was a victim of ligature strangulation and was dead when she was submerged in the bathtub water while Bryce (5'9" and 190 pounds with blue eyes and gray hair)[763] and Bobby (5'8 ¾" and 140 pounds with blue eyes and brown hair)[764] were strangled while their heads were underwater, water being found in their lungs.[765] In his medical examiner reports, Dr. Clayton Dean, who had ordered the autopsies, stated Bryce died of asphyxia, rope strangulation, and drowning, Virginia died from ligature strangulation, and Bobby died of asphyxiation, rope strangulation, and possible drowning.[766]

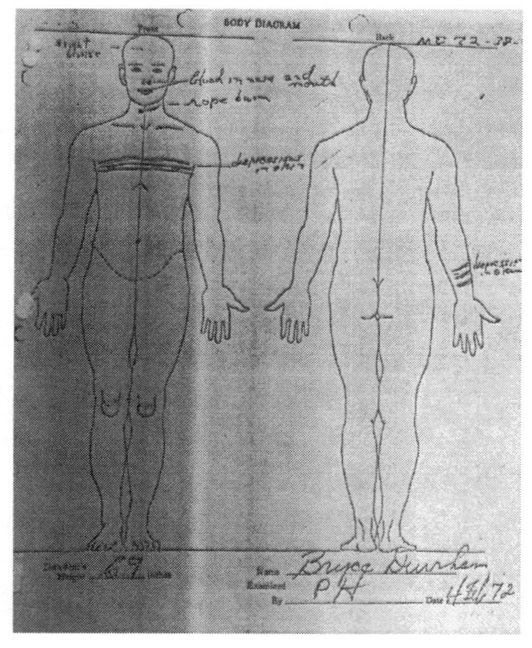

The left side of Bryce's nose was bloodied, bruised, and badly cut, and there was blood in his nose and mouth. Three parallel depressions were in the skin on the back of his right wrist, and rings of bruises extended from his right wrist up his right forearm in approximately two-inch intervals. He also had a short gash on the side of his right forearm. Three linear marks or depressions extended across the width of his upper chest, near the nipple-line, and three similar rows of linear marks were across his belly (not noted in the autopsy body diagram but visible in photos). These (and perhaps the three parallel depressions on the back of his right wrist) were likely made by his body being draped over the shower door track on the edge of the bathtub. He had a six-inch rope burn around the front and left side of his neck and a one-inch, superficial contusion (i.e., bruise) on his right forehead, possibly having been hit on the head with a blunt instrument. His scalp and skull revealed no evidence of disease or injury. His fingernails were clean, but his fingers had fingerprint ink on them (presumably from being fingerprinted by law enforcement). He had subconjunctival petechiae (caused by bleeding and manifested as tiny purple, red, or brown dots, each about the size of a pinpoint, just under the clear surface of the eye),

[ooo] Klutz was the father-in-law of future Watauga County Sheriff Len Hagaman. [Sources: Genealogical research by author; Hagaman, Len. In-person interview with author. May 19, 2023.]

[ppp] The author attempted to obtain more pristine copies of the Durhams' autopsy reports, but all such records housed at the NC Office of the Chief Medical Examiner prior to 1976 were lost in a fire. [Source: NC Office of the Chief Medical Examiner. Phone call with author. July 31, 2024.]

indicating possible mechanical compression of the neck and jugular veins (e.g., choking or strangulation). There were no deep hemorrhages in the strap muscles of the neck beneath the rope burn, but his middle ears were hemorrhaged. Toxicology reports ruled out the presence of "a wide variety of drugs and chemicals," including alcohol, acetone, and barbiturates. No diseases were found that would account for illness or death. His teeth were in relatively good repair. His lungs were congested and edematous (i.e., abnormally swollen) and blood was present in many areas of the lungs. The gross appearance and the microscopic characteristics were typical of freshwater drowning. His stomach held a "relatively large quantity of food material, including well-masticated portions of corn, squash and light-colored meat resembling chicken." The sinusoids (tubular spaces for the passage of blood) in his liver were mildly congested with blood. There was a relatively small amount of well-digested material in his small intestine, and his colon contained a moderate amount of fecal material. His bladder contained about 10 milliliters of clear amber urine. "Either the strangulation as evidenced by the rope burn and the noose or the aspiration of water as indicated by the lungs and history would have been adequate to have caused death."[767]

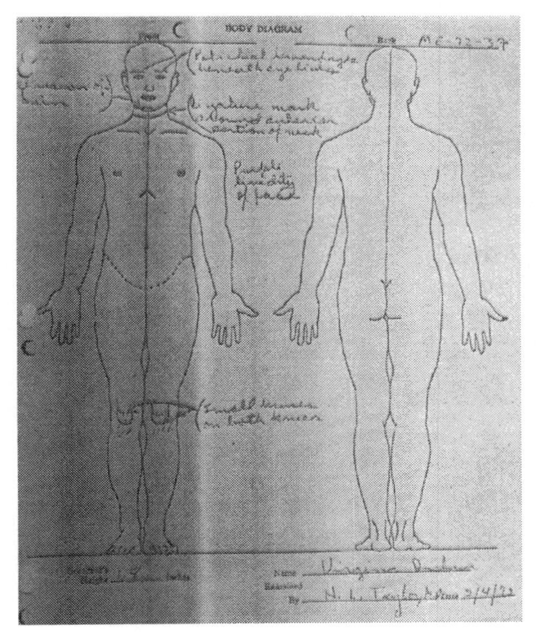

Like Bryce, Virginia had been struck in the face and her nose was bloodied, particularly her left nostril, with abrasions extending down to her left upper lip and the left side and underside of her chin. In contrast to Bryce's autopsy results, Virginia's strap muscles did exhibit a small amount of hemorrhaging underneath the ligature strangulation mark around the anterior (i.e., front) of her neck. Her thyroid cartilage and hyoid bone (the small horseshoe-shaped bone in the middle of the neck at the base of the mandible) were intact. She had petechial hemorrhages beneath her eyelids. Her lungs were congested but not edematous, and there was no edema fluid in her trachea or bronchi. Toxicology studies were negative for blood ethanol or other volatiles. Smears of the vagina were negative for acid phosphatase activity, meaning there was no presence of semen. She had small bruises on both knees and purple lividity of her face, lividity being the discoloration of the skin that occurs after death and is associated with the post-mortem phase of livor mortis. She was also found to have Hashimoto's thyroiditis, an autoimmune disorder affecting the thyroid gland. Her body was in full rigor mortis, meaning her muscles had stiffened. Her stomach contained "a large quantity of partially digested food, corn, squash, [and] white meat."[768]

Bobby's autopsy stated he had obvious ligature marks (rope burns) on his neck (7" long and ¼" wide) and face (about 3" long and ¼" wide on either side of his mouth, indicative of his being gagged prior to his death). There were petechial hemorrhages in the skin and conjunctiva (interior) of his eyelids, in the undersurface of his scalp, and in his larynx. There were also petechial hemorrhages on the front and left side of his chest (¾" in diameter) and a parchment abrasion (i.e., a pressure abrasion caused by a slow, prolonged compression of the skin by a blunt object[769]) on the

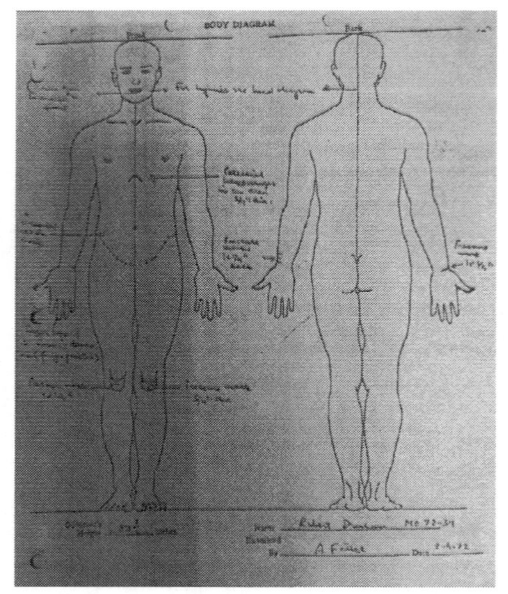

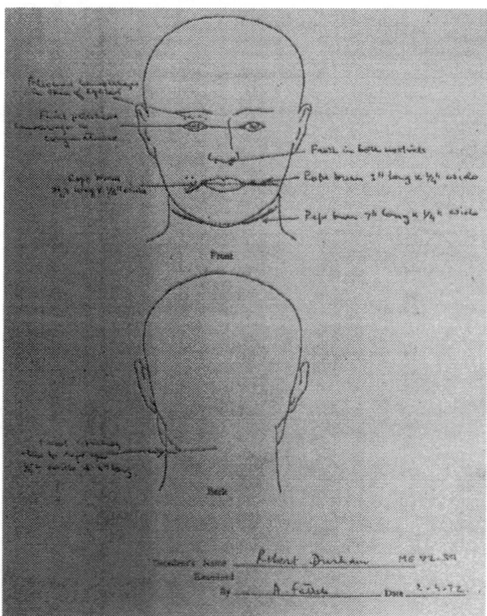

right side of his abdomen (½" in diameter and perhaps caused by his body lying across the shower door track on the edge of the bathtub), and he had pressure marks on both wrists and both knees. The ones on his wrists were on the same sides as his thumbs (perhaps indicating his hands had been bound together). The left wrist had three parallel linear marks, each 1¼" long. The right wrist had one mark 1¼" long. His fingertips showed evidence of being fingerprinted. The front of his lower gum was lacerated, and both nostrils were filled with froth. He had severe pulmonary congestion and edema. There was presence of froth in his air passages, congestion of his visceral (internal) organs, and hemorrhages in his middle ears. Toxicology reports showed the absence of alcohol, barbiturates, or other volatiles. The surface of his heart was glistening. Both of his lungs were large and ballooned and retained their shape when they were removed from his body. The surfaces of the lungs were glistening and had a mottled purplish color. The trachea and bronchi contained a considerable amount of froth. His stomach contained 100 grams of whitish digesting food, but no water. His bladder contained 2.5 cubic centimeters (milliliters) of clear urine. It was noted, "It is entirely possible that the decedent might have been strangled while his head being held underwater, and that drowning might have contributed to the acceleration of death."[770]

There were no signs of resistance on the part of the victims. "None of the corpses bore defensive wounds, which led the coroner to surmise the Durhams had been slain by more than one assailant." If there had been "a lone assassin…more evidence of a life-or-death struggle would have been present. The family had seemingly been overpowered with lightning speed."[771]

COPY 1
FOR STATE HEALTH DEPT.

MAR 6 1972
REGISTRATION DISTRICT NO. 95-00 LOCAL NO. 17

NORTH CAROLINA STATE BOARD OF HEALTH
OFFICE OF VITAL STATISTICS – RALEIGH
MEDICAL EXAMINER'S
CERTIFICATE OF DEATH

8174

650

DECEASED

1. Name of deceased: First: Baxter Middle: Bryce Last: Durham
2. Date of death: 2/3/1972
3. Sex: Male
4. Color or race: Cau.
5. State of birth: N. C.
6. Date of birth: 11/12/1920
7. Age (in years last birthday): 51
8a. Place of death: County: Watauga
8b. City or town: Boone
8c. Name of hospital or institution: Rt. #3
8d. Inside city limits: no
9a. Usual residence: State: N. C.
9b. County: Watauga
9c. City or town: Boone
9d. Street address or R.F.D. No.: Rt. #3
9e. Inside city limits: no
10. Married, never married, widowed, divorced: Married
11. Surviving spouse: — —
12. Citizen of what country?: U.S.A.
13. Social security number: 238-20-2213
14a. Usual occupation: Owner Auto Dealership
14b. Kind of business or industry: Automobile
15. Father's name: Coy Durham
16. Mother's maiden name: Collie Crabb Durham
17a. Informant's name and address: Mrs Ginny D. Hall, 57 Greenway Village, Boone, N. C.
17b. Relation to deceased: Daughter

CAUSE

18. Part I. Death caused by:
(a) Immediate cause: Asphyxia due to rope strangulation and drowning.
Interval between onset and death: Immediate
(b) Due to, or as a consequence of:
(c) Due to, or as a consequence of:

963X

19. Part II. Other significant conditions:
20a. Autopsy: yes
20b. M.E. or other:
20c. If yes:
21a. Accident, suicide, homicide, undetermined, natural causes, or pending: Homicide
21b. Describe how injury occurred: Rope around the neck.
21c. Time of injury: Month 2 Day 3 Year 72 Hour 10:00 p
21d. Injury at work: No
21e. Place of injury: Home
21f. City or R.F.D.: Boone County: Watauga State: N. C.

CERTIFIER

Medical examiner certification: On the basis of the examination of the body and/or the investigation, in my opinion, death occurred on the date and due to the cause(s) stated.

22a. Death occurred (hour): 10:00 p.m.
22b. The decedent was pronounced dead: Month 2 Day 3 Year 1972 Hour
22c. Date signed: 2/7/1972
23a. Signature: [signature] MD
23b. Address: Boone, N. C. 28607
23c. Medical examiner of (specify county): Watauga

BURIAL

24a. Burial, cremation, other: Burial
24b. Date: 2/6/1972
24c. Name of cemetery or crematory: Pleasant Home Cemetery
24d. Location: Lomax, Wilkes Co., N. C.
25. Funeral home: Reins-Sturdivant of Boone, Inc., Boone, N.C.
Signature of funeral director: [signature] License no. 1929
Signature of embalmer: James M. [signature] License no. 873
27. Date rec'd by local reg.: 2-7-72
Signature of registrar: WATAUGA COUNTY HEALTH DEPARTMENT

MEDICAL EXAMINER: After you have initiated the Certificate of Death, give copies 1 & 2 to funeral director when body is released, and route copy 2 to Chief Medical Examiner. If cause of death is pending, file Supplemental Report of Cause of Death (Form VS 8A) when the additional information has been obtained.
FUNERAL DIRECTOR: Take copies 1 & 3 to local or sub-registrar for signature. When signed, file copy 1 with local or sub-registrar and retain copy 3 as your burial-transit permit.

FORM 8X
5-71

COPY 1
FOR STATE HEALTH DEPT.

MAR 6 1972

NORTH CAROLINA STATE BOARD OF HEALTH
OFFICE OF VITAL STATISTICS – RALEIGH
MEDICAL EXAMINER'S
CERTIFICATE OF DEATH

REGISTRATION DISTRICT NO. 95-00 LOCAL NO. 15

8176

650

DECEASED

1. NAME OF DECEASED: Virginia (First) Dare (Middle) Durham (Last)
2. DATE OF DEATH (Month, Day, Year): 2/3/1972
3. SEX: Female
4. COLOR or RACE: Cau.
5. STATE OF BIRTH (If not in U.S.A., name country): N. C.
6. DATE OF BIRTH: 10/24/1926 1927
7. AGE (in years last birthday): 45 44
8a. PLACE OF DEATH – COUNTY: Watauga
8b. CITY OR TOWN: Boone
8c. NAME OF HOSPITAL OR INSTITUTION (If not in either, give street and number): Rt. #3
8d. INSIDE CITY LIMITS (Specify yes or no): no
9a. USUAL RESIDENCE (Where deceased lived. If institution, residence before admission) – STATE: N. C.
9b. COUNTY: Watauga
9c. CITY OR TOWN: Boone
9d. STREET ADDRESS OR R.F.D. NO.: Rt. #3
9e. INSIDE CITY LIMITS (Specify yes or no): no
10. MARRIED, NEVER MARRIED, WIDOWED, DIVORCED (Specify): Married
11. SURVIVING SPOUSE (If wife, give maiden name): n/a
12. CITIZEN OF WHAT COUNTRY?: U.S.A.
13. SOCIAL SECURITY NUMBER: 245-34-0202
14a. USUAL OCCUPATION (Kind of work done during most of working life, even if retired): Bookkeeper
14b. KIND OF BUSINESS OR INDUSTRY: Automobile Dealership
15. FATHER'S NAME: Calvin Church
16. MOTHER'S MAIDEN NAME: Jennie Eller Church
17a. INFORMANT'S NAME AND ADDRESS: Mrs Ginny D. Hall, 57 Greenway Village, Boone, N. C.
17b. RELATION TO DECEASED: Daughter

CAUSE

18. PART I. DEATH CAUSED BY: (Enter only one cause per line for (a), (b), and (c))
(a) IMMEDIATE CAUSE: Ligature strangulation. — APPROXIMATE INTERVAL BETWEEN ONSET AND DEATH: Immediate
CONDITIONS, IF ANY, WHICH GAVE RISE TO IMMEDIATE CAUSE (a), STATING THE UNDERLYING CAUSE LAST
(b) DUE TO, OR AS A CONSEQUENCE OF:
(c) DUE TO, OR AS A CONSEQUENCE OF:

963X

19. PART II. OTHER SIGNIFICANT CONDITIONS CONTRIBUTING TO DEATH BUT NOT RELATED TO CAUSE GIVEN IN PART I (a)
20a. AUTOPSY (Specify yes or no): yes
20b. M.E. OR OTHER
20c. IF YES, WERE FINDINGS CONSIDERED IN DETERMINING CAUSE OF DEATH
21a. ACCIDENT, SUICIDE, HOMICIDE, UNDETERMINED, NATURAL CAUSES, OR PENDING (Specify): Homicide
21b. DESCRIBE HOW INJURY OCCURRED (Enter nature of injury in Part I or Part II, Item 18): Rope around the neck.
21c. TIME OF INJURY – MONTH: 2 DAY: 3 YEAR: 72 HOUR: 10:00
21d. INJURY AT WORK (Specify yes or no): No
21e. PLACE OF INJURY (At home, farm, street, factory, office bldg., etc.) (Specify): Home
21f. CITY OR R.F.D.: Boone COUNTY: Watauga STATE: N. C.

CERTIFIER

MEDICAL EXAMINER CERTIFICATION: On the basis of the examination of the body and/or the investigation, in my opinion, death occurred on the date and due to the cause(s) stated.

Amended 4-18-72

22a. DEATH OCCURRED HOUR: 10:00 P.M.
22b. THE DECEDENT WAS PRONOUNCED DEAD – MONTH: 2 DAY: 3 YEAR: 1972 HOUR: —
22c. DATE SIGNED (Month, Day, Year): 2/7/1972
23a. SIGNATURE: [signature]
23b. ADDRESS: Boone, N. C. 28607
23c. MEDICAL EXAMINER OF (Specify county): Watauga

BURIAL

24a. BURIAL, CREMATION, OTHER (Specify): Burial
24b. DATE: 2/6/1972
24c. NAME OF CEMETERY OR CREMATORY: Pleasant Home Cemetery
24d. LOCATION (City, town, or county) (State): Lomax, Wilkes Co., N.C.
25. FUNERAL HOME – NAME / ADDRESS: Reins-Sturdivant of Boone, Inc., Boone, N.C.
26. SIGNATURE OF FUNERAL DIRECTOR: Barney S. Hampton — LICENSE NO. 1929
27. DATE REC'D BY LOCAL REG.: 2-7-72
SIGNATURE OF REGISTRAR: WATAUGA COUNTY HEALTH DEPARTMENT
SIGNATURE OF EMBALMER (If embalmed): James M. Penny — LICENSE NO. 873

MEDICAL EXAMINER: After you have initiated the Certificate of Death, give copies 1 & 2 to funeral director who, if body is released, and route copy 2 to Chief Medical Examiner. If cause of death pending, file Supplemental Report of Cause of Death (Form VS 8A) when the additional information has been obtained.
FUNERAL DIRECTOR: Take copies 1 & 3 to local or sub-registrar for signature. When signed, file copy 1 with local or sub-registrar and retain copy 3 as your burial-transit permit.

FORM 8E
5-71

COPY 1
FOR STATE HEALTH DEPT.

MAR 6 1972
REGISTRATION DISTRICT NO. 95-00 LOCAL NO. 16

NORTH CAROLINA STATE BOARD OF HEALTH
OFFICE OF VITAL STATISTICS – RALEIGH
MEDICAL EXAMINER'S
CERTIFICATE OF DEATH

8175

X 650

DECEASED

1. Name of deceased: First: Bobby — Middle: Joe — Last: Durham
2. Date of death: 2/3/1972
3. Sex: Male
4. Color or race: Cau.
5. State of birth: N. C.
6. Date of birth: 5/2/1953
7. Age (last birthday): 18
8. Place of death: County: Watauga — City or town: Boone
9. Usual residence: State: N. C. — County: Watauga
Name of hospital or institution: Rt. #3 — Inside city limits: no — City or town: Boone
10. Married, never married, widowed, divorced: Never Married
11. Surviving spouse: — —
Street address or R.F.D. No.: Rt. #3 — Inside city limits: no
12. Citizen of what country?: U.S.A.
13. Social Security Number: 247-78-5794
14a. Usual occupation: Student
14b. Kind of business or industry: College
15. Father's name: Baxter Bryce Durham
16. Mother's maiden name: Virginia Dare Church Durham
17a. Informant's name and address: Mrs Ginny D. Hall, 57 Greenway Village, Boone, N. C.
17b. Relation to deceased: Sister

CAUSE

18. Part I. Death caused by:

9103X

(a) Immediate cause: Asphyxiation due to strangulation and possible drowning. — Interval between onset and death: Immediate
(b) Due to, or as a consequence of:
(c) Due to, or as a consequence of:

19. Part II. Other significant conditions:
20a. Autopsy: yes

21a. Accident, suicide, homicide, undetermined, natural causes, or pending: Homicide
21b. Describe how injury occurred: Rope around the neck.
21c. Time of injury: Month 2, Day 3, Year 72, Hour 10:00 p.m.
21d. Injury at work: No
21e. Place of injury: Home
21f. City or R.F.D.: Boone — County: Watauga — State: N. C.

CERTIFIER

Medical examiner certification: On the basis of the examination of the body and/or the investigation, in my opinion, death occurred on the date and due to the cause(s) stated.

22a. Death occurred: 10:00 p.m.
22b. The decedent was pronounced dead: Month 2, Day 3, Year 1972
22c. Date signed: 2/7/1972
23a. Signature: [signature] — Address: Boone, N. C.
23c. Medical examiner of county: Watauga

BURIAL

24a. Burial, cremation, other: Burial
24b. Date: 2/6/1972
24c. Name of cemetery or crematory: Pleasant Home Cemetery
24d. Location: Lomax, Wilkes Co., N.C.
25. Funeral home: Reins-Sturdivant of Boone, Inc., Boone, N.C.
26. Signature of funeral director: Barney S. Hampton — License No. 1929
Date rec'd by local reg.: 2-7-72
27. Signature of registrar: WATAUGA COUNTY HEALTH DEPARTMENT
Signature of embalmer: James M. Pennington — License No. 873

FORM 81 3-71

MEDICAL EXAMINER: After you have initiated the Certificate of Death, give copies 1 & 2 to funeral director who, if body is released, and route copy 2 to Chief Medical Examiner. If cause of death is pending, file Supplemental Report of Cause of Death (Form VS 8A) when the additional information has been obtained.
FUNERAL DIRECTOR: Take copies 1 & 3 to local or sub-registrar for signature. When signed, file copy 1 with local or sub-registrar and retain copy 3 as your burial-transit permit.

CHAPTER 5

A HARD FAREWELL

When Bobby Durham and his Watauga High School classmates graduated on June 2, 1971, the commencement speakers' addresses centered around the theme of "Turn, Turn, Turn,"[772] a nod to the popular song of the same title, which the folk-rock band The Byrds made famous in 1965.[773] The lyrics, mostly taken from the third chapter of the biblical Book of Ecclesiastes included:

A time to be born, a time to die
A time to plant, a time to reap
A time to kill, a time to heal
A time to laugh, a time to weep

A time to build up, a time to break down
A time to dance, a time to mourn
A time to cast away stones, a time to gather stones together

A time to kill…a time to die…a time to weep…a time to mourn. No one could have imagined on that celebratory night what a reality these select words would become for Bobby and his parents exactly eight months and one day later.

The brutal slayings of the Durham family invoked community grief and concern, which was summarized in the following editorial that appeared in the *Watauga Democrat*:

The Community Mourns

"We share the general sorrow occasioned by the tragic deaths of Mr. and Mrs. Bryce Durham and son, Bobby Joe, when their home was invaded Thursday night.

"Of all places, we would have least supposed that a Boone home would have been pillaged and its occupants slain. That the wave of indiscriminate crime which has been sweeping the nation has come here to take the lives of a prominent local business man, his wife and son has occasioned grief and at the same time has brought uneasiness to householders.

"Sheriff's officers, augmented by agents of the State Bureau of Investigation are working diligently to identify and bring to justice the person or persons responsible for this heinous crime, and we feel their efforts will soon meet with success. Then, the guilty will no doubt be punished to the degree befitting the atrocious act.

"The Democrat family extends sympathy to the bereaved daughter, other relatives of the deceased and to business associates in the bereavement.

"Meanwhile, Boone citizens have been made more aware of the common dangers that lurk in the darkness, so long as these felons are at large. Many have taken a second look at firearms, unused for many years in some cases, have made their door locks more secure and have taken every logical step toward preventing burglaries.

"The old precept that 'a man's home is his castle' has come into question of late, but we hear that a lot of people still believe that and are aiming to do whatever they can to protect their abodes and their families."[774]

Additional expressions of the community's grief and sympathies were demonstrated in the form of memorials. Exactly two weeks after the evening of the murders, the Boone Rotary Club conducted a special tribute to the Durhams. Club President Lee Barnett read a statement from their bulletin: "Our hearts are saddened tonight by the absence of fellow Rotarian Bryce Durham, who was dedicated to Rotary and all business and civic affairs right up until the night of his death."[775] Within a few months after the tragedy, Bobby was individually honored when Boy Scout Troop 109, sponsored by the Boone United Methodist Church, established the Bobby J. Durham Memorial Fund to assist scouts in their summer attendance at Raven Knob Scout Camp in Mount Airy,[776] where Bobby had served as a counselor.[777]

BOONE — Bobby Durham, 19, died Thursday. Funeral 2 p.m. Sunday at First Baptist Church. Burial Pleasant Home Baptist Church, Wilkes County.

BOONE — Bryce Durham, 51, died Thursday. Funeral 2 p.m. Sunday at First Baptist Church. Burial in Pleasant Home Baptist Church Cemetery in Wilkes County.

BOONE — Mrs. Bryce Durham, 45, died Thursday. Funeral 2 p.m. Sunday at First Baptist Church. Burial in Pleasant Home Baptist Church Cemetery in Wilkes County.

The Durhams' obituaries in brief. [The ages stated for Bobby and Virginia are incorrect and should have been 18 and 44.] (Source: The Charlotte Observer, February 5, 1972)

After the autopsies were completed, the bodies of Bryce, Virginia, and Bobby Durham were transported to Boone's only funeral home at that time – Reins-Sturdivant – which had left its old downtown location and moved eastward to a newer, more modern, 12,000-square-foot facility about a half mile from Troy and Ginny Hall's residence.[qqq] Funeral director Barney Hampton worked with Ginny to gather information for the death certificates and to plan the arrangements. Three silver caskets, identical in style, were selected, and Ginny provided the burial clothing with the exception of a white garment purchased for Virginia from the funeral home. Hampton was instructed to publish out-of-town obituaries in newspapers in Asheville, Charlotte, Mount Airy, and Winston-Salem.[778] Ginny phoned her aunt Gayle and asked her to inform everyone she would not be receiving anyone at her trailer; rather, she had reserved a room at the funeral home.[779]

Certain ensuing behaviors contradicted the solemnity of making funeral arrangements, particularly for three murdered loved ones. At some point, someone removed the traditional funeral home floral arrangement denoting a family member's passing and threw it under the Halls' trailer. On Saturday, February 5, Troy reportedly went to a men's clothing store in Boone to acquire a suit to wear to his in-laws' funeral. The store owner

[qqq] In 1987, the funeral home left this facility, and the Boone Police Department began its occupancy there; the two briefly shared the space, and as of 2024, the police department remains there. It is ironic that the space which held the Durhams' bodies in their caskets later housed some of the officers involved in the investigation of their murders. [Source: "One-Stop Convenience?" *The Charlotte Observer*, Charlotte, NC, July 16, 1987, p. 2B.]

inquired if the sale would be cash or charge, and Troy said charge. When the owner asked for his address, Troy replied, "Do you want my present or my new address? I'll be moving to the house up on the hill"[780] – this, the same house Bryce Durham swore Troy would never spend a night in.

At the Durhams' Saturday evening viewing, with the bodies of Bryce, Virginia, and Bobby lying in repose at the front of the funeral home's cathedral-like chapel,[781] Troy and Ginny sat on a bench to the side. Some observers felt Troy exerted control over Ginny, making sure no one talked to her.[782]

The triple funeral service was held at 2:00 PM on Sunday, February 6 at the Durhams' place of worship, First Baptist Church in Boone.[783] Snow began falling within the hour before the service, which was officiated by the church's minister, Rev. Robert Mann, who had only assumed the pastorate there a month earlier,[784] and Rev. Joe Crews, former pastor of Bannertown Baptist Church in Mount Airy, which the Durhams attended prior to moving to Boone. The main sanctuary and balcony were nearly filled with Watauga County residents, including a majority of the business community[785] as well as family, friends, and former neighbors from Wilkes and Surry counties. Among those present were "a group of Boy Scouts from Mount Airy for whom Bobby Durham had once been a leader," and a large number of his Watauga High School graduating class. The Boone Rotary Club furnished pallbearers for the service.[786] Cecil and Mildred Small were among those in attendance.[787]

Funeral home tents at the Durhams' graves

After the service, Barney Hampton lined up and led the processional. Three light gray hearses, at least one of them borrowed from Reins-Sturdivant's facility in North Wilkesboro,[788] carried the bodies to the Pleasant Home Baptist Church Cemetery in the Lomax community of Wilkes County, where they were viewed at graveside by 500-600 people.[789] Despite the undertaker's best concealment efforts with mortuary makeup,[790] bad bruises remained visible on Virginia's face and neck, and, according to one observer, the fingers on one of her hands looked to be broken as if a door had been slammed on them. Although medical examiners had found no signs of resistance, and crime scene photos seem not to reveal trauma to her fingers, this suggested to the viewer that Virginia had been a fighter who had endured a brutal struggle. Bryce had a noticeable bruise on his forehead, and rope burns were still evident on Bobby's neck.[791] Bobby's friend, Gary Edmisten, recalled the heavy makeup used on Bobby's face gave it a hauntingly wax-like appearance.[792]

Following the graveside service, husband, wife, and son were buried in the cemetery, only a fifth of a mile and almost within sight of Coy and Collie Durham's house.[793][rrr] The Durhams had come home. Their physical bodies having been laid to rest, the disposition of their earthly possessions was soon to follow.

[rrr] To the present day, Durham family members keep the memories of Bryce, Virginia, and Bobby alive by maintaining flowers on their graves and by sharing fond memories of them at family get-togethers. [Source: Sean Kipe, Imperative Entertainment, *In The Red Clay*, podcast audio, Season 2, Episode 6: *Beneath the Chestnut Tree*, January 6, 2023, http://intheredclaypodcast.com.]

CHAPTER 6

THE PAYOUT

Five days after the murders, Durham family friend and attorney John C. W. Gardner, Sr. of Mount Airy, North Carolina was appointed by the Watauga County Superior Court as Executor of Bryce's and Virginia's estates and Administrator of Bobby's estate (as Bobby had no will). Gardner did not anticipate any distribution of assets in less than six months and said they could be tied up for perhaps as long as a year. Although Bryce had a lock box when the family lived in Mount Airy, no such box was found among the banks in Boone. Gardner had hoped to find one "containing a portfolio of all the Durhams' assets and liabilities, such things as deeds, insurance policies and stock certificates." He stated, "We have found some deeds to property, a few insurance policies for comparatively small amounts, but nothing like the accumulation of records I would have expected to find."[794][sss]

Bryce's and Virginia's unaltered wills were dated January 10, 1964 and had been executed in Mount Airy when they were still residents of Surry County. They had named one another as their primary beneficiary, but in the event of both of their deaths, Ginny and Bobby were to be equal beneficiaries. Because Bobby died intestate, nineteen-year-old Ginny was left as the sole heir.[795] Gardner, who drew up Bryçe's and Virginia's 1964 wills inquired among attorneys in Mount Airy, Wilkesboro, North Wilkesboro, and Boone, but turned up no later wills. Gardner had heard rumors the Durhams planned to change their wills, but neither of them had mentioned that to him.[796] Bryce's brother Bill contacted two hundred lawyers in an attempt to locate the new wills, but to no avail.[797] The SBI also later looked into this claim and likewise found no new wills.[798] The "dollar will" that had been such a big topic of discussion at the dealership and within family circles could not be found.[ttt]

[sss] At some point after the murders, two boxes of papers disappeared from the dealership and were never found. SBI Agent Wally Hardwick, Jr. was to have picked them up, along with an officer from the Boone Police Department or the Watauga County Sheriff's Department, but Sheriff Ward Carroll stated he had no knowledge of the boxes. Reportedly, when Ike Eller and authorities went to the dealership's safe, wills and unnamed items belonging to Bryce Durham were missing. When Bryce's brother Bill went to the dealership the day after the murders, he observed the open "vault."[Sources: Watauga County Sheriff's Office investigation file 118-H-1/2/3; Durham, Bill. Interview with Len Hagaman, Kelly Redmon, Carolynn Johnson, Wade Colvard, Larry Wagner, & Rufus Edmisten. August 6, 2019; Eller, Tom. Phone interview with author. July 14, 2022.]

[ttt] What none of the Durhams or Halls likely understood was that, even if a new will had been located and validated, Ginny would still have ended up inheriting all three estates. In the event of Bryce's and Virginia's deaths, although the new will would have only left Ginny $1 from their estates and everything else would have gone to Bobby, by virtue of Bobby also dying and without a will, Ginny would have come into possession of everything he had. The actual order of death of the three victims, even if known or ascertainable, would also have made no difference. If Bobby died first, and if Bryce and Virginia named no contingent beneficiary in the event that Bobby predeceased them, the end result

Approximately five days following Gardner's appointment, preliminary inventories of Bryce's and Virginia's estates were announced with an estimated total value of $107,585.[799] More detailed and accurate information was provided in the 90-Day Inventories that were subsequently filed, reflecting a revised total value of $73,934.79 for all three estates. A final account was provided to the Clerk of the Watauga County Superior Court on April 25, 1973, which showed the total combined value of all the estates' personal property assets (including receipts not reflected in the 90-Day Inventories) to be $128,439.26.[800]

The personal property of all three estates, prior to the settlement of estate debts, was comprised of a number of assets, including more than $67,000 in various life insurance policy proceeds being paid to their estates (the largest payouts being from Metropolitan Life Insurance Company in the amounts of $35,000 for Bryce, $10,000 for Virginia, and $5,000 for Bobby), checking and savings account balances, various interest and dividends on escrow accounts, certificates of deposit, stocks, etc., various refunds (e.g., unearned insurance premiums, telephone service, and tax refunds), assorted other small collections, a $225 Social Security burial allowance for Bryce, and $1,000 of household and kitchen furniture.[801] *[By authority of the Uniform Simultaneous Death Act, which provided that, if the insured and the beneficiary died at the same time, insurance policy proceeds reverted to the insured's estate, this was true of Bryce's and Virginia's estates. "Almost all of Bryce's insurance policies named Virginia as his beneficiary, and almost all of her policies named him as her beneficiary."[802]]*

Another asset from Bryce's estate was the Modern Buick-Pontiac dealership, which had remained closed since the day following the murders[803] (or for about a week, according to service manager Dean Combs[804] or since Tuesday, February 8 when Gardner "came to Boone to file the wills for probate and qualify as executor"[805]).[uuu] For a brief time, Troy and Ginny entertained the thought of running the dealership themselves, and the night after the funeral, they arrived at the home of sales manager, Ike Eller and his wife Frances. *[The Halls were driving one of the new cars from the dealership. This is likely the black car Troy's and Ginny's neighbors, Chester and Minnie Nelson, saw them arrive home in later that night[806] and may be the same car that General Motors, which owned the new car vehicle inventory at the dealership, made Troy return.]*[807] Troy told Ike he wanted him to continue working at the dealership once he [Troy] took it over.[808] The following day, the Ellers went to Boone and met Troy at the dealership, where Ike turned over around $3,800 to him. This was money Ike said he had as a result of selling some used cars at the dealership, and he had not had a chance to give it to Bryce and Virginia before they were killed, so he gave it to Troy instead.[vvv] Frances Eller brought a car back to the dealership and gave the keys to Troy. She had

would have been the same. [Sources: Henson, Jack (retired attorney). Personal communication with author. April 8, 2023 & June 2, 2024.]

[uuu] Bryce Durham's father Coy and brother Bill, alongside Troy Hall, were present at the courthouse in Boone when Bryce's will was probated. Bill's later recollection of the proceedings was blacked out and supplanted by his memory of being in such close proximity to Troy. [Source: Durham, Bill. Interview with Len Hagaman, Kelly Redmon, Carolynn Johnson, Wade Colvard, Larry Wagner, & Rufus Edmisten. August 6, 2019.]

[vvv] Ike Eller's assertion about the $3,800 was contrary to the way the Durhams conducted business. Bryce had told family members that Ike would never handle a dollar of money, but when Ike made a sale, he would send the buyer to Virginia, and she would receive the money when the title was transferred. This was substantiated by service manager Dean Combs, who stated it would not have been customary for the sales manager to have taken money home after a sale and brought it back the following day. "I don't believe Virginia would have stood for that 'cause she [was] too strict." According to Combs, Virginia, Bryce, and Bobby were the only ones he ever saw carry the money. Ike would later change his story, saying he gave nothing to Troy but instead gave this money to attorney John Bingham. He also stated the money was comprised of some down payments on cars. [Sources: Combs, Dean. Interview with

instructed her husband to give all the money to Troy and be done with him.[809] At some later point in time, there were hard feelings between Troy and Ike because Troy thought Ike might be trying to buy the dealership.[810] After the murders, Ike never returned to Boone to work but remained in Wilkes County.[811]

Despite Troy and Ginny having approached Gardner about allowing them to run the dealership, they "eventually agreed with his decision to sell [it],"[812] and Gardner stated, "We hope to get the business back in operation promptly and to sell it as quickly as we can." He added "that GM [had] agreed to 'give us a reasonable time.'"[813]

Bryce's ownership of the dealership was in the form of 6,000 shares of common stock in the company, each share valued at $10.00 for a total value of $60,000. Mack Brown, Sr. purchased the dealership on February 29, 1972 for $49,625 and, in accordance with the terms of the Contract of Purchase and Sale, $9,500 of the purchase price was "placed in escrow to provide for the payment of certain contingent corporate obligations, including additional assessments for ad valorem taxes, State and Federal income taxes, and like matters," including any liability developments. From the portion of the purchase price placed in escrow, Bryce's estate paid Brown $2,040.43 in settlement of contingent liabilities that were outstanding on the date of the sale. Based on the terms of the Contract of Purchase and Sale, Brown had the option to take over the cars on Bryce's lot and did so because he needed the inventory. Estate records show that Ginny, as the sole beneficiary, was the one who entered into the contract with Brown,[814] but it is believed Troy was the driving force behind their end of the deal. In meetings to discuss the sale, it seemed to one who was present that Troy controlled Ginny, and that she appeared to not really know what was taking place.[815]

Brown operated the business under the Modern Buick-Pontiac Co. name for about thirty days until its new name, Brown Pontiac-Buick Co., took effect.[816] The grand re-opening of the dealership transpired on May 12 and 13, 1972, and several former Durham employees, including Dean Combs, continued their employment, with Brown adding other staff.[817][www]

The debts owed by the Durham estates totaled $66,089.83 and included paying off their house with the Watauga Savings and Loan Association (the mortgage being satisfied on September 1, 1972), federal and state income taxes, court and attorney's fees, and inheritances taxes, the payoff of a $4,041.20 note to the Bank of Pilot Mountain, and Watauga Ambulance Service and funeral expenses, including casket sprays and grave markers.[818]

After all the estates' debts were paid, the final combined value of personal properties stood at $62,349.43. This consisted of $48,383.41 in personal property (including his shares of stock in the dealership) from Bryce's estate, $9,340.79 in personal property from Virginia's estate, and $4,625.23 in personal property from Bobby's estate. This total was the amount distributed to Ginny Hall. In addition to personal property, real property was estimated (likely tax-valued) at $40,000 ($30,000 for the Durham home and lot in the Brushy Fork Township of Watauga County and

---

Red Lyons. July 5, 1989; Eller, Ike. Interview with Arlie Isaacs. January 16, 1975; Eller, Ike. Interview with Red Lyons & Fred Myers; Notes compiled by Gayle Durham Mauldin.]

[www] Brown continued to operate the Pontiac-Buick dealership from its East King Street location until he built a larger facility that became known as Mack Brown Chevrolet. The old building was eventually demolished as part of a widening of U. S. Highway 421.

Former Durham employee Barry Hudler (far left) beside Mack Brown, Sr., new owner of Bryce Durham's former automobile dealership in Boone, NC (Source: www.unexplained-mysteries.com)

$10,000 for fifty acres of unimproved land near Fries in the Old Town Magisterial District of Grayson County, Virginia).[819]

The Durham house was sold, along with some of the furniture, including bedroom suites, on October 3, 1972 for approximately $13,500, which was $16,500 less than the estimated $30,000 value of the real property as listed on the 90-Day Inventory.[820] Presumably, the price was affected by the difficulty of selling a house where such horrors had occurred.

At the time of the house sale, Troy Hall did not want to sign the final paperwork without having one more opportunity to go back inside the house. When the attorney asked the buyer if that would be okay, the buyer said he would accompany Troy, and in doing so, he witnessed Troy enter the kitchen, remove all the drawers, and look inside, under, and behind them. Troy also crawled inside the cabinets and looked around. In a bedroom, he pulled out all the dresser drawers, pulled out the dresser itself, and looked and felt around. The SBI shared this information with Bryce's sister Gayle Mauldin, who believed Troy was still looking, unsuccessfully, for a copy of an altered will.[821]

In December 1976, Ginny sold the acreage in Virginia for approximately $20,500. The deed stated this property was comprised of sixty-five acres on or near the New River and that Ginny had obtained it by will from her parents,[822] although when the estate was settled in 1972, it was estimated to be only fifty acres. At that time, the value of the property was estimated to be $10,000, so when Ginny sold it, she realized approximately $10,500 above the earlier estimated value.[823] She reportedly applied the proceeds of this sale toward building a house.[824]

SUMMARY OF DURHAM FAMILY ESTATES

Category	Estate of Baxter Bryce Durham	Estate of Virginia C. Durham	Estate of Bobby Joe Durham	All Estates Combined
90-Day Inventory - Personal Property Assets	$ 69,376.23	$ 2,681.40	$ 1,877.16	$ 73,934.79
Final Account - Receipts	+ 38, 973.80	+ 10,331.04	+ 5,199.63	$ 54,504.47
Total Personal Property	$ 108,350.03	$ 13,012.44	$ 7,076.79	$ 128,439.26
Less Disbursements for Estate Expenses	- 59, 966.62	- 3,671.65	- 2,451.56	- $ 66,089.83
Balance Distributed to Ginny Sue Durham Hall (April 25, 1973)	$ 48,383.41	$ 9,340.79	$ 4,625.23	$ 62,349.43 *

*** In addition to this amount, Ginny Sue Durham Hall was the sole heir/devisee of the following real property:**

- **House and one-acre lot in Brushy Fork Township, Watauga County, NC – Sold on October 3, 1972 by Troy Hall and wife, Ginny Sue Durham Hall to Donald Joseph Kidder and wife, Geraldine T. Kidder, for approximately $13,500 [Deed Book 133, Page 478 (Office of the Register of Deeds, Watauga County, North Carolina)]**

- **Approximately 65 acres of vacant land in Old Town Magisterial District in Grayson County, VA – Sold on December 27, 1976 by Ginny Sue Durham (divorced) to T. P. Kirby for approximately $20,500 [Deed Book 163, Page 198 (Office of Clerk of Circuit Court, Grayson County, Virginia)]**

In consideration of the sale prices of both the house and its lot in North Carolina and the land in Virginia (approximately $34,000) combined with the disbursement she received from her family's personal estates ($62,349.43), Ginny ultimately inherited approximately $96,349.43. One source reported it more concretely as "a net total of $134,000."[825] *[Depending on the inflation calculator used and inputting 1976 for the sale of the Virginia property and 1972 for the remaining property, that is roughly $660,000 in 2024 currency. Or, if the $134,000 net total is accurate, it could be as much as around $964,000 today. It was erroneously reported the combined estate value totaled almost $200,000.*[826] *Another source stated Ginny inherited nearly $250,000*[827] *in 1972 currency – approximately $1.8 million in 2024 currency – but that is a gross exaggeration.]*

The only point of contention noted in the estate records between Executor Gardner and Troy and Ginny Hall concerned the gravesite monument for Bryce, Virginia, and Bobby. In a December 1972 letter addressed to "Troy and Ginny Sue," Gardner wrote:

"Bryce Durham was a friend of mine, as was your mother. The estates are substantial. I have given you copies of Statutory authority authorizing me as Executor to place a suitable monument at their gravesites. I do not feel that the stones you have selected are suitable considering the station in life of your father, mother and brother, and considering the other attendant factors and circumstances.

"I have advised you that Mrs. Church *[Virginia's mother]* and the elder Durhams *[Bryce's parents]* have spoken several times with the Clerk of Superior Court of Watauga County about a suitable monument.

"I called Mr. [Orville] Foster, the Clerk of Court, today after receiving the order which you have placed and he feels, as I do, that some more fitting monument is indicated and agrees that as Executor it is in my discretion as to the amount that shall be spent for this purpose.

"While I do not intend to expend a large sum of money for a monument, I do feel that something larger than you have ordered is indicated. Accordingly, I have called Mr. [Worth] Bare at the Reins-Bare Monument Works [in North Wilkesboro] and have advised him to take no further steps toward completing the monuments you have ordered. I have asked Mr. Bare to come by my office with his catalog and I intend to place an order for one large monument to be placed at the head of the three gravesites and I intend to order three appropriate footstones to be placed at the foot of each grave. I would anticipate that an appropriate monument along these lines can be obtained for something between $500.00 and $1,000.00

"I am sorry that we have not seen eye to eye on this matter, but I assure you that I intend to continue to discharge my legal responsibilities as Executor and personal representative with respect to these estates and I hope that you can understand why I am forced to take this action."[828]

[Although Gardner, in his official capacity, was only required to communicate matters of the estates to Ginny as the sole heir and beneficiary, the fact that he chose to address this letter to both Troy and Ginny seems telling and may indicate he sensed Troy had influenced Ginny in the selection of an inferior monument.]

Ultimately installed at the gravesites was a substantial granite monument, polished on all sides, and simply carved "DURHAM." Three footstones were placed in the ground at the base of the monument, one for Bryce, one for Virginia, and one for Bobby.[829] Their estates having been settled and their earthly belongings disbursed, their lifespans were commemorated in stone by their birth and death dates, the latter sadly identical for all and forever telling of their shared demise.

Durham Tombstone at Pleasant Home Baptist Church, Roaring River, NC (Photo by author)

Durham Footstones (Photos by author)

PART II:

THE FIFTY-YEAR INVESTIGATION

CHAPTER 7

THE PURSUIT BEGINS

As news of the murders spread nationally, Boone Police Chief Clyde Tester received numerous letters, some containing rough language and some suggesting how to bring the guilty parties to justice. One writer from Flagler, Colorado advocated the return of public hangings and public whipping posts to counteract the nation's lax treatment of criminals: "The criminal too often…shrugs off the thought of conviction and sentencing with a feeling that his suffering will be at a minimum 'even if I get caught.'" The writer continued: "A crackdown on criminals will not save the lives of the Durham family, but if the public will get tough and assist law enforcement agencies in bringing criminals to justice, then it might be that we can save the lives of potential victims of such heinous slaughtering."[830]

In response to this, Joy Elvey Lamm, wife of Boone attorney Charles Lamm, Jr., wrote a letter to the editor of the *Watauga Democrat*, stating, in part:

"I was both appalled and saddened by your editorial of Thursday, February 17, 1972, which was titled 'Letters Protest Murders.'

"I believe that a journalist's duty is to report facts and encourage reason. It was therefore shocking to find you quoting a crude, inflammatory letter from a man in Colorado to support your own emotional biases concerning the handling of the Durham murder case. I wonder why his opinions are the basis of your lead editorial rather than the opinions of our Watauga citizens. And why must you quote statistics on criminals in another state to support your theory that 'there are some who will never make good citizens'? Just what is the point you're making in this editorial? It seems to me that you're trying to persuade the citizens of Watauga County to take the law into their own hands – to 'get tough,' as you put it….

"In the case of the Durham murders, I feel that Sheriff Carroll and Chief Tester must be commended in particular. They have acted wisely in not giving in to the demands for sensational stories by the press, and especially in not persecuting suspects upon whom they have no substantial evidence of guilt. They have not acted on the impulse of their outrage and it is important that the community at large follow their lead.

"We do not need vigilantes or hanging parties in the night. Rather we need somehow to reach the conscience of anyone who knows the facts, who knows truths he fears to tell, concerning the Durham murders. We need to speak to those involved about the horror of their atrocity; for

it will be locked up in their bodies and their souls, hounding their days and sleepless nights for the rest of their lives until they confess what it is they know.

"For those of us who are innocent, let our lives be examples of loving concern for all men, rather than examples of seething hatred and bitterness. Hatred cannot bring back the Durham family; but the spirit of love can keep us from brutalizing one another in the future.

"I cannot believe that mankind will ever find the 'hangin' tree' a better solution to its ills than the Sermon on the Mount."[831]

Another newspaper editorial called upon the North Carolina General Assembly to retain the death penalty as a discouragement of capital crime. "On the outside chance that such maniacal murders as those in…Boone will have at least to face the prospects of death by the state, we believe that capital punishment should remain on the books. The fiendish people who committed the triple murder in Boone are poor prospects ever to be turned loose again in society, assuming they will be captured…."[832]

And that was the question. How soon would these fiends be captured?

Although the Watauga County Sheriff's Department had jurisdiction over the Durham crime scene, Sheriff Ward Carroll and his five deputies were stretched thin by the murder investigation, Carroll working an average of sixty hours per week, and each of the deputies averaging seventy to seventy-five.[833] As a result, Carroll gave approval for the Boone Police Department to work the case alongside the sheriff's office.[834] Meanwhile, the State Bureau of Investigation remained faithful in its supporting role to these agencies, and the North Carolina State Highway Patrol also provided assistance.[835] The investigation became a truly collaborative effort with officers and agents working on it continuously and "in constant contact while checking out each new lead,"[836] hundreds of which took the lawmen over many miles throughout Western North Carolina and into the adjacent states[837] of Tennessee and Virginia.[838]

During the early days of the investigation, as many as eight SBI agents[839] were "constantly running down leads in connection with the case."[840] SBI Director Charles Dunn and his assistant, Haywood Starling,[841] both visited Boone,[842] and Dunn sat in the Durham house for hours "just trying to figure out what happened."[843] Teams of specialists in chemical analysis, ballistics, and procedures were dispatched from Raleigh[844] as well as a mobile SBI crime lab from Chapel Hill.[845] By the Saturday morning following the murders, seven SBI agents were on the scene, and three more were en route via helicopter, perhaps including two top physicists from the state crime laboratory who arrived later that day. Among the additional agents who District Supervisor Red Minter called in were John Parker[xxx] and Bob Thomas, both of whom were from Watauga County but based in Asheville. Although Agent Charlie Whitman had come from Lenoir to assist in the case, he was scheduled to attend polygraph training and needed to leave Boone. In light of this, Minter informed Parker and Thomas their help was needed.[846] The team of SBI agents worked well into the night trying to piece together clues in the Durham home.[847]

[xxx] Parker's father, Rev. J. K. Parker, Jr., of Boone, had led the invocation at Bobby Durham's high school baccalaureate service in May 1971. [Source: "WHS Students To Don Caps, Gowns," *Watauga Democrat*, Boone, NC, May 27, 1971, p. 1]

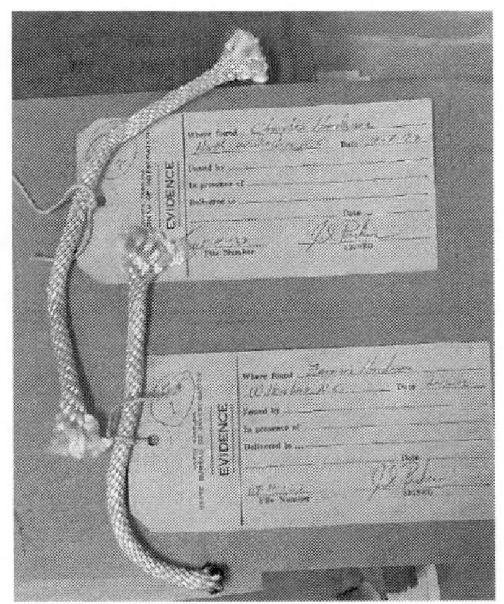

Rope comparisons in evidence (Photo by author)

Technicians began looking for fingerprints and other physical evidence,[848] and investigators soon announced substantial evidence had been gathered, including five sets of fingerprints.[849] In the end, more than two-hundred and forty-six prints, including more than two-hundred fingerprints, were lifted from the Durham house and vehicle, including the inside of the right vent glass of the GMC "Jimmy."[850] Among the identifiable prints were those of Bryce Durham on the doorframes of an upstairs bedroom, the upstairs sewing room, and a quart jar on the kitchen table. Bobby Durham's prints were found on a metal box in the basement. *[Could this have been the breadbox that potentially held cash or important documents?[851] At a later probable cause hearing, the district attorney asked Troy Hall if he had ever bothered the breadbox downstairs, and he said he had not.[852]]* Assistant District Attorney Tom Rusher's palm print was on the doorframe of Bobby's bedroom. A palm print and fingerprint on a door jamb were matched to Craven G. Ford, an Appalachian State University student from Burlington, North Carolina, who was perhaps a school acquaintance of Bobby Durham, Ginny Durham Hall, and/or Troy Hall.[853][yyy] Four simultaneous fingerprints – from the index, middle, ring, and little fingers of a right hand – were lifted from the bathroom wall beside the bathtub, about three feet off the floor. It would take years to determine those prints belonged to the medical examiner, who had apparently bent down to examine the bodies and placed his hand on the wall.[854] During his three to four days in Boone, John Parker did some preliminary work to identify suspects and motive but did not turn up anything and returned to Asheville.[855] Later on, he logged rope samples from two hardware stores in Wilkes County to compare to the rope found around Bryce Durham's neck.[856]

Canvassing of homes near the Durham house continued the day after the murders.[857] The investigation even spilled onto the Highway 105 Bypass down the hill and in front of the Durham residence. Officers stopped motorists to ask if they had traveled that route or seen anything the night of the murders.[858] Neighbor Dean Combs felt particularly pressured by SBI agents who, if Combs was home, would visit him three or four times a day and would hit him with questions so fast he did not have time to respond before they asked another. Combs became so aggravated with their persistence that he sent his wife and daughter to his mother's home. He assumed he was considered a suspect for a while, particularly since he had recently returned to his native Watauga County from Cincinnati and had begun working at the Durhams' dealership.[859] The SBI also questioned some of Bobby Durham's friends, including sixteen-year-old Jackie Vines, who he had briefly dated. Jackie's parents and her Boone Police Chief uncle, however, were very protective of her, and at a certain point in time, her parents, fearing for her safety, would no longer consent to her being interrogated.[860]

[yyy] Craven Ford was enrolled at Appalachian State University between 1968 and 1974. The author's attempts to contact Ford via telephone, e-mail, and Facebook proved unsuccessful. [Source: Rhododendron (yearbook), 1970, Appalachian State University, Boone, NC, https://www.ancestry.com/discoveryui-content/view/252880774:1265?tid=&pid=&queryId=3a784b9303f77f27689df14ec222ff5d&_phsrc=rKl34154&_phstart=successSource; https://www.linkedin.com/in/craven-ford-a2087280/.]

Despite the theft of the GMC "Jimmy" and the presumed theft of silver pieces, both of which were left behind by the killers, Sheriff Ward Carroll stated he did not believe robbery was a motive[861] because a canvas Northwestern Bank deposit bag *[some sources erroneously state there were two bags[862]]*, which Bryce was known to have sometimes but not always carried between his dealership and home,[863] was found lying in the open on a dining room chair.[864] *[When neighbor Paul Allen accompanied George Baker, Clyde Townsend, and Troy Hall to the residence, he had seen it on a table.[865] One report stated the bag was on the floor,[866] while another said it was in the living room.[867] Johnny Tester recalled seeing it on an end table.[868]]* Depending on the source, the bag contained either a few[869] or several hundred dollars,[870] believed to be the dealership's daily receipts.[871] According to a statement made by a former bank employee, the Durhams made daily visits there, presumably to make deposits.[872] Because there was a steep incline at the drive-through window at the bank, both bad weather and the Durhams' late departure from the dealership likely prevented them from getting there to make that day's deposit,[873] and it is possible the bank may have even closed early because of the inclement weather. A savings account passbook with some money stuck in it was also found untouched in the house.[874]

Based on the knowledge that greed, revenge, and passion are most typically reasons for murder, Sheriff Carroll quickly concluded the Durham murders were motivated by a combination of greed and revenge.[875] Carroll believed these were "grudge"[876] or revenge killings but did not elaborate.[877] While he did not completely rule out robbery as a motive,[878] he believed the messy condition of the home's furnishings was indicative "the killers were intent on destroying rather than searching for something."[879] Other investigators, including SBI District Supervisor Red Minter, believed the crime could have involved robbery,[880] and the killers simply overlooked the money bag.[881] SBI Agent Wally Hardwick, Jr. and some fellow agents were convinced robbery *was* the motive and stated "it would not have been necessary for the slayers to 'tear the place apart' unless they were looking for something on the order of a strongbox or a wall-type safe."[882] Some who believed the robbery theory thought perhaps one of the Durhams had been handled roughly and died as a result, and the robbers then killed the other two Durhams to eliminate them as witnesses.[883] Bryce Durham's brother Bill said he would not discount the possibility of a grudge killing as his brother had been threatened [in the past] with bodily harm by a disgruntled customer while in business in Surry County.[884]

SBI Director Charles Dunn shared that investigators had been considering several possible motives for the murders:

- "A 'grudge' killing stemming from personal animosity against [Bryce] Durham...or against the entire Durham family."
- "Robbery, involving either professionals or amateurs, because of the manner in which the house was ransacked."
- "A 'cult' or 'ritual' assassination carried out by mentally disturbed persons or persons crazed by drugs."

Dunn stated if the murders were due to a grudge, "then there is a strong possibility that the daughter [Ginny Hall] may be in danger. We are concerned for her safety."[885] Consequently, the SBI assigned agents to follow and watch Troy and Ginny Hall as well as Bryce and Virginia Durham's extended relatives. This was primarily for their protection in the event they might also be targets, and the surveillance continued for a period of months.[886]

Law enforcement officers began checking "local crime records and the recent activities of offenders with histories of violent and anti-social conduct."[887] Numerous officers also spent the next few days scouring the woods and questioning neighbors around Poplar Grove Road, where the "Jimmy" had been abandoned. Carroll Garland, who was the Assistant Vice President and Cashier at the Northwestern Bank in Boone, lived near this location, and the SBI used his home as a sort of headquarters for a few days. Garland fearfully wondered if he might also be a target due to the fact that, in his capacity as a banker, he had been associated with the Durham dealership and, only a day or two before the murders, had participated with Bryce Durham in a conversation with a disgruntled young black man whose car had been repossessed. The young man's race gave Garland pause due to what Troy Hall claimed to have heard during the alleged phone call from his mother-in-law regarding black intruders.[888][zzz]

Within days of the murders, race was also the basis for a news article that stated, "Police today hunted the three black men…."[889] Sheriff Ward Carroll told the press, "We have some good clues. We hope to have early arrests, and we are definitely investigating blacks,"[890] although he stated to one newspaper, "Negroes are no more suspects than anybody else."[891] Carroll was also reported as saying "the identities of the three men being sought [were] known, and he [hoped] to have them in custody by Monday. 'The investigation has definitely centered on these three Negro men.'"[892] An unidentified investigator tempered Carroll's comments, stating "hopes for an early arrest were 'optimistic.'"[893] Carroll felt the newspapers were working against law enforcement,[894] and a day later, he denied making those statements, saying he had been misquoted: "I have not mentioned that to no paper nor to nobody. It's none of your business who we're looking for or when we're looking for them. We are running a law enforcement department. We are trying our best to find the people responsible for killing these three victims. The status of the investigation is that we have the SBI here and the Boone Police Department and the Highway Patrol – they are cooperating real good. At this time we have no special suspects in mind."[895] This was echoed by SBI Agent John Parker, who said he had "nothing at this time" to tell and that "a lot of rumors were circulating in the county, but 'rumors are what most of them are.'"[896] Carroll further told the press, "We're just still investigating. I'm not going to make many comments on this. We've got to solve this thing someway."[897] SBI District Supervisor Red Minter guardedly stated, "About all I can say at this point is that the investigation is continuing." He added that the bureau, which had established its local operations center at Appalachian State University's police department offices, was still digging but arrests were not imminent.[898]

SBI Agent Charlie Whitman stated the scope of the investigation had been widened into "other counties and outside the state," which suggested "a conspiracy reaching beyond Boone and Watauga County." Whitman did not disclose those locations, but "sources close to the investigation said SBI agents [had] questioned people in Avery, Mitchell, and Surry counties [North Carolina], and that the [other] state involved [was] Tennessee."[899] The expansion of the investigation into these other locations also suggested "the possibility of a conspiracy involving two, three or perhaps four persons," and the only way SBI Director Charles Dunn believed one person could have acted alone

[zzz] About five or six weeks later, the SBI put an initially skeptical Garland under hypnosis at his bank office. Afterwards, he was amazed he could remember so many details, including the color of Virginia Durham's shoes the last time he saw her. [Source: Garland, Carroll. Personal interview with author. April 5 & 7, 2022.]

was "if the Durhams had been incapacitated to some extent by drugs." When asked if there was any evidence of immobilizing drugs being administered to the family, Dunn had no comment. He added, "We have gathered a considerable amount of evidence, much of which we feel will be important in our continuing investigation of the case." Yet Dunn admitted they had not uncovered anything strong enough to lead to an arrest.[900]

According to Charlie Whitman, several people had been interviewed, including Ginny Hall, as the Durhams' sole heir, and Troy Hall and Cecil Small because they were the first people to see the Durhams' bodies, but he said the investigation had "not centered on any one person," and the SBI had not reached the point of feeling legally compelled to advise any person that evidence pointed to that person as a prime suspect. "We are not pointing an accusing finger at anyone," Whitman stated.[901]

Ginny became upset by some of the questions asked by law enforcement, and she went to Cecil and Mildred Small's home in tears. When Troy came to return pliers and a screwdriver to Cecil and found his wife in turmoil, he asked, "What am I going to do? They just aggravate her to death." Cecil advised him, "Well, they ain't but one thing for you to do, Troy. Go up there and get you a lawyer. See what your lawyer says." "You know any of 'em?" Troy asked. Cecil said, "Yeah, I know 'em all, but hell, I wouldn't recommend none of them. But go up there and pick you one."[902]

Following Small's advice, and having overheard agents say he [Troy] and Ginny had committed the crime, the Halls retained Boone-based attorney Stacy Eggers, Jr.[903] After answering authorities' questions the night of the murders, Troy had refused to speak with them again.[904] He and Ginny also refused to be fingerprinted, and, on the advice of Eggers, they refused requests from the SBI to submit to polygraph tests. Law enforcement officials all agreed "the Halls were unwilling to talk in depth about the case."[905] Troy pretty much limited his statements to two subjects – the alleged phone call from his mother-in-law and discovering the bodies with Cecil Small.[906] Sheriff Ward Carroll felt Troy would talk to him at times when he would not talk with the SBI,[907] and the SBI declared Troy and Ginny uncooperative.[908] SBI Director Charles Dunn said "I believe they could help us a lot if they would. I know they have been under great stress, but I trust they will talk to our agents in time."[909] The next time Boone Police Chief Clyde Tester went to speak with Ginny, she said, "My lawyer told me not to answer any of your questions."[910] By the first week of March, however, Eggers informed Carroll and Tester "the Halls would cooperate any way they could," and the two officers met with them on March 1, 1972 in Eggers' law office and in his presence and interviewed them for about three hours.[911] *[No notes pertaining to this interview exist within the Watauga Sheriff's Office investigation file.]* Troy's and Ginny's fingerprints were eventually obtained through their attorney's office, but they consistently refused additional requests to submit to polygraph tests.[912]

Despite the fact that, only months after the murders, Cecil Small was commended by the North Carolina Association of Licensed Detectives for his part in the Durham Case,[913] he came under suspicion because he was a neighbor and acquaintance of Troy and Ginny Hall, and because he and Troy had discovered the murdered Durhams. Cecil and his wife Mildred were scrutinized and questioned,[914] and the office at Mildred's workplace sent for her to speak with Sheriff Carroll and Chief Tester. They asked if she was sure Cecil was at home that night. "Well, certainly I'm sure," she told them. Similar to Dean Combs's experience with investigators, Cecil also felt provoked by their questions, saying, "If they ask you a question, they won't give you time to answer it 'til they're asking you another question."[915]

Combs recalled seeing Cecil a time or two at the dealership prior to the murders,[916] and a Greenway Trailer Park neighbor of Cecil's had been fired from the dealership for theft and had reportedly threatened the Durhams. This man, said to have also been a close friend of Cecil's and a rival of Cecil for meanness, was willing to do anything for a few dollars and was absent from home the night of the murders. According to his wife, when he returned home the following morning, he told her he "had taken care of some business."[917]

Characterized by some as an attention-seeking bumbler, who relished interjecting himself as a witness to or participant in historical events and dramatic criminal activity, some questioned Cecil's credibility. He maintained for years that Lee Harvey Oswald did not assassinate President John F. Kennedy in 1963. Cecil said he was in Dallas, Texas that day and gave Oswald a ride after Kennedy was shot, but Oswald was too calm to have just committed such a crime.[918][aaaa] Claims like this caused some to wonder if Cecil had merely been a "useful idiot" in the Durham Case, unwittingly "lured to the scene to establish an alibi and solidify [a particular] narrative of the crime."[919] Perhaps Troy Hall had manipulated Cecil for his own purposes, hand selecting him because of Cecil's naivete and/or his detective credentials, which might give law enforcement a sense that Cecil had some degree of "policing" ability and would have noticed things about the crime scene that would prove useful. Perhaps Troy intended Cecil to be an eyewitness to his feigned shock and surprise and to divert any suspicion away from himself. Although public opinion was that Cecil and Troy had carried out the murders, Cecil was not sure if law enforcement suspected him, and, unlike Troy, he submitted to a polygraph test.[920] SBI agents stated Cecil's results showed "no deception."[921]

Although some wondered if Cecil could have been an accomplice in planning the Durham murders and benefited financially, authorities never indicated they thought he had prior knowledge of or took part in the murders. Retired Boone Police Sergeant Jeff Rucker believes Cecil was used rather than being a principal in the case.[922] There is also no outward evidence of Cecil having a financially enhanced lifestyle subsequent to the murders. In 1987, he and his wife were still living in the same 8' x 30' trailer they had lived in at the time of the 1972 murders.[923] Although his widow Mildred died at a life care center in 2015, she had continued to live modestly in the same trailer park.[924]

Whatever Cecil's involvement, he would be perpetually plagued by the Durham Case. He stated he would never forget the night he discovered the Durhams' bodies...and the public would not let him. According to Cecil, he could not go anywhere – not a store or a service station – without someone saying, "There's that man that killed them Durhams!" Cecil added, "People are calling all the time. I've had calls ever since it happened. Every year around February, they continue until I quit answering the phone. They don't let me forget."[925]

[aaaa] Cecil "avowed to his dying day" that the man he had given a ride to "was none other than Lee Harvey Oswald," and he was so insistent and persistent with his story that the Federal Bureau of Investigation finally interviewed him in 1967 but later decided not to pursue the matter further "because Small's memory of Dallas streets and landmarks wasn't accurate." According to FBI records, one federal agent stated, apparently post-1977, "That's quite a witness. Maybe he knows where Elvis is living." Cecil's story regarding Oswald was never verified. [Sources: Michael Capuzzo, *The Murder Room* (New York: Gotham Book, Penguin Group, Inc., 2010), 84-85. https://www.kingauthor.net/books/Michael%20Capuzzo/The%20Murder%20Room/The%20Murder%20Room%20-%20Michael%20Capuzzo.pdf; "Man said he had chance encounter with Oswald," *The Charlotte Observer*, Charlotte, NC, January 5, 1992, p. 2D. http://www.kenrahn.com/JFK/The_critics/Whitmey/Small.html. The Trail Went Cold, podcast Episode 234 – The Durham Family Murders, July 14, 2021, http://trailwentcold.com/2021/07/14/the-trail-went-cold-episode-234-the-durham-family-murders/. Charlie Peek, "Dying Words: Oswald Was Innocent, N. C. Man Says," *Winston-Salem Journal*, Winston-Salem, NC, January 4, 1992, pp. 13 & 15.]

According to Mildred Small, she and her husband "lived in pure hell" after the murders. Beginning the night following the triple homicide and for more than a decade afterwards, particularly whenever news articles announced the reward money had increased, the Smalls received mysterious and threatening calls at their trailer home, sometimes three or four a day. Although Cecil would sometimes inquire as to the caller's identity, they never knew who it was other than a man disguising his voice in a low, gruff manner. Sometimes the caller would tell Cecil that his [Cecil's] hands were bloodied the same as the caller's and ask him to meet so they could talk it over and strike some sort of deal. Cecil told the caller on more than one occasion, "To hell with you! I don't make no damn deals with nobody!" On another occasion, the caller said to Cecil, "When they get that reward up, you'll tell them who it is, won't you?" When the caller threatened Cecil by saying he knew where he lived, Cecil defiantly responded, "I'll be waiting for you." At other times, the caller threatened to take Mildred as a means of getting Cecil to cooperate with him. Over time, both of the Smalls answered the phone, cursed the caller, told him to never call again, and slammed down the receiver. Mildred told an interviewer, "Honey, I've done more cussing since this took place." As a result of the threats, Mildred began carrying mace and a knife, and Sheriff Ward Carroll recommended Cecil carry a gun. Cecil stated to the same interviewer, "He [the anonymous caller] just ain't got the nerve to come here. He ain't showed up yet."[926]

In 1972, the Smalls had law enforcement put a temporary tracer on their phone, but oddly, while the tracer was in place, they received no calls; when it was removed, the calls resumed. According to the Smalls, only they, Sheriff Carroll, Boone Police Chief Clyde Tester, and the telephone company representative had knowledge of the tracer, although word somehow leaked out, even to the point of one of Mildred's co-workers asking her about it the day after it was installed. This prompted the Smalls to suspect many of the calls were being made by local law enforcement, which they already had a dim view of.[927] The Smalls were generally put out with both the sheriff's department and the police department. According to Mildred, "The durn law – pardon my English and my impression of them – ain't got sense enough to pinpoint anyone…." When an investigator came to interview residents of the trailer park, the Smalls said he [the investigator] was scared to death and afraid he would get shot. He enlisted Cecil to accompany him, and during what turned out to be an all-day commitment, Cecil said the investigator sat in the car while he went door to door asking questions. Once Cecil had cleared the way, the investigator would join him. Cecil ultimately accompanied the investigator to Charlotte, Statesville, and Marion, North Carolina.[928]

Sales manager Ike Eller was questioned about the Durham Case less than forty-eight hours after the murders by Bryce Durham's immediate family, particularly by Bryce's sister Gayle Mauldin, and later by investigators. Because Eller's phone number was unlisted, the Durham family asked a patrolman to go to his home and request him to come to Bryce's parents' house. Eller arrived there around 10:00 AM on Saturday, February 5. Gayle met him outside and brought him into the house where she introduced him to her parents, Coy and Collie Durham and her brother and sister-in-law, Ralph and Lucille Durham. None of the family had previously met Eller, and Collie Durham invited him to sit beside her. Over the course of the next two weeks, Eller visited the Durham house twice more to answer the family's questions. But again, Eller's answers were not always consistent,[929] and this caused Gayle and her husband Charles to be suspicious of him.[930] Within a couple of weeks after the murders, although previously admitting to these things, Eller denied having read Bryce's and Virginia's revised will – "the dollar will"[931] – and he denied having changed the dealership locks, stating they must have been changed before he began his employment there.[932] He also refuted Virginia's claim that he had shared knowledge of Troy Hall's family members with her. According to Eller, he did not realize their identities until they walked into the funeral home. "My God," he said, "I thought I would die when I saw who they were."[933]

About a week after the murders, Troy Hall gave his brother Ray a gun, approximately four inches long and black with a wooden handle. Ray had it in a shoebox, and he took it out of his car and into his trailer where he showed it to his wife Kay. He told Kay it had belonged to Bryce Durham. Kay would later state that, although she did not know what Ray did with the gun, she believed he returned it to Troy.[934] Ginny would later state she was not aware of Troy or Ray having any guns that belonged to her parents; she had her father's hunting guns but no short guns. She said her mother had carried a gun while making deposits when they lived in Mount Airy, but she had no knowledge of her carrying one in Boone.[935] However, Gayle Mauldin knew both Bryce and Virginia carried pistols. Bryce had obtained his through the sheriff's department in Mount Airy and showed it at one point to Gayle's husband, telling him he could get one for him too.[936] Bryce's good friend[937] Dallas Coe, a Surry County law enforcement officer, had acquired Virginia's pistol, which she carried in her purse. After the murders, Bryce's gun was not found.[938]

Shortly after this incident with Ray Hall, Ike Eller was reportedly also in possession of some of Bryce's guns – a few deer rifles and some pistols. According to Gayle Mauldin, Eller took the guns to Wade Houck, a gun dealer and preacher who lived about a mile up Highway 18 and near the Hall family in Wilkes County. According to Houck, as indicated in Gayle's notes, Eller left the guns with Houck to have them appraised and came back later to retrieve them. Eller allegedly told Houck he was from Roaring River and worked as Bryce's manager at the dealership, but oddly, he also said his surname was Durham, and he was Bryce's brother. These were guns Bryce had taken from Mount Airy to Boone and kept locked in a cabinet, and it is unclear how Eller came by them unless Troy or Ginny had taken them from the gun cabinet in the Durham home and given them to him. When Charles and Gayle Mauldin learned about this from Houck, Charles suspected Eller may have been involved in the murders, and the guns may have been part of his payoff.[939] *[Eller's son Tom finds this account unbelievable. He says his father was a gun collector and had hundreds of guns, and it would have made no sense for him to take guns to someone else for appraisal when it was more likely individuals would come to him for that purpose. He also does not believe Troy Hall would have ever given his father any guns, nor would his father have accepted them.[940]]*

On the night of February 10, 1972, "law enforcement agencies created a traffic jam in front of Modern Buick-Pontiac Company in Boone by stopping all cars traveling in both directions. They asked motorists if they had happened to be passing that particular point in the highway between 8 p.m. and 9 p.m. the night of the killings. This set off what turned out to be unfounded speculation that perhaps the investigation had linked the murders with some occurrence at the automobile dealership." Meanwhile, SBI District Supervisor Red Minter stated no arrests had been made or were imminent.[941]

While the investigation was underway, the Boone Rotary Club, the Watauga County Board of Commissioners, the Watauga County Automobile Dealers Association, and members of the Boone Area Chamber of Commerce and Merchants Association offered a $4,000 reward ($1,000 each) for information leading to the arrest and conviction of the killers. With the assistance of other groups, the reward soon grew to $7,000, and on February 11, 1972, Governor Bob Scott offered an additional $5,000 reward from the North Carolina Police Contingency Fund. By early March, the total reward stood at $14,500 (the largest amount offered in North Carolina in many years). By late March, several of Bryce Durham's cousins had contributed, and the overall reward soon grew to

$17,050. Although some leads did eventually result in arrests *[see Chapter 10]*, authorities said no money would be released until convictions were obtained.[942]

In late February, more than two weeks after the murders, law enforcement officers were no closer to solving the case, and although they had followed many leads, none led to new developments. They urged "all local citizens who have any information that might 'shed light on the murders' to contact the Watauga Sheriff's Department immediately." Sheriff Ward Carroll stated, "I'd personally appreciate any assistance the general public can give us on breaking this case and bringing the guilty party to justice."[943]

One month after the murders, law enforcement officials "termed the case 'highly complicated.'" Although they were "still following up on every clue and every report" – "many leads requiring as much as 24 hours research" – these had been "followed to no avail," and there had been little progress made. Sheriff Carroll stated, "This is the number one crime being investigated in the state right now…and…we are intensifying the investigation." Carroll also stated that confidentiality might be possible for any potential informants. On Saturday, March 4, relatives of Bryce Durham visited the Watauga County Sheriff's Department to discuss the case with Carroll and SBI agents.[944] In late March, Carroll reported there were no new developments, and he once again implored the aid of the citizenry: "We need the help of anyone and everyone in Watauga County and the entire area to help us halt this malicious criminal and bring justice to the slayers of this Watauga family."[945]

This plea for assistance would soon take a rather unorthodox turn….

CHAPTER 8

DIVINATIONS OF A DUTCHMAN

E. J. Durham, Sr.
(Courtesy of Frank Jolley)

Although the murders devastated the Durhams' surviving relatives, the case also seemed to have a unifying effect, particularly within the extended Durham family, which did everything they could to help solve the case and bring justice for their loved ones.[946] This was the number one priority of Bryce's parents and siblings and of his cousin, Erastus Jones "E. J." Durham, Sr. of Winston-Salem, North Carolina,[947] who, for a brief period, had been jointly involved with Bryce in a business venture.[948] E. J. Durham, Sr. was "very upset about losing his very good friend." After his cousins' murders, he traveled to Boone, introduced himself to key figures, and "poured a lot of energy and money into the investigations," including $5,500 in reward funds.[949]

In March 1972, E. J. Durham, Sr. contacted James Bolton, Jr., a Charlotte, North Carolina real estate broker, about Marinus Bernardus Dykshoorn *[pronounced Dikes-horn]*, a Holland-born immigrant and clairvoyant, who reportedly had helped Massachusetts authorities in their pursuit of the Boston Strangler in the 1960s "and had worked with similar success on other investigations in the United States and abroad."[950] Dykshoorn had also been in discussions about possibly assisting with the 1970 MacDonald Case, which concerned the murders of Dr. Jeffrey MacDonald's pregnant wife and two daughters at Fort Bragg, North Carolina.

Dykshoorn was a short, stocky, middle-aged man with piercing blue eyes and bushy eyebrows, who dressed in business suits, white shirts, and ties, and spoke with a thick Dutch accent. He was considered to be good-humored, compassionate, highly intelligent, and "extravagantly unique."[951] He had "assisted officers on at least five other murder cases in North Carolina,"[952] and was the only parapsychological researcher endorsed by the government. E. J. Durham, Sr. desired his help in finding new leads, and Bolton, a student of clairvoyance and a supporter of Dykshoorn, was instrumental in getting him to take the case.[953] According to Bolton, "[Dykshoorn] does not seek publicity and he works confidentially. He is able to follow the paths of criminals and retrace their moves regardless of the time lapse." Bolton added that Dykshoorn was "able to give physical descriptions of the guilty persons and [had], in three cases…led officers to the home of the criminal."[954]

M. B. Dykshoorn (© Art Hill - USA TODAY NETWORK; with permission)

According to Dykshoorn, he had had the gift of extrasensory perception (ESP) since a very young age, and although he never understood exactly how it worked, he had "the ability to see the unknown future and the unfamiliar past" and used his five senses to do so. "When I'm on a murder case, I'm no longer myself – I become the victim. I see, hear, and smell everything he did before he was murdered." Dykshoorn attributed his past successes to his ability to concentrate, which resulted in mental pictures related to whatever he was investigating. He emphasized that he was not about black magic or hocus-pocus, and although he did not rely upon tea leaves and Ouija boards, he did utilize a divining rod to aid his concentration. In this case, the rod was a piano wire bent into a loop, and he held an end of the wire in each hand. According to Dykshoorn, the wire had no power of its own, but if he was on the right track, the loop would swing back and forth, and it would stop if the trail he was following turned cold. He said he did not necessarily need the wire, but it made things easier by helping control the mental images and pictures he received.[955]

M. B. Dykshoorn and his divining rod

Finding murderers was not Dykshoorn's favorite use of his talents, but it played a large part in his career. At a crime scene, his preference was "to go to the place where it happened and reconstruct [it] through the eyes of the victims." "I look in the last four or five minutes before he or she died and…I will actually see the murderers and feel what they do," he said. In the case of a victim who had been strangled, he said he felt it around his own throat. After seeing the murderers through the victims' eyes, he would "track them to where they are living." His preference was to pursue psychiatrically deranged murderers rather than contract killers associated with organized crime.[956]

Although Dykshoorn guaranteed nothing and charged no money for assisting with criminal investigations, he said he had been successful in the past and would be again in the future. He made it clear that he did not tell stories or what people wanted to hear; he would only state facts – the things that his gift saw. He was also adamant that he did not solve cases. As the middleman, he merely provided investigators with clues to help find criminals; it was up to them to verify the information.[957]

Convinced Dykshoorn "could solve the case in a few hours," James Bolton, Jr. wrote to Sheriff Ward Carroll recommending he invite Dykshoorn's assistance.[958] Dykshoorn flew to North Carolina from his home in North Miami Beach, Florida, and E. J. Durham, Sr. covered his $300-$400 of expenses. Dykshoorn initially denied involvement in the case but later admitted it[959] to Charlotte-based television news station WBTV, which questioned him as he addressed a Charlotte civic club.[960]

When Sheriff Carroll was asked by a reporter if Dykshoorn would be helping with the case, "Carroll's immediate reaction was 'Who told you that? How'd you find out about it?' Recovering, the sheriff then refused to confirm or deny that Dykshoorn's aid [had] been sought in the case which he admitted [was] 'at a standstill.'"[961]

On March 23, 1972, Dykshoorn "spent more than five hours in Boone,"[962] some of which was in the Clyde Townsend Road neighborhood,[963] and E. J. Durham, Sr. and James Bolton, Jr. were present when Dykshoorn walked through the Durham home.[964] Dykshoorn believed five persons were involved in the crime and they came from "out of this location, perhaps to the west of here."[965] He told officers the first two of the intruders came to the front door and knocked. He said Virginia Durham knew them and gave them entrance.[bbbb] A third man, larger in stature, came in later and did most of the killing. They exited through the back door. A fourth man never went into the house but was an accessory to the crime. A fifth man was indirectly involved.[966] Dykshoorn said one or two of these individuals "are either now in custody or soon will be." He further stated "supporting evidence would turn up in two weeks or less" and three arrests would be made.[967] Dykshoorn never said the case would be solved and only mentioned arrests.[968] *[According to one (probably erroneous) news report, Dykshoorn "gave Watauga County sheriff's officials the name of the person he said was responsible for the slayings,"[969] although if this is true, it seems to have been an unproductive lead as it was never mentioned elsewhere.]* Aside from the murder scene, "Dykshoorn, with uncanny accuracy, pinpointed the exact location at which the Durham's ["Jimmy"] had been ditched."[970]

Dykshoorn knew the things he did were controversial and that, to many people, the words "clairvoyant" and "kook" were synonymous, but he was firm in his belief that his gifts and abilities were legitimate.[971] Some, however, were dubious of Dykshoorn, including a sheriff's spokesman who said, "That fellow snooped around some, and it was all very interesting to watch. But we don't know how much real good it did. Certainly, he didn't come up with the killers' names or addresses. My own belief is that you don't often catch a killer with a crystal ball."[972]

[bbbb] According to Virginia Durham's niece, Jerri Bumgarner Waddell, the SBI likewise believed the intruders were individuals the Durhams more than likely knew, and when they knocked on the door, they were allowed entrance. [Source: Edwards, Diana (Virginia Durham's great-niece). Phone interview with author. October 14, 2023.

CHAPTER 9

EVERY THEORY KNOWN TO MANKIND

Crystal balls and clairvoyance aside, many people, including citizens in both Boone and the Durhams' former home of Mount Airy, had made up their own minds that Troy Hall was involved in his in-laws' murders. The word circulating in Mount Airy was that Troy had the murders carried out.[973] Some, adhering to the philosophy of following the money as a solution to the crime, speculated Troy had planned the murders to acquire the Durham family estate. His refusal to submit to a polygraph test only added fuel to the suspicion.[974] Others, because of Cecil Small's accompaniment of Troy into the Durham home on the night of the murders, continued to believe him complicit.

But beyond suspecting eyes being cast upon Hall and Small, a variety of other theories regarding motive were put forth, many by the public, but all in the form of conjecture.[975] According to SBI Agent Charlie Whitman, "Just about everything brought to our attention was purely speculative." In the words of then North Carolina Attorney General Rufus Edmisten, "When something like that happens…every theory known to mankind will pop up."[976]

One theory was that Bryce Durham may have been targeted because of hard feelings resulting from business deals. Rumor had it Bryce experienced professional difficulties before moving to Boone.[977] As a car dealer, he had "many business transactions, both positive and negative," including repossessing cars.[978] Bryce had lived and worked in a number of locations, and "his range of acquaintances – any one of whom might bear him some long-standing grudge, real or fanciful – was extensive."[979] A theory offered by a North Carolina citizen in a handwritten letter to the Watauga County Sheriff's Office was that Bryce had perhaps exhibited a superior attitude in dealing with the public, and a dissatisfied customer, feeling he had gotten a "raw deal," became enraged and vindictive, gathered a few friends, went to the Durham home, and murdered the family. The writer suggested that putting the Durhams face down in the bathtub may have been "symbolic of the 'put down' feeling that the customer received from Mr. Durham."[980]

Another theory held that Bryce had been silenced because he "had revealed the ringleaders of a car dealership scam in Surry County that involved rolling back the miles on vehicles' odometers before selling them to unknowing customers…." According to Rufus Edmisten, this was a theory held by SBI Agent Larry Wagner, whose judgment was described as "spot-on."[981] However, Edmisten dispatched an SBI agent to Mount Airy to specifically look into this possibility, and he found no information to corroborate Bryce ever having done such a thing.[982] The dispatched agent may have been Wagner himself, who, alongside fellow SBI Agent Steve Cabe, made several trips to Mount

Airy, where they spoke with Bryce's attorney, Carroll Gardner, the brother and law partner of John Gardner, who handled the Durham estates. The agents inquired if Bryce may have been involved with stolen cars or odometer rollbacks, but they found no evidence of it. According to Wagner, "We were trying all the theories we could."[983]

The rollback of odometers was actually a longtime, common practice among many used car dealers. While odometer tampering was unethical, no consumer-protecting laws were in place to address the practice until passage of certain state and federal acts between 1969 and 1973.[984] Although a machine used for rolling back mileage, along with instructions and accompanying instruments, was found at Bryce's dealership after his death,[985] the instruments may have been inside the building prior to his purchase of the dealership and may have belonged to and been utilized by a predecessor. Mechanic Lester Reece, who worked for Bryce between 1969 and 1971, never knew of anyone at Bryce's dealership to run back miles.[986] Ginny Durham, however, affirmed that her father had miles rolled back, and she drove vehicles on several occasions to a garage in Wilkes County where a man accomplished it.[987]

Some suggested Bryce was killed because local used car dealers who were already established prior to his arrival in Boone resented an "outsider" horning in on their turf,[988] but when asked about this in 1976, Ginny remembered no such conflict.[989] In fact, other Boone car dealers were put on alert that they might also be potential targets of the Durhams' killers.[990]

Without any supporting evidence, one individual claimed Bryce was laundering money through his car dealership for the Mafia and would not pay them, so they killed him.[991] Likewise, with no supporting evidence,[992] some surmised Bryce may have been involved in other criminal or drug-related activity – perhaps using cars to smuggle drugs,[993] such as one-hundred-pound bags of marijuana,[994] which brought deadly consequences to him and his family. Mention was also made of him possibly being involved in illegal horse and farm dealings in Mount Airy,[995] where a big drug ring operated, but Bryce's reputation "as a very strait-laced" individual and the absence of any illegal transactions among his dealings made that theory unlikely. The SBI disproved Bryce was criminally involved in anything in Mount Airy.[996] "There was [also] a theory because of the manner in which [the Durhams] had been killed that professional hit men had been involved, [but] authorities could find no evidence of anyone who would want the family killed."[997] A related theory was that Bryce bought the dealership using high interest funds borrowed from possible associates of organized crime, and when he failed to pay what was owed them, they murdered him.[998]

After Bryce acquired the dealership in late 1969 and moved to Boone in advance of his family, he seemed lonely and became good friends with John Pritchett, a customer of his predecessor. Pritchett had ordered a truck from G. C. Greene, Jr. in August 1969, but due to a GMC strike and Greene selling the dealership, Bryce had to fulfill the transaction. Bryce went out of his way to do little things for Pritchett, including adding extras to the truck. Late one Friday night, after all the staff had gone home, Pritchett stopped by the dealership, and Bryce opened up and confided in him. According to Pritchett, when he asked Bryce what prompted his move to Boone, Bryce shared that things had gotten rough for him because a ring of auto thieves from Virginia was stealing cars in the northeastern portion of the country and changing the titles in Mount Airy. Bryce "apparently loaned money on these stolen cars." These thieves were from Grayson, Carroll, or Patrick, all Virginia counties bordering North Carolina and in close proximity to the Durhams' former homes in Mount Airy and Galax, Virginia, and they had threatened Bryce's life.[999] Bryce told Pritchett he was scared to death of these people and wanted to move away because of them. Pritchett thought

Bryce seemed very much afraid of what was likely to happen, and he doubted Bryce ever shared any of this with anyone else in Boone. Pritchett did not believe Bryce was involved with these title scams, saying, "No, I don't think he ever did anything wrong in his life."[1000]

When asked if she was aware of her father being involved in gambling or stolen cars, Ginny Durham mentioned to Boone police officers that a stolen car was discovered on her father's lot and another car belonging to her father had been stolen.[1001] *[Retired Watauga County lawman Jerry Vaughn, who worked on the Durham Case, did not believe Bryce was involved with stolen cars or had any illegal dealings.[1002cccc]]*

Some, including extended family members,[1003] believed Bobby Durham had never been targeted for murder, but that Bryce and Virginia were the intended victims, and the killers would have been surprised to discover Bobby at the residence, having expected him to be at the university ballgame that night with his friends. If true, the killers would have had prior, inside knowledge of Bobby's plans.

Others wondered if Bobby[1004] or Troy Hall, as college students, were involved in drug deals and owed someone money.[1005] By the early 1970s, illegal drugs were appearing more frequently in North Carolina, including Watauga County; the first drug charge ever made at Appalachian State University occurred in 1969. That same year (and exactly one week after Bryce Durham purchased the car dealership), SBI Director Charles Dunn visited Watauga High School and said he knew a "pusher" was on campus. The principal stated the school had a "drug traffic problem," although it was limited to three or four percent of the student body, which equated to around thirty-five students.[1006] By the start of 1970, Boone police officers had received training in narcotics.[1007] In 1971, twenty-one drug arrests were made in Watauga County, resulting in ten convictions for possession of marijuana; other cases involved possession of LSD, hashish, and cocaine. Despite several drug education endeavors, that year was believed to be the first in the county's history during which more people had been charged with and convicted for drug possession than unlawful liquor possession.[1008] But those who knew Bobby best discount this as he was not a rebellious son nor known for riotous living. His circle of friends did not consume alcohol let alone drugs.[1009] As one friend stated, Bobby had probably never had a drink or tried drugs in his life.[1010] "Lawmen checked into the associates of young Bobby Joe Durham,"[1011] and the SBI also disproved the theory.[1012]

Also eliminated was the prospect that one of a couple of house burglary gangs in Wilkes County may have been involved. Although there was no plausible reason to believe this was true, six SBI agents spent about a year investigating the possibility.[1013]

Some felt the murders had been carried out with military-style precision,[1014] employing the use of a rope or ropes, the victims "placed side by side, bent over at the waist in a tub with their heads submerged in water," absent of gunshot and cutting wounds. Wild rumors suggested the Green Berets, who had been scheduled to hold the skiing demonstration for Bryce's Rotary Club the evening of the murders, were involved,[1015] having knowledge of "the [military] type of knots used

---

[cccc] In contrast, Bryce Durham's maternal half-uncle, Dewey Veach, had been a used car and salvage dealer in the 1920s and was jailed after being "charged with wholesale theft of automobiles, trucks, and auto accessories." Veach pleaded guilty and was sentenced to one to three years in the state prison. [Sources: "Two Charged With Wholesale Thefts," *The Landmark*, Statesville, NC, September 10, 1928, p. 1; L. J. Hampton, "Pair of Thieves Chased, Caught," *Winston-Salem Journal*, Winston-Salem, NC, September 18, 1928, p. 3; "White Gets Two Years On One Count," *The Landmark*, Statesville, NC, November 15, 1928, p. 1; "Dewey G. Veach" (obituary), *Winston-Salem Journal*, Winston-Salem, NC, August 21, 1961, p. 2; Genealogical research by author.]

on the ropes to restrain the victims"[1016] and having killed people in Vietnam in similar fashion.[1017] Most of these soldiers in training were "veterans of fighting in Southeast Asia,"[1018] and had served in the U. S. Army during World War II, Korea, and/or Vietnam; many were members of the Special Forces/Green Berets.[1019] Some wondered if one of their local military exercises had gotten out of control.[1020] "Men with such special services training who were in the Boone area at the time of the murder[s] were checked out, but...nothing came of it."[1021] Despite this being a dead end,[1022] more than thirty men with military backgrounds had their inked prints compared to the finger and palm prints lifted from the Durham house and vehicle.[dddd]

In the wake of the Charles Manson "family's" killings of actress Sharon Tate[1023] and others in California a few years prior to the Durham murders, and recalling headlines of ritualistic killings, others theorized drug-crazed hippies may have committed the crime,[1024] much like the ones the Green Beret physician, Captain Jeffrey MacDonald, claimed murdered his family at Fort Bragg, North Carolina in 1970,[1025] almost exactly two years prior to the Durhams' killings. But the likelihood of homicidal maniacs being in Boone in the midst of a winter storm and randomly selecting the Durham house, perched on a steep, almost unnavigable hill, and the possibility of individuals under the influence of narcotics carrying out such a well-orchestrated crime held little credence. According to former SBI Agent John Parker, the Durhams were not arbitrarily chosen by their killers,[1026] and Rufus Edmisten dismissed the idea that a drug-addled person could carry out such precise murders[1027] or some random person would be driving down the 105 Bypass on a snowy night in Boone and suddenly decide to go rob that particular house. In the words of former Georgia Bureau of Investigation Agent Bob Ingram, who was to contribute to the case many decades later, "Did [the killers] happen to drive off the highway and find this house in a snowstorm? Did a couple of wild, crazy, drugged-out teenagers do this? No!"[1028]

Some of the most fantastical theories included Virginia Durham having had an extramarital affair and she and her family being killed by her jilted lover,[1029] and a stressed-out Bobby killing his parents over embroiled political differences or other issues. Certainly, with the Vietnam War still on, unrest was being seen on a nationwide scale, and young people, who felt unseen and unheard were rebelling and protesting, but the suggestion that Bobby killed his parents over such matters and then called Troy Hall to help him in the aftermath, and that Troy subsequently killed Bobby seemed preposterous.[1030]

[dddd] Among the most interesting of those with military backgrounds whose prints were considered in the Durham Case were William Bradford Bishop, Jr. and Charles Darrell Odorizzi. Bishop, a former U. S. Foreign Service officer, allegedly killed his wife, mother, and three sons in Bethesda, Maryland in 1976 and then drove their bodies to North Carolina where he burned them in a shallow hole in Tyrrell County. He subsequently abandoned his car in the Great Smoky Mountains of Tennessee near the Appalachian Trail. Although Bishop was removed from the FBI's "Ten Most Wanted Fugitives List" in 2018, he is still being pursued. Odorizzi served in the U. S. Army and later worked undercover with the FBI to help thwart a 1984 assassination attempt on Honduras President Roberto Suazo Córdova. [Sources: Watauga County Sheriff's Office investigation file 118-H-1/2/3; https://en.wikipedia.org/wiki/Bradford-Bishop; "Commando Helped Blow Lid Off Alleged Plot to Kill a President," *The Washington Post*, August 15, 1985 (online). https://washingtonpost.com/archive/politics/1985/08/15/commando-helped-blow-lid-off-alleged-plot-to-kill-a-president/d8b787e-a57d-4d4b-b96a-6512ed7b4644/; "FBI Holds 8 in Plot on Honduras," *The Washington Post*, November 2, 1984 (online), https://washingtonpost.com/archive/politics/1984/11/02/fbi-holds-8-in-plot-on-honduras/1eba4304-7048-4d8d-af86-83f30e2fd60f/.]

Cecil Small being interviewed in front of the Durhams' former home in 1978.

Rumors also circulated in both Wilkes and Watauga counties that there had been incidents of abuse and estate inheritance in-fighting involving extended members of the Durham family, and, while Cecil and Mildred Small believed Ginny Durham Hall to be innocent, they believed another Durham family member from out of town had come to Boone and carried out the murders.[1031] Cecil also had other opinions about the murders, one being that the person he felt was lurking in the shadows of Bobby Durham's bedroom on the night he discovered the bodies was actually waiting for Troy and Ginny Hall to arrive so he could kill them as well. Cecil theorized that, following Virginia Durham's phone call, this assailant was expecting Troy and Ginny to arrive at the Durham home alone and was watching for them. When Cecil's car approached the house, the assailant would not have thought much about it because Cecil's car was white and so was Troy's but when the killer saw two men exit the car (Cecil and Troy) rather than a man and a woman (Troy and Ginny), he would have questioned the identity of the second man. Subsequently, not knowing who Cecil was and who else might be in the car, the killer and his accomplices, if they were still in the house when Troy and Cecil entered, remained hidden and silent.[1032]

Cecil carried his theory about the murders a step further following a rather odd encounter. About a month after the Durhams were killed, Cecil's father died in Burlington, North Carolina, and Cecil and his wife Mildred attended the funeral there. They shared a car ride from the church to the cemetery with a woman who was a friend of Cecil's stepsister. The woman was married to a Spaniard, and she said she knew all about the Durham murders. She stated her husband and another Spanish man went as accomplices with a third man – a Durham relative – to the Durham house in Boone where they forced Virginia to make the call to Troy and Ginny to lure them to the house where they would be unsuspectingly murdered, resulting in five victims rather than three. Supposedly, the primary killer (i.e., the third man/Durham relative) needed money and was in debt to the two Spaniards. The Smalls subsequently concluded Virginia had considered the Spaniards to be colored – even black, thus explaining why she mentioned their race to Troy on the phone.[1033]

Sometime after the murders, Cecil also had a conversation with an unnamed Wilkesboro chainsaw and lawnmower repairman whose place of business was across the road from Carolina Mirror, where Troy Hall's brother Claude was employed, and this is believed to have been the Trading Post, which was owned and operated by Ralph Frazier, father of Troy and Ray Hall's close friend John Frazier, who worked for his father at the establishment. Cecil came to believe the rope(s) used in the murders had been acquired from a boatyard in Wilkesboro, and Frazier's business establishment reportedly sold such rope.[1034] According to Mildred Small, Claude Hall stood in her and Cecil's yard and stated he could "throw a rock or spit right hard" into the yard of the person who committed the murders.[1035] It is unclear who Claude was referring to. Since Claude was in Boone at the time of his statement, and Troy was a neighbor to the Smalls, perhaps he was insinuating he thought Troy was the killer or someone who lived near Claude's home in Wilkes County. Alternatively, perhaps he was speaking of someone living or working in close proximity to his own workplace, which may have alluded to and or implicated John Frazier.

The Smalls, like Sheriff Ward Carroll before them, further believed the murders to be grudge killings, that the ransacking of the Durham house was the result of the killers searching for something like a will or deed, and that it was made to look like a robbery. Cecil also chauvinistically theorized the "Jimmy" must have been driven away from the Durham home by a woman who was unfamiliar with four-wheel drive, thus explaining why the vehicle ended up in a ditch.[1036]

These multiple theories aside, an unexpected development was on the horizon that would take the Durham Case in a new direction and shape its trajectory for the next two years.

CHAPTER 10

THE ASHEVILLE BOYS

Sheriff E. Y. Ponder (Source: Front Page Detective)

Among the law enforcement agencies in other North Carolina counties that reached out to contribute to the Durham investigation was the Madison County Sheriff's Department headed by Sheriff Elymas Yates "E. Y." Ponder.[eeee] Prior to the murders, Ponder had become concerned about the growing frequency of break-ins in Madison and neighboring counties. With each new report, he and his deputies began to realize "certain cars were observed near the sites of the break-in[s] with highly suspicious regularity." Accordingly, Ponder established "a corps of 'car watchers'.... Key 'lookout men' were provided with descriptions of the suspect cars and were asked to notify sheriff's headquarters...the moment they were seen." This community watch effort proved effective during a break-in on February 8, 1972 and led to the arrest of four young men, including twenty-two-year-old Dean Chandler, of Enka, North Carolina.[1037]

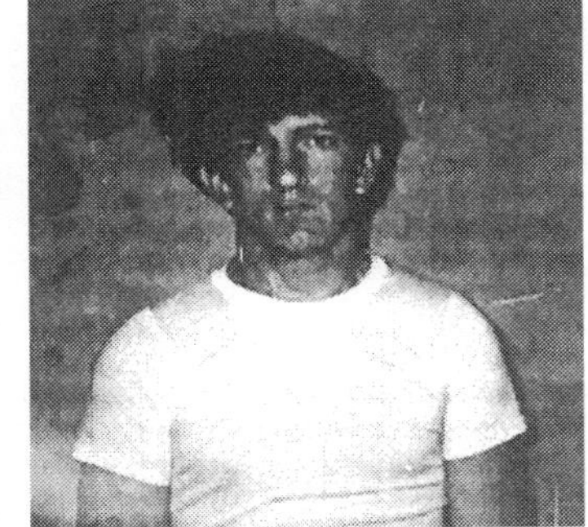

Dean Chandler (Courtesy of Watauga County Sheriff's Department)

Because of what had transpired in Boone only five days earlier, Ponder wondered if the break-in suspects could have played a role in the Durham Case.[1038] The same day as the February 8 break-in, he informed Watauga County Sheriff Ward Carroll "he had some suspects under observation and some clues that seemed to fit into the [Boone] puzzle."[1039] Ponder carefully questioned the four apprehended men but was unable to link them to the Watauga crime. Still, the arrests proved useful as they afforded the opportunity to investigate these men's contacts and associates. This enabled Ponder, Buncombe County Sheriff Tom Morrissey, and Yancey County Sheriff Kermit Banks[1040] to uncover an Asheville-based, "highly organized ring of breaking and entering and larceny artists which had apparently been working in 'shifts' in several counties" throughout western North

[eeee] E. Y. Ponder and his younger brother, Zeno Ponder, oversaw the Democratic Party-affiliated "Ponder machine," which dominated politics in Madison County for three decades amidst claims of ballot box tampering. [Source: "Ponder machine," Wikipedia, https://en.wikipedia.org/wiki/Ponder_machine.]

Carolina, including Buncombe, Henderson Madison, Yancey, Caldwell, and Watauga.[1041] They were accused of breaking into around one-hundred residential and commercial buildings and stealing television sets, stereo equipment, watches, shotguns, rifles, pistols, knives, and assorted other merchandise.[1042]

Jerry Cassada in 1966 (As published in The Asheville Citizen)

On March 1, using information provided by Dean Chandler, the three sheriffs and their officers collaborated to carry out "a series of pre-dawn raids" which resulted in the arrests of eight men, two of whom were twenty-two-year-old Jerry Ray Cassada *[pronounced Cassidy[1043]]* and twenty-three-year-old Eugene Clarence Garren.[ffff] Cassada and Garren were charged with breaking and entering and larceny.[1044] As with the previous arrestees, Sheriff Ponder questioned these men concerning the Durham murders, but again, without success.[1045]

By mid-April 1972, while a certain degree of fear lingered, life for Boone citizens had commenced its return to normalcy. Gun sales were dropping, and the streets were once again filling with shoppers and tourists. While conversations regarding more mundane topics like the weather had been supplanted by "murder talk" in early February, it was quieter now with only occasional

---

[ffff] Jerry Cassada and Eugene Garren were no strangers to trouble with the law. Throughout the 1960s, Cassada had been convicted of operating a motor vehicle without a proper driver's license, carrying concealed weapons, assault with a deadly weapon, breaking and entering, larceny, receiving stolen property, theft, and forgery. In 1962, he escaped from a prison camp road gang in the vicinity of Avery and Mitchell counties, and in 1965, he unsuccessfully attempted another escape. In 1966, he was imprisoned at Burnsville, NC and was sentenced in 1969 to Central Prison in Raleigh. Supposedly, in a transcript of a court case against Cassada, he was described as evil, a loose cannon, and a ticking time bomb, who would lash out for no apparent reason. People would cross the street to avoid walking past him and frequently reported his threats to the local police out of fear for their safety and lives. In 1966, at the age of sixteen, Garren was one of seven youths arrested in connection to an auto-theft ring that stole thirty-four cars in West Asheville, primarily from shopping center parking lots. The cars had not been taken for re-sale or profit, but for drag racing and joy riding, and many were wrecked or damaged. Garren pleaded guilty to charges of temporary larceny of automobiles and aiding and abetting in temporary larceny. He was sentenced to a hefty seven and half years, with the presiding judge recommending the sentence be served at a first-offenders camp. He served his time at Craggy Prison in Asheville. In March 1970, Garren was charged with rape and held on a $750 bond. [Sources: "Police Court," *Asheville Citizen-Times*, Asheville, NC, September 17, 1960, p. 10; "Two Are Held On 2 Counts Of Entering," *Asheville Citizen-Times*, Asheville, NC, November 22, 1961, p. 5; "1 Escapee Caught, Another At Large," *Asheville Citizen-Times*, Asheville, NC, August 30, 1962, p. 3; Court Listener, Jerry Ray Cassada v. State of North Carolina, https://www.courtlistener.com/opinion/286509/john-henry-hewett-v-state-of-north-carolina-r-l-turner-warden-central/?q=&court_ag=on&order_by=score+desc; "Escape Try Adds Time To Sentence," *Asheville Citizen-Times*, Asheville, NC, November 6, 1965, p. 3; "2 Asheville Men Charged In Postal Check Thefts," *Asheville Citizen-Times*, Asheville, NC, April 14, 1966, p. 36; "Sentence Given For Assault," *Asheville Citizen-Times*, March 18, 1969, Section Two, p. 1; "Post-Conviction Review Denied," *Asheville Citizen-Times*, Asheville, NC, May 30, 1969, p. 13; Post by username "lorimommy3," https://unexplained-mysteries.com/forum/topic/262185-unsolved-triple-murder-north-carolina-1972/page/38/#comments, October 4, 2015; "Seven Boys Charged: 34-Car Theft Ring Reported Broken Here," *Asheville Citizen-Times*, Asheville, NC, December 8, 1966, pp. 1 & 30; "Convicted Youth Cancels Appeal," *Asheville Citizen-Times*, Asheville, NC, January 17, 1967, p. 17; Watauga County Sheriff's Office investigation file 118-H-1/2/3; "Probable Cause Is Found In Robbery Case," *Asheville Citizen-Times*, Asheville, NC, March 26, 1970, p. 38.]

outspoken ruminations about the killers and if they would ever be caught.[1046] Meanwhile, Sheriff Ward Carroll and his investigators, along with the SBI, had just about exhausted all leads in the case,[1047] and Carroll was observing the outcome of the raids his fellow sheriffs had conducted. Like Sheriff Ponder, Carroll was hopeful there might be a link to the Durham Case.[1048]

Dean Chandler was out of jail, but not for long. The FBI had been investigating his possible connection with two auto thefts that occurred the month before in Tennessee. Both cars had been subsequently taken across the state line to North Carolina, which were federal offenses.[1049] The week of April 17, 1972, Chandler and seventeen-year-old Ellen Plemmons Shelton[gggg] were stopped by Asheville city detectives upon being found together in one of the stolen cars.[1050] Shelton was ultimately charged with being a juvenile delinquent involved in aiding and abetting Chandler in the interstate transportation of a stolen motor vehicle and was placed on three years' probation.[1051] Chandler was returned to jail, and on April 18, Sheriff Ponder, having missed two phone calls from Chandler, called the jail in Asheville and was connected to him. The conversation reportedly went as follows:

PONDER: "You've got something to say to me?"

CHANDLER: "Yes, sir. It's about that Boone thing you were asking me about."

PONDER: "The Durham murders?"

CHANDLER: "That's right, sir. If you'll come down here, I'll talk some about it."

PONDER: "Well, last time we talked about that, you didn't know anything about the Durham Case. If you want to tell me another lie, I've got no time to waste on you, but if you want to tell me what God loves, the truth, I'll come on over and listen."

CHANDLER: "I'll tell you the truth, Sheriff."[1052]

"Later that afternoon, Sheriff Ponder, in the company of SBI Agent Charlie Whitman, Buncombe County Sheriff Tom Morrissey, and Operations Officer Bob Parker, listened to Dean Chandler's astonishing story." Chandler conveniently distanced himself from the murders by prefacing his story with a statement that he was not one of the Durhams' killers. He then shared that, sometime past, he had been arrested, convicted, and incarcerated for the federal charge of stealing Social Security checks. He had been paroled ten years prior to his anticipated release date with a warning that, if he got into trouble again, he would have to make up those ten years. Chandler knew "a number of larceny counts were beginning to stack up against him and that if even one could be made to stick, he faced revocation of parole" and those ten additional years in prison. Chandler wanted to cut a deal. He promised to provide a break in the Durham Case if the larceny charges against him and his wife Anne could be dismissed or not prosecuted. The officers promised nothing, but Chandler continued with his story in a signed and sworn statement.[1053] On April 22, 1972, at the Buncombe County jail in Asheville, Chandler's entire statement was reiterated in an interview taped by

---

[gggg] At the time of this incident, Dean Chandler was married but dated and occasionally lived with Ellen Shelton, who was separated from her husband. [Sources: "Free On Bond, Man Arrested Second Time," *The Asheville Citizen*, Asheville, NC, September 25, 1968, p. 19; Anonymous source. Phone interviews with author. September 17, 2022 & October 15, 2022, and email communication with author, September 27, 2022; Notes compiled by Gayle Durham Mauldin, Watauga County Sheriff's Office investigation file 118-H-1/2/3.]

Whitman in the presence of Ponder, Sheriff Ward Carroll, and Bob Roberts, the Chief Investigator for the Buncombe County Sheriff's Department.[1054]

Chandler said that Jerry Cassada was in need of money, so the two of them met on the afternoon of February 2, 1972 to discuss plans to burglarize some homes and how to implement those plans the following day. They agreed to work together and to recruit Eugene Garren to go with them. They decided the three of them would meet the following morning at Jay and Jan's Restaurant in Asheville.[1055]

On February 3, because Chandler's wife Anne wanted to use his car that day, she went with him to the restaurant and sat in the car with their children while he met with Cassada, who had already arrived with Garren, and a big boy named Dewey, who neither Chandler nor his wife said they knew until that day, and who turned out to be Dewey Coffey.[hhhh] Cassada told Chandler that Garren and Coffey wanted to be included, and Cassada asked Chandler to case some houses that day, saying he would give him a share of whatever they took in. Afterwards, they all left, Chandler with his wife and their children in his white 1965 Plymouth and Cassada, Garren, and Coffey in Cassada's red 1965-1967 Ford sedan. They reunited around 10:00 AM at the Burger Hut just outside of Marion, North Carolina and remained there until around 10:30 AM. From there, Cassada, Garren, and Coffey went toward Burnsville, North Carolina while the Chandlers went on their way to case homes for the others to burglarize – something they had previously done together on occasion. About two miles up the road, Cassada stopped Chandler and asked if he had any gloves in his car. Chandler checked but did not, so Cassada pulled out in front of him and stopped at a little store on the right side of Highway 221 where he bought several pairs of brown cotton gloves.[1056]

In the meantime, the Chandlers journeyed to Boone. Because Chandler had never been there, he did not want to get too far off the main roads as it would have made giving directions to his associates more difficult. Once they neared the Boone town limits, they came to an intersection and turned left *[presumably from Highway 105, which Chandler referred to as 221 – 105 doubling as a truck route for 221[1057] – onto the 105 Bypass]* and between half a mile and two miles later, he saw a house off the road, sitting high on a bank, but he could not get his car in the driveway, so he circled (turned?) around and decided not to "bother with…that house." Chandler drove on and saw what he believed to be an apartment building with a cluster of four or five houses on the hill to the left *[presumably the Clyde Townsend Road community, including the Durham house, which is approximately one mile from the Highway 105/105 Bypass intersection]*. Chandler estimated the time at this point to be 1:30 or 2:00 PM. Chandler drove up the "driveway" *[presumably Clyde Townsend Road]* beside the apartment building, where he saw some people, but he did not pay any attention to them, nor did they seem to notice him or to find his presence peculiar. Off of that road, Chandler saw two additional driveways that turned left *[presumably the lower one leading to Clinard Wilson's house and the upper one leading to the Durhams' house]*. Chandler pulled into the lower one, but when he saw a second house *[presumably Bill Norris, Jr.'s house]* behind the initial house *[presumably Clinard Wilson's house]* on that driveway, he backed out and then proceeded to the upper driveway. At that house *[presumably the Durham house]*, which he described as a large, newer built brick home with some green on it, he blew his horn three or four times, and with no response, along with the absence of [chimney] smoke, he assumed the house was unoccupied. *[Ordinarily, Chandler*

[hhhh] Coffey's surname was also reported as Ramsey, but the mix-up was attributed to his mother's remarried surname being Ramsey. [Source: "4th Durham Suspect Brought to Carolina: Surrenders Before Maryland Officials," *Watauga Democrat*, Boone, NC, May 1, 1972, p. 1.

would have exited the car and knocked on the door of the house. If no one answered, the presumption would be no one was at home; if someone did answer, he would inquire where such and such a person lived in the neighborhood. However, because it was very cold, with fine snow blowing and snow on the ground, he did not want to get outside, and he stayed inside his car and blew the horn instead.] Afterward, he went to the top of the hill and saw a house sitting up on the bank to the right *[presumably the Dean Combs home]*, but since he did not see many close houses further back, he figured it would be possible for Cassada and the others to hit a couple of the houses that were in close proximity to one another. He then came back down to the main road *[presumably the 105 Bypass]*, and "not hardly a quarter of a mile below that, [he] found the road that turned to the left" *[presumably Greer Lane]*. Shortly after, he saw another road that turned back to the left *[presumably Laurel Fork Road]*. He believed that road might lead to the back of the houses he had just driven among, so he followed it for three or four miles, but found that not to be true.[1058] *[Had Chandler turned left off of Laurel Fork Road onto what is now Fox Hill Road, he would have reached the dead end that was more or less directly behind and below the houses he had cased.]*

Around 2:30 or 3:00 PM, the Chandlers left Boone to rendezvous once more with the others at the Burger Hut around 4:00 PM. Once there, Chandler asked Cassada if they had hit any houses, and Cassada replied they had not. They had only entered one home, but because coffee was boiling, a bathroom door was shut, and the radio was playing, "they got the hell out of there." *[Although this would not have been in Boone, it was oddly reminiscent of the experience of Durham neighbor Clara Wilson the morning of the murders when she heard someone in her house while she was in the bath with the radio playing.]* Cassada said "he would have to make a hit at Boone," and he asked Chandler if he had found any houses. Chandler affirmed he had identified some and proceeded to give Cassada directions to them. He knew Cassada normally did not hit houses that were close together, but Cassada said he would look it over, and since it would likely be dark by the time they got there, they might hit two of the houses. Chandler then told Cassada he could park his car where a road turned down left and walk back through the woods to the houses.[1059] *[This may indicate Chandler did have knowledge of present-day Fox Hill Road after all or simply felt they could cut through the woods off of Laurel Fork Road.]*

The group concluded its meeting and agreed to meet again at 9:00 PM. In the meantime, the Chandlers drove from Marion toward Hickory, North Carolina to kill time and look for other houses to hit in the future. Around 8:45 or 9:00 PM, the Chandlers returned to the Burger Hut to wait for Cassada, Garren, and Coffey, but when they had not arrived by 10:30 PM, they became worried that the trio might have been picked up and jailed, and they decided to head toward Boone. Because the weather was snowy and windy, Chandler drove slowly and closely observed each car they met. Around 10:45 or 11:00 PM, and about fourteen miles down the road, they met Cassada's car coming down the mountain in the opposite direction on Highway 221 at an intersection near the Avery County line. Chandler made a U-turn and began following Cassada, flashing his lights several times to get him to stop. Cassada eventually pulled over, leaping from the car and "brandishing a pistol," which he put away only after Chandler shouted out to identify himself. As Chandler approached Cassada's car, Cassada asked, "What's the matter with you? Don't you know you can get killed that way?" When Chandler inquired what was wrong, Cassada told him he [Cassada] had messed everything up. After a few minutes of conversation, Cassada told Chandler to have his wife drive their car the rest of the way and for Chandler to join him and the other men in his car. Cassada was in the driver's seat, and Garren, who had been in the front, moved to the back with Coffey, relinquishing the front passenger seat to Chandler. Chandler said they all seemed nervous, and

Cassada highly so. They all resumed the trek toward Marion with Chandler's wife following Cassada's lead.[1060]

Along the way, Cassada reiterated that he had "really [messed] up." Chandler asked if he had shot someone. Cassada said no, but he had fired once and needed to get rid of the gun unless Chandler wanted to buy it; Chandler declined. Cassada was driving too fast for the condition of the roads, so after a few miles, at Chandler's request and for fear of attracting attention and being pulled over, he stopped and let Chandler take the wheel. Cassada then began conversing with Garren and Coffey, asking them if they each still had their gloves, which they did. Cassada asked Garren if he had his fingerprints inside the Jeep (presumably a reference to the Durhams' GMC "Jimmy"), and Garren said he did not think so even though he had taken one glove off to start with. When Coffey asked, "Are they all dead?" Cassada replied, "I did my part, did you [do] yours?" [Coffey] said, "Yes." When Cassada asked Garren if he touched anything inside, Garren said no, but he should have brought the silver as it might have some fingerprints. Cassada said he did not think so and that the silver was not worth fooling with. Cassada asked about fingerprints on the rope, and Coffey (later stated to be Garren) said he felt they were safe and that if the rope was fingerprinted, more prints than theirs would be found. Cassada asked Coffey if he ripped the telephone out, and Coffey said yes, unless there was an extension. Cassada said he did not think there was. Cassada and Garren shared the belief that not all of the people they had seen lived in the house – that "some of those people were the neighbors." Cassada said they must have called the law. Garren commented, "We could have got out," and Cassada replied, "We could have, but the others might have seen us. It's best the way we did." According to Chandler, Cassada was not providing many details about what exactly had transpired, but Cassada "seemed to think that something had attracted the neighbors' attention, and they came over." *[Could this have aligned with the allegation that neighbor Bruce Faw had gone to the Durhams' door to seek assistance with his stuck vehicle and had seen and heard people inside the house despite the fact no one answered the door?]* Cassada also stated if those people had waited five minutes, it would have saved them and us too. Garren asked Cassada if he thought anyone saw their car, and Cassada said no, that he had parked it out of the way so no one could tie it to their presence in the house. Chandler said he had no idea where the car was parked, but their normal procedure was to park it within a quarter of a mile of their target house so they could reach the car in the event something happened and yet have it far enough away that passersby and neighbors would not be suspicious.[1061]

The conversation between Cassada, Garren, and Coffey continued back and forth about one thing and another until the cars reached Jay and Jan's Restaurant around 12:00 or 12:30 AM. Chandler went inside to have coffee, Coffey and Garren went to Coffey's car, which had been parked all day at the restaurant, and Cassada remained in his car. When Chandler returned, Cassada requested that he and his wife, if asked by anyone, say that he [Cassada] was in Asheville on the night of the murders, and the Chandlers agreed to do so. Cassada recommended that Garren and Coffey also say they were in Asheville, telling them they would need an airtight alibi for the period of time between dark on February 3 until 12:00 or 1:00 AM the morning of February 4. Before leaving the restaurant parking lot, Garren and Coffey said they would be sure to do that and to come up with alibis that had them at different places rather than together.[1062]

Cassada said he wanted to go home and change clothes, and he asked Chandler to wait at the restaurant. After about twenty to thirty minutes, Cassada returned and asked Chandler if he still lived on the mountain that was part of his [Chandler's] father-in-law's property in Buncombe County. Chandler said he did most of the time, and Cassada asked him to take a paper bag of his old clothes – a pair of brown pants and a blue shirt – and burn them, and for Chandler's wife to make sure he did. (Another piece of clothing Cassada had been outwardly wearing was a green Army field jacket.) Chandler agreed and did so the following day, burning the items in a large trash barrel below his house. Chandler's wife – apparently despite having heard Cassada's request – asked him what he had burned, but he did not tell her. *[The day after Chandler's statement, he directed officers to this location, and "they recovered several fragments of charred cloth."]*[1063] Cassada had also encouraged Garren and Coffey to dispose of their clothing from that night, and they said they would. According to Chandler, Garren was wearing a green and white checked CPO ("chief petty officer") jacket *[Chandler could not recall any of Garren's other clothing]*, while Coffey was dressed in a blue or green service station-type uniform with a matching shirt and pants *[Chandler said Coffey wore no coat]*. When the group arrived back at Jay and Jan's Restaurant and Chandler saw Coffey under streetlights as he [Coffey] was exiting Cassada's car, he noticed Coffey's shirt sleeves were wet from the cuffs up to a little past his elbows, the front of his shirt had wet splatters, and his pants were soaked between his knees and his waist. Chandler asked Coffey if he had fallen, and Coffey said no.[1064] *[Could Reed Trivette's testimony of seeing three men standing near the 105 Bypass on the night of the murders correspond with Cassada, Garren, and Coffey? And could Trivette's recollection of two of the men he saw dressed in military-style overcoats correspond with Cassada's army field jacket and Garren's "chief petty officer" jacket?]*

Oddly, it seems Chandler told officers a different version of his story at some point: "After the arrests, it [was] alleged, one of the suspects [presumably Chandler]...took the officers to the spot below and behind the Durham dwelling, where the tire tracks of the getaway car were found early in the investigation. According to the statement which the informant allegedly gave lawmen, he drove two of the suspects to this particular spot *[presumably the dead end of present-day Fox Hill Road]*, from which they allegedly planned to climb the steep incline to the rear of the Durham residence, for the purported purpose of burglarizing the premises. The informant has reportedly said he left his companions at the foot of the hill and drove away. After waiting the prearranged length of time, he returned *[presumably to Poplar Grove Road]* to pick up his associates. As he was driving along the road, the informant allegedly found them scrambling out of Bryce Durham's jeeplike car, which was in the ditch with lights and motor still running. His companions got into the informant's auto and he drove them away."[1065]

Regarding the rope at the crime scene, Chandler said it was something they frequently used during break-ins, and it was always in one of their cars. He said they employed it for whatever purpose was needed, including tying up guns and tying down trunk lids. He described it as 3.5'-4' long, ¼" in diameter, brownish white in color, and in the form of something like a plow line with about an 8" diameter loop tied on one end. When used for carrying guns, they would run the single end of the rope through a gun's trigger guard and then back through the loop. Chandler said that, sometime after the Boone incident, he and Cassada were in another home taking guns, and Chandler told Cassada he needed the rope. Cassada replied that "if [they] ever saw that rope again, it would be in court, but [he] hoped to hell he never saw it again." Chandler said he never saw the rope again after February 3, and that he had to cut a cord off of a blind to use instead of the rope.[1066]

Chandler stated the gun Cassada had that night was a .22-caliber, six-shot, single action, western style Ruger revolver, and he assumed it was the gun Cassada said he fired in the Durham house because it was the one Cassada pulled when Chandler flagged him down on the highway and the same one Cassada asked Chandler if he would like to buy that night in the car. Chandler said Cassada later told him he did sell it to someone. Chandler said when he, Cassada, Garren, and others worked together in the past, they agreed that any one of them not carrying a gun would stay outside and do the driving; no one would enter a house without a gun. He said they never discussed what they would actually do if someone caught them in a house other than they would not shoot them. Most of the guns they carried were stolen, and if a gun was traced back to a break-in that any of the three of them were charged with, it would not be a good thing for authorities to also discover that gun had been used to kill someone. Chandler said he carried Cassada's .22 revolver at one point for a two-week period and Garren also had a .22 revolver, while Coffey carried a .38 with a two-inch barrel.[1067]

Chandler was originally to have gotten a share of whatever Cassada, Garren, and Coffey took from the house they hit. Cassada never mentioned this or talked about anything they took from the house in Boone, yet on February 4, Cassada, who previously had no cash, had $140 or $150 on him. Cassada did not say where he got it, and Chandler did not ask.[1068]

A few days after news of the Durham murders was released, Chandler asked Cassada what the problem had been that night. Cassada laughed and said Chandler knew him better than that. Chandler explained to Cassada that he was asking so he would know what to say if he was ever picked up and questioned. Cassada replied, "Well, if you don't know anything, then there isn't nothing you can tell them, is there?" "No," said Chandler, "I guess there isn't."[1069] Chandler also asked Garren about the events of the night of February 3. Garren asked if Cassada had not told him, and Chandler said no. Chandler asked, "Did you all kill them people?" Not giving a direct answer, Garren said it was useless and he could understand getting rid of one person so they could have exited the house before two other people arrived.[1070]

Dean and Anne Chandler separated, and sometime afterward, Anne encountered Cassada on the street in downtown Asheville. Cassada informed her Dean had signed around twenty-five statements against him for breaking and entering. He asked Anne if Dean had ever told her what happened the night of February 3, and she said he had not. Cassada warned her if anything happened regarding the case in Boone, he would take Dean with him. Anne replied she did not know what he was talking about *[which is curious since Anne was reportedly with her husband, jointly casing homes in Boone for Cassada and the others to rob]*. Cassada told her they had broken into a house in Boone, and while they were inside, they heard someone coming and hid. A man entered the home, and they were going to wait for him to leave, but when it became apparent he was not leaving, Cassada jumped out from behind him and began to choke him to unconsciousness. He then realized he had killed the man and was trying to decide what to do with his body. In the meantime, another man and a woman entered, who Cassada thought might be neighbors, and Cassada and his accomplices had to get rid of them as well.[1071] Anne asked if Cassada shot anyone, and he told her no, but he got rid of them, and one shot was fired in the struggle. When Anne asked how he got rid of the people, he told her to never mind and if she said anything, she would be mixed up in it and guilty of the crime as well. Cassada knew Anne was on five years' probation for cashing government checks, and he told her if she said anything, she would go to jail and lose her children. From that point onward, being somewhat afraid of Cassada, Anne stayed away from him.[1072] At one point, Anne informed her aunt, Viola West, that Cassada had threatened her [Anne], saying he was going to kill her. Cassada also reportedly told someone "that before he would take all the blame, he was going to fix some other people."[1073]

On April 24, 1972, Boone-based Assistant District Solicitor Tom Rusher told reporters more than two-hundred individuals had been questioned in connection with the Durham Case, and he predicted a break would soon occur.[1074] Speaking to the Boone Rotary Club that Bryce Durham had been a member of, Rusher also stated more than twenty SBI agents had worked on the case, with five of those being permanently assigned, and that the SBI had used "'every piece of scientific equipment available to them' in carrying out 'a very intensive investigation.' He said he felt all local lawmen working on the case had done everything possible in an attempt to find the criminals and 'get enough evidence to bring about a criminal prosecution.'"[1075] That same day, arrest warrants were issued for Dean Chandler, Jerry Cassada, and Eugene Garren.[1076] The following day, April 25, around 4:30 AM, based on Chandler's statement, Cassada and Garren were each charged with three first-degree murders, and Chandler was charged with three counts of accessory before the fact.[1077]

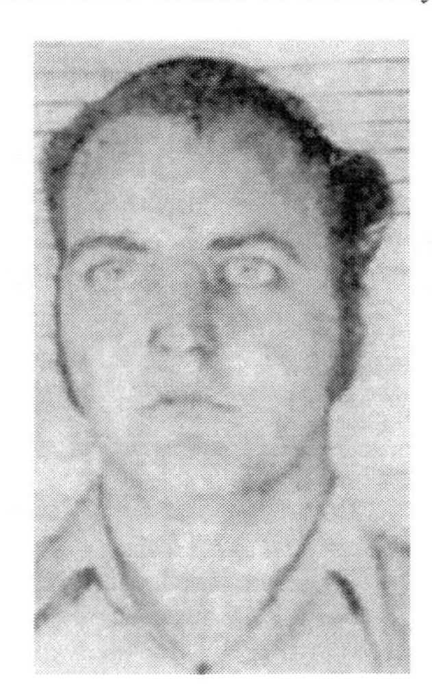

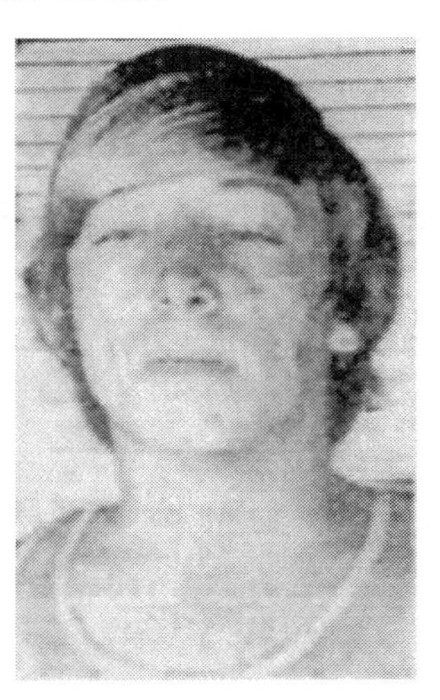

Left to Right: Dean Chandler, Jerry Cassada (Source: Front Page Detective), & Eugene Garren (Source: Startling Detective).

"Officers from sheriff's departments in Buncombe, Watauga, Madison, and Caldwell counties took part in the arrests, assisted by members of the State Bureau of Investigation." These included Sheriff Tom Morrissey of Buncombe, Sheriff Ward Carroll of Watauga, Sheriff E. Y. Ponder of Madison,[1078] Sheriff S. Ray Moore of Caldwell, and SBI Agent Charlie Whitman. Boone photographer George Flowers was also present.[1079] Chandler was already in the Buncombe County jail on the earlier charges of stealing a credit card and was being held without bond on an FBI retainer while agents continued their investigation into his connection with the two Tennessee auto thefts.[1080] "Cassada and Garren were rousted from their homes…neither was armed nor offered resistance,"[1081] and they were also placed in the Buncombe County jail.[1082] Sheriff Carroll stated "it was about agreed that the motive for the murders was breaking and entering and larceny, and that apparently the Durhams had been taken by surprise by their assailants."[1083] Another account reported Carroll saying "it appeared the murderers were engaged in looting the Durham house that night when the Durhams 'came in on them' unexpectedly.'"[1084] The SBI reiterated the latter viewpoint, saying the deaths appeared to have been the result of panic after the Durhams surprised the suspects while they were breaking and entering.[1085] *[This theory, however, did not align with the food and drinks that the family had been consuming in the den prior to their murders. If the Durhams had arrived home and surprised the intruders, they would not have prepared a snack for themselves afterward.]* When news of the arrests reached the attention of Troy Hall's brother Ray, he showed no surprise, but when Ray's wife Kay spoke to Ginny Hall about it, Ginny expressed her belief these men were innocent.[1086]

Jerry Cassada escorted by SBI Agent Charlie Whitman (Source: Front Page Detective)

Chandler, Cassada, and Garren were reportedly taken from the Buncombe County jail and then "whisked before daylight [via Lenoir, North Carolina]...and booked... in the Watauga County (Boone) jail,"[1087] although SBI District Supervisor Red Minter later stated Cassada and Garren would remain in Lenoir "because the Watauga County jail was 'inadequate to hold them,'[iiii] [and] as far as he knew, Chandler was still in the Buncombe County Jail."[1088] Another news report stated Sheriff Morrissey of Buncombe County turned the men over to Watauga County Sheriff Ward Carroll, "who subsequently ordered the suspects confined at undisclosed locations,"[1089] but which apparently turned out to be the "federally-approved" Caldwell County jail in Lenoir.[1090] "This separation of the prisoners reinforce[d] earlier, unofficial reports that Chandler became an informer while in custody and implicated the [others] in the murders."[1091]

Following the arrests of these men, two questions surfaced. One was why authorities felt they had the right men in custody when those charged were white and Virginia Durham had allegedly stated the intruders were black? Sheriff Carroll's reply was that Troy Hall was actually unsure about what his mother-in-law told him.[1092] Also, investigators had conducted a thorough vacuuming of the crime scene and no "negroid" hair was found,[1093] although it was possible for such evidence to have been lost during the poor containment of the crime scene. The other question was if shots were actually fired in the Durham house on the night of the murder as clairvoyant M. B. Dykshoorn had said. "A key investigator confirmed...that at least one bullet hole had been found," and Sheriff Carroll "admitted finding bullet holes."[1094] Crime scene photos substantiated the presence of one bullet hole in the paneled wall of the Durhams' den, indicating the intruders may have fired a warning shot to intimidate or bring the Durhams under control. The bullet was believed to have been fired above the chair where Bryce Durham was sitting, and therefore perhaps fired over his head.[1095]

Although Dykshoorn would later claim to have reconstructed and solved the Durham murders,[1096] and although he was named as an honorary sheriff in two North Carolina counties,[1097] the extent to which his clairvoyance actually assisted in the arrests was debated. At least three individuals felt it was negligible. Despite E. J. Durham, Sr. having no regrets about engaging Dykshoorn and calling him a wonderful man and very fine gentleman, he dismissed the clairvoyant's role, stating he did not believe Dykshoorn had anything to do with the arrests, and that he had said the killers lived in Boone rather than Asheville.[1098] *[In fact, Dykshoorn had stated the perpetrators were from outside of Boone, perhaps coming from the west, and Asheville is southwest of Boone.]* SBI District

---

[iiii] In 1970, the Watauga County jail had been declared to be "an old jail and not very secure" and "ruled substandard" by a state inspection team. [Source: "New Jail Is Proposed To Watauga Officials," *Watauga Democrat*, Boone, NC, January 8, 1970, pp. 1 & 2.]

Supervisor Red Minter felt Dykshoorn made no contribution whatsoever, saying, "None of his clues led to the arrests. Most anyone could have told us what he did."[1099] Minter said Dykshoorn "had not told the SBI anything about the case that couldn't have been found in newspaper accounts."[1100] Sheriff E. Y. Ponder said although "he had heard that Dykshoorn was pretty much on target," the Asheville arrests were based "on hard evidence, not supernatural prophecies."[1101] Dykshoorn admitted he was not perfect and sometimes missed things because he did not always understand what he saw. In the end he was "accurate enough to be unsettling" but erred enough "for the skeptic to breathe easy."[1102]

Subsequent to the arrests and speaking on Dykshoorn's behalf during a newspaper interview, his wife Cora stated investigators "had not one clue when they started and my husband gave them the whole thing, like they had it on a platter." She stated her husband was able to go back in time to the last five minutes of the victims' lives and then follow the killers after the murders. Mrs. Dykshoorn added that her husband "involve[d] himself in about one murder case a month" and provided his services for humanitarian reasons. She said he agreed to take on the Durham Case on the conditions that his involvement receive no publicity, that officers cooperate fully, and that he be contacted immediately in the event of arrests. She said Sheriff Carroll had promised to call but did not, which was a breach of their agreement. "My husband kept his promise; he kept his mouth shut, and it's not nice the way he was treated."[1103]

Dykshoorn's prediction of arrests within two weeks or less following his visit to Boone did not align with the April 25 arrests of the men on the murder charges, but it did align with their previous arrests related to burglary and the stolen property ring. Some felt this alignment was proof Dykshoorn knew what he was talking about. His attribution of the murders to a group of four to five individuals also seemed to be substantiated when a reliable but anonymous law enforcement investigator "indicated that a fourth suspect may be arrested soon."[1104] This suspect turned out to be twenty-one-year-old Henry Dewey Coffey, a resident of Leicester near Asheville and formerly of New Jersey.[1105]

Dewey Coffey (Source: T. C. Roberson High School Yearbook,

A warrant was issued for Coffey for three counts of murder, and a widespread manhunt for him ensued. His parents lived in Asheville and told police they had not seen their son in about two months;[1106] he was believed to be in Virginia or staying with a girlfriend in the Washington, D. C. area. On April 26, Coffey surrendered himself to police in the Oxen Hill Precinct of Prince Georges County, Maryland, saying, "I think they want me down there for murder."[1107] Coffey had never previously been booked for a crime[1108] and had only ever had "a few traffic violations."[1109] Authorities declined to say whether Coffey was suspected of being directly involved in the murders or of being an accomplice. Sheriff Ward Carroll, Boone Police Chief Clyde Tester,[1110] and SBI Agent Wally Hardwick, Jr. transported Coffey from Maryland to the Watauga County[1111] jail, arriving there on April 28. He was transferred to the Caldwell County jail the following day to join fellow suspects Cassada and Garren.[1112] After these Asheville suspects had been pictured in the newspaper, Troy and Ginny Hall's former Greenway Trailer Park neighbor, Chester Nelson, recognized some of them as having been at the Halls' trailer.[1113]

In early May 1972, SBI Agent John Parker investigated the employment histories of Eugene Garren and Dewey Coffey. Between 1968 and January 1972, Garren worked four different jobs, including construction, paving, and fencing. He had the reputation of a good, hardworking, and very reliable employee, and one employer described him as "a pretty nice boy." The week of the Durham murders, he worked a few days for the fencing company, but not on Thursday, February 3, the day of the murders. The following day he worked two hours. His employer stated Garren's hours on those two dates were reflective of the fact their work was limited due to the cold weather and the work was completed.[1114]

When Agent Parker met with individuals in Dewey Coffey's former place of employment (a plumbing company), Coffey's supervisor stated he had been a good, dependable, punctual employee who never laid out of work. Both the supervisor and a co-worker of Coffey stated Coffey had worked on the day of the Durham murders. Coffey and his co-worker had gone out on a call in Enka, North Carolina that morning and on another call in nearby Arden that afternoon, which they partially completed. They returned to their shop around 5:00 PM, and because the roads were somewhat bad and the weather cold and snowy, they went to a service station, where Coffey put tires with snow treads on his Mustang. Coffey dropped off his co-worker at home around 6:00 PM. (The service station attendant, who described Coffey as a quiet man who did not drink or cause trouble, may have even finished changing Coffey's tires as late as 7:00 or 8:00 PM.) *[Coffey's presence at work on the day of the murders contradicted Dean Chandler's statement that Coffey had accompanied him, Cassada, and Garren that day in Marion and that Coffey had gone with Cassada and Garren toward Burnsville.]* The following morning, February 4, Coffey picked his co-worker up at the normal time, and they returned to Arden to complete the job from the previous day. News of the Durham murders was circulating, and Coffey and his co-worker discussed the information being put out by the media, but the co-worker said nothing was unusual about Coffey that day. The co-worker knew Jerry Cassada and that Cassada and Coffey were good friends. Coffey left his job in late February stating his father was sick and he lived in the Washington, D. C. area. He also said he had a friend in trouble in jail and was going to try to get him out.[1115]

In May 1972, District Court Judge James E. "Peck" Holshouser, Sr. considered petitions asking him to name court-appointed lawyers for Chandler, Cassada, and Garren, who had filed affidavits of indigency, claiming they were financially unable to hire defense counsel.[1116] Coffey also completed financial papers but did not request a court-appointed attorney.[1117] The availability of criminal lawyers in Boone was limited due to the fact that Stacy Eggers, Jr. had been retained by Troy and Ginny Hall, John H. Bingham was associated with the settlement of the Durhams' estates and was ineligible for appointment, and John Livingston Williams, who had moved to Boone from Surry County and knew Bryce and Virginia Durham, said he would not accept appointment.[1118]

Ultimately, the court-appointed attorneys were Robert Lacey of Newland, representing Chandler (who was not present in court[1119][iiii]), Charles Lamm, Jr. of Boone representing Cassada, and C. Banks Finger, Jr. of Boone representing Garren. Coffey's family hired his attorney, Ted West, of Lenoir. The preliminary hearing for the four, which had been scheduled for that same day was

[iiii] Chandler's absence was likely due to the fact that, unbeknownst to the other defendants, he was being charged differently as an informant, although he may also have been ill. A "Jail Account" invoice in the amount of $5.00 from Dr. Len Hagaman, Sr. (father of future Watauga County Sheriff L. D. Hagaman, Jr.) to the Watauga County Commissioners reveals he treated Chandler on May 11, 1972. On September 12, 1972, the commissioners were billed $3.00 for penicillin for treatment of Chandler's abscessed tooth. [Source: Watauga County, NC Clerk of Court's Office, Criminal File #72-CR-1078, State vs. Dean Chandler.]

delayed until they could confer with their lawyers.[1120] Judge Holshouser then asked the attorneys to "get together and decide whether they wanted to ask for a preliminary hearing." Coffey told the court he had already spoken with West at the Caldwell County jail and had decided to ask for a preliminary hearing. Cassada and Garren nodded to indicate they would like the same.[1121] As an additional point, Assistant District Solicitor Tom Rusher told Judge Holshouser his office was strictly opposed to the setting of bond, and Cassada, Garren, and Coffey were subsequently returned to the Caldwell County jail.[1122]

The rescheduled date for the preliminary hearing was not initially agreed upon and it was anticipated it might "not be held for some time since the attorneys [would] have to travel some distance in most cases to be in contact with their clients and [would] need time to become better acquainted with their defense."[1123] Eventually, though, after the attorneys consulted with District Solicitor Clyde Roberts the preliminary hearing was rescheduled for June 15.[1124]

In light of these developments, it was finally revealed that Chandler was no longer in the Buncombe County jail but under tight security in the Watauga County jail and was being charged differently than the other three defendants. While Cassada, Garren, and Coffey were charged "with having a direct hand" in the murders, Chandler was charged with three counts as an accessory before the fact of murder,[1125] having cased the Durham house and counseled with the other three.[1126] This "confirmed what observers in the case had suspected: that Chandler may have informed on the other three, thus breaking a deadlocked case which had kept scores of investigators in several Western North Carolina counties without a clue for nearly twelve weeks." It was also revealed Chandler served as an informant in the earlier burglary and stolen goods ring case resulting in the arrests of Cassada and Garren, and Chandler would testify as a state's witness when that case came to trial.[1127] Chandler feared going to the state penitentiary, saying he would not last a week as others would be waiting there to kill him.[1128]

On June 15, 1972, the probable cause hearing for the four suspects was held at Watauga District Court[kkkk] before an audience of around four hundred spectators. With the exception of several brief recesses and just over an hour-long lunch break, the hearing lasted from 9:30 AM to almost 6:00 PM. District Court Judge J. Ray Braswell presided, and the prosecution was led by District Solicitor Clyde Roberts and Assistant District Solicitor Tom Rusher. Their contention was that Chandler and his wife cased the Durham home for burglary and Cassada, Garren, and Coffey killed the Durhams when caught in the house. The defense argued Chandler manufactured his story implicating Cassada, Garren, and Coffey because he was seeking immunity from prosecution for other crimes, and when he "failed to obtain 'absolution,' he decided not to cooperate.[1129] Chandler did, in fact, refuse to testify at the hearing.

The witnesses subpoenaed in Cassada's and Chandler's cases were:

- Darrell Miller, an inmate within the North Carolina Department of Corrections in Wake County.[1130] *[Miller had been arrested alongside Chandler in February 1972, charged with a Madison County break-in.[1131]]*
- Sheriff E. Y. Ponder of Madison County[1132]
- Sheriff Tom Morrissey of Buncombe County[1133]

[kkkk] Although the Watauga County Clerk of Court's office graciously pursued with the North Carolina State Archives the author's inquiry regarding an audio recording or transcript of this probable cause hearing, no record of these materials could be found, and they may never have existed.

- Claude E. Gillikin, Jr. of the SBI in Raleigh[1134]
- Dr. Clayton Dean of Boone[1135]
- William J. "Bill" Roberts of the Buncombe County Sheriff's Department (administrative operations)[1136]
- Jack V. Staggs of the Buncombe County Sheriff's Department (criminal investigation bureau)[1137]
- Gray A. Burleson of the Buncombe County Sheriff's Department[1138]
- Charles E. Whitman of the SBI in Lenoir[1139]
- James Forrester Dotson of Dotson Plumbing Company in Asheville[1140]
- Charles D. Chambers of the SBI in Enka[1141]
- Michael L. Lewis of the SBI in Arden[1142]
- Ronnie Taylor of the Amoco Service Station in Biltmore[1143]
- Mrs. Dean (Elizabeth Anne) Chandler of Asheville[1144]
- Troy Hall of Wilkesboro[1145]
- Ginny Durham Hall of Wilkesboro[1146]
- Ellen Shelton of Asheville[1147]
- Cecil Small of Boone[1148]

Anne Chandler was a surprise witness but also a reluctant one, who stated she only lived off and on with Dean Chandler. Judge Braswell told her she would have to testify as to what Cassada had said, but she could stop short of incriminating herself. He also mentioned the possibly of placing her in jail to give her an opportunity to think it over, but he determined that would not be necessary. After consulting with her husband's attorney, when questions were asked regarding her and her husband's activities, Mrs. Chandler availed herself five to seven times of the Fifth Amendment, which permits a person to withhold testimony that may tend to incriminate oneself. She did, however, state that Cassada "had once warned her not to say anything about the Durham killings." Mrs. Chandler recounted how Cassada threatened her and her children on an Asheville street in March or April, telling her if she "spilled anything" to authorities about the Boone case, he would take her and her husband down with him and she would be charged and lose her kids. She testified Cassada told how he and Garren and Coffey were burglarizing the Durham house when someone came in and surprised them. One of the guys choked a woman, and then two men came in, and they [Cassada, Garren, and Coffey] "had to get rid of them" too before they could make their getaway. *[This differed from Mrs. Chandler's April 22 statement that Cassada had choked a man first, followed by two others – a man and a woman.[1149]]* Mrs. Chandler said one of the three intruders choked the three Durhams to death, but if she named which one did the choking, it was not noted in news reports. "Judge Braswell ruled Mrs. Chandler's testimony…could only be used as evidence against Cassada and not as a basis for probable cause against Garren or Coffey."[1150]

At the joint agreement of the defense attorneys (other than Coffey's), Garren, Chandler, and Cassada had taken lie detector tests. The attorneys also agreed in advance of the tests that, regardless of the results, "good or bad, favorable or unfavorable," they would be introduced at the hearing. SBI Agent Claude E. Gillikin, Jr., the bureau's top polygraph examiner,[1151] administered the extensive tests, asking three key questions: 1) Did you kill any member of the Durham family? 2) Were you present when members of the Durham family were killed? 3) Do you know who killed members of the Durham family? Although the tests were inadmissible as evidence, Gillikin testified he was satisfied from the defendants' responses "that they were not lying when they denied the Durham slayings."[1152]

The state's case relied on Chandler's April 22 statement to Sheriff Ward Carroll and SBI Agent Charlie Whitman, and "a great portion of the [hearing] was taken up" by the transcript of that statement. Carroll testified nearly one and a half hours[1153] by reading aloud the transcript of his interview with Chandler, saying Chandler admitted to having worked with Cassada, Garren, and Coffey in housebreaking activities and that he directed them to the Durham neighborhood on February 3 after being assigned by the others to case houses for them to hit. Chandler said he and his wife had come to Boone the day of the murders "to look over houses for burglary possibilities for Cassada, Garren, and 'a boy named Dewey,'" and he described the location of the Durham house and its color, although the color he stated was incorrect.[1154] Chandler denied being in Boone and going to the Durham house on the *night* of the murders.[1155] "He said he didn't find out about the killings until later in the night when he met the others after being separated from them for several hours." He "said the other men indicated that they had killed some people who had found them in the Durham house," and "they told him to say he had been in Asheville that night if he were asked."[1156] Chandler also said Cassada "seemed very nervous [and] kept talking about how to get rid of a gun and said, 'If those people had waited five minutes, they could have saved themselves and us too.'"[1157]

Chandler's attorney, Robert Lacey, cross-examined Carroll and brought up the point that Chandler had mentioned the color green on the Durham house, where green did not exist in any form.[llll] He pointed out as incompetence the fact that the transcript of Chandler's statement contained references to "inaudible" words. He asked Carroll why his [Carroll's] conversation with Chandler prior to Chandler's official statement was not also taped, and Carroll stated he did not know. Lacey asked the same question of Whitman, who said the conversation with Chandler prior to his statement consisted of preliminaries, including informing him of his rights and advising him as to what charges might arise as a result of his statement.[1158] Lacey argued the statement had been obtained illegally and Chandler had only made it because Carroll promised him the large reward fund. Carroll denied making any such promise, although he did say that, before Chandler's statement was taken, he had told Chandler about the reward, shown him some of the checks, and told him he would be eligible for the $14,000. *[The preceding April, Carroll had stated the arrests resulted from an informant, although he did not state the informant had been Chandler, and he added that the reward money would not be "doled out until after there had been a conviction in the case."* [1159] *In contrast to those who questioned Carroll's actions, only about six weeks prior, the Boone Optimist Club had named him "'Lawman of the Year'...in recognition of his service to the county.* [1160]*]* Judge Braswell ruled Chandler had made the statement voluntarily and it could be used as evidence against him but not against the other three defendants.[1161]

Defense attorneys also suggested Sheriff E. Y. Ponder "had brought Chandler to Boone and familiarized him with the area and the Durham home before he made his statement. Carroll conceded Ponder told him by telephone that he [Ponder] had brought 'some person' over to Boone in an automobile and showed him the Durham house, among other things. This telephone call was received, said Carroll, before Chandler made his detailed statement involving Cassada, Garren, and Coffey."[1162] The sheriffs denied Ponder "told Chandler about the reward to persuade him to testify and then drove him to the Durham house to make certain he got his story straight."[1163]

[llll] In a 1978 televised investigative special about the Durham murders, the Durham home, at least by that time, did have light green window shutters and light green trim on the garage doors. [Source: *Special Edition of WBTV News*, Charlotte, NC, March 1978.]

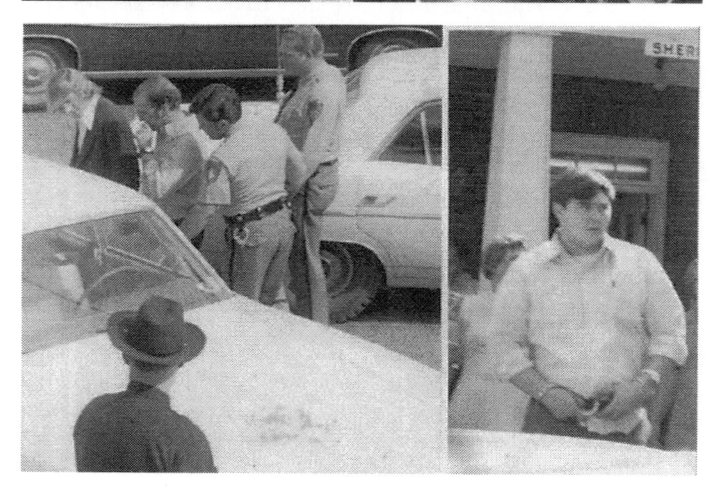

Asheville area suspects being escorted in Boone, NC by law enforcement officers. Top: Eugene Garren; Middle: Eugene Garren (L) and Jerry Cassada; Bottom: Garren & Cassada (L) and Dewey Coffey. (All images courtesy of the George Flowers Collection, Digital Watauga Project)

Troy and Ginny Hall also testified at the hearing and were questioned by each of the attorneys. The topics directed to Troy included the layout of the Durham home, Bryce Durham's habits, money matters, a gun collection believed to have belonged to Bryce, the alleged telephone conversation with Virginia Durham, the condition of the home on the night of the murders, and knowledge (which Troy said he had none) of the presence of a "breadbox" in the basement and its contents. Troy was also asked "about his association with the Durhams, when he and his wife last ate at the Durham home, and what, if anything, was missing from the home after February 3."[1164] Troy told of receiving the mysterious phone call between 10:10 and 10:30 PM and reiterated his understanding that "the whispering voice" made mention of "niggers." He also told of going to the Durham home with Cecil Small and discovering the bodies with their heads submerged in the bathtub. Troy's and Ginny's testimonies "added little to what they had already told officers."[1165]

Medical Examiner Dr. Clayton Dean testified Bobby and Bryce Durham were choked with a rope until they were unconscious and then put in the bathtub where they drowned. He said Virginia Durham had also been choked with a rope but had no water in her lungs.[1166]

Virginia Durham's niece, Jerri Bumgarner Waddell, attended the probable cause hearing, driving from her home in Greensboro. She recalled being unnerved when one of the defendants pointed at her and said to someone in the courtroom, "She looks like Virginia. Is she Virginia's sister?" The person being spoken to asked something along the lines of, "How do you know that? I thought you said you didn't see her," the implication being that the defendant had denied seeing Virginia Durham. Waddell was further rattled after being followed by someone from the hearing back to her home in Greensboro, particularly after verifying she had not been tailed by SBI agents for protection purposes as usual.[1167]

At the conclusion of the hearing, Judge Braswell found the state had produced insufficient evidence and no physical evidence to link Garren and Coffey to the murders, and the charges against them were dropped. Assistant District Solicitor Rusher "said somewhat sadly, 'We are aware of the deficiencies in the state's case.'" Coffey was released from custody, but Garren remained in jail on the felonious breaking and entering charges he faced in other counties. Because the hearing was not a trial, double jeopardy was not applicable and left the door open for Coffey and Garren to be recharged if additional evidence was discovered later. Braswell *did* find probable cause against Cassada and Chandler, ruling the evidence provided by the Chandlers was sufficient to hold Cassada for trial for murder and to hold Chandler for trial as an accessory. If convicted, Cassada would face the death penalty and Chandler three life terms. Cassada and Chandler "were bound over to Watauga Superior Court for grand jury action." The judge's rulings "brought tears" to Garren's wife and "an angry outburst" from Cassada's wife,[1168] Frances.[1169] During one of the breaks, Mrs. Cassada had encountered Bryce Durham's brother-in-law and sister, Charles and Gayle Mauldin, and said to them, "It wasn't my family that killed your family. It was your own family." The Mauldins did not respond but were puzzled as to why neither Cassada nor his wife took the stand to offer an alibi that might clear him.[1170] *[Jerry Cassada reportedly told his wife about participating in the murders, and they eventually divorced. His former sister-in-law stated he told his wife if she ever said anything about it, he would kill her. Eugene Garren also reportedly told his mother about his own involvement. Cassada allegedly had no reason to kill the Durhams and only wanted what was in their house.]*[1171]

On July 18, 1972, Jerry Cassada was taken to the district court in Boone for his bail bid, which was set by Judge Braswell at $50,000; no bond was set for Dean Chandler.[1172] Earlier that same month, in Buncombe County, Chandler pleaded guilty to stealing the two automobiles in Tennessee and was sentenced to five years in a federal penitentiary as well as a second five-year term for probation violation, to run concurrently with the auto theft charge. His attorney requested he be moved from the Watauga County jail to a Florida prison for security reasons,[1173] but he remained in Watauga County while Cassada, unable to post bail,[1174] was returned to the Caldwell County jail. In early August 1972, Chandler was convicted in Yancey County of breaking and entering and larceny in connection with an incident that occurred on February 5, two days after the Durham murders.[1175] For that conviction, he received an eight to ten- year prison sentence.[1176]

On August 14, 1972, Bryce Durham's brother Bill hired Gray Burleson, of Asheville, to help investigate the case. Burleson was an investigator and deputy sheriff with the Buncombe County Sheriff's Department.[1177] The day after he was hired, Burleson visited Anne Chandler, who had requested to see him. She told Burleson she was "disgusted and scared and did not know what to do any more" or who to trust. Dean Chandler's trial had been scheduled for September 18, and she wanted to talk to Burleson about it as she was not sure what was going to happen with Dean. Burleson told Anne he did not believe events had happened the way Dean told them, and she agreed, saying it had to be someone in Boone who set things up, and it had to be planned in advance. Anne said she believed that person to be Troy Hall.[1178] She did not believe robbery was the motive in the Durham Case, finding it odd that pieces of silver were taken while the bank deposit bag and guns were left behind. She also felt robbers could have accomplished that goal without killing anyone.[1179]

Burleson suggested to Anne she knew how it happened, and she said she only knew half the story and would have to talk to Dean to get his opinion about telling the entire story so Burleson could work on obtaining corroborating physical evidence. Eager to have this off her mind, Anne asked Burleson if he could take her to see Dean in jail, and Burleson did so and spoke with him as well. Dean said he "wished to stick with the statement he had already given." When Burleson told Dean he did not believe that statement, Dean asked him why, and Burleson replied he knew that was not Dean's method of operation. Dean said he didn't understand why Burleson did not believe his story because everyone else did. When Anne stated Dean thought he was going to get the reward money, Dean affirmed it. Burleson disagreed and asked Dean why he believed that. Dean said because Troy Hall was the sole benefactor of the estate *[in actuality, Ginny Hall was]*. This prompted Burleson to ask if Dean knew Troy, and Dean said he did, even before the probable cause hearing, but he did not want to discuss it. Dean said no one would believe him if he changed his story, and he felt no one would convict him on the basis of his current story…that he would go to Federal prison to serve his sentence for his conviction on other charges in Yancey County, he would serve two years, and he would get the Durham reward money. Burleson reiterated his belief Dean would never get the money, and Dean said if he did not, "it would not be his heels sticking out of the bathtub." Dean also told Burleson, "You know too damn much." Anne again encouraged Dean to tell what he knew, and she would tell what she knew, but Dean said he would take his chances at the September 18 trial. He added that if that didn't work out, then he might get back in touch with Burleson, and he said he would take a lie detector test on that date. On the return trip to Asheville, Anne told Burleson, "He will never get that money. I wish I could get this through his head." She added that her half of the story would make no sense without Dean's. She indicated she would be willing to speak with the SBI after September 18, adding "she was damned if she did and damned if she didn't."[1180]

Meanwhile, Anne's aunt, Viola West, informed Burleson that, in late July 1972, Anne had returned to the home she and Dean had shared on Milk Sick Cove Road on property owned by Anne's father in Candler, North Carolina at the time of the Durham murders. Anne went there to retrieve some clothing and took along Mrs. West's ten-year-old daughter, Leona. When they returned to Mrs. West's home, Leona asked why there were bloody clothes in the attic, including a pair of men's trousers with blood on the legs and a pair of women's slacks with blood on the front. Late that night and the following night, Mrs. West witnessed Anne burning clothing in the wood stove inside her basement apartment. Mrs. West also found inside an old buffet chest an eighteen-inch-long mask made from a leg of a dark blue, perhaps polyester, pair of women's slacks, with holes cut out for the eyes, nose, and mouth, carefully sewn at the top and cut with pinking shears around the bottom. Detective Burleson picked up the mask from Mrs. West and turned it over to SBI Agents Charlie Chambers and John Parker, who also went to Mrs. West's home and retrieved ashes from the stove in which Anne had burned the clothing. The two agents additionally obtained a search warrant for the former Chandler home, where they retrieved clothing and a pair of handcuffs which they submitted to the SBI lab for analysis.[1181] *[The outcome of this analysis is not indicated in the Watauga County Sheriff's Office investigation file, but presumably did not result in any concrete connections with the Durham Case.]*

On August 22, 1972, Burleson and Agents Chambers and Parker met with Jerry Roberts of Weaverville, North Carolina. On December 9, 1971 (approximately two months before the Durham murders), Roberts' trailer had been broken into, and several guns were stolen. One of these was a rifle, which Roberts carried with a sling made from a white, nylon rope about five feet long. The rope had been taken along with the guns. Dean Chandler had admitted to Burleson in January 1972 that he, Jerry Cassada, and Eugene Garren broke into Roberts' trailer and took these guns. Roberts was shown the rope found around Bryce Durham's neck, but he could not identify it as being the same rope he used as a sling for his rifle. Roberts and Burleson agreed to try and find another piece of Roberts' rope for comparison in a lab.[1182]

When Burleson next saw Anne Chandler on August 28, 1972, she said she had received a letter from Dean affirming he was sticking with his original story until after the September 18 trial. Dean asked her to come to Boone until the trial was over. She did not think that to be a good idea, although she did plan to visit him on September 5 and would continue to try to get him to change his mind about telling the real story.[1183]

On September 2, 1972, while Bryce Durham's brother Bill and brother-in-law Charles Mauldin were in Boone, they witnessed a white, blonde female in her early twenties enter the jail to visit Dean Chandler. When Bryce's sister, Gayle Mauldin, followed up on this with Sheriff Ward Carroll, Carroll told her the young woman was Cheryl Mullikin, a friend of Anne Chandler's from Michigan. The Mauldins reported these details to Burleson, who then questioned Anne about Mullikin. Anne seemed surprised when the name Cheryl was brought up. She said Cheryl's surname was "Mullins," and that Dean and another man had picked her up in December 1971 when she was hitchhiking, and that Cheryl and Dean subsequently lived together for a while in an Asheville trailer park.[1184] After the Durham murders and Chandler's incarceration, Mullikin frequented the City Café in Wilkes County where she phoned Chandler daily at noon. Troy Hall's father was also a frequent patron of the café and reportedly sat with young girls there.[1185]

As a seventeen-year-old, Cheryl Ann Mullikin (sometimes reported as "Milliken") and fifteen-year-old Tonya Rose Fisher had run away from their Shepherd, Michigan homes and were hitchhiking to Florida. After about eight days, they arrived in North Carolina, where they were arrested for prostitution in Statesville in December 1971, less than two months prior to the Durham murders.

Also arrested were two Mitchell College students – James Kenneth Leitch[mmmm] and Samuel Jones Thomas III – who were charged with "operating a bawdyhouse" at the residence the men shared. When officers arrived there following a call from the college "that something 'out of the ordinary' was going on at the house," they discovered the residence filled with around twenty-five young men, two of whom were engaged in sexual intercourse with Mullikin and Fisher. The young women stated they had an agreement "about monetary reimbursement" with the boys who were running the house. Mullikin, Fisher, Leitch, and Thomas were incarcerated.[1186] Days later, at a district court hearing, the charges against Mullikin, Leitch, and Thomas were dismissed.[1187] Soon after, Mullikin evidently became involved with Dean Chandler, and she left Asheville in February 1972. Anne Chandler told Burleson that Mullikin had gone to Boone for Dean's trial and was prepared to testify on his behalf that he was with her on the night of the Durham murders. She added that Mullikin was staying in a motel and daily visiting Dean in jail. Anne also shared with Burleson she now remembered that, on the night of the murders, she [Anne] was in Dean's rental trailer in Asheville. She also stated she was presently being followed everywhere she went by an unknown person, and Dean did not want Burleson coming around her anymore. Anne concluded their conversation by telling Burleson she would call him if she needed him, and she would be present at Dean's trial. She also told Burleson that Ellen Shelton – the teenaged girl who had been arrested with Chandler in April 1972, only a about a week before he was charged with the Durham murders, had turned state's evidence against him.[1188]

Ellen Plemmons Shelton was the daughter of Jay and Jan Plemmons, who owned Jay and Jan's Restaurant in Asheville. The restaurant was open 24/7, and Shelton worked there as a waitress. After all the local bars and nightclubs closed around 2:00 AM, patrons would congregate at the restaurant in large numbers. Shelton told SBI Agent John Parker she had often seen Dean Chandler, Jerry Cassada, and Eugene Garren together in her parents' restaurant, and although she knew that Dewey Coffey (who she described as a well-mannered, quiet loner) knew all three of those men, she could not recall seeing him with them. She said Chandler was usually at the restaurant in the mornings with his wife and in the evenings with his girlfriend, and he and Cassada were normally together. Shelton stated Garren, like Coffey, was well-mannered, whereas Chandler would "fly mad real quick." She said Cassada was mean and had once used a chain to attack a man in the restaurant's parking lot. Shelton knew of two meetings these men had with Troy Hall in January 1972, during one of which $500 was passed around, and Shelton's parents said they saw Troy come into their establishment about a week before the murders. *[More than fifty years later, however, Shelton had no recollection of seeing, meeting, or knowing Troy Hall or of his presence in the restaurant.]*[1189]

Shelton worked the restaurant's graveyard shift and normally finished around 11:30 PM or 12:00 AM, although she sometimes hung around afterwards and chatted with her fellow employees. February 3, 1972 was a friend's birthday as well as a snowy night, so a group had stayed late at the restaurant. According to Mr. and Mrs. Plemmons, around midnight on February 4 (which would have been just hours after the murders in Boone), Cassada, Chandler, Garren, and Coffey came into their restaurant, and Cassada's pants were wet, and his sleeves were wet up to his elbows. The men claimed their car had slidden off the road in the snow and offered that as an explanation for the wet clothing. *[This was contrary to Chandler's story, which stated it was Coffey's clothing that was wet*

[mmmm] James Kenneth Leitch was later a political science major at Appalachian State University in Boone, NC (as was Troy Hall) and graduated there in 1973. [Sources: "Morrison-Leitch Nuptials Said In Afternoon Ceremony Today," *Statesville Record and Landmark*, Statesville, NC, September 1, 1973, p. 7-A; James K. Leitch Facebook page, https://www.facebook.com/jkleitch/about_overview.]

and that Cassada did not enter the restaurant following their return to Asheville that night. Shelton only remembered Chandler, Garren, and Coffey being together and that Cassada and Chandler's wife and girlfriend were absent. Shelton could not recall for sure, but she did not believe Coffey appeared to be wet that night.] Either that same night or the following night, Chandler sold some items to Jay Plemmons, including a sword and a piggy bank in the shape of an antique car that was branded with the name of Bryce Durham's car dealership. Guns were also offered, but Mr. Plemmons declined to purchase them as he did not like or collect them. When Mr. Plemmons and his wife subsequently learned of the murders in Boone, they immediately contacted the Asheville Police Department and turned these items over to them.[1190nnnn]

Although they were completely willing to cooperate with authorities, Mr. and Mrs. Plemmons were very nervous and feared for their daughter's life because of certain individuals in Asheville. Ellen Shelton reportedly never went anywhere by herself – not because she feared the "Asheville gang" (which consisted of people she was familiar with) but the "Wilkes County gang," (which consisted of people unknown to her). Despite her and her parents' belief that Dean Chandler and his associates had killed the Durhams, Shelton was in the company of Chandler two months after the murders when she was arrested alongside him in April 1972 on other charges. *[Reflecting on that many decades later, she attributed her keeping company with Chandler to being a wild teenager who apparently did not care he was a potential murderer.]* Following Chandler's arrest in the Durham Case, Shelton visited him on one occasion at the jail in Boone. She had even ridden once with Chandler and other Asheville associates and knew these guys were primarily engaged in theft. Based on her observations and understanding, they typically went to totally empty houses, entered through back doors, stole mostly guns and coins, and then departed. Shelton was willing to provide more information once more arrests had been made, and she stated that, once everything was over, she could find the gun with a 5½" barrel that Chandler used in the Durham house. Although she never actually saw the gun and had never previously known Chandler to carry a gun, she heard things while waiting tables at the restaurant and understood it was hidden in a wall in the basement of her parents' restaurant, behind a chest-type freezer. As an aside, Shelton did not believe Cecil Small had taken part in the murders but was a victim of circumstance. According to her, among the rumors circulating at the time were that Bobby Durham's head had, at one point during the attack, been placed in the commode, that Dewey Coffey had thrown up after the murders, and that the killers were unable to locate the money they were searching for in the Durham home – hundreds of thousands of dollars supposedly sewn inside the bottom of Bryce Durham's den chair.[1191]

Meanwhile, Gray Burleson told the extended Durham family to be patient, that some people from Wilkes County would soon be locked up. He also stated his belief Dewey Coffey did participate in the murders and claimed to have a witness that could tear Coffey's alibi all to pieces, but he also said a man who looked like Coffey – Richard Penley – had been with Dean Chandler to Michigan, where Chandler's cousin, Clarence Chandler, had lived in addition to Dean's former girlfriend Cheryl Mullikin. It was suspected Clarence may have participated in the murders, but that Dean would never implicate his kin.[1192oooo] In late February 1972, an informant had reported to the Captain

[nnnn] As of 2022, neither the Asheville Police Department nor the Buncombe County Sheriff's Office had a sword or antique car bank or record of either item in their files. [Sources: Sarver, Aaron (Public Information Officer, Buncombe County Sheriff's Office, Asheville, NC). E-mail to author. December 4, 2022. Zack, David J. (Chief of Police, City of Asheville Police Department). E-mail to author. October 24, 2022.]

[oooo] Although Dean Chandler and Clarence Chandler shared the same surname and apparently knew one another, the author's genealogical research finds no familial relationship between the two.

of Detectives at the Asheville Police Department overhearing a conversation between Penley and a man named Robert Earl Lee in which they talked about committing the Boone murders.[1193]

There was other talk of Troy Hall in connection with Asheville. Some believed he was acquainted with Cassada, Chandler, Garren, and Coffey via a shared involvement with stolen goods. A neighbor of Anne Chandler's was willing to swear she had seen Troy at Anne's apartment more than once, driving a small white car (Troy drove a small, white Oldsmobile at that time). Gray Burleson believed that a couple driving a 1970 or 1971 white Cadillac, who had been spotted going into Anne's apartment to see her, were Troy and Ginny Hall, and Ginny's family provided Burleson with a large picture of her to see if she could be identified.[1194]

On September 18, 1972, District Solicitor Clyde Roberts presented the cases of Cassada and Chandler to a grand jury at the Watauga County Superior Court. Witnesses called to testify in Cassada's case – and also Chandler's case, with the exception of his wife – were:

- Watauga County Sheriff Ward Carroll[1195]
- Charlie Whitman of the SBI in Lenoir[1196]
- Mrs. Dean (Anne) Chandler of Asheville[1197]
- Wallace E. Hardwick, Jr. of the SBI in Boone

The grand jury was comprised of Harold Edmisten (foreman), eight carryover members from the previous term, and nine newly appointed members.[1198] Thirty-one-year-old Edmisten had never previously served on a jury, and when he wound up as foreman and was tasked with getting the other jurors to work together, he found it to be "a madhouse" and "stressful to no end." This was also the first service for twenty-three-year-old jury member Sherry Reese, a married mother of two, who was "scared to death" and found the experience terrifying, wondering if the killers might also come after the jury. Although the jurors were allowed to go home each night, they were instructed not to discuss the case with anyone. Edmisten left each day with a terrible headache, and by the time the jury was released altogether, he was "totally whipped." The jury members were sequestered in the jury room for two to three days and, while they were shown photographs, including ones of the Durhams' bodies in the bathtub, they were not involved with any of the courtroom activities, nor did they hear individual witness testimonies. Rather, information was relayed to Edmisten to present to the jury for consideration, but he found it nearly impossible to achieve anything because they were not provided sufficient information to make a decision.[1199]

In the end, however, before Judge Sam J. Ervin III, the jury[1200] issued three true bills of indictment each for Cassada and Chandler.[1201] Both were indicted for first-degree murder, whereas in April, Chandler had only been charged with being an accessory before the fact of murder.[1202] No explanation was given for the change in the charges against him.[1203] Later in September, Chandler stood trial in Madison County and pleaded guilty to breaking and entering and larceny as well as possession of stolen goods in connection with a February 5 break-in and robbery. He was sentenced to two eight-to-ten-year sentences to be served concurrently with the other state and federal sentences that had already been set. Cassada had similarly been charged with three counts of breaking and entering and larceny of homes in Madison County, but the same day Chandler was convicted, District Solicitor Clyde Roberts recommended the Madison County charges against Cassada be nol prossed with leave. Roberts' reasoning was not reported.[1204] In October 1972, sureties from Buncombe County posted Cassada's bond in the amount of $15,000 on the condition that Cassada would appear before the Watauga County Superior Court in Boone on January 15, 1973 to answer the charge of three counts of murder.[1205]

By late December 1972, with her husband in federal prison in Tallahassee, Florida,[1206] Anne Chandler had disappeared or otherwise gone into hiding, perhaps in Asheville. Some believed she may also have gone to Florida with her children and a "black-headed boy," leaving behind her car and all their clothing. Anne's mother, Lucy Sutton, who feared Anne would be killed, told Gray Burleson she would try to locate her and persuade her to tell everything she knew. Mrs. Sutton had heard conversations between Anne and others and said she knew Anne was "right in there."[1207]

By this time, Gray Burleson and Clyde Roberts felt "things [were] beginning to happen, and Burleson was inclined to believe two cars were used in conjunction with the murders – a white Ford or Chrysler Plymouth that sat at the bottom of the Durhams' driveway with three people, one of whom was Anne Chandler, and possibly Jerry Cassada's red car. In exchange for her testimony, Roberts was willing to seek immunity for Anne from a judge. Instead, it seems Anne was sent to prison on a federal probation charge.[1208]

In January 1973, Bryce Durham's parents, Coy and Collie Durham, apparently explored the possibility of filing a civil suit against Troy Hall, but Gray Burleson believed it would prove unfruitful.[1209]

At the one-year mark of the murders in February 1973, the *Watauga Democrat* reported citizens had been reminded of the crime, which had not been "completely solved." Detective Jerry Vaughn, of the Watauga County Sheriff's Department, stated the Durham Case was by "no means closed and that the extensive investigation [was] still continuing."[1210]

By May 1973, Dean Chandler was still serving his federal sentence in Florida for forgery, mail theft, and auto theft, and would not be eligible for parole until June 30, 1974. If not paroled, he would be eligible for release July 8, 1976; if he served his full term, he would be released October 31, 1977. Meanwhile, Cassada had remained free on bond[1211] until he was jailed in Asheville following a misdemeanor conviction.[1212]

The weekend of June 2-3, 1973, Chandler, having filed a motion in February for a speedy trial,[1213] was returned to Boone to go on trial for the Durham murders.[1214] Following correspondence and legal agreements between District Solicitor Clyde Roberts and a Florida prison official, temporary custody of Chandler was granted to North Carolina authorities,[1215] and Watauga County Sheriff's Deputies Johnny Carroll and Jerry Farmer[pppp] transported Chandler from Tallahassee to Boone.[1216]

The individuals who were subpoenaed as defense witnesses for Chandler were:

- Clarence Chandler of Marshall, North Carolina[1217]
- Susan Davis of Asheville[1218]
- Terry Hunter of Asheville[1219]
- Edd Biddix of Asheville[1220]
- Deborah Plemmons of Asheville[1221]

[pppp] Johnny Carroll was the son of Sheriff Ward Carroll, and Jerry Farmer was a brother-in-law to SBI Agent Bob Thomas, who helped investigate the Durham Case. [Source: Personal knowledge of author.]

Terry Hunter and Edd Biddix were members of a band at the Hideaway Club in Asheville, which Dean Chandler and Ellen Plemmons Shelton had frequented, and Biddix was a future husband of Shelton. At the time, Deborah "Debbie" Plemmons was married to Shelton's brother and worked as a server at Jay and Jan's Restaurant.[1222] The subpoenas for Clarence Chandler and Susan Davis could not be served because neither could be located despite searches being made for them. According to Sheriff E. Y. Ponder of Madison County, he personally knew Clarence Chandler and knew he had not been seen in that county for the past eight months. Ponder stated he last saw Chandler in March 1973 in Lavonia, Georgia, where Chandler was employed by Thompson Produce and where the Lavonia Police Department would know him.[1223][qqqq]

After "'conferences with law enforcement officers' over the past several weeks had left the state with no grounds on which to try Chandler," the state, on the morning of June 4, 1972,[1224] elected not to prosecute him. District Solicitor Clyde Roberts "told Superior Court Judge B. T. Falls of the decision, asking for a nol pross [sic] with leave, meaning that the case could be reopened at a later time. Roberts told the judge the slayings [were] still under investigation."[1225] Chandler was remanded to federal authorities and returned to Tallahassee to continue serving the sentence he had received for his prior convictions.[1226]

By July 1973, it seemed charges against Cassada would also be dropped. "Authorities [were] generally agreed they did not have the evidence necessary to convict any of the accused. Some…indicated they [felt] the wrong people were arrested in the first place."[1227] Sheriff Ward Carroll concluded that the "prompt arrest" of Chandler, Cassada, Garren, and Coffey may have been a mistake. "I'm not saying flatly that they didn't do it, mind you," Carroll stated, "but frankly, in the light of later developments, we might have done better to keep them under surveillance." Carroll said he was inclined to "'look in another direction' for the guilty party or parties,"[1228] and he emphasized "the case was 'still very much open,' and that the investigation [would] continue, as it [had] continued, without letup."[1229] He planned to hire two additional deputies, adding, "I don't have enough manpower to assign one or two men to the case full time, but when I get the new deputies, I except to put a lot more time on this thing. It's a bad case." Investigative emphasis had "shifted away" from and beyond the four men, but District Solicitor Roberts "declined to disclose in what direction the investigation" was headed other than to say, "some of the impressions formed earlier have now changed."[1230]

Cecil Small said a fellow private detective in Asheville called him and said, "Y'all may think you got the right boys, but you don't. They're mean as hell, but they're charged with misdemeanor[s] and stuff like that, but that's all."[1231] Sheriff Carroll, however, returned to his prior belief in the guilt of the four men. He defended the charges and felt the Chandlers' statements gave officers plenty of grounds for the arrest warrants. Carroll stated, "We know how and when they went up and came off the hill, but we can't offer identification by anyone that will place the men in the house." Carroll said they needed more evidence and again stated his intention to hire two additional deputies to help continue working on the case.[1232] Carroll seemed put out that the case against the Asheville suspects was going south, and he lashed out at a reporter: "This don't concern you or the newspapers. You

---

[qqqq] Ponder erroneously referred to Clarence Chandler as "Charles" Chandler. In 2022, the Lavonia Police Department stated they had no record of Clarence Chandler. [Sources: Watauga County, NC Clerk of Court's Office, Criminal Files #72-CR-1078, -1079, -1080, State vs. Dean Chandler, Subpoena, May 17, 1973; Lavonia Police Department. Facebook message to author. September 2, 2022.]

out-of-town reporters have hampered our investigation. And if you give me any trouble, I'll lock you up."[1233]

Unlike Carroll, Boone Police Sergeant Arlie Isaacs and Watauga County Sheriff's Deputy Jerry Vaughn did not believe the Asheville suspects were involved in the murders or had even been to Boone and felt there were too many holes in their story. Still, they did not say much to Carroll about their misgivings, and Vaughn was not about to disagree with his boss. Rather, they wondered if Carroll had more information or evidence than they were aware of, and they waited to see how things would unfold. Vaughn personally believed these suspects had been a long-standing pain in Sheriff E. Y. Ponder's neck in terms of break-ins in his jurisdiction, and Ponder, eager to have them put away, saw the Durham murders as an avenue by which to accomplish that. Vaughn also felt Carroll was eager to solve the Durham Case and was unduly persuaded by Ponder that the Asheville men were the culprits.[1234]

Meanwhile, "the SBI had never confined its probe to the four accused men,"[1235] and this turn of events also revealed "a strained relationship between the SBI and the sheriffs involved" in the pursuit of the Asheville suspects. One of the sheriffs bitterly complained off the record that "the SBI had sabotaged their case by giving some of the results of its investigation to defense attorneys." Jerry Cassada's lawyer, Charles Lamm, Jr. "recalled that he did get help from the SBI in preparing Cassada's defense. 'If I had a question, they'd answer.' But [SBI Director Charles] Dunn [said] there [was] 'no evidence' that the SBI cooperated more with Lamm than with any other defense attorneys." Additionally, "Dunn neither confirmed nor denied a report from a very high source in the state government that the SBI had been almost ready to make a different arrest when the sheriffs arrested the four Asheville men." Dunn called the Durham Case "the most intensive crime investigation in North Carolina history," [and stated] the SBI [was] still alert to any new leads about the case, but there [were] no agents working on it [at that time.]"[1236] Similar to the SBI, Virginia Durham's siblings and extended family thought Sheriff Carroll had jumped the gun in arresting the Asheville suspects.[1237]

In November 1973, Gray Burleson reported to the Durham family that the SBI was investigating another angle that might tie into the case. He also said he wanted to coordinate with them and see if any new leads might match up. Burleson stated that District Solicitor Clyde Roberts did not want to lose the case on a technical error, and he hoped an arrest would be made by December 1, although he did not indicate who might be arrested.[1238]

In January 1974, in a sparsely attended proceeding that "took less than two minutes,"[1239] the state officially dropped its case against Jerry Cassada, District Solicitor Roberts stating that "two years of investigation had not produced sufficient evidence to bring the case to trial." Watauga Superior Court Judge J. W. Jackson granted Roberts' motion for a nol pros with leave, "meaning that the case could be reopened at a later date."[1240] Like Chandler, Cassada had filed for a speedy trial. In Cassada's case, which would also have been true for Chandler's, Roberts said he had no choice but to bring the case to trial or to take a nol pros with leave.[1241] *[Another account, however, erroneously stated that filing a motion for a speedy hearing was not available to Cassada because he was free on bond, "while Chandler was in federal prison in Florida, and the pending murder charge curtailed his (recreational and educational) privileges there."[1242]]* Sheriff Carroll vowed to continue the investigation "for the next ten years if we're still in business."[1243] Later, Carroll, a staunch Democrat, implied the dropped charges were politically motivated, the result of a Republican prosecutor.[1244]

In September 1974, Jerry Cassada, during an approximately two-and-a-half-hour interview at his home in Asheville with Boone Police Chief Clyde Tester and Captain Arlie Isaacs, stated he did not know Troy Hall or the Durham family, and he had no part in the Durhams' murders. He said Sheriff E. Y. Ponder had Dean Chandler make up the story placing him [Cassada] in Boone, and Dean and Anne Chandler never told the truth and only wanted the reward money. Cassada offered to help any way he could to clear his name, even if it meant returning to Boone or taking another lie detector test. On the same day as Cassada's interview, Captain Isaacs also spoke with Eugene Garren about two blocks from Cassada's residence, and Garren stated much the same as Cassada had.[1245]

In October 1974, Dean Chandler spoke with Captain Isaacs, telling him Sheriff Ponder and Sheriff Tom Morrissey told him they knew Jerry Cassada, Eugene Garren, and Dewey Coffey killed the Durhams, and they needed a statement from someone in order to charge them with the murders. Chandler said Ponder and Morrissey offered him immunity and the reward money and said they would break one of the three men after the arrests. According to Chandler, Ponder and Morrissey then told him the story of what happened and took him to the Durham house in Boone, although "they had to ask someone where it was before they could find it." Chandler said he went along and told the story, making believe Cassada, Garren, and Coffey were the murderers. Chandler said he could not change his story for fear of being tried for a false report, but everything he told Sheriff Ward Carroll had been provided to him [Chandler] and was false. Chandler stated he never saw Troy or Ginny Hall or the Durhams, he knew nothing about the murders, and he, Cassada, Garren, and Coffey had nothing to do with them.[1246] Four months later, in February 1975, Isaacs told Chandler that if he [Chandler] knew anything about the Durham murders, he [Isaacs] would take him to see the North Carolina Attorney General and assure his immunity so he could get the reward money. Chandler, who was not in jail at that time, admitted he would like to have the money, and if authorities wanted him to tell more lies, he could do so, but he did not have any knowledge of the murders. Chandler stated, as before, that the story had been supplied to him and he simply retold it because he had been facing twenty years in prison and saw the story as a way out. Chandler expressed his willingness to take a lie detector test or anything else authorities wanted if it would help, but he told Isaacs, "You will never solve it until you forget the story I have told."[1247]

Court-appointed attorney Robert Lacey reflected on his representation of Dean Chandler: "He started to tell me something about a murder one time *[Lacey did not indicate whether this concerned the Durham murders or if he even knew]*, and I stopped him. I said I don't want to know that. I'm not going to let you tell me that because I know that the state doesn't have enough evidence to cause you any problems, and I don't want to go to my grave having to hold that secret. And I stopped him, and I don't know now what he wanted to tell me. I justify that by knowing that he was a psychopathic liar in the first place. So, whatever he told me might or might not have been true, but I didn't have to carry the burden anyway."[1248][rrrr]

In 1976, Eugene Garren was arrested in Asheville for possession of heroin with intent to sell.[1249] By 1977, Dean and Anne Chandler were divorced, and Anne remarried that year.[1250][ssss]

As late as March 1978, Sheriff Ward Carroll still believed there was a connection between the Asheville suspects and the murders. By that time, the Boone Police Department and North Carolina

---

[rrrr] Dean Chandler was reportedly highly intelligent and "the kind of crazy" that got away with things because he was so smart. [Source: Chandler, Sean and anonymous. Text messages to author. March 4, 2024.]

[ssss] Anne Chandler died in 2014 at the age of 65 in Asheville, NC "following a long battle with cancer." [Source: https://www.grocefuneralhome.com/obits/elizabeth-anne-brocklesby/.]

Attorney General Rufus Edmisten believed the information leading to the men's arrest "was simply jailhouse talk." According to Edmisten, "They thought they had their people, and that was just total bunk. Those people were finally released, and it was then back to zero again."[1251] Carroll appeared to be "the only investigator…still [looking] to the Asheville area for a break in the case."[1252] In later years, forensic psychologist Richard Walter (who once briefly worked on the case) stated that, in light of the release of the Asheville suspects, he "would argue that the system worked [because] innocent men were not prosecuted."[1253]

In April 1982, Baxter Bryce Prevette,[1254] of the Roaring River community in Wilkes County, was arrested "in connection with the alleged manufacture of illegal drugs worth millions of dollars in at least five laboratories in the county."[1255][tttt] Prevette was a nephew of E. J. Durham, Sr., who had brought clairvoyant M. B. Dykshoorn to Boone following the murders and had contributed heavily to the reward fund. Prevette had been named for his second cousin, Baxter Bryce Durham, and like his cousin, he went by the name Bryce. While Bryce Prevette was in prison for drug charges, he met a man named Baxter Dula, Jr., from Lenoir, North Carolina,[1256] who was in prison for the 1980 murder of a furniture worker.[1257] Dula claimed a man named Bobby Cassada told him he had helped murder the Durhams, and Dula told that to Prevette, who, in turn, informed Bryce Durham's sister, Gayle Mauldin. At Prevette's request, Mauldin contacted SBI Agent Steve Cabe to speak with Prevette.[1258] It is unclear if or how Bobby Cassada may have been related to Jerry Cassada, or if Dula was referring to Jerry Cassada by the wrong first name.

In 1989, local citizen John Paul Brown told the Watauga County Sheriff's Department that, on the night of the Durham murders, February 3, 1972, he was in the lobby of the Daniel Boone Hotel in downtown Boone. At that time, Brown was teaching school at West Wilkes High School at Millers Creek in Wilkes County. He was either just divorced or in the process of divorcing and was temporarily living at the hotel. Around 10:45 PM, as he sat in the lobby waiting to watch the 11:00 PM news, the front door opened, and a large, clean-shaven man, about 6'2" and 220-225 pounds with brown hair,[uuuu] a flat-top haircut and wearing an Eisenhower military jacket and dark, army green, wool slacks with a windbreaker draped over his arm walked in. The man came and sat beside Brown on a couch and said, "It's a lot colder here than it is in Statesville." Brown took this to mean the man had perhaps just arrived in Boone from there. The man's face was flushed, and he smelled heavily of alcohol. He pulled out a half-empty pint bottle and offered Brown a drink. Brown declined, after which the man went to the desk to register for a room. Meanwhile, Brown moved from the couch to a single seat closer to the television. When the man returned, he chose a single seat close to Brown and asked if he was going to watch television. Brown said yes, and the man

---

[tttt] Bryce Prevette and his brother Leo were among sixteen men indicted for "involvement in a Wilkes County drug conspiracy believed to be responsible for producing and distributing illegal drugs [specifically methaqualone] worth millions of dollars nationwide." In 1993, seventeen people were indicted for more than fifty offenses "in connection with an alleged drug [specifically cocaine and marijuana] distribution ring in Guilford County," NC. Twelve of these seventeen were members of this Prevette family – all Durham cousins – including Bryce Prevette, one of his sons, his brothers Alfred, Carlyle, and Leo, six of Carlyle's children, and a son-in-law of Carlyle. [Sources: Kenneth Haynes. "16 Indicted Anew in Far-Reaching Drug Case," *Winston-Salem Journal*, April 14, 1982, p. 13; "Drug-Charge Indictments," *News & Record*, Greensboro, NC, July 7, 1993 (updated January 25, 2015) (online), https://greensboro.com/drug-charge-indictments/article_cecaebb9-0bbb-5fd2-9e6e-bc423386a26d.html; "Drug-Charge Indictments," *News and Record*, Greensboro, NC, July 8, 1993, p. B4B; "Family drug bust in High Point," *Asheville Citizen-Times*, Asheville, NC, July 9, 1993, p. 2B; https://findagrave.com/memorial/220137578/carlyle-prevette.]

[uuuu] Although Jerry Cassada had brown hair, he was 5'8" tall and weighed 170 pounds. [Source: Watauga County Sheriff's Office investigation file 118-H-1/2/3.]

indicated he would watch it with him, but the man then got up and said he would be right back. The man went to use the pay phone inside the hotel, at which point Brown arose and retired to his room, hoping to avoid any further interaction with the man. The following morning, Brown drove to Wilkes to teach, and that afternoon, as he and two fellow teachers traveled together back to Boone, the Durham murders came up in conversation. This was the first Brown had heard of the murders, although he knew of the Durhams from having been in their dealership when looking to purchase a car, and he had specifically dealt with Virginia. Bryce had gone to college with Brown's sister, and Brown had seen Bobby on the golf course. After learning of the murders, Brown concluded the man he had encountered at the hotel the night before may have been involved. He reported his hunch to Sheriff Ward Carroll and suggested he follow up on it. When that did not happen, Brown communicated with SBI District Supervisor Red Minter, but as far as Brown knew, no one ever pursued the matter. Clarence Price and his wife Billie, who managed the hotel, did not believe the man was involved or would do something like that, telling Brown the man had previously been a guest there and had confided in them about his domestic problems. Brown believed the Prices were mistaking the man for someone else. About a month later, when Jerry Cassada's picture was published in a newspaper following his arrest for the Durham murders, Brown saw it and was absolutely, positively convinced Cassada was the man from the hotel lobby.[1259]

Sometime later, Brown had a carpenter working for him by the name of Sonny Burkins, from Baltimore, Maryland, who had spent some time in a penitentiary, possibly in Baltimore and possibly for murder. Burkins was arrested for drunk driving and jailed at Boone. By this time, Dean Chandler had also been placed in the Boone jail and shared a cell with Burkins. Brown, while visiting Burkins on two or three occasions, encountered Chandler and spoke with him quite a bit. Chandler admitted he had been charged with the Durham murders. Burkins told Brown that Chandler told him Cassada received $50,000 for killing all three Durhams, and Chandler received $35,000 for his role. Afterwards, Cassada and Chandler met somewhere and had a bad argument, almost getting into a fight, and Chandler then drove straight to Asheville in a souped-up 1970 Pontiac.[1260]

While Brown believed he saw Cassada at the hotel on the night of the murders, another similar sighting was reported. According to the Durhams' neighbor, Clinard Wilson, the photographer who had been at the Durham house (presumably George Flowers) told him that, the day after the murders, a stranger had come into his photography shop in Boone. The man did not purchase anything but only looked around. When Jerry Cassada's photograph was published in the newspaper, the photographer said he was the same man who had been in his shop.[1261]

Another identity comparison was made between Cassada and a young man who was reportedly a friend of Troy Hall's, although some have discounted any depth of relationship between them. Tim Moore was from Wilkes County, the son of a furniture manufacturer, and lived in the affluent Finley Park community across from Troy's friend "Babes" Lowe. In November 1972, nine months after the Durham murders, twenty-three-year-old Moore, "a collector of swords and knives," died of hemorrhagic shock following a stab wound to the right side of his groin. He had been cleaning a samurai sword and accidentally cut himself, severing the femoral artery. The incident occurred at his trailer home on Highway 194 near the Sands community of Watauga County around 11:15 PM, and Moore "attempted to drive himself to the Watauga County Hospital but passed out. A woman with him drove him to a nearby service station. An attendant at the station drove Moore on to the hospital," where Moore died.[1262] The night of his death, "two boys" were seen leaving the trailer, and Troy later commented that "he had hold of that 'knife' about two weeks before this."[1263] When Moore died, Watauga County Sheriff's Deputy Jerry Vaughn was amazed at the near identical resemblance Moore bore to Jerry Cassada.[1264] Moore's death was jointly investigated by the Watauga County Sheriff's Department and the State Bureau of Investigation, and an autopsy was performed.[1265]

Additionally in 1989, Jerry Cassada and Dean Chandler, resurfaced when an inmate at the Women's Prison in Raleigh, North Carolina reported another woman had seen the two men walking around Asheville, bragging about killing someone and talking about the murders in Boone.[1266] In June of that year, mention of these men reoccurred when Roy Dale Cornell, whose uncle, Jerry Cornell, lived near the Durhams' house at the time of the murders, stated that, around March 1972, he had been in the bullpen on the third floor of the Caldwell County jail with Dean Chandler, Jerry Cassada, and Eugene Garren. Cornell was being sent back to prison for a parole violation and breaking and entering, and the three men were being held, charged with the Durham murders. Cornell stated the men were bragging about the murders and how they were going to get away with it. According to Cornell, the men talked about how they choked the Durhams and placed them in the bathtub. The "big guy" among the three said there was supposed to be money in the house, but they did not get all they were supposed to. Cornell believed this encounter to have occurred after the trio had had their probable cause hearing, but that did not transpire until June 1972.[1267] Also, Chandler was never held in the Caldwell County jail with Cassada and Garren, although Dewey Coffey was. At 6'2" and 295 pounds,[1268] Coffey was the largest of the three, so perhaps Cornell's mention of the "big guy" was a reference to Coffey.

Following his release in the Durham Case, Jerry Cassada went on to retire from the International Paper Company, and eventually moved to Pomaria, South Carolina where he faced a charge of assault and battery with intent to kill in 1979, and where he died in 2003.[1269] Eugene Garren resumed life in the Asheville area, worked for the city's water department, and died in Black Mountain, North Carolina in 2006.[1270] Dean Chandler died in Arkansas in 2008,[1271] and Dewey Coffey, having moved to Alexandria, Virginia and worked for the Architect of the United States Capitol in Washington, D. C., died in 2010.[1272] None of the "Asheville boys" lived past the age of sixty.

CHAPTER 11

REDIRECT

At the time of the Durham murders, Boone native Rufus Edmisten was living in Washington, D. C. and working for United States Senator Sam J. Ervin, Jr. from North Carolina.[1273] Despite the fact Edmisten had been away for a number of years, he subscribed to his hometown newspaper, the *Watauga Democrat*. When he saw the February 1972 headlines announcing the Durhams' horrible demise, he picked up the phone and called Boone Police Chief Clyde Tester to find out more details.[1274] He also phoned Watauga County Sheriff Ward Carroll, who, referring to the magnitude of the case, told Edmisten, "We got us a big 'un."[1275]

The case was, indeed, a big one – so big that, when the accused men from the Asheville, North Carolina area were released due to insufficient evidence and the case against them crumbled, the disappointment felt by the Watauga County Sheriff's Department was equally mammoth. Although "the anxiety that developed in the Boone area immediately after the murders [had] dissipated considerably…there [was] still a deep interest in seeing that the guilty persons [were] convicted and punished."[1276] But there seemed to be few other leads to pursue, and the investigation began to wane.

In June 1973, Sheriff Carroll had stated his intention to soon hire two additional deputies to "intensify his department's investigation into the killings,"[1277] but on September 5, 1974, due to an ongoing staff shortage and at a loss of where to turn after his firmly held Asheville theory failed to materialize, he turned the investigation of the Durham Case and all interviews over to Boone Police Captain Arlie Isaacs,[1278] who had joined the department in 1969. Isaacs was a smart law enforcement officer, was good at his job, and had good instincts.[1279] Several months after the murders, he completed hundreds of classroom hours in the areas of laws of arrest, narcotics, criminal investigation, and police public relations.[1280][vvvv]

Boone Police Department Captain Arlie Isaacs (Courtesy of the Isaacs Family)

Meanwhile, SBI Agent Charlie Chambers passed his agency's mantle in the case to Agent Larry Wagner,[1281] who grew up in Surry County,

[vvvv] In November 1974, the local Jaycees presented Arlie Isaacs with the Outstanding Young Law Enforcement Officer award at their meeting at which newly elected North Carolina Attorney General Rufus Edmisten was the keynote speaker. [Source: "Gets Jaycee Lawman Award," *Watauga Democrat*, Boone, NC, November 28, 1974, p. 1.]

North Carolina – former home of the Durhams – and served as a North Carolina Highway Patrolman prior to joining the bureau in 1974. Wagner was sent that same year to Boone, where the Durham Case became part of his portfolio until his reassignment in 1977. Wagner worked closely with Isaacs and Len D. "L. D." Hagaman, Jr. (future Watauga County Sheriff), who became a Boone policeman in 1976. Hagaman was serving in the U. S. Army when he, like Rufus Edmisten, read about the Durham murders in their hometown newspaper. The trio of Wagner, Isaacs, and Hagaman handled the bulk of the investigation and interviewed numerous individuals. Isaacs devoted many long hours to the case, even at home outside of office hours. On occasion, he would receive a suppertime phone call from Bryce Durham's mother, Mrs. Collie Durham, to see if he had any new leads.[1282]

Meanwhile, Troy and Ginny Hall did not initially return to school following the murders[1283] and, by April 1972, had moved to the Mulberry community of Wilkes County.[1284] Troy's brother Claude sent their brother-in-law, Bob Gryder (husband of their sister Dorothy), to move Troy's and Ginny's trailer from Boone to Gryder's yard.[1285] Claude went to Boone himself to retrieve Troy's inoperable Ford Thunderbird. Cecil Small had tried unsuccessfully to charge the battery, but with "fire jumping all over the distributor," he felt the distributor cap was cracked or busted and that parts might be needed, so Claude hooked a chain to the car and pulled it away.[1286] Something undisclosed later happened between Troy and Gryder's daughter (Troy's niece), and Gryder told Troy "to move his ass out."[1287] Troy's brothers-in-law hated him, and Ginny did not care for Troy's parents. She felt them to be arrogant and spent no time around them.[1288]

Troy was a controlling person, who would not allow money to be spent unless he believed it was necessary. Always scheming for a dollar,[1289] he went into the real estate and construction business, building houses with his brothers Ray and John. Ray was president of Carolina Construction Company of North Wilkesboro, Inc., and Troy was the secretary.[1290] By July 1973, Troy and Ginny jointly owned five properties, including a new split-level house (not unlike her parents' house in Boone), which they moved into. Their old Thunderbird had been replaced by a bright yellow Camaro,[1291] and Troy drove an orange Porsche with a black convertible top.[1292]

After the settlement of her family's estates, despite the fact Ginny was their sole heir and beneficiary, Troy took control of those assets.[1293] When Ginny gave the deed for her parents' property near Galax, Virginia to her mother's brother, Wayne Church, for safekeeping, Troy almost struck her, but his brother Ray stopped him.[1294] Ginny reportedly deposited the estate proceeds into joint accounts she shared with Troy, and he subsequently withdrew them. In one instance he is said to have redeposited money into a new joint account in his and his father's names.[1295] Troy quickly ran through Ginny's inheritance,[1296] reportedly leaving her penniless[1297] or at least with barely enough money to finish school.[1298] "After Troy started his construction business" and defaulted on a loan, [Ginny] "gained access to the money, and that's how she was able to pay off her school."[1299] Troy allegedly used Ginny's money to expand his construction business,[1300] "build his mama and daddy a big fine house"[1301] as well as a house for one of his brothers,[1302] and fix up his sister Lois's house.[1303]

Like most people, Ted Brown, who had known Troy since their early elementary school days in Wilkes County and later only in passing, learned of the Durham murders the morning after they occurred. About a year after his discharge from the U. S. Army and for about six weeks in the spring of 1974, he took a job mixing brick mortar for a house Troy and Ray were building in northern Wilkes County. According to Brown, Ray was the brick mason, but Troy seemed averse to manual labor. Brown's most telling memory of Troy – a "Kodak moment" as he calls it – was on a particular Friday evening and payday. A tired and sweaty Brown hesitantly mentioned to Troy that he needed to be paid, and Troy asked him to get in the passenger side of his orange Porsche. Sitting behind the wheel, Troy reached behind the seats and retrieved a three-ring binder of company checks. Brown had known for a long time that Troy was a person of interest in the Durham Case, and as Troy prepared to write the paycheck, Brown impetuously commented, "I guess it's really tough being watched by the SBI all the time." Troy paused, lifted the pen from the checkbook, made a swirling motion with it, and stared straight ahead out the windshield. Seemingly deep in thought and oblivious to the grandeur of the setting sun and pink and yellow horizon before him, almost as if he were momentarily transported to a different place, he said to Brown, "It's like playing chess. You have to think three to four moves ahead at all times." He then casually returned his attention to writing the check.[1304]

Another of the Hall brothers' employees, Billy Lee Denny (a black man), who, as of January 1975, had worked for them for two years, noted that, while Ray rarely spoke, Troy was always talking about how to do things and get away with them. According to Denny, Troy once pointed at a boy and commented he would shoot him. When Denny asked why, Troy replied because he could get away with it. Denny stated that Troy frequented the "colored section" of Wilkes County, where he had several black friends, and was "into everything," including drugs and stolen goods. At the time investigators interviewed Denny, he stated that, just within the past two weeks, Troy had trafficked drugs.[1305]

Near one of their work sites, the Hall brothers had house trailers for rent,[1306][wwww] and a witness observed perverse behavior there, particularly when irreputable women would visit the job site and the nearby trailers. Troy also had access to a house on Country Club Road in North Wilkesboro. This same witness knocked on the door of the house, and a naked Troy, in the company of a likewise naked young woman, answered it while continuing to engage in sexual intercourse.[1307] Sex was reportedly central to Troy's ego,[1308] and there were rumors that he, alongside others, made amateur

---

[wwww] One of the Hall brothers' trailer tenants was Jeff Van Meter, whose brother, Wally Van Meter, was married to June Ella Neff, former wife of Ray and Troy Hall's brother John. In 1984, Jeff Van Meter (who was then living in Charlotte, NC) and Jorge Felix Aragon, of Miami, FL, were among seven people indicted "for conspiracy to smuggle large amounts of marijuana and cocaine from South America to Wilkes County." The drugs were imported from Colombia, offloaded in Florida, and driven to North Carolina. The arrests resulted from the FBI's "Wilco" investigation. Both men pleaded guilty and agreed to testify in future drug cases in exchange for reduced sentences. "Van Meter pleaded guilty to tax evasion and intent to distribute more than 1,000 pounds of marijuana, [and] prosecutors recommended he receive a fifteen-year sentence. The government agreed to drop a conspiracy charge against him and to place him in the federal witness protection program." Co-defendants, James Alvin "Mickey" Rhodes and Garvey Martin Cheek, Jr., both of Wilkes County, were charged with multiple instances of possession and distribution of cocaine and marijuana. Troy Hall was a character witness for Rhodes who received a fifty-year sentence without parole. Cheek was sentenced to seventy-five years without parole. [Sources: https://www.findagrave.com/memorial/127106109/jeffrey-dennie-van_meter; North Carolina, U. S. Marriage Records, 1741-2011 for June Ella Neff, Wilkes, Marriage Register (1874-1979), https://www.ancestry.com/discoveryui-content/view/12060136:60548?ssrc=pt&tid=170690419&pid=252392614256; https://www.findagrave.com/memorial/107043303/june-ella-van_meter; Kay Hall, interview with Clyde Tester & Arlie Isaacs, February 15, 1975, Watauga County Sheriff's Office investigation file 118-H-1/2/3; "Trial, sentencing for drug smuggling defendants," UPI Archives, July 19, 1984 (online), https://www.upi.com/Archives/1984/07/19/Trial-sentencing-for-drug-smuggling-defendants/2609459057600/; United States of America, Appellee v. James Alvin Rhodes, a/k/a Mickey Rhodes & Garvey Martin Cheek, Jr., Appellants, U. S. Court of Appeals for the Fourth Circuit, argued March 6, 1985 & decided December 26, 1985, https://law.justia.com/cases/federal/appellate-courts/F2/779/1019/106000/.]

pornographic films, using hidden cameras within this same house to record unwitting female subjects.[1309] This house was likely the same location where Troy reportedly brought a prostitute, invited married men to have sex with her, and then, through two-way mirrors, filmed them for blackmail purposes.[1310] Troy also allegedly made pornographic films to ship to California,[1311] and there were rumors of his watching such films and of homosexual activity. Ginny knew Troy had been unfaithful to her,[1312] that he had a hard time remembering which woman he was with, and that he was evasive with her due to his infidelities.[1313] In early 1974, Troy had a falling out with his friend John Frazier over a girl Frazier was dating, and Troy "cut in" on him.[1314] Troy was thought to be oversexed[1315] and was known to have strange relationships with women, treating them as objects and sexually abusing them with "reckless abandon."[1316] He was too rough,[1317] and he reportedly turned one woman against sex because of his behavior.[1318]

In the summer of 1973, after a fifteen-month absence, Ginny had resumed her studies at Appalachian State University and remained continuously enrolled until she graduated with a Bachelor of Science degree in History in 1974. Although it had been a hardship, she drove from North Wilkesboro to Boone to attend her university classes. Troy was enrolled at ASU from the fall of 1969 until 1975 and falsely claimed to have graduated with degrees in political science and business.[xxxx] For the next three years, he worked alongside his brother in their construction company.[1319]

In September 1974, Boone Police Chief Clyde Tester and Captain Arlie Isaacs went to Wilkes County to interview Ginny and were waiting on her when she arrived home from work. She initially informed them she would not speak with them until Troy arrived home around 8:00 or 9:00 PM, but she went inside and called him and then returned to say she would proceed with the interview. When the officers asked if she knew anyone who had trouble with her parents, she stated that, when they lived in Mount Airy, a man would come to their house, always accompanied by a big man, but she was unsure what they wanted. She said her parents had problems in Boone with parts missing from the dealership, and her father took a man named Dave Miller *[employed as the parts manager at the dealership*[1320]*]* to court over a labor dispute, her father hiring attorney John Bingham.[1321]

Ginny shared that she and her parents got along very well, and she and Troy had Christmas pictures taken with her family. She said she had been in her parents' house on Saturday, January 29, only five days before the murders, and said her brother Bobby was a really quiet boy, and he would frequently play cards on the coffee table. The officers told Ginny about Troy showing people photographs of nude subjects, including himself, in various sexual acts, and that similar pictures were reportedly seen on the walls of their trailer in Boone. Ginny stated she had no knowledge of it. The officers mentioned Bobby having dated a girl a week before the murders *[a reference to Bobby's date and conversation with Jackie Vines]* and telling her he and his parents did not like Troy and things were so bad he could not talk about it. Ginny said she did not know what that would be. She confirmed Bill Overcash[yyyy] and "Babes" Lowe had formerly lived with Troy. She also said Ray Hall and his wife were frequent visitors of theirs in Boone, and Ray and Troy built houses together.[1322]

[xxxx] Troy did not graduate nor receive a degree there. [Source: Pitts, Grace (Appalachian State University Registrar's Office). E-mail to author. March 23, 2022.]

[yyyy] Either Ginny or the reporting officer misstated Charlie Overcash's given name as "Bill." Charlie Overcash was, in fact, Troy's roommate. [Sources: Overcash, Charlie. Phone interview with author. March 19, 2022; Henson, Wayne (friend of Charlie Overcash). Facebook message to author. March 15, 2023.]

By this time, Troy arrived home – some two to three hours earlier than the arrival time Ginny had suggested to the officers. Troy acknowledged knowing both Tester and Isaacs but looked at them as if he could kill them both. He was quite upset and had little to say. When asked several questions about the supposed phone call from his mother-in-law and about what he saw in the Durham house the night of the murders, he stated he would have to look back at his notes to see what he had previously said. Isaacs asked Troy what had caused him to jump back at the den door just prior to him and Cecil Small entering the Durham home. Troy said his brother was twelve years old before he saw a police car, and ever since he [Troy] had been a little boy, their father taught them to always take care of their own problems. This was not an answer to the question Isaacs asked, but when Isaacs repeated it twice more, Troy gave the same answer each time. When the officers asked Troy about the nude photos, he stated he would not call any of the sexual activities depicted in those photos bad unless they involved animals. He added that he did not care what people thought about him, and they could call him a queer or whatever as long as he knew he was not. This was the end of the approximately three-hour interview.[1323]

A week later, Tester and Isaacs returned to the Halls' home and once more awaited Ginny's return from work. Upon seeing the officers, she said, "Looks like you all are going to be here waiting on me every Friday." She seemed nervous and upset. Tester and Isaacs told her they did not want to come in, but they needed to clear up some things concerning her and Troy, and the best way to accomplish that would be with a polygraph test, which they could arrange any time or anywhere. They told her she could discuss this with Troy, and Ginny said they could call back the following Monday evening, and she would let them know. She stated Troy and his brothers knew nothing about the murders.[1324] When the officers called back as instructed, Troy told them he and Ginny would not submit to a polygraph as he had studied polygraph tests and learned they were only about seventy percent accurate.[1325]

Rufus Edmisten (Source: Wikipedia; public domain)

While still in Washington, D. C., Rufus Edmisten had vowed if he ever got back to North Carolina, he would do something about the Durham murders.[1326] At the time, though, he never realized what an important role he would play in the investigation.[1327] In November 1974, he was elected North Carolina Attorney General, a position he held for a decade and from which he oversaw the State Bureau of Investigation and made the Durham Case a top priority.[1328] In January 1975, he stated "he would appoint a special prosecutor for the case if necessary."[1329] Edmisten "had strategy sessions" with Sheriff Ward Carroll and met with Boone Police Chief Clyde Tester,[1330] and he provided the Boone Police Department with investigative files.[1331] He also assigned SBI Agents Larry Wagner and Charlie Whitman[1332] full-time to the case and ensured it was on the SBI's radar for the entire ten years he was attorney general. Additionally, "the SBI would sometimes assign agents with no knowledge of the case and tell them to look at it with fresh eyes."[1333] According to Joe Momier, supervisor of the SBI district office based in Hickory, North Carolina, this rotation of agents had been happening as early as 1972, the year he was employed.[1334] At one point in time, some twenty agents had been assigned to the case.[1335]

In February 1975, Sheriff Carroll, Chief Tester, Captain Isaacs, and Agent Wagner interviewed Troy and Ginny Hall at their home in Wilkes County in the presence of Troy's parents. Troy and Ginny declined to answer any questions previously asked of them or any questions relative to their relationships with the Durhams. Ginny denied ever discussing with her university laundry co-workers anything about her mother wanting to get her fired or changing the locks on the Durham home. Both Troy and Ginny stated they would like to see the murders solved, but again, they would not take polygraph tests.[1336]

In March 1975, after meeting with members of the Durham family in Wilkes County, Rufus Edmisten reviewed all the SBI files regarding their loved ones' murders, and he thought almost nightly about the case. As a result, he "stepped up the [SBI's] probe"[1337] and stated "a new approach [would] be used in the investigation,"[1338] although he "declined to say how the new approach would be different."[1339] Edmisten became convinced the Asheville men did not commit the Durham murders," and he said, "It is our intention to accumulate the evidence and build a case that will stand up in court."[1340] Edmisten met with SBI Director Charles Dunn, asking that "we start over and go back and redo the investigation from the very beginning." He said he would leave it to Dunn's discretion to determine how many agents would be assigned to the case. At one point that year, Agent Steve Cabe, who later served with the Wilkes County Sheriff's Department, was assigned alongside another agent to review the case and follow any new leads. They worked on it for about eight months but came up empty handed.[1341] Although Edmisten conceded the SBI was "unbelievably busy [and] just worked to death," he said, "I find it personally appalling that we have these murderers of innocent people running around loose somewhere, maybe in North Carolina." Haywood Starling, assistant SBI director for investigations confessed that, although the Durham Case had never been closed and that "agents, although busy, [had] worked sporadically on the [case] in recent months…more active cases have had to take precedence." Starling was more cautious than Edmisten about the previous suspects from Asheville and "declined to comment on their guilt or innocence."[1342] Edmisten also promised, as far as legally and practically possible, to guarantee confidentiality, immunity, and physical protection to any witnesses who might offer assistance He "called on the general public to step forward with any information they may have [and stated], 'I will meet anywhere, anytime with anybody who has any information to offer.'"[1343]

Edmisten also asked Governor James E. "Jim" Holshouser, Jr., another Boone native, to increase the state's reward money in the case from $2,500 to $7,500, the maximum allowed by law.[1344] Holshouser declined the request based on his concern that "such an action might appear that he was giving special treatment to his hometown."[1345]

Also, in March 1975, at her apartment in Wilkes County, Boone Police Chief Clyde Tester and Captain Arlie Isaacs interviewed Ray Hall's wife, Kay Hall.[1346] Kay told the officers she and Ginny hated to see the case reopened, and Kay stated she had heard Troy might be planning to put Ginny in a mental institution, after which her [Ginny's] testimony would be no good in court.[1347] Troy had taken out an insurance policy on Ginny, and Ray had taken one out on Kay, with the beneficiaries of the latter policy being Troy and Ray's and Troy's father.[1348]

Two and a half hours later, the same officers interviewed Ray Hall. Nervous and smelling strongly of marijuana, he sat in the backseat of the officers' car with the door open. He stated he knew nothing of the murders and on that night, he and his mother had been working on water pipes at a trailer park. *[In 1972, within hours of the murders, Ray had told his wife Kay to tell officers he had been working that night on a furnace at his mother's. Even that had deviated from the story he told Kay a few hours earlier about his car breaking down and being at a service station in Lenoir.]* Although Ray told the officers he would speak with them any time they came, he said he would not submit his fingerprints unless his parents and brothers would submit theirs. He stated that, maybe after Ginny had a breakdown and was put into a mental institution, everybody would be happy. He asked the officers if they had evidence against Troy and Ginny, why they didn't "arrest them and give them their day in court?"[1349]

In May 1975, Rufus Edmisten, while in Lenoir, North Carolina, stated he was very confident the Durhams' murderers would soon be apprehended,[1350] and by June, he announced the reward money had been boosted to a total of $17,000 through "a collective effort by his office, the Boone Police Department and the Watauga County Sheriff's Department."[1351]

Troy and Ginny Hall separated in late July 1975 after less than four years of marriage, although Ginny had known she "had to get out of there" (i.e., away from Troy and out of their marriage) as early as the day after her family's funeral when she overheard Troy and his brother Ray discussing sending her to a mental hospital. But their conversation had also strengthened her resolve because she did not want Troy to succeed in doing that to her,[1352] and despite her initial impetus to leave him, she was determined to carry on in the interim. In January 1976, Ginny "began proceedings in Wilkes County for a division of property." She claimed she had advanced money to Troy that he promised to pay back but had not. She "sought to have the courts rescind deeds she had signed allowing [Troy] to sell jointly owned properties [and] alleged that funds belonging to her were fraudulently used by [Troy] because her signature was obtained under duress," although neither she nor her attorney elaborated further. In March 1976, after "a drawn-out dispute," Ginny requested "these actions be dismissed on grounds that she and [Troy] had reached a satisfactory property settlement."[1353] The provisions of the settlement included Troy relinquishing all right, title, and interest in Ginny's real property in Virginia, and Troy and his brother Ray agreeing to give Ginny a one-half, undivided interest in three lots of land in West High Acres (a subdivision in Wilkes County) and a one-fourth, undivided interest in a certain lot on new U. S. Highway 421 in the Reddies River Township of Wilkes County. Troy also agreed to endorse notes of certain individuals to Ginny, and to give her an Encyclopedia Britannica set that was in his possession as well as the contents of an old bus parked on Country Club Road in Wilkes County, the "contents being personal property once belonging to her parents" and other items belonging to Ginny. Troy further agreed to transfer to Ginny all proceeds coming to him from the foreclosure sale of West High Acres lots if those proceeds were $1,000 or less; if the proceeds exceeded that amount, Ginny would receive $1,000 plus half of any amounts over $1,000. Troy agreed to convey to Ginny all his right, title, and interest in a sixteen-foot tri-hull boat, trailer, 110 horsepower Chrysler engine, and tape deck that went with the boat. In return for all these things, Ginny agreed to relinquish her right, title, and interest in and to any other real or personal property held now or in the future by Troy.[1354]

Prior to February 1976, Ginny had relocated to Forsyth County, North Carolina, and when she filed for divorce on August 5, 1976 in Yadkin County, Troy was still living in Wilkes County, his address being that of his brother Ray on Country Club Road in Wilkesboro. Troy accepted a summons and the verified complaint for divorce on August 31, 1976, and he responded on September 1.[1355] He did not contest the divorce, and "a division of property had been worked out earlier in a series of conferences in Wilkes County."[1356] The divorce was sought on the grounds of one year's separation,[1357] and Ginny had separated from Troy because of the physical and mental abuse she suffered at his hands.[1358] Cecil and Mildred Small understood that Troy had, at some point, "beat the hell out of her, and she ended up in the hospital."[1359] The divorce was finalized September 15, 1976, and Ginny resumed the use of her maiden name.[1360] Some of Ginny's relatives, who had never liked or trusted Troy, were thrilled she had finally gotten away from him.[1361]

In June 1976, Troy's acquaintance, A. C. Greene, Jr. and his brother, Edward Greene, were murdered.[zzzz] Three days before his body was found, A. C. had last been seen alive at the Midway Sunoco service station on East Main Street in Wilkesboro,[1362] which was owned by Reggie Colvard,[1363] a close friend of Ray and Troy Hall.[1364] There was "some speculation that the brothers were killed because they knew something about" the unsolved Durham murders. "Others speculate[d] that the brothers were murdered by people connected with illegal drug traffic. John [Vanderford], district supervisor for the State Bureau of Investigation at Hickory, said…he [did] not rule out either possibility, though most officers lean[ed] toward the second theory."[1365] SBI Agent Larry Wagner, who was continuing his investigation into the Durham murders was also assigned to work on the Greene Case.[1366]

Being a native of Watauga County and the son of Boone businesspeople, Bill Norris, Jr., who had been one of the Durhams' neighbors at the time of their murders, knew the Greene brothers. Around the same time the brothers went missing, Norris became frightened and stopped answering his phone because a caller told him he would be next. By this time, Norris was working part-time as a Watauga County deputy sheriff, and someone also made a call to the sheriff's department threatening him and stating he [Norris] knew too much about the Durhams. Norris was on weekend National Guard maneuvers in West Jefferson, North Carolina, and authorities notified him there about the threat. Meanwhile, sheriff's deputies and federal and/or state agents went to Norris's Boone apartment, retrieved his wife Darlene,[aaaaa] informed her of the threat, and questioned her extensively about the Durhams and the Greene brothers. They also accompanied her to West Jefferson to pick up her husband, and they returned the shaken couple to their home in Boone. For a two-week period, officers conducted a stakeout at their home and followed them everywhere they went in order to keep a protective eye on them.[1367]

By late September 1976, the reward money in the Durham Case had grown to $18,000,[1368] and in November 1976, Watauga County prosecutor Clyde Roberts obtained a judge's order for a SBI agent to obtain the finger and palm prints of Troy Hall's sister, Lois Hall Sebastian, of the Traphill community, at the Wilkes County Sheriff's Department. In the application for the order, Roberts stated Sebastian was a suspect in the murders and a sister to other suspects. He wrote, "Investigations reveal that she was in Boone with another suspect every night for one week prior to the murders. Ms. Sebastian was actually within the crime residence after the murder[s]. Ms.

[zzzz] A. C. Greene, Jr. was shot in the head, and his bound body was found in the trunk of his car on a dirt road off of Highway 421 between Boone and Wilkesboro, just a couple of hundred feet from the Watauga County line. The day following his murder, his younger brother, Edward Greene, of Boone, was murdered. He was shot four times – once in the head and three times in his right side – and his throat was slashed twice. His legs had been taped, and his hands were taped behind him. His body was found in the back of his shag-carpeted van, parked in one of the bays at a car wash on U. S. Highway 321, about seven miles north of Lenoir. It was determined Edward had been killed inside his van and robbery was not a motive as money and other valuables were found inside the van. Although Edward was murdered the day after his brother, his body was discovered first. [Sources: "Killers Hunted in 4 Counties," *The Charlotte Observer*, Charlotte, NC, June 5, 1976, p. 1; "Reward Set In Slayings," *Statesville Record and Landmark*, Statesville, NC, June 21, 1976, p. 10-A; "Man Guilty Of Trying To Buy Killer," *The Charlotte Observer*, Charlotte, NC, May 18, 1978, p. B1; "Convict On Trial In 1976 Killings Of 2 Brothers," *The Charlotte Observer*, Charlotte, NC, September 19, 1978, pp. 1B & 6B; State of North Carolina v. Jackie Rand Robinette, Court of Appeals of North Carolina, February 6, 1979, https://www.leagle.com/decision/1979886251se2d6351836; Watauga County Sheriff's Office investigation file 118-H-1/2/3; "Man Is Charged In Dynamite Case," *The Herald-Sun*, Durham, NC, July 15, 1976, p. 5B; "Pair Exonerated in Bombing Attempt Case," *Statesville Record and Landmark*, Statesville, NC, March 11, 1977, p. 3-B; Dennis Whittington, "Greene Brothers' Deaths, Aborted Drug Deal Linked," *Winston-Salem Journal*, Winston-Salem, NC, June 9, 1977, p. 1; Wagner, Larry. Phone interview with author. December 22, 2022.]

[aaaaa] This was Norris's second wife, who he married in August 1975.

Sebastian has thus far refused any cooperation with investigators and declined voluntarily to be fingerprinted." SBI Agent Steve Cabe served Sebastian with the court order.[1369] At one point, Sebastian's husband, Troy Sebastian, said he knew who committed the murders, and although there was no further information regarding that inside the Watauga County Sheriff's Office investigative file, the SBI spoke with him but learned nothing of ultimate value.[1370]

In December 1976, Boone Police, including Chief Clyde Tester, Captain Arlie Isaacs, and Officer L. D. Hagaman, Jr. visited Ginny (now divorced from Troy) at her apartment in Winston-Salem, North Carolina. Her roommate Cindy answered the door and then let Ginny, who was upstairs at the time, know the officers wished to speak with her. When Ginny came downstairs, she immediately asked them to leave.[bbbbb] After repeating the directive three or four times, the officers rose and went to the door. Isaacs reminded her that, the last time they met, he had promised to come back if any new leads or information had surfaced. "Ginny, we are back," he stated. This prompted Ginny to invite them to have a seat, telling them she would speak with them. She told them she had been in bed all day with the flu, and when they suggested they come back when she was feeling better, she said no, since they were already there, she wanted to get it over with. She also said she was tired of hearing the same thing over and over and would not answer any questions she had previously been asked. Isaacs asked her if, since her divorce from Troy, she had any different outlook on his or any of the Hall family's involvement in the murders. Ginny said she did not believe the Halls were capable of it, and she did not believe Troy would have done something like that and put her through all she had suffered. When asked who she thought might be involved, she mentioned a wrecker driver from Mount Airy who had gotten into a rift with her father between 1966 and 1968 and verbally threatened him. She expressed disdain about her Durham relatives' claims of having knowledge about Troy's and Bryce's relationship with one another. She stated her father did not let others know what was going on, and he had had a falling out with his relatives over his sister Gayle's multiple marriages and divorces.[ccccc] When Tester asked Ginny if she feared being arrested, she said she did when she and Troy were fingerprinted and every time something appeared in the newspaper. She said officers had done a really sloppy job handling the crime scene, with spectators running in and out like it was a museum, and she could have criticized them many times in the media, but she chose not to so as not to hamper the investigation. She further stated she had requested police protection but was denied by Sheriff Ward Carroll. She said no one offered her any assistance during that critical time. When the officers asked her if they could return following any new developments, she told them no, but she provided them with her phone number so they could call instead. The officers later noted that, during this two-hour interview, Ginny's demeanor "would change from...pleasant and laughter to a real sarcastic tone of voice," and that she seemed really nervous and upset at times, especially when her brother Bobby's name was mentioned. Ginny told the

---

[bbbbb] Years later, Hagaman shared that he and his fellow officers had harassed Ginny during the course of their investigation, even to the extent that she would no longer speak with him. In 2022, when he told her, "Ginny, I know it's been hard on you," she responded, "I understand you were doing your job." [Sources: Hagaman, Len. In-person interviews with author. May 19, 2023 & January 16, 2024.]

[ccccc] Gayle Durham was first married in 1952 to Harold Gilbert Hayes; they divorced in 1958. Gayle next married Bernard Foy "Bud" Smitherman in 1960; they divorced in 1965. By 1971 she had married her last husband, Charles Augustus Mauldin. [Sources: Marriage Register (1874-1979), Wilkes Co., NC, June 4, 1952, https://ancestry.com/imageviewer/collections/60548/images/42091_343633-00454?pId=11835011; https://ancestry.com/discoveryui-content/view/2671717:1115; Marriage License/Certificate No. 1564, Office of Register of Deeds, Yadkin County, NC, January 9 & 31, 1960, https://ancestry.com/discoveryui-content/view/13491838:60548; https://ancestry.com/discoveryui-content/view/2760986:1115?ssrc+pt&tid=170690419&pid=252430501104.]

officers she never thought about her parents and Bobby being murdered and tried to wipe it out of her mind, only thinking about their absence at Christmas time.[1371]

By March 1977, as part of Attorney General Rufus Edmisten's intention to keep fresh eyes on the Durham Case and fresh thoughts about it coming, SBI Agents Dave Keller and Lewis Young were sent from their posts in northeastern North Carolina to Boone. Thirty-two-year-old Keller and twenty-seven-year-old Young were sent with informal instructions to find some new leads as ones from the preceding five years had not led to a resolution of the case. Upon their arrival in Boone, the agents situated themselves near the Watauga County Sheriff's Department and the Boone Police Department and spent their initial days on the case introducing themselves to key officers in each of these agencies, sharing what they already knew, asking for additional information that might be valuable to their investigation, and generally getting up to speed on all that had occurred since 1972.[1372]

Keller and Young also went through the SBI's immense Durham Case files in the district office in Hickory, North Carolina to determine where preceding investigators had or had not been. Because the two men were the third wave of agents assigned to the case, they faced some inherent challenges. "It's not like you were cutting fresh ground…where you might discover something," Young recalled. "That's the frustrating part. Whatever we were doing, that row had already been plowed once before, and we were probably going to get the same answers. We were struggling to come up with something." The pair also encountered individuals, including Durham family members and friends, who were exasperated that the "real killers" had not been identified and that, with the assignment of each new round of agents, they were having to start from scratch and be subjected to the same line of questioning over and over. People who had likely already been interviewed several times seemed to be getting sick of talking to the SBI, and Keller and Young found that to be particularly true of Ginny Durham, who came across as irritated, fed up, and disinclined to speak, even to the point of stonewalling.[1373]

Meanwhile, Troy Hall was still high on the list of suspects when the agents arrived in Boone and the pair discussed him often. While they purposely intended to shift their focus away from him in order to explore other possibilities, it was a difficult task. As Young recounted, "We had a hard time keeping our minds off of the son-in-law," and they felt they should interview him if only for background purposes. Troy and Ginny had split by this time, and Troy was out of the immediate area. Aside from Troy, Keller and Young did develop a new lead concerning a black man residing in Boone, who, as a customer, had had an argument or disagreement with the Durham dealership, but the lead went no further after the man was interviewed. Although Young enjoyed working on the case and found it intriguing and wanted to continue with it, after about two to three months, his supervisor needed him back in eastern North Carolina. The Durham Case had been designated as Keller's and Young's sole focus, and even after Young's departure and Keller's resettlement into the SBI's northwestern district, Keller was told to continue giving his full attention to the case until further instructed.[1374]

In April 1977, Peter Hurkos, of Los Angeles, was recommended to Boone Police Chief Clyde Tester by a service representative from a Raleigh, North Carolina fingerprint company, who had contacted Hurkos. A professional psychic, Hurkos, for a fee of $5,000, and utilizing pictures of the victims, suspects, and witnesses and a map of the area around the crime scene, would reportedly be able to identify the killers.[1375] Born Pieter van der Hurk in the Netherlands, Hurkos "allegedly manifested extrasensory perception (ESP) after recovering from a head injury and coma caused by a fall from a ladder." After coming to the United States, he "became a popular entertainer [who performed] psychic feats before live and television audiences." Throughout the 1960s, Hurkos was reported to have come close to identifying the Boston Strangler, to have found the Stone of Scone that had been stolen from Westminster Abbey, and to have identified Charles Manson to police after doing what turned out to be an inaccurate "reading" in the home of victim Sharon Tate. He also claimed Adolf Hitler was alive and residing in Argentina. Billed as the "world's foremost psychic detective," he appeared in a 1970s film in which he shared his psychic readings concerning Bigfoot. Hurkos, however, was widely refuted, and his errors were documented. Although he claimed to have solved twenty-seven murders in seventeen countries, critics called his cases "pure bunk," and some detectives said he "contributed no information unobtainable in newspapers."[1376]

That same month, a black man named Beauford Whittington, of the Wilkes County, North Carolina prison unit, was interviewed. Whittington, whose prints were among those checked against the Durham Case prints, had previously reached out to speak with Boone Police Chief Clyde Tester concerning his [Whittington's] suspicion that another black man and others had killed the Durhams because those individuals "were out that night." But Whittington never followed through with the conversation because Sheriff Ward Carroll had come along (perhaps implying Whittington spoke to him instead of Tester). By this time, Whittington understood the man he suspected (perhaps the same one interviewed by SBI Agents Keller and Young) had been checked out, and he no longer believed this man or any of the blacks in Boone were involved.[1377]

Having completed her university degree, Ginny Durham taught for a time at West Yadkin Elementary School in Yadkin County, North Carolina[1378] and she remarried sometime after April 20, 1977,[ddddd] her second husband being Steven Roger "Steve" Mackie, a native of Yadkin County and a graduate of Yadkinville High School, Gardner Webb College in Boiling Springs, North Carolina, and North Carolina State University in Raleigh.[1379] At one point the Mackies moved to Everett, Washington and were associated at various times with addresses in Yadkinville, North Carolina, Slidell, Louisiana and Chester, Richmond, and Mechanicsville, Virginia. They eventually made their home in Elkin, North Carolina.[1380]

Steve Mackie (Source: Gardner Webb University Yearbook, 1968)

In May 1977, Ginny told WBTV News of Charlotte, North Carolina she did not grant interviews on the subject of her family's murders. By March 1978, the news station had again attempted "to contact her in person, by telephone, and by certified mail," but she never acknowledged their inquiries. Troy Hall similarly ignored their telephone calls and certified mail.[1381]

In June 1977, Rufus Edmisten commented on the murders of A. C. Greene, Jr. and his brother Edward Greene, which had occurred a year earlier. "Those boys were killed in a drug deal that went bad," Edmisten stated. He also said the case might be related in some way to the Durham murders as investigators had determined A. C. once worked for Bryce Durham at his dealership. "Edmisten added, however, that investigating officers [were] not viewing the Durham and Greene cases as one and [were] pursuing each separately."[1382]

[ddddd] This was the date of Steve Mackie's Yadkin County, NC divorce from his first wife, who he had married in June 1972. [Source: North Carolina, U. S. Divorce Index, Ancestry.com, https://www.ancestry.com/discoveryui-content/view/409995:1115?ssrc=pt&tid=170690419&pid=252358662595.]

Later that same month, Edmisten spoke to the Wilkes County Democratic Party Convention at the county courthouse in Wilkesboro, where Coy Durham and his daughter Gayle Mauldin were seated in the front row. "Edmisten discarded some prepared remarks and turned his attention directly to them. 'As long as I am attorney general there will never be a time when I stop searching for the cruel murderers of your family. That's a pledge I make to you.'" Following the convention, Edmisten stated his assignment of two SBI agents to the case on a full-time basis had resulted in some new leads, and he was optimistic the case would be solved. "This is one of the most intensive investigations in the history of this state," he said.[1383]

In November 1977, the SBI announced its reopening of the Durham Case, along with other unsolved "dramatic homicides."[1384] A special "murder task force" or "murder squad" comprised of "some of the state's top criminal investigators"[1385] was formed by Attorney General Edmisten as part of the SBI to work on fifty-seven of "North Carolina's unsolved murders,"[eeeee] with the Durham Case being at the top of their list.[1386] As before, Edmisten's plan was to assign fresh SBI agents to cases they had never worked on and had no knowledge of, with instructions "to treat those old cases as if they had just occurred." He said the agents would be "given a free hand to develop new leads."[1387] That December, SBI Agent Max Bryan stated he was working on four cases, including a 1966 unsolved triple homicide in Henderson County,[fffff] but the Durham Case "was taking most of his attention."[1388]

Edmisten also stated he was soon anticipating arrests in the murders of the Greene brothers: "We're getting very close to making some arrests in the case. People up there are petrified over the case – people's lives are at stake. This is probably the most brutal unsolved murder case that we've got." Edmisten went on to say he considered the Durham Case "to be the top unsolved murder case in the state, [and] he listed the Greene brothers' case as the second most important unsolved case."[ggggg]

[eeeee] Another source quoted Edmisten as saying the murder squad would handle "more than 100 unsolved murders. [Source: Dennis Whittington, "Arrests Expected In 1976 Murders," *Winston-Salem Journal*, Winston-Salem, NC, November 5, 1977, p. 13.]

[fffff] This was the triple murder of Vernon Shipman, Charles Glass, and Louise Davis Shumate. Although unconnected to the Durham murders, the two cases shared similarities – a frightened community commencing to lock its doors while wondering who the killer was; rumors circulating; a poorly-preserved, circus-like crime scene; the case "hindered by ogling crowds of onlookers" and cars full of "curiosity seekers" driving by within days; a lack of forensic capabilities; missing evidence; unsolved after fifty years (as of 2016); and no incentive to invest resources into a case with no one left to convict. [Source: Derek Lacey, "1966 triple murder still sends shock waves through Hendersonville," *Hendersonville Times-News*, July 18, 2016 (online), https://www.goupstate.com/story/news/2016/07/18/1966-triple-murder-still-sends-shock-waves-through-hendersonville/4570754007/.]

[ggggg] In 1978, Jackie Rand Robinette and Michael Dean Keller were indicted for the murders of the Greene brothers, which authorities believed stemmed from a drug deal gone bad. According to Robinette, he and Keller lured A. C. Greene to Robinette's farmhouse in Alexander County, NC. Greene supposedly owed Robinette between $300,000 (the street value of nine pounds of heroin) and $400,000 for past drug deals, and the purpose of the meeting was to rob Greene to recover some of that money. As Greene reached for a gun, Keller shot him. The next day, in Caldwell County, Robinette and Keller met with Edward Greene, who was looking for his brother. Robinette shot Greene four times, and when he did not die immediately, Keller cut his throat with a pocketknife. [Sources: "Man Guilty Of Trying To Buy Killer," *The Charlotte Observer*, Charlotte, NC, May 18, 1978, p. B1; "Convict On Trial In 1976 Killings Of 2 Brothers," *The Charlotte Observer*, Charlotte, NC, September 19, 1978, pp. 1B & 6B; State of North Carolina v. Jackie Rand Robinette, Court of Appeals of North Carolina, February 6, 1979, https://www.leagle.com/decision/1979886251se2d6351836; "Convict On Trial In 1976 Killings Of 2 Brothers," *The Charlotte Observer*, Charlotte, NC, September 19, 1978, pp. 1B & 6B; Watauga County Sheriff's Office investigation file 118-H-1/2/3; "Man Is Charged In Dynamite Case," *The Herald-Sun*, Durham, NC, July 15, 1976, p. 5B; "Pair Exonerated in Bombing Attempt Case," *Statesville Record and Landmark*, Statesville, NC, March 11, 1977, p. 3-B;

Both were among five "high-priority cases" in northwestern North Carolina, which was served by the Hickory district SBI office.[1389] Speaking specifically about the Durham murders, Edmisten stated, "I am not discouraged on the case. I'll never give up. Someday we'll solve that crime."[1390]

In March 1978, the *Special Edition of WBTV News* debuted and included a segment led by reporter Bruce Bowers, who examined the unsolved Durham murders.[1391] Bowers, a native of Wilkes County,[1392][hhhhh] had first reported on the case the morning after the murders when he traveled to Boone and spoke with Watauga County Sheriff Ward Carroll. In 1976, Bowers joined WBTV, where he proposed the news special.[1393] Carroll appeared on Bowers' 1978 program, sharing, "This has been a case where we just didn't have much evidence or anything to go on…," but he stated he and his officers had worked really hard and had a case file about six inches thick. Bowers told Carroll some individuals inside the State Bureau of Investigation felt the Watauga County Sheriff's Department had "muffed the case," and Carroll responded, "I don't think the sheriff's department has muffed the case at all because the SBI was called in just as soon as we found this information that the people had been put in the bathtub, and they was the ones that started working real hard on it. They brought their laboratory over here, and they stayed on it for days and days and days, and the sheriff's department has not muffed the case."[1394]

In the same news special, Rufus Edmisten stated, "We've interviewed hundreds of people. There's stacks of materials that'd go to the ceiling of this room on the Durham murder case, and I'm thoroughly convinced that sometime it will be solved…and I'm not going to rest until [it is]."[1395] One motivator for Edmisten was to bring closure to Bryce Durham's family, particularly his parents, Coy and Collie, who continued to live in Wilkes County. The elder Durhams were heartbroken, frustrated, and anguished,[1396] and within a month after Edmisten was sworn in as Attorney General, Mrs. Durham phoned him. "Mr. Edmisten, I know you're a good man. I wonder if you would help us try to find out who did this? I just want the answer before I die."[1397] This was one of forty to fifty contacts Edmisten had with the Durhams over the years.[1398] Any time he got within fifty miles of Wilkes or Watauga counties, Mrs. Durham had an uncanny way of knowing about it,[1399] and she and her family, as well as others, would ask him about the case. As Edmisten wrote in his memoir, "I routinely flew to Wilkesboro on my way to Boone, and the Durhams sometimes met me at the airport there. Mrs. Durham was a lovely silver-haired lady with azure eyes and hands that had seen a lot of work. Mr. Durham was a dignified, characteristically stoic mountain man, and seemed happy to have his wife do the talking."[1400]

The elder Durhams also participated in the WBTV news special. Mr. Durham stated, "It's been awful hard on us, but we have managed to live this far. But I do hope and pray that we'll live to see

---

Dennis Whittington, "Greene Brothers' Deaths, Aborted Drug Deal Linked," *Winston-Salem Journal*, Winston-Salem, NC, June 9, 1977, p. 1

[hhhhh] Brent Reeves (Bruce Bowers' first cousin) and Troy Hall attended grade school together, graduated from high school together, and knew one another at Appalachian State University. Reeves and his wife also lived in the Greenway Trailer Park in Boone at the same time Troy and Ginny Hall and Cecil Small resided there, and they had some interactions with Small. According to Reeves, his father [Rev. Garland Reeves] and uncle, Blaine Reeves, had had some minor business dealings with Bryce Durham a few months before the murders. Blaine Reeves' wife, Ozena Durham Reeves, was a first cousin to Bryce Durham. [Sources: Brent Reeves, e-mail to Tim Bullard, August 11, 2010, Watauga County Sheriff's Office investigation file 118-H-1/2/3; https://www.findagrave.com/memorial/71868086/garland-reeves; York, Debbie. "Cold Weather-Cold Hearts," 2012, unpublished; Genealogical research by author.]

Coy & Collie Durham participating in a 1978 interview

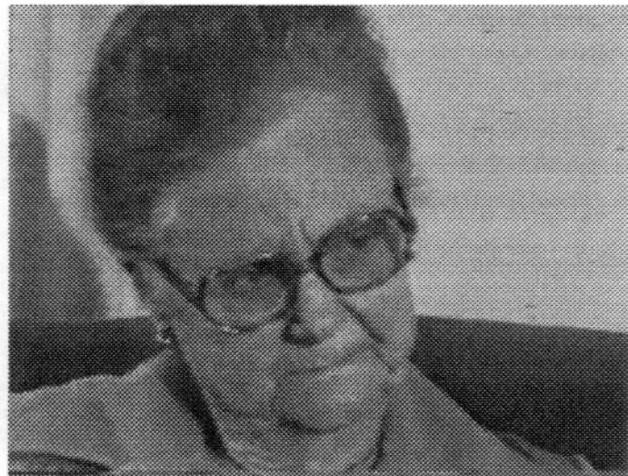

that murder solved." Mrs. Durham added, "They're still loose; they're out there free, and never been anything done. And they's someone a-listenin' to me right now, I know they's someone listenin' to me has some information, or they know of someone has some information that could solve this case. And they's a reward of about $17,000 just waiting for someone to give a tip that'd break this case. And I wish that they would please help us."[1401]

Around this same timeframe, Boone Police Captain Arlie Isaacs, along with Chief Clyde Tester, Officer L. D. Hagaman, Jr., and SBI agents, were prepared to arrest Troy Hall, but Sheriff Ward Carroll prevented them from doing so, at least in part because such an arrest for a crime committed one mile from Boone's town limit was outside of the Boone Police Department's jurisdiction. The Boone Police Department and the SBI did not discuss the development of probable cause with Carroll, and it is possible Carroll, unbeknownst to the other agencies, which were busy interviewing hundreds of people, may have also been considering arresting Troy and would have done so if he had had enough probable cause. This would have been done in consultation with the District Attorney, who was kept in the loop. While authorities had frequently discussed the possibility of arresting Troy, and while there may have been grounds for taking him into custody for more in-depth questioning, there was simply not enough probable cause to warrant charges by any of the investigating agencies. Interviewing Troy was extremely difficult as he would not disclose anything to incriminate himself or would completely shut down and refuse to answer questions.[1402] According to Hagaman, "Troy was Troy.... He knew what to do. He was a shrewd operator."[1403]

In 1978, as Boone Police Captain and (by now) Assistant Chief Arlie Isaacs prepared to run for Watauga County Sheriff[1404] on a platform that included his commitment to continue prioritizing the Durham Case, his election committee published a promotional article with the following remarks:

Along with the dates December 7, 1941 and November 22, 1963, no citizen of Watauga County can ever forget where they were on the night of February 3, 1972. On that cold, snowy night sometime between 8:30 and 11:00 p.m., Bryce Durham, his wife Virginia, and their son Bobby were murdered in their home....

Six years have now passed. No one has since been arrested for the Durham murders. The perpetrators of the most horrible crime in Watauga County's history are still at large.

But the Durham case must never be closed as long as the murderers remain free. And it should not be forgotten that the Watauga County Sheriff's Department has primary jurisdiction for the investigation of this case. True, the State Bureau of Investigation is presently looking into the case. But the SBI is designed to serve only to assist local law enforcement agencies, not to serve as a police force in their own right. The Watauga County Sheriff's Department has still today in 1978 not only primary jurisdiction, but also primary responsibility for the investigation of this case. And if the case is ever broken, the Sheriff's office should issue the warrants. It remains today the duty of the Watauga County Sheriff's Department to be an active partner in this investigation.

There is no other unsolved crime in Watauga County that is more important than this case. It should be given top priority. And if Arlie Isaacs is elected Sheriff, he is pledged to give this case the time and attention it deserves and to work closely with other law enforcement agencies that are looking into this case also.

The family of Bryce Durham has waited for over six years for the killers of their loved ones to be caught. Put yourself in their shoes. If it had been your family, would you want the investigation ever to stop?[1405]

In another campaign ad, Isaacs stated to voters that "professionalism in law enforcement is…the highest duty for any officer in any department…. Law enforcement has changed drastically in the past ten years…. Technology and new breakthroughs in the science of criminal investigation require officers to look upon their work as a continually changing profession." Isaacs also acknowledged that "a new breed of criminals and criminal activities is emerging that is both smart and organized."[1406] In the end, however, Isaacs was unsuccessful in his bid for sheriff against incumbent Ward Carroll in the May 1978 Democratic primary. Oddly enough, another Democratic candidate who Carroll defeated in the same primary was none other than Cecil Small, whose campaign ad stated he was a bonded private detective and security officer, approved by the North Carolina State Bureau of Investigation.[1407] Carroll, who had been sheriff since 1966,[1408] not only won the primary but also the general election and would continue in the sheriff's office for an additional four years.

As of July 27, 1979, roughly seven and half years after the Durham murders, the fingerprints of more than four-hundred individuals had been compared to the prints lifted from the Durham home and vehicle. While some of the prints taken were for elimination purposes – to eliminate the victims' prints as well as those of non-suspects who had been in the Durham home, entered the crime scene, possibly touched the Durhams' vehicle, etc. – other prints were from suspects. Among those whose prints were compared were Durham and Hall family members, local law enforcement officers, SBI agents, other crime scene responders, Modern Buick-Pontiac Company employees, men with military backgrounds, and more than 140 individuals with criminal records/associations, some of whom were known for systematically ransacking residences, removing items (including sterling silver), using a pillowcase or suitcase from the residence to carry their loot, wearing gloves, and leaving behind little physical evidence.[1409]

By October 1979 – about two years after its inception – Rufus Edmisten's "murder squad" task force had been quietly disbanded for lack of funding – the result of "a spiraling crime rate and a department budget that [had] not climbed nearly so rapidly. Edmisten said the murder squad was a victim of tightening purse strings within his department. He asked the General Assembly…to pay for 37 new agents over [a two-year period] but received money for only four people." According to Edmisten, "I could not in good conscience have a squad working on unsolved murders when so many new ones are popping up." Edmisten added that the squad had to be decentralized because recent murders, which had better chances of being solved, had to take priority. Also, requests from local law enforcement agencies for homicide investigation assistance from the SBI had increased 23%, whereas the SBI's manpower had increased by only 2%. The task force had successfully "obtained six court convictions," and Deputy SBI Director Harold E. Elliott said the remaining unsolved cases had been "distributed among the bureau's eight regional offices" for agents to work on as time allowed – with one exception…that of the Durham Case. Max Bryan, the agent overseeing murder investigations, stated that an agent remained assigned to the Durham investigation. According to Bryan, "Needless to say, if you've got a triple murder in your boss's hometown, you're going to be working on it." Despite the budgetary setback, Edmisten expressed optimism, stating almost identically as he had two years earlier, "I will never rest until this case is solved," and "I'm not discouraged on the case. I'll never give up – someday we'll solve the case."[1410]

In late January and early February 1982, on the occasion of the tenth anniversary of the deaths of Bryce, Virginia, and Bobby Durham, family members were still hopeful the mystery would be solved, and investigators insisted there was reason for that hope, confidently stating "that eventually the killers – whoever they are – will face justice." That confidence had been expressed by investigators for a decade, but no one could or would say when that justice would be administered.[1411] The anniversary generated much media attention, which garnered responses from those involved in the case.

Watauga County Sheriff Ward Carroll stated the Durham Case was open and still under investigation, although he admitted he and his department had not "been working on it too much lately" due to an absence of recent breaks. "It's the worst murder case we've ever had in this county. I'd hate to see it go unsolved." Carroll stayed the course with his assertion that charging the Asheville men with the murders a decade earlier had been on point. He expressed this in a statement that began confidently but then trailed off with an acknowledgement of additional possibilities: "In my opinion, I made the right arrests. I thought they were involved. We just didn't get the right cooperation to get them convicted…unless the Mafia was involved in it, and those cases are hard to solve. But there is some evidence pointing that way."[1412]

Attorney General Rufus Edmisten had a passion for solving all cases, and he was embarrassed the Durham murders remained unsolved, especially since they occurred in his home county. He had begun putting together the framework for his 1984 gubernatorial bid and leading the effort to solve the Durham Case would bolster his law-and-order image.[1413] He once more expressed optimism the case would be solved despite it being the most baffling and one of the most frustrating cases he had ever encountered. "We've spent hundreds of thousands of hours on this. We've involved law enforcement from all over the Southeast. We've run leads as far away as California and to foreign countries. Never in the eight years I've been attorney general has a case been discussed as much as this one. [It] is our number one priority. It's the largest file we have. This is a cold-blooded murder that happened in my hometown. I don't care where I am or what I'm doing, I'll never give up. Someday, sometime, someone will come forward or do something that will solve this case. Someone in the Boone area knows something about it, and I just wish they would come forward."[1414] Edmisten also stated, "This is one of those cases where we have just almost enough to close it, but not quite enough. We have to be very careful because suspicions will not stand up in court."[1415] Edmisten added that "after all these years, there is only a single theory and a single set of suspects 'that works.' But he declined to outline the theory. 'We've had investigators check different scenarios, but nothing else works. There is just the one scenario that makes any sense, and there is nothing we have learned as yet to dissuade us from that.'"[1416]

Despite Sheriff Ward Carroll's continued belief that the Asheville men were involved, Max Bryan of the SBI's Raleigh office said the four had been "pretty well eliminated as suspects." Bryan further stated, "I really think that it will be solved. There is some one thing or another that we haven't seen yet – or aren't looking at right. One day we are going to see it and everything is going to fall into place."[1417] SBI Agent Charlie Whitman of the Hickory office was now in charge of the case, and in the preceding few months, Edmisten had assigned a second unnamed agent to assist Whitman.[1418] By this time, a motive of robbery was "no longer given much credence." While Max Bryan did "not entirely discount robbery," he asked, "Why would you go out and rob someone on a night when it was impossible to get around?"[1419]

Over the course of the past decade, Bryce Durham's extended family had contributed thousands of dollars to the reward fund, hired investigators as well as the Dutch psychic Dykshoorn, and believed an answer to the case would be found. Mrs. Collie Durham stated, "That's what I live for. If I didn't hope anymore, I would have to just give up and die." Mrs. Durham and her daughter, Gayle Mauldin, said they had their own suspicions but were afraid to share them publicly.[1420]

When the *Winston-Salem Journal* began compiling its article commemorating the tenth anniversary of the Durham murders, Troy Hall was living out of state and could not be reached for comment. Ginny Durham Mackie had an unlisted phone number, and when a reporter went to her home, her husband Steve answered the door saying, "Why do you people dredge this thing up every year? You never went through anything like this, so you don't even know what it is like. You are just trying to sell papers."[1421] When the article appeared, Ginny was very upset,[1422] believing "it pointed a finger right at her." The article also mentioned Steve, and he did not like that, vowing to put a stop to it. Afterwards, the Mackies paid a visit to Ginny's uncle and aunt, Charles and Gayle Mauldin. Upon their arrival, Gayle invited them to come inside. Both Ginny and Steve seemed nervous, and Ginny expressed her uncertainty she would be welcomed. Gayle encouraged Ginny to let her call the law so Ginny could tell them what she knew and get it over with. "They wouldn't listen to me; they wouldn't believe me," Ginny replied. "I'll stand right by you. They will," Gayle assured her. After a little more conversation, Ginny agreed, and Gayle phoned Rufus Edmisten, who said he could come the following day, agreeing to meet at Ginny's paternal grandparents' home. Gayle warned Ginny the authorities would be rough on her and would want her to take a polygraph test. Ginny said she knew that and would do so if Gayle would be with her. Gayle reassured her she would stick with her through it all. Gayle reiterated the polygraph test a few more times, and Ginny agreed she would submit to one. The following day, Edmisten came, along with SBI Agent Charlie Whitman. Seated around Collie Durham's coffee table – according to Gayle's recollection of the meeting – Ginny stated, among other things, "Let's suppose Troy introduced Daddy to the wrong people, I would say from Lenoir, and that night, Daddy was the payoff man, and Troy tricked him, and Daddy didn't know what it was all about, so they murdered him." At the conclusion of this initial meeting, Ginny and Gayle spoke privately in a bedroom, and Gayle witnessed Ginny be overcome with emotion for the first time since before she had met Troy. Grabbing her aunt by the shoulders, Ginny said, "Gayle, they weren't hard on me at all. I've never been so surprised." Gayle assured her, "They'll get hard. They'll bear down on you."[1423]

Later, in a letter to Gayle, Ginny wrote, "I think that maybe someone that Troy [and others] was mixed-up with in something illegal helped them. Also I think maybe Lenoir is the link instead of Wilkes County." Ginny had been speaking with SBI Agent Charlie Chambers and suggested he talk with Ray Hall's ex-wife Kay regarding the people they knew in Lenoir when they were married.[1424]

[Before the murders, Ray Hall had worked for insurance agent Bill Luck in Morganton, North Carolina.[1425] At Ray's request, Luck agreed to hire John LaRue, with whom Ray had attended high school in Wilkesboro. LaRue was a large man, approximately 6'1" and 230 pounds, who reportedly would do anything Ray instructed him to. Luck felt LaRue was "not quite all there" as he "would stand and stare into outer space."[1426] After the Durhams were murdered, Luck said Ray seemed really nervous and would not talk about anything. When Ray and LaRue began drinking heavily, Luck let both of them go.[1427] Ray's wife Kay was certain LaRue drove a white, four-door 1966 Ford, and almost daily, he was either at their house, or Ray was at LaRue's in Lenoir.[1428] (Could LaRue's car be the 1965-1966 white, four-door Ford that Lester Johnson saw near the Durham home on the night of the murders? Could LaRue's stature correspond with one of the large men Reed Trivette witnessed standing that night along the 105 Bypass?) LaRue's brother, Brady Jack LaRue of Thomasville, North Carolina, became a suspect in the Durham murders. Brady Jack was involved in the 1972 and 1973 Wilkes County shooting deaths of three victims. After pleading guilty of manslaughter, he was eventually sentenced to ten years[1429] in Central Prison in Raleigh, North Carolina.[1430][iiiii] It could be that Brady Jack LaRue was the same Central Prison inmate who SBI Agent Charlie Whitman stated confessed to a cell mate that he had been present "when his friends shotgunned the Durhams in a robbery gone bad." This confession was problematic in that the Durhams had not been shot, and the man making this claim had been arrested and was already incarcerated on the night of the murders.[1431]]

Agent Charlie Chambers was planning to meet with Ginny at her home in Yadkinville, North Carolina, and Ginny extended an invitation to Gayle and her husband Charles to be present at that meeting. She thanked Gayle for her friendship during the preceding month and stated, "I try to stay calm and objective when I talk to the agents, but inside I'm a mess."[1432] After the next meeting, however, Ginny became more relaxed, and after a total of three meetings at Ginny's house, Gayle prepped Ginny to take a polygraph test in Hickory, North Carolina, even planning for just the two of them to ride together, but then the authorities never followed through. Agent Charlie Whitman commented, "We have to handle her [Ginny] with kid gloves. It's like getting a kitten to drink milk.

[iiiii] Brady Jack LaRue was shotgunned to death in 1986 by his son-in-law following a dispute about the custody of LaRue's grandchild. According to the son-in-law, LaRue was a dangerous man, and he "was scared to death of him." [Source: "High Point man charged in slaying," *The News and Observer*, Raleigh, NC, January 22, 1986, p. 2C; "High Point Man Is Acquitted," *Winston-Salem Journal*, Winston-Salem, NC, September 14, 1986, p. B2.]

If you do too much, she'll run away." After that, Ginny did not want Gayle's presence, and Gayle had no knowledge if authorities met with her again. The next time Gayle saw Ginny was the following year at a hospital where Ginny's Grandfather Durham was a patient. While there, Ginny told Gayle about being hypnotized and said she could remember everything they asked about.[jjjjj] About a week later, Ginny went to see Gayle but missed her. According to Gayle, "That's when it all *[presumably their communication and/or relationship]* was ended."[1433]

On the maternal side of her family, Ginny's Uncle Wayne and Aunt Ronnie Church were good to her, and Wayne always stood up for her,[1434] but Ginny became estranged from other relatives, particularly those on the Durham side.[1435] Her grandparents, Coy and Collie Durham, and her Aunt Gayle always believed if Ginny told everything she knew, she could solve the murders.[1436] Some Durham family members vacillated in their opinions regarding if or how Ginny may have been involved,[1437] and Ginny believed Gayle was the driving force behind her [Ginny's] paternal grandmother wanting her to be "gotten" for the murders. *[Even years later, after Rufus Edmisten lost his gubernatorial bid in 1984, Ginny said her Durham grandparents wrote to Edmisten's Attorney General successor, Lacy Thornburg, trying to convince him to prosecute her.]*[kkkkk] Ginny said she tried several times to swallow her pride and see her Durham relatives, but they made it difficult for her and were rude to SBI Agent Charlie Whitman. Immediately following the 1972 funeral in Boone, her uncle, Bill Durham, had placed her paternal grandparents in the same car as her and Troy, and Collie Durham was upset by this uncomfortable pairing. Even though Ginny visited her Durham grandparents two or three times after the murders, she had conflict with them regarding the burials of her parents and brother, and things went further south from there.[1438]

On another occasion in the early 1980s, Rufus Edmisten traveled from Raleigh to speak with Ginny in Winston-Salem. According to Edmisten, a steel blue and cold-eyed Ginny never intimated during the interview that she had any notion of Troy being involved in the murders and stated she certainly had no part in it, asking Edmisten, "Do you think I would want my own mother, and my own father, and my brother killed?" Appearances aside, Edmisten left the interview satisfied Ginny had no direct involvement in her family's murders. Rather, he believed her to be a pained young lady with a heavy burden on her shoulders, and he felt it was unfortunate she had been married to Troy Hall, to whom she had been somewhat of a captive. Edmisten and the attorney from his office who had accompanied him to the interview discussed it all the way back to Raleigh, the attorney perceiving Ginny to be a traumatized, bewildered, and grief-stricken person, who did not exhibit the behavior of an accused criminal. Decades later, Edmisten stated, "I have to feel sorry for Ginny Sue," and he reaffirmed his belief that she "was under Troy Hall's spell. He was such a compelling figure…. We've seen that happen – sort of the Stockholm Syndrome…. I really believe that she was under his spell. She had nothing to do with the planning or commission of this crime." Edmisten further stated Ginny "just wishes that somehow she could get it behind her, but I doubt she ever will. But I do not think that she had a thing to do with it.[1439]

Some of Ginny's maternal relatives also maintained her innocence but speculated she may have known something was going on. Her first cousin, Jerri Bumgarner Waddell, did not believe drugs were Ginny's "cup of tea," but Waddell likewise knew something was not right and Ginny was not

---

[jjjjj] Years later, Ginny recounted how she had undergone hypnosis, which, in her assessment, did not help. [Source: Mackie, Ginny Durham. Interview with Carolynn Johnson & Wade Colvard. December 7, 2020.]
[kkkkk] Ginny's grandfather, Coy Durham, died in 1983, about a year and a half prior to Thornburg's 1985 assumption of the office of Attorney General, so this statement could only pertain to her grandmother, Collie Durham.

herself. Family members on both Bryce's and Virginia's sides wondered if and/or believed Troy had kept her drugged or medicated to a degree of numbness or oblivion regarding what was happening around her.[1440]

As early as the day before her parents' and brother's funeral, Ginny expressed her unwillingness to discuss their murders with Durham relatives, and she admonished them to not speak with the press or provide them with a photograph of her mother.[1441] In the summer of 1973, she continued turning away the media when she learned a caller at her home was a reporter and "said tonelessly, 'I don't want to talk about it,' and shut the door."[1442] Present Sheriff Len Hagaman believes Ginny pushed away and refused to talk because she did not want to relive her family's tragedy "over and over and over."[1443]

Watauga County Sheriff Ward Carroll described Ginny as a short-tempered woman who could talk hateful, but like Edmisten, he did not believe she was involved in the murders. He believed she may have suspected Troy's involvement but feared he would kill her or have her killed.[1444] *[When someone asked Ginny if she was afraid of Troy, she said she was still alive because she did not know anything.[1445]]* Sheriff Hagaman believes Ginny was genuinely scared of Troy and shut down because she was under his influence and control. Captain of Investigations Carolynn Johnson concurs and, after speaking with Ginny, does not feel she "had any part with Troy."[1446] Still, Hagaman suspects Ginny knows things she has chosen not to reveal for whatever reason.[1447] He believes she is still fearful and does not want to open that door.[1448]

Watauga County Sheriff Red Lyons (Source: Watauga County Sheriff's Office)

In November 1982, Republican candidate James Carlton "Red" Lyons defeated Democrat incumbent Ward Carroll for the sheriff's job, much to Carroll's ire. Subsequently, the six-inch Durham murder file Carroll had spoken of a few years earlier went missing, and Lyons was left bare-handed regarding the case. According to Lyons, "Carroll had kept an 'extensive' file with photos and information. The file was taken. I don't know by who, or why, but it has not been here since I've been here, and we have searched and searched for it." Lyons expressed that "he wanted the file back, wherever it was…. It is not my file, but I feel that it is the county's property, paid for by the citizens of Watauga County." According to Carroll, "he had kept a large file on the case, but the last time he said he saw it was at the sheriff's department." Carroll stated, "It used to be in a file in the investigator's office. I don't know where it is now."[1449][lllll] Still, politically motivated dissatisfaction with Lyons's election seemed intent on leaving him with nothing to go on.[1450][mmmmm]

Former Watauga County Sheriff's Deputy Jerry Vaughn, however, discounted the claim that the file went missing upon Carroll's departure from office. He remembered working with it at the time he

[lllll] Within the Watauga County Sheriff's Office files is an empty manila envelope labeled "Durham Case," the outside of which contains the following handwritten note by Lyons: "This is the only folder turned over to me when I took office – 12-6-1982. No contents within. James C. Lyons." [Source: Watauga County Sheriff's Office investigative file 118-H-1/2/3.]

[mmmmm] The SBI was not obligated and, in fact, was legally prohibited from providing the Watauga County Sheriff's Department with copies of the SBI's Durham Case files as a replacement for those records missing from Watauga County. However, it is possible the Watauga County Sheriff may have been granted permission to review the SBI files within an SBI facility. [Source: Wagner, Larry. Phone interview with author. September 19, 2023.]

left the sheriff's office with Carroll, and that another deputy, who transitioned from Carroll's staff to Lyons's staff, recalled seeing it in the basement of the jail after Lyons assumed office. Vaughn stated the file took up about ten to twelve inches of shelf space and contained primarily hand-written notes, along with a few reports that had been typed up for District Attorney Tom Rusher.[1451]

In 1982 or 1983, Agent Charlie Whitman took the SBI's Durham file to an FBI profiler and spent twelve hours with him. The profiler complimented the well-compiled documentation and said he believed the killer(s) "probably felt comfortable in the house."[1452] The interpretation of "comfortable" could mean, but not necessarily, that the killers had prior familiarity with the house, or perhaps that killing strangers was not as stressful as killing someone familiar, or that they did not feel hindered or threatened with discovery during the course of their activities while in the house. The profiler also shared, "The longer the perpetrator can go without confessing to anybody, the easier it becomes, and finally it's like you've got an out-of-body experience that there is someone else doing this."[1453]

In 1983, after an extended illness, Bryce Durham's father, Coy Durham, died.[1454] Bryce's mother Collie continued to spend every day contemplating the murders.[1455]

A year later, the SBI, still regarding the Durham Case as a top priority, stated a new lead had developed, although no additional details were provided.[1456] By 1985, Watauga County Sheriff Red Lyons had begun rebuilding his department's Durham murders investigation file. He was hopeful the case could be solved, but he admitted it had been difficult: "We really just don't have much to go on."[1457]

CHAPTER 12

SECOND WIND

For approximately six years, there were no notable developments in the Durham Case, and in early 1989, some of those who had played key roles in the investigation, though now retired, expressed their ongoing thoughts about it.

Former Sheriff Ward Carroll still felt the four men arrested from the Asheville area in 1972 may have been the right suspects. "You just don't know," he stated. "We worked on it for years. The way they planned it and everything, I could have had the right guys. It has been real hard to solve."[1458] *[Even at age ninety-one, shortly before his death in 2009, Carroll expressed his continued belief that the four men from the Asheville area he charged were responsible, and Troy Hall "put them up to it."[1459]]*

Former Boone Police Chief Clyde Tester shared that he thought about the Durham Case "all the time," saying, "I am still interested as much as ever. It has bothered me more than any other case. I feel like, even though it's went all these years, it can still be solved."[1460]

Former SBI Agent Charlie Whitman also reflected on the case: "I cannot recall another case which has intrigued me as much as this one has. In my career I have investigated a vast number of homicides, and with this case there are so many facets and so many unanswered questions. There have been so many theories, and it's hard just trying to establish a motive. I don't know of a plausible motive to this day. It was a rather heinous crime, the most heinous I've ever seen, and I'm not satisfied that we have even hit the right theory. I feel like there is somebody out there that has some knowledge but may not realize that they have the knowledge. Somebody out there knows something, and we are looking for any kind of assistance. We've kind of come with our hat in our hands asking for help from somebody...anybody."[1461]

In contrast to Tester's and Whitman's optimism, Durham family friend and attorney John C. W. Gardner, Sr. remained skeptical. "The case was quite shocking to all of the people around here. As far as if they'll ever solve the case, I doubt it very seriously."[1462]

But 1989 heralded a renewal in law enforcement's commitment to solve the murders of Bryce, Virginia, and Bobby Durham. Sheriff Red Lyons remained positive about the case and set a goal to raise public awareness and community involvement. Lyons was determined to solicit additional pledges to the $17,000 reward fund,[1463] hoping more money would lead someone with information to talk. The goal was to increase the reward to $50,000 with the help of area residents, businesses, and family members.[1464] Shortly after, in response to a request submitted by Lyons,[1465] North Carolina Governor Jim Martin upped the state's share to $15,000[1466] ($5,000 per murder, which added $10,000 to the original $5,000 authorized by Governor Bob Scott in 1972).[1467] This brought the total reward to $27,000.[1468] Lyons thought the state's boost to the reward money might also encourage others to contribute, perhaps even enough to increase the total to $70,000 or $80,000.[1469] Lyons added that, "unless the reward fund gets to a high enough figure or there is a 'death-bed confession,' the case may never be solved."[1470]

Lyons believed the Durham triple homicide was very well planned and he was positive it was not a one-man crime. He described it as the most "mysterious murder case in all of western North Carolina,"[1471] and said it was being examined "in every direction you can think of; it's just like an octopus [with] a lot of different ways to look at it."[1472] Not wanting "to settle for what information they [had] on the Durham murders and...determined to find more," Lyons stressed, "This is not a closed issue. Somebody has to know something. We are looking for someone who knows something that they would like to tell me in confidence...."[1473] According to Lyons, "I hear someone talk about the case at least twice a week, but in my six-plus years here, I have not had one thread of information come to me that would even start me to begin an active investigation," which was also prevented, in part, by an ongoing lack of manpower within the sheriff's department.[1474]

Although Crimestoppers was already operating internationally, Boone Police Chief Zane Tester (who had recently succeeded his father Clyde in that position) and Sergeant Jeff Rucker had established it in Boone around 1987, with Rucker being the program coordinator. Witnessing its success with local cases, they approached their board about utilizing the program to work on the dormant Durham Case and received enthusiastic feedback. Boone Crimestoppers subsequently got the case back into the public consciousness, and people in the community began discussing and remembering it on a regular basis.[1475] In conjunction with Sheriff Lyons, Boone Crimestoppers also explored nationwide exposure for the case via NBC,[1476] and the investigation files of the sheriff's office indicate communication with writer/director/producer Laura Verklan of Paramount regarding the production company's television show *Hard Copy*.[1477] Staff from another, similar "info-tainment" news magazine show, *A Current Affair*, were only days away from traveling to Boone to do a story about the Durham murders. They had asked to enter the Durham home, but the occupants were in the midst of remodeling and construction projects and asked the crew to delay their visit by a week. This proved unacceptable, and the producers of the show canned the project. Had it gone forward, they were prepared to interview several individuals, including knocking on Troy Hall's door.[1478]

By mid-1989, the reward had reached $40,000, which Lyons said was "nothing to sneeze at" and appetizing "enough to make some interested person talk."[1479] Authorities were hopeful this "shot in the arm" toward solving the case might continue gaining steam, and Lyons said the case would not be closed until the guilty person or persons were brought to justice. While Lyons acknowledged resolution of the Durham Case "would be a major accomplishment for any law enforcement officer," he wanted no pats on the back, only to see the murders solved.[1480] Lyons and Officer Delmus "Del" Williams worked hard on the case as did Paula May, who eventually rose to Chief Deputy, in which capacity she supervised all divisions, including investigations.[1481]

Also, in mid-1989, former WSOC Channel 9 investigative reporter Bruce Bowers, from Charlotte, who had covered the Durham Case on at least two prior occasions, went to Boone and put together a one-minute clip providing a short sequence of events from the night of the murders. The clip was to air on television stations across North Carolina and four other states, including Georgia and "some targeted areas in Virginia and Tennessee." According to Bowers at the time, "I firmly believe that this case is going to be solved. This is a case where it took two to three people to do the crime. Somebody had to have heard about it, and someone knows some information. We are hoping that the clip will trigger a memory in someone's mind. Somehow justice needs to be done."[1482]

Bruce Bowers setting up a Crimestoppers shot
(Photograph by Jamey Fletcher. Image courtesy of the Historic Boone Collection, Digital Watauga Project.)

(L-R) Gayle Mauldin & Collie Durham; (As published in the Watauga Democrat)

The extended Durham family was pleased with Sheriff Lyons's initiative, and Bryce Durham's sister, Gayle Mauldin, stated, "We just heard it was going to be reopened or renewed and we're just so thankful. We've always told them, 'Don't let it die down, don't let it die down.'"[1483] Mauldin, along with her brother, Bill Durham, and their mother, Collie Durham, traveled to Boone to offer their assistance. Mrs. Durham "started to perk up after hearing the news that there was renewed interest in the investigation…pulled herself together to make [the] trip…and said [to her daughter], 'Let's go to Boone for a day and see what we can stir up.'" The trip would be Mrs. Durham's first meeting with Sheriff Lyons and with Chief Tester.[1484] Both Mauldin and her mother had begun their own investigation, even interviewing

Bill Durham (As published in the Watauga Democrat)

people the same week the murders had occurred, and they dedicated years of their lives to getting the case solved.[1485] Like Lyons, Mauldin believed the reward increase was "the incentive for someone to come forward."[1486] Bill Durham added, "As the family, we appreciate the effort and logistical approach everyone is taking. Watauga County and the city of Boone can be proud of these men. Sheriff Lyons is a very efficient and capable man. I think he is approaching this in a way that I think will get results."[1487] Mauldin also remarked, "We have just been praying for something to renew the interest. It hurts. We watch the news and see it on the news, and it still hurts, yet we have got to be happy that there is still interest." Despite having "many unanswered questions," Mauldin and her mother still had "high hopes of the case being solved."[1488] Mauldin said of her mother, "It's all she really talks about. She just wants to see it solved."[1489] Mauldin further stated, "All we know is the end results. We want to know who and why. I can't imagine anyone who would want to hurt them. They were good Christians. Once this is solved, we feel they can rest in peace."[1490]

While Sheriff Lyons and Police Sergeant Jeff Rucker acknowledged community interest in the case remained strong, solving the case would still be a challenge.[1491] According to Rucker, "I think the case is ready to be solved.[1492] We have a lot of work ahead of us. It has taken some time because the case is so immense. We are just getting a foothold. The wheels are just beginning to turn.[1493] It's time to make things right. Somebody out there has the answers.[1494] We're confident and hopeful about this. And any little bit of information can help."[1495] This was not just any case to Rucker; it was personal because he had attended Watauga High School with Bobby Durham, and it became increasingly more so as he came to know Bobby's paternal grandmother and his aunt and uncle, Gayle and Charles Mauldin. Interaction with the family was a motivator for Rucker.[1496]

That same year (1989), a committee met at the Boone Police Department to discuss the Durham Case, and this was comprised of SBI Agents Dave Keller, Steve Wilson, and Charlie Whitman (by then retired), Sheriff Red Lyons, Boone Police Captain Arlie Isaacs, Boone Police Sergeant Jeff Rucker, and Boone Police Chief Zane Tester.[1497] Joe Momier, supervisor of the SBI's district office in Hickory, North Carolina, stated that "new action in the case 'is just another attempt. If it works, it's great; if not, well, at least we tried.'"[1498]

Former SBI Agent Charlie Whitman discussing how Virginia Durham was strangled.
(As published in the Watauga Democrat)

In addition to the bolstered reward fund, there were other encouraging developments that could potentially help solve the case. First, the SBI was on the verge of utilizing a new fingerprint identifying computer, and unidentified prints found inside the Durham house and vehicle would be run through it. Second, Lyons had learned a woman driving a car matching the description of a car belonging to the Durhams was spotted near the crime scene shortly after the murders.[1499] This was a reference to Boone resident Jerry Harrison's witnessing of a vehicle like the Durhams' and a blonde-headed woman using the phone booth at the Union 76 station at the corner of Highway 105 and the 105 Bypass on the night of the murders. Sergeant Jeff Rucker had hoped that, if the woman was local, and under no definitive assumption she was connected to the murders, she would come forward with information that might prove helpful.[1500] In March 1989, Harrison also shared that a Mrs. Baird,[nnnnn] an employee at Farmer's Hardware in Boone, had sold a rope the morning of February 3, 1972 to A. C. Greene, Jr., the reported drug dealer and sometime acquaintance of Troy Hall.[1501]

By April 1989, Gayle Mauldin had come to suspect that Troy Hall and Cecil Small may have been at the Durham house the night of the murders, not in response to the alleged phone call from Virginia Durham, but because they had carried out the killings and then got stuck while leaving the scene. Gayle believed that, had they not gotten stuck while backing down Clyde Townsend Road, no one would have known about the murders until the following day when someone else would have discovered the bodies.[1502] A few months later, a caller to Boone Area Crimestoppers stated John Hall was a brick mason and had done some work for the caller's mother in Lenoir, North Carolina about ten years prior. The caller stated John said he bet his brother [Troy Hall] committed the murders.[1503]

Also in April 1989, local resident Coaker Triplett visited Sheriff Red Lyons to inform him of Mrs. Sue Lukens, who had worked as a secretary for Triplett at the time of the murders, and who had since relocated to Lebanon, Tennessee. Triplett shared that Mrs. Lukens believed her son, Warren Lukens, may have played a role in the murders.[1504] In a subsequent phone conversation with Lyons, Mrs. Lukens stated her son (aka Luke Warren) was on drugs, was a Hells Angel, and had a tattoo on his arm that read "Born to Raise Hell." She said he was a mean person who frightened her, and he was absent the night of the murders. He returned home during the early morning hours of February 4, 1972 and then disappeared for several days afterward. Mrs. Lukens claimed her son had spent time in a psycho ward of a Nashville hospital in 1988, had been charged with several crimes in North Carolina, and had been tried and acquitted of two murders in Colorado. Lyons checked into Warren Lukens' background and did find a criminal record for him in North Carolina but nothing to substantiate the information concerning Colorado. In the end, Lyons found none of this information to be of any value in the Durham Case.[1505]

That same year, an Appalachian State University professor reported to the Watauga County Sheriff's Department that he and another person from ASU were discussing the murders, and this person said they knew who committed the crime but had been unwilling to tell Sheriff Ward Carroll

---

[nnnnn] This was most likely Mrs. Della McGuire Baird, whose daughter, Glenda Baird Vance, states her mother was the only saleslady by the surname of Baird at Farmer's Hardware at that time. Mrs. Vance, however, never heard anything about her mother selling a rope the morning of the murders and does not believe it to be true. Mrs. Vance's husband, Phil Vance, was the fellow Rotarian who followed Bryce Durham to and from the Rotary meeting the evening of the murders and was able to account for the timing of Bryce's return to his dealership. [Source: Vance, Glenda. Phone conversation with author. January 28, 2023.]

anything. The informant also shared that a Vietnam veteran had been working in the university's food services but left town the Monday after the murders. A neighbor to this man said he had been killing animals in the same manner the Durhams had been killed – tying them up and drowning them – and he had learned these methods in Vietnam. The informant had forgotten the veteran's name but said Boone Police Captain Arlie Isaacs knew it. At the time, the SBI had reportedly said this man fit the profile of the Durhams' murderer. It was also possible the man had had dealings with the Durhams and/or their dealership.[1506] *[No further information regarding this individual is located within the Watauga County Sheriff's Office investigation file.]*

Beyond these random pieces of new information, there was another development that transpired in 1989 and involved the most incredible stories concerning the Durham murders that had surfaced since the sworn statement of Dean Chandler seventeen years earlier. And, oddly enough, they once more involved "the Asheville boys"….

CHAPTER 13

THE TALES OF "PAPA BARE"

In July 1989, Paul Bare, a former garage owner[1507] and a prison inmate in Taylorsville, North Carolina wrote a letter to the Watauga County Sheriff's Department. Known by some as "Papa Bare,"[1508] what he was prepared to share was no Goldilocks story. Bare wrote, "Since you have offered a reward for the name of the woman in the Bryce Durham deal, the first name is Della White or Wyatt.[ooooo] Her husband's name was R. D. Wyatt or White. I have forgotten the last name. Also, I know a little more info on the deal."[1509] In September 1989, Sheriff Red Lyons interviewed Bare in prison. Bare said he knew who killed the Durhams, and that Troy Hall put "money in a man's hand on the street to get to R. D. Wyatt, who then set up the deal through two other men."[1510]

R. D. Wyatt was from Asheville and had been in trouble with the law since the age of sixteen. Between 1955 and 1960, he was arrested for tire slashings, assault, breaking and entering, larceny and receiving, possession of burglary tools, and robbery.[1511] Wyatt was also known for writing bad checks, flim-flam deals, and auto thefts.[1512] In June 1962, he escaped from a Mitchell County, North Carolina prison camp road work gang,[1513] and in September that same year from an Avery-Mitchell county prison camp near Spruce Pine, North Carolina.[1514] In August 1962, Jerry Cassada – one of the Asheville men previously charged with the Durham murders – escaped from the same Avery-Mitchell prison camp.[1515] In 1969, while living on the same Asheville street as Cassada, the two were charged with breaking into a home and stealing more than $1,000 worth of guns. Both men pleaded guilty to receiving stolen property,[1516] and both received five to eight-year sentences.[1517] Between 1969 and 1971, Wyatt escaped twice more but was recaptured each time.[1518]

At the time of the Durham murders, Bare was living in Wilkes County and had a black 1960 four-door Chevrolet for sale.[ppppp] The car had large tires and had been souped-up with two four-barrel carburetors for transporting whiskey. According to Bare, Della Wyatt and another woman came to him inquiring about the car. He took them on a ride up Highway 268, running the car 125-130 miles per hour, and the women agreed the car was fast enough. They left and returned the following day, January 31, 1972 (three days before the Durham slayings), with a check for part of the money – around $750. They wrote the car's serial number on the check and promised the check was good,

---

[ooooo] Contrary to what Bare wrote, there seems to be no reward that was specifically offered by the sheriff's department for the identification of a woman, although Bare may have been referring to the department's desire to identify the woman Jerry Harrison had seen at the phone booth alongside what appeared to be the Durhams' vehicle on the night of the murders. Concerning Bare's uncertainty about the spelling of Della Wyatt's name, her maiden name was White, and her married name was Wyatt, making her name Della White Wyatt. [Source: https://www.findagrave.com/memorial/45260013/della_wyatt.]

[ppppp] In this interview Bare said around 1984, a man in Raleigh, NC told him this car was still in existence, stored in an outbuilding near Burnsville, NC. [Source: Bare, Paul. Interview with Red Lyons. September 23, 1989, Watauga County Sheriff's Office investigation file 118-H-1/2/3.]

but they asked Bare not to cash it as they did not want it run through the bank. They took the car and said someone would come later for the title, with cash in exchange for the check. Later, Jerry Cassada and another man came from Boone (or Deep Gap, also in Watauga County) and gave Bare the needed cash in exchange for the check, plus an extra hundred dollars. Cassada did not want the title in his name, so it was put in the other man's name. The unnamed man saw that Bare also had a souped-up Chrysler for sale that he wanted, and he came back later and got it.[1519] *[Could Dean Chandler have been the unnamed man, and could the souped-up 1970 Pontiac that Sonny Burkins said Chandler told him he was driving the night of the Durham murders (see p. 168), actually have been the souped-up Chrysler that Bare was selling?]*

Paul Bare

In 1972 or 1973,[qqqqq] Bare was in a Burnsville, North Carolina prison unit. His incarceration there may have stemmed from his being charged with assault with a deadly weapon with intent to kill following his October 1971 shooting of a man in Wilkes County.[1520] While in Burnsville, Bare met fellow inmate R. D. Wyatt. Wyatt was a good friend of the unnamed man who had bought the Chrysler from Bare, and he asked Bare if he knew him. Bare affirmed he did. A few days later, Wyatt was sent to the hospital in Raleigh, and Bare followed shortly after because he was partially disabled with Hodgkin's disease[1521] and needed cancer treatments. Once reunited in Raleigh, Wyatt told Bare he had arranged the attack on the Durhams and had enlisted the help of Cassada, "the old lady" (referring to Wyatt's wife Della[rrrrr]), and two black men from Wilkesboro, one with the surname Redding – a son of Tom Redding and a brother of Tommy Redding – who was from the primarily black Cairo community of Wilkes County and who fled to California immediately after the murders. *[The only other known son of Tom Redding and the only known brother to Tommy Redding was James George "Jimmy/Jimmie" Redding, a U. S. Marine Corps Sergeant in Vietnam, who did live for an extended period of time in California.* [1522]*]* Wyatt said they used a four-wheel drive Jeep to go so far and then the Chevrolet from there on out. This may have been a reference to the taking of the Durhams' GMC "Jimmy" to Poplar Grove Road and then using the Chevrolet that Della Wyatt had purchased from Bare as the getaway car. Bare's understanding was that Della Wyatt drove the car.[sssss] Wyatt further stated their

---

[qqqqq] At one point in his interview with Sheriff Lyons, Bare said this prison meeting with Wyatt occurred in 1982 or 1983, but then said no, he meant 1972 or 1973. [Source: Bare, Paul. Interview with Red Lyons. September 23, 1989, Watauga County Sheriff's Office investigation file 118-H-1/2/3.]

[rrrrr] At the time of the Durham murders, R. D. Wyatt was 32 years old, and his wife Della was 53. Despite the twenty-one year difference in their ages, Della's previous two marriages and divorces, her eight children, her poverty, and the fact that R. D. was widely feared, they remained together for a long period of time, and Della is said to have worshipped R. D. At the time of Paul Bare's 1989 interview, he believed Della to be living in Burnsville, North Carolina and said she had a boyfriend by the last name of Whisnant, who had been in prison and who had written phony statements about Bare in an unsuccessful attempt to have the FBI prosecute him [Bare] on other charges. Bare stated Della "used to come around with 'some of them' running up to Detroit on their drug buy." In later life, Della Wyatt was a churchgoer and a nursing home dietician, dying in 1992 as a 74-year-old great-grandmother. R. D. Wyatt died at age 79 in 2019. [Sources: Bare, Paul. Interview with Red Lyons. September 23, 1989, Watauga County Sheriff's Office investigation file 118-H-1/2/3; Rudy, Jennifer Bradley (granddaughter of Della Wyatt). Facebook messages to author. March 23, 2024; https://www.findagrave.com/memorial/45260013/della_wyatt; https://www.findagrave.com/memorial/203150756/r_d-wyatt.]

[sssss] Della Wyatt reportedly did not have a driver's license; nonetheless, she is said to have driven and been in a vehicle accident in 1966. [Source: Rudy, Jennifer Bradley (granddaughter of Della Wyatt). Facebook messages to author. March 23, 2024.]

payoff was $160,000 in dope money taken from the Durham house, and Troy Hall knew where the money was located. Wyatt told Bare they left behind the money that belonged to Bryce Durham's dealership. Wyatt also told Bare that Troy initiated "the job," told Wyatt what to do and how to do it, and suggested what times of day would be good to go in. Bare said Wyatt told him how the murders were carried out, but Bare had forgotten those details in the ensuing seventeen years, other than one of the men was already in the house when the Durhams arrived home, and Wyatt talking a lot about a bathtub. Troy was never to be implicated in any of this, and Wyatt and others tried to keep quiet about his involvement. Bare said Wyatt never mentioned Ginny Hall, and Bare did not think she was involved. Bare had knowledge of Troy being badly involved in "some shaky business," including breaking and entering and larceny in Wilkes County and other locations. He said Troy was hurting people and causing a lot of trouble.[1523]

According to Bare, he originally met Bryce Durham through a mutual friend, Haggie Faw,[1524ttttt] who ran the Chevrolet dealership in Wilkes County, and over a sixteen-month period, Bare had made two or three trips hauling used cars for Bryce. Bare said Bryce had a man from Galax, Virginia bring the vehicles from up north to Galax, and then Bare would take them to his garage and work on them before taking them on to Boone. When Bryce needed a repair done on a car prior to anyone else seeing the problem, he would have Bare fix it before it went to the car lot and before the title arrived. Then it would appear as if the car had just been brought in and prospective buyers would not know the difference. Bare said he had run thousands of miles back on vehicles for Bryce and many others. In fact, Bare said he ran the miles back on every car he repaired for Bryce, but he acknowledged that was common practice at the time and most car buyers presumed that was the case.[1525] *[Bare is likely the man whose name Ginny Durham could not remember when she stated to investigators she drove vehicles to a Wilkes County garage on several occasions for her father to have the mileage rolled back.[1526]]*

Bare claimed that, even before he met Wyatt in prison, he and a lot of people knew Bryce was dealing in large quantities of drugs with "some big people from up north." The drugs were not marijuana or cocaine but "truck driver's pills" – RJS's (the "RJS" stamp representing the pharmaceutical division of the R. J. Strasenburgh Company), Deximol, Dexedrine, Benzedrine, etc. According to Bare, Bryce got the drugs from a Wilkes County man who lived down Highway 268 and who later got into trouble around 1979 or 1980 for some stolen merchandise out of the Chrysler motor division in Delaware. *[Could this be a reference to one of Bryce Durham's Prevette cousins who lived at Roaring River (which corresponded with Highway 268) and who were later convicted of drug trafficking? (see p. 167). On the other side of their family, these same Prevette's had cousins who, at least in the 1940s, lived in Delaware and were charged with operating illegal liquor stills.[1527]]* Bare further claimed drugs were flown into Boone from Dover, Delaware and the airplane would land at the small airstrip near the Watauga County Hospital. The pilot of the plane lived in a farmhouse between Trade and Mountain City, Tennessee. Bare said Bryce would then put several thousand dollars' worth of packaged cases of drugs in a parked car with a tag on it, and then a man would come for the car and drive away in it.[1528]

[ttttt] Haggie Faw was a first cousin once removed to Bruce Faw, who lived behind the Durham family on Clyde Townsend Road. Haggie Faw worked for the Gaddy Motor Company for seventeen years and also for Empire Cadillac-Oldsmobile. For several years, he was both an assistant coroner and an employee of the Wilkes County Sheriff's Department. [Sources: Genealogical research by author; https://tributearchive.com/obituaries/2162759/Haggie-William-Faw.]

In 1982, a decade after the Durham murders, Bare (then living at Laurel Springs in Ashe County, North Carolina) was indicted alongside a man named Gary Miller for kidnapping and first-degree murder in the 1981 disappearance and death of Lonnie Gamboa. Gamboa had been executed because he owed a large drug debt "to cocaine dealers supplying Western North Carolina." His frozen body was retrieved from the Ore Knob Mine shaft in Laurel Springs.[1529] Miller was a native of Boone and, in 1967, had moved to Asheville, where, although he had no dealings with Jerry Cassada, Dean Chandler, Eugene Garren, and Dewey Coffey, he knew who they were by sight, and Garren's sister Pam worked for Miller at a drive-in theater he acquired in 1976.[1530] Miller first came into contact with Paul Bare around 1974, after which "things went real crazy." Over time, the two became well acquainted and were jointly involved in "some pretty serious things." In addition, Miller pleaded guilty to the drug-related kidnapping and murder of Tommy Forester (whose body, like Gamboa's, was found in the Ore Knob mine shaft), and the kidnapping of Forester's girlfriend, Darlene Callahan, who Miller and others reportedly trafficked, forcing her into prostitution in Chicago.[1531] Miller pleaded guilty to two second-degree murder charges and three first-degree kidnapping charges and was sentenced to forty-five years in prison.[1532] Bare was convicted and sentenced to life in prison with the possibility of parole after twenty years.[1533] Miller would later state it had been Bare, along with two other men, one of whom was from Tennessee and connected to the Dixie Mafia, who murdered Forester.[1534]

In November 1981, a month prior to the murders of Gamboa and Forester and the kidnapping of Callahan, a drug-related shootout occurred at Miller's home on Moffitt Branch in Buncombe County, North Carolina. The incident was investigated by Donald Cole, a criminal investigator with the Buncombe County Sheriff's Department, and Miller was arrested and charged with trafficking cocaine and possession with intent to distribute. According to Cole's official sworn statement, Miller initially discussed the shooting with him, but "Miller's next statement to the officer was of the death and murders of the Durham family in Boone." Some hours later, when Cole and Officer Herb DeWeese interviewed Miller, "Miller told about the people involved in the Boone murders in detail…." It is unclear why Miller chose these particular moments to bring up the Durham Case, and it is unknown what he shared, but after his June 1982 capture in Caldwell County, North Carolina for the Forester, Gamboa, and Callahan crimes, he made an additional statement at the Ashe County Detention Center. According to Ashe County Sheriff Richard Waddell, Miller spoke to him in the presence of Chief Deputy Gene Goss for a period of four hours, during which "Miller…stated that he knew who did the Durham murders in Boone. He stated that [Jerry] Cassada, who was arrested and turned loose, was one of the people and there was two colored men from Wilkes County helped him. That one of the colored men was now living in California and the other one was living in Wilkes County. Miller stated that Bryce Durham was one of the largest drug dealers in the area, and that he (Miller) himself had bought hundreds of pounds of marijuana from him."[1535] Miller later refuted this as completely false and said he never made that statement, that he was not involved in the purchase, use, or sale of drugs until early 1974 – a good two years after the Durham murders – and that he never knew Bryce Durham or purchased any drugs from him. Miller attributed the earlier statement to an Alcohol, Tobacco, and Firearms (ATF) Agent who Miller said never spoke with or interviewed him. Miller asserted it as common practice for law enforcement agents to fabricate things to pit defendants against one another and for competing law enforcement agencies to seek notoriety as the star in a particular case or to vie for bigger budgetary slices.[1536]

Sometime during his association with Paul Bare, Bare had told Miller how the Durham murders unfolded, although Bare's story differed from what he would tell Watauga County Sheriff Red

Lyons in the later, 1989 interview from prison. Bare told Miller that Bryce Durham was part of a pervasive and widespread ring of new and used car dealers – primarily associated with General Motors – that stretched from Chicago and Texas to Alabama, Florida, North Carolina, and the northeastern United States. This ring reportedly laundered money and went to a great deal of expense and extremes (including murder) to keep their car dealership connections quiet. They controlled much of the drugs being brought into the country and were heavily involved in the importation and distribution of what was known as "airplane dope" as opposed to "boat dope." (Miller asserted Bare "was really big in the marijuana business including plane loads and boat loads."[1537]) This dope was primarily marijuana as, in 1972, it was almost impossible to pull together substantial quantities of cocaine due to the absence of large labs and cartels. The dope Bare claimed Bryce was involved in was marijuana being flown in a DC-3 airplane from Colombia to the North Carolina mountains, where some airports were considered "friendly," selling fuel and allowing offloads, or where local law enforcement might provide protection.[1538] Because the DC-3's cargo hold would be so heavily filled – often fifty percent over its payload – it could barely get off the ground, and it only had enough fuel to reach, at most, areas just shy of the Virginia border without having to refuel. Once landed, a number of logistics ensued. Whoever was designated as the money man would enlist other men to offload the cargo into one or more tractor and trailer semitrucks, which would then be driven to other distribution locations. Meanwhile, drug dealers who were prepared to pick up their individual loads would sit in their vehicles at various locations such as restaurant parking lots and wait to receive a code via pager to call someone or go somewhere. As they were notified, each would drive their vehicles to the semitrucks and take turns picking up their individual loads. Each pickup would be arranged in such a way that there was no interaction between them, and all of this transpired quickly so everyone involved could get away from the "hot area" and spread out. Much of the plane's cargo would ultimately be placed in cars purchased at auction by various automobile dealers and transported to their lots. It was not uncommon for haulers with eight or ten cars going down the road to have some of the car trunks loaded with drugs. According to what Bare told Miller, Bryce was heavily involved in the distribution of marijuana *[a contradiction of Bare's 1989 interview, in which he stated Bryce was not involved with marijuana but with pills]*. Miller felt Bryce may have moved to Boone at the direction of the car dealers' ring (perhaps on the heels of his previous work in Mount Airy) for the purpose of carrying out their activities, and although the scope of his "assignment" was unknown, it was believed he placed drugs into cars being sent to other locations rather than selling drugs locally.[1539] *[These allegations of drug trafficking via cars on haulers actually align with the reported activities of Troy Hall, who Bryce had discovered was placing drugs inside the glove boxes of cars at his dealership that were being taken to auction. See p. 30.]*

Sometime not long before the Durham murders, Bare said Bryce had been the ground and money man for a particular planeload of marijuana, valued at $3 million, that was flying into nearby Ashe County. *[This is problematic because the airstrips in Ashe County – one at Nathan's Creek and one at Jefferson – were not established until 1976 and 1977, respectively...well after Bryce Durham had been murdered. Airports did exist, however, in Avery, Caldwell, McDowell, and Watauga counties.[1540]]* Bare told Miller that, for this particular load, Bryce had contracted Jerry Cassada, Dean Chandler, Eugene Garren, and Dewey Coffey – all alleged to be serious, hardcore individuals – as the offloaders of the cargo, and they were to be paid $1,000 each. When a freak snowstorm occurred, the plane – perhaps at Bryce's behest – was rerouted to a clear area such as Marion in McDowell County, North Carolina, where another crew of offloaders was likely on standby. When the plane was diverted, Bryce did not inform the Asheville men, and when the four arrived in Ashe

County to find no plane, they were angry and wanted their money. Bare was one of the individuals who was supposed to pick up a quantity of the offloaded marijuana in Ashe County, and when he connected with the four men from Asheville, he suggested they go get their money from Bryce. It is unlikely the men knew where Bryce lived, so Bare, described as a sort of mechanical genius, drove them in his self-engineered four-wheel drive van (a rarity in 1972) to the Durham house in Boone on the night of the murders. *[This is another contradiction as Bare later told Sheriff Red Lyons he was in jail the night of the murders.[1541]]* Bare claimed to have remained inside the van while Cassada, Chandler, Garren, and Coffey, perhaps high on Dilaudid (an opiate painkiller and, in this story, their drug of choice) entered the house and committed the murders. Bare's claim to have been the driver was common among criminals, many portraying themselves to have only "held the horses." In addition to the $1,000 each had anticipated being paid, the four Asheville men had in mind to take whatever quantity of money they found in the Durham house, even in excess of what they were originally promised. Based on Bare's estimation of the $3 million dollar value of the plane's cargo and lacking the knowledge that Bryce had gone to meet the plane in the alternative location and paid for the cargo, they anticipated finding a huge sum of money in the house, perhaps as much as the entire $3 million. With this in mind, the men ransacked the house and brutalized the Durhams in an effort to make Bryce reveal the money's location.[1542]

In 1984, while Gary Miller was incarcerated in the Buncombe County jail, he shared a cell with another inmate, who had been arrested on a separate charge and who he understood was one of the two men who had been charged with the Durham murders in 1972. Miller claimed to have previously known Cassada and his associates by sight, but he was not entirely sure of this man's identity. Although the man was called by another name, Miller came to believe he was probably Jerry Cassada. This cellmate (referred to here as "Cassada") knew Miller had been associated with Bare and assumed Miller was "higher on the food chain" than Bare and might know how he, Chandler, Garren, and Coffey were able to walk free. "Cassada" told Miller he had fully expected them to receive the death penalty due to the brutality of the murders. "Cassada" also related to Miller that, although they had had court-appointed attorneys, other attorneys (who may not have been on record) arrived on the scene and told him ["Cassada"] and his co-defendants to keep their mouths shut – to not say anything about the case then or ever. "Cassada" told Miller one of his co-defendants was a leak and had planned to testify against him and the others, but he later recanted and decided not to say anything. Although this would have been Dean Chandler, Miller understood "Cassada" believed it was Eugene Garren. At any rate, "Cassada" told the attorneys he was going to take care of the snitch, and they told him he was not to do anything, that that was part of the deal. Although the attorneys for Cassada, Chandler, and Garren had been court-appointed, Miller understood "Cassada" believed someone had put up money for their defense to get them off, and he wanted to know if Miller knew who had done that. Miller did not, but based on hearsay and conversations with others, he came to believe there was no will on the part of the state to prosecute the case, and the state did not want to convict the men because either the case may have brought out Bryce Durham's interaction with them, and they wanted to "paint" him as being really clean, and/or the ring of car dealers had gotten to someone in the court system – perhaps one of the prosecuting entities – with "a sack full of money." The fact that the snitch had recanted may have also given prosecutors an out, claiming they had no case without that testimony. Although Garren and Coffey were released after the probable cause hearing in June 1972, Cassada and Chandler were indicted for the Durham murders and were to have stood trial separately in 1973, but their cases were never prosecuted. Miller, however, did not understand this to be the case from his cellmate, who indicated, albeit erroneously, they had actually been tried and found not guilty. Miller believed this explained

"Cassada's" willingness to speak freely about the case and to state he had been at the Durham house – that because of double jeopardy, he could never again be tried for the murders. "Cassada" told Miller he and his accomplices found no money in the Durham house. He repeated emphatically, "There was no money! There was no money there! There was no money in the house!" Miller related to "Cassada" some of the details Bare had shared with him. One of the pieces of information concerned the allegation that Bryce had met the plane at the alternative location with the large quantity of money the killers had hoped to find and had used it to pay for the cargo. Upon learning this, an extremely indignant "Cassada" told Miller that Bryce deserved what he got – that he should have made arrangements to inform them of the plane's diversion, and that he should have paid them something for their trouble, even if not the full amount. It had been a "bad, bad, bad mistake" for Bryce not to have paid them in order to keep them quiet and pacified.[1543]

An anonymous source believes Bare's implicating of R. D. and Della Wyatt and Troy Hall may have stemmed from his being wronged by them in some way unrelated to the murders, and he may have been seeking revenge, his accusations against them being the only weapon at his disposal – "If you're in prison, it's sort of hard to reach out with a telephone cord and wrap it around somebody's neck." Because Bare told authorities he had some additional information he could share if or when he got out of prison, that may have been indicative of a vendetta he wanted to settle; otherwise, he might have offered it straightaway to secure an early release. Regarding Bare's other story involving the Asheville suspects, he reportedly kept the van that he claimed to have driven them to Boone in, as well as the tires that were on the van, understanding authorities might have taken photographs of the tire prints. He may also have retained items brought out of the Durham house by the four killers and left in the van after Bare took them to their vehicles in Asheville or wherever their drop off point was. Although these items may have been of little or no monetary value, Bare, if need be, could have used them, along with the van and the tires, as his "get out of jail free card," by telling authorities what had happened that night, implicating the four other men, and sticking to his claim of only being the driver with hopes of immunity or reduced charges.[1544]

The contradictions told by Bare cast a measure of doubt on his truthfulness, causing one to wonder if his accounts were more fable than fact. During Bare's trial for Lonnie Gamboa's murder, ATF Agent Tommy Chapman was questioned about Bare's credibility. Chapman testified Bare had volunteered to be an informant and his relationship with Bare, which began in the late 1960s, had deteriorated by 1972 because of Bare's lies. Chapman affirmed Bare told a lot of stories, "told a lot of things about people [that] never turned out to be correct" and led him on "a lot of wild goose chases."[1545]

Initially, no one would talk to Paul Bare about the Durham Case, and if he had been released from prison, he may have told authorities more.[1546] But Bare had been implanted with a pacemaker shortly before his interview with Sheriff Red Lyons, and a month later, he collapsed in his prison yard. Despite resuscitation efforts, he succumbed to a heart attack,[1547] and the remainder of what he knew – if anything – died with him. There would be no more tales – tall or otherwise – told by "Papa Bare."

CHAPTER 14

"NOT A COW IN TEXAS"

In the early 1990s, while forensic psychologist Richard Walter was teaching at Methodist University in Fayetteville, North Carolina,[1548] he was contacted by three or four SBI agents, including Richard Lester, who asked him to review the Durham Case, and he agreed to do so pro bono.[1549] Walter was a co-founder of The Vidocq Society, a "members-only crime-solving club in Philadelphia, Pennsylvania" named for "Eugène François Vidocq, a legendary nineteenth century French detective and former criminal who used his knowledge of the criminal mind to look at cold case homicides from the psychological perspective of the perpetrator." At the society's meetings, "law enforcement officials from around the world presented cold cases for review" by the society and sought the expert advice of its members, which included "current and former FBI criminal profilers, homicide investigators, various forensic scientists, psychologists, and coroners."[1550] According to Walter, The Vidocq Society's conclusions were "successful about eighty-five percent of the time," although "a relatively low rate of" the society's suggestions led to conviction.[1551]

Throughout the years, Ginny Durham Mackie received periodic case updates from law enforcement, including the Watauga County Sheriff's Department and the State Bureau of Investigation. She was particularly receptive to former SBI Agent Charlie Whitman while less so to others.[1552] In 1991, she completed a questionnaire for Richard Lester and Richard Walter regarding Troy Hall's pre- and post-crime behaviors, although most of the questions had previously been asked by Whitman. Because this was nineteen years after the fact, Ginny could not recall many details about Troy's behavior in the nine-month period preceding the murders, but she did provide some details concerning his later behavior. According to Ginny, Troy particularly trusted his brother Ray, their mother, and their sister Lois, and he maintained contact with them, while to a lesser extent with brothers Claude and John. Ginny stated Troy was secretive both before and after the murders and had private conversations in the car with Ray. After the murders, Troy kept a locked box. Ginny also expressed a willingness to travel to meet with Walter, but the SBI, which would have facilitated the meeting, experienced a budgetary issue that prevented it.[1553]

Walter presented the Durham Case files and crime scene photos to a couple of dozen Vidocq Society members for discussion. The murders evoked reminiscences of the 1959 Clutter family murders in Holcomb, Kansas as described by Truman Capote in his book *In Cold Blood.* Walter told the group the Durham Case was "a wonderful case [with] all sorts of drama," and he stated, "As it happens, the killer was rather obvious. This kind of killer always thinks he's smarter than he really is." According to Walter, "the killer knew the local roads and mountains and the Durham house." When asked by a member who the killer was, Walter declined to provide a name but replied, "I have a theory. We'll see if the state police are savvy enough to go forward with it." According to Walter, despite problems in the Halls' marriage and Ginny's family pressuring her to leave Troy, "police never considered him [Troy] a major suspect."[1554]

This, however, is contrary to what most law enforcement officers have expressed, and Walter was not alone in his suspicion of Troy Hall. In fact, according to former Attorney General Rufus Edmisten, Troy was suspected from the beginning, in part because of his rough background in Wilkes County and the impression that he was not leveling with everyone.[1555] At the very least, Troy was a person of interest, and his involvement in the murders was a firmly held belief of Boone Police Chief Clyde Tester and of Sheriff Ward Carroll,[uuuuu] who felt Troy was behind the murders. According to Carroll, Troy was smart as well as a rough character capable of murder and a lot of other things.[1556]

Retired law enforcement officer and private detective Jerry Vaughn, who worked on the Durham Case for many years, said people tried to link Troy to the murders as early as mere days after they occurred. Officers even watched him and his associates with binoculars during Wilkes County stakeouts, but there was never enough evidence to prove his involvement. Vaughn understood officers wanted to arrest Troy, but he believed Troy would have "dried up," and they would have never gotten anything out of him. Vaughn knew this from firsthand experience as he had personally met Troy, and he refused to talk. Still, Vaughn was among those who believed Troy played a part in the murders, and that his motivation for doing so was the revision of the Durhams' wills.[1557]

Based on what others (perhaps including extended Durham family members and Bryce Durham's attorney Carroll Gardner) told SBI Agent Larry Wagner,[vvvvv] Troy wanted the inheritance that would come...upon the death[s] of his father-in-law and mother-in-law.... They despised him. He was from the other side of the tracks and part of a rough and tumble family from Wilkes County. They thought Ginny could do better. She rebelled and lived with Troy before marrying him. Troy was bitter by this shoddy treatment. He saw a way to get his hands on a lot of money.[1558] According to Wagner, Troy was arrogant, uncooperative, self-confident, and assured. "He thinks he is very smart, and obviously he is. He is capable of murder. We found evidence of his reading some interesting books in college. He had a pattern of checking out books about explosives and crimes and the perfect murder." Troy once told his school acquaintance Roger Dick (who Wagner interviewed) that he knew how to get away with the perfect crime.[1559][wwwww] SBI Agent Richard Lester believed Troy was one of the killers,[1560] and belief in Troy's guilt was reiterated as recently as a 2022 interview with current Watauga County Sheriff Len Hagaman: "I think from day one, he has been involved, whether directly or indirectly, I don't know."[1561]

Among those who personally knew Troy and suspected his involvement in the murders were some of his own family members and as early as the morning after *(see p. 98)*. Troy's brother-in-law, Bob

---

[uuuuu] Troy always claimed that a day or two after the murders, Sheriff Carroll read him his rights. [Source: Mackie, Ginny Durham. Interview with Carolynn Johnson & Wade Colvard. December 7, 2020.]

[vvvvv] According to Wagner, the interview(s) with Carroll Gardner were very telling and are on file with the SBI office in Hickory, NC. [Source: Wagner, Larry. Phone interview with author. December 22, 2022.]

[wwwww] Author Charles Heatherly's notes indicate Dick's first name as "Robert," but it was actually Roger. Mr. Dick preferred not to speak with the author stating, "That was a long time ago and their [sic] is not much I remember about Troy." [Sources: Wagner, Larry. Interview with Charles Heatherly. December 18, 1987; Dick, Roger. E-mail to author. July 7, 2022.]

Gryder, said he did not believe Troy and his brother Ray could have murdered the Durhams, but he thought Troy may have hired it done.[1562] Ray Hall's former wife Kay stated Ray never indicated to her whether he was involved in the murders, but she believed if Troy planned the murder, he "would let someone else do his dirty work."[1563]

Ike Eller believed Troy could have committed the murders because he was mean, was always mad at his in-laws, and knew the right people to involve,[1564] and the first time Eller met with Bryce Durham's family following the murders, he said "Troy Hall did it. He killed them over that dollar will."[1565] After the murders, Eller and his wife were certainly uneasy about Troy and Ray Hall and instructed their son Tom to steer clear of them.[1566]

During the murder investigation, John Hall would not talk, and authorities had to acquire his and Ray Hall's fingerprints involuntarily.[1567] At one point, Sheriff Len Hagaman obtained a judge's order to obtain non-testimonial identification from Ray in the form of hair, saliva, and palm prints. Ray was reluctant. His attorney informed him he must comply, although he did not have to make a statement. The process took about five minutes, during which Ray never spoke.[1568] Neither John's nor Ray's prints matched any of the prints lifted from the Durham house.[1569]

Both the SBI and the Watauga County Sheriff's Department expressed interest in interviewing Troy further, but he never cooperated. SBI Agent Charlie Whitman traveled outside of North Carolina at one point to interview him, but without success.[1570] Sheriff Len Hagaman attempted to interview Troy on probably twenty occasions between 1976 and 1983, but Troy refused to speak and ordered him off the premises.[1571] According to Hagaman, "We didn't find anything out about Troy…he wasn't going to reveal anything. He was a very smart guy…. He [knew] the right things to say; he always did."[1572] This is echoed by former Boone Police Sergeant Jeff Rucker: "[Troy] was that smart – to be a step ahead if necessary."[1573]

Former Georgia Bureau of Investigation Agent and White County (Georgia) Chief Deputy Bob Ingram, who worked on the Durham Case many years later, suspected someone in the Durhams' inner circle set up their murders, and that someone was Troy Hall. When asked how certain he was about Troy, Ingram said, "Well, about 98%, if that's a good number." Like other investigators before him, Ingram also desired to interview Troy and told Watauga County Sheriff's officers, "He won't have a bowel movement for a month…after I talk to him, and he may not confess, but he's damn sure gonna know that I know."[1574]

Among the few people who maintained Troy's innocence were Cecil and Mildred Small. Although Cecil had expressed uncertainty in 1987 about Troy's involvement, two years later he stated Troy was an honest man. "Everybody says, 'Oh, Troy had a hand in that.' Troy didn't no more have a hand in that thing than [my cat] had." Mildred stated she would stake her life on his innocence. "Troy Hall was not that kind of person."[1575]

When interviewed three years after the murders and informed about the reward money, Troy's brother John stated "if he [John] did know anything…he probably would not tell," and "he didn't know when Troy and Ray did that murder, or if they had it done," but he did not think they could have.[1576] Troy was the favorite uncle of at least one of his nieces, who stated he was one of the best people she had ever met, and he was not involved [in the murders].[1577]

While Troy's and Ray's close friend, John Frazier, acknowledged the Halls had grown up in a "white liquor county" and disliked the law, and while Troy talked rough, he did not believe Troy or

Ray could kill anyone.[1578] On the contrary, Troy's friend, "Babes" Lowe, who claimed he had severed ties with Troy before the Durham murders, believed Troy was the type of person who could certainly pull off this type of crime.[1579] Some, however, wondered if Lowe and/or Frazier could have played a role in the murders. Those who knew Lowe well are confident he would not have been involved, and due to his family's wealth, would not have benefitted financially by doing so.[1580] Those who knew Frazier, who is said to have occasionally exhibited evil, Charles Mansonesque eyes[1581] and whose nickname was "Flim Flam," are less certain about him. He was much closer to Troy and Ray Hall than anyone else[1582] and has been described as crazy, perhaps somewhat sadistic, and willing to do anything for a thrill – at least at the time of the murders.[1583][xxxxx]

Immediately following the murders and until the present day, both sides of Bryce and Virginia Durham's family suspected and believed Troy Hall was involved. As one relative put it, "There's not a cow in Texas if he didn't have something to do with it."[1584]

[xxxxx] John Frazier died in 2005 at the age of sixty-one.

CHAPTER 15

PSYCHICS REVISITED

By February 1992, the reward money in the Durham Case had reached $50,000. The case remained open, and law enforcement officers had not given up on solving it,[1585] but unlike the banner year of 1989, during which several new pieces of information were offered by various informants, the past few years had proven barren. In 1990, the Watauga County Sheriff's Department received word from the Hickory, North Carolina Police Department that an anonymous caller had claimed a male Hickory resident was selling cocaine, had been involved in drugs and a Buick dealership in Boone in February 1972, had a .45-caliber gun, and "shot the man and other people." Who the victims were is unclear, but obviously not the Durhams as none of them were shot.[1586]

In June 1992, Bryce Durham's ninety-two-year-old mother, Collie Durham, died at her home in the Roaring River community of Wilkes County.[1587] Despite her and her late husband's fervent hopes, neither of them got the peace and closure they sought, and they died without ever knowing who killed their loved ones.[1588] Rufus Edmisten would later write, "I truly regret that I was not able to fulfill Mrs. Coy Durham's dying wish and solve this mystery."[1589]

More than twenty years had passed since clairvoyant M. B. Dykshoorn attempted to identify the Durhams' killers, and more than fifteen years had passed since psychic Peter Hurkos was recommended to the Boone Police Department when, in 1993, in the absence of other leads, the Watauga County Sheriff's Office,[yyyyy] in conjunction with the SBI, considered asking psychic investigator Noreen Renier, of Maitland, Florida, to review the case. Several years prior, Boone Police Sergeant Jeff Rucker had heard that Renier worked with a police artist on an unsolved Orlando, Florida case in which Renier provided a vehicle tag number she had envisioned via whatever "source" she had tapped into, thereby solving the case. Rucker subsequently contacted Renier, and during their conversation, she enquired if he had any evidence from the Durham crime scene she could touch. Renier employed psychometry, which entailed her physically holding something (preferably a metal object) that had belonged to a victim or that a suspect had left at the scene. To Rucker's knowledge, the only physical items being held from the night of the murders were the rope left around Bryce Durham's neck and Bryce's eyeglasses, which had presumably been knocked from his face. Renier responded positively to the possibility of putting the glasses on and seeing who and what Bryce had seen, then giving those details to a police artist who could sketch them. Rucker also researched some of Renier's credentials, and although he described her

[yyyyy] Sometime between 1991 and 1993, the Watauga County Sheriff's *Department* became known as the Watauga County Sheriff's *Office*.

"as reputable and very accurate while assisting law enforcement agencies with unsolved cases," he discounted utilizing her "due to his personal religious convictions." Rucker had been warned about and unnerved by the fact that the taped interview associated with the Orlando case revealed audible voices of an undetermined source (perhaps some spiritual realm?) speaking in addition to Renier's voice. Rucker did not want to involve himself in anything contrary to his Christian beliefs, although the decision ultimately belonged to the Watauga County Sheriff's Office, which still held jurisdiction over the Durham Case. By 1993, Renier had lectured at the FBI Academy in Quantico, Virginia, predicted the assassination attempt on President Ronald Reagan, and made appearances on such television programs as *Inside Edition*, *Joan Rivers*, *Geraldo*, *48 Hours*, and *America's Most Wanted*. In her renewed discussions with the sheriff's office, she did not want to know any details of the crime other than what type of crime it was and the victim's first name. She offered in-person consultations in Florida or by telephone, and based on her findings, a local police officer would produce a sketch of the suspect. Her fee in 1993 was $650, but because Rucker had initially contacted her about the Durham Case many years before, she was willing to reduce the fee by $100. Law enforcement agencies in Florida, New York, Virginia, and Ohio recommended Renier to the SBI, variously stating she was reputable, undisputedly credible, amazingly accurate, and honest. The only hesitant feedback came from a professor at the University of Virginia at Charlottesville, who stated Renier tended to be "publicity conscious," on which basis the university had distanced itself from her.[1590]

In the end, the sheriff's office decided against utilizing Renier's services, in part because they felt Dykshoorn's earlier attempt had been unfruitful, but Sheriff Red Lyons did give a similar opportunity that same year to Barbara Finney of Lynchburg, Virginia. This was Finney's first official attempt to solve such a case. She worked from photos but admitted it was problematic because, in addition to "a rush of information contained within the photos," she picked up "psychic garbage" from everyone who had previously touched the photos. Self-described as "very empathetic," Finney said she keyed in on feelings and emotions, while warring with logic and reason. Finney said the most significant image that came to her was that at least one of the Durhams' killers wore a straw cowboy hat and habitually rolled up packs of cigarettes in his sleeve, and she told Lyons she would try to draw a sketch of the man. Photos of the deceased Durhams upset Finney, but because of her great love for animals, she was particularly disturbed by a photo showing the small dog that had survived the attack. She did not believe the dog was allowed to live because the killer was an animal lover but because it was randomly "left in the lurch." Finney's other thoughts included the name "Fred Bell," who she felt might play a role in solving the case, and that the killer may have been a former friend of one of the Durham children or a jilted boyfriend who blamed the family. Finney admitted, however, that at least fifty percent of her statements were likely "garbage based on [her] own personal prejudices and opinions" influenced by other similar cases she had seen, heard, or read about. She shared that psychic abilities could also be heavily influenced by subconscious opinion. Finney told Lyons she hoped her mistakes and initial failure did not deter him from using psychics, and she confessed she worked better in situations involving an individual who was lost or being held captive, with the possibility of saving his or her life. Regarding the Durham murders, she stated, "This is a very strange case, and I am surprised that other cases with a similar modus operandi have not turned up again in 20 years.... It bothers me that someone could do stuff like that and get off scott free [sic]. In fact it enrages me." She added, "I have not totally given up on your case as...I frequently get answers in unexpected dreams. I still feel the answer and reason is bizarre, and the person is mental. Those of us who think rationally have a hard time figuring out the evidence left by the irrational. To us it makes no sense."[1591]

In the Watauga County Sheriff's Office Durham Case file, immediately following Barbara Finney's communication with Sheriff Lyons, are handwritten notes. The author of the notes is not identified, but the notes could presumably be Finney's. Titled "First Impressions," the notes include the following thoughts:

- The letters "F, E, and R" had flashed through the author's mind but had no meaning attached as yet.
- The author had feelings the murders were linked to organized crime; abnormal sexual behavior was involved, with either a victim or a killer being gender confused or gay; the killer enjoyed the murders, getting sexual gratification or a deep satisfaction in the way the victims died; a sleazy business motive (e.g., drugs, gambling) may have been involved; and the killer, in a blind rage and with irrational thought, felt a need to retaliate for something.
- The author thought the killer might be a relative of a minor figure in local government, and the killer might be living in another state in fear of capture, or already be dead, or be serving time for a lesser, unrelated crime.
- The author had not yet seen any crime scene photographs and was expecting to be disturbed by them and to see at least one of the victims in a near fetal position.[1592] *[Since Finney did view photos of the Durhams, if these were her notes, perhaps they were submitted prior to her seeing them.]*

While these otherworldly avenues led nowhere, the Watauga County Sheriff's Office had not given up on the Durham Case and would next turn to a grave for answers.

CHAPTER 16

TO EXHUME OR NOT TO EXHUME: THAT WAS THE QUESTION

Benny Staley (Source: 1968 West Wilkes High School Yearbook)

All in all, the 1990s were a wash for the Durham Case with the exception of one promising lead involving a dead man's fingerprints. In 1993, the late Benny Staley, a native of Wilkes County, North Carolina and son of a Baptist preacher, became a focal point in the case.[zzzzz] Early on, Staley had had run-ins with the law and dropped out of high school in 1968, having "developed a taste for fast cars and…[speeding] along 'ol' country roads' with little regard for the law or his future." Described as a pretty rough and reckless young man who was "always into something," he joined the Marine Corps in 1970, spent time at bases in North Carolina and South Carolina, and earned some meritorious commendations. Although Staley was stationed at Camp Lejeune in Jacksonville, North Carolina, some three-hundred miles east of Boone, it was rumored he had been seen in Boone the day of the murders. His military record noted that he was in training in Jacksonville on January 31, 1972 (three days before the Durhams were killed), but if he took some leave days afterward, it is possible he could have traveled to Boone.[1593][aaaaaa]

An eye of suspicion was further cast on Staley due to his association with Phil Fausnet,[1594] a 6'6," more than 260-pound man, who was nicknamed "California" because he had relocated to his mother's native Wilkes County[bbbbbb] from the west coast where he had been a Hells Angel.[1595]

[zzzzz] Ginny Durham Mackie stated she had no knowledge of Staley. Troy Hall's friend, "Babes" Lowe had at least heard of Staley through other friends, who told Lowe that Staley was a "very cocky type individual." Ted Brown clearly remembers that, when he worked for Ray and Troy Hall in the spring of 1974 in Wilkes County, Staley's wife, Donna Combs Staley, periodically visited with the Hall brothers at their construction site while on her lunch break. [Sources: Whitman, Charlie. Phone conversation with Sheriff Red Lyons. December 7, 1993, Watauga County Sheriff's Office investigation file 118-H-1/2/3; Lowe, William Asa. Interview with James C. Lyons. June 27, 1994, Watauga County Sheriff's Office investigation file 118-H-1/2/3; https://www.tributearchive.com/obituaries/2163299/Donna-Combs-Staley; Brown Ted. Phone conversation with author. June 10, 2022.]

[aaaaaa] There is no indication in the Watauga County Sheriff's Office investigation file as to what Staley's military record showed regarding his presence in camp from February 1 through February 3.

[bbbbbb] Fausnet was a second cousin to Willie Clay Call, one of Wilkes County's most renowned moonshiners, who was labeled by Federal ATF agents as "The Uncatchable," and to Willie Clay's brother, Norman Call, a former mayor of Wilkesboro. [Sources: Genealogical research by author; https://www.callfamilydistillers.com/new-page; Monte Mitchell, "One of Wilkes' best known former moonshiners dies at 73," *Winston-Salem Journal*, Winston-Salem, NC, August 7, 2012 (updated April 16, 2021; online), https://journalnow.com/one-of-wilkes-best-known-former-

Fausnet had reportedly been an offender since the fifth grade, and beginning in 1962, his rap sheet included burglary, parole violations, reckless driving, drug possession, possessing illegal firearms, grand theft auto, resisting arrest, smuggling merchandise, receiving stolen property, drunk driving, extortion, and arson, including setting fire to a former policeman's house and car. He was in prison several times doing both federal and state time and was suspected in California of conspiracy to commit murder, conspiracy to commit arson, dealing in large quantities of imported dope, firing a shot at the home of a police officer, and burning down parole and bail bonds offices.[1596] Fausnet was described as a mean, dangerous, violent, and very vengeful person who had done harm to others. He had residences in Munich, Germany, North Carolina, and Hong Kong, and a great many assets, including a Porsche,[1597] and he drove a Volkswagen bug.[1598] *[Could this be the Volkswagen bug that was seen the week before the murders making several trips on present-day Fox Hill Road, which dead-ended at a field behind and below the Durham home?]* In 1970, after having been notified by the Wilkes County Sheriff's Department that Fausnet was "armed and dangerous," Boone policemen arrested him in front of the local bus terminal and charged him with carrying a concealed weapon – a "pen pistol" that was "a spring-operated single-shot weapon" resembling a slightly larger than normal fountain pen. He carried it in his "right trouser pocket, and [it] was loaded with a solid point .22-calibre bullet." Fausnet had been seen previously and often around the Appalachian State University campus.[1599]

Over a period of time, various people contacted the Watauga County Sheriff's Office with information concerning Staley and Fausnet. According to one individual, who was around eighteen years old and hanging out with Staley, Fausnet, and others when news came out about the Durham murders in 1972, Staley and Fausnet acted very strange. The informant believed they were the killers and added that the pair loved to fight and hurt people. Another person reported overhearing Staley brag about criminally related activity, which caused him to wonder if Staley had played a role in the Durham murders. Yet another individual heard Staley and Fausnet discussing the murders of five people in an unknown location.[1600]

After his 1974 military discharge, Staley returned home to Wilkes County and eventually became manager of the Hardee's restaurant in North Wilkesboro. Although his military service had matured him to a degree, "he still had a wild streak [and] could be violent, especially if he was drinking or felt he had been insulted." Over the next several years, Staley was arrested for assault with a deadly weapon, breaking and entering, larceny, and possession of marijuana. In 1975, he was convicted of safecracking, breaking and entering, and larceny at the City Café in Wilkes County and was sentenced to prison. He appealed the case to the North Carolina Supreme Court and was granted a new trial because "the judge had inadvertently prejudiced the jury by remarks he made during the trial." In 1977, Staley was convicted once more and sentenced to twelve years in prison. He appealed again and was out of jail awaiting a court hearing when he was killed in a nighttime automobile accident in 1978. While traveling along North Carolina Highway 268 about one mile east of North Wilkesboro, he hit a bridge abutment, which caused his car to become airborne and strike an embankment opposite the bridge. The car overturned several times, and Staley was thrown from the vehicle and died instantly from head injuries. Moments later, a car traveling in the opposite direction ran over him and dragged his body about sixty-five feet down the highway.[1601]

---

moonshiners-dies-at-73/article_6056fea6-4d9c-5a3c-ad70-bad627a04a53.html; "Five Arrests Made By Marshal's Office," *The Greensboro Record*, Greensboro, NC, October 19, 1948, Section B, p. 1.]

In 1993, fifteen years after Staley's death, Sheriff Red Lyons contacted the National Personnel Records Center in St. Louis, Missouri to obtain Staley's fingerprints to "either clear or confirm" his involvement in the Durham triple homicide,[1602] but this evidently did not prove to be fruitful, nor did checking with other sheriff's departments, the SBI, and the U. S. Marine Corps.[1603] In 1994, stating it "would be beneficial to law enforcement," Tom Rusher, District Attorney for the 24th Judicial District, with the involvement of the Watauga County Sheriff's Office, filed a petition asking Wilkes County Superior Court Judge Julius A. Rousseau, Jr. to order the exhumation of Staley in order to obtain his fingerprints and palm prints. Although the petition did not specifically name the Durham Case, it referred to a "serious unsolved felony crime" in Watauga County.[1604] Sheriff Lyons and Wilkes County Sheriff Dane Mastin declined to identify the case the petition pertained to, but other law enforcement sources told *The Journal-Patriot* in Wilkes County the felony crime referred to the Durham murders.[1605] Investigators also informed Staley's family of the connection to the Durham Case. The petition worried and upset the family,[1606] and they stated their intention to fight the exhumation.[1607] Judge Rousseau "agreed to continue the case after attorneys for Staley's family asked for time to prepare their case opposing the request."[1608][cccccc]

It was eventually determined the Watauga County Sheriff's Office had overlooked "a less dramatic alternative" to exhumation – the possibility of acquiring Staley's prints from the State of North Carolina Department of Corrections (DOC) based on Staley's criminal record. The DOC was ultimately able to fax Staley's fingerprints to the sheriff's office. Although the fingerprints did not match those lifted from the Durham crime scene, District Attorney Tom Rusher said Staley was not ruled out as a suspect because his palm prints were unobtainable and because investigators had other evidence indicating Staley's involvement. Due to Staley's death in the automobile accident, "his palms probably were badly scraped and would not yield useful prints, even if the body had not already decomposed." Also, H. D. Caudill, Jr., president of Reins-Sturdivant Funeral Home in Wilkesboro, had previously told the Watauga County Sheriff's Office that Staley's fingers were "leather-like,"[1609] and the deterioration rate and decomposition of Staley's corpse – potentially affected by moisture and fungus – would have also been a determining factor as to the usefulness of his prints.[1610] Rusher thought the odds of getting useful prints were remote and "did not warrant disturbing the grave and paying at least $2,000 to have the body reburied."[1611]

When Bryce Durham's sister, Gayle Mauldin, had learned investigators had new evidence and planned to exhume Staley's body, she was initially thrilled and "hoped this would be the tie-in." When nothing came of it, she stated, "This is really bursting the bubble."[1612] One more disappointment. One more dead end….

[cccccc] Around the same time that talk began publicly circulating about Staley's possible exhumation, the Wilkes County home of one of Staley's associates, Henry Minton, was blown up one night after having gasoline poured all around it, and Minton was badly burned. Benny Staley's sister-in-law relayed this information to the Watauga County Sheriff's Office and also shared her concerns for the safety of her mother. In June 1994, Virginia Durham's great-niece, Diana Edwards, phoned the Watauga County Sheriff's Office to seek information about the court order for Staley's exhumation. She stated that older family members, having heard news of the investigation, were concerned about the case, although the specific concerns were not outlined in the phone message. [Sources: Genealogical research by author; Watauga County Sheriff's Office investigation file 118-H-1/2/3.]

CHAPTER 17

OLD CASE, NEW MILLENIUM

Considering Dean Chandler's sworn statement in the 1970s, Paul Bare's tales in the 1980s, and the exploration of Benny Staley's possible involvement in the 1990s, one would think the various versions of how the Durham murders transpired would have petered out, but the 2000s and 2010s would yield their own.

In 2001, in a "he said she said she said" scenario, a confidential informant who was a prison guard in Morganton, North Carolina met with Captain Paula May at the Watauga County Sheriff's Office and reported that he worked with a new female prison guard, who lived in Caldwell County, North Carolina. During a conversation, the informant mentioned to the female guard he was from Watauga County, and they began discussing people they knew from the area and things that had happened in Boone. The female guard said she knew something about the Durham murders and then proceeded to tell the informant a female friend from Caldwell County told her a woman named Janie Edmisten (aka Elaine Chapman)[dddddd] was the one who knocked on the Durhams' door the night of the murders. Edmisten reportedly told the Durhams her car had broken down, and she asked if she could use their phone. When the Durhams gave her entrance, unnamed men who were with Edmisten also entered. Edmisten then left the house and waited in the car with the understanding that the men were going to rob but not kill the Durhams. The informant encouraged the female guard to share these details with authorities, but she refused, saying she had been "burned" by law enforcement when she cooperated with them in the past when she and her husband ran a poker house. The female guard was also hesitant to speak out because she was "scared to death of those people" (the murderers). Edmisten was described as an attractive woman who traded sex for drugs, particularly cocaine, and who cohabited with men in the Lenoir/Morganton area. She served time in prison and was associated, both directly and indirectly, with a number of individuals who were involved with gambling, moonshining, shootings, murder, assault, arson, theft, vandalism, breaking and entering,

---

[dddddd] Elaine "Janie" Chapman was unmarried and two weeks shy of her 18th birthday at the time of the Durham murders. She later married and divorced, her surname being "Edmisten" at the time of this 2001 report. Edmisten was known to fabricate stories and place herself in scenarios that she had nothing to do with. She reportedly did this to see who she could trust. If the stories she made up got circulated, she would know who told them. The woman from Caldwell County who reportedly provided the female prison guard with information concerning Edmisten's involvement in the Durham murders was allegedly involved with Edmisten's husband, which ensued in conflict between the two women. Edmisten died as a great-grandmother in 2021. [Sources: Genealogical research by author; Minton, Michelle (Elaine Chapman Edmisten's daughter). Facebook messages. April 12, 2024; https://www.bennettfuneralservice.com/obituaries/Margaret-Janie-Chapman-Edmisten?obId=20785555#/obituaryInfo.]

larceny, and stolen vehicles. According to a former Caldwell County Sheriff's Deputy, these individuals were known to be very rough criminals.[1613] In the end, this trail led nowhere.

Mark Shook succeeded Red Lyons as sheriff in 2002. As Lyons passed the torch to Shook, the Durham Case file was still minimal, consisting of a folder, a handful of photographs, and the rope that had been around Bryce Durham's neck. An attempt to get copies of files from the SBI in order to beef up the sheriff's office file were, according to Shook, unfruitful due to it not being a priority of the SBI.[1614] Around this same time, the Boone Police Department was helpful in turning their Durham Case files over to the sheriff's office.[1615] Shook's primary focus, though, was on current crime, including the busting up of ever-increasing methamphetamine labs in Watauga County. Still, during Shook's administration, Captain Brian Tolbert worked on the Durham Case to an extent.[1616] A few calls came in offering leads, but upon investigation, they were found to be unproductive.[1617]

In 2004, a confidential informant suggested to the Watauga County Sheriff's Office that it look into the 1983 deaths of two Wilkes County men – Gary Keith Huffman and Carl Cockerham – as a possible connection to the Durham murders. Huffman was a chicken farmer who lived on Dragway Road, ten miles west of Wilkesboro, and Cockerham was his friend and helper as well as a poultry processor at Holly Farms. On December 2, 1983, Cockerham was visiting Huffman at his home, and the two had been watching television. Sometime between 11:30 PM and 1:30 AM, both men were stabbed multiple times in their chests and backs, and Huffman's house was set on fire. The confidential informant stated Huffman was shot and Cockerham was stabbed with a sword, but news sources mentioned no shooting or sword…only that both men had been stabbed. Whether a sword was involved is uncertain, but death by sword was reminiscent of the accidental sword death of Troy Hall's acquaintance, Tim Moore, in 1972. The motive for Huffman's and Cockerham's murders is believed to have been drug related.[1618] There is no indication in the Durham investigation file that any connection was established between the Durham murders and the murders of these two men, which remain unsolved.[1619]

Watauga County Sheriff Len Hagaman (Source: North Carolina Sheriffs' Association)

In 2005, a caller identified only as "John" phoned the Watauga County Sheriff's Office, saying he had new information regarding the Durham murders. Not wishing to say more on the telephone, he was to come into the office that afternoon. There is no indication of further information from this potential informant.[1620]

When Len Doughton Hagaman, Jr. was elected as Watauga County Sheriff in 2006, the Durham Case was one of the first things he focused on.[1621] Sheriff Hagaman (historically known as "L. D." but also referred to as "Len") originally began working on the case as a Boone policeman in 1976, and when he took office as sheriff, he took an inventory of evidence in the Durham Case. Although he recognized there were holes in the case file, he stated the investigation was still active and ongoing. "Several investigators from various agencies convened to review old crime scene photographs, and case files were reviewed with notations and an open discussion followed. New ideas and strategies were then formulated." According to

Hagaman, "There have, from day one, been persons of interest but as in any homicide, developing persons of interest into suspects is often easier said than done. I can say that we continue to have leads and are actively looking at and following up on these leads. I can also say that many of these leads have occurred within the past two years. We discussed with the SBI lab the potential of DNA with a specific piece of physical evidence *[the rope left around Bryce Durham's neck]*. It was determined that the piece of evidence had been exposed to elements that made DNA analysis very difficult." Also, there was no blood and no bodily fluids to subject to DNA testing. Hagaman further stated, "It should be noted that every year since the homicide...all fingerprints have been resubmitted for comparison. To date, there are latent prints that have yet to be identified."[1622] Retired lawmen, including Boone police officers Zane Tester and Willie Watson and former SBI Agent Charlie Whitman, were also assisting Hagaman's force with a fresh look into the case. Whitman stated the rope found around Bryce Durham's neck "is still accounted for," and there were "still pictures that could be introduced."[1623]

In 2009, journalist Tim Bullard, who was writing a book about the murders, was in touch with Bill Durham, Bryce Durham's only surviving sibling, and informed him Sheriff Hagaman was working on the case. Durham was retired and had been living in Wilmington, North Carolina about thirty years, and he subsequently contacted Hagaman, writing, "Our family has long given up real hope of this case solving. To learn that even a little law enforcement interest still exists is encouraging. I wish I had the key to this case. Enforcement has long had everything we know. But strong opinion still abounds." Durham further stated that, after so many years and the consuming nature of the case, he had to disentangle himself from it, but he would welcome the opportunity to meet with Hagaman and "to be as helpful as possible toward any investigative work" Hagaman's office might wish to conduct. Hagaman responded, reminding Durham of having met him many years prior when Hagaman was a Boone police officer. He told Durham he would like to review the case with him and others. He also shared that Dee Dee Rominger, his Captain of Investigations, was looking into an individual from neighboring Ashe County who claimed he had killed seventeen people over the years. Although this individual was only fourteen at the time of the Durham murders, Hagaman felt it was worth exploring.[1624][eeeeee]

In 2011, Sheriff Hagaman planned to hold a meeting with the case's various stakeholders, including Rufus Edmisten, former SBI agents Larry Wagner and Charlie Whitman, retired Boone Police Department Captain Arlie Isaacs, and reporter Tim Bullard. Hagaman also assigned Captain Dee Dee Rominger to the cold case, and they met together to discuss "best practices, strategies, and coordination" for reactivating the Durham Case. According to Hagaman, Rominger participated in an intense "Cold Case" school of instruction (taught, in part, by national and international cold case experts), "exhibited a fresh and focused approach to the case," and devoted many hours to its investigation, including the resubmission of several pieces of evidence to the SBI.[1625] Although Rominger did not work on the case full-time, she reexamined the investigative file and followed up on any new leads that came in. She and Hagaman also aimed to make sure the latent fingerprints

---

[eeeeee] This was likely a reference to Ashe County resident Freddie Hammer (born 1958), who killed a Philadelphia police officer in 1978, was suspected but never charged in the murder of another Ashe County man in 2005, killed his nephew by marriage in 2007, and murdered three men at a Grayson County, VA Christmas tree farm in 2008. [Sources: Monte Mitchell (*Winston-Salem Journal*), "Slain man's family awarded $14.9 million," *The News and Observer*, Raleigh, NC, March 13, 2011, p. 2B; Wesley Young, "Freddie Hammer case to air on Sunday," *Winston-Salem Journal*, Winston-Salem, NC, June 15, 2024, pp. A1 & A4.]

lifted from both the Durham house and vehicle (including a common thumbprint that was found on the underside of a plate that may have been flipped as well as the vent window[1626] of the GMC "Jimmy") were periodically run by the SBI through the FBI's Automated Fingerprint Identification System (AFIS). This was done annually for many years, but without any matches.[1627] Initially that process had been very labor intensive,[1628] but as time passed, technological advancements in automation enabled print comparisons to be accomplished in seconds.[1629] Despite these advancements, there were still no answers in the Durham murders. Rominger and Hagaman also intended that the rope left around Bryce Durham's neck the night of the murders be further explored. Unfortunately, the SBI lab informed Rominger the rope could not be tested for DNA because it had been submerged in water.[1630]

That same year (2011), the Watauga County Sheriff's Office spoke with Sam Round, who was thirteen at the time of the murders and a friend of Bobby Durham, both being members of the same Boy Scout troop. At a February 1, 1972 meeting, Round told Bobby he needed transportation to a subsequent event. Bobby told Round to call him on February 3, and Round attempted to do so beginning at 8:00 PM, but he got a busy signal. He continued to call in ten to fifteen-minute intervals, finally giving up at 9:30 PM, and never having encountered anything but a busy signal each time. He learned about the murders at school the following day.[1631] Round's account has possible bearing on the time of the Durhams' arrival home (believed to be around 9:00 PM), Troy Hall's account of the supposed phone call from Virginia Durham between 10:10 and 10:30 PM, the disabling of the Durhams' phone(s), and the timing of their murders.

Even after Rufus Edmisten had left his Attorney General position, served as North Carolina's Secretary of State, and launched his law firm in Raleigh, he never lost sight of the Durham Case and his desire to have it solved. This murder hit close to home, and of all the cases he assigned agents to, he wanted this one solved the most. He spent more personal time – thousands of hours[1632] – on the case than any other during his career, and it was also the most baffling. "I kept it in my mind all the time."[1633] By 2011, however, Edmisten's earlier optimism had waned. He doubted the case would be solved and believed it would remain an eternal mystery.[1634]

On the occasion of the fortieth anniversary of the murders in 2012, Troy Hall did not respond to an interview request left at his office by the *Winston-Salem Journal*,[1635] and when the paper attempted that same year to contact Ginny Durham Mackie, her husband Steve "said his wife did not wish to talk, but that she had cooperated with the SBI and it would be great to find out who did it, if they are still alive." He further stated, "After all the time she spent in the past with the State Bureau, being put under hypnosis, there was nothing she knew to help. I can tell you right now she has nothing left to say. Every minute that goes by, every hour that goes by, makes it harder to solve. Everybody wants closure."[1636] *[Ginny remained consistent in her unwillingness to give interviews and reportedly posted a notice on her front door telling would-be inquirers she had no wish to speak to anyone about the case.[1637] In 2015, she told a Watauga County Sheriff's Office investigator that an SBI agent had advised her to let it go, close the door, and live her life.[1638] In more recent years, she has only occasionally expressed to relatives a desire to talk about the murders, saying she still does not understand the "why" of it all.[1639]]*[ffffff]

[ffffff] In October 2022, the author reached out via certified mail to Ginny Durham Mackie to inform her of his intention to write this book and to ask if she would consider speaking with him. Although she received the letter, she never responded. The author likewise reached out to various members of Troy Hall's family but received no responses.

When interviewed in 2012, Rufus Edmisten believed the murders resulted from a professional hit job that required more than one person to hold two men underwater in the bathtub, especially with Bobby Durham being a strong, teenaged boy.[1640] "I've always believed that this was a contract killing," Edmisten stated,[1641] although his opinion about that would change within the following decade *(see p. 454)*.[1642] Former SBI Agent Charlie Whitman concurred that was a possibility but questioned why the entire family would be slain as part of a contract killing.[1643] He also wondered why a contract killer would have gone to the trouble of staging the scene to look like a burglary versus just going in, killing the victims, and then leaving.[1644]

Also, in 2012, Sheriff Len Hagaman, stated that more than two-hundred individuals (a figure that actually had not changed since 1972 and 1989[1645]) had been interviewed through the years, and he had "plans to re-interview some of the key people, who may or may not be suspects."[1646]

That same year, a woman contacted Sheriff Hagaman and writer Tim Bullard to share some of her intuitions about the Durham Case. She felt a woman who was known by the murder victims was somehow involved, and it may have been a sister (to whom?). The murders may have stemmed from a problem or issue that this woman had with the family. She also felt the victims, and particularly "the wife" (presumably referring to Virginia Durham), did not want the case solved because there was something they did not want to be discovered. Another individual called the Watauga County Sheriff's Office to say he had built chicken houses for relatives of Troy Hall, and that, in 1967, one of the family members had stated it would be cool to pull off the perfect murder.[1647]

Additionally in 2012, North Carolina private investigator Edward Lankford independently took on the Durham Case in response to his aged father's desire to know who killed the Durhams. Lankford's father had been a grade school pupil of Bryce Durham's father Coy in Wilkes County and repeatedly expressed how he wished the mystery could be solved. After a six-month examination of the case, Lankford believed he had identified a Durham neighbor as the murderer. This was based, in part, on Lankford's conversation with Ginny Durham Mackie, who stated her family and this particular neighbor had been at odds because the neighbor had shot and killed the Durhams' cat. Lankford came to believe this neighbor disliked the Durhams and wanted them out of the neighborhood, and, purposely waiting until a bad winter's night could help cover his movements, he went to their house to rob them and frighten them so badly they would move away. Lankford theorized that, after the Durhams arrived home, the neighbor, donning a ski mask and carrying a .22-caliber pistol, raised a garage door and entered the house. Surprising the Durhams, he forced them to go room to room and empty the contents of drawers to reveal where they kept their money. As the ransacking progressed, no money was found, and when the Durhams recognized the intruder's voice, he was left with no choice but to kill them, even though murder had never been his intention. Lankford believed the neighbor hit Bryce in the face with the pistol, breaking Bryce's glasses and knocking him unconscious if not killing him outright. Following this, Lankford supposed that Bobby struggled with the intruder as Virginia ran to the kitchen phone and placed a call to Troy and Ginny. According to Lankford, Ginny told him her family always referred to this particular neighbor as "the neighbor" rather than by his name, and Lankford believed that, rather than Virginia hushedly telling Troy "*three niggers* are beating Bryce and Bobby," she said "'*the neighbor*' is beating Bryce and Bobby." Lankford believes that, had Ginny answered the call and heard her mother make mention of "the neighbor," she would have immediately known the identity of the man her mother was referring to. Lankford also theorized the intruder then caught Virginia on the phone and struck her in the face with the pistol while simultaneously and accidentally pulling the trigger, thus firing the bullet that was found in the den wall paneling. Lankford further believed the intruder found inside the house a piece of rope (which Ginny told Lankford Bobby used for practicing knot-tying as an Eagle Scout)[gggggg] and placed it around each of his victims' necks, pulling each body, one by one, to the bathroom and putting them in the water-filled bathtub. Finally, Lankford believed the neighbor took the Durhams' GMC "Jimmy," drove it to Poplar Grove Road and abandoned it, and then walked two miles back to his own home on Clyde Townsend Road, ducking temporarily into the phone booth at the Union 76 station at the corner of Highway 105 and the 105 Bypass when he thought someone had spotted him. The neighbor could have foregone the taking of the "Jimmy" and simply walked back to his house from the Durham home, although perhaps the thought was that he took the car to throw authorities off the trail of a neighbor, who would have had no need for a getaway vehicle. A final basis for Lankford's identification of this neighbor as the murderer was that Ginny told him [Lankford] that, when she was having the phone service disconnected from the Durham house following the murders, the phone company told her she would either have to turn in the telephones or pay for them. When she went to the house to retrieve the phones, they were gone. Someone told her to check with "the neighbor" (i.e., the killer), and when she went to his house to ask if he had the phones from the Durham house, he did, and he gave them to her. No explanation was offered as to why he would have taken the phones, and if that *was* the case, he would had to have taken the phones after crime scene photos were taken which show telephones still inside the house.[1648]

After Lankford pieced together what he thought had transpired and who had killed the Durhams, he presented his hypothesis to Ginny, and according to him, she believed it made sense, so much so that she called former SBI Agent Charlie Whitman. Lankford subsequently presented his thoughts to Whitman, and Lankford said Whitman also found the hypothesis plausible. Finally, Lankford presented his theory to the Watauga County Sheriff's Office and to Captain Dee Dee Rominger, in particular, and she followed up on some of its elements, specifically in regard to the conflict that had allegedly resulted from the Durhams' neighbor shooting their cat. Ginny had also imparted this pet-shooting incident to law enforcement officers on two separate occasions, years apart, stating the neighbor claimed their cat was messing with his dogs, and her father had confronted the neighbor about the shooting. Ginny further shared that her father told her to stay out of the backyard anytime the neighbor was around. Rominger found this to be new information never previously introduced in the case. By this time, the neighbor in question had been deceased more than thirty years, but Rominger spoke to his widow, whose health was in decline. Other than the statements both Lankford and Rominger said Ginny made to them, there was no evidence supporting these claims.[1649]

In November 2012, Ginny and her husband, Steve Mackie, spent several hours at the Watauga County Sheriff's Office, meeting with Rominger and Whitman. Ginny acknowledged Whitman had been good to her. It had been a long time since she had spoken with law enforcement, but she was cooperative and willing to speak with Rominger, in part, because she had never previously been interviewed by a female officer. This was Rominger's only face to face meeting with Ginny, and she assured Ginny she did not intend to interrogate her but merely wanted her to share what happened the night her family was killed. Ginny recounted the details of her mother's alleged phone call, of Troy answering the phone and afterwards telling her that Virginia had stated that "niggers" had Bobby and Bryce, and of Troy asking if Virginia would play a joke on them. She retold how their car would not start, how Troy enlisted Cecil Small to take them to her parents' house, and how

---

[gggggg] After viewing photos of the rope found at the crime scene, Bobby's former scout master confirmed this was a common type of rope for scouts to have and to practice with. [Source: Sale, Arvil. Facebook message to author. February 12, 2023.]

Troy had her wait at the bottom of the driveway while he and Small proceeded to the house. She shared with Rominger and Whitman that, in the early days of the case, Sheriff Ward Carroll took her and Troy to look at a bronze-colored car to see if they recognized it, and how she believed that was actually a ploy for someone else to identify the two of them. She expressed her belief that warrants were issued for the men from Asheville so that authorities could get her and Troy on the stand. She recalled testifying at the men's probable cause hearing and that she was repeatedly asked if the outside light of her parents' home was on or off the night of the murders, but she could not say as it had not been visible to her from where she remained inside Cecil Small's car. She told Rominger and Whitman she had no part in the murders but felt former investigators did not believe her and thought she was withholding evidence to protect Troy. Despite her difficulties with Troy and her split from him, Ginny stated she had no reason to believe he participated in the murders. She shared that she never believed the theory that the Green Berets killed her family, and she did not know how that theory originated. She stated that, although she found no indication her father owed any money, she did wonder if he had any business dealings that were not above board. Ginny discussed family dynamics and shared that her mother's side of the family was kind to her and never accused her of being involved in the murders. She said Durham relatives were ashamed and embarrassed that Bryce died in a suspicious manner and were concerned that his reputation not be marred. Ginny was less bothered by this and merely wanted to know the truth.[1650]

In March 2013, Ginny shared additional information with Rominger, stemming from Charlie Whitman asking her about her childhood in South Carolina – something she had never been previously asked about. Under what remain mysterious circumstances, sometime between mid-May and mid-July 1962,[hhhhhh] Bryce, Virginia, Ginny, and Bobby showed up unexpectedly at the Wilkes County, North Carolina home of Virginia's mother, Jennie Church. It was around 3:00 AM and, with only the clothes on their backs, they had fled South Carolina. Over the course of the next three days, Bryce and Virginia met several times with Wilkes County resident Tal Pearson,[iiiiii] who Ginny believed had some involvement with loan companies, and who she said her father had worked for at some point. Anytime Virginia's brother, Wayne Church, or his wife Ronnie entered the room where the three were meeting, the trio would cease their conversation. Also, during this time, Virginia borrowed a dress, reportedly for an appointment with an attorney, although Ginny was not

---

[hhhhhh] Although Ginny believed this to have happened as she finished the fifth grade, which would have been between mid-May and mid-July 1963, this is not possible as Tal Pearson, who her parents met with in this account, died in January 1963. [Sources: Mackie, Ginny Durham. E-mail to Captain Dee Dee Rominger. March 26, 2013, Watauga County Sheriff's Department investigation file 118-H-1/2/3; https://www.findagrave.com/memorial/68205198/tallie-joseph-pearson

[iiiiii] Tal Pearson owned and operated "a successful and prosperous local supermarket and wholesale grocery business at the corner of Highways 115 and Old 60 in North Wilkesboro," NC. In 1956, he was involved "in promoting the sale of sugar to illegal distillers." Pearson, along with others, was indicted for "conspiracy to possess sugar for the unlawful purpose of distilling illegal whiskey" and other charges. He was described as "the 'kingpin' of moonshine activities in this area." He spent a year in an Atlanta, Georgia prison, where his attorney observed he "had become 'mayor' of the facility and was 'running the place.'" Pearson had been convicted of similar sugar-alcohol charges as early as 1940. In 1949, he was the selling agent for the auction of a farm owned by Troy Hall's parents. [Sources: "Convicted On U. S. Count: Three Fined For Failing to Make Complete Reports On Sugar Sales," *The Charlotte Observer*, Charlotte, NC, June 14, 1940, p. 15; "In Wilkes County Roundup: 3 More Men Arrested On Bootlegging Charges" and "Bootleg Capital: Crackdown," *The Herald-Sun*, Durham, NC, July 5, 1957, pp. C2 & D8; https://www.findagrave.com/memorial/68205198/tallie-joseph-pearson; Russ Pearson, "The moonshine era in Wilkes," *The Wilkes Record*, North Wilkesboro, NC, Watauga County Sheriff's Office investigation file 118-H-1/2/3; Tal Joe Pearson, Appellant v. United States of America, Appellee, U. S. Court of Appeals for the Fourth Circuit, 1959, https://law.justia.com/cases/federal/appellate-courts/F2/265/167/63115/; "At Auction" ad, *The Journal-Patriot*, North Wilkesboro, NC, July 28, 1949, p. 6.]

convinced that was the real reason. After this three-day period, Bryce and Virginia left Ginny and Bobby with Virginia's mother for two weeks.[1651]

Ginny stated that, during the Durham family's transition period between Florence, South Carolina and Mount Airy, North Carolina, Virginia traveled during warm weather back to South Carolina to sign paperwork and close out their home there. It was dark by the time she returned to Mount Airy, and Bryce, Ginny, and Bobby went outside when she arrived. The windshield of the car Virginia was driving had been destroyed. Although Virginia said a rock had hit it, Ginny and Bobby agreed that it looked as if it had been hit with a baseball bat. Broken glass was all across the car as well as in the interior, especially on the floor.[1652] After this incident, Virginia began carrying a gun, and because there were some sketchy people in Mount Airy, Bryce carried one as well.[1653]

Ginny also recalled her father having lots of meetings with Ford dealers in Galax, Virginia, Darlington, South Carolina, and Mount Airy, North Carolina. She stated Ford and General Motors sent individuals to her father to borrow money, and he took chances loaning it. She said her father never discussed finances with her or Bobby, but she thought he may have borrowed money from untraceable sources.[1654]

In a 2015 recap of the Durham Case, Sheriff Len Hagaman said a triple homicide was unique, and the fact it occurred on a night with horrible weather in an unusual length of time made it even more peculiar. On top of that, a motive had never been firmly established.[1655] He also reported his office had been in touch with Ginny Durham Mackie and she had been "very cooperative."[1656][jjjjjj] In January of that year, Ginny shared with the Watauga County Sheriff's Office that a woman had contacted her and wanted to meet in person regarding information the woman had about the Durham Case. Ginny declined the meeting but told the woman she would provide the woman's phone number to authorities so she could speak with them instead. Later, former SBI Agent Charlie Whitman received a call from a Knoxville, Tennessee area phone number. The caller was the same woman who had spoken with Ginny. She initially claimed to be Ginny but then told Whitman her name was Elizabeth. The woman claimed her ex-husband told her who killed the Durhams but said no one would listen to her. Ginny had found the woman to be strange and did not understand things the woman shared with her, including her instruction to Ginny "to check out Facebook pages." The woman also supplied a couple of men's names, telling Ginny she knew them, and making mention of bodies buried in a Lowe [family?] swimming pool in the Finley Park community of Wilkes County.[1657]

A month later, a local citizen reported to the Watauga County Sheriff's Office that his daughter had been in a Raleigh, North Carolina jail with a woman named Darlene Chandler, who, by this time, was believed to be residing in Michigan. Chandler had told her cellmate that a man, also surnamed Chandler and by that time already deceased, had killed the Durhams, and he had stabbed his wife or girlfriend to shut her up, presumably about the Durham Case. The Chandler man had allegedly worked for Bryce Durham.[1658] *[Darlene Vicknair Chandler (1967-2013) was referring to her husband, Dean Chandler, one of the Asheville men, who had been indicted for the Durham murders in 1972 and subsequently released (see Chapter 10). There is no indication Dean Chandler ever worked for Bryce Durham at his car dealership or elsewhere, other than Paul Bare's claim that*

[jjjjjj] In later years, SBI Agent Wade Colvard also found Ginny to be cooperative. Although he described her as "very sensitive" and "very guarded about who she speaks with," he felt they got along great and seemed to have easy conversations. [Source: Colvard, Wade. Phone conversation with author. August 1, 2023.]

Bryce had hired Dean, along with Jerry Cassada, Eugene Garren, and Dewey Coffey to offload drugs. Dean and Darlene Chandler were married in 1989, and the woman mentioned as being stabbed was actually Darlene herself. Darlene Chandler had been sentenced to prison in North Carolina in 1997 for larceny, forgery and uttering, credit card fraud, and eleven habitual felon charges.[1659]]

In August 2015, Ginny Durham Mackie told the Watauga County Sheriff's Office she did not know how her father had been financially able to independently own a car dealership. Ginny stated even though Bryce only had a small amount of money in his checking account, he would never have considered asking his father, Coy Durham, for money. She also reiterated that she found it strange her paternal grandparents and aunt had been obsessed with preserving her father's reputation.[1660]

That same year, a woman called the sheriff's office with a new lead, stating she had "recovered some potential physical evidence."[1661] The woman, a resident of coastal South Carolina, had been closing up the home of her late grandparents in Wilkes County, North Carolina. During this process, she came across some items in a certain location of their garage that she had always been told to stay away from as a child. It is believed these items belonged to her uncle by marriage, Benny Staley, who had been suspected in the Durham murders *(see Chapter 16)*. The woman's mother, Linda Combs Garwood,[kkkkkk] was a sister to Staley's wife, Donna Combs Staley, and the woman wondered if Staley may have been involved. The woman provided the sheriff's office with a black, hard-shell case, known as "The Original Trav-L-Bar," a portable travel bar produced between the 1950s and 1970s. It contained two-fifths of liquor, four glasses, a jigger (a measuring tool), a strainer, a spoon, and a tray (all instruments being metal) along with an insignificant car registration and envelope (both bearing the name of Benny Staley's father, Warren Staley), some work gloves, and some other inconsequential items, including a photograph of Donna Combs Staley. The hope was that her uncle's fingerprints might be lifted and compared with those from the Durham Case. The items were processed by the sheriff's office and then submitted to the State Crime Lab for further analysis.[1662] This same woman also found a length of rope matching the diameter and color of the rope left around Bryce Durham's neck, but the weaves were different.[1663] In the end, both the travel bar and the length of rope proved to be dead ends.

[In the summer of 1972, Durham next-door neighbor Clinard Wilson reportedly found a piece of rope in a doghouse, and it was supposedly the same type of rope used in the murders. Wilson reported the rope to the Watauga County Sheriff's Department, and officers picked it up after two or three reminders to do so. No follow-up of this is mentioned in their investigative file.[1664] Another source states it was neighbor Dean Combs who, while mowing the Durham yard in the late spring or summer of 1972, found this rope (approximately three feet in length) inside an unused doghouse behind the Durham home, and that Combs called the Watauga County Sheriff's Department, and detectives retrieved the rope. According to Combs's brother Jerry, however, Combs was unable to mow yards due to his heart condition, and it was Wilson who found the rope, not Combs.[1665]]

In June 2015, Bryce Durham's brother Bill Durham and nephew Jeff Mauldin had provided the Watauga County Sheriff's Office with their DNA samples. Ginny Durham Mackie followed suit,

---

[kkkkkk] In 2015, Ginny Durham Mackie told the Watauga County Sheriff's Office she had spoken with former SBI Agent Charlie Whitman about a November [2014] meeting with a Garwood lady in Wilkesboro, NC. This likely refers to Linda Combs Garwood. [Source: Watauga County Sheriff's Office investigation file 118-H-1/2/3.

providing her DNA that October.[1666] These samples were collected in case some future testing of the rope from the crime scene might provide an opportunity for comparison.[1667]

In 2016, a local citizen informed the Watauga County Sheriff's Office of a tractor theft ring that had been active in the county in the late 1980s and involved four men with troubled pasts who lived less than a mile from the Durham residence. One of the men had been a high school classmate of Bobby Durham. Although the citizen did not know if these men were connected to the Durham Case, he had stated his suspicions much earlier to former SBI Agent Charlie Whitman, but at that time, Whitman had discounted them, reportedly still holding to the theory that black men had committed the murders. After Whitman's death, the citizen shared the same information with a man who had assisted Whitman and was told by him it was a good theory. Likewise, the citizen stated Whitman's widow, Pat, had encouraged him to share his suspicions with the authorities. Captain Dee Dee Rominger subsequently discussed this with Ginny Durham Mackie.[1668]

Despite all of these new leads and theories, which were generally fruitless,[1669] by 2019, resolution of the almost fifty-year-old case seemed doubtful. Some of the primary investigators had died, and some of the involved people had moved. Although the Durham Case had remained on the radars of Rufus Edmisten, Charlie Whitman, and Len Hagaman, it had once more become stagnant. According to Hagaman, "For a long time, we hit a brick wall."[1670] But what occurred next would rock the decades-long, stop-and-go investigation, introducing an entirely new cast of characters and setting the stage for what some would consider the final curtain to fall.

CHAPTER 18

BITS AND PIECES

In 1978, Rufus Edmisten had told WBTV News in Charlotte, North Carolina, "The key [to solving this case] is that some individual sometime will slip up, and they will tell somebody something that will lead us to the trail because we have every facet ready if we just get one little piece of evidence."[1671]

When asked in 2009 (twenty-seven years after the murders) if the killers could be prosecuted if they were identified, former SBI Agent Charlie Whitman said, "There is no time limit on murder. It could be fifty years from now. It doesn't make any difference.... So, the case is still alive, and as I said, it may take fifty years."[1672] Fifty years. In retrospect, what a fitting prediction that would be, counting the years since 1972. And someone did tell somebody something.

Bob Ingram
(Courtesy of Bob Ingram)

Native Bostonian and former U. S. Marine Robert "Bob" Ingram served with the Georgia Bureau of Investigation (GBI) in its Thomson, Georgia field office from 1972 until his retirement in 2000, at which time he moved to Cleveland, Georgia.[1673] In 2011, he was asked to serve as Chief Deputy for the White County (Georgia) Sheriff's Office. In February 2019,[1674] veteran newspaperman and author Phil Hudgins, of Gainesville, Georgia, contacted Ingram to inquire about his knowledge of the late Billy Sunday Birt,[1675] a notorious criminal and a leader of northeast Georgia's Dixie Mafia. At the time of Birt's death, he was serving multiple life sentences, including ones for the brutal 1973 robbery, torture, and murders of Reid and Lois Fleming in Wrens, Georgia. Ingram had been the lead investigator on the Fleming Case[1676] and had helped put Birt on death row for it in 1975. Hudgins was conducting research for *Grace and Disgrace: Living with Faith and a Dixie Mafia Hitman*,[1677] his upcoming book about Birt from the perspective of Birt's former wife, Ruby Nell Lee Birt, with the assistance of Birt's youngest son, Billy Shenandoah "Shane" Birt.[1678] When Hudgins asked to interview Ingram, Ingram agreed, inviting him to the White County Sheriff's Office on February 6, 2019.[1679]

Hudgins had embarked on his book project a year prior at the behest of Shane Birt,[1680] who asked to accompany Hudgins to his interview with Ingram.[1681] When Hudgins asked Ingram if he could bring Shane with him, Ingram considered this a peculiar request and was hesitant about how he could speak openly with Hudgins about Billy Birt's criminal history in front of Birt's son. Still, he told Hudgins to bring Shane. Ingram would speak with him in the lobby of the sheriff's office and then make a final determination whether he would allow him to be present during the interview. After being introduced to Shane, conversing with him for a few minutes,[1682] and determining he was not interested in "glorifying his father's actions,"[1683] Ingram was impressed that he was a genuine and sincere person. He agreed that Shane could sit in on his interview with Hudgins, but he told Shane he could not speak, and Shane complied. Hudgins recorded his two-hour interview with Ingram, and they bade farewell.[1684]

As Shane was leaving and shaking Ingram's hand, he told Ingram he had visited his father in prison almost weekly[llllll] since 1987 when he was sixteen and able to drive until his father's death in 2017 – a period of thirty years. He also shared that he had a lot of information his father told him. This intrigued Ingram as he knew from personal interaction that Billy Birt rarely talked. Realizing the importance of hearing what Birt had told his son and hoping to gain new information that might help close any of the unsolved murders that had been attributed to Billy Birt and his associates, Ingram invited Shane to return at a later date. Because Hudgins had introduced Ingram and Shane, and because Hudgins asked to sit in on the follow-up interview, Ingram reciprocated.[1685]

On April 30, 2019, in the interrogation room at the White County Sheriff's Office and in the presence of Hudgins and Mike Walsingham, Assistant Special Agent in Charge for the GBI, Ingram interviewed Shane. Their time together was prefaced by Ingram stating that the purpose of the interview was to clarify as specifically and in as much detail as possible, the events and circumstances surrounding several deaths and missing persons cases where foul play was suspected, both in North Georgia and other locations, in which Billy Sunday Birt and others were involved.[1686] A specific goal of Ingram was to inquire about a list of homicides that had been compiled by retired Alcohol, Tobacco, and Firearms (ATF) Agent Jim West in the 1970s. These homicides had been previously investigated by West, Sheriff Earl Lee of Douglas County, Georgia, GBI Agent Ronnie Angel, "and numerous other lawmen." Ingram felt "if Shane could shed light on murder cases still on the books – more than four decades after [Billy Birt] was imprisoned for the last time – then [he] wanted his help."[1687] Ingram vocalized his hope that, by working together and comparing and compiling information each of them had received, whether confirmed or unconfirmed, they might clear cases and thereby enable victims' families to know what happened.[1688]

Ingram told Shane he had a lot of specific cases he wanted to run by him to see if he recalled anything his father may have shared about them, but he made it clear he did not want to be suggestive in any way, and he allowed Shane the opportunity to first recount all the things he had knowledge of, most of which Shane said had been told to him by his father and his uncle, Bobby Birt.[1689]

Three sessions, interrupted only by breaks, were conducted on the same day. In the first session, Shane recounted the things his father had told him in a "bits and pieces" fashion.[1690] During the second session, Ingram questioned Shane about specific cases Ingram had knowledge of and tried to dovetail them with details Billy Birt had disclosed.[1691] Although Shane knew nothing about some of the cases in West's report, he was familiar with others. While some did not coincide with the way Shane said his father had explained them, others "were spot-on accurate."[1692] Ingram stated that the

---

[llllll] In 2024, Shane stated the frequency of his meetings with his father to have been at least twice a month and sometimes weekly. [Source: Birt, Shane. In-person interview with author. March 6, 2024.]

cases Shane had no knowledge of could be ones that merely had occurred during the timeframe Billy Birt was most active and may have been misattributed to him.[1693]

When the third part of the interview began, Ingram asked Phil Hudgins and Mike Walsingham if either of them had any questions for Shane. Walsingham asked Shane to further expound upon a case Shane previously mentioned concerning snowfall and involving Billy's Birt's criminal associate, Billy Wayne Davis, and $80,000. Walsingham, however, had conflated two different cases, and Shane corrected him, stating that the case involving snow was an out-of-state case. "I know it wasn't in Georgia.... When he [Billy Birt] got there to do the job, he said that while he was in the house or in the area, said it started snowing.... But after they got in the house, said the snow fell. He said it was almost a foot...and...I know it was a murder. I know it was out of state...I know the snowfall near about trapped him in the house."[1694][mmmmmmm]

Based on additional details Shane would share at a later date, this information seemed to be the first mention by him of any case approximating that of the Durham Case, but at this time, the information was scant and a connection to the case seemingly had not yet been made. When Ingram asked Shane if he had any idea when this occurred, Shane said it was the early 1970s. When Ingram asked if Billy Birt had said who he killed or how he killed them, Shane replied with two back-to-back, yet seemingly contradictory sentences. "No, he didn't tell me that. I'm sure he did, but daddy wouldn't tell the whole story." *[Perhaps these were two successive but separate answers to Ingram's two successive and separate questions, as in, "No," Billy Birt did not say who he had killed, and "I'm sure he did" say how he had killed them but without providing all the details.]* Shane then reiterated that his father would only tell bits and pieces, "and then, throughout the day, you might get another bit or piece. Or when you come back, he might give you another bit or piece."[1695]

At the conclusion of the three-session April 30 interview, the participants had covered a total of twenty-four cases and thirty-eight victims. Ingram and Shane agreed they would conduct a follow-up interview as needed. Two and a half weeks later, after Shane called to say he had remembered something else, a subsequent interview occurred on May 17, 2019, and more specific information concerning the Durham Case surfaced. Following is a transcription of the portions of this interview pertaining to the Durhams:[1696][nnnnnnn]

INGRAM: This is a follow-up interview to a previous interview that occurred on April the 30th, at which we will be discussing crimes involving Billy Sunday Birt – Shane's dad – and others, and this interview was requested to provide additional information, and Shane, if you would just begin.

SHANE: Daddy told me story a long time ago, and I thought for a long time it was Durham, North Carolina. But it was not Durham, North Carolina; it was a family named Durham in North Carolina. This was the case that Daddy told me that when they got there, it had started snowing, but while

---

[mmmmmmm] Shane's prior mention of a snowfall, preceding Walsingham's revisitation of the subject, was not captured in recordings of the first or second portions of the April 30 interviews, although the recording of the second portion had cut off before that portion was concluded. Either Shane mentioned snowfall during the second portion, and it got cut off, or he brought it up in an unrecorded side conversation – perhaps during a break – prior to the third portion of the interview.

[nnnnnnn] The process of obtaining the recorded interviews with Shane Birt and Billy Wayne Davis was both laborious and time-consuming. Rather than summarizing these interviews and merely telling readers what was said, the author has chosen to include full transcriptions of the Durham Case-related portions of these interviews in this chapter and the subsequent chapter so that readers can see for themselves the manner and order in which questions were asked and answered and form their own opinions.

they was there, said the snow fell so hard they almost didn't make it out. And the man was a car salesman, and there was three of 'em. Uh, and the, uh, *(4-second pause)* the, the, the, I, I know all three of them were killed. And there was daddy, Bobby Gene, Billy Wayne, and Charlie were the ones that was there.

INGRAM: Let's, just for a moment, identify those four people by their full names.

SHANE: Yeah. There was my daddy – Billy Sunday Birt, Bobby Gene Gaddis, Billy Wayne Davis, and Charlie Reed.

INGRAM: Okay, and they were the persons who committed the crime.

SHANE: They were the persons who committed the crime.

INGRAM: And how many victims were there?

SHANE: There was three.

INGRAM: Three victims. Okay.

SHANE: Yes sir.

INGRAM: Go ahead.

SHANE: And evidently, what ticked daddy off about the crime, the crime should have never been committed because the money that was supposedly there wasn't there. You know, the people didn't have much at all or what they were supposed to have at the house was not there.

INGRAM: How did your father get information about these people having money?

SHANE: It was either a nephew or a son-in-law or might have been both.

INGRAM: Who talked to who?

SHANE: Who talked to daddy.

INGRAM: Okay. Who talked to daddy about – daddy being Billy Sunday Birt – about these people having a large sum of money.

SHANE: Having or keeping money at the house.

INGRAM: So, the purpose in going there was to rob them.

SHANE: To rob 'em.

INGRAM: And you said they did not have the money.

SHANE: They did not. They had some money, but daddy said it was nothing.

INGRAM: And now, was this in a residence or a business?

SHANE: This was in a residence.

INGRAM: And this was in North Carolina.

SHANE: North Carolina.

INGRAM: Where they were having snow.

SHANE: They almost didn't make it out because of the snow.

INGRAM: And the family's name that was killed was Durham.

SHANE: Durham.

INGRAM: I'm assuming D-U-R-H-A-M.

SHANE: I would say.

INGRAM: Durham. Okay. Do you know what town or what area of North Carolina?

SHANE: No, just in the mountains.

INGRAM: In the mountains. Do you know what timeframe this would have occurred in, approximately what year?

SHANE: I would say '72 or '73.

INGRAM: So, '72, '73 'cause your dad was incarcerated in '74.

SHANE: That's right.

INGRAM: Now, did he say how the people were killed?

SHANE: No. I took it to be about like the Wrens couple.

[Here Shane was referring to the murders of Reid and Lois Fleming in Wrens, Georgia (see Chapter 19). Shane would explain five years later that he took the Durhams' deaths to be about like the Flemings' deaths because his father was badly bothered that both crimes were heinous and involved torture.[1697]]

INGRAM: Now, tell me what that means – like the Wrens couple.

SHANE: Probably, tied and either strangled or, you know, just something to get the information out of 'em – tortured.

INGRAM: Tortured. Okay, that's the word we were trying to determine. Tortured to tell where the money was.

SHANE: That's right.

INGRAM: Now, did he describe the victims to you as far as what the race [was]? Were they white?

SHANE: They were white.

INGRAM: How about male or female?

SHANE: [They] had the mom. I took it to be the wi..., husband and wife and, and adult kid.

INGRAM: Husband and wife and adult kid. Did they say the gender of the kid? Was it male or female?

SHANE: Don't know.

INGRAM: And this was in a residence? You believe it to be a residence.

SHANE: I know it was a residence.

INGRAM: Did they say how much money they did end up getting?

SHANE: No, but whatever it was, it couldn't have been much.

INGRAM: Did he ever tell you how the people were killed – the method used to kill them?

SHANE: No, sir.

INGRAM: But you're assuming, based on what happened at Wrens [GA] and also what happened in Winder [GA], that where people had money and he went in and robbed them, if they didn't tell him, they were tortured.

SHANE: That's right. These people here – I know it's a gory detail – but you gonna find a family that's got their fingernails snipped. I know for a fact that daddy didn't tell me that and to mislead.

[Shane had previously shared with Ingram that his father told him about a crime during which something was forcibly put under a victim's fingernail. Shane was uncertain which case this pertained to, but after reviewing Reid Fleming's autopsy, Ingram found that Fleming's left thumb nail was split and showed a recent hemorrhage. Ingram considered this to be proof that Billy Birt was at the Fleming house.[1698]]

INGRAM: Yeah. Well, let me tell you, you are absolutely correct because I stand corrected. When I told you I didn't recall that from the Fleming [case], the autopsy revealed that. So, that confirms and verifies what your father told you.

SHANE: Yeah.

INGRAM: 'Cause you told me in the previous interview if it wasn't the Flemings, it was someone else because that's a detail he told me and that's something I would remember...

SHANE: Yeah.

INGRAM: ...that I think you said scissors...

SHANE: Scissors.

INGRAM: ...were forced up under...

SHANE: ...up under...and snipped

INGRAM: ...their fingernails...

SHANE: ...and snipped.

INGRAM: ...and snipped, yeah, as part of the torture.

SHANE: That's right. And I would say then, if they did it in Wrens, you might want to check these people up here.

INGRAM: In North Carolina.

SHANE: In North Carolina. And that's what I was telling Phil [Hudgins] coming up here is there's a lot of my information that's broken. But the reason it's broken, my wife or my kids would get up and they'd go to the vending machine or go to the bathroom, and daddy would talk. And then, when they'd come back, he'd just shut up, and if he didn't get the opportunity to say it again, that's just the end of the conversation.

INGRAM: How many times would you have visited your dad?

SHANE: Oh, hundreds.

INGRAM: And usually when he would talk to you about crimes that he had committed, or others had committed with him, it was in bits and pieces.

SHANE: Just in bits and pieces.

INGRAM: And primarily when you were alone with him.

SHANE: That's right.

After a brief diversion to other topics, the discussion again returned to the Durham Case:

INGRAM: Mike, do you have anything you want to ask him about that North Carolina case that he just described? That's something we should be able to find.

WALSINGHAM: Yeah, that would be. I mean you say mountains, but I guess that kind of, [inaudible] that's uh...

INGRAM: The western half of the state.

WALSINGHAM: Yeah, which would be consistent if it was on this side.

INGRAM: And with the snow to have fallen, it would require mountains for it to, for a foot of snow to fall in a day or a short time, and they almost got trapped. So, I think the timeframe early seventies, that about snow in a short amount of time, and three victims in a residence, uh...

WALSINGHAM: Yeah, I think that's good detail that we can work with on that.

SHANE: Well, wait, the man owned a car dealership.

WALSINGHAM: That's right.

INGRAM: That's probably a good point. You know, I asked you a question, and I want you to rethink this. I just wonder, and you told me, you said a relative of that family is the one that provided the information to uh.... You said a nephew or somebody like that...

SHANE: Yeah.

INGRAM: ...provided the information.

SHANE: And see, and when I started talking to Phil, all the stories are jumbled for the most part, and there for the longest time I thought that it was a nephew or a son-in-law of the Wrens victims that set them up, but it wasn't. So that means it was a nephew or a son-in-law of another story, and all these stories are about in the same timeframe.

INGRAM: That Wrens case is almost a template as to how crimes were committed when people have money and that information was put into the hands of your dad, and then he would take some of his associates, and they would go in and rob the people in what we term now to be a home invasion – they just force your way in, torture the people, get their money, kill them so there's no witnesses, and now you can almost say any case that resembles that would be a case to look at.

SHANE: Yeah. Well, this, this case here, it was right around the Wrens case because it was just shortly before it, well, it had to be shortly before...but, what I'm saying is both of them was told to me near about the same time. It might have been the same visit or something like that.

INGRAM: Well, they're very similar.

SHANE: Yes.

INGRAM: You have more than one victim. You have information that they have money. You had forced entry. You had torture. And you had death. But yeah, it's very interesting 'cause I'm seeing that commonality in these cases, and that tells me something. It tells me that any open case in the southeastern United States will be something to look at...

After other discussion, the conversation briefly resumed concerning the Durham Case:

INGRAM: Do either of you *[Hudgins or Walsingham]* have questions about the North Carolina case?

HUDGINS: I've got a question. How did you determine it was not Durham, North Carolina but the name was Durham, the people?

SHANE: Well, I was sitting there thinking and it just come to me.

[Regarding how Shane came to determine "Durham" was the surname of the victims rather the city of Durham, he elaborated later that same month by saying while he and his wife were watching the 1988 movie Bull Durham, about the Durham Bulls, a minor-league baseball team in Durham, North Carolina, he "realized that his dad was talking about the last name of these people."[1699]]

INGRAM: Yeah. And what's happened is that thirty years of conversation with your dad, you have kind of categorized it, indexed it...

SHANE: Uh-huh.

INGRAM: ...and periodically your memory kind of gets a little bit more specific....

SHANE: Yeah. Well, when daddy would talk to you, he'd pronounce a word and then he'd say, "Do you understand what I said?" And a lot of times he'd make you say it back to him.

[Billy Birt suffered from a speech impediment.]

HUDGINS: Because of his speech.

WALSINGHAM: Because of his speech.

INGRAM: Yeah.

SHANE: And so, there's a lot of times that you're just driving down the road and, I don't know why, but something that he said just pops back into your head.

INGRAM: Well, and like I said, it's just when you started talking about cases, things reminded me and popped in my head, and then what Mike [Walsingham] and I try to do is take it all on, piece it together, and overlay it and see and then retrieve old records....

Based on these details that Shane Birt said his father provided concerning the Durham Case, Bob Ingram summarized the main takeaways as follows:

- Billy Sunday Birt, Billy Wayne Davis, Bobby Gene Gaddis, and Charles David "Charlie" Reed committed a triple homicide in a residence in the mountains of North Carolina around 1972 or 1973. *[At some point – outside of the April 30 and May 17 taped interviews with Bob Ingram – Shane stated he was surprised his father named his accomplices. "Why Daddy gave me names of everybody involved, I don't know, because it was real, real rare for him to give me everything like that."[1700]]*

- The victims were a man, a woman, and an adult child by the surname of Durham. *[According to Shane, "If anybody ever said that Daddy said he killed a grandmother or grandfather or a man and his wife, they're lying. He would never say, 'The people I killed was a husband and wife.' No. He would say a man and woman or two men and a woman."[1701] This, however, contradicts Shane's statement in the May 17, 2019 interview, in which he said the victims were a "husband and wife and adult kid." Of course, perhaps his father did not use those exact words, and the husband-wife relationship was Shane's own assumption or interpretation, or he received that detail from some other source.]*

- The male victim ("the husband") owned a car dealership. *[During the first session of his April 30, 2019 interview with Bob Ingram, Shane, while discussing the murder of Reid Fleming, who was a semi-retired used car dealer, stated that he knew Fleming was not the only car dealer his father had killed, but he did not elaborate or provide names. During the second session of the interview, Shane stated that his "daddy despised car salesmen" and there were several car dealers in surrounding states who had been his father's victims.[1702]]*

- The victims were bound, strangled, and tortured. *[Up to this point, Shane never mentioned drowning.]*
- The crime had been arranged by a nephew and/or son-in-law of the victimized family, who spoke to Billy Birt.
- Robbery was the motive, but the killers did not get the amount of money they were told they would find. *[It was subsequently related that Billy Birt wanted to return to North Carolina to "kill that S.O.B." (i.e., the nephew or son-in-law who set it up), "but heat from authorities was too high in town following the murders, [and] he couldn't risk being arrested or shot."[1703]]*
- Birt and his accomplices almost got trapped in a snowstorm.

[During the course of his four-year book collaboration with Hudgins between 2018 and 2022, Shane participated in some interviews with Hudgins alone in which Shane later revealed additional memories of what his father told him regarding the Durham Case – memories he never shared during his interviews with Bob Ingram. One was that Billy Birt and his accomplices were specifically in a four-wheel-drive vehicle. This, however, would later be contradicted by Billy Wayne Davis, who stated he and his accomplices had driven a two-wheel-drive vehicle to North Carolina.[1704]]

At the time of the May 17, 2019 interview with Shane, none of the participants "immediately drew a connection to" the murders of Bryce, Virginia, and Bobby Durham in Boone, North Carolina,[1705] but Shane had provided enough detail to indicate such a case existed.[1706] After this interview, Hudgins and Ingram almost simultaneously conducted online searches[1707] using "some key words from Shane Birt's details…something like 'triple murder in North Carolina mountains'" or "unsolved triple homicide mountains North Carolina Durham," and both were led relatively quickly to the Durham Case. Hudgins discovered it first, finding a 2012 article from "the *Winston-Salem Journal* that recapped the cold case on the fortieth anniversary of the murders. It presented details of that night that matched Shane's bits and pieces, fitting perfectly, like a jigsaw puzzle." Hudgins believed it to be exactly what Shane's story referred to,[1708] and Ingram subsequently "found a report about a case in Boone that lined up with the story." According to Ingram, "Everything that Shane had provided…[was] corroborated with an actual unsolved crime in North Carolina."[1709]

Top to Bottom: Billy Birt, Billy Wayne Davis, Bobby Gaddis, Charlie Reed
(All images courtesy of Bob Ingram.)

CHAPTER 19

A TEMPLATE FOR MURDER

Bob Ingram next "began to recall the organization and methodical steps taken in the Wrens, Georgia case early in his career, even down to how the offenders were dropped off and fled in the victims' vehicle so their own was never spotted at the scene." Ingram believed "the Fleming case in Wrens was almost a template or boiler plate to what happened in Boone."[1710]

On Sunday, December 23, 1973, Ingram, who was then a rookie GBI agent, received a call to go immediately to Wrens to join other investigators. Upon arrival, he met Hugh Fleming, who had found the bodies of his parents, seventy-five-year-old Reid Oliver Fleming, Sr. and seventy-three-year-old Lois Robinson Fleming, inside their home. Reid Fleming had owned R. O. Auto Parts and Fleming Ford Sales in Wrens, and as a semi-retired car dealer, he kept a small inventory of vehicles for sale across the road from his home. Mr. Fleming was also a Sunday School teacher. When he failed to appear at church that morning, his son went to investigate and made the horrific discovery. The Flemings' wrists and ankles had been bound with strips of sheets. An extension cord was additionally used to bind Mr. Fleming's wrists. The couple had been gagged, and metal coat hangers were around their necks. The cord to an electrical drill was also wrapped around Mr. Fleming's neck. The coat hangers had been fashioned into ligatures that had been twisted multiple times so that pressure was repeatedly applied to their necks, then released and reapplied. Mrs. Fleming, dressed in her nightgown and bathrobe, was face down on a bed, her head hanging off the corner. Mr. Fleming was face up on the floor next to the bed. A distance of about two feet separated their faces from one another.[1711] The Fleming strangulations would be remembered for decades as two of the most gruesome murders in Wrens history.[1712]

There were no signs of forced entry, but the Fleming home had been ransacked and was in total disarray. Every drawer, cabinet, and location had been gone through;[1713] even an upright piano had been partially disassembled.[1714] Still, nothing seemed to be missing from the house; jewelry was strewn about, and a diamond ring remained on one of Mrs. Fleming's fingers.[1715] The dirt floor in their smokehouse had several holes, and empty fruit jars laid nearby, along with slips of adding machine tape with various calculations. The Flemings' vehicle was found abandoned one and a half miles from their home.[1716]

Autopsies determined the time of death was between 10:00 and 11:00 PM the previous night. Mr. Fleming's autopsy revealed he had died from quite abusive strangulation. He had severe abrasions and contusions around his throat and multiple hemorrhages around his throat, face, and scalp. Additionally, there were abrasions on his right ear and cheek and multiple contusions around his eyes. Other head injuries were possibly a result of multiple impacts of his head against the floor. One of his fingernails appeared to have a hemorrhage underneath it, as if something had been jammed under the nail as a means of torture. "Mrs. Fleming's death also resulted from strangulation." Her eyes were bulging and hemorrhaged, and her tongue pushed forward. A bruise on her neck had resulted from the friction of the coat hanger, and blood and fluid were found in her nose and mouth.[1717]

The number of local law enforcement personnel in Wrens was small, so they relied on the GBI to investigate the case. The GBI determined the Flemings were fine, salt of the earth, family-oriented, church-going people with no known enemies, and they ruled out revenge as a motive. They also ruled out sexual motives and determined greed was the cause. The GBI was also able to determine the empty fruit jars in the smokehouse had contained money the Flemings sealed inside and then buried in the dirt floor. They concluded the Flemings had been targeted victims of a robbery, they had been bound and tortured as a way of revealing the location of their hidden money, and they had ultimately been murdered. The Fleming Case was a real whodunit, and although the GBI was not sure where to begin looking for the guilty parties, it was evident the killers were older, very clever, experienced offenders with criminal sophistication, demonstrating a high level of planning and organization and taking care not to be detected or leave physical evidence.[1718]

A break in the case came when a man named Elvis Larry Bethune contacted a Cobb County, Georgia investigator about some items he had discovered in the trunk of a Cadillac brought to him by Billy Wayne Davis, with whom Bethune partnered in an auto body shop in Austell, Georgia. On December 19, 1973 – three days before the Fleming murders – Bethune joined Davis at a car auction in Macon, Georgia after which Davis asked him, "Do you want to make some money?" According to Davis, Bethune was kind of down and out and in bad financial straits and was always asking him how he could make some easy money. Bethune expressed interest in Davis's proposal, and Davis told him to follow him. They drove to Wrens, where Davis pointed out both a white house and "Jerry's Shell," a gas station and pool hall. Davis said he had information that the old man who lived in the house used to run a Ford dealership and reportedly had up to $50,000 in a bedroom dresser drawer. Davis and Bethune stopped at the Shell station where Davis spoke to the owner, Jerry Haymon, who Davis previously knew from card games. Haymon's nearby home was the other intended target.[1719]

Returning to the white residence, Davis told Bethune that entering the house would probably require breaking a window, which might awaken the residents, and they would likely have to kill them. According to Bethune, Davis asked him if he thought he [Bethune] could kill someone, and Bethune said no. Bethune thought Davis did not fully trust him, and after discussing the late hour, Bethune said he needed to get home. According to Bethune, all of this, paired with the fact that lights were on inside the house and an extra car was there, led Davis to tell him they would have to consider the job at another time.[1720]

Three days later, on Saturday morning, December 22, 1973, Davis brought to Bethune a Cadillac he had been driving and wanted to swap it for the Nova Bethune had been driving. The exchange was made, and the following day, Sunday, December 23, Bethune opened the trunk of the Cadillac and discovered several items including a pistol, a shotgun, a change purse containing a number of half dollars, cigar boxes holding rolls of pennies with "J. W. Haymon" written on some of the wrappers, a pair of gloves, and two flashlights. When Bethune saw Davis later that day and mentioned finding items in the car, Davis asked what they were, and Bethune showed him.

According to Bethune, Davis looked inside the change purse, zipped it back up, and put it in his pocket. He told Bethune to dispose of the other items, saying they could get them into some serious trouble or could connect him [Davis] to a serious crime. Bethune, however, saved the items in case he might need them to hold against Davis in the future. According to Bethune, "I had figured that one of these days I would have to save my life through something that I had on Billy hisself, and that's the only reason I kept the stuff…." When Davis later asked Bethune if he had gotten rid of the items, Bethune lied and told him yes. By this time, Bethune had heard on the radio about the murders in Wrens, and he afterwards contacted authorities. The items Bethune found in the Cadillac were quickly determined to have been stolen from the residence of Jerry Haymon. Knowing Haymon's residence was also in Wrens, Bethune told an investigator he believed he "could hand him a man [Davis] on a murder charge." Although Bethune was afraid of Davis and wanted the law's protection in exchange for his testimony, he believed if Davis could be put away, it would end a lot of the crime in and around Mableton, Georgia.[1721]

Meanwhile, word came to Bob Ingram concerning a man named Carswell Tapley, an alcoholic timber cruiser who managed a deer camp on a farm owned by his employer, George Leisher, near Sandersville, Georgia. Leisher resided in the Marietta, Georgia area where he was a used car lot owner and business partner of Billy Wayne Davis. Leisher was reportedly known to keep his eyes and ears open regarding financially well-off people who might be targeted for robbery, and according to Leisher, Davis asked him to locate such places in Sandersville and Washington County.[1722] Tapley claimed Leisher asked him if he knew of any people who kept large amounts of money and said Leisher specifically inquired about Wrens, the Flemings, and Haymon. At that time, Tapley did not know of anyone, but when he did acquire this information, he shared it with Leisher, saying he heard Mr. Fleming had $55,000-$60,000 in his house. Leisher said that was worth looking into, and he[1723] passed Tapley's phone number on to Billy Wayne Davis. Leisher told Davis that Tapley had some houses he wanted hit for money, and that whoever called should inquire about buying some hogs, and that would be Tapley's cue to talk. Davis said he would pass this information to someone he knew (who Tapley and Leisher referred to as the "boys up yonder"), and someone would contact Tapley. A man named "Jim Gordon" subsequently got in touch with Tapley, and the two met on Wednesday, December 12, 1973 in Louisville, Georgia, from which point they drove to Wrens. There, Tapley pointed out the two targets – the Fleming and Haymon homes – and stated the Fleming home contained between $60,000 and $70,000.[1724]

Ten days after this meeting, the two homes were robbed, and the Flemings were murdered, and both Carswell Tapley and George Leisher wondered how the crime went down and who had been involved. Tapley said he knew Billy Wayne Davis was a crook because Leisher had told him Davis's "bunch were just as dangerous as a cocked pistol." Tapley also said Leisher told him that "when he heard tell of a job being done with coat hangers and drop cords, he knowed exactly who done it" – Davis, "Gordon," and another man – and that these same men had robbed the bank in Stapleton, Georgia. Davis had told Leisher on one occasion that he [Davis] knew someone from Winder, Georgia who could make anyone tell him anything he wanted with the use of a coat hanger. Leisher was well aware of Davis's ties to Winder as Davis received quite a few phone calls from there, and Leisher had traveled there with Davis to buy cars. But Davis also met with other people there outside of the automobile business. He frequented a little beer joint outside of Winder and talked to guys there, including one who Leisher believed had a speech impediment *[which was true of Billy Birt]*. Leisher did not believe Davis committed the Fleming and Haymon crimes but put someone on those jobs – likely some guys from Winder. When Leisher was shown photographs, he did not recognize one of Bobby Gaddis, but he identified Billy Birt as a man who had met with Davis numerous times. Tapley eventually came to believe Birt had killed the Flemings with coat hangers, and he believed Davis was the driver.[1725]

Meanwhile, Larry Bethune was also trying to sort out who had put this together for Davis and how the Fleming and Haymon crimes had occurred. Bethune was convinced Davis had a partner who Davis counted on quite a bit and who pulled jobs with him. Bethune thought Davis might even have two partners, but he did not know their identities. Because Bethune knew George Leisher was in business with Davis prior to Bethune meeting Davis, he wondered if Leisher might have helped set people up for Davis. According to Bethune, "He depends on somebody, and it is just a feeling that I got. Somebody is helping him on this." Bethune said Davis knew several people in Winder, and although Bethune initially did not think Davis would have taken more than one person to Wrens due to having to further split the "profits," he came to believe Davis, Billy Birt, and Bobby Gaddis were the guilty parties – two men killing the Flemings and one man burglarizing the Haymon house. Investigators showed Bethune photographs of several men, and, just like Leisher, although he did not recognize Gaddis, he identified Birt as an associate of Davis. Bethune also held an interesting opinion regarding the order that things transpired. He believed Bobby Gaddis (not Billy Birt or Billy Wayne Davis) discovered Jerry Haymon's safe on Friday night, December 21 (after Haymon and his wife departed that same night for a trip to Texas) but had no tools to open it. Nonetheless, other items were taken that night – the pistol, shotgun, coin purse with silver dollars, and cigar boxes containing rolled pennies – the same items that were in the Cadillac Davis brought him the next day, Saturday, December 22, and that Bethune discovered when he opened the trunk on Sunday, December 23. Bethune believed Davis, Birt, and Gaddis returned to Wrens on Saturday night with the proper tools to open Haymon's safe *[Bethune said Davis and several others who Davis knew had the skills to peel or rip a safe]*, and they also robbed and killed the Flemings that same night. When asked by an investigator if he thought Davis was "the type fellow that would just plunder around a place for two or three hours and be caught while he was…digging around and looking for [money] in buildings," Bethune said yes. "If there's money concerned, Billy [Davis] would do anything."[1726]

Bethune did not believe Davis had been in the Haymon house that Friday night because, when Bethune first mentioned the items in the trunk to Davis, Davis asked what they were, and when Davis took the change purse, he looked inside to see what it contained as if he had no prior knowledge of it. Still, by Davis instructing Bethune to dispose of the other items, Davis was obviously aware of what had transpired, even if he had not been there himself. Bethune also said Davis was not the type of person who would take small stuff (including guns), which could not be sold as they might tie him to a murder. Bethune stated that Davis went for "money, stuff that counts, not this stuff that was in the trunk of this car…." Another reason Bethune believed a partial robbery took place at the Haymon house that Friday night is that, when Davis brought the Cadillac to him on Saturday, Davis had no cash. Davis owed money for a truck and attempted to give Bethune a check, which Bethune rejected. When Davis returned on Sunday, however, he had a roll of hundred-dollar bills.[1727]

By the time Bob Ingram interrogated Carswell Tapley and George Leisher, both had been promised immunity,[1728] and Ingram was eventually able to use their testimonies, along with that of Larry

Bethune and the items from the car trunk, as leverage against Billy Wayne Davis.[1729][oooooo] Based on the materials Davis had asked Bethune to dispose of, Ingram was convinced Davis had knowledge of and involvement in the Fleming murders. According to Ingram, "I told him he was going to be tried in a rural county where he had killed two good citizens, lifelong residents. He could take all of it, or he could take his part of it."[1730] By this time, Davis, Billy Birt, and Bobby Gaddis were serving time in federal prison for robbing the bank in Loganville, Georgia in early 1974. Ingram interviewed Davis on multiple occasions between September 1974 and January 1975, ultimately confronting him with evidence. When Ingram first explored the possibility of interviewing Davis, Davis's attorney, Richard Still, had told Ingram "his client was concerned with the murder case in Cobb County *[which referred to Davis being indicted for the 1973 shotgun slaying of used car salesman Harold Amell[1731]]*, and if a deal could possibly be worked in relationship to that case, it might assist Davis talking" to Ingram about the Fleming homicide. Ingram told Still he had no knowledge of a Cobb County case or anything to do with that area, that Davis was involved in the Fleming case, and developing evidence showed Davis was in Wrens when the Flemings were murdered. Ingram also shared that the district attorney had already stated that, for complete, truthful testimony, Davis would be granted immunity in the Fleming and Haymon cases. The following month, Davis told Still he [Davis] could be of no assistance with the Fleming murders, but Still related to Ingram that immunity in both the Amell and Fleming cases "would probably cause his client to provide the investigative officers with information in the Wrens [Fleming] case."[1732] In October 1974, Davis told Ingram and Jefferson County (Georgia) Sheriff Zollie Compton he could assure them of a conviction in the Fleming Case and would provide that information after getting a disposition in the Amell Case. In December 1974, Davis said he would provide them with a written and taped statement as to his involvement and the subjects involved in the actual commission of the Fleming murders after details could be worked out with his attorney and the District Attorney.[1733] Ingram felt Davis "was the best hope for charging and convicting the other three" [Billy Birt, Bobby Gaddis, and Charlie Reed],[1734] and in exchange for immunity from prosecution, Davis, as well as Carswell Tapley and George Leisher, agreed to testify for the state. In January 1975, Billy Wayne Davis finally provided a statement regarding the murders of Reid and Lois Fleming,[1735] which he would testify to when Billy Birt came to trial the following June.

On January 31, 1975, thirteen months after the Fleming slayings, Birt, Gaddis, Reed, and William Eugene Otwell (who was alleged by Carswell Tapley to be "Jim Gordon") were indicted by a Jefferson County grand jury and charged with "burglary, armed robbery, and murder." Birt and Gaddis were already in prison, and Reed and Otwell were subsequently arrested. An interview with Otwell proved fruitless as he denied any knowledge of or involvement in the Fleming and Haymon cases. He denied ever being in Wrens, Louisville, or Jefferson County at any point in his life, and he said he had never used the alias "Jim Gordon" nor used a code phrase concerning hogs. Otwell offered to take a polygraph exam and sodium pentothal ("truth serum") to prove his innocence, and he said the only person who could implicate him or falsely accuse him was Davis. *[Otwell had knowledge of criminal activity involving Davis, but nothing in the Fleming Case summary indicates Davis was the one who implicated Otwell.[1736] Because the only testimony connecting Otwell with the crime came from Carswell Tapley, who was a co-conspirator who had been granted immunity, that testimony was deemed insufficient to try Otwell, and charges against him were dropped in*

oooooo Although Larry Bethune was initially suspected of participating in the Fleming murders and the Haymon burglary, a polygraph examination cleared him of both. However, the polygraph examination results for Bethune, Carswell Tapley, and George Leisher all demonstrated some level of deception.

December 1975.[1737]*]* When asked why Otwell would have gotten involved with Birt in the Fleming and Haymon cases, Davis said Otwell would have either gotten a percentage of the take or he was working with Birt, either returning a favor or out of fear of Birt. Davis said he introduced Birt to Otwell in 1971, and Otwell had several business transactions with Birt. Davis said he had also seen Birt and Reed exiting Otwell's office in Austell.[1738] As with Otwell's interview, the interview with Charlie Reed was similarly unhelpful. The day following Reed's February 25, 1975 arrest, Bob Ingram told him the state had good evidence in the Fleming Case, but Reed said he was not involved and asked to speak with an attorney before making further statements, at which point the interview was terminated.[1739]

At trial in 1975, a "pale and nervous" Billy Wayne Davis, "recount[ing] from memory," provided "a lengthy statement" consisting of the same information he had previously told Bob Ingram, denying his presence at the Fleming home and implicating Birt, Gaddis, and Reed. Davis testified nearly four hours, and Birt's defense attorneys, cross-examined Davis the majority of that time.[1740] Details of how the Fleming robbery and murders transpired came to public light, although the details provided by Davis differed from those that Birt subsequently testified to. Without question, Carswell Tapley had passed information concerning the Flemings and their money to George Leisher. According to Davis, a couple of days after receiving the information from Leisher, Billy Birt was at Davis's car lot in Austell and told Davis if he ever ran across any information like that, he would pay him well for it. Davis gave Birt Tapley's number, and Birt gave it to another source (presumably "Jim Gordon") to have the information checked out. A couple of weeks later, Birt told Davis "they" had contacted Tapley, who had pointed out a couple of places in Wrens – the home of an ex-Ford dealer, who supposedly had $70,000 in a bedroom dresser drawer, and a gas station that housed a pool hall, the owner of which was in the liquor business and did a lot of gambling.[1741]

As Larry Bethune had previously shared, Davis acknowledged that he took Bethune to Wrens on Wednesday, December 19, 1973, and Davis said he pointed out the places that Birt informed him of. That Friday, December 21, 1973, Davis said Birt called and asked him to meet him in a hotel room. When Davis arrived, Gaddis and Reed were also there. Birt said they were going to Wrens to take care of some business but needed a nicer, late model car, and Birt also asked to borrow Davis's pistol. Davis said he obliged both requests. On Saturday morning, December 22, 1973, Davis said Birt came to him saying he had been to Wrens and talked to Jerry Haymon and checked things and everything looked okay. Birt wanted a different car since the one he was driving had already been seen in Wrens. Davis then took the Cadillac from Birt and traded it for the car Bethune was driving. Bethune opened the trunk and found the items previously described. He asked Davis about them, but Davis had no knowledge of the items. Davis took the change purse and told Bethune to put the other items up and he would instruct Bethune later what to do with them. When Davis asked Birt about the items, Birt said to get rid of them as they came from a burglary in Wrens (which implied some degree of robbery had occurred at the Haymon home the prior evening). Birt asked Davis to meet him later that night, and they agreed to meet at the intersection of I-20 and Highway 11.[1742]

Around 2:00 AM on Sunday, December 23, 1973, Birt, Gaddis, and Reed met Davis at the agreed upon location, and, according to Davis, Birt said they had trouble in Wrens and had killed the old couple. They tortured the man trying to get the wife to tell where the money was, and after they choked him to death in her presence, she said the money was buried in fruit jars in the smokehouse. They then decided to kill Mrs. Fleming to eliminate her as a witness. Davis asked for his pistol back, and they realized they did not have it and needed to go back to Wrens to get it as Davis said it could likely be traced back to him. While Reed continued on to Winder, Davis, Birt, and Gaddis headed back to Wrens. The men stopped along the way to urinate beside the road, and their car broke down. When two passersby stopped to help, Davis walked behind the car so he would not be seen and later laid down on the back seat of the car so that the men assisting them only saw Birt and Gaddis.[pppppp] Once they were back on their way, their car was still having difficulty, so when they got to the Fleming house, Birt pointed Davis toward the garage to get tools to fix the car. Birt went in the house to look for Davis's pistol while Gaddis remained in the car to keep it running so the battery would not die again. Birt did not find the gun in the house, so they drove to where they had left the Flemings' car and found it on the seat of the car. Leaving Wrens to head home, Davis said Birt and Gaddis provided more details.[1743] On Saturday evening, December 22, 1973, Bobby Gaddis had stopped by Mr. Fleming's car lot to inquire about and test drive a pickup truck, and Gaddis was later identified by a nearby resident who was present and had witnessed that interchange.[1744] That night, the attack on the Flemings began, and here again, accounts diverge of what happened next.

En route back to the I-20 and Highway 11 intersection, Davis said Birt and Gaddis described the events of that evening. Birt, Gaddis, and Reed had gone to the Fleming home around 8:00 PM. Mr. Fleming was watching television, and Mrs. Fleming was already in bed. They knocked on the door, and Gaddis told Mr. Fleming he wanted to purchase the truck he had test driven earlier. When Mr. Fleming asked them to return during daylight hours, they forced their way in, put a gun on Mr. Fleming, took him into the bedroom, and bound the couple. Gaddis stood watch over them while Birt and Reed drove their getaway car and the Flemings' Ford to a side road away from the Fleming home and then returned together in the Flemings' car. Over the course of several hours that night, the attackers ransacked the home but found nothing of great value. Davis said Birt and Gaddis told him "with mirth" how they repeatedly beat and tortured the Flemings and slowly strangled them with wire coat hangers and electrical cords to make them divulge the location of their hidden money. They laughed and joked about how "Mrs. Fleming was hard of hearing, but that her hearing improved considerably when a coat hanger was tightened about her throat." Davis also stated Birt told him how he, Gaddis, and Reed had taken turns strangling the elderly couple. Davis claimed he was sickened by their account but was afraid to show any emotion and kept quiet out of fear of what Birt, Gaddis, and Reed might do to him.[1745] Davis added Birt, Gaddis, and Reed wore old, cotton, brown work gloves during the crime, which was their normal method of operation.[1746] After their return to the I-20 and Highway 11 intersection, with Birt and Gaddis following him in a separate vehicle from that point, Davis said he drove to Austell, where Birt paid him in cash for a car for Birt's son.[1747] Finally, Davis testified Birt and Gaddis told him they took $4,000 from the Flemings' smokehouse.[1748] According to Davis, if "they" had taken more than $10,000, "we" (which presumably included Davis) were to get 10% and Carswell Tapley wanted 10%. Anything under $10,000, "they" kept it all.[1749]

[pppppp] When Bob Ingram interviewed these two men, they individually stated they had seen and assisted two white stranded motorists, which corresponds with Birt and Gaddis. The two later testified they "had seen something like 'clothing or packages in the rear seat,'" perhaps a reference to Davis lying in the back seat. [Sources: Chance, Edgar and John Allen. Interviews with GBI Special Agent R. F. Ingram. January 25, 1973. Investigative Summary, Mr. and Mrs. R. O. Fleming Case #70-0302-01-73; Murderpedia: Billy Sunday Birt, https://murderpedia.org/male.B/b/birt-billy-sunday.htm#:~:text=Billy%20Sunday%20Birt%20was%20born,in%20North%20Georgia%20in%201938.&text=Even%20with%20Birt's%20reputation%20as,Fleming%2C%20in%20Wren%2C%20Georgia

In his own defense, Birt, "pale and nervous" like Davis before him, denied any involvement in the robbery and killing of the Flemings, claiming he had never even heard their names until after they were murdered, had never been to Wrens before his arraignment, and had not robbed the Haymon home.[1750] Birt testified he went to Davis's car lot on December 20, 1973 to buy his son a car for Christmas. The one he selected needed body work, and Davis agreed to have that done by Christmas Eve. However, at 2:30 AM on Sunday, December 23, Davis arrived at Birt's home in Winder to tell Birt he was about to leave town, "and if Birt wanted the automobile, he would have to come to the lot in Austell and get it now." En route, Birt said Davis asked him to look in the glove compartment for Davis's pistol, and when it was found to be missing, "Davis turned around and started toward Athens, stating that he had to go to Wrens." Birt said the car developed fan belt trouble and, after they cut a piece off the belt, the car failed to start. The two passersby stopped, and Birt went with them to get jumper cables, telling them he and Davis were headed to Florida.[1751] *[This account would also align with the testimony of the two passersby that they saw only two men, although in this instance, that would be Birt and Davis rather than Birt and Gaddis. Another account states both Davis and Bobby Gaddis were with Birt and hid in the back seat at Birt's request "'because he'd beat them to within an inch of their life' for screwing up a simple robbery, which, unfortunately, turned into two murders." According to Birt's son, Billy Stonewall "Stoney" Birt, his father was angry with Davis and Gaddis for being late to their rendezvous and because Davis had lost his gun. Billy Birt pistol-whipped them while Charlie Reed held them at gunpoint. According to Stoney, his father went into damage control mode, and the men proceeded to the Fleming house, where Billy Birt observed what Davis and Gaddis had done to the Flemings, but where the missing gun was not located.[1752] In Shane Birt's version of this story, something sparked a fight between his father, Davis, and Gaddis at the Fleming house, and his father beat them there. According to Shane, it was Charlie Reed's gun that was misplaced and had to be retrieved rather than Davis's.]*[1753]

Afterwards, Birt said he and Davis drove to where a Ford (the Flemings' vehicle) was parked. There, Davis retrieved his pistol, and then they proceeded to Davis's car lot in Austell where Birt paid Davis for the car for his son. Birt then returned to his home in Winder, arriving there around 9:30 or 10:00 AM on December 23. Birt had four alibi witnesses, including his wife Ruby Nell, his mother-in-law, and two friends who testified he was at his home in Winder from 6:00 PM until after 11:00 PM on December 22, and he did not leave the house until Davis arrived at 2:30 AM on December 23. According to Ruby Nell Birt, none of the four witnesses lied that Birt had either been seen or was with them that evening and night in Winder, although she acknowledged he could have left their home later on, after she was asleep, which she said "wasn't unusual. He left most nights. He seldom spent the whole night at home."[1754]

According to Stoney Birt, his father thought the Fleming attack was a bad idea from the start, and he refused to participate. In this version (which contradicts Billy Birt's profession to have never been to Wrens or to have never heard of the Flemings until after their murders), Davis approached Birt around September 1973 and told him about a handful of jobs he had been exploring. Among these were the home of Jerry Haymon, a retired businessman who "had a large safe and a lot of gold coins," and who would be out of town with his wife; two pill houses; and the home of the Flemings, who were rumored not to put their money in banks. Because Davis had been responsible for organizing the May 1971 robbery of Drs. Warren and Rosina Matthews in Marietta, Georgia, and because that had gone so wrong, culminating in their murders,[qqqqqq] Birt was skeptical and doubted the reliability of Davis's information regarding these newly proposed hits, especially when he learned the Haymon and Fleming houses had been cased for Davis by William Otwell, who had allegedly provided Davis with information regarding the Matthews home. Still, Birt agreed to go with Davis to explore these potential jobs. In Birt's assessment, the Haymon house was a good prospect because it held silver and gold pieces and guns and would afford a larger yield, plus Haymon would be gone. The two pill houses were no-brainers because the occupants would never report their robberies to law enforcement without implicating themselves in their own illegal activities. But Birt doubted Reid Fleming would have much money, and he was concerned the Fleming home, being in the middle of town, could draw too much heat. According to Birt, his dissent regarding the Fleming job resulted in an argument with Davis, who was determined to rob the Flemings. Birt told Davis if he [Davis] wanted to hit the Fleming house, then do it, but it would be without his assistance.[1755] At that point, Birt said he and Reed split from Davis and Gaddis, and that evening, he and Reed robbed the Jerry Haymon home and the two pill houses while Davis and Gaddis carried out the Fleming robbery and murders. According to Stoney Birt, prior to this time, none of his father's Dixie Mafia boys in Winder (which Davis was not a part of) had killed; Billy Birt was the only one who had killed among them, but that changed when Gaddis, who shared a sadistic streak with Davis and who was the only one of Birt's gang who looked up to Davis, cast his lot with Davis and helped him kill the Flemings.[1756]

Regarding Davis's testimony about Birt, Gaddis, and Reed taking $4,000 from the Flemings' smokehouse, Bob Ingram says Birt, in 1976, while "looking straight at him," told him, "You, know, we got $40,000, not $4,000."[1757] *[Ingram, admitting that anything is possible, says there is a slim chance Birt was not at the Fleming house and received a cut of this money after the fact, which is why Birt had knowledge of the total amount taken, but he believes Birt was there, participated in the murders, and knew specific details about the money because he was the one who dug it from the smokehouse floor and removed it from the fruit jars.[1758] According to Ingram, this, along with Shane Birt's recollection of his father telling him he had forced a pair of scissors underneath one of his victim's fingernails, which aligns with Reid Fleming's autopsy, are independent pieces of corroboration that confirm Birt killed the Flemings. In a variation of this story, Stoney Birt says his father and Charlie Reed made that $40,000 burglarizing the Jerry Haymon house and the two unoccupied, "big-ticket" pill houses in the Wrens area that night while Davis and Gaddis went to the Fleming house and "spent all night trying to prove themselves by coming up with more than the $4,000 the [Flemings] had, and they thought it would impress my dad, but it went the other way."[1759] Stoney says his father would never have told Ingram he and his accomplices took $40,000, and that Ingram conflated the $40,000 taken from the Haymon and pill houses with the $4,000 taken from the Fleming smokehouse.[1760]]*[rrrrrr]

[qqqqqq] The Marietta, GA home of Drs. Warren and Rosina Matthews had been robbed on two prior occasions, one of which occurred in August 1970 when gunmen took jewelry. Billy Wayne Davis, Doyle Ray Henderson (whose prints were, at one point, compared to those in the Durham Case), and Frank Ray Conway (a former Marietta and Atlanta police officer) were charged with that robbery. The doctors armed themselves in case this happened again, which it did on May 7, 1971. Davis reportedly brought this second job to Billy Birt's attention as it was on Davis's side of the state, and he assured Birt he had cased the Matthews residence and familiarized himself with their schedules. Davis said it would be an easy job, and he anticipated they would clear $70,000. [Sources: Birt, Billy Stonewall. *Rock Solid: The True Story of Georgia's Dixie Mafia.* (2017), pp. 118-119; Birt, Ruby Nell (as told to Phil Hudgins), *Grace and Disgrace: Living with Faith and a Dixie Mafia Hit Man* (YAV Publications, Asheville, NC, 2022), p. 117.

[rrrrrr] One newspaper account stated the Flemings were robbed of less than $100. [Source: Beau Cutts & Don Hicks, "Matthews," *The Atlanta Constitution*, June 29, 1979, p. 5-C."]

Billy Birt's trial had begun June 23, 1975, and five days later a jury convicted him.[1761] Bobby Gaddis and Charlie Reed would subsequently be convicted in later trials – Gaddis in August 1975 and Reed in November 1975. In the end, Birt and Gaddis were each found guilty of two counts of murder (for which they received sentences of death by electrocution on each count), two counts of armed robbery (for which they received sentences of life imprisonment on each count), and one count of burglary (for which they received sentences of twenty years of imprisonment). Reed was found guilty of all the same charges and received the same sentences with the exception of receiving life imprisonment on each count of murder rather than death.[1762]

As Bob Ingram reflected on the Fleming Case and other crimes involving Birt, Davis, Gaddis, and Reed, he compared them to Shane Birt's revelations and newspaper accounts of the Durham Case. By this time, Ingram's law enforcement career had spanned 40+ years, during which he had investigated more than five-hundred homicides. By the time he learned of the Durham Case in 2019, he had come a long way in terms of experience and knowledge since his rookie days in the early 1970s. Perhaps most notably, he had been educated about the value and importance of behavioral evidence.[1763] Ingram had come to understand repeated behavioral patterns could be used as evidence to identify criminals, and he had learned Birt, Davis, Gaddis, and Reed were experienced criminals who demonstrated such patterns. According to Ingram, although behavioral evidence cannot be picked up and placed in a bag like physical evidence, it is just as important, and the following patterns point to older, cautious, more experienced offenders with lengthy criminal histories and who may have served prison time:

- They would come in advance to the targeted location in a vehicle to conduct surveillance and case the residence, including identifying what types and how many vehicles their victims had.

- When they were ready to commit their crime, they would cleverly return in a different vehicle in case their previous vehicle had been observed. Once they confirmed a vehicle belonging to their victims was at the home, the driver would drop off his accomplices in close proximity to the home and usually within walking distance. This prevented anyone seeing the intruders' car at the crime scene.

- The driver would then go to a predesignated location a mile or two from the home and park and wait.

- The homes they targeted showed no signs of forced entry, leading to the conclusion that their victims opened their doors – a behavior not uncommon in rural, historically low-crime locations, particularly in the 1970s, when homeowners infrequently locked their doors.

- Each of the intruders was always armed, and when victims opened their doors, they forced their way inside. Although armed, the intruders did not typically use their weapons because guns make noise and draw attention.

- Once inside the home, the intruders would first disable the phone and then incapacitate their victims by binding and gagging them. This allowed them to both control and torture the victims while ransacking the premises, searching for whatever they were looking for, and it prevented the victims from escaping.

- They would torture the victims to locate money and then kill them to eliminate them as witnesses. They also took care to ensure they did not leave much physical evidence such as fingerprints.

- Once the robbery and murders had been accomplished, the intruders would take their victims' vehicle, drive it to the predesignated location, abandon it, and then flee in their getaway car.[1764]

Because a modus operandi of Georgia's Dixie Mafia was to seek information about individuals who kept large sums of money and then go rob them, Ingram's conclusion was that the Durhams had been targeted for robbery just like the Flemings. Both homes had been ransacked, and both had their phones disabled. The Durhams and the Flemings had been bound, tortured, and strangled. "In each case, one of the victims was a car dealer. In each case, a driver apparently dropped the killers off at or near the victims' home and then drove to a predesignated location." In both instances, their homes were right off of main roads where anyone might have noticed a strange car, and the victims' cars were found abandoned one to two miles away from their homes, the killers having stolen them in order to return to their own vehicle. In Ingram's estimation, almost everything was the same and pointed, behaviorally, to the same killers. According to Ingram, "The cases are almost identical," or as Phil Hudgins wrote, "They're like bookends."[1765]

CHAPTER 20

TURNING POINT

On May 20, 2019, within a day of reaching his conclusions, Bob Ingram phoned the Watauga County Sheriff's Office, not merely to provide a tip, but to boldly state that he knew who was responsible for their long unsolved triple homicide. He left a message saying he needed to speak with the sheriff and that he had specific information regarding the Durham murders that would make a trip to Georgia worthwhile.[1766] Ingram was unsure how he would be received. He had worked other cold cases and had been rebuffed by some law enforcement agencies who felt they were too busy or budgetarily constrained to bother with fifty-year old mysteries. As Ingram said, the Watauga County officers did not know him from Adam's housecat and could have thought he was some nut job who had no idea what he was talking about. But the Watauga County Sheriff's Office was very interested and took Ingram's call seriously.[1767]

The following day, Sheriff Len Hagaman and Captain of Investigations Carolynn Johnson returned Ingram's call, and Ingram recounted for them his interviews with Phil Hudgins and Shane Birt and the background details of the Fleming Case and its similarity to the Durham Case. Ingram informed the officers he had no prior knowledge of the Durham Case, but there was no doubt in his mind the four men named by Shane were the Durhams' killers. Ingram wanted a team from North Carolina to travel to Georgia and stated Shane was available for an interview. Hagaman agreed that everything Ingram shared seemed to fit.[1768] According to Hagaman, this was an "out of left field" revelation and "a much-needed turning point for the Durham Case,"[1769] taking it in a direction he never imagined.[1770]

After Ingram laid out his thoughts in detail, all of which was new information and involved names of individuals that Watauga County authorities had never previously heard of, Hagaman and Johnson told him they wanted their State Bureau of Investigation to be involved, and they would need time to do some things and to locate certain individuals.[1771] Hagaman and Johnson straightaway began reviewing old details of the Durham Case and "immediately began to investigate the new leads."[1772] Hagaman also made plans to phone Chris Laws, Special Agent in charge for the SBI's Northwestern District, and he also called retired SBI Agent Larry Wagner (who had investigated the case in the 1970s alongside Hagaman) about this Dixie Mafia revelation.[1773]

On July 10, 2019, the Watauga County Sheriff's Office "sent a contingent" to the White County (Georgia) Sheriff's Office to hear Bob Ingram conduct a case consultation, during which he presented the facts and behavioral evidence from both the Fleming and Durham Cases.[1774] Watauga County was represented by Hagaman, Johnson, Wagner, and SBI Agent Wade Colvard, who was new to the Durham Case. From Georgia, alongside Ingram, were GBI Agent Mike Walsingham and Captain Clay Hammond, head of the White County Sheriff's Office Criminal Investigations Division. Ingram used the first hour to lay out the Fleming homicide. He subsequently showed pictures of the Flemings and of Billy Birt, Billy Wayne Davis, Bobby Gaddis, and Charlie Reed and presented their criminal backgrounds. He also outlined a chronology of murders that one or more of these men were confirmed to have committed between 1971 and 1973, a window of proximity to the 1972 Durham murders and the 1973 Fleming murders. Ingram wanted the visiting officers to understand that these men were active before, during, and after the Durham murders and to know what kinds of crimes they had committed and how dangerous they were.[1775] After a thorough two-to-three-hour briefing, Ingram provided the Watauga County officers with a thick packet of information, including everything he had covered as well as DVD copies of his April 30 and May 17 videotaped interviews with Shane Birt.[1776]

At the conclusion of the case consultation, as they walked out the door together, Bob Ingram had a brief interchange with Larry Wagner, the individual he felt he best related to. *[Wagner was likewise impressed with Ingram and felt him to be "on the ball."[1777]]* Ingram asked Wagner what he thought, and Wagner replied, "This has got to be it. It's the best information we've had." At this point, in Ingram's mind, it was Watauga County's case. He was at their disposal and offered to help any way he could, but it was not his responsibility to tell them what to do or how to do it. The Watauga County officers told Ingram they would look into it all. From reading newspaper accounts of the Durham Case, Ingram was aware of the four men from Asheville, North Carolina who had been charged with the murders decades earlier, and he believed the Watauga County officers were wanting to cautiously proceed with this new information in order to ensure no similar mistake was repeated.[1778]

Captain Carolynn Johnson subsequently compiled a list of potential interviewees that included Ruby Nell Birt (Billy Birt's ex-wife), Shane Birt, Stoney Birt, Billy Wayne Davis, Deborah Wester (Davis's girlfriend), Troy Hall, Ray Hall, John Hall, Ginny and Steve Mackie, and Gary Morgan (who, alongside SBI Agent Wally Hardwick, Jr., had discovered the Durhams' abandoned GMC "Jimmy"). Johnson also reviewed Bryce, Virginia, and Bobby Durhams' autopsies.[1779]

On July 16, 2019, Len Hagaman, Larry Wagner, Carolynn Johnson, Wade Colvard, and Evidence Specialist Deputy Patrick Anderson visited the SBI's district office in Hickory, North Carolina, where they reviewed portions of the tremendously large Durham Case file. Wagner used this opportunity to refresh his memory, especially as it related to the interviews he had conducted. That same day, the Watauga County Sheriff's Office began looking into the prison dates for Billy Birt, Billy Wayne Davis, Bobby Gaddis, and Charlie Reed as well as the status of latent prints from the Durham Case, and what steps to take next.[1780] Hagaman also contacted retired law officer Jerry Vaughn, who had continued to work on the Durham Case as a private investigator and had maintained his own case notes at home. Because of the limited investigative file at the Watauga County Sheriff's Office, Hagaman had a plethora of questions for Vaughn, sometimes phoning him in the wee morning hours to pick his brain about some detail or another.[1781] On July 17, 2019, Johnson and Colvard interviewed Pat Whitman, widow of retired SBI Agent Charlie Whitman, and on July 22, Johnson noted a visit to the Watauga County Public Library to look into Durham crime scene photographs taken by the late George Flowers.[1782]

Between July 29 and September 20, 2019, the FBI and GBI sent inked fingerprint impressions for Birt, Davis, Gaddis, and Reed to the North Carolina State Crime Laboratory in Raleigh. These prints were compared to two-hundred and seventeen unidentified latent prints lifted during the Durham Case, which had been sent to the laboratory by the North Carolina State Archives in 2013. *[More than a year later, in October 2020, the laboratory reported to the Watauga County Sheriff's Office that no matches were found.[1783]]*

On August 6, 2019, at the North Carolina Sheriff's Association office in Raleigh, North Carolina, Len Hagaman, Chief Deputy Kelly Redmon, Carolynn Johnson, Wade Colvard, Larry Wagner, and Rufus Edmisten met with and interviewed Bryce Durham's brother Bill and Bill's son Steve. Among other things, Bill related that he and Bryce had been good buddies and saw each other weekly in Mount Airy, North Carolina, where they enjoyed trout fishing, but Bill had an office job in Greensboro, North Carolina and once Bryce moved to Boone, they lost their frequent contact. Bill described Bryce as successful and a good money manager, who used banks for his money rather than fruit jars (as in the Fleming Case). He added that Bryce was not a rich man and did not have a lot of money in the bank. At one time, Bill and Bryce had discussed a business partnership, but it never materialized. Although Bryce was the sole owner of the dealership in Boone, Bill said Bryce had the financial backing of some wealthy individuals in Mount Airy. Bill stated that even though Bryce's dealership was successful – one customer paying for a Pontiac with a shoebox of cash – he did not believe Bryce kept money at his house and certainly not several thousand dollars.[1784]

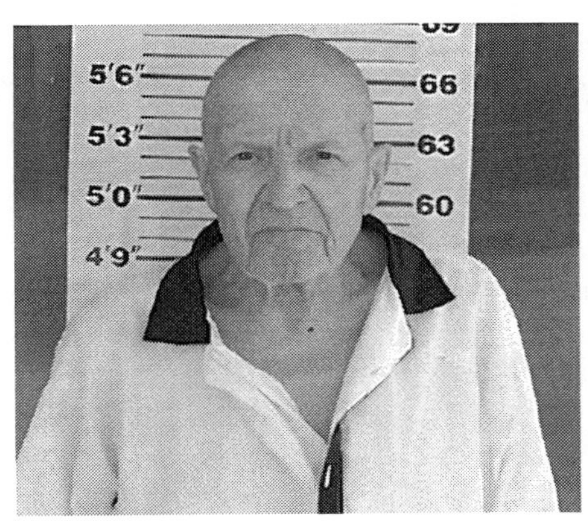

Billy Wayne Davis (Source: Georgia Department of Corrections)

On September 29, 2019, after three days of phone tag and messages, Ruby Nell Birt respectfully declined the Watauga County Sheriff's Office request for an interview.[1785] The following day, Hagaman, Johnson, and Colvard returned to Georgia to conduct their own interviews beginning with then seventy-eight-year-old Billy Wayne Davis[ssssss] at Central Prison in Macon, where he was serving a life sentence for the murder of a man named Charles "Mac" Sibley, Sr. By this time, Davis had been in prison forty-five years.[1786] According to Hagaman, Davis was beginning to show some physical evidence of his age, although not much mental deterioration, and Hagaman felt him to be "a smart cookie."[1787] During the hour and a half interview, Davis extensively discussed his quarter century career in the used car business, his attendance of automobile auctions in Atlanta and Alabama alongside out-of-state car dealers, and his acquaintance with car dealers in Raleigh and Cherokee, North Carolina. Davis also recounted first meeting Billy Birt, Birt's speech impediment, and how he let Birt borrow cars. Although he stated he and Birt had not been "real tight," he shared that the two of them had robbed banks together, how Birt tried to enlist his help in other jobs, and how Birt would go after anyone with money. He described Birt as a tough character, who was mean and crazy and the person to contact if you wanted someone killed. He said Birt tied up his robbery victims and would torture them if need be. Davis also stated that Birt claimed he [Davis] was present during the Fleming

[ssssss] The four Durham Case-related interviews with Billy Wayne Davis were audio recorded, but the recording of this first interview (September 30, 2019) is the only one that has not been released. It was recorded by Agent Wade Colvard and is presumably part of the SBI's files, which are inaccessible to the public. Sheriff Len Hagaman and Captain Carolynn Johnson made no recordings of their own, so the only record of this initial interview available to the author is within Johnson's handwritten notes.

murders, but Davis said Mr. Fleming was a nice old man, and he would never have harmed the Flemings. Davis liked talking about himself, but as it related to the Durham Case, he said he did not remember any job that Billy Birt did in the snow, and he had no knowledge of the Durham murders. Although Davis was familiar with Durham, North Carolina, he did not recognize the name of Bryce Durham or the Hall surname. Davis was focused on getting out of prison, stating how much he wanted parole, and wanting to know how the officers could help him.[1788]

Stoney Birt
(Courtesy of Stoney Birt)

The following morning, October 1, 2019, Hagaman, Johnson, and Colvard, along with GBI Agent Nic Johnson, met with Billy Birt's son Stoney in Winder, Georgia. Johnson had pre-arranged the meeting but had only stated it concerned an old case in North Carolina. Stoney gave the officers an extensive rundown of his father's life and crimes but remained unaware that the purpose of the interview was specifically related to the Durham murders in Boone.[1789] In fact, Stoney had never heard of the Durhams and had no knowledge of his brother Shane's interactions with Bob Ingram.[1790] Stoney told the officers his father's areas of operation included Georgia, Alabama, North Carolina, South Carolina, Tennessee, and Florida. He had robbed banks in all those states (the majority being in Georgia), and he and his associate, Harold Chancey, had run moonshine in the Carolinas. Stoney believed North Carolina was the only place his father was ever indicted on a whiskey charge, which was later dropped. Stoney did not recall any other specific jobs his father did in North Carolina. Johnson shared they had received information concerning a story Billy Birt had told about being in the cold and snow, and Stoney said the only story he knew along those lines concerned his father being in the cold in Montana and almost dying – a story Stoney had published in one of his books about his father. Johnson stated they had a case in North Carolina that was similar to the Fleming Case, but they did not know if Billy Birt was necessarily involved. Stoney asked if coat hangers or cinder blocks had been used (a reference to the murder of Harold Chancey's stepfather, Jim Daws, which was attributed to Billy Birt). Stoney stated coat hangers and electrical cords had been used in the Fleming Case and that Billy Wayne Davis and Bobby Gaddis were guilty of those murders. He suggested that the officers speak to Davis. According to Stoney, the investigators "left after two hours with nothing of any substance 'cause I didn't know anything."[1791]

Later that same day, Hagaman, Johnson, and Colvard interviewed Billy Wayne Davis's girlfriend, Deborah Wester, who had known Davis close to twenty years and gave the officers some good insights into his mental condition and personality. Although she had not seen him for three to four years, she had spoken with him by phone. Wester stated Davis's mind had started going bad a year earlier, and he had begun telling crazy stories and repeating himself. She said he was confused about what he claimed was an upcoming parole hearing that was actually not scheduled until 2021. Although mentally declining, he was physically quite strong and fit, constantly working out and jogging. *[This was contrary to Hagaman's assessment of Davis as showing some physical evidence of his age but little mental deterioration.]* Wester stated Davis was very intelligent and smooth, and he cared what others thought of him, wanting to be perceived as a compassionate family man. In reality, however, she described him as having no empathy or sympathy for anyone, probably not caring about closure for victims' families, and being only concerned with getting out of prison. *[Wester's portrayal of Davis also stood in sharp contrast to his self-assessment the day before, when he told the same officers he did not understand why anyone would want to kill somebody else for money, and he felt sorry for anyone who got killed.*[1792]*]* Wester further described Davis as a cold, soulless individual without heartstrings, who was not even upset by the overdose death of his own wife, claiming she had ratted him out and that a "snitch belongs in a ditch."[tttttt] Although Davis came from a good Christian family, Wester said he did not believe in God and did not feel reformed. At times, when Wester had asked Davis about some of his victims, he told her if he shared that information, he would have to kill her. She said Davis remained a very dangerous man inside of prison, retaining connections on the outside and successfully enlisting other inmates to do things for him, and she felt he would be even worse if released. Regarding Billy Birt, Wester said Davis told her he did not know Birt was going to kill people, and he said Birt tortured others, not him. Although Davis would admit to being "with the guys," he would deny murdering anyone. Still, Wester said, Davis admitted to counterfeiting, robbing banks, committing numerous arsons, selling stolen vehicles, making liquor with Birt, playing poker, gambling, and killing individuals who did not pay them. Davis also told of hiring someone to kill another individual, and when the hitman came to claim his pay for the accomplished "job," Davis killed him and kept the money. When Wester asked Davis how he slept at night, he said he laid down, closed his eyes, and slept just fine. Although Davis did not trust law enforcement, he told Wester he would talk and cooperate with the GBI if he could get out of prison immediately. Wester had no recollection of Davis ever mentioning North Carolina.[1793]

When Carolynn Johnson and Bob Ingram communicated by phone in late November 2019 (two months after the initial Davis interview), Ingram inquired as to how the interview went. Johnson said not well, and they got nothing from him other than him saying something to the effect that he might be able to help with the Durham Case if they could get him out of prison. Still, Johnson indicated she felt Davis knew something, and Ingram replied, "Of course he does. He did it."[1794] Ingram believed the North Carolina investigators' lack of success in their attempt to get Davis to discuss a connection to the Durham Case could be attributed to them never having dealt with nor being able to fully fathom a criminal like Davis or Billy Birt. According to Ingram, while an officer might read about such types, he or she could serve in law enforcement for years and still never encounter them face to face. Ingram said it was hard for him to do justice to the characters and activities of these men when trying to describe them to others. Ingram also believed interviewers between the ages of thirty and fifty (such as Johnson and Colvard) had less success with Davis; it helped "to be in his ballpark." At this point, Ingram was inclined to meet with Davis himself, particularly since the North Carolina authorities had made no headway, but he was initially very reluctant about going alone because he had only intended to assist Watauga County authorities with the case, and he did not want to step on their toes or have them think he was attempting to take control of it. But Sheriff Hagaman and Captain Johnson told Ingram they had no problem with him speaking to Davis, and they appreciated his help. At the additional encouragement of his good friend, GBI Agent Mike Walsingham, Ingram relented. Walsingham, knowing of Ingram's former

[tttttt] Davis's former associate, Larry Bethune, stated Davis was abusive to his wife and saw Davis beat the hell out of her one night, knocking her to the ground. [Source: Bethune, Elvis Larry. Interview with Joe Chambers, Lt. Penn Jones, Jefferson County (GA) Sheriff Zollie Compton, and Agents Jimmy Davis & C. W. Herndon. February 27, 1974. Investigative Summary, Mr. and Mrs. R. O. Fleming Case #70-0302-01-73.]

work with the GBI and his history and familiarity with these criminals[uuuuuu] (including his insights into and ability to talk to them), felt Ingram had the best shot of anyone with Davis. Ingram set up the appointment and notified the Watauga County Sheriff's Office of the same. Although Ingram had stated he would attempt to interview Davis between Thanksgiving and Christmas (2019), the interview did not actually occur until almost a year later.[1795]

On October 21, 2020, "armed with a deep knowledge of [Davis, Birt, Gaddis, and Reed], their methods and their cases," Ingram drove three hours to speak directly with then seventy-nine-year-old Davis.[1796] Sometime between September 30, 2019 and October 21, 2020, Davis had been moved from Central Prison in Macon, Georgia to Augusta State Medical Prison in Grovetown, Georgia, reportedly due to his age and health, potentially including the early stages of Alzheimer's disease. Ingram wanted "to see if Davis would corroborate Shane [Birt's] account from his father." According to Ingram, speaking with Davis alone was a more successful approach. Ingram felt he understood Davis's personality and described him as a no-nonsense "tough hombre," not easily intimidated and not susceptible to "stroking." Davis was a very matter of fact and non-confrontational individual who just sat there and listened; he was not a conversationalist and disliked small talk. According to Ingram, it was ineffective to simply ask Davis what he knew; the only way to get him to talk was to be prepared, direct, and factual, letting him know that you know what happened, that he was involved, and that you have evidence to support it. He would only talk if he had respect for and fear of you.[1797]

This was the first time Ingram had seen Davis in forty-five years, and he was not sure if Davis would recognize him as they both had aged; Davis certainly did not look the same as the last time they met. Although Davis told Ingram he had worked out for the past twenty-five years, tried to walk three hours a day, and only took medication "for people that work out," Ingram felt Davis was frailer and had somewhat mentally deteriorated due to very mild dementia, which manifested in slower thinking and response time as well as some degree of confusion.[1798]

In their initial discussions, Ingram recounted Davis's criminal history, and Davis affirmed his recollections of the bank robbery in Loganville, Georgia that landed him in prison, the Mac Sibley Case that earned him a life sentence, and the Fleming Case in Wrens, Georgia, in which he testified against Billy Birt, Bobby Gaddis, and Charlie Reed. Ingram showed Davis old photographs of Birt, Gaddis, and Reed and discussed their behavioral patterns and their modus operandi for home invasions, particularly that of the Fleming home. In response, Davis commented that Ingram had done his research and homework.[1799]

Ingram and Davis discussed Birt extensively – his nature and temperament, his speech impediment, his brutality, and the fact that Birt resented Davis testifying against him, was hell-bent on getting back at him, wanted to kill both Davis and Bobby Gaddis, and regretted not doing so. Ingram and Davis agreed Birt was a dangerous man and "the meanest man" either of them had ever dealt with. Ingram commented that both Birt and Davis were mean individuals who no one would mess with, and Davis affirmed it. Although Davis claimed not to be as bad as Birt, he agreed with Ingram that the two of them together [Birt and Davis] were really dangerous.[1800]

[uuuuuu] Ingram, upon his GBI retirement in 2000, had been dubbed in a newspaper article as the man who "broke the back of the Dixie Mafia." [Source: Jack Warner, "End Of An Era: GBI's class of '72 retiring, led by acclaimed agent," *The Atlanta Journal-Constitution*, Atlanta, GA, July 30, 2000, p. F3

Davis said violence and killing people never suited him, and he claimed he never accompanied Birt during a murder, stating the only thing that had interested him was bank robbery because it did not require killing anyone. When Ingram asked Davis to estimate the number of Birt's murder victims, Davis replied, "Oh, God, they ain't no telling," but when pressed by Ingram, Davis guessed forty-five but also said Ingram's number of fifty-two to fifty-four was realistic. Davis said Birt told him about some of the murders, but he learned about most of them from the newspaper "like everybody else." Davis said Birt was a pretty smooth individual until he began taking pills, at which point he became hard to deal with. Davis added that Birt became paranoid and thought everyone was out to kill him.[1801]

At one point, Davis was curious as to what case Ingram wanted to discuss with him but then said it did not matter – that whatever it concerned, he had gotten right with the Lord and no longer associated with criminal types. Davis also said he was dumb to have done the things he did, and he had too much confessing to do. When Ingram asked him where he would go after he died, Davis replied, "I'm going to heaven with my mother and father. Most certainly I am. It don't matter how I die or where it's at. That's where I'm going."[1802]

Twenty-two and a half minutes into the hour-long interview, Ingram introduced the Durham Case, and following are chronological (although not always immediately consecutive) excerpts from his conversation with Davis specifically pertaining to those murders:[1803]

INGRAM: February the 3rd – listen to me – 1972. That was forty-eight years ago. Okay. Forty-eight years ago. This was a Thursday, okay? Okay. Bill Birt and some other people – listen to me – went up to North Carolina, okay? They went up to North Carolina. Boone, North Carolina, up in the North Carolina mountains. Boone. Listen to me. Listen to me. They went into a house with a car dealer, like the Wrens case, former car dealer. Same scenario. Go into the house, rob the people, right? Tie 'em up, make 'em tell them where the money was.... But they went into this house, just like in Wrens, knocked on the door, forced their way in,[vvvvv] got the three people in the house, these three people, okay?

DAVIS: Right.

INGRAM: Father, mother, son, okay? Hear me out. Tied 'em up. Tied 'em up. Put their heads in the bathtub.

DAVIS: Hmm.

INGRAM: Oh, yeah. But this is how he [Billy Birt] operated. Tortured 'em, strangled 'em, tortured 'em to get the money in that house. Okay.... They drive up there. They rob these people. They kill these people. They don't get the money they thought, okay? When they go to leave – listen to me – there's a severe snowstorm, okay? They almost get trapped. They almost get trapped. They barely get out of there 'cause the car they took from the house was a four-wheel drive Jimmy. And had it not been, they wouldn't have got out of there. And they drove it to where the person was driving the getaway vehicle, okay?

[vvvvv] No one knows for sure how the intruders entered the Durham home or if they knocked on the door or forced their way in, so this was presumptive on Ingram's part.

DAVIS: Uh huh.

INGRAM: You, Bill Davis, can help me with that case. And I know – listen to me – you're kind of doing this, like, "What do you mean?" Well, what I mean, you know about it, okay? You know about the case. You can help me with the case. And that's why I came and made this three-hour trip, okay? Now, listen to me, listen to me. The Wrens Case, the Flemings, the elderly couple in the house, you know what I'm talking about?

DAVIS: Yes sir.

INGRAM: Yeah. It's '73. December of '73. Same deal, okay? They were put out at the house. The getaway vehicle was a mile or two away. They do the robbery and the murder. They leave in the victim's car, the Fleming car; they leave in it, okay? Hold on, hold on. It's important that you see this. They leave in the Fleming car. That's the one they leave in, and they abandon it. They abandoned the car, they get in the getaway car, and they leave.

DAVIS: Yes sir.

INGRAM: Okay? [Are] you following me so far? You understand what I'm saying, okay? I know all about the Fleming case and that, the details of it, everything that happened, who did what, everything, the participants and how it happened. They tied 'em up, they strangled 'em with coat hangers, tortured 'em, made 'em tell where the money was in the smokehouse in those fruit jars. Follow me?

DAVIS: Yes sir.

INGRAM: Yeah, okay? But then this one in Boone, I tell you about the Fleming one because this one in Boone is the same case, same people. Same case, same people is what I'm saying. In Wrens, there were two victims, right?

DAVIS: Yes.

INGRAM: Right? In Boone, there were three victims, right here, that I'm showing you.[wwwwww] Tied up, same way.

DAVIS: What a waste.

INGRAM: Sir?

DAVIS: I said what a waste.

INGRAM: Well, Bill, a lot of people died, and it was a waste. It was tragic.

DAVIS: Yes.

INGRAM: ...I came here to clear this up for these people's family and parents.

[wwwwww] Ingram says he showed Davis photos [Source: Ingram, Bob. Phone interview with author. May 27, 2023.]

DAVIS: They're from where? South Carolina?

INGRAM: Boone. Boone, North Carolina.

DAVIS: North Carolina.

INGRAM: Boone, North Carolina. This is almost fifty years ago. Bill, you know about this, okay? And I know that because I'm not here just on a whim. I'm here because I've talked to a lot of people. You've already said this. You've said, "You, sir, you've done your homework. You've done a lot of research. You know what's going on." So, I'm not here just to say maybe or possibly or could. I know that Bill Davis knows about this case. Okay? I know that. And it's something you'd remember. When you went up there that day, okay, on this, you almost didn't get out of there because of the snowstorm. And that's something that you can really remember. And this, here's the house. That's the house.

DAVIS: And that's in North Carolina?

INGRAM: Boone, North Carolina.... Tell me what you remember about this. This Boone, North Carolina case. Think. Take your time.

DAVIS: Wasn't he related to them people?

INGRAM: Okay, you just said something important, Bill Davis. The person who set this up was related to 'em. Do you hear what I just said?

DAVIS: Yeah, I heard.

[During this exchange, when Davis asked, "Wasn't he related to them people?" Ingram associated that with Shane Birt's claim that a nephew or son-in-law of the Durhams had set up their murders. Unfortunately, Ingram did not follow up with clarifying questions such as, "Who do you mean by 'he'?" and "Which people do you think he was related to?" Rather, Ingram immediately assumed Davis was referring to Troy Hall and his relationship to the Durhams. Of course, most people who have investigated the Durham Case believe Troy Hall helped set up his in-laws' murders; still Davis never mentioned Troy Hall by name in any of his interviews, and it would have been better to have asked follow-up questions to confirm exactly who he was referring to.]

INGRAM: Okay. Now tell me what you remember. The person – listen to me, listen carefully – the person who set this up to do this job was related to them.

[Ingram was again referring to Troy Hall.]

DAVIS: Well, it had to have something to do with Billy Birt.

INGRAM: Yeah. Something to do with who?

DAVIS: Billy Birt.

INGRAM: Billy Birt.

DAVIS: Yeah.

INGRAM: Yeah. Did Billy do this?

DAVIS: I'm quite sure he did. But I wasn't there.

INGRAM: I didn't say that.

DAVIS: I understand.

INGRAM: I didn't say that. We're gonna get to that in a minute. Just hold tight. Sometimes – listen to me, Bill Davis – sometimes you drove the car.

DAVIS: I have done that before....

INGRAM: I know you have driven the car in these jobs sometimes. Okay. And you were off at a distance, you put them out, you were off at a distance, and they came out. You may not have been present – listen to me –...

DAVIS: Uh huh.

INGRAM: ...when these people were killed, but you know about it.

DAVIS: Yes.

INGRAM: I know you do. I know you do. But the thing that I want you to think, this is fifty years old. It's hard to remember. I know that. I know it is. It's hard for me. I know it's hard for you.

DAVIS: Terrible sometimes.

INGRAM: Well, you still got your mind. You still got it. But here's my point. When this happened, when y'all went up there, you got hit with a big snowstorm, okay? And that's something you can remember, and you say, "What are you talking about?" Well, it was so big that you almost didn't get out of there. What I mean is the car that was parked there, it was a four-wheel drive Jimmy. You know what that is.

DAVIS: Uh huh.

INGRAM: Yeah, of course you do. You're a car dealer. You probably know more about cars than I ever thought I knew. But that Jimmy there, after they robbed and killed these three people, that Jimmy barely got them out of there and they drove to the getaway vehicle. I think Bill Davis was driving that vehicle. Now hold on, hold on.

DAVIS: I'm trying to think.

INGRAM: I know you're trying to think. I can see the wheels turning.

DAVIS: Uh huh.

INGRAM: Okay? Because at first you said, "Well, I don't know what you're talking about," and I'm trying to give you things, Bill, to refresh your memory. Trying hard. But the snowstorm is one thing. These three people that they went in on, Bill [Birt] and others, because there was more than one at Wrens, and this is just like the Wrens Case, just like it. They tied 'em up, they tortured 'em, and the reason they tortured 'em was for what?

DAVIS: For the money.

INGRAM: For the money, to find out where the money was. Because if they didn't see the money, they tortured 'em to find out where it was. Because, see, the jobs they were doing were because they were told these people had money. And see, they didn't select Boone, North Carolina by throwing a dart at a map. That ain't how it happened.

DAVIS: No.

INGRAM: How would it happen? How would a job be set up?

DAVIS: Well, you'd have to have some information on it.

INGRAM: Thank you. You'd have to have some information. Somebody set this up, and you said something important to me. You said somebody had to give this information to Bill Birt. Had to.

DAVIS: Oh, yeah. He didn't know people like that [*or* up there].

INGRAM: Right. Well, he wouldn't know somebody up in Boone, North Car-.... Like he wouldn't know somebody in Wrens, Georgia. Because everybody's then, "What are these people doing in Wrens? They're from Marietta and Winder. How did they find Wrens?" Well, I know how they found 'em. Carswell Tapley at that deer camp was running his mouth to George Leisher. And George Leisher told you. And you told Billy Birt. And that's not me creating that. That's in sworn testimony by everybody. That's what happened. Am I right? You follow me?

DAVIS: Yes sir.

INGRAM: Okay. I mean everything I've said so far is...

DAVIS: Yeah, you're right on course.

INGRAM: Right on the money.... This case up in Boone, so, they get up there, they do the job, the snow hits, they barely get out of there. I mean, in Boone, North Carolina, when snow hits, it ain't like Marietta and Austell where we get two inches. They get two feet in one evening. So, this stuff hit hard. They barely got out of there. But these are the three people, Bill, that were killed...

DAVIS: Uh huh.

INGRAM: ...in their house.

DAVIS: What a waste.

INGRAM: Total waste. Well, the Fleming Case was a waste.

DAVIS: Well, all of 'em are...

INGRAM: Yeah.

DAVIS: ...when you kill somebody.

INGRAM: ...So, tell me what you know about this case. Tell me what you know. 'Cause it's important that I clear this up for this family and put this to rest. And that's why I'm here.

DAVIS: The only thing that I could possibly help you with is that I know that he [Billy Birt] killed them. And they went in the house and done it. I don't know how they got in. I didn't ask, didn't want to.

INGRAM: How'd they get in the Fleming house?

DAVIS: Through the front door.

INGRAM: Knocked on the door. And they opened it and what?

DAVIS: So that might be the way they did then.

INGRAM: They, you said...

DAVIS: I don't know.

INGRAM: Well, wait a second. But you know he did this?

DAVIS: Yes. He...

INGRAM: Okay.

DAVIS: ...absolutely did it.

INGRAM: ...You knew about this.

DAVIS: Yes.

INGRAM: Oh, I know you did. You knew about the Boone, North Carolina case. You knew about going up there to do a job, and Bill Birt robbed and killed 'em. And I'm gonna tell you something. I'm convinced you drove the car. Oh yeah.

DAVIS: I could have.

INGRAM: Oh, I know you could have.

DAVIS: That's just what I did, but...

INGRAM: Yeah, I know it's what you did. You drove the car and Bill Birt.... Well, who was with Bill Birt? Was Gaddis with him?

DAVIS: Yes.

INGRAM: So, it was Gaddis and Birt. Who else? Who was the third one that went in the house?

DAVIS: The other one was, uh, Charlie Reed.

INGRAM: Charlie Reed. Charlie Reed, Bobby Gaddis and Bill Birt went in that house, and you drove the car.

DAVIS: Yes. That [was]...

INGRAM: And you regret what happened to those people?

DAVIS: Oh Lord, yes.

INGRAM: Because you knew when Bill Birt went in, he wasn't leaving until they were dead.

DAVIS: Yep.

INGRAM: ...Who set this up? Who set this up? Think, because that's why I'm here. Who set this in motion? You said something earlier. But who set this up?

DAVIS: Well, it had to...normal inclination would be Billy Birt, but I think he had some help with it.

INGRAM: Okay, but who was the one that gave the information that these people had money to Birt? Or to whoever? Was it given to you?

DAVIS: No.

INGRAM: Okay, if it was given to Birt...

DAVIS: It was him.

INGRAM: It was given to Birt, but who gave it to him?

DAVIS: Mmm. I'm not sure.

INGRAM: Okay. You're not sure, but...

DAVIS: No.

INGRAM: ...what did you tell me earlier? Did you tell me earlier it had to be somebody who knew these people...

DAVIS: Yeah.

INGRAM: ...and possibly a....

DAVIS: Had to be.

INGRAM: Did you say a family member or not? I don't want to put words in your mouth. Did you say that?

DAVIS: Yes, I did.

INGRAM: You said a family member.

DAVIS: Yes sir.

INGRAM: Do you know who the family member was?

DAVIS: I, I don't think it was a woman. I think it was either him or him.

[Davis seemed to be referring to the photos of the Durhams and saying the person who supplied the information was not a woman (Virginia) but was "him or him" (pointing to Bryce and Bobby). This indicates Davis was confused about victims versus perpetrators.]

INGRAM: Okay. Okay. Okay.

DAVIS: But I don't know that.

INGRAM: Okay. You don't know who it was, but why did you say.... Was that a lucky guess, or why did you say you thought it was a family member? Somebody had to provide information to Bill Birt. I mean, Bill Birt doesn't know Boone, North Carolina. You don't either.[xxxxxx]

DAVIS: No.

INGRAM: You just know it was a job...

DAVIS: Right.... They never have settled that case?

INGRAM: This case is not solved.

DAVIS: It's not?

INGRAM: No.

DAVIS: All of 'em are Durham?

INGRAM: All of 'em are dead. Yeah. They've been dead a long time. This boy was only nineteen *[actually eighteen]* years old.... If you could tell me who set this up, it would be a big help.

DAVIS: I'm going to have to do some homework on that. I don't know, and uh....

INGRAM: Well, ain't no homework to do. You just got to use your memory. Is your memory pretty good?

DAVIS: Not as good as it was.

INGRAM: No, it's not as good as it was. But you have control of your faculties, don't you? I mean you...

DAVIS: Oh, yes.

INGRAM: ...you know what's going on. You know what you're doing.

DAVIS: Yes.

[xxxxxx] This was another assumption on Ingram's part. There was no proof whether Billy Birt was familiar with Boone or anyone who lived there. In fact, in subsequent interviews, Davis would state he [Davis] had been to Boone on several occasions.

INGRAM: Yeah. You got good intelligence as far as I'm concerned. You understand. You understand the most important thing. Right and wrong and who did what?

DAVIS: Where did the Durhams actually come to recognition, I guess?

INGRAM: This Durham case here, the gravestone of these three people, what happened was one of Billy's sons – listen to me – one of Billy's sons who had been talking to Billy in prison – not Stoney, but the young one that you don't even know, Shane, the youngest one. He was an infant when you guys got locked up. But as he was growing up – listen to me – as he was growing up, Bill Birt, he would come visit his dad. Shane would come visit his dad, Bill, and Bill would talk to him in bits and pieces.... I remember that he [Billy Birt] was so smart with, he would never tell you a story from beginning to end. Never. He would tell you things in pieces, bits and pieces, little bits and pieces. And what he would do, he would give you information in bits and pieces. And that's what he did to his son. And he told his son about this. This. Okay.

DAVIS: Uh huh.

INGRAM: He told his son about it. And then when his son wanted to get right, he came to me and said, "Let me tell you what my dad told me." So, I knew all about the Wrens Fleming Case. So, I took that one and put this one on top of it, and I said same people did it. So that's how we get to this. You follow me?

DAVIS: Yes.

INGRAM: Follow me?

DAVIS: Uh huh.

INGRAM: Okay. So, the two cases are, I won't say they're identical, but almost. They're very, very similar. The only difference is there's three victims here where there was two in the Fleming Case. But the same way, the same reason, the same purpose. The Fleming Case was set up with information. This case was set up with information. Three were put out. Who'd you tell me were put out at the house here? You said who? You said Gaddis.

DAVIS: Gaddis.

INGRAM: Who? Reed. Charlie Reed, Bobby Gaddis, and Billy Birt.

DAVIS: Charlie Reed, Bobby Gaddis, and Billy Birt.

INGRAM: Billy Birt.

DAVIS: Right.

INGRAM: Who drove the car? Bill Davis. You just told me you did.

DAVIS: I probably did.

INGRAM: You did. No, you didn't say probably. You said you did drive it and put 'em out, and then they came to you and told you what they had done. How much money did they get?

DAVIS: It was a wad of it, but I don't know the exact amount...

INGRAM: Okay. Okay.

DAVIS: ...or how much I got. I got some money out of it, but I don't...

INGRAM: Right, right.

DAVIS: I don't know the total.

INGRAM: Right, right. Well, sometimes they didn't tell you the truth.

DAVIS: Yeah.

INGRAM: ...You remember the snowstorm?

DAVIS: Uh huh. Oh, yeah.

INGRAM: Huh?

DAVIS: Yes sir.

INGRAM: Yes sir. Almost didn't get out.

DAVIS: That's right.

INGRAM: Yeah. You remember the snowstorm?

DAVIS: Uh huh.

INGRAM: Okay. You remember the house?

DAVIS: The house is vaguely familiar.

INGRAM: Vaguely familiar. Remember the people?

DAVIS: Uh, this one. *[referring to the photo of Bryce Durham]*

INGRAM: You remember the man?

DAVIS: Yes.

INGRAM: But you don't remember these two? *[referring to photos of Virginia and Bobby Durham]*

DAVIS: No.

INGRAM: But you remember there were three of 'em, right?

DAVIS: They was, yes.

INGRAM: Yeah. Okay. And you remember you got a wad of money?

DAVIS: Yes, we did.

INGRAM: Okay. All right. What kind of car did you drive that night, you remember? Think.

DAVIS: I think it was a Chevrolet.

INGRAM: What kind?

DAVIS: Probably a 70 model. The one with the slanted trunk on it.

INGRAM: Okay. Chevrolet?

DAVIS: Uh huh.

INGRAM: With the slanted trunk, '70s model. So, was it a two-wheel or four-wheel drive?

DAVIS: Oh, it was two.

INGRAM: You were lucky to get out with a two-wheel drive with that snowstorm.

DAVIS: *[laughing]* I know.

INGRAM: You remember those mountains?

DAVIS: Uh huh.

INGRAM: ...Is everything you told me true today?

DAVIS: To my knowledge, it is.

INGRAM: Okay, true and correct to the best of your knowledge and your memory?

DAVIS: Yes.

INGRAM: Okay. Anything you want to ask me?

DAVIS: Yeah, when we going home?

INGRAM: I don't know. That's the parole board's decision. But I...left it with you.... I said, "You want me to tell the parole board you cooperated or not, leave it alone or tell 'em?" And you said, "Tell 'em." So...I will tell the parole board because I know who they are. I know the members of the parole board. I will tell 'em you cooperated with this case and helped me clear it up.

DAVIS: Well, I certainly appreciate that.

INGRAM: Okay.... You were the driver in this one, just like you were in the Wrens Case. You were the driver in both of them, right? Yes or no?

DAVIS: Yes. Yes.

[It is curious that Davis confessed to being the driver in the Fleming Case when he testified decades earlier that he only met Billy Birt, Bobby Gaddis, and Charlie Reed after the trio had killed the Flemings and departed Wrens.]

INGRAM: Okay. All right. All right, sir. Thank you very much...

Despite Davis's mild dementia, Ingram believed him to be "totally aware and cognizant of what was going on" and capable of understanding the questions he asked him. According to Ingram, "This [was] a man who had good recollection.... He [was] not as clever as he was, but [he] still [had] it.... He understood clearly and specifically everything we talked about...." Because their main discussion had been focused on an almost fifty-year-old case, it was natural for Davis to have difficulty recalling specifics, but according to Ingram, "He knew plenty. He knew a lot about the case.... Was he able to provide specific, precise detail? No. But was he able to give a good general description of what occurred and who was involved? Yes, and he did.... But did he reveal it all? Of course not, and that [wasn't] his nature."[1804]

The day after this interview, Ingram called the Watauga County Sheriff's Office to inform them of the results, and he also sent them a copy of his audio-recorded conversation with Davis, again offering to continue helping any way he could.[1805]

One month later, on November 16, 2020, Sheriff Len Hagaman and Captain Carolynn Johnson returned to the White County Sheriff's Office in Cleveland, Georgia, this time to meet with Bob Ingram and Shane Birt. Aside from sharing some general, historical background about himself (including his personal methamphetamine addiction between 1998 and 2003), his father, and their family, Shane recounted the things he had previously told Ingram that his father had shared with him about the Durham Case, but with some new details:

SHANE: The first thing I ever heard about the Boone case, the closest he [Billy Birt] ever come to being caught was a snowstorm. And he said while he was there doing a job, said the snow fell and he said, "Son, we almost didn't get away." And he said if the man hadn't drove the truck *[a reference to the GMC "Jimmy"]* home, he said we wouldn't have got away.

INGRAM: He said if the man hadn't drove the truck home; who are you referring to?

SHANE: The victim.

INGRAM: Tell us what you remember your father told you. Don't add, don't subtract anything, but tell us what your dad told you about that case.

SHANE: That was it in the beginning. He was just telling me about the snowfall.

INGRAM: The first time – I want to be clear – the first time your dad mentioned the case we're here talking about, is that he said that there was a bad snowstorm and almost got trapped, and the man not bringing the vehicle home, that they wouldn't have got out.

SHANE: They wouldn't have got away.

INGRAM: When did you hear about that case again?

SHANE: It's really hard to say, because whenever we'd go see my dad....we would get thirty minutes at a time....

INGRAM: When we talked the last time, you said that more of this has come back to you.

SHANE: That's right.

INGRAM: Okay, let's piece it together, and let's go from the snowstorm, and he didn't tell you where it was, did he?

SHANE: That come – I don't know when the conversation was – but "Durham" come up, and uh....

INGRAM: How did that come up?

SHANE: We was talking, and daddy said, "Durham." And I said, "Durham, North Carolina?" And he said, "No, son." He said, "The people's name was Durham."

INGRAM: Okay, and this is in a separate conversation from the snowstorm.

SHANE: This is in a separate conversation, and this was probably, I would say I'd be in my early or mid-twenties or somewhere around in there.

INGRAM: So, this was twenty-five years ago or more.

SHANE: Yeah.

INGRAM: So, what did this next conversation consist of?

SHANE: He said it was in Boone, like Daniel Boone.

INGRAM: Oh, he said...this is the first time I've heard you say this.... So, because of his speech impediment, he had to clarify...

SHANE: He had to make sure that we knew what he was talking about.

INGRAM: The first time he mentioned it was about the snowstorm, the vehicle to get out of there. The second time he mentioned Durham, the name....

SHANE: I can't say the second time because daddy didn't talk like that. When daddy really opened up to me, it was after I was on drugs and me and my wife was divorced, and this was in the real early 2000s.... After I was divorced and I was straight and had a right mind to me, I would go see my dad.... Daddy would tell me about different cases. And why he would tell me about North Carolina the way he did, I really don't know.... And now, the North Carolina case, daddy was mad about that case, and if you ask me could I positively tell you who set it up, no, but do I know if it was a son-in-law or a nephew, 100%. Either one of those.

INGRAM: How do you know that?

SHANE: Because that's what daddy said. Because daddy said that, if he had time to go back and do it over, he *[the person who set up the murders]* wouldn't be alive today because he was the sorriest SOB that ever lived. Said those people should have never died and said that they didn't have anything there.... He said that the people in Boone had nothing, and he was assured of that.

INGRAM: He was assured of what?

SHANE: That they didn't have anything as far as the money, the wealth or anything for him to be there.

INGRAM: But that's what he was told.

SHANE: That's what he was told.

INGRAM: And you don't know by who.

SHANE: It was either a son or a son-in-law. *[Shane likely meant to reiterate "nephew" or son-in-law.]*

INGRAM: He told you that.

SHANE: He told me that.

INGRAM: What did he tell you he did in the crime? Describe for us what you remember he told you.

SHANE: Oh boy. Dad and Billy Wayne and Otis – this crime is the reason that Otis went crazy. *[A reference to Otis Reidling, Jr., one of Billy Birt's inner circle.]*

INGRAM: This crime.

SHANE: This crime here is the reason Otis went crazy.

INGRAM: Otis being Otis Reidling.

SHANE: Otis Reidling.

INGRAM: Okay.

SHANE: My Uncle Bob [Birt], not my dad, but my Uncle Bob told me that – I always called him "Otie" – said Otie was going down the road and said a woman out of North Carolina jumped on his hood, and Otie wrecked his car. So, the reason Otis went crazy was because of this.... Otis's wife called dad – which was my dad's niece – and said, "You've got to come and get Otis." And Otis was on top of the house hugging the chimney, saying the ghost was coming to get him. Well, Otis was only twenty-one years old, so he was just a kid. But dad said, evidently, they was at the house when the people come in, and said that the first person to die was the wife, and said the reason that she died is the son wouldn't watch a mother die without giving up what was in the house. And said the second one to die was the son because a daddy wouldn't watch his son pass away without giving up what he knows. And said the last one to die was the dad. And daddy told me, he said with the snow and the lack of money and just the fact that killing people for nothing, and daddy didn't have to have much of a reason to kill you, but if he killed somebody for money, the minimum charge was $5,000, and dad told me, he said that the money was not there, and said that if the man hadn't drove a truck home from his dealership, and why dad either hated car dealers or targeted car dealers is beyond me, but evidently the man was a car dealer in Boone.

INGRAM: How were these people killed? Did he ever say?

SHANE: He didn't say. I don't know if they was shot, but later on, I understand that they was drowned.

INGRAM: Who told you that?

SHANE: That was Phil. *[Referring to author Phil Hudgins]*

INGRAM: Phil did. Okay. But your dad didn't tell you that?

SHANE: My daddy never told me that.

INGRAM: Did he say anything about how they were able to control the people? There were three victims, you said.

SHANE: No, but the first thing daddy would do is either tie 'em up, either with rope or coat hangers, either one of the two. Now, I don't know anything about your case...

INGRAM: Yeah, just don't tell us what you've heard; tell us what your dad told you.

SHANE: But if it was coat hangers, it was my dad. 100%. But my dad did tell me that, uh, and I do think this *[pointing to the silver on the table beside him]* is from the house.

[On September 1, 2020 – six weeks prior to this interview with Shane Birt – Bob Ingram had phoned the Watauga County Sheriff's Office, informing them that Shane had called him and GBI Agent Mike Walsingham and wanted them to see Ruby Nell Birt's china cabinet filled with silver that her husband, Billy Birt, had given her. Ingram requested photographs of the silver that had been taken from the Durham home and left in the GMC "Jimmy" the night of the murders so that a comparison might be made.[1806]]

INGRAM: Who committed the crime?

SHANE: It was my dad, Billy Wayne Davis, and Otis Reidling.

[The mention of Otis Reidling, Jr. being a participant in the Durham murders was a first and was a deviation from Shane's previous mention of Charlie Reed as an accomplice.]

INGRAM: Okay. Was Bobby Gaddis with them?

SHANE: And Bobby Gaddis.

INGRAM: Bobby was with them?

SHANE: Bobby was with them.

INGRAM: Okay. Now how does this silver that you're pointing to fit in?

SHANE: That was the only thing really worth taking.

INGRAM: Now, who had this silver? Who did you get it from?

SHANE: I got it from my mom.

INGRAM: Okay. And who did your mom get it from?

SHANE: My mom got it from my dad.

INGRAM: Okay. Did your mom tell us a couple of months ago, when you invited us to the house, when she got that?

SHANE: Yes. It was late '72, early '73.

[In 2024, Bob Ingram stated that, based on this 1972-73 timeframe, he knows with certainty that the silver in Ruby Nell Birt's possession came from the Durham house, but without proper identification and documentation of the pieces, no one can know this for sure. Considering the Durhams were murdered in February 1972, Shane's statement that his mother received these silver pieces in "late '72, early '73" means, if Billy Birt really did take silver from the Durham home, a number of months passed before he gave them to his wife. Why the delay? Could this passage of time actually indicate that Billy Birt brought the silver from a different, later crime scene, unrelated to the Durhams? In 2024, Shane stated his mother told him his father had returned home after being gone three or four days and gave the silver to her as a peace offering to assuage her being upset at his extended absence. If this timeframe is correct and really was connected to the Durham Case, then Billy Birt would have given the silver to his wife in early 1972, likely between February 6 and 7, which would be three or four days after being in Boone, and this does not align with Shane's previous statement of "late '72, early '73."[1807] Billy Birt was certainly back in Winder by February 14 (eleven days after the Durham murders) as that is the date he testified on behalf of Otis Reidling, Jr. when Reidling was on trial for the January 10 robbery of a Winder jewelry store.[1808]]

INGRAM: Okay. '72 or '73. And she got this from...

SHANE: She got this from my dad.

INGRAM: ...Bill Birt. And there's this plus a lot more at the house.

SHANE: That's right.

INGRAM: She'd be willing to let anybody look at it or...

SHANE: Yeah. Any time, and the thing about it is, is that there's all this; there's twenty or thirty more pieces. There's bigger pieces; there's smaller pieces. I brought this right here because, if this was in the [Durham] house, people's going to remember this. *[Shane lifted a sugar bowl, which was distinctively silver on the outside and gold-colored on the inside.]* You understand what I'm saying? And this piece here *[lifting and showing a creamer]*, and you can tell it's quality.

INGRAM: It's so unusual...

SHANE: And this right here *[lifting a spoon or utensil]*, it's got "Princess Pattern" on it. And this right here is just a big tea kettle *[lifting it]*. What I tried to do is just bring what I know that people would recognize, and the first thing I would recognize is this *[referencing the sugar bowl again]* 'cause it's got a gold...

HAGAMAN: Uh huh. It's unusual.

INGRAM: How certain are you that your father committed this crime in Boone, North Carolina?

SHANE: 150%, 200%, if we'd get 1000%, I'm 1000%. You know, it's no question.

INGRAM: Did he tell you out of his own mouth that he did it?

SHANE: He told me out of his own mouth that he did it. He told me that out of his own mouth, that the only reason the person that set it up is still alive because he didn't have time to kill him.

HAGAMAN: To kill the…?

SHANE: The person who set it up. Daddy was dead set on going back and [reckoning?]. But daddy was arrested just several months after this, and the heat was on.

[Billy Birt was actually not arrested until April 1974 – more than two years after the Durham murders.]

INGRAM: It's very important to us, the information that put this whole thing in motion came from somebody.

SHANE: Yes.

INGRAM: 'Cause your dad didn't know anybody in Boone. Did that information go to your dad or Billy Davis?

SHANE: I think the information went to Billy Davis because Billy, from what I understood, I'm 98% sure that Billy Davis drove up, and I'm 98% sure that my dad drove back.

[This is the first recorded mention of Billy Birt driving the getaway car back to Georgia, although just one day later, in a separate interview with the same officers, Billy Wayne Davis mentioned the same thing.]

INGRAM: That's important what you just said. Billy Davis drove the car there. Now hold on. Who got out at the house?

SHANE: Who got out at the house was Billy Wayne Davis, my dad, and Otis Reidling. At that time, I want to say that Bobby Gene was the getaway driver because Bobby Gene was the getaway driver in most everything my dad ever done. Now, if Billy *[Shane apparently meant to say Bobby]* was not the getaway driver, it had to be Billy Wayne.

INGRAM: Okay. So, it was either Bobby Gaddis or Billy Davis that drove the car.

SHANE: That's right.

INGRAM: Now, do you know the method your father used to put people out? How did that happen, or did he tell you? If he didn't tell you, I don't want…

SHANE: No, he never told me how he dropped anybody off or anything like that….

INGRAM: When you first told me about this, neither one of us knew about any case in North Carolina.

SHANE: No.

INGRAM: Once you told me, you told me about the snowstorm, you told me about they almost got trapped, you said the mountains of North Carolina, but you didn't know anything about Boone.

[Shane's recollection of his father's mention of Boone, as stated earlier in this interview, apparently transpired after his earlier interviews.]

SHANE: The way this right here come about is, about three or four days after our first interview, I was sitting at the house, and I was watching TV. And *Bull Durham* was on, and I was sitting there, and when it said "Bull Durham" or I read "Durham," I was thinking, "Where do I know that name from? Durham, Durham, Durham, Durham." And it was a couple of hours, and it might have been the next day, it hit me, and I called Phil [Hudgins], and I said, "Phil, I know where 'Durham' is." And I said "Durham" wasn't a place, "Durham" was the people…. That's when we called you back, and I said, "Hey, I do know that it was 'Durham.'"

[Only moments earlier in this same interview, Shane had told a different version about how he knew the victims' surname was Durham, saying, "We was talking, and daddy said, "Durham." And I said, "Durham, North Carolina?" And he said, "No, son." He said, "The people's name was Durham."]

HAGAMAN: So, they were told that there was money at the house, you think, or…?

SHANE: They was told that they was money. Evidently, my dad thought that if you had a car lot, if you sold a car for cash, that cash had to go somewhere. And I knew they was a car dealer. And so, that is actually what my dad was looking for.

HAGAMAN: Did he happen to say what amount was supposedly at the house? Was it a couple of hundred dollars? Was it…?

SHANE: No, it had to be $20-, $30-, $40,000 before my dad would look at it, especially outside of Georgia.

INGRAM: Where did you come up with this relative is the one that set it up? Is that something your dad told you?

SHANE: That's something that my dad told me. If you go back and you listen to our interviews, I kept talking about a nephew or a son-in-law in the Wrens case. And I knew that it was there because daddy always cussed the nephew or son-in-law. He cussed him 'til the day he died. And after "Durham," and just going back and thinking, and it hit me….

JOHNSON: You said usually he charges somebody about $5,000; that was a minimum. So, at a bare minimum, people had to pay that, and then what they would maybe get out of the house was just what the group got to keep? Is that how that worked?

SHANE: That's right.

INGRAM: Your dad told you there were three victims and the order in which they were killed.

SHANE: The order in which they was killed.

INGRAM: Tell me that again – the order.

SHANE: That was first, the mom; second, the son; and third, the dad.

INGRAM: Okay. And that was to get others to talk.

SHANE: That was to get others to talk.

[By this time and by some means, Shane had become aware of the gender of the adult Durham child that had been murdered – something he did not know in May 2019. In 2024, Shane was less definite about the order in which the Durhams were killed, stating that he does not know if his father told him the exact order and that he does not like to speculate about it. According to Shane, once the first one drowned, everything was on the table and all of them had to go – a son is not going to watch his mother die, and a father is not going to watch his son die without giving up information. Shane says his father told him this because it was proof that what was promised to be in the house was not there – that after the first one died, if they had anything of monetary value, it would have come out, and it did not. "If there was any money there, a dad ain't gonna watch his boy get drowned and not spill his guts; he's gonna tell you everything down to the least. He's gonna offer everything he can offer you, and if there's nothing to offer, three people just died in vain, and that's exactly what happened in Boone."[1809]]

INGRAM: The Durham Case, you said, made him mad.

SHANE: To absolutely no end.

INGRAM: To the point he wanted to kill the person who put this thing in motion.

SHANE: Exactly.

HAGAMAN: Did he mention anybody's name, the son-in-law's name?

SHANE: He never mentioned the son-in-law's name or nephew's name, but daddy always told me he was the most worthless SOB that ever walked the face of the earth. The only reason daddy did not go back is because the heat was so hot up there. In daddy's mind...if he went back at any given time, they'd have got him.

INGRAM: It's real important to me that, based on your relationship with your dad and knowing all these people, you think that either Bobby Gaddis or Billy Davis drove that car.

SHANE: That's right. The reason I say Bobby Gaddis was driving the car, on 90% of the bank robberies, Bobby Gene drove the car. And Bobby Gene was a big guy, and he couldn't move good, and they always either called him "Big Boy" or "Fat Boy." And so, Bobby Gene very rarely went into a bank because he was noticed, and he very rarely went into a house.

INGRAM: Well, he couldn't move quick.

SHANE: He couldn't move quick....

HAGAMAN: Back to the nephew or son-in-law...did your dad ever mention his name or what he did?

SHANE: Daddy never mentioned his name. I know that he was a young guy, but my dad never mentioned his name.

HAGAMAN: So, your dad got upset because what was in the house, that evidently whoever this person was told him, was not there.

SHANE: ...was not there. And not only that is daddy never said anything about money or anything like that, but the money never come through....

JOHNSON: Meaning that he got stiffed the $5,000?

SHANE: I don't know, but I do know that the only reason he's still alive is 'cause you all had a lot of heat up there. And evidently he never left there.

HAGAMAN: The nephew or the...

SHANE: Yeah.

INGRAM: Let me ask you an important question, and you've given us some excellent information and some details. This is very important to me. Has anybody fed you information or given you information about this case in North Carolina other than your dad?

SHANE: No, other than Phil.

INGRAM: What did Phil tell you? That's important.

SHANE: Uh...*[Shane struggled without success for well over a minute to recall things Phil Hudgins may have told him and stated he was trying to go through thirty years of information and everything he had said in this interview.]*

INGRAM: Did anything you tell us today come from Phil?

SHANE: No. I know everything come from dad. I know the "Durham" come from dad. I know that Boone come from dad. I know the snowstorm come from dad.

INGRAM: See, that's interesting the way you remember that 'cause you were watching *Bull Durham*, and then you said Daniel Boone, and then you said the snowstorm.

SHANE: No, the way everything got started was the snowstorm, 'cause daddy was telling me that the snowstorm was the closest he ever come to getting trapped or getting caught.

INGRAM: Did they say they drove that vehicle away from the house?

SHANE: They drove that vehicle away from the house.

INGRAM: Okay.

HAGAMAN: The one that he *[Bryce Durham]* had brought home.

SHANE: The one that he had brought home.

INGRAM: Okay. And they were in the house waiting on 'em when...

SHANE: They was in the house waiting on 'em...

[More than three years later, Shane said he did not recall that his father was already in the house waiting for the Durhams.[1810]]

INGRAM: Did he say what time it was?

SHANE: He didn't, but I think they *[the victims]* was late.

INGRAM: Okay. Was it daylight or dark?

SHANE: No, it was dark 'cause it was late, and daddy said when they got there the snowstorm hadn't started, and by the time...

INGRAM: You're talking about when your dad got there.

SHANE: When my dad got there.

INGRAM: But when the people got there...

SHANE: ...got there, the snowstorm just had started or hadn't started yet, but by the time they left, daddy said that the snowstorm, he said, son, he said when you walked outside, he said you couldn't see nothing but white. He said that it was snowing that hard.

INGRAM: So, do you know what they did with that vehicle they drove from the house?

SHANE: They just left it.

INGRAM: Okay. They left it.

SHANE: Yeah, and that's what I was saying is, this stuff here *[pointing to the silver]*, I'm near about 100% positive y'all will have a match, but if it is, God smiled on you because my daddy wouldn't take jewelry off of any victim. My dad wouldn't take anything that he...

INGRAM: Why?

SHANE: Because it would always be linked back to him. But this stuff here, I'm 99-100% positive.

INGRAM: Well, your mom told us, told you and me, she got it around '72 or '73.... I don't know how she remembered that....

SHANE: Well, for some reason, the silverware always comes up in my mind when we talked, and how dad told me, I don't know.

INGRAM: Did he tell you it came from there?

SHANE: We had silverware that come from there. Now, I don't know if it was this, but it's got to be this because that was the only silverware that ever come back to my house.

INGRAM: Okay.

SHANE: Period.

INGRAM: To your mom's house.

SHANE: To my mom's house....

INGRAM: I think we've covered what he knows, and I'm very careful about being suggestive in any way or adding to it. I don't want to do that. I want to say this on the record. The impression I got from Shane the day I met him eighteen months ago was he's genuine, he's sincere, and he's not going to add or subtract anything from what he mentioned, and he's certainly, certainly not trying to glorify what his father did.... Are you going to allow us to take this *[the silver]* to North Carolina?

SHANE: Yes, you can take all that.

INGRAM: So that family members can look at it and see if it's...

SHANE: Now, there's a couple of plates, there is a tea pitcher that's a little bit bigger than this....

HAGAMAN: Why do you think your dad was talking to you all along? Did he talk to any other of your family other than you?

SHANE: ...Daddy had a little more faith in me than he [once] did.

INGRAM: We have a lot of faith in you. I think he confided in you. You know, a lot of people have said a lot of things, but I believe in my heart that you're the most truthful and honest without trying to embellish or glorify what your dad did. You're just trying to tell it straight.... Is everything you've told us the truth?

SHANE: Everything I've told you is the truth, and everything I've told you is exactly what my dad's told me.[1811]

The following day, November 17, 2020, Bob Ingram, Len Hagaman, and Carolynn Johnson once more visited Billy Wayne Davis, and Ingram recapped some of the things he and Davis had previously discussed.[1812] This interview lasted a little over one hour, and following are the chronological excerpts related to the Durham Case:[1813]

INGRAM: *[referring to his previous visit with Davis one month earlier]* We talked about the Wrens Case, and then about halfway in, I said, "I'm here with a purpose, and if you'll allow me to, I wanted to tell you what that purpose was." And that purpose was the case with the big snowstorm. Remember, we talked about that?

DAVIS: Uh huh.

INGRAM: And there was a heck of a snowstorm that came all at once, and you said, and Bill Birt said, "I don't know if we're going to get out of here." You remember that?

DAVIS: Yes.

INGRAM: And when you said that to me, and I asked you the question, and I'll see if you remember, I said, "Were you driving a two-wheel drive or a four-wheel drive?" What did you tell me?

DAVIS: Gosh, I don't know if I can remember that one or not. I probably was driving an old model coupe.

INGRAM: A Cadillac...

DAVIS: Yeah.

INGRAM: When you say coupe, a Coupe de Ville, or...?

DAVIS: It would have been back then. I think that's what it was.

INGRAM: It was an early 70s...

DAVIS: Yes sir.

INGRAM: ...and it wasn't brand new, but it was in good...

DAVIS: Whatever it was, it was something I just picked up off the lot.

INGRAM: Picked up off the lot. And that's what you drove to North Carolina.

DAVIS: Yes sir.

INGRAM: Now, who drove it back from North Carolina?

DAVIS: The last time I seen it, Birt was under the wheel, so...

[Davis's mention of Billy Birt driving the car back to Georgia was something he had not previously shared,[1814] although it had been stated by Shane Birt the preceding day.]

INGRAM: Okay. Birt was under the wheel, and knowing him, if he's with a group of people, he's going to want to drive. Am I right?

DAVIS: Well, yeah, they enjoyed...

INGRAM: Well, he was good behind a wheel.

DAVIS: Yes, he was.

INGRAM: ...Let me ask you something. When you got there, was it snowing, or did it start after you got there?

DAVIS: I believe it was spittin' a little bit.

INGRAM: Spittin', and then it...

DAVIS: And the bottom fell out. *(chuckling)*

INGRAM: The bottom fell out. Now who actually went in the house? Who were the ones that went into the house? Think a minute. You've got your skull cap on. That'll help you think.

DAVIS: I'm gonna need more than that for these *(chuckling)* kind of questions. *(chuckling)*.

INGRAM: You're gonna need more than that. Well listen, I'll help you if we can work together to get this straight, okay?

DAVIS: Okay.

INGRAM: Alright. So, tell me who went in the house, or who got put out at the house?

DAVIS: I don't even remember but two people that was there.

INGRAM: Okay, well, tell me who they were.

DAVIS: Birt and Gaddis.

INGRAM: Birt and Gaddis. And you were behind the wheel.

DAVIS: Yes, but I didn't stay as long as they did.

INGRAM: You didn't stay long. You put them out, and where'd you go?

DAVIS: I went uptown for a little bit to see somebody I hadn't seen in a long time...

INGRAM: Okay.

DAVIS: ...that was a straight, honest person. He wasn't into what we was.

INGRAM: Okay. Okay. Alright...

[Although follow-up questions were asked about this later in the interview, it is surprising none of the officers immediately asked Davis for the identity of the person he said he went to see.]

INGRAM: And then when did you go park the car where they could find you?

DAVIS: Uh, probably...I couldn't tell you what year it was. I don't even know what year we went up there.

[This was not an answer to the question Ingram asked, but in his next question, Ingram followed Davis's lead regarding timeframe.]

INGRAM: Okay. Okay. Give me a ballpark. Give me a ballpark if you don't know exactly, 'cause it's been a long time ago.... When was it in terms of, you know, what timeframe? Is it around the timeframe of the Wrens Case? Is it the same timeframe?

DAVIS: It was probably one of those, but, it's uh...

INGRAM: Now, the Wrens Case was '73...

DAVIS: Yes.

INGRAM: ...down in Wrens.

DAVIS: I remember that one.

INGRAM: Oh, I know you do 'cause you testified in that one.

DAVIS: Uh huh.

INGRAM: And you knew a lot. That's the old couple. And then up in North Carolina there were how many victims? Three? Or you remember?

DAVIS: I couldn't tell you...

INGRAM: Okay.

DAVIS: ...not and be accurate about it.

INGRAM: Yeah. What was the purpose in going up there...to North Carolina?

DAVIS: The purpose was for the robbery.

INGRAM: For robbery, and then after the robbery, Bill Birt always what? What'd he always do?

DAVIS: He always left a body.

INGRAM: Left a body. And why is that?

DAVIS: So, they couldn't tell on him.

INGRAM: So, they couldn't tell on him, couldn't identify him. So, he always robbed 'em and killed 'em. But that location where those people were in North Carolina, that location was targeted.... You understand what I mean by targeted?

DAVIS: Yes, I understand that.

INGRAM: Well, I know you do. What does targeted mean to you?

DAVIS: It means that if I'm going to rob you, you're the target.

INGRAM: Yeah, if I'm going to rob you, you're the target. So, what you knew going up there that there was somebody up there with some money...and that's what you were told, right?

DAVIS: I was told that the family that lived there had money.

INGRAM: The family that lived there had money. And who told you that?

DAVIS: Billy Birt.

INGRAM: Billy Birt. Now, how did he learn that?

DAVIS: I don't know who told. I tried to stay away from that part of it.

INGRAM: Oh, I know you tried to stay away from that part of it, but Birt, see, remember, I'm gonna go back. I'm gonna jump back. I'm going over here before we go forward, okay?

DAVIS: Okay.

INGRAM: In the Wrens Case – now hear me, 'cause you hit it right on the head. In the Wrens Case, Carswell Tapley, he was that old drunk at the deer camp. You follow me?

DAVIS: Right.

INGRAM: And he told Leisher that this old couple had money. Retired car dealer had money. He told Leisher, and Leisher told you. Follow me!

DAVIS: I'm trying. *(chuckling)*

INGRAM: You tracking me?

DAVIS: I guess.

INGRAM: Okay, you're tracking me.

DAVIS: Maybe.

INGRAM: Maybe?

DAVIS: Maybe.

INGRAM: Well....

DAVIS: We're talking about something that happened fifty years ago.

INGRAM: Oh, I know we are, but your mind's still working, not as good....

DAVIS: It is, but not near as good as it once was.

INGRAM: Oh, neither is mine. Neither one of us got the minds we used to have, but yours is still good; it's tracking. Tapley runs his mouth at the deer camp, he tells Leisher, Leisher tells you, and you tell Birt. Am I right?

DAVIS: That may be the way it went, but I couldn't swear to it, but I know he talked to 'em.

INGRAM: Right, and then Birt got you, Gaddis, and Reed, and you all went to Wrens.

DAVIS: Right.

INGRAM: Right?

DAVIS: Yes sir.

INGRAM: Okay. You drove. You, you drove down. Who drove back?

DAVIS: Birt did, I....

INGRAM: Birt drove back. That's right. 'Cause, remember, hold on, remember when you stopped to pee...

DAVIS: Uh huh.

INGRAM: ...on that hill at the chalk mine, and the alternator went out, remember? It wouldn't crank.

DAVIS: Yeah, I understand.

INGRAM: And Birt got the two guys to jump the car off, and you all went on. And remember, you had to go back because you left a gun there?

DAVIS: I think we did go back, but I ain't sure it was for a gun.

INGRAM: Why? What were you thinking?

DAVIS: Well, we didn't really need one.

INGRAM: Didn't need a gun?

DAVIS: Huh uh.

INGRAM: Why?

DAVIS: They'd done done all the damage you could do.

INGRAM: Yeah, the people were tied up and strangled.

DAVIS: Uh huh. But of course, they followed up with having a gun in their hand when they went in the door.

INGRAM: Of course. Yeah, they had to get control.

DAVIS: Right.

INGRAM: And that's typical in what I call a – I don't know if you use this word – but when you invade somebody's home and go into their home, you've got to have a gun to control them, but then you tie them up; you don't need the gun.

DAVIS: Right.

INGRAM: And you tie 'em up to control 'em and – this is a hard word – I'm going to use it because it's right – to torture 'em.

DAVIS: Oh yeah, Birt was good at that.

INGRAM: He was good at torturing people.

DAVIS: Uh huh. *[faintly]*

INGRAM: And why did he do that?

DAVIS: To get money, if they was any money there.

INGRAM: To get the money if there was any money there. And if it wasn't visible, he was gonna make 'em tell him where it was.

DAVIS: Uh huh.

INGRAM: And in Wrens, you remember, the money was buried in those jars...

DAVIS: Uh huh.

INGRAM: ...outside, remember?

DAVIS: I was told that. I never seen it (where the)...

INGRAM: And remember, you said you got $40,000, I mean 4, but Birt told me you all got $40,000.

DAVIS: I can't remember the exact figure, but it was lower than what we expected.

INGRAM: Now, let me ask you something. Did they get the amount of money they expected from North Carolina?

DAVIS: Hmm. I can't even remember that case.

INGRAM: Yeah. Well, there's a lot of cases, and it's hard to keep 'em straight, and as you told me, this is fifty years ago, and I can't remember every detail.

DAVIS: Right.

INGRAM: But you can remember some things, right?

DAVIS: Oh, yeah, yeah.

INGRAM: Not everything, not every detail. And I understand there's a lot of jobs that were done, and different people involved at different times. You were the guy that supplied the cars to do the jobs.

DAVIS: That was my job only.

INGRAM: Yeah, well, and to drive, and to put people out.

DAVIS: Well, I drove when Birt wasn't in the car. He liked to drive too.

INGRAM: But this case up in North Carolina, I want to be clear, who went into that house that you put out at that house? Who went into it? Think. You said who?

DAVIS: Let me see. Gaddis was there.

INGRAM: Okay. Who else?

DAVIS: And Birt, of course.

INGRAM: Birt. Okay. And who else?

DAVIS: And...Charlie Reed.

INGRAM: Charlie Reed. So, three went in the house.

DAVIS: Right. That I know of.

INGRAM: Well, you would know 'cause you put 'em there.

DAVIS: Yeah, I drove 'em there.

INGRAM: You drove 'em there, put 'em out.... Now how did they get to you from the house? How did they get from the house to you where you were parked, waiting?

DAVIS: I think he sent one of them to get me.

INGRAM: Sent one of 'em to get you?

DAVIS: Yeah. Charlie Reed maybe. But it's been so long I can't...

INGRAM: How much money did they get out of that house?

DAVIS: I'm not exactly sure. Birt always pinched it, whatever he got, and then...

INGRAM: Pinched it? You mean, he didn't tell people exactly what he got.

DAVIS: Yeah.

INGRAM: Now you got some of the money?

DAVIS: Yes.

INGRAM: For driving. How much?

DAVIS: Gosh, you ask hard questions. *[chuckling]* And you know, it's been a long time ago.

INGRAM: Oh, yeah. But let me tell you something, Bill Davis. When I talked to you a month ago, you know what I said?

DAVIS: What was that?

INGRAM: He ain't as sharp as he used to be, but he's still sharp. You've still got a good mind and a good body. Oh, and neither one of us have the mind or the body we had, but, you know, we've still got something left.

DAVIS: I was at one time, but I'm not as sharp, as you well know, today, as I was back then.

INGRAM: Let me ask you something. How much money come out of that house? Did they get as much as they thought out of that house?

DAVIS: I think they got more, but they didn't let it be known.

INGRAM: They got more, but they didn't let it be known. Did they kill the people?

DAVIS: Yes.

INGRAM: How'd they kill 'em?

DAVIS: Shot 'em.

INGRAM: Shot 'em? Okay.

DAVIS: Now, what case we talking about here?

INGRAM: Hold on. Hold on. We're talking about the case in North Carolina at the snowstorm. Don't confuse them, okay? 'Cause there's plenty of people that were shot, I know that. But the case in North Carolina, were the people tied up?

DAVIS: I couldn't tell you.

INGRAM: Okay. Were they killed?

DAVIS: Yeah, they was killed.

INGRAM: Okay, there were no witnesses. Do you know how they were killed?

DAVIS: Yes, they shot 'em.

INGRAM: Shot 'em. Okay.

DAVIS: You could claim that on just about everything he [Birt] ever done.

INGRAM: What, that he shot 'em?

DAVIS: Yeah. Shot people that he robbed.

INGRAM: Okay. And you're saying they went, they robbed 'em and killed 'em. Okay.

DAVIS: Yeah, they killed 'em.

INGRAM: Yeah, you know, but were you in the house when they killed 'em?

DAVIS: No.

INGRAM: Okay. So, do you know how they killed 'em? How, how he killed 'em?

DAVIS: I heard shots.

INGRAM: Okay. How far away from the house were you when he killed those people?

DAVIS: About two or three blocks.

INGRAM: Okay.

DAVIS: If I remember correctly, they was a church up there.

INGRAM: A church?

DAVIS: Or a building that looked like a church.

INGRAM: A church or a building that looked like a church that wasn't far away.

DAVIS: Uh huh. (inaudible)

INGRAM: Okay. How bad was the snowstorm when you drove out of there?

DAVIS: Oh, it wasn't as bad as it was when I got to Atlanta, but it was coming down good.

INGRAM: Okay. Was the Coupe de Ville two-wheel or four-wheel drive?

DAVIS: I'm pretty sure it was a two-wheel.

INGRAM: Two-wheel drive, so you had a hell of a time in that snowstorm.

DAVIS: Uh huh.

INGRAM: So, you drove up there and you came back, and do you remember the timeframe this happened in? The year frame?

DAVIS: No. All I can tell you is when we got on the road to come back, it was dark.

INGRAM: Dark. Okay. So, this happened at night?

DAVIS: Uh huh.

INGRAM: Okay.

DAVIS: I remember the lights; had to turn the lights on to see (this?)

INGRAM: Okay.

DAVIS: Keep people from running into you and you running into them.

INGRAM: Right, right. You remember the Fleming Case? Was this in close proximity to that timeframe? Yes or no, or do you remember?

DAVIS: Fleming *[as if trying to recall]*

INGRAM: The Fleming Case was in the Wrens. That was the name of the man and woman, Mr. and Mrs. Fleming, but in the Wrens Case, you drove in that one.

DAVIS: Who was it? Do you know?

INGRAM: No, what I'm saying is the Wrens Case, when that couple was...

DAVIS: Oh, the old man and his wife.

INGRAM: ...tied up and strangled. Yeah, the old man and his wife killed. Yeah, you drove in that one, and put them out. That's the one with the fruit jars and the smokehouse that had the money in it.

DAVIS: I'm pretty sure I drove in it...

INGRAM: Yeah.

DAVIS: ...but I can't remember the details.

INGRAM: Well, I know you did 'cause you told me you did back then.

DAVIS: Well, if I told you that...

INGRAM: Well...

DAVIS: ...well, I remembered it at that time.

INGRAM: Yeah, I understand, and it's fifty years, and anybody would have a tough time remembering fifty years ago, but what's important here is not only was it fifty years ago, but a lot was going on then. There were a lot of crimes being committed and a lot of people being killed. Is that fair?

DAVIS: Right.

INGRAM: Yeah. And the people involved in most of them were Birt, Gaddis, and yourself.

DAVIS: Yes.

INGRAM: What else do you remember about North Carolina? I don't want to be suggestive in any way to you, but on a zero to one hundred scale – you understand what I mean, zero to one hundred?

DAVIS: Uh huh.

INGRAM: How sure are you that Birt and Gaddis and Charlie Reed went in that house and killed those people in that North Carolina house in that blinding snowstorm?

DAVIS: Well, no doubt to me that they did, but Charlie Reed, I don't know that he entered the house.

INGRAM: Okay. But Gaddis and Birt...

DAVIS: ...'cause if anybody stayed out, it would have been him [Reed].

INGRAM: Okay. How much money did they get?

DAVIS: It's hard to say. One time it's one amount and *[chuckling]* a hundred miles later it's two or three.

INGRAM: So, you're telling me when you're traveling, the amount of money they're telling you they got changes.

DAVIS: Uh huh.

INGRAM: And Birt would keep some of it and not tell you.

DAVIS: Right.

INGRAM: But you always got some money for participating.

DAVIS: Oh, yeah, he'd kick you down a little something.

INGRAM: Do you mind if these North Carolina folks ask you a question or two?

DAVIS: Not at all.

HAGAMAN: You said earlier, when you drove the car to the North Carolina mountains, that you drove downtown and that you went to see a friend. Who would that have been? Do you know? In Boone.

DAVIS: Yes, I think I do. It's, uh...

[It is unfortunate that Davis was cut off here and not given time to complete his thought. Instead, as seen in the next statements, Ingram, as he did in the previous month's interview, immediately assumed Davis was speaking of Troy Hall, and in the event Davis was about to say someone else's name, that moment was lost as the conversation turned to Hall. Just a few statements later, however, Davis said he could not remember the name of the person he visited – not even Troy Hall.]

INGRAM: *[to Hagaman]* Have you got a picture of him?

HAGAMAN: *[to Ingram]* Huh?

INGRAM: *[to Hagaman]* You got a picture of Hall?

HAGAMAN: *[to Ingram]* No.

JOHNSON: *[to Ingram]* No.

DAVIS: I can't remember his name.

INGRAM: *[to Hagaman]* I'd just ask him straight out if he knows.

HAGAMAN: *[to Ingram]* Yeah. *[to Davis]* Do you know a guy by the name of Troy Hall?

DAVIS: Hall?

HAGAMAN: Uh huh.

DAVIS: No sir.

INGRAM: Think. Don't answer that quick. Think. Think.

DAVIS: It usually pops in my head if I know 'em but...

INGRAM: Young guy, back then. Young guy, Billy, younger than you.

DAVIS: Where'd he work?

HAGAMAN: He actually was going to school. He was in college.

DAVIS: University of Georgia?

HAGAMAN: No, it's at the university in Boone, North Carolina – Appalachian State. He and his wife both went to school there.

DAVIS: So, we killed 'em there?

HAGAMAN: No, no, no. I asked you if you knew a guy by the name of Troy Hall in Boone. You said that you drove around before you went back, and you said you met a friend or were meeting a friend, or something along those lines.

DAVIS: That name really don't ring a bell, but it must have the day I talked to you, or I wouldn't have said what you said I did.

HAGAMAN: Okay.

DAVIS: But I cannot place him right at the moment.

HAGAMAN: I understand. Okay.

INGRAM: *[to Hagaman]* What about this building he's talking about in close proximity to the house? Is there anything...

HAGAMAN: *[to Ingram]* The church?

INGRAM: *[to Hagaman]* ...that resembles that? A building that he had said that there's a church-like building...

HAGAMAN: *[to Ingram]* Yep.

INGRAM: *[to Hagaman]* ...in close proximity. There is?

HAGAMAN: *[to Ingram]* Uh huh.

INGRAM: *[to Hagaman]* That's important. *[to Davis]* Tell me about that church – now, I don't want to put words in your mouth – you said that you put Gaddis, and Birt, and Reed out at the house. You don't know if Charlie Reed went in the house, but you said you know Gaddis and Birt did.

DAVIS: Uh huh *[very faintly]*

INGRAM: Okay? And you said you drove – you think it was a Cadillac Coupe de Ville, right?

DAVIS: Uh huh.

INGRAM: Okay. And you said that there was a church or a building like a church close by that you said, did you park there, or did you remember it?

DAVIS: I can't tell you if I parked there or not. I don't even know where that place is at now. Back then I would have.

INGRAM: No, but your memory is good. Your memory is good because you said there was a church or church-like building close to it, right?

JOHNSON: Two or three blocks.

HAGAMAN: Yeah.

INGRAM: Is that right? That's what you just said a few minutes ago. Are you thinking?

DAVIS: *[chuckling]* Yeah, I am on that one. I usually get 'em right away, but...

INGRAM: Well, but listen. You're close to eighty years of age. Your mind still works. It's just not as fast.

DAVIS: Well, it's sure slowed down a lot.

INGRAM: You haven't missed one word I've said, have you?

DAVIS: No sir, but the problem is bringing it back. I forget what it is and what it was done for.

JOHNSON: Can I ask you something that might help bring it back? It was customary for you guys, once you dropped them off at a house, they would meet you driving the people's car from the house, right?

DAVIS: Uh huh.

JOHNSON: So, can you remember anything about them getting a vehicle stuck in the snow? Did that cause a problem, or were you with them when they got stuck, or how'd you find 'em? Maybe that rings a bell?

DAVIS: I really don't understand that.

INGRAM: Here's what she asked you – very important. She said when you'd put 'em out at the house, you'd leave...

DAVIS: Uh huh.

INGRAM: ...and go away. And the reason you did that is so your car wouldn't be seen there.

DAVIS: Right.

INGRAM: Right? That makes sense. Alright. Now, when they left, they took the car that was there at the house to come meet you.

DAVIS: Uh huh.

INGRAM: Okay. Right?

DAVIS: Right.

INGRAM: That's what they did. Alright. Did that vehicle they were in get stuck? Or do you remember?

DAVIS: I recall some vehicles getting stuck, but I can't put a...

INGRAM: Okay. I just thought of something. Was there any silver? When I mean silver, I mean plates, a tea kettle, a coffee deal, silverware. Was any of that come out of that house?

DAVIS: Goodness. I can't tell you if they brought anything out of there. They had a roll of money and was countin' it in the back seat while I was driving, but, as far as other items, I can't put my finger on it.

[Counting money would have happened after the crime, and although Davis said Birt drove the car back to Georgia, Davis says here he (Davis) was driving.]

INGRAM: Okay.

DAVIS: And I would have that one because there's money involved in it.

INGRAM: Well, you were paying attention to the money and not the other stuff.

DAVIS: Right.

INGRAM: Which I understand completely, but when they came out of the house, did they tell you they killed those people? Or was that just a known given?

DAVIS: Oh, I'm sure he told me. He always liked to brag about what he'd done.

INGRAM: He tell you how many people?

DAVIS: No, I don't think so. I really can't recall that house and that kind of money.

INGRAM: But you used the word family. Did he kill a family?

DAVIS: I don't even know if it was a family that lived there.

INGRAM: Do you know, possibly, what the occupation of the person was that lived there?

DAVIS: And where was that at?

INGRAM: Boone, North Carolina. The snowstorm. Remember the snowstorm. Focus on that. You know, there's two things happening, and I'm gonna say it and you correct me if I'm wrong. There's two things happening here. You're eighty years old, and your memory is not as good as it once was. Right?

DAVIS: It's just about gone.

INGRAM: Well, it ain't gone 'cause you still got plenty, and we're gonna find out here. But the other thing, there was so many of these they're getting confused. Right or wrong?

DAVIS: Right.

INGRAM: Right. We got so many crimes, so many cases, so many people killed, that we've got 'em confused. And then the age factor, but I keep saying this, you're very sharp.... You said you haven't missed a word I've said. Not one word. And is anything I've said not the truth?

DAVIS: Oh, no. (or I don't know)

INGRAM: It's all true.

DAVIS: Yes sir. Well, I assume that it is.

INGRAM: No, no. Don't assume it. True or false?

DAVIS: It's true.

INGRAM: Okay. That's all I'm asking you. And we had that understanding.

DAVIS: But if we're talking about something that I don't know nothing about, and you say something, how can I say that it was true or false?

INGRAM: You can't do that. But you remember clearly what we're talking about, and that's the robbery/murder where there was a snowstorm up in Boone, North Carolina.

DAVIS: Uh huh.

INGRAM: That part you remember.

DAVIS: Uh huh.

INGRAM: Yes?

DAVIS: Yes.

INGRAM: Okay. And you remember driving, and you remember who was with you. Right? Yes or no?

DAVIS: Yes.

INGRAM: Okay. And you also remember that they came out with a roll of money that they were countin' or whatever.

DAVIS: I think they did. Yes sir.

INGRAM: And Birt told you that who was ever in that house was dead. He killed 'em.

DAVIS: Uh huh. I remember that.

JOHNSON: What would happen if somebody didn't pay the money that they said that they would for a job?

DAVIS: Well, sometimes he'd [Birt would] leave, sometimes he wouldn't.

JOHNSON: My understanding is there was a monetary amount that Birt charged people.

DAVIS: Right.

JOHNSON: Do you remember how much that was?

DAVIS: I don't know how much, but it was a pretty good pile of it.

HAGAMAN: Let me ask you a follow-up question. You said that Billy had a temper. You know, he would get mad easily. When you all were driving back to Atlanta, was he upset that the money that was there was not what he understood there to be, like, he was told one thing – he was told there was a lot of money, and when he left, did he say anything about, "Well, they ripped me off," or "I didn't get as much as I was told," or whatever?

DAVIS: Oh, yeah, he was very paranoid about that, about somebody beating him out of some money.

INGRAM: What we need to do, I think, is get really down to the nitty gritty and the bottom line. And here's the bottom line: That crime didn't happen by accident.

DAVIS: No, not at all.

INGRAM: Somebody set it up.

DAVIS: Uh huh.

INGRAM: And whoever set it up – listen to me – had to be close to those people. Had to. 'Cause they had to know who they were, where they lived, and how much money they had. Right?

DAVIS: Right.

INGRAM: Because Bill Davis, Bill Birt, Bobby Gaddis, Charlie Reed, just didn't drive up there and find this house by accident. You knew where the house was. These people were targeted. In other words, they were targeted to be robbed and killed by somebody. And we've been talkin' around a circle here, but somebody close to those people set that up.

DAVIS: Yes, in my opinion they did.

INGRAM: Oh, there's no opinion about it. We know it. We both know it because that's how things work, and that's how you people operated. If you received information that people had money, they were going to be robbed and killed. True or false?

DAVIS: True. It's what they got the information for.

INGRAM: That's what they did. Do you, Bill Davis, know where the information came from to rob and kill those people in Boone, North Carolina?

DAVIS: I don't know who set it up. No.

INGRAM: Well, who do you think set it up, if you don't know for sure?

DAVIS: I'm thinking it was Bill's buddy. I was trying to think of his name.

INGRAM: Bill who? Bill Birt?

DAVIS: Yeah, his friend.

INGRAM: Bill Birt's friend?

DAVIS: He lived there. He didn't live in Winder, but he lived close to it.

INGRAM: And knew these people?

DAVIS: Yes.

INGRAM: And that they had money?

DAVIS: Well, yes.

INGRAM: The information came to Birt or to you?

DAVIS: No, it come to Birt.

INGRAM: It come to Birt?

DAVIS: Right.

INGRAM: But you knew that somebody set this up, that knew where those people lived, who they were, and that they had money. 'Cause you knew where you were going, right?

DAVIS: Yeah, I didn't know all them people, but the names...

INGRAM: When you dropped them at the house, were the people already home or did they come home afterwards?

DAVIS: I couldn't tell you that, I really couldn't.

INGRAM: Okay. But you put 'em out, and then you...

DAVIS: I mean, I could have told you, yeah they..., but I don't do that.

INGRAM: No, you've never been one to tell me something wasn't correct, wasn't right.

DAVIS: If I know something about it, and I can tell you, I do that, but if I can't, well I can't.

INGRAM: Are you absolutely certain that the people you named committed that crime that we're talking about where these folks live in Boone, North Carolina?

DAVIS: Yes sir.

INGRAM: Okay.

DAVIS: In fact, he bragged about it all the time.

INGRAM: Okay. Did Bill like to torture people?

DAVIS: Oh, yeah. That was his main thing.

HAGAMAN: What did you all talk about that night after the killings, coming back to Atlanta?

DAVIS: That's another one I don't know *[chuckling]*, uh.... He drove and, uh...

INGRAM: He brag about the crime?

DAVIS: No, not that one he didn't. He usually does, but he didn't about that one.

[Here Davis contradicted himself. Moments earlier he stated that Birt "bragged about it all the time."]

INGRAM: Yeah. Was he mad driving?

DAVIS: Oh, yeah, yeah.

INGRAM: Was he mad about the money he got? Did he get the amount that he wanted or not?

DAVIS: I don't know.

INGRAM: You don't know. But he gave you some; he gave everybody some.

DAVIS: Yeah.

INGRAM: Yeah. How much did you get?

DAVIS: It was small. It wasn't much. I think a thousand dollars.

HAGAMAN: Let me ask one more question. When you let them out at the house, was there another vehicle in the driveway, or do you remember?

DAVIS: Sometimes it would be, it wouldn't be. I often got nervous because when we'd pull up in there, if some other car pulled in behind you, you killed or you get in the woods or you do whatever you do, but you hope you don't get caught, but you do.

INGRAM: If somebody else had driven up, you'd have killed them. It's that simple. That's how you guys operated. There were no living witnesses.

DAVIS: Yeah.

INGRAM: We're here, and we came back for one reason. Remember when I talked to you a month ago, we talked about the Fleming Case, and we put that aside – the Wrens Case. That's aside, put away. That's done, over with. But I told you my purpose was to talk to you about a case up in North Carolina, remember?

DAVIS: Uh huh.

INGRAM: And then I told these folks, and we all said we need to come back, and we need to talk to him and find out right from him, but I'm repeating myself, but there's a reason. There's two things going on here. You're not as sharp as you once were, right?

DAVIS: Oh, no.

INGRAM: But you still got a good brain and a good body.

DAVIS: Well, sometimes I think I do, and other times I think I don't.

INGRAM: Well, I think you do, 'cause you made a heck of a comment. You listened to me and said, "Boy, you have done your homework, and you have done your research, and you absolutely know these cases and have studied 'em." And that's why, when I notified them, I wanted them to hear from you, 'cause you and I ain't got long left, my man…. You regret what happened in North Carolina, don't you?

DAVIS: Oh, yes. I regret everything I ever done in that line of work.

INGRAM: Yeah. But you got a lot of cases that you've been involved in, and it's hard to remember which is which. Is that fair?

DAVIS: Yes, it is.

INGRAM: Yeah. But there's no doubt about the one in North Carolina. Is there?

DAVIS: No.

INGRAM: Okay.

DAVIS: Not at all.

INGRAM: Yeah.

DAVIS: No, sir.

INGRAM: *[to Hagaman and Johnson]* He's got a good brain.

HAGAMAN: *[to Ingram]* Oh, yeah.

INGRAM: *[to Hagaman]* It's...

HAGAMAN: *[to Ingram]* Sharp. *[to Davis]* When you all left there during the snowstorm and everything, and you almost maybe got caught, how did you drive back, or which highway did you take back to Atlanta? Do you remember? Was it a rural road or a main highway or what? Do you remember?

DAVIS: Well, in the beginning it was rural, and then I got on the highway.

HAGAMAN: Okay. As you were leaving?

DAVIS: Yes...

HAGAMAN: Okay.

DAVIS: ...after we left.

INGRAM: You don't remember the silver at all coming out of that house?

DAVIS: I don't remember it. It could have been there now.

INGRAM: Of course...

DAVIS: I don't know.

INGRAM: ...it could have. Yeah, you were one of four people.

JOHNSON: Do you remember worrying about getting caught because of the snowstorm?

DAVIS: Yes. 24/7.

JOHNSON: I guess that would be on anything. That makes sense. *[chuckling]*

DAVIS: *[chuckling]* Yes, ma'am. Was mine. It wasn't the other guys'. But it certainly was mine.

INGRAM: Did you ever get stuck?

DAVIS: Got put in jail one time, but it was for speeding, reckless driving.

INGRAM: I'm talking about that night you come out of there. I can just imagine a blinding snowstorm at night. Did the car ever get stuck that night?

DAVIS: I don't remember that getting stuck.

INGRAM: Okay, that's fine. You can only tell us what you remember. *[to Hagaman]* Anything you want to hit him with straight up? I think just go for the gold.

HAGAMAN: Do you remember where you met them after they'd left the house? Do you remember where they were or how you picked them up?

DAVIS: Well, we always had it established where we was going after it.

INGRAM: That's a good point. Before you ever got to the house, you knew where you were gonna pick 'em up.

DAVIS: Right.

HAGAMAN: Do you recall specifically where that place was that you were gonna pick 'em up?

DAVIS: Ooh, that'd be a rough one there. I know some of the streets up there, but they probably are gone by now.

HAGAMAN: How many times have you been to Boone, North Carolina?

DAVIS: Well, I've been up there a few times.

HAGAMAN: Did you have family or friends up there?

DAVIS: Yes, both.

HAGAMAN: Both?

DAVIS: Uh huh. My mother's father, he was from borderline to Carolina.[yyyyy]

[Unfortunately, the officers failed to explore this answer more thoroughly. When Davis affirmed he had both family and friends in Boone, the natural follow-up question, which was never asked, would have been "Who were they?"]

INGRAM: Billy, I'm gonna ask you something as we conclude. I'm gonna be straight with you. You knew the man who set this up. Listen to me. You knew the man who set this up in Boone, to put this whole thing in motion. He was a young fellow, and he was part of that family.

[yyyyy] Davis's maternal grandfather, Bart Bearden, was a native of Gilmer County, GA, approximately thirty miles from the Georgia-North Carolina state line. [Source: Genealogical research by author.]

[Ingram was again thinking of Troy Hall.]

DAVIS: Part of the family that lived there? Or part of Birt's family?

INGRAM: I don't know. I'm asking. (One of) them. But you, Bill Davis, knew the person who set this up, 'cause you knew people in Boone. Right?

DAVIS: Uh huh.

INGRAM: Okay. And you knew him. And you might not know his name, but you know that he's the one that gave the information that these people would have money. It's true.

DAVIS: Uh huh. And he lived in Boone?

INGRAM: That's right.

DAVIS: ...set up robberies and...?

INGRAM: That's right.

DAVIS: Is he still alive?

INGRAM: Yeah.

DAVIS: Hmm. Is he in jail?

INGRAM: No. He needs to be. I want him in jail. We want him in jail. That's where he belongs because it would have never happened had he not put it in motion. You follow me?

DAVIS: Yes. Absolutely on that one.

INGRAM: Oh, absolutely on it. I'm on the money. 'Cause, remember, *[Davis previously referring to Ingram]* you said something that you don't come unprepared. If you come in here, you know what you're talking about. And I know what I'm talking about.

DAVIS: Well, have you got any leads, ways to arrest him, or make charges?

INGRAM: I can damn sure get a picture and bring a picture of him to you and see if it's the guy.

DAVIS: Were they from there or here?

INGRAM: There. You'd recognize his picture, wouldn't you?

DAVIS: Yes. I think I would.

INGRAM: Yeah, I do too. That's what we need to do. Can I come back? Or are you tired of me?

DAVIS: *[chuckling]* No, I'm not tired of you, sheriff.

INGRAM: I'm willing to come back with these folks with a photograph and let you look at it, and you tell me, yes or no, that's the man that set it up. Somebody set it up. You didn't happen on that house by accident.

DAVIS: Huh uh.

INGRAM: You knew where you were going. You knew who the people were. You knew where they lived. You knew they'd have money.

DAVIS: Uh huh.

INGRAM: Oh, yeah.

JOHNSON: And you would do your homework as far as making a plan, right? To see where the house is, where to drop people off, where to pick people up or meet, right?

INGRAM: You know the two things we got in common, me and you?

DAVIS: *[chuckling]*

INGRAM: We're old. You know the other thing?

DAVIS: What is that?

INGRAM: We prepare.

DAVIS: Yeah, (inaudible).

INGRAM: That's what she just said. You're not going somewhere unprepared.... *[to Hagaman and Johnson]* We need to come back with a photograph.

JOHNSON: *[to Ingram]* Yeah, we can do that.

INGRAM: *[to Johnson]* Yeah? Of when he *[referring to Troy Hall]* was of the age.

JOHNSON: *[to Ingram]* Yeah.

DAVIS: That was in Boone, North Carolina?

INGRAM: Oh, yeah, absolutely. We know what we're talking about, the four of us in this room, we know, but see, I get the fact that I want you to know and everyone to know in this room that I understand fully and completely we're both old, we both aren't as sharp as we used to be, but there's a lot of stuff that you've done that you've gotta figure out in your mind which goes with which. You follow me?

DAVIS: Right. Right.

INGRAM: And it's hard.

DAVIS: Yeah, it is.

INGRAM: It is hard 'cause there's so much.

JOHNSON: But what sucks is, while you're answering for things that you've done, this guy, if he did that, if he hired you guys to do this, has been scot free and living it up large all these years.

INGRAM: And he needs to be in jail. And you can help us.

DAVIS: Well, I will if I can.

JOHNSON: We'll bring you some pictures.

INGRAM: Absolutely.

DAVIS: Does he live in Boone?

INGRAM: He...

JOHNSON: Not anymore.

INGRAM: ...used to, but he lived there at the time. You'll know who he is when you see his picture. You mark my words. It'll come back. You're saying, "How can you even predict that?" Because I know you. That's how I can predict it.

DAVIS: Well, we'll give it a try and see what I...

INGRAM: Absolutely. It's worth a try. You got anything you want to ask us?

DAVIS: Yeah, when are you gonna get me out of here? *[chuckling]*

INGRAM: I told you I'd write the parole board. I'm gonna tell 'em that you cooperated, and you were truthful. You cooperated and you were truthful. You had my word on that, and I will keep it.

DAVIS: Well, that's all we can do.

INGRAM: Well, that's all we can do. Can't make any promise whatsoever.

DAVIS: But you got more persuasion than most people do.

INGRAM: Yeah. Well, I told you I'd write them and say the two things. You were cooperative and truthful in a case that we're trying to solve in Boone, North Carolina, and that I appreciate it.

HAGAMAN: Let me ask one question. Have you ever heard of a name of Bryce Durham, or Virginia Durham, or Bobby Durham, or Ginny Sue Durham, or Troy Hall? Do you know any of those folks?

DAVIS: Not right off. If I knew something about 'em, I might know...

INGRAM: *[to Hagaman and Johnson]* I think pictures are gonna speak a hundred...there's so much that has transpired, so many people that have died, that it's really difficult to unravel this. It really is.

JOHNSON: *[to Ingram]* Well, and maybe with old pictures of, like, the house and the area might trigger something that could be of help to us.

DAVIS: Uh huh.

INGRAM: *[to Johnson]* Yeah, he's willing, but he's like me. We'd both better do it pretty quick. It's not something that can wait. *[to Davis]* You don't mind if we come back?

DAVIS: No, not at all. You people are dead on the money all the time, every time I've talked to you, and that means a lot, especially when it's you that was on the line. You know what I mean?

The following month, on December 7, 2020, Captain Carolynn Johnson and SBI Agent Wade Colvard met with Ginny Durham Mackie and her husband Steve for approximately three and a half hours. Ginny told the officers she had tried to assist with the investigation all through the years, but no one listened to her or asked for her help until 1985. Ginny examined the silver pieces the officers had brought from Georgia, but due to the passage of time and there being so many different patterns of silver, she could not state with certainty whether they had or had not belonged to her family. She said the pattern did not match, but the teapot being shown to her looked like one her family had with the exception of it (i.e., the one she was examining) being heavier. Regarding the recent claims of the Dixie Mafia's involvement in her family's murders, Ginny stated she had never heard of Billy Birt, Billy Wayne Davis, or Charlie Reed, although she indicated the name Bobby Gaddis might be familiar. She asked about brothers Stoney and Shane Birt and the books they had written or were in the process of writing and was curious why this was taking place now[1815] (presumably meaning after the passage of so many years).

At the request of the Watauga County Sheriff's Office, Bob Ingram arranged a subsequent meeting with Billy Wayne Davis for the primary purpose of showing him a lineup of photos, including one of Troy Hall – a critically important step. "They wanted to see if Davis would recognize Hall nearly fifty years after the murders."[1816] At the beginning of this August 3, 2021 interview with Ingram, Sheriff Len Hagaman, and Captain Carolynn Johnson, Davis stated he was in fairly good physical shape for his age *[Hagaman noted Davis was shuffling more, but was not tired[1817]]*, and his mental faculties were good. Davis said he felt good and understood what was going on. Following are chronological excerpts from this interview that pertain to the Durham Case:

INGRAM: Do you know where Boone, North Carolina is?

DAVIS: I know where Boone is, yes.

INGRAM: And you've been to Boone in your life?

DAVIS: Yes, I've been through there.

INGRAM: When the sheriff asked you last time, you said you'd been up there a few times in the car business.

DAVIS: Uh huh.

INGRAM: Is that right?

DAVIS: Yes.

INGRAM: Did your business, in the car business, ever take you up to Boone?

DAVIS: I don't recall that it did.

INGRAM: Now, you told the sheriff our last interview – and I'm not putting words in your mouth – but you told the sheriff that you had been to Boone a few times, and I believe you were asked, and you referred to the car business. Is that correct or is that incorrect? Or do you remember?

DAVIS: Well, uh...

INGRAM: Think it through.

DAVIS: And what are you asking me specifically?

INGRAM: What I'm asking you specifically, did you go up to Boone on some occasions for some car business, either to buy or sell or go to a dealership or an auction or whatever? Did your business take you to Boone, in other words?

DAVIS: Yes, it has.

INGRAM: Okay. Okay. That's what I was getting at, and...I'm bad about this. If my question's not clear, you tell me, "Hey, be specific." I'm trying my best and I know you are too. Do you recall what the business in Boone would have been related to cars?

DAVIS: I don't understand the question. The latest two cars that he had in...?

INGRAM: No. Okay, my question is when you went to Boone, you just said it had to do with business, and that business you were in was the car business.

DAVIS: Yes, sir.

INGRAM: Okay. Do you recall anybody you dealt with or any dealerships up there in Boone or any sales, specifically.[zzzzzz]

DAVIS: My uncle, but he's not there any longer; he's dead.

INGRAM: Who? Your uncle?

[zzzzzz] If Davis conducted business with a car dealership in Boone, NC it would not have been a solitary incident of a Carolina car dealer transacting with an associate of Georgia's Dixie Mafia. In December 1972, federal authorities charged Greenville, SC car dealer J. L. Cannon (who previously owned a dealership in Asheville, NC and moved his business to Greenville in 1968) with conspiring "with two Georgia men during a time when Cannon's Chevrolet dealership in Greenville was on the financial rocks in 1970." The two men were Kenneth Royster and his first cousin Harold Chancey, both of Winder, GA and both known to Billy Birt, Chancey being a long-time bootlegging associate of Birt. Cannon allegedly conspired with Royster and Chancey to illegally "transport stolen cars across state lines," from Cannon's car lot to Winder. "Royster was eliminated as a defendant...when the judge declared a mistrial as to him," but Cannon and Chancey were convicted. Only five months prior to this case, Chancey and two other Georgia men had gone on trial in U. S. District Court in Columbia, SC "on charges of illegal moonshine whiskey operations involving at least four Georgia counties and Greenville County in South Carolina." This moonshine case at one point involved Billy Birt and resulted in the disappearances and deaths of several potential witnesses in Georgia. [Sources: J. L. Cannon (photo caption), *The Asheville Citizen*, Asheville, NC, July 26, 1968, p. 14; "Greenville Auto Dealer Closes," *The State*, Columbia, SC, March 26, 1970, p. 8-D; Hugh E. Munn, "Moonshine Suspects Tried," *The State*, Columbia, SC, July 18, 1972, p. 15-A; Douglas Mauldin, "Conspiracy Case: Prosecutors May Put Up 15 Witnesses," *The Greenville News*, Greenville, SC, December 12, 1972, p. 34; Douglas Mauldin, "Federal Court Jury May Begin Cannon Case Deliberations Friday," *The Greenville News*, Greenville, SC, December 15, 1972, p. 26; Douglas Mauldin, "Greenville Car Dealer Convicted," *The Greenville News*, Greenville, SC, December 17, 1972, p. 2A

DAVIS: Yes.

INGRAM: What was his name?

DAVIS: Bearden. J. W. Bearden, my mother's brother.[aaaaaaa]

INGRAM: Okay. J. W. Bearden?

DAVIS: Right.

INGRAM: What did he have up there? An auction, a dealership, or just some cars?

DAVIS: He was mainly used cars, but he kept top of the line cars.

INGRAM: *[to Hagaman]* Does that ring a bell? Bearden?

HAGAMAN: *[to Ingram]* No.

INGRAM: *[to Hagaman]* We'd have to go back in time and do some huntin'.

DAVIS: He stayed on the road in that area a good bit, and it was a good area to buy cars in, especially if you had a dealership.

INGRAM: This is a difficult question and do the best you can. Do you have any idea from your recollection how many trips or times you went to Boone?

DAVIS: Gosh, it'd be hard to say. It's on up there.

INGRAM: Again, I don't want to put words in your mouth, but several trips to Boone?

DAVIS: Oh, yes. We'd go up there and look the inventory over and then try to make a deal on some of the cars. And they was as glad to see us as we was them.

INGRAM: Do you remember when we were here last time and we talked to you about a case in Boone in which, now let me just refresh your memory a little bit. It was a bad, severe, blinding snowstorm up in Boone, and you and Bill Birt, Bobby Gaddis, Charlie Reed – that same crowd that was involved in Wrens and in the Fleming Case, that case that you and I are familiar with, and we're not going to rehash that. You even said to me, "You've done your homework." Well, we've

---

[aaaaaaa] Davis was close to his uncle, Jess Willard "J. W." Bearden (1930-2021), who started J. W. Bearden Used Cars in Marietta, GA in the 1950s. They did a lot of business together and visited one another's homes, and their individual car lots were only a couple of miles apart on Bankhead Highway. Together, the two men would attend the Atlanta Auto Auction in Red Oak, GA, and Bearden also attended the Sand Mountain Auto Auction in Boaz, AL. These two locations – Atlanta and Alabama – align with the auction locations Davis mentioned attending in his September 2019 interview with North Carolina law officers. There is no indication Bearden ever had a business in Boone, NC, and his son has no knowledge of him ever traveling to Boone. Any records that might prove transactions between Modern Pontiac-Buick, Inc. (Bryce Durham's dealership) and Billy Wayne Davis or J. W. Bearden were reportedly seized by law enforcement (perhaps the SBI). The author's query regarding the records of another long-time Boone car dealership from the late 1960s and early 1970s was fruitless as they had already been destroyed. [Sources: "Manager driven to sell used cars," *The Atlanta Journal-Constitution*, Atlanta, GA, January 16, 1992, p. G9; Genealogical research by author; Anonymous text messages to author. March 14, 2024; Bearden, Dwight (J. W. Bearden's son). Facebook messages to author. March 15, 2024.]

done our homework on this – what happened in Boone – went up there in this blinding snowstorm. Remember, you told me that you were driving the car?

DAVIS: Yes. What part of North Carolina is that in?

INGRAM: That's way up in the mountains, up in the northwest. Way up in the mountains. And you know Boone, 'cause if you've been up there, and I've been there, you don't drive fast over in Boone, North Carolina because the roads are…

DAVIS: Oh, yeah.

INGRAM: And it's very, very…

DAVIS: Are they still in that kind of shape?

INGRAM: Yes. They've got asphalt, but you ain't going fast in Boone, North Carolina…. It's a slow go to get there, and it's winding roads, and in the wintertime, it's got some ferocious weather – cold and snow…. It's a mess and it's hard driving and it's rough sledding, if you know what I mean. So, I want to refresh your memory. I want to tell you this is important…. When you got up there, the weather was okay, but when you got there, that snowstorm hit. Remember I asked you about driving. I said, "Was it hard to get out of there?" And what'd you tell me?

DAVIS: I told you it was almost impossible. You was better off to park your vehicle and wait for it to clear up, but you never know how long it is.

INGRAM: Alright, let's get to it…. After those people were killed in that house, you had no choice but to get out of there. Okay, you're thinking a minute, but you understand what I just said, right?

DAVIS: Uh huh.

INGRAM: Uh huh. And when they came out of that house and they got to you, who left driving the car? Who drove it up there, first of all? Who drove the car up there?

DAVIS: I would say that I drove it up there.

INGRAM: Okay. You would say you drove it up there. Alright. Who drove the car when you left? It's gonna be one of two people.

DAVIS: Probably Birt.

INGRAM: Okay. Probably Birt. He was good with an automobile.

DAVIS: Yes, he was.

INGRAM: Very good. He could drive, and he was an old liquor man, so he knew how to drive…. When you left Boone, who was in the car?

DAVIS: It's been so long I can't remember.

INGRAM: Well, think for a minute. You know *you* were there, right?

DAVIS: Yeah, I know I was there. Birt was there, but...

INGRAM: Okay. Was Gaddis there?

DAVIS: I'm not sure he was there.

INGRAM: How about Reed?

DAVIS: Reed was usually around.

INGRAM: Yeah. And Gaddis was too, wasn't he? Would it be fair to say that Gaddis was a gopher for you and Birt? He'd do whatever you all told him?

DAVIS: Most of the time.

INGRAM: He wasn't real smart was he?

DAVIS: No.

INGRAM: Gaddis.

DAVIS: But let's face it, none of us were.

INGRAM: The two of you [Birt and Davis] killed lot of people. Is that true?

DAVIS: Well, it was with him.

INGRAM: How about with you?

DAVIS: No, I didn't go out and kill any people [unless] it's a situation where you got to do it....

INGRAM: So, I want to make sure I'm correct. You drove the car to Boone.

DAVIS: Well, that's possible because I drove a little, but Birt would rather drive than he would let somebody else drive.

INGRAM: I know, but somebody had to put those people out at the house.

DAVIS: I would say it was him.

INGRAM: Okay. Put 'em out at the house.

DAVIS: Well, I know it was him because I wouldn't have done that.

INGRAM: Hold on. Did you go in the house or stay in the car?

DAVIS: No, they had a car.

INGRAM: They had a car. You talking about the car that they got from the house? Is that what you're saying?

DAVIS: Well, I guess it is.

INGRAM: No, no. Now, you said a little earlier you drove to Boone. Is that right?

DAVIS: I've drove to Boone before, yes.

INGRAM: Okay. And who put them out at the house?

DAVIS: Whoever was driving.

INGRAM: Was that you or Birt?

DAVIS: Most of the time it was him.

INGRAM: Okay. Most of the time it was him. You're not certain or you are certain?

DAVIS: I'm not certain.

INGRAM: Okay.

JOHNSON: I think what he's asking is, if you drove up to Boone and you typically weren't one of the ones that was going in the house to do those things, then would you have been the one that set them out at the house and then met with them or picked them up later?

DAVIS: That's mostly it.

JOHNSON: What would we be missing from that?

DAVIS: That's about all you ever heard around him, so what else could you mention?

JOHNSON: Well, there was some things we were kind of wanting to clear up about that case in Boone in the winter, so if you set them out at the house, do you remember where you picked them up or how that worked if they had the other car and then you would have met them or...

DAVIS: Gosh, they was so much of that stuff going on, I couldn't tell you.

JOHNSON: How did it normally work?

DAVIS: They was no normal with 'em.

INGRAM: What's real important, what she asked you, and you've said this in a roundabout way – they were put out at the house – the people who robbed and killed those folks at that house, okay. And then they left that house in a vehicle to meet you. Are we...?

DAVIS: Yes.

INGRAM: Is that right?

DAVIS: That's true.

INGRAM: Okay. That's true. Alright, and I think between all three of us, we'll get this all figured out – four of us. And I want you to do this and you've done it. When I am not clear, and you don't understand me, tell me. Let me know. But when you waited for them and they showed up in a vehicle, okay, when you left Boone, did they tell you how much money they got?

DAVIS: I doubt that they did, the exact amount.

INGRAM: Okay. See, in Wrens, they didn't tell you the exact amount 'cause you told me $4,000; Birt told me $40,000.

DAVIS: Yeah. Well, they was bad about doing that anyway.

INGRAM: Okay. How much money did they pay you for your vehicle? That was your vehicle they were in...

DAVIS: Yes.

INGRAM: ...one of the vehicles off the car lot. Do you remember what kind of car it was?

DAVIS: Yes, it was a Cadillac.

INGRAM: Okay. It was a Cadillac. Did they give you some money from that job you did in Boone, robbing and killing those folks?

DAVIS: Do what now?

INGRAM: Okay. Did they give you some money from that job when you went up there and robbed and killed those folks up in Boone, did they give you some money for using your car and driving?

DAVIS: Oh, yes, they did.

INGRAM: Okay. How much?

DAVIS: It would have been a small amount. Whatever they had on 'em.

INGRAM: Give me an approximate amount.

DAVIS: Well, it was different every time.

INGRAM: Okay.

DAVIS: Say, if they come to your house and they shoot you, when they go out the front door, whatever you had on you went to them.

INGRAM: Do you recall the last time we were here, the sheriff asked you about a landmark close by. He asked you a question about a church. Do you remember, in the vicinity of that house, a church?

DAVIS: I don't even remember the church, what it looked like.

INGRAM: Yeah. I think I'm correct you said there was a church close by, though. You remember?

DAVIS: Yeah, there was.

INGRAM: Okay. I'm not asking you to describe it, I'm just asking you if you remember one. You do?

DAVIS: I remember that they had one.

INGRAM: How far from the house did you park your car to meet them? She [Johnson] asked you a question. You usually would park away from the house.

DAVIS: Uh huh.

INGRAM: Okay. Tell me why you did that.

DAVIS: Well, I didn't want to be seen.

INGRAM: And do you remember how far away from the house you parked when they came and met you?

DAVIS: Yes, it wasn't far away at all.

INGRAM: Give me an approximate distance.

DAVIS: I don't know, let's put it on a mile, mile and a half, two miles, somewhere in that vicinity.

INGRAM: Okay. Wow. Right. That's right on point. Yeah. You have an incredible mind. And let me tell you what you told me that made me realize something. You said there's a lot of stuff that happened, and it's hard to remember which is which, which one I got this amount of money, but you remembered you were driving a Cadillac, you parked a mile, mile and a half away so you wouldn't be seen, you put them out at the house. I want you to think for a minute. Just think it through. Who did you put out at the house?

DAVIS: I'm not sure I put anybody out. I don't even know who killed 'em except for Birt, but he had some help doing that.

INGRAM: Oh, of course he did.... Do you know how many victims there were in that house? You're shaking your head. How many?

DAVIS: Most of the time, I'd see 'em in grocery stores and stuff like that. Just normal people...

INGRAM: Yeah, but how many victims did they kill in that Boone house? How many people did they rob and kill?

DAVIS: Boone?

INGRAM: Yeah, in Boone, North Carolina where that blinding snowstorm was. Okay?

DAVIS: Uh huh.

INGRAM: Where you drove the Cadillac and you put Birt and some others out, and they robbed and killed those folks, okay? And it was tough to get out of there because of the snowstorm. What my question is how many people did they kill in that house?

DAVIS: However many was in it. I don't know.

INGRAM: Was there more than one?

DAVIS: Of course, yes.

INGRAM: Do you recall what his profession was, the man that they killed, what he did?

DAVIS: He worked for one of them factories around there.

INGRAM: Factory?

DAVIS: Yes, but he was a preacher.

INGRAM: A preacher?

DAVIS: Yes, he certainly was.

INGRAM: Were there family members there with him?

DAVIS: Yeah, he carried his wife with him, even his grandmother, but that was not on a hit.

INGRAM: Was that a target? Was that a hit? In other words, was he targeted to be robbed and killed?

DAVIS: Well, you see, back then that place was still dry. You couldn't go to a liquor store. You had to find you a supplier. So, yes, they killed 'em off pretty regular.

INGRAM: Do you know the method they used to kill those people, how they killed them?

DAVIS: They shot 'em with a gun.

INGRAM: Shot 'em with a gun.

DAVIS: Right. Or, now, some of this is what I was told. And I wasn't there. I don't know if that's true or not.

INGRAM: Well, you were there, but you were in a car.

DAVIS: Well, it could've been.

INGRAM: Yeah.

DAVIS: But several of his [Birt's] escapades, he'd want somebody to drive 'em and drop 'em.

INGRAM: Oh, sure. Yeah, had to. And you've already said that they were dropped out so the person puttin' 'em out wouldn't be seen. When they showed up where you were waiting on 'em, were they in a vehicle?

DAVIS: Yes, they would be.

INGRAM: Okay. Yeah. Do you know where the vehicle came from they were in?

DAVIS: Come from the Winder area, but I don't know where it was at. See, Birt grew up there.

INGRAM: Where?

DAVIS: At Winder.

INGRAM: Winder, yeah, Barrow County. No, I'm talking about, after the crime, what kind of vehicle were they in?

DAVIS: Whatever they picked up.

INGRAM: Okay.

JOHNSON: Do you remember them getting a vehicle stuck?

DAVIS: They could have. I'm sure they did.

JOHNSON: Do you remember anything like that?

DAVIS: No.

INGRAM: Do you know who put that crime in motion, who set that crime up? Do know who would have set that up – that crime?

DAVIS: Yeah, he's dead too.

INGRAM: He's dead too?

DAVIS: Yeah.

INGRAM: Who is it?

DAVIS: His name was West, but I don't know where he lived or who he was related to.

INGRAM: Was he related to the family?

DAVIS: I don't know.

INGRAM: Did you set that up?

DAVIS: No, I didn't set it up.

INGRAM: Who set it up, put it in motion?

DAVIS: Uh, Billy Birt.

INGRAM: Billy Birt. You remember me showing you some pictures of the victims, and you said you recognized the man. You remember that? The male victim.

DAVIS: Yeah, I remember that.

INGRAM: Okay. Okay. That's good. I've still got those pictures I think. I think they were pictures out of the newspaper.

DAVIS: I don't see how I remember stuff like that.

HAGAMAN: You're doing well.

INGRAM: Well, this is fifty years ago. You're doing better than...you're doing fanta-...you're doing tremendous.

DAVIS: No, I shouldn't have never done any of it.

INGRAM: Well, I know you have regrets now for all of it. I know you do. I'm convinced of it. Birt did too, believe it or not, and as ruthless and as violent as he was, he had tremendous regrets.

JOHNSON: But for what it's worth, it's a big help to us now to be able to at least bring some closure to some of these family members who had no idea what happened or have wondered their whole life like, why or what, so it just at least can answer some questions for these people, so thank you for doing this.

DAVIS: Uh huh.

INGRAM: I get the fact that you don't want to have to relive this.

DAVIS: I'm not going to.

INGRAM: I know you're not, and you don't want to, and I understand that 'cause you want to be able to go to sleep at night. I understand that. I know you do, but she's touched on something really important and powerful. Sometimes we just want to close the book and put an end to this, and what I mean put an end to it, where we just don't have to keep going over the same old [song?]. But you think Birt is the one that set this thing up?

DAVIS: Oh, of course, yes.

INGRAM: Okay. *[to Johnson]* Have you got a picture you wanted to show him?

JOHNSON: *[to Ingram]* So, we were never able to find a picture of "our friend" Mr. Hall.[bbbbbbb] The only thing I've got is just an old newspaper clipping, but...

INGRAM: *[to Johnson]* Is he in it?

JOHNSON: *[to Ingram]* [No].

INGRAM: *[to Johnson]* Hall's not?

JOHNSON: *[to Ingram]* Nope. He refused to take any high school or college pictures.[ccccccc]

INGRAM: *[to Johnson]* Have you got the victims' pictures there?

[bbbbbbb] Although the Watauga County Sheriff's Office Durham Case file contained no early photograph of Troy Hall from circa 1972, it did (since 2011) contain one of him from his 2005 driver's license. The first photo Ingram ever saw of Hall was when the author showed him one in April 2022. The author also mailed a letter to Davis at Augusta State Medical Prison and included photos of Troy Hall, and without identifying the subject of the photographs, asked Davis if he recognized the man pictured. There is no guarantee Davis ever received the letter and no reply was ever received.

[ccccccc] Johnson did not indicate how she knew Troy Hall refused to take high school or college pictures. In fact, at least one high school picture of Hall exists *(see p. 27)*, which appeared in a 1978 televised special about the Durham Case.

JOHNSON: *[to Ingram]* Yeah.

INGRAM: *[to Johnson]* Let's show him that, and let's see if he remembers what he told me.

JOHNSON: Do either of those look familiar to you? *[showing Davis pictures of Bryce and Bobby Durham]*

DAVIS: I don't know. Let me look at it. *[reading the caption]* ...Bobby Joe Dur-ham.... Did they ever put them in jail?

JOHNSON: No, but this was the father and son that Billy killed. The father and son that we think Billy Birt killed. And there was a female; the mom was at the house too. And that's why we're just trying to find some answers and closure for the family.

INGRAM: *[after locating the pictures he had]* Here's the three victims. Take a look at 'em and study 'em for just...

DAVIS: [Bryce?] Dur-ham...

INGRAM: These are the three that were killed.

DAVIS: ...Virginia Dur-ham...

INGRAM: That name ring a bell? Durham?

DAVIS: I've never seen 'em before.

JOHNSON: Which, if you drove the car and set them out, you probably wouldn't have.

DAVIS: I would certainly remember 'em if they were [in?] that area and doing stuff.

JOHNSON: These people were in Boone.

INGRAM: These are the three in the house that were killed, and I showed you those pictures, I showed you that picture last time, and you said – you didn't tell me how – but you said, "I recognize him." I don't know if you remember that or not.

DAVIS: Bryce Durham. Does he have a business in Winder?

INGRAM: No, he's got one in Boone, or he had one in Boone. This man – and I don't think there's any reason to hold back here – this man had a car dealership in Boone. Okay? And you told me in the last interview that you recognized him. You didn't say how or when or where, but you said he looked familiar.

DAVIS: I hope I never see none of 'em no more, but, you know, you gotta live with it.

INGRAM: Oh, I understand, and you don't really...they're all dead, they were murdered. They were tortured, they were killed in their house in Boone, North Carolina, and you drove the car, and Birt and whoever else you put out were the ones who killed them. I'm certain of that. And I'll tell you why I'm certain of it, Bill Davis. I'm certain of it because Birt's youngest son told me that. He told me that his dad told him everything that ya'll did from beginning to end.... Shane turned out to be a pretty good fellow, and he wanted to right the wrong of his daddy 'cause his daddy told him all this in prison. Told him about this killin' and who was there and what they did and everything. 'Cause Billy Birt was notorious for torturin' people. Am I right or wrong?

DAVIS: No, he loved to torture 'em.

INGRAM: He loved to torture people, and he loved to rob them. He would torture them to get the money, find out where the money was, and then he killed everybody so they wouldn't be able to identify him, so there were no witnesses. That was his MO. That's the way he did business. Right?

DAVIS: Right.

INGRAM: Okay. And on some of these, you were with him. Right?

DAVIS: Very few, but yes.

INGRAM: I understand. Some of them you...I didn't say all of them. I didn't say that. I said some of them, you were with him, and Gaddis was with him on some, and Reed was with him, so was Otis *[referring to Otis Reidling, Jr.]*, right? On some.... But we're trying to get this cleared up, and we appreciate you helping us, but we want to get all the details that you can remember. I know you just told us, you said you were in a Cadillac that came from your dealership. Do you remember Birt saying who set this up? Who's the one that set it up? Which person that got you all to the house and killin' the folks?

DAVIS: I don't remember the names of even who it was.

INGRAM: *[to Hagaman and Johnson]* Is it okay if I just ask, specifically?

HAGAMAN: *[to Ingram]* Sure.

JOHNSON: *[to Ingram]* Yeah.

INGRAM: Was it a relative?

DAVIS: He was good at killin' relatives.

INGRAM: But I'm talking about the relative who set this up. Does the name Hall ring a bell to you?

DAVIS: Hall.

INGRAM: *[to Hagaman and Johnson]* What's his first name?

JOHNSON: *[to Ingram]* Troy Hall.

HAGAMAN: *[to Ingram]* Troy.

INGRAM: Troy Hall.

DAVIS: Troy Hall.

INGRAM: The son-in-law of these people.

DAVIS: No, I never had any dealings with him whatsoever.

INGRAM: Okay. Do you remember, after this crime was committed, a phone call being placed by anybody in the group? A phone call to somebody saying that it was done.

DAVIS: No, I don't.

JOHNSON: If Billy took on a job like this, would you come up or go to the area a day or two before and scope anything out, or would you just get what information, he would get what information he needed and just go do it? How would that usually work?

DAVIS: I'm not sure.

JOHNSON: Well, did you go watch people for some time before anybody would get set out and they would rob 'em and torture 'em and kill 'em, or did they just go do it? Or did it depend?

DAVIS: No, I think you got it right the first time.

JOHNSON: Okay. So, sometimes they would watch and see.

DAVIS: [Yes?]

JOHNSON: Do you remember anything about that, being in Boone, watching anybody or seeing how they operated or what they did?

DAVIS: No, I wouldn't allow them people around my home.

JOHNSON: So, when you guys got in the car and came up to Boone in North Carolina...

DAVIS: Yes.

JOHNSON: ...do you remember how long you guys stayed that trip? Was it like a day or....?

DAVIS: I didn't even know they had such a leadership from that side.

INGRAM: Right.

DAVIS: Yeah. If they's a lot of people around that specific area, and some people claim that Birt didn't kill all them people, that that's why he got killed. I don't know.

INGRAM: *[showing Davis a picture of the Durham house]* That house look familiar?

DAVIS: No.

INGRAM: *[to Hagaman and Johnson]* This is so difficult. Fifty years.

JOHNSON: *[to Ingram]* Yeah.

INGRAM: *[to Hagaman and Johnson]* So difficult.

HAGAMAN: See where it was snowing there, in that picture? Where it was slick?

JOHNSON: If you could think really hard and remember anything about the vehicle that they drove away from the house...

DAVIS: Yes.

JOHNSON: ...I guess to either come meet you or get up with you. They got it stuck. We know that. But do you remember anything about how they got it either unstuck or got away from the vehicle, or did you have to go get 'em from where they got stuck? Do you remember anything like that?

DAVIS: I sent a pull truck over there to get it out of his screw-up.

[It is unfortunate the officers did not further explore how and where Davis obtained a tow truck as well as his mention of "'his' screw-up" in an attempt to identify the individual whose screw-up Davis was referring to.]

JOHNSON: A pull truck? Oh, like a tow truck?

DAVIS: Yeah.

JOHNSON: So, I'm wondering if you're thinking of the same one, 'cause this one, it looks like it got stuck and stayed stuck.

DAVIS: Yeah.

JOHNSON: And you wouldn't have had time to maybe call a tow truck 'cause...

DAVIS: No...

JOHNSON: ...I imagine you were needing to get out of there.

DAVIS: Quick.

INGRAM: I don't want to put words in your mouth. I'm not gonna do that, and there's so much that happened in this timeframe, these years when they were runnin' and gunnin' and robbin' and killin', that it's like Shane had the same problem separating the cases from what his dad had told him. There's so much that went on and this was so long ago and some of it confusing. Yes or no?

DAVIS: Yes.

INGRAM: You're older, it's hard to remember this, and you're trying your best to do that, and each time you've told us basically the same thing, but there's been some confusion. There has been. As you've told me, you've got a good mind, you've got a good body, but it's not what it once was. Your memory, when I first met you in 1973-'74-'75, was unbelievable.... That's why I was counting on you here. I was just counting to try to say remember what you can, and you've done that in bits and pieces. You've done the best you can. I mean, I don't know if you can do any better. I don't know.

DAVIS: I hope I can't.

INGRAM: Hope you what?

DAVIS: Cannot.

INGRAM: You know, I detect something, and I think these guys too. Some of this you don't want to remember.

DAVIS: That's right.

INGRAM: No, I know I'm right, and it's not that you can't remember it; you don't really want to remember three people – a man, his wife, and his son – being murdered in a house in Boone. But it damn sure happened, and you were involved in it. Yes or no? Sir?

DAVIS: What?

INGRAM: Go ahead. Look at it. Study it. Make sure. *[perhaps again referring to a picture of Bryce Durham]*

DAVIS: No, that's not him. He's dead anyway. He's one of the few that died without gunplay and all the...

INGRAM: Who's that?

DAVIS: This guy right here.

JOHNSON: He died without gunplay?

DAVIS: Yeah, he helped a little bit. I think his wife did most of it. I'm not sure.

INGRAM: Why, when they went in the house, would they tie people up? Why would they do that?

DAVIS: To keep 'em from hollerin' and screamin' and noise level mostly.

INGRAM: Did they do it to control 'em so they couldn't run away?

DAVIS: Well, they could have done it for that.

INGRAM: Did they always bring guns to these jobs to control people with a gun?

DAVIS: Yes.

INGRAM: They had guns then, didn't they?

DAVIS: Oh, yeah.

INGRAM: Alright, let me ask you something. If you know, tell me; if you don't, tell me. Do you know how these people were killed in the house?

DAVIS: You mean...

INGRAM: The method how they were killed.

DAVIS: Like somebody broke in their house and shot 'em.

INGRAM: Well, they went into the house. Did they torture these people?

DAVIS: I don't know. I wasn't there.

INGRAM: Well, you were there, but you weren't in the house.

DAVIS: Right.

INGRAM: Right. You were outside in a car, and you see, you've already told us you were a mile, mile and a half, two miles away in a car waiting for them to come. Did they come to you? The captain [Johnson] asked you, after getting stuck, did they come to you in a vehicle that came from that house? Yes or no?

DAVIS: It would have just about had to have been, yes.

INGRAM: Well, I mean, that makes sense, does it not, if you put them out?

DAVIS: No, no. Not at all.

INGRAM: No what?

DAVIS: No one.

INGRAM: No, no. You drove up there in the Cadillac, and you put them out, and then you told us that when you left, Birt drove. Isn't that what you said?

DAVIS: Bus roll. *[Davis seemingly misheard "Birt drove" as "bus roll."]*

INGRAM: Birt. Listen to me. You drove up there in the Cadillac. It was your vehicle, right?

DAVIS: Right.

INGRAM: Yes?

DAVIS: Yes, I drove a Cadillac...

INGRAM: Alright, you drove up. You put 'em out. Okay? They commit the crime. They take the vehicle from the house and come and meet you. And then you said Birt drove home. Yes or no?

DAVIS: That's probably the truth. I'm not sure, but, uh...

INGRAM: Well, I mean, it's the best you can remember, and that *is* what you told us, you know. You remember the blinding snowstorm, the bad snow, how hard it was to get out of there?

DAVIS: I remember some, uh, weather like that, yes.

INGRAM: Yeah, weather like that, okay. Well, there aren't many cases... Let me ask you this. I just realized this. Is there any other case you've been involved in your whole life, Bill, where there was a bad snowstorm, or is that the only one?

DAVIS: I think that's the only one.

INGRAM: Okay. Well, that helps.

DAVIS: You don't have that many here in the South anyway.

INGRAM: That's something Shane told me that his dad told him. Do you remember the name Durham, the name of the people that were killed? You remember that name?

DAVIS: No.

JOHNSON: But would it be uncommon for you to know people's names or not know people's names if you were going to do something like that?

DAVIS: No, I wouldn't think so.

INGRAM: *[to Johnson]* No, they killed others they didn't know who they were.... *[to Hagaman and Johnson]* Why don't you guys be as specific as you need to be, 'cause I think we all understand, the four of us, there is some confusion.

JOHNSON: *[to Ingram]* Yeah, I think that's the hardest thing is maybe so much is running together.

INGRAM: *[to Hagaman and Johnson]* I sit here, and I say to myself, here I am asking him stuff to be specific about fifty years ago...and sometimes we, investigators, almost expect and demand too much out of witnesses or suspects.... *[to Davis]* Bill, you know more about this case here in Boone, North Carolina than you're willing to tell us. I know that, and you know that, and I respect that because some of this you don't want to relive and go over again. I understand that, and I respect it, and you've given us all you're gonna give us. Am I right or wrong?

DAVIS: You're right.

INGRAM: I know I'm right. I know you, and I can talk to you and look at you and tell there's just some things that you just don't want to go there.

DAVIS: Yeah, you're correct about that.

INGRAM: Well, 'cause you've done a hell of a lot, sir, and some of it you just want to let it stay where it's at. True or false?

DAVIS: That's true.

INGRAM: True. That's the most specific answer you've given and never had to equivocate. There's just so much in your background, and I'm not going to force you. I'm not gonna do it. *[to Hagaman]* Sheriff, I think you and the captain need to ask anything on your mind. Anything.

HAGAMAN: When you all left Boone and when it was really snowy and everything, did Birt say anything about being ripped off – that he was mad because somebody didn't pay him off for that particular job? I understood that he was upset because he didn't find or get the money that he was supposed to in the house, and so he was mad at this Troy Hall fellow that set 'em up, that we think that set the killing up.

DAVIS: Hmm.

HAGAMAN: Do you recall him ever being mad about somebody ripping him off? That is, Billy Birt.

DAVIS: Yes. He should have been killed years ago.

HAGAMAN: Yeah, but was he ever upset at a job that he did that they didn't get paid, or...

DAVIS: Yeah, that's what I'm talking about.

HAGAMAN: Okay. And do you know if it was in relation to this particular case where the snowstorm was?

DAVIS: No, I haven't seen any in there that leads straight to him. I'll put it that way.

INGRAM: What do you want to ask us? I've known you off and on for almost fifty years – a long, long, long time – and I know how you are. You'll talk to a point, and then you don't want to talk no more about certain things.

DAVIS: Yes, sir.

INGRAM: Certain things you want to leave them where they lie.

DAVIS: Well, do you think that works?

INGRAM: Works? It works for you, sir, because you have to live with yourself, and you have to go to sleep at night.

DAVIS: That's what I'm getting around to...

INGRAM: I know. Mr. Davis, sir, you have done a lot of shit in your day.

DAVIS: But I've never been accused of murder. I mean, I've been accused, but I've won the cases.

[This was not entirely true as Davis had been convicted of the murder of Mac Sibley.]

JOHNSON: Do you feel like that's what we're accusing you of here?

DAVIS: Oh, no.

JOHNSON: Okay.

DAVIS: Them days are over, but they used to be.

JOHNSON: Are you worried that if you say something to us that we will add on to your sentence?

DAVIS: Well, it does cross my mind, yeah.

INGRAM: Sure it does.

DAVIS: And I try to be honest anymore, but I tried that stuff, just making everything my way.

INGRAM: *[to Hagaman and Johnson]* He's one of the smartest criminals you'll ever meet in your life, and he won't acknowledge that, but I will. *[to Davis]* I am not trying to blow smoke up your ass, Mr. Davis, sir, you are a very smart, clever man.

DAVIS: Well, I appreciate that, but I didn't use it the right way if I am a smart, clever man.

INGRAM: I know. You have tremendous regret what you did in your life. I know that. You do. If you had it to do over again, you'd do it different. You'd use that brain power another way....

JOHNSON: Will you make me a promise?

DAVIS: *[laughing]* I don't know.

JOHNSON: If you ever change your mind about remembering or talking about anything to do with the Boone case and the snow, would you write it down for me?

DAVIS: Yeah, I'll write that down for you.

INGRAM: *[to Johnson]* You know, you might, captain, seriously, you've just touched something very valuable. You might want to correspond with him. It might be easier for him to write it than to say it.

JOHNSON: Would that work? Can I write you letters, and you write me letters back?

DAVIS: There's some points there, yeah.

HAGAMAN: And understand too, what she was saying originally, we're not looking to really put anybody, a lot of people are deceased that were involved in this on both sides – on the perpetrators and law enforcement. Our main point is to try to bring to the family, what's left of them, some closure so that they can put this behind them too. This has been weighing on them for a long time as to who did what, and that's all we're trying to do – bring some closure to it. So far as us adding any charges, that's not our goal here. Our goal is to help bring closure to the family.

DAVIS: Well, that's the way it should be,

HAGAMAN: Thank you, and thank you for saying that, 'cause you're right.

[Hagaman believed Davis was worried he was going to be charged with the Durham murders, and when the officers told him that was not the case and they were only there for closure, Davis seemed relieved.[1818]]

INGRAM: And we know what you did. We know you drove the car. We know who did this. I also believe you know that these people were killed because, as you told me already, you said, look, if they went into here to rob 'em, they're gonna torture 'em, they're gonna kill 'em. They ain't leaving no witnesses. That's how they operate.

DAVIS: Yes, sir.

HAGAMAN: Do you remember when, in any of the things where Billy Birt was involved or any of the others, did they take things from the house? Not just cash. Did they ever take any, like, jewelry, or guns, or watches, or silverware, or anything like that? Do you remember them ever bringing anything like that from a house?

DAVIS: Yeah, they did it all the time.

HAGAMAN: Oh, did they? Okay.

DAVIS: Yes, sir.

HAGAMAN: Uh, what? Mostly just the silverware or just whatever they could get their hands on?

DAVIS: Whatever they think could get 'em twenty-five or fifty dollars to...

HAGAMAN: Did you ever see any silverware that they took?

DAVIS: Yeah.

HAGAMAN: Do you remember where it came from? Did they...

DAVIS: Some of it come from the local churches.

INGRAM: Did any of it come from places they robbed and killed people?

DAVIS: Right.

INGRAM: Okay. *[to Hagaman]* It's a good question, sheriff. *[to Davis]* Anything else you want to ask or tell us?

DAVIS: Yeah, when you gonna get me out of here?

INGRAM: It'll be a while probably.

DAVIS: Okay. *[laughing]*

INGRAM: I told the parole board that you cooperated and helped, so, you know, we'll see what happens.

Based on Shane Birt's recollections and Billy Wayne Davis's interviews, the Watauga County Sheriff's Office moved ahead with publicly declaring Billy Birt, Davis, Bobby Gaddis, and Charlie Reed as the Durhams' murderers and closing the Durham Case. On December 16, 2021, Sheriff Len Hagaman met with Chris Laws, Special Agent in charge for the SBI's Northwestern District, and a media specialist,[1819] perhaps in preparation for the February 8, 2022 Watauga County Sheriff's Office press release announcing the closure of the case.

Bob Ingram was certain Davis was in Boone that night with Birt, Gaddis, and Reed, and he believed it was Davis who was responsible for their arrangements.[1820] According to the *White County News* in Georgia, Ingram's "wealth of insight on reviewing evidence, suspect interviews, and the behavioral signs that can be missed by an untrained eye...[as well as his] skill set developed from decades in law enforcement was critical to bring the [Durham] case to a close."[1821] Author Phil Hudgins, who felt he [Hudgins] had been given more credit in the press than he deserved for helping solve the case, acknowledged it was Ingram who should be credited. According to Hudgins:

- "It was Bob Ingram who made three trips to the prison in Augusta to interview Billy Wayne Davis, the only survivor of the four murderers.

- "It was Bob Ingram who got Davis to confess – twice – to the Boone murders.

- "It was Bob Ingram who worked on this case for two years, prompting Sheriff Len Hagaman of Watauga County, North Carolina, to finally declare the case closed…."[1822]

From the time Ingram first contacted the Watauga County Sheriff's Office in May 2019 to inform them of the connection he had made between Georgia's Dixie Mafia and the Durham murders until the sheriff's office issued its press release in February 2022, two years and nine months had passed, a period of time during which Ingram did a lot of prodding, hoping to move the case along as, according to him, "it was *the* most major deal in Boone in the last one-hundred years, crime wise…."[1823]

A breakdown of the intervals within that timeframe are as follows:

➢ **May 2019:** Bob Ingram initially contacts the Watauga County Sheriff's Office

Two months pass

➢ **July 2019:** Len Hagaman, Carolynn Johnson, Wade Colvard, and Larry Wagner meet with Ingram in Georgia.

Two months pass

➢ **September 2019:** Hagaman, Johnson, and Colvard travel to Georgia to interview Davis and others.

Thirteen months pass

➢ **October 2020:** Ingram interviews Davis alone and reports back to the Watauga County Sheriff's Office.

One month passes

➢ **November 2020:** Ingram, Hagaman, and Johnson interview Shane Birt as well as Davis.

Nine months pass

➢ **August 2021:** Ingram, Hagaman, and Johnson interview Davis again.

Six months pass

➢ **February 2022:** Watauga County Sheriff's Office press release.

When asked what other investigatory steps or actions the Watauga County Sheriff's Office took during these intervals of time, Sheriff Hagaman stated, "We probably weren't following up as quickly as we could," but their attention to other pressing matters and some budgetary constraints prevented it.[1824] In the spring of 2021, Hagaman and Captain Carolynn Johnson had planned another trip to Georgia to interview Billy Wayne Davis, but in the midst of this timeline, on April 28, the sheriff's office suffered the tragic loss of two of its officers, who were shot and killed on the same day in the line of duty. The return to Georgia was put on hold until the following August.[1825]

INTERLUDE

CHAPTER 21

THE REINVENTION OF TROY HALL

Although the 2019-2021 developments in the Durham Case directed investigators' attention to Georgia, that was not all that had been transpiring in the Peach State. Within a couple of years following Troy and Ginny Hall's 1976 divorce, and as the Durham murder investigation continued in North Carolina, Troy moved to Georgia, where he seemingly embarked on a self-reinvention, assuming the name Justin T. Hall. But reimagining himself was not a foreign concept. When he first introduced himself to Ginny's family in 1971, he had taken on the persona of a former military school student, the son of a wealthy stockbroker father who lived in Florida and owned a Learjet.

Justin Troy Hall
(Sources L-R: Watauga County Sheriff's Office; Georgia Government Transparency and Campaign Finance Commission; tributearchive.com)

In light of their close relationship, it came as no surprise that Troy's brothers Ray and John also relocated to Georgia. Similar to Troy's assumption of a new identity, John sometimes used the name "John Hall Carrington," and although he lived in Georgia for periods of time, he retained a residence in North Carolina.[1826] Of the three brothers, John was thought to be "more natural" and "more real." He was also considered to be more handsome – big and tall – while Troy was described as short and scrawny.[1827][ddddddd] Troy and Ray were particularly close, one not acting or having knowledge of

[ddddddd] Troy's 2005 driver's license indicates he was 5'9", 145 pounds, and had green eyes. [Source: Watauga County Sheriff's Office investigative file 118-H-1/2/3.]

something without the other's involvement.[1828] In the early days following the Durham murders, newspaper articles occasionally and erroneously reported Troy's name as "Ray Hall"[1829] and even as "Ray A. 'Troy' Hall."[1830] As Troy's trusted older brother, Ray was faithful to support him, even when he knew Troy's grandiose ideas (including thoughts at one time of being a "movie guru" and traveling to Hollywood[eeeeeee]) would never amount to anything. According to one observer of the brothers' relationship, Troy did whatever Ray instructed him to do, and Ray's support and involvement amounted to him running Troy's life.[1831] Another observer saw it differently, saying Troy was good at telling everybody else, including Ray, what to do. This same observer, however, never saw the two in any heated discussions or arguments and admits Troy was not a tyrant who constantly ordered Ray around. Regardless of who called the shots and when, the brothers were unquestionably loyal to one another.[1832]

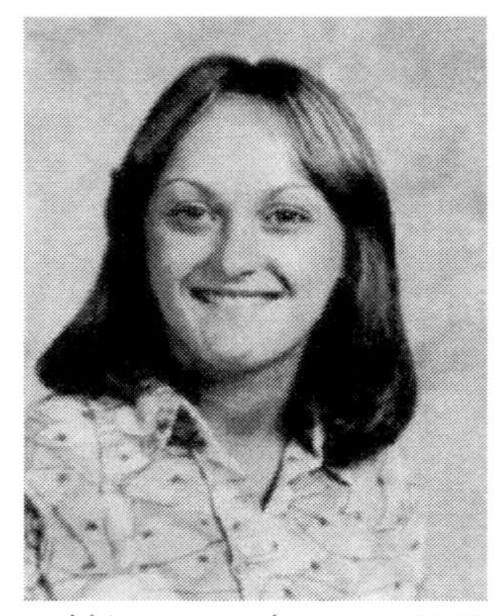

Debbie Foster (Source: 1976 Wilkes Community College yearbook)

No matter the extent or success of Troy's self-reconceptualization, drama seemed to follow him. By early 1979, he was dating fellow Wilkes County, North Carolina native Debra Lynn "Debbie" Foster, who had either relocated to or was visiting Georgia.[1833] On January 6 that same year, twenty-one-year-old Foster was killed as she tried to cross the busy, six-lane Buford Highway in DeKalb County on foot and was struck by one car and run over by another.[1834][fffffff] Some claimed she fell out of another moving vehicle[1835] and was struck by four separate cars, two of which fled the scene and two of which stopped.[1836] SBI Agent Larry Wagner was told Foster was running away from Troy's apartment at the time of her death.[1837] Some believe her passing to be one more example of a mysterious death linked to Troy, who reportedly was the beneficiary of a $100,000 insurance policy he had on Foster.[1838] Foster's father believed Troy killed her.[1839]

In June 1979, six months after Foster's death, Troy, now going by "Justin," graduated with a Juris Doctor degree from John Marshall Law School in Atlanta[1840][ggggggg] and was admitted to the Georgia State Bar that same month,[1841] reportedly having passed the bar exam on his first attempt.[1842] Within the following year, Troy reportedly worked for the federal government as the prosecutor in a "trust

---

[eeeeeee] Between 1994 and1995, a for profit corporation, Motion Pictures International, Inc., was registered with Justin T. Hall as the agent with a principal address of 1932 N. Druid Hills Rd. NE #100, Atlanta, GA. [Source: https://opengovus.com/georgia-business/915600.]

[fffffff] The author's Open Records Requests to acquire law enforcement reports concerning Foster's death from the DeKalb County (GA) Sheriff's Office, the Doraville (GA) Police Department, and the Chamblee (GA) Police Department proved unsuccessful as no records could be found. [Sources: DeKalb County Sheriff's Office, Records Section. E-mail to author. July 30, 2024; Michelle Oneil, Records Department, City of Doraville, GA. E-mail to author. July 30, 2024; Chamblee Police Department. Phone call with author. August 1, 2024.]

[ggggggg] The school verifies the 1979 graduation date, although Troy stated he attended law school between the ages of 27 and 30 (1978-1981). At the time of Troy's graduation, John Marshall was not accredited by the American Bar Association and would not be until 2005. Ginny Durham Mackie affirmed Troy's lack of a bachelor's degree, stating that the State of Georgia allowed individuals to obtain a law degree without one. [Sources: John Marshall Law School Registrar's Office, Atlanta, GA, phone confirmation to author, March or April 2022; Letter from David Lipsig, M.D. to Patrick Meriwether, Esq., October 15, 2012, p. 5, Gwinnet County, Georgia Superior Court, Civil Action File #12-A-06853-10, Melanie Hall, Plaintiff v. Justin Hall, Defendant, February 4, 2013; https://en.wikipedia.org/wiki/Atlanta%27s_John_Marshall_Law_School; Mackie, Ginny Durham. Interview with Carolynn Johnson & Wade Colvard. December 7, 2020.]

territory."[1843] He would later falsely tell associates he had been the Attorney General of Palau,[1844] an island country located in the Micronesia region in the western Pacific Ocean.[1845][hhhhhhh] While working there, he is alleged to have somehow finagled his way to Washington, D. C. – perhaps as part of an official delegation – to attend the January 1981[1846] inauguration of President Ronald Reagan.[1847]

In 1980, Troy found himself involved in a lawsuit related to alleged insurance fraud. One of the spec homes he built in or near Atlanta burned to the ground, and he was accused of setting the fire to collect the insurance. At the civil court hearing, Troy reportedly stated he did not need the insurance money because he had $100,000 from his in-laws (presumably a reference to the Durham estates). Ginny Mackie was subpoenaed in the case to testify whether Troy's claim about the $100,000 was true, and the district attorney from the Georgia county in question told her to mention her parents. Ginny subsequently went to the courthouse in Wilkes County, North Carolina and provided video testimony. This was her last contact with Troy.[1848]

Between circa 1982 and 1984, Troy worked as an Assistant District Attorney in the six-county Southwestern Judicial District of Georgia, based in Americus.[1849] In that capacity, he served alongside another Assistant District Attorney, R. Rucker Smith (later Chief Judge of the Southwestern Judicial Circuit).[1850] The two men worked under the direction of District Attorney John R. Parks, and, although Smith and Troy were not close friends, they got along well and had a pleasant professional and personal relationship. According to Smith, Troy seemed to do a good job and exhibited no character or behavioral problems. The two men handled criminal hearings, trials, grand juries, and related matters.[iiiiiii] Each had independent caseloads, but they occasionally worked together on the same matters.[1851] When North Carolina SBI agents paid a visit to the District Attorney (presumably Parks) and made it known Troy was being uncooperative in the Durham Case, the District Attorney called Troy in and ordered him to cooperate, perhaps including taking a polygraph test. When Troy refused, he was dismissed from his position.[1852] Smith knew Troy was divorced, but he had no knowledge of Troy's in-laws' murders or of Troy's dismissal due to a North Carolina investigation of the murders. When Troy left his position to move to the Atlanta area, he and Smith maintained contact for a few years, Smith visiting Troy's house in Dacula and occasionally speaking with him about case referrals or general legal matters. Smith recalls Troy

---

[hhhhhhh] Kim Batchelor, followed by Ron Stock, were appointees of the Trust Territory of the Pacific Islands (TTPI). Stock served from 1979 to 1981, when the Republic of Palau gained its independence, and was succeeded by Robert "Bob" Ferm, who was employed by the Republic of Palau, and thus their first Attorney General. Ferm held the office from September 1981 through December 1982, and his colleague Walter Urban was there in an acting capacity into the spring of 1983. Neither Ferm nor Stock have any recollection of a Justin Troy Hall in Palau while they were in office. Troy's alma mater, John Marshall Law School, currently has its Micronesian Externship Program, which "places students in legal offices throughout the Commonwealth of the Northern Marianas, the Federated States of Micronesia, the Republic of Palau, and the Territory of Guam." The program began in the summer of 2007, but perhaps something along those lines existed at the time Troy was a student at the law school. [Sources: Ferm, Robert. Emails to author. July 20, 2022. Stock, Ron. Phone conversation with author. November 15, 2022; https://johnmarshall.edu/micronesian-externship/; "At The Crossroads: John Marshall Law School's Global Community," *The Atlanta Lawyer,* Professor Kathleen Burch, https://bluetoad.com/publication/?i=100138&article_id=972220&view=articleBrowser.]

[iiiiiii] Seemingly, the only case that Troy prosecuted as an Assistant District Attorney and that made the news was a 1982 child rape case that resulted in a mistrial. [Sources: Rick Rountree, "Man Tried in Child Rape Case," *The Macon Telegraph*, Macon, GA, May 25, 1982, p. 8A; Rick Rountree, "Judge declares mistrial in child rape case," *The Macon News*, Macon, GA, May 26, 1982, p. 6B.]

was dating a girl named Deborah,[1853] had a nice home, drove a Mercedes convertible, and seemed to have resources beyond what he was paid as an Assistant District Attorney.[1854]

In the mid-1980s, Troy returned to North Carolina to testify as a character witness for Mickey Rhodes, of Wilkes County, who had been charged with multiple instances of possession and distribution of cocaine and marijuana *(see footnote on p. 173)*. Troy took the stand at Federal District Court in Charlotte, where reporter Bruce Bowers was covering the story. In 1978, Bowers had hosted and led the investigative reporting for WBTV's news special about the Durham Case. At that time, Troy had been unresponsive to the television station's request for an interview, but he and Bowers were now in the same courtroom. After his testimony, Troy left the courthouse and sat on a bench outside. Bowers followed him and introduced himself. Troy replied, "I don't have any…I…I've gotta go, I gotta go, I gotta go." Bowers, who is of the opinion that Troy was involved in his in-laws' murders, had never seen anyone make such as quick exit.[1855][jjjjjjj]

Troy subsequently established a law practice in Lawrenceville, Georgia, listing entertainment and sports law as specialties,[1856] and, by 1986, he sought to hire an attorney with one to two years of experience in workman's compensation, social security, and/or insurance.[1857] He hired attorney Richard M. Loftis and formed a partnership under the name of "Hall and Loftis."[1858] Loftis was a former public defender in DeKalb County, Georgia, resigning that position after four years to return to private practice.[1859] In 1981, Loftis had defended Decatur, Georgia native James Samuel Walraven (dubbed the "The Bathtub Strangler"), who was convicted, indicted, and suspected, respectively, in three separate Atlanta-area cases of young women who had been strangled and whose bodies had been placed in the shallow water of their bathtubs[1860] – cases unrelated but eerily similar to the way Troy's in-laws had been murdered.

It was erroneously rumored that Troy had been married to a woman named Annette Pearson[kkkkkkk] prior to his marriage to Ginny Durham, and that Annette died under mysterious circumstances.[1861] Annette was actually the first wife of Troy's brother Ray, with whom she had one son before Ray, described as "a blue-collar construction worker," left the marriage in 1966. Ray and Annette divorced in December 1967 following the birth of their second son. Annette eventually remarried, her new husband legally adopting her sons by Ray Hall. After her second husband's death, Annette's health began to deteriorate. In August 1997, her third husband reportedly heard a gunshot while working in their kitchen, and he found Annette's body in a chair in their bedroom with an open Bible and note in hand. A gunshot wound to the chest indicated she had taken her own life; she was fifty at the time of her death.[1862] After his divorce from Annette, Ray Hall married Katrina "Kay"

[jjjjjjj] Troy's new name "Justin Hall" was reportedly discovered in a ledger associated with the federal indictment of Rhodes and others, but investigators failed, at least initially, to associate that name with Troy Hall. [Source: Rucker, Jeff. Phone interview with author. October 4, 2023.]

[kkkkkkk] The Watauga County Sheriff's Office case file on the Durham investigation contains a note that, before his marriage to Ginny, Troy was married to a niece of an Edie Andrews. This is likely Edie Crysel Andrews, a native of Wilkes County, whose husband, Dean Andrews, was a salesman for Andrews Chevrolet Co. in Boone, NC. The case file reference to Edie Andrews' niece is likely a reference to Annette Pearson Hall. Edie Andrews' grandmother was a sister to Annette Pearson Hall's grandfather, making Edie and Annette second cousins rather than aunt and niece. Annette Pearson was a first cousin once removed to Tal Pearson, who had met with Bryce and Virginia Durham when they fled South Carolina in 1962 *(see p. 225)*, and Annette was a niece of Forest Church (her mother's brother), who had gotten Bryce Durham into the auto loan business. [Sources: Watauga County Sheriff's Office investigation file 118-H-1/2/3; Genealogical research by author.]

Stogner, a California native, who he was married to at the time of the Durham murders, but who he was separated from by March 1975.

Carmen Wells Shackelford (Source: 1975 DeKalb College yearbook)

In 1984,[1863] Troy began a relationship with Duluth, Georgia native Carmen Wells Shackelford, a blue-eyed, blonde divorcee who taught middle school. Carmen was the mother of a teenaged daughter, who, like Carmen's former husband, had dwarfism.[1864] Carmen told a friend she met Troy while they were pumping gas, and that she, dressed in "her little skirt," flirted with him like crazy.

Described by this same friend as "flouncy and bouncy" but not dumb, Carmen, in fact, was very book smart and graduated from high school in Lawrenceville, Georgia a year early in 1972.[1865] Carmen's parents, Randall and Betty Tanner Wells, had divorced when she was young. Her father remarried, and he and his second wife died in 1967, the result of a murder-suicide in DeKalb County, Georgia.[1866] Meanwhile, Carmen's mother married Eugene "Gene" Reeves, Jr., with whom she had another daughter, but the pair divorced prior to Carmen's marriage to Troy on March 1, 1987.[1867]

Another rumor concerning Troy was that he was in a relationship with one of the daughters of *Hustler* magazine publisher Larry Flynt,[1868] which seemed reasonable considering Troy's pornographic interests, but this was apparently conflated with the fact that Carmen's stepfather, Gene Reeves, Jr., was Flynt's defense attorney during Flynt's 1978 obscenity-related legal battle in Gwinnett County, Georgia. During the trial, both Flynt and Reeves survived being shot in Lawrenceville. Reeves had graduated in 1964 from John Marshall Law School in Atlanta,[1869] the same school Troy later graduated from, and over the course of his career, Reeves was a civil and criminal trial lawyer, twice president of the Gwinnett Bar Association, a deputy sheriff and investigator with the Gwinnett County Sheriff's Department, and a magistrate judge. Notably, in 1975, Reeves, a friend of Billy and Ruby Nell Birt, had helped defend Birt at his Jefferson County, Georgia trial for the murders of Reid and Lois Fleming of Wrens, Georgia. Members of the Birt family had collected money to retain Reeves, and one of the witnesses who testified on Birt's behalf regarding his alibi was Brenda Wages, a sister of Dennis Wages, who was married to Ruby Nell Birt's sister Betty. Five years later, Brenda Wages would become the second wife of Gene Reeves, Jr.[1870] In 2019, Billy Birt would be alleged as one of the killers of Troy's first in-laws, and the murders of the Flemings would be compared to the murders of the Durhams.

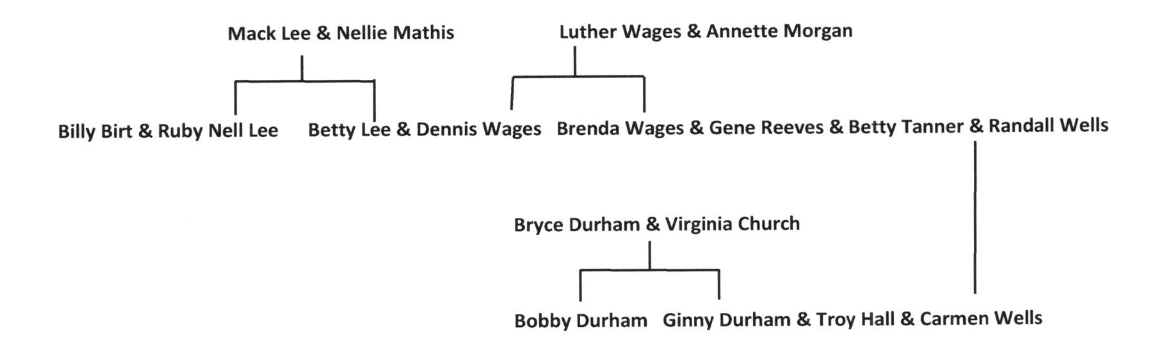

Around 1990, Troy learned that DUI and defensive driving schools were lucrative and, with the help of his brother Ray, he immediately endeavored to establish four of them in Georgia, including Lawrenceville (where Troy's law firm and other businesses were headquartered), Tucker, and Smyrna. To help run the schools, Troy employed his wife Carmen, his mother-in-law Betty Reeves, and a handful of others and paid for their certifications, which included training in alcohol and drug intervention – somewhat of an irony considering Troy's previous alleged drug use and trafficking. When establishing the location of the schools, Troy looked for stand-alone structures, such as an old extermination building in Snellville, Georgia, that could be tax write-offs. He also looked to open his schools in close proximity to existing, successful driving schools owned by others in a ploy to take business from them. In one instance, he purchased a former Huddle House that stood in the parking lot of a shopping center where another school was located but made sure his school would be the first one encountered as patrons entered the lot. Individuals looking to enroll in a driving school would think the first one they encountered was the only one located there. Although the State of Georgia had no regulations preventing this, it did not curtail complaints about Troy's "shenanigans" from other Gwinnett County area school owners whose feathers he had ruffled.[1871]

In another move exemplary of both Troy's intelligence and his strategic use of it, he chose the name "A-1" for his schools so that, whenever one searched for such a school within a directory, his would be the first to appear alphabetically. He also put his school's name and contact information on a van and parked it in front of one of the schools, thus leading potential students to select the school on the mistaken belief it provided a shuttle service. To further enhance his business, Troy sent one of his employees weekly to the local court to retrieve a list of the names and addresses of those who had recently been arrested for driving under the influence. Misappropriating letterhead with the Georgia State logo, he then mailed certified letters to those individuals instructing them they were required to enroll in one of his driving schools. This prompted further complaints from his competitors within the industry, and the state eventually put a stop to it.[1872]

Troy repeatedly pushed the boundaries of the state's regulations, using his knowledge as an attorney to defend his actions as mere interpretations of those regulations. The state would then have to clarify or amend their regulations to prevent further misinterpretations. According to a former employee of Troy's, "He was slick. He was real, real slick." While he was technically doing everything by the book, he was simultaneously taking advantage of loopholes the state had not yet addressed, and once they called him on a certain action, he would test them with another. Because Troy "fought back tooth and nail," because continual clarifications of regulations took time and money to hire attorneys, and because it became political, the state eventually shied away from him and left him alone. As one of the competing school owners said, "We couldn't get away with it; if it was us, they'd be all over us, but he [could] get away with that kind of stuff.... We're not Justin T. Hall."[1873]

While Troy was the boss overseeing the schools, his brother Ray signed employee paychecks. In fact, Troy never put his schools in his own name but put them in the names of family members. "Therefore," a former employee recalls, "he [Troy] didn't have to be investigated. He had to make sure he had everything sewn up." The same former employee recalls Troy being "in cahoots" with others and remembers thinking, "This man must lay awake at night thinking all this stuff. He has a mind like a bear trap.... I never underestimated him, for sure.... This man stayed on top of stuff. He always had a way around things."[1874]

Troy's law partner, Richard Loftis, continued working with him for a couple of years until February 1992,[1875] and among other responsibilities, he was tasked with handling DUI cases and representing Troy's driving schools. Troy was allegedly an incompetent attorney, who failed to perform any legal work for the duration of his partnership with Loftis. Rather, his days were spent overseeing the driving schools. Determined to monopolize the DUI driving school industry, Troy began branching out, eventually owning most of the schools in the metro-Atlanta area, including Decatur and Fulton County. A former employee likened him to McDonald's with a franchise on every corner. "He wanted to take over.... He was like a powerhouse in the business."[1876]

Whatever his daily business activities, Troy always engaged in them in the company of one female companion or another. Carmen suspected him of having an affair with a particular woman, and the extensive sexual proclivities he had demonstrated in North Carolina continued in Georgia, where his house was alleged to be equipped with mirrors and recording devices. He reportedly had multiple girlfriends and intimate partners, and he enjoyed telling others about his sexual escapades.[1877] Troy seemed to prefer manageable, subservient women who were beholden to him and who he could control. This was reflected in his alleged bringing of Asian women to the United States and grooming them to be part of his household and business interests. This was also evidenced in his relationship with Carmen, who had difficulty standing up for herself. In one friend's assessment, as long as Troy supported her and provided her with the things she wanted, Carmen, in her own self-interest, was willing to look the other way where it concerned his unscrupulous activities. She obeyed Troy's instruction and more or less played by his rules.[1878]

Troy and Carmen Hall separated around January 1, 1991,[1879] and Troy filed for divorce that March.[1880] Law partner Richard Loftis, represented Troy in the early phases of the divorce and through the emergency temporary relief hearing. Because Loftis lacked legal experience in divorce at that time, Troy subsequently retained an attorney with that specialization.[1881] During the divorce proceedings, Troy fired Carmen, her mother Betty, and others.[1882] Meanwhile, Carmen stated she was entitled to an equitable division of Troy's law practice, his chain of A-1 DUI and Defensive Driving Schools, Troy's construction company – Homes by Troy Hall, Inc. (which his brother John was given free rein to operate) – and all other assets, including property on Lake Lanier in Georgia, property in North Carolina, and insurance proceeds (reportedly $1 million[1883]) from the burning of their residence at 2091 Harbins Road in Dacula.[llllll] She also claimed entitlement to alimony, to a 1981 Cadillac El Dorado, and to sole ownership of their marital residence – a condominium at 1200 Country Court in Lawrenceville – as well as all the residence's furniture, furnishings, fixtures, and equipment.[1884]

In February 1992, Carmen filed a motion for emergency temporary relief, claiming Troy had fired her from the driving school, where she had been employed as an instructor, thereby depriving her of her only source of income, and that he had not provided her with any financial support. She also claimed he had cut off her utilities and was "selling off marital assets."[1885] In March, Carmen claimed Troy and his attorneys were attempting to transfer assets.[1886] That same month, Troy filed four motions to prevent Carmen and her attorney from making any direct or indirect reference in a jury trial to certain subjects, which he claimed would be prejudicial in the minds of the jurors. Among these potentially prejudicial subjects were Troy's sexual relations prior to his marriage to

[llllll] The burning of Troy and Carmen's home in Dacula may be the one recorded as occurring on Harbins Road at 12:07 AM on October 5, 1988. [Source: "Fire Calls In Gwinnett," *The Atlanta Journal-Constitution*, Atlanta, GA, October 7, 1988, p. 7.]

Carmen (on the basis that these were immaterial and unnecessary to the disposition of their divorce case, and that by Carmen's prior knowledge of these encounters and her marriage to Troy, she had "excused such events"). Also among the potentially prejudicial subjects were the deaths of Troy's in-laws by his first marriage and any attempt to introduce evidence possibly suggesting Troy as a suspect in their deaths, which Troy claimed would be "outrageously and unreasonably speculative…highly prejudicial," and irrelevant to his and Carmen's divorce case.[1887] Carmen had told a friend that Troy confided in her at some point during their relationship, saying that he had been a murder suspect, but beyond that, the friend believes Troy remained tight-lipped, and Carmen knew no details of the Durham murders.[1888]

Ultimately, their divorce settlement stated, among other things, that Troy was to pay Carmen $10,000 in alimony within ten days, an additional $5,000 after one year, an additional $5,000 after two years, and a final $10,000 after three years. As an equitable distribution for Carmen's property claims arising from their pre-martial relationship from 1984 to 1987, monthly mortgage payments of $750 for the condominium Carmen resided in would be deducted from the final payment. As part of the final settlement, Carmen, contrary to her claims the preceding May, stated she had no knowledge Troy had any proprietary interest in the driving schools, and she waived claims to certain assets, including Troy Hall Construction Company, Troy Hall Construction Company-Drywall Division, Homes by Troy Hall (including several houses and lots), A-1 DUI & Defensive Driving Schools (five locations), Ray Hall Construction Company (including houses and vacant lots), various properties in Georgia and North Carolina, the house Troy was residing in in Camden Forest and its furnishings, two Corvettes, a 1984 Jaguar XJS, 1984 Pontiac Fiero, 1979 Mercedes 450 SL, Mercedes 420 SEL, 1991 Cadillac Allante, 1948 Buick, 1983 Jaguar, and Ford pickup, a Spirit ski boat, furniture and furnishings at 255 Langley Drive, a new construction company Troy had formed, two new DUI & Defensive Driving Schools, a new insurance agency, and certain bank accounts and finances. Carmen confirmed she and Troy, prior to their marriage, had signed an agreement in February 1987 acknowledging certain real property was "the sole and exclusive property of Ray Hall," and she waived claims to it. This included four tracts of land in Gwinnett and DeKalb counties, several pieces of heavy equipment – backhoes, tractors, trailers, loaders, lowboys, pickups, and a 1979 SL450 Mercedes. Carmen was granted possession of her Cadillac and their Lawrenceville condominium and its furniture and furnishings with the exception of a mantel clock, an ivory chess set, clothing, jewelry, and any other personal property belonging to Troy. Likewise, Carmen would retain ownership of her personal belongings, clothing, and jewelry. A separate confidentiality agreement was included in the judgment but not filed for public record. If Carmen violated the agreement, she was to pay Troy $10,000, and if Troy filed an action against her and she was found not to be in violation, he would pay her an additional $10,000.[1889]

Troy and Carmen had no children together, and after their divorce, Carmen married auto mechanic Terry Wright.[1890] She eventually became a recluse and a devout Christian, while her new husband, though a good man, struggled with a gambling addiction. The two of them obsessively hoarded rabbits, which overtook and destroyed their townhouse. When Wright died of a massive heart attack, those who knew how heavily Carmen depended on him wondered who would take care of her. According to a friend, Carmen "was a sweetheart, [who] just encountered some crazy people and some crazy times."[1891] Carmen died of colon cancer in 2019.[1892]

On June 1, 2002,[1893] Troy married his third and last wife, Melanie Ann Giles, who was twenty-six years his junior,[1894] and who he had begun dating and living with shortly after she earned a bachelor's degree from the University of Georgia in 2000.[1895] Melanie's aunt, Laura Lee White was

Troy's close associate for more than twenty years and worked at one of his DUI and Defensive Driving Schools.[1896] Troy and Melanie had a son, Grant Tristin Hall, in 2007.[1897] At that time, they lived in a condominium at 4226 Baverton Drive in Suwanee, Georgia, a property Troy had purchased in December 2006 with nearly $246,000 in funds gifted to him by his brother Ray, the funds being derived from insurance proceeds for a house fire at Ray's home at 3788 Sweet Bottom Drive in Duluth. Ray had deeded the Baverton Drive property solely to Troy, and it was conveyed as a gift with Troy making no payments to any lien or mortgage holder or to Ray. *[Troy would deed the property back to Ray in September 2012.]*[1898]

Meanwhile, Troy was involved with political lobbying, and between 2006 and 2017, he contributed nearly $25,000 to the campaigns of various Republican candidates (including Mitt Romney) running for both state and federal offices.[1899] In 2007, as attorney for A-1 Driving School and under the name of Justin Hall, he wrote a letter to *The Atlanta Constitution* advocating the blocking of a bill that would allow traffic violators to have their drivers' licenses reinstated upon completion of an online course[1900][mmmmmmm] – likely an attempt to protect his own financial interests by forcing offenders to enroll in brick and mortar schools such as his own. Between 2008 and 2010, Troy was registered as an active lobbyist with the Georgia Government Transparency and Campaign Finance Commission (formerly known as the State Ethics Commission), representing the Driving Educators of Georgia (DEOG). During those years of activity, the only expense he submitted was a $100 meal on March 20, 2008, during which he hosted Georgia State Senator Donald Kenneth "Don" Balfour II.[1901]

Between 1987 and 2011, Troy was affiliated with multiple businesses, both S and C corporations, partnerships, and/or limited liability corporations (LLCs) in Georgia (most since dissolved), primarily using the name Justin T. Hall. In some instances, he was listed as a registered agent, a role he may have merely filled as an attorney on behalf of various clients without having any ownership or interest in those businesses. In the following instances, however, he and/or his brothers Ray and John held official positions:

- United Financial Leasing, Inc.[1902]
- Troy Hall Construction[1903]
- Homes by Troy Hall, Inc.[1904]
- A Advocacy Atlanta Law Firm of Justin T. Hall, PC[1905]
- Justin T. Hall, Atty.[1906]
- Law Firm of Justin T. Hall[1907]
- Public Adjusters, Inc.[1908]
- A-1 Counseling, Inc.[1909]
- A-1 Driving School, Inc.[1910]
- Chamblee DUI & Defensive Driving School, Inc.[1911]
- Secret Witness Detective Agency, Inc.[1912]
- Creative Insurance Company[1913]
- North Wilkesboro Services, Inc.[1914]
- Leased Centers of Georgia, LLC[1915]
- Hall & Loftis[1916]
- Drive Now[1917]

[mmmmmmm] Troy's wife Melanie wrote a similar letter a month later. [Source: "Don't take it easy on DUIs," *The Atlanta Journal-Constitution*, Atlanta, GA, March 19, 2007, p. A10.]

In addition to his business ventures, Troy amassed a substantial amount of property, which may have included personal residences, vacation homes, businesses, rentals, and apartments. Of these thirty properties, nineteen were also associated with his brother Ray and one with his brother John. Ray and John independently held additional properties. Between the three brothers, their holdings were located in Dacula, Norcross, Duluth, Lawrenceville, Palmetto, Lilburn, Berkeley Lake, Gainesville, Suwanee, Forest Park, Jonesboro, Athens, Snellville, Conyers, Oakwood, Buford, Canton, East Point, and Peachtree Corners, Georgia; Seneca, South Carolina; Hickory, Wilkesboro, North Wilkesboro, Conover, and Newton, North Carolina; and Westchester, Illinois.

Aside from his property holdings, Ray Hall owned and operated a number of DUI and defensive driving schools (typically under the name of "A-1") in Lawrenceville, Marietta, Conyers, and Buford, Georgia as well as one in Seneca, South Carolina. At one time, Troy was listed as the Chief Financial Officer for the school in Lawrenceville. Meanwhile, John Hall (aka Carrington) owned and operated a contractor's business in Seneca.

While many of Troy's and Ray's businesses operate(d) at 225/255 Langley Drive in Lawrenceville, Ray's home at 3788 Sweet Bottom Drive in Duluth has been, at one time or another, listed as the residence of Troy, Ray, Ray's last wife, Josephina "Josey" Elley Hall (from the Micronesian island of Kosrae[1918]), and John Hall Carrington as well as the business address for A-1 DUI Defensive Driving School, Driving Educators of Georgia, Wayne Capital Investors, LLC, My Rich Girl's Closet, LLC, Troy Hall Construction, Thomas Gearin Plumbing Co., Josey's Something Special, and Ray Hall Incorporated (maker of residential cabinets).[1919]

This colonial style, two-story, six-bedroom, nine-bath, 18,020 square-foot home with a four-car garage and a private 608 square-foot swimming pool was built in 1995 by Troy Hall Construction, Inc. (Ray Hall, CEO). Sitting on a 1.21-acre lot that Ray purchased in 1993 for $45,000, it is valued at approximately $2 million.[1920] In May 2011, Troy, his wife Melanie, and their son Grant moved into this home, which they shared with Ray and Ray's wife and daughter. Reportedly, the two halves of the house in which each family lived were mirror images. Troy had no ownership in the property.[1921]

Hall Residence in Duluth, Georgia

Troy and Melanie Hall separated in August 2012[1922] and divorced the following month in Gwinnett County, Georgia.[1923] Their ensuing settlement drama became so litigious it spanned the course of more than five years. Troy, the boy from the wrong side of the tracks in Wilkes County, North Carolina, who once lived in a trailer park and persistently vowed at age twenty in 1972 that "he would get money someday" and show the people back home, now occupied a mansion and seemingly achieved his goal of wealth. But he would soon claim to have lost that wealth...along with his mind.

During the divorce proceedings, Troy stated he had numerous physical ailments, including Parkinson's disease, that greatly impaired his ability to work outside the home, and as of September 2011, he had resigned as an employee and officer at A-1/DUI Defensive Driving School. By August 2012, he had exhausted his sick leave, and he subsequently applied for Social Security Disability. He stated his health prevented him from maintaining his businesses, including Hall Holding Company, and that his brother Ray was the owner and manager of those businesses. He also said he owed Ray approximately $1 million in loans and notes for various business enterprises, and he had to borrow funds from Ray to pay his attorney's fees.[1924]

According to Troy, on Friday, September 14, 2012, Melanie and her attorney "sent over a settlement agreement that would completely bankrupt him." Ray went with him to see Troy's attorney, who advised Troy not to sign the agreement. A day later, Melanie brought over a new agreement, not substantially different from the first, and Troy claimed it would have cost him approximately $1 million – money which he said he did not have.[1925] In this agreement, Melanie relinquished her interests in properties in Duluth, Suwanee, Jonesboro, Athens, Forest Park, Snellville, Decatur, Gainesville, and Riverdale, Georgia. She further relinquished her interests in Hall Holding Company, LLC, United Financial Leasing, Inc., Troy Hall Construction, Inc., and A-1 DUI and Defensive Driving School, A-1 Driving School, Inc. The agreement stated both parties had divided to their mutual satisfaction bank, stock, and retirement accounts as well as furniture, furnishings, fixtures, equipment, and all jointly owned personal property. Melanie, however, was to retain exclusive ownership of her jewelry and was entitled to a Yorkshire Terrier named Vegas. Troy was to pay Melanie $300,000 as a property settlement as well as assume responsibility for $30,000 of American Express charges incurred by Melanie that year. Melanie was to retain a 2007 Lexus RX350, while Troy would retain a 2002 Lexus SC430. Both parties would have joint custody of their son, with Melanie having physical custody. Troy was to be exclusively responsible for the cost of their son Grant's four-year college education, including tuition, books, fees, room, and board, and he was to maintain an Edward Jones account in the amount of approximately $75,000 for that purpose. Troy was to assume responsibility for their son's health insurance and healthcare expenses and maintain insurance policies on his [Troy's] life totaling $3,750,000, naming the Grant T. Hall Life Insurance Trust as the beneficiary. The yearly premiums for these policies were estimated to be a total of $16,000, which Troy would pay. Upon Troy's death and until Grant reached the age of twenty-five, the trust was to provide Melanie with an annual stipend of $50,000 per year, payable in quarterly installments. Additionally, Troy was to pay Melanie $4,167 per month in child support until Grant was eighteen or had graduated from high school, and an additional $4,167 per month in alimony for a five-year period, as well as assume responsibility for tax on the alimony payments and maintain Melanie's health insurance premium for a three-year period. Troy was to also pay $5,000 to Melanie's attorney.[1926]

One of the articles within the settlement agreement stipulated, among other things, that each party was entering into it freely and voluntarily, had read each page carefully before signing, had "ascertained and weighed all the facts and circumstances likely to influence their judgment," and clearly understood and assented to all the provisions of the agreement. Despite the fact both Troy and Melanie signed the settlement agreement,[1927] one month later, on October 17, 2012, Troy filed a motion to set aside the agreement and the final judgment and decree on the basis he was (and had been) mentally ill and incompetent and "incapable of managing his estate and entering into contracts." The motion further stated Troy did not experience any "lucid intervals" as defined by Georgia law, he was unable to comprehend the value of his current assets and his inability to be employed, and his incompetency to manage his financial affairs put him in a treacherous position of being permanently in contempt of the settlement agreement because he was and would forever be incapable of performing those obligations. The motion requested the court to appoint a guardian to handle Troy's affairs.[1928]

In support of this motion, Troy's attorney submitted an October 16, 2012 affidavit from Dr. David S. Lipsig, an Atlanta psychiatrist, who had conducted an almost four-hour psychiatric evaluation of Troy four days prior to assess his "psychiatric condition and cognitive capacity in order to determine his competency to contract." When Troy arrived on time for his appointment with Lipsig, in the company of his brother Ray, "he was alert and oriented to person, place and situation," but he did not know the date or time. "He was dressed appropriately and appeared to have appropriate hygiene. He shuffled his steps when he walked and had a noticeable tremor that greatly affected his ability to write. He looked older than his stated age [of sixty]. He was friendly and cooperative…[and] made appropriate eye contact. His speech was low in volume and difficult to understand at times. Although he answered the questions asked, he would provide different answers at times when the same question was asked…."[1929]

Lipsig's multipage assessment included Troy's historical background (which made mention of his previous two marriages but no mention of his former in-laws' murders), his current life, and his health (including his psychiatric history and treatment, medical history, and twenty-three separate medications he was taking). According to Troy and medical records, he suffered from a long list of conditions:

- Parkinson's disease (late stage)
- Depression
- Anxiety
- Asthma (chronic obstructive)
- Bronchiectasis (chronic with acute exacerbation)
- Dementia/Memory Loss
- Extensive Sinus Disease
- Obstructive Pulmonary Disease
- Speech problems
- Balance problems
- History of Hepatitis
- Double Hernia (requiring surgery)[1930]

Troy told Lipsig that, in December 2010, he began struggling to remember people's names. The following month, his pulmonologist was concerned he had Parkinson's disease, and this was confirmed by a neurologist, who stated the disease was progressing rapidly. Troy subsequently began experiencing a lot of anxiety and was placed on a number of medications. He told Lipsig he and Melanie had a perfect marriage until he told her about his diagnosis, after which point he believed she became distant and spent less time around him. Troy subsequently hired a private detective and accused his wife of an extramarital affair. He reportedly suggested couples counseling, which did not materialize, and in July 2012, he gave Melanie an ultimatum about their marriage. Six days later, Melanie filed for divorce, and according to Troy, she withdrew and charged a total of $70,300 from a variety of accounts, some of which she had no authorization for, including individual accounts in his name alone and a credit card business account belonging to his brother Ray. Troy stated he did not initially contest the withdrawals because he did not wish to sue the mother of his child. The two then hired their respective divorce attorneys.[1931] At one point, Troy had sought representation from a former law associate and begged him to reduce his retainer fee and hourly rate, claiming he had fallen on hard times. The attorney declined.[1932]

Troy recalled extended arguments with his wife the weekend she brought him the settlement agreement, and he said that Sunday, September 16, 2012, he was on multiple medications and was extremely anxious, feeling as if ants were crawling inside him and he needed to get out of his own skin. He doubled his antidepressant and took a high dosage of Valium for anxiety. The remainder of the day was unclear to him other than "snapshots" of time he recalled. He remembered looking at the settlement papers but did not read them and, although he signed them, he did not recall doing so. He stated he had hallucinations that "the walls were moving in and out, as if they were breathing," he heard a buzzing sound, and he felt as if things were not real, as if he was watching himself on television. He also felt suicidal and had planned to take a gun from his safe and place it in his mouth. He knew his life insurance policies excluded suicide for the first two years but was aware the exclusion would end on October 31. He shared that he felt suicide would be his only logical choice as it would financially provide for his son and wife and, due to the fact "he could no longer work and only had several hundred dollars to his name," it would prevent him from being a burden to Ray, who was financially supporting him. Lipsig asked Troy why he had given Melanie approximately $300,000 from the sale of a townhouse and why he had waited until this time to contest the divorce settlement, but the answer Troy provided was he had only considered not killing himself within the preceding week. Ray did not know until days later that Troy had signed the papers, and when he asked why he signed, Troy said, "I just don't know what else to do." He later saw Troy crying, gun in hand. In a later, more lucid moment, Troy realized signing the agreement had been a mistake.[1933]

Troy told Lipsig he had never previously seen a psychiatrist or received any form of therapy or counseling. He denied any history of psychiatric hospitalizations and had only previously been on antidepressants for a brief period in the 1990s. He stated there was no history of psychiatric, drug, or alcohol problems in his family other than his father's alcoholism, and there was no family history of completed suicides. He said he had no history of legal difficulties, DUIs, or arrests and had never filed for bankruptcy.[1934]

Troy stated he had "felt sad most days" since early June, and he had difficulty maintaining sleep, no interest in pleasurable activities, feelings of guilt and worthlessness, decreased energy and concentration, loss of appetite, and suicidal ideations. "He denied ever having any homicidal ideations." He described his typical routine as going to his room for the night around 8:00 PM, falling asleep around 9:30 PM without difficulty, waking up around 4:30 AM and lying in bed thinking, going back to sleep between 6:30 and 7:00 AM, and getting up at 9:30 AM. Ray cooked his breakfast, and he took his medications with a Coke to help prevent nausea. He showered and shaved once every two days and would spend most of his days sitting and watching television. He might eat a piece of fruit for lunch and another piece of fruit for dinner. He typically did not leave the house, and he did not venture outdoors as it made his asthma worse. He quit driving a year prior (in 2011) after having sneezed and passed out on two occasions. He did not perform any chores around the house and had no social activity other than Ray taking him out to lunch on rare occasions. Troy stated when he tried to go out with his wife, she refused.[1935]

During Troy's evaluation, Lipsig administered the Folstein Mini-Mental State Examination to determine cognitive impairment. Troy scored 21 of 30 possible points, an indicator of mild impairment.[1936] The nine missed points consisted of three for being unable to recall the season, date, or day of the week; three for failure to recall three objects after three minutes; and three for being unable to serially state sevens. He was unable to spell "world" backwards but could recall four digits forward and three digits backward. He could name the current U. S. President and could name his predecessors back to George Bush, Sr. [sic]. He demonstrated an ability to think abstractly by interpreting proverbs. "When asked what he would do if he found a stamped, addressed envelope on the street, he responded, 'Pick it up and stick in the mailbox depending on the condition of the envelope.' When asked what he would do if he were in a crowded movie theater and a fire broke out, he responded, 'Get my family to the door then yell fire.' When asked if there was any concern regarding yelling 'fire,' he responded, 'Not if it's a real fire.' When asked to describe a similarity between an orange and a ball, he responded, 'They both are circles.' When asked to describe a similarity between a bird and an airplane, he responded, 'Both can fly.'" When tested for malingered (i.e., exaggerated, feigned/faked) cognitive problems, "he scored adequately" so that Lipsig "did not find any evidence that [he] was malingering," and that "malingering was not a significant issue with this evaluation."[1937]

Troy "cried throughout a large portion of the evaluation," and Lipsig believed he was exhibiting symptoms of severe depression and anxiety. Lipsig also believed Troy "had so many risk factors for suicide," he recommended he be hospitalized due to safety concerns. Troy "was resistant to this idea and said that he would not commit suicide." Upon Lipsig's recommendation, Ray Hall subsequently drove Troy to the in-patient psychiatric Peachford Hospital in Atlanta where he was voluntarily admitted for further evaluation and treatment. Ray and Lipsig also agreed the gun should be removed from the home, and Ray stated it would be done.[1938]

Lipsig concluded "with a reasonable degree of medical certainty, there was sufficient evidence that Mr. Hall was not competent to sign a contract at the time of this evaluation." He also stated Troy did poorly on the cognitive portion of his evaluation, and "these cognitive deficits were significantly below what would be expected for his level of education." Lipsig said some of Troy's medications had "the potential to interfere with cognition," and the effects of them could be compounded through drug interactions when taken together. Lipsig also concluded that, although he had not evaluated Troy on the day he signed the divorce papers, there "was sufficient evidence to support that his condition was as bad, if not worse, at the time he signed [them]."[1939]

In November 2012, motions were filed to hold Troy in contempt for failing to pay alimony, to incarcerate him for the same, and to delay the ruling on Troy's request to set aside the divorce settlement so that Melanie could conduct discovery and obtain an expert to support her denial of

Troy's allegations.[1940] In a December response to the contempt motion, Troy again stated his inability to pay due to his mental incapacity, adding that he had already liquidated all his assets in order to pay Melanie the lump sum of $300,000 in an effort to comply with the court's order.[1941] That same month, another motion was filed to hold Troy in contempt for failing to pay child support and to incarcerate him for the same.[1942]

In January 2013, Melanie filed a motion for attorney's fees, stating she was a stay-at-home wife and mother during her marriage to Troy, and she was never employed other than assisting in the operations and management of Troy's businesses or real property holdings. She stated Troy had "assets, businesses, [and] real property holdings to pursue this litigation," and she requested the court to award her $20,000 in temporary attorney's fees to defend the litigation.[1943]

Meanwhile, various motions had been filed regarding questions to be answered, documents and other evidence to be produced, and the scheduling of depositions of both parties. Among the more unique things Melanie requested Troy to produce were any materials related to any surveillance or investigation of her conducted by Troy or anyone on his behalf, any materials in Troy's possession or being held by anyone or any entity related to her conduct (including notes, cards, letters, photographs, recordings, e-mails, and clothing), any gifts or documentation of gifts to or from any person Troy had had sexual intercourse or a sexual relationship with other than Melanie since their marriage date, documents related to any periods of time Troy had rendezvoused with any woman in a hotel or motel room, duplex, apartment, house, condominium, lodge, or cabin since January 1, 2007, current and expired or cancelled passports Troy had possessed in the past five years, and any documents related to gambling, including amounts and dates of wagers and amounts of money won or lost.[1944]

In response to Melanie's interrogatories, Troy listed his possible witnesses as Ray Hall (who would testify to his observances of Troy's physical and mental condition when the settlement was signed, Troy's estates, and any relevant business transactions between him and Troy), attorney Margaret Washburn (who would testify to her observances of Troy's physical and medical condition when the settlement was signed), and a private investigator (who would testify regarding his surveillance of Melanie). Troy further stated he might call as expert witnesses Dr. David Lipsig (who would testify regarding Troy's mental condition), Dr. Lawrence Kaplan (a pulmonologist who would testify regarding Troy's physical and mental condition), pharmacist Bill Mason (who would testify regarding drug interactions associated with the combination of medications prescribed to and taken by Troy), and attorney Dan Britt (who would testify regarding business transactions between Ray's and Troy's business entities, the liens Ray had on Troy's interests in the businesses, and the legal problems associated with the life insurance plans that the divorce settlement had set forth). In addition to Lipsig and Kaplan, Troy stated he had also been treated by Karina Barrantes, C.M.A. (a certified medical assistant), Mark Harris, M.D. (a neurologist), Daniel Eisenman, Ph.D. (a neuropsychologist), and Prof. Daniel Jeanmonod, M.D.,[1945] (a Swiss neurosurgeon).[1946]

Melanie had intended to video Troy's deposition on January 24, 2013, and Troy's attorney, Patrick "Leh" Meriwether, was to take Melanie's deposition once Troy's was completed, but the afternoon prior to the deposition, Meriwether, submitted a second affidavit from psychiatrist David Lipsig. The affidavit was preceded by a letter from Meriwether to Melanie's attorney and began, "I ask that you read this letter with a spirit of compassion and try to understand that we are not simply litigating over procedural issues or money – there is potentially a man's life at stake." The letter went on to say Lipsig indicated Troy was totally incapacitated and at high risk for suicide, and that, if he was forced to proceed with a deposition or trial, "he could be faced with hospitalization or worse." Meriwether wrote, "I cannot in good conscience subject my client to a proceeding that might kill him without the prescribed safeguards in place. I am faced with the additional, ethical issue of representing a client in need of a guardian, and you understand that until such time a guardian is appointed, I cannot even proceed with settlement discussions.... I have no choice but to take all measures to protect my client's life, in addition to his legal position." Meriwether further stated he "could not consent to a videotaped deposition. Subjecting this fragile man to the added stress of video scrutiny is unnecessary and could even push him over the edge."[1947]

Attached to Meriwether's letter was the second affidavit from Lipsig, which stated he found Troy to be mentally ill with significant cognitive impairments, lacking "sufficient understanding or capacity to make significant, responsible decisions," and incapable of managing his estate. Lipsig stated that, "unless proper management is provided," Troy's property "will be wasted or dissipated," and he had concerns about Troy proceeding with the divorce case "without being under the care of a psychiatrist and therapist to treat his severe depression." Lipsig said Troy had "anxiety, confusion, poor focus, and poor short-term memory associated with dementia, depression, and multiple prescribed medications." He added, "There are no foreseeable limits on the duration of such incapacity." Lipsig's findings were based on a further evaluation of Troy, which Lipsig considered to be an addendum to his report from the preceding October. For an hour and a half on January 18, 2013, and for an additional one hour and ten minutes on January 21, Lipsig interviewed Troy, and he spent a total of fifty minutes interviewing Ray Hall on those same dates. Troy arrived with Ray at Lipsig's Atlanta office and, according to Lipsig, Troy 'was alert and oriented to person and situation...to city and state, [and] to the day of the week, [but] he was not aware of the season, date, month or year, [and] he did not know the name of the building, area or county where the evaluation took place." Troy believed it was December prior to Christmas, and when he would leave the office, he frequently became confused about where to return and had to be redirected. Lipsig stated Troy was appropriately dressed and "appeared to have fair hygiene. He wore an oxygen nasal cannula connected to an oxygen tank that he wheeled into the office. He shuffled his steps when he walked and had a noticeable tremor that greatly affected his ability to write. He looked older than his stated age [of sixty-one]. He made appropriate eye contact. His speech was low in volume and difficult to understand."[1948]

Lipsig obtained Troy's medical, pharmacy, and Social Security records from various providers, and interviewed and obtained information from neuropsychologist Daniel Eisenman, Ph.D., who had seen Troy on three occasions in November 2012 in order to evaluate him, but who had never treated him. Eisenman stated Troy had been having problems with his memory since January 2011 and struggled with forgetting recent events, information he had read, details of conversations, and names of familiar people as well as misplacing items (e.g., placing mayonnaise in the freezer), entering a room and forgetting his intended action, and not understanding how to use his computer. Troy told Eisenman he required assistance with keeping track of appointments, driving, meal preparation, and managing his medications and finances, and that Ray was his main caregiver. During the tests Eisenman administered, he found Troy to be pleasant, cooperative, motivated, and making an effort, but his repetition capabilities were impaired, and he had significant difficulty sustaining attention. Eisenman determined Troy demonstrated "evidence of a mild Parkinson's related cognitive impairment," and he had "significant problems with the acquisition and registration of new information." His ability to retain information ranged from average to mildly impaired, although his retention capacity was enhanced when information was presented more than once. Troy also exhibited dysfunction in verbal reasoning and staying on task during complex verbal reasoning. He also demonstrated weakness in the areas of global cognition, verbal fluency, divided attention, and visual perception reasoning. Eisenman also found Troy to be significantly depressed and told him he might need assistance with certain tasks, that he needed continued follow-up with a neurologist, and that he could benefit from continued psychotherapy. Multiple severe psychosocial stressors were determined to include his Parkinson's disease diagnosis, his wife's alleged infidelity, being served with divorce papers, being unable to work due to illness, financial stressors, and the legal issues involved with his divorce.[1949]

During Lipsig's more recent evaluation, Troy stated that, following his three-day admission to Peachford Hospital in October, he believed he had gone to a therapist but was unsure of the dates or duration of his treatment. He said he "did not find the therapy to be helpful [and] he was unsure if he was currently seeing a psychiatrist." Lipsig learned three psychiatric medications had been filled at a pharmacy and had been prescribed by different providers. By this time, Troy was taking a total of twenty medications, and Lipsig was very concerned when he learned Troy was responsible for keeping track of his medications and the system he was using could be prone to mistakes. Lipsig stated the medications could cause sedation, contribute to Troy's confusion, and negatively impair his cognition.[1950]

When Lipsig asked Troy how he had been doing since October, Troy stated he was having a lot of difficulties, feeling severely depressed, sad, hopeless, and worthless on a daily basis. He had difficulty sleeping, decreased energy and appetite, lack of interest in activities, feelings of guilt, and problems with concentration. When Lipsig asked if he was having suicidal thoughts, Troy responded, "Not like I was. I mean I want to see how the court case comes out. I want to see my son grow up." Troy then began to cry. Lipsig asked him if he had thought about suicide in the event the case did not go his way. Troy answered, "I haven't thought about it. I just try to stay positive." Still, he admitted that the court case caused him to be very anxious. As in October, Troy "denied ever having any homicidal ideations." Although he was at times tearful, Troy would, at other times, "have a flat affect," which Lipsig stated was "typically seen in someone with Parkinson's disease." Troy shared he was having frequent problems with hallucinations, sometimes believing he heard his son giggling in the next room when his son was not actually in the house. At other times he believed his ex-wife and son "were in the room sleeping at night, [and] if he needed to get up, he would be careful not to wake them." After some time, he would realize they no longer lived there. He would also mistake a dream for reality or believe a conversation had taken place when it had not. In terms of concentration and memory, he would forget numbers such as his bank card PIN and would enter a room multiple times, forgetting what he was looking for. He stated he was unable to follow the plot of a television show or movie. He continued to live in Ray's home in Duluth, and although Melanie and Grant had moved out, he shared the house with Ray, Ray's wife, Ray's daughter and son-in-law, and Ray's sister-in-law and her three sons. Troy related his daily activities: Ray would wake him at 6:30 AM, Troy would brush his teeth and then share a breakfast with Ray that Ray had prepared; then Troy would brush his teeth again. Afterwards he would go downstairs, take his medication, and try to watch television but would forget the storyline. Lipsig noted Troy's thoughts then became "very tangential" and disorganized, providing "a story or answer that had little relation to the question asked." Troy told of his sister [Lois] dying of cancer and his paralegal (a close friend) dying of a stroke. When redirected, Troy "would attempt to provide an answer to the question asked" but would often say "he did not remember or recall." Troy told Lipsig he sometimes ate lunch and sometimes skipped it altogether. Sometimes he tried to clean up. He usually had a banana sandwich for dinner at 6:00 PM and would afterwards sit in front of the television. He would go to bed at 8:00 PM but would wake up four or five times a night.[1951]

Troy once again took a Folstein Mini-Mental State Examination, this time scoring 18 (down from the previous 21) of 30 points. Points were deducted for failing to correctly answer questions about the year, season, date, month, time, and place, for failing to repeat three objects, to recall three objects in three minutes, to state serial sevens, to spell "world" backwards, to repeat a sentence, and to follow a three-stage command. He was able to recall three digits forward and two digits in reverse. As in October, he was asked what he would do if he found a stamped, addressed envelope on the street and what he would do if he was in a crowded movie theater when a fire broke out. This time he answered the first question by saying, "Just probably walk on," and the second question by saying, "If I had my son or somebody with me, I would exit and yell 'fire' by the exit. If by myself, I would just yell 'fire.'" As before, he stated an orange and a ball were both round, and a bird and airplane both flew, and he could name Barack Obama as the current president and George Bush, Jr. [sic] as the previous president, but no further back. He again demonstrated the ability to think abstractly by interpreting proverbs. Once again, a separate test and other questions indicated Troy was being open and honest, and there was no evidence of malingering – something Eisenman also confirmed from his time with Troy.[1952]

Ray Hall told Lipsig he believed Troy was going to kill himself at the time of the previous evaluation in October but did not believe Troy felt that way anymore. He confirmed Troy's constant moments of confusion and gave an example of Troy believing he had a meeting with someone and Ray calling that person only to confirm he or she had not even spoken with Troy. Ray stated that, although Troy could easily tell a story from the distant past, he would often forget to eat breakfast, forget what he was doing, confuse dreams with reality, and often need to be redirected from an idea. When Troy tried to copy papers, he would copy the wrong ones and put them together incorrectly. Ray tearfully told Lipsig "how difficult it was to see [his brother] like this," and said he felt Troy was very depressed and incapable of managing his own affairs. He said Troy was focused "on his son being looked after."[1953]

On February 4, 2013, in response to the letter from Troy's attorney and the second affidavit from Lipsig, Melanie agreed to postpone Troy's deposition until an independent medical exam could be obtained, but Troy's attorney refused to consent to such an exam due to Troy's incompetence. On the basis that this refusal demonstrated bad faith on the parts of Troy and his counsel, Melanie then filed a motion requiring Troy to have an independent medical examination with a psychologist and psychiatrist of her choosing and to produce all medical, psychological, and pharmacy records. This motion also revisited the fact that Melanie had previously filed contempt motions against Troy for failure to pay court-ordered child support and alimony, and this failure to pay was a conspiracy meant to bankrupt her. Melanie stated Troy knew she had not been employed since she had graduated from college, after which she immediately began dating and living with him. Meanwhile, Troy continued "to spend hundreds of dollars to litigate this issue, while failing to pay support for his child." As a result, Melanie put him and his attorneys on notice she intended to file a frivolous litigation suit against them.[1954]

On February 20, 2013, Troy filed a motion to dispute Melanie's previous claims that he had "assets, businesses, [and] real property holdings to pursue this litigation," and he again stated he had, with the assistance of family members, liquidated all his assets to pay Melanie $300,000 in cash. He further stated she had received $5,000 toward her lawyer's fees, and she had paid her lawyer an additional $20,000 by using his and Ray's American Express credit cards. Troy stated Melanie also used a company account to take an additional $10,000, she had received more than $30,000 from their joint banking accounts, and she received a paid-for car and around $120,000 in jewelry. Finally, he once more reiterated that his disability and unemployment prevented him from paying further attorney's fees for Melanie.[1955]

The following day, the court ordered Justin Troy Hall, aka Troy Justin Hall, aka Troy Hall, aka Justin Hall to present himself to Dr. Julie Rand (a forensic psychiatrist), and Dr. Adriana Flores (a forensic psychologist), for examination and evaluation, to fully cooperate with them, to promptly pay them for their services, and to provide them with his medical history, documents, providers, medications, and treatments, including records from Peachford Hospital or clinics in Zurich.[1956] Dr. Rand and Dr. Flores, who were, by this time in private practices, had both previously worked at Atlanta's Georgia Regional Hospital, one of the state's six psychiatric hospitals. Dr. Rand had, for many years, worked as one of the lead evaluators on the hospital's forensic unit for patients who were found incompetent to stand trial or to assess them for criminal responsibility or insanity.[1957] Dr. Flores had also worked many years on the forensic unit, primarily to evaluate, train, do group therapy, and testify in court regarding persons who had been determined to be criminally insane or not guilty by reason of insanity.[1958] Dr. Rand and Dr. Flores were to determine Troy's competency at the time he signed the divorce settlement in September 2012, his current competency, whether he was capable of understanding the nature and object of the court proceedings, and whether he comprehended his own condition in reference to the proceedings in the Superior and Probate Courts of Gwinnett County.[1959] Records do not indicate if they actually met with or evaluated Troy.

By this time, the case had been heavily litigated, and the judge stated, "This case is going to get back on track. Counsel are going to reasonably confer and do their best to maximize the efficiency of these proceedings."[1960] Troy had become so litigious that the judge issued an order requiring him to litigate in good faith. For her part of the litigation, Melanie subpoenaed third party insurance providers for three past property fire claims and life insurance applications showing assets Troy owned at or around the time of the divorce filing. After the court required a deposition from Troy, he claimed to be too ill to sit for it, and he settled his case against Melanie.[1961]

On March 11, 2013, some modifications were made to the settlement agreement, mostly pertaining to Troy's maintenance of life insurance policies benefitting trusts for his son, making Troy the sole proprietor of any funds left over from the Edward Jones account for his son's college expenses, and prohibiting Troy from filing for further modifications for a four-year period. The court ordered Troy to pay $50,409, which included $8,391 for arrearages of child support, $16,668 for arrearages of alimony, $2,850 for reimbursement of his son's unpaid medical expenses, and $22,500 for attorney's fees and costs of litigation. Melanie's motions for contempt were denied, and Troy's motion to set aside the settlement agreement was also denied.[1962]

Troy agreed to take no action to modify his support obligations for four years,[1963] but in March 2017, almost four years to the date of their divorce, he filed a petition to modify the final judgment and decree on the basis that his circumstances had changed and he was destitute. He stated he had exhausted all financial means to pay child support, including selling all of his assets and spending all his resources on his son. He further said his Parkinson's disease had worsened to the point he was reliant on 24-hour supervision, and he had a feeding tube and was on oxygen. He claimed his only source of income was Social Security Disability, which was paying a portion of the child support. Because he had to hire an attorney to petition the court for a reduction in child support, he also sought to be awarded those attorney's fees.[1964] Troy and Melanie then entered a "Final Consent Order on Modification Action," which consisted of several modifications. The divorce settlement also excluded Melanie from making any future claims for alimony, and it relieved her of any obligations to perform work or functions at A-1 DUI & Defensive Driving School, Inc.[1965]

In May 2017, because Troy had failed to willingly comply with the final modifications to their settlement, Melanie filed a motion for contempt against him. On the basis that he had previously alleged almost the exact same circumstances in his March 2013 attempt to set aside the final judgment and decree of divorce that had resulted in the original modification, she asked the court to dismiss his March 2017 petition for modification, and she sought to recoup her attorney's fees and expenses.[1966] Melanie did not believe Troy's circumstances had changed, but there had been one noteworthy probate action in Gwinnett County which had pronounced Troy as incompetent. Troy indicated, however, that he was later adjudged to be once more competent. Troy had made changes to the insurance policies, but Melanie did not know if he was competent when those changes were made, and even if the changes were valid, she believed them to not comply with the agreed upon terms. As a result of this dispute, both parties agreed full access to all probate actions involving Troy in Georgia, and specifically Gwinnett County, be given to each of their attorneys.[1967]

In late June 2017, Melanie filed a motion for a Gwinnett County Superior Court judge to hear the case, but it was denied in July. The motion stated she and Troy had "a history of litigation that involves a complicated set of allegations, including but not limited to, that Justin Hall fraudulently transferred all marital and separate individual assets to his brother, Ray Hall, or other persons for the purpose of avoiding equitable division of property and alimony expenses in his divorce." That same month it was verified Troy was an inactive member in good standing of the Georgia State Bar and there was no record of public disciplinary action between January 1991 and June 2017.[1968]

In August 2017, a summary of Troy's income and expenses showed he earned $1,894 in Social Security Disability or Retirement Benefits and had $325.31 in a Wells Fargo account. His Social Security benefits for 2016 totaled $22,666.80. His monthly expenses totaled $2,616.72 and consisted of health insurance for himself ($379.68), health and dental insurance for his son ($136), life insurance premiums ($1,441.04), a cell phone bill ($40), grooming expenses ($50), and miscellaneous out of pocket medical, household, and grocery expenses ($450).[1969]

In February 2018, it was outlined that Troy's total monthly income was $2,148 from Social Security Disability. Based on the pro rata shares of his and Melanie's combined income, Troy's portion of the basic child support obligation was determined to be 44.55% or $400 per month.[1970] In March 2018, it was determined Troy would pay that amount to Melanie (who, by this time, had moved to Alpharetta, Georgia[1971] and had been working five years as a home healthcare software implementation consultant[1972]), and he would continue providing health insurance coverage for their son as well as pay for 100% of their son's health care expenses not covered by insurance.[1973] In addition to these determinations, it was ordered Troy would reimburse Melanie $12,625, which she had paid for their son's 2017-2018 school year at Notre Dame Academy,[1974] a private Catholic school for grades K-12 in Duluth,[1975] and the reimbursement would be paid in twelve consecutive monthly installments of $1,052. He was also to cover tuition, uniforms, books, fees, etc. or reimburse Melanie for any of those items she paid. He was to pay the same for the 2018-2019 school year and was to pay tuition directly to the school. Melanie was to continue to be exclusively entitled to her son's Social Security benefits, and Troy was to pay 100% of the premiums for all life insurance policies required by their original divorce settlement and to give Melanie access to information regarding those policies. It was noted Troy had converted a designated college account into a 529 plan at Edward Jones for their son, and it was ordered that the account be used exclusively for their son's education, that Troy could make no withdrawals or changes to the account without Melanie's notarized signature, and that Grant would be the sole beneficiary of the account in the event Troy died before Grant reached college age.[1976]

Although the Probate Court of Gwinnett County had, at one time, designated Ray Hall as guardian over Troy's person and property, Troy now affirmed he was of sound mind, legally competent to contract, was satisfied with his attorney, that there were no pending probate actions regarding him, and that he had no legal guardian.[1977] With his assets possibly hidden or transferred, and with a generous reduction in monthly child support payments from more than $4,000 in 2012 to $400 in 2018, the competency of Troy Hall seemed to have conveniently rebounded.

Following the allegations from Georgia that Billy Birt, Billy Wayne Davis, Bobby Gaddis, and Charlie Reed had murdered the Durhams, one thing that made the seven-month interval between May 2019 (when Bob Ingram first contacted the Watauga County Sheriff's Office) and December 2019 so critical was that it was a window of time during which Troy Hall might have been confronted with the fact that Birt reportedly implicated a nephew or son-in-law of the Durhams. According to Sheriff Len Hagaman, when he and his office learned of Birt's alleged statements that May, they intended to speak with Troy, but before that could happen, Troy died[1978] on December 19, 2019.[1979] According to Captain Carolynn Johnson, Troy had been hard to locate,[1980] in part, due to his name change and the fact "that some people still feared him," and by the time the Watauga County Sheriff's Office located his last known address, he was deceased.[1981][nnnnnnn] As stated on his death certificate, Troy succumbed to a sudden heart attack at the age of sixty-eight in Duluth, Georgia and was pronounced dead on arrival at the Gwinnett Medical Center.[1982] When Hagaman informed a still fearful Ginny Durham Mackie of Troy's death, she seemed genuinely relieved.[1983][ooooooo]

[nnnnnnn] In fact, the Watauga County Sheriff's Office, as indicated by their own investigative records, were already aware of Troy's new name and his last known address at least by late 2011. [Sources: Comprehensive background reports and Georgia driver's license details for Troy Justin Hall/Justin Troy Hall, Watauga County Sheriff's Office investigation file 118-H-1/2/3.]

[ooooooo] Ginny subsequently looked up Troy's obituary. Although she did not recognize him in the accompanying photograph, the names of his parents and siblings were accurately listed. [Source: Mackie, Ginny Durham. Interview with Carolynn Johnson & Wade Colvard. December 7, 2020.]

PART III:
AWAY DOWN SOUTH IN DIXIE

CHAPTER 22

THE EVOLUTION OF A HITMAN

When it was alleged that Billy Sunday Birt, Billy Wayne Davis, Bobby Gene Gaddis, and Charles David "Charlie" Reed had carried out the murders of Bryce, Virginia, and Bobby Durham, the four Georgia men's names were unfamiliar to the Watauga County Sheriff's Office. Who, exactly, were these men?

By the mid-1960s, in Winder, Georgia – some 250 miles southwest of Boone, North Carolina – "a loose group of locals [had] learned how to rub two quarters together and make a dollar without working,"[1984] thus forming what would become known as northeast Georgia's sect of the Dixie Mafia. Their activities "quickly escalated,"[1985] and its members made "their fortunes and destinies with liquor, fast cars, amphetamines, murder, burglary, and armed robbery."[1986]

Billy Sunday Birt was born in 1937[ppppppp] to a poor sharecropping family.[1987] His mother named him after the renowned Christian evangelist Billy Sunday in hopes her son would one day also become a preacher.[1988] From childhood, Birt was afflicted with a heavy speech impediment.[1989] He received little formal education, and when he was nine, his father died suddenly. At age thirteen, he quit school and took a job at a sawmill. At sixteen, he committed arson,[1990] and this was the beginning of a criminal trajectory very different from the life his mother had dreamt for him. Also at sixteen, Birt married his twelve-year-old first cousin once removed, Ruby Nell Lee,[1991] and he obtained a good job at a rock quarry. By 1955, he was involved in the manufacturing and hauling of bootleg whiskey. In 1960, he committed his first murders.[1992] In 1966, he learned "he could make more money from a gambling house robbery in one night than he could working at a rock quarry in six months."[1993] His future would no longer involve "moving dirt or busting rocks."[1994]

As Birt dove deeper into the underworld, he needed to establish an inner circle, and he handpicked a group of loyal and trusted friends and relatives to assist him, including Bobby Gaddis and Charlie Reed.[1995] These men were Birt's "soldiers," who followed him and his orders, and all of them would, at various times, commit crimes together in assorted groupings. "He would choose which of his boys was best suited for whatever he was going to hit, and only at the last minute would he bring them in and prepare them for what he needed each man to do. They…learned through trial and error what worked for them and what didn't. They all knew what each other's faults and character flaws were."[1996] Birt, however, was the only one who set up their jobs.[1997]

[ppppppp] At the time of the Durham murders in 1972, Billy Birt would have been 34 years old, Billy Wayne Davis and Bobby Gaddis 30 years old, and Charlie Reed 25 years old.

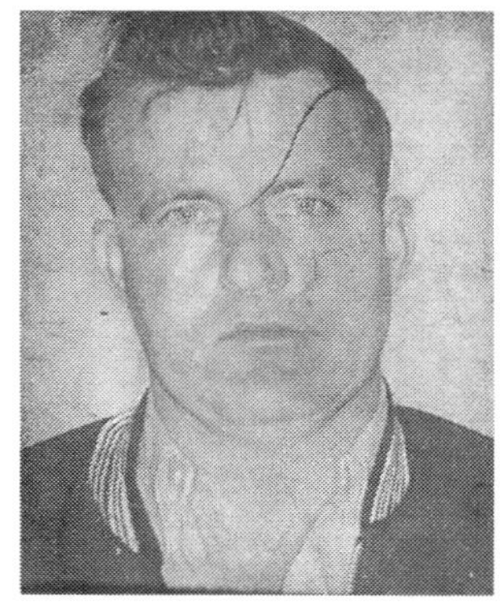

Billy Sunday Birt (Courtesy of Special Collections and Archives, Georgia State University Library)

By 1967, at the age of thirty, the stocky and muscular[1998] Birt had transformed from a heavy equipment operator to a "full-blown criminal" and was the man who walked among all the local kingpins and was welcomed into their circles.[1999] Because Birt was the trusted "go to" for anything illegal that money makers needed done,[2000] he became the de facto leader of the Dixie Mafia sect based in the farming town of Winder. That same year, Birt added murder for hire to his resume,[2001] and murders soon "started piling up." While Birt's "in-house" rate for contract killings was $5,000, outsiders paid $10,000. Birt gained a reputation as someone who could discreetly get things done, no questions asked, for a price.[2002] He "was the most trusted hitman in Georgia" and "was the man to call because he was good at what he did." "It was lucrative work."[2003]

Bobby Gaddis (Courtesy of Bob Ingram)

Between 1963 and 1967, Bobby Gaddis had been arrested for speeding, driving without a license, auto larceny, larceny from a house, and passing fraudulent checks.[2004] In 1966, he had been held on charges of armed robbery and assault with intent to murder.[2005] Sometimes publicly referred to as "Big Boy,"[2006] he was the most recognizable of their group, "barrel-chested"[2007] and weighing around 340 pounds. Despite his physical size and strength and his "non-flinching resolve while executing a robbery, hit, or heist," Gaddis was considered the weakest member in terms of his sadistic nature and lack of intelligence.[2008] Within inner circles, he was known as "Big Dummy" because his counterparts thought him stupid and laughed at him whenever he tried to assume leadership of their group during Billy Birt's incarcerations. According to Birt's son Stoney, because of Gaddis's deficits, there was no job for him to do but drive getaway cars, sometimes while wearing a wig as a disguise. Stoney states Gaddis was "cruel and sadistic in all kinds of ways. He didn't mind throwing a turtle in boiling water and watching [it] come unraveled instead of cutting its head off."[2009] Stoney also describes Gaddis as a dog and as a sexual predator and pedophile, who was abusive to women, children, and animals. Stoney sums up his opinion of Gaddis as the worst person he ever knew – an S.O.B. who "needed killing."[2010]

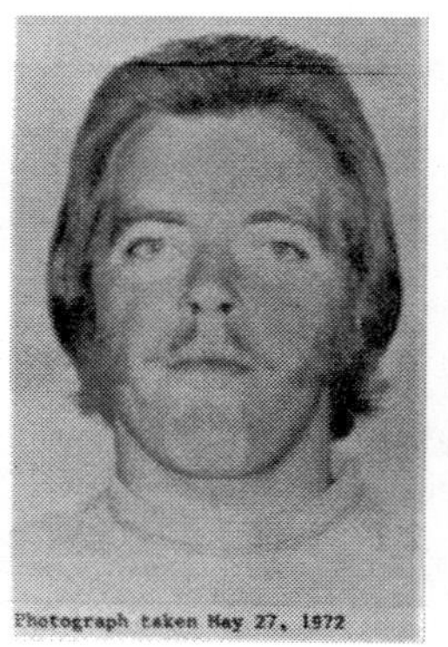

Charlie Reed (far right image courtesy of Bob Ingram)

In contrast to Gaddis, Charlie Reed was small in stature, good-looking, and a ladies' man. He was a welder by trade and first met Billy Birt at the latter's pool hall in Winder. The two clicked, and Birt felt he could trust him. Reed ended up serving Birt like a true soldier, comrade, and friend, who "kept his mouth shut to the end.... He was a damn good gangster" and took orders well, but he was also a self-starter, who could figure things out. According to Stoney Birt, although Reed "was cold as ice [and] capable of anything," he never killed anyone but would watch Birt do it.[2011] Still, Reed, like Birt and Gaddis would be convicted of murder.

Billy Birt fronted and planned his criminal activities out of his pool hall,[2012] where, in 1967, he was introduced to the fourth alleged killer of the Durham family, Billy Wayne Davis,[2013] "a known gambler...thug...hoodlum,"[2014] and self-serving opportunist from Cobb County, Georgia.[2015] Davis, following a stint in the U. S. Army and a series of jobs, including working as a fireman, had begun his criminal career in the mid-1960s with counterfeit money. He was one of several men arrested in November 1966 for his participation in what was believed to be a $2 million counterfeit money seizure.[2016] At the time, it was "called the biggest bogus bill crackdown in the history of the South."[2017] He was convicted a year later in Atlanta and given a three-year probated sentence.[2018] Davis may also have already killed thirty people by the time he met Birt,[2019] but "he didn't advertise the fact that he was a hitman because he only killed for money" that belonged to his victims as opposed to money paid by a client. "If he found out a man had $10,000, he'd kill him."[2020]

Billy Wayne Davis
(L-R: First & second images courtesy of Special Collections and Archives, Georgia State University Library; third image courtesy of Bob Ingram)

Davis was a well-dressed, educated man, who had a relatively privileged life and a more affluent and connected family than Birt's.[2021] He "kept himself presentable and looked like he could have been an advisor to the governor."[2022] Davis's refinement stood in sharp contrast to Birt, whose "speech impediment and gruff exterior stood out like a sore thumb."[2023] Despite these differences, Davis was impressed by Birt's bravado and the team he had assembled in Winder; Birt immediately liked Davis and was impressed with his business sense.[2024] "Birt...looked up to Davis as being the man with all the connections, the man who could put everything together, and a man that was extremely smart."[2025]

The two men's similar criminal backgrounds and mindsets led to a collaboration. "They talked and soon realized that they both could benefit from doing business together. Davis was a wealth of information,"[2026] and Birt learned he "was connected to a lot of big money people" on the west side of Georgia[2027] – influential individuals such as politicians, doctors, and lawyers,[qqqqqqq] who Birt could not reach. Davis, on the other hand, fit in seamlessly with them and "had his finger on the pulse of those with money and power."[2028] He thrived on inside knowledge and cash,[2029] and he "liked to have things done rather than do them himself."[2030]

According to Birt, Davis "had some lawyers working with him that would sell him information on people who kept money in their homes. Until I met Davis, I never thought about all a lawyer knowed about where big money was hid. But I damn sure found out. Billy Wayne Davis had lawyers lined up to sell him information. And if it turned out to be good information the lawyer would get 20 percent."[2031]

This kind of insider knowledge opened up a whole new avenue of income for Birt, and his "association with Davis broadened their territory. Davis had connections in other parts of the state, so he set up jobs in areas where the Dixie Mafia had never operated."[2032] He also had access to informants who provided him with the names and addresses of individuals known to keep large sums of money, guns, or jewelry in their homes.[2033] Davis additionally knew who carried large amounts of money with them and where all the big poker games would take place.[2034] Ninety percent of the information regarding big hits – who had big money, who had filed for bankruptcy – came from Davis.[2035] Davis also "came up with several of the banks to rob, people and places to hit, jobs that sometimes led to murder."[2036]

Broadly speaking, Davis was the brains who often set up their crimes, and Birt was the brawn. While both were dangerous and had interchangeable roles, Davis was more cunning, scheming, and conniving; Birt more ruthless, violent, and deadly.[2037][rrrrrrr] For the next seven years, the pair made a lot of money together, initially transporting stolen goods and eventually robbing many banks as well as poker games in west Georgia and other states.[2038] They and their associates "criss-crossed north and middle Georgia, indiscriminately robbing homes and businesses and killing the occupants to eliminate witnesses."[2039]

Birt and Davis were "tornadoes,"[2040] and theirs "would be the beginning of a partnership that would lead the two men down a long and dark path of robbery, extortion and murder."[2041] They were of the same ilk and caliber in terms of intelligence and cold-bloodedness. Neither "seemed to…have a conscience when it came to getting the job done." They "were willing to go all the way to secure power and money, and they would kill at the blink of an eye to silence an eyewitness or informant."[2042] Cobb County, Georgia District Attorney Tom Charron described the pair as "ruthless killers," and a Cobb County detective agreed, stating, "You can't get much meaner than these guys were. They'd kill even when they didn't have to. It became a habit with them."[2043] According to

---

[qqqqqqq] Davis's associate Larry Bethune believed judges were among Davis's connections: "I have always figured he had friends everywhere.... He said don't worry if you get into it; I will get you out of it." [Source: Bethune, Larry. Interview with Chief Knowles, Sgt. C. H. Morris, Lt. W. P. Jones, Capt. J. W. Reed, and Joe Chambers. Undated. Mr. & Mrs. R. O. Fleming case file #70-0302-01-73.]

[rrrrrrr] Although Billy Wayne Davis claimed he was not comparable to Billy Birt, Bob Ingram believes Davis and Birt were the leaders and the nucleus of their group. According to Ingram, there is no distinction between Davis, Birt, Gaddis, and Reed in terms of their capacity to kill and torture. Ingram states they would do anything necessary to get the money or information they were seeking. Still, Ingram is of the opinion that Birt was "mean as hell" and the meanest of the group. [Sources: Sean Kipe, Imperative Entertainment, *In The Red Clay*, podcast audio, Chapter 11: *Something Old, Something New*, October 20, 2020, http://intheredclaypodcast.com; Davis, Billy Wayne. Interview with Bob Ingram. October 21, 2020; Ingram, Bob. In-person interview with author. April 19, 2022.]

Bob Ingram, "…the two of them together were extremely dangerous because one [Davis] was very clever, very smart, very manipulative, and the other [Birt] was just flat out dangerous, and when they ran together, they cut a wide path."[2044]

Even so, Davis did not fit the mold of Birt's Dixie Mafia associates as he "wanted to have a hand in all aspects of it." He also did not fit in with Birt's inner circle.[2045] He lacked comradery with them and did not associate with them on a regular basis.[2046] Some of Birt's long-time friends mistrusted Davis from the start and were reluctant to accept him. Birt's own brother, Bobby, despised Davis and thought him a coward. But Birt ignored their warnings, seeing Davis's statewide connections as money-making opportunities.[2047] Birt would write, "Davis was a real good talker so we used him as a talk man. I probably trusted him more than any other man I worked with because he was a damn good back man…."[2048] Still, Birt "never considered Davis a member of his group," and although Birt and Davis did some things together and sometimes in company with Birt's "boys," Birt also continued with separate jobs utilizing only his original gang,[2049] and Davis maintained his separate criminal connections and activities in west Georgia.

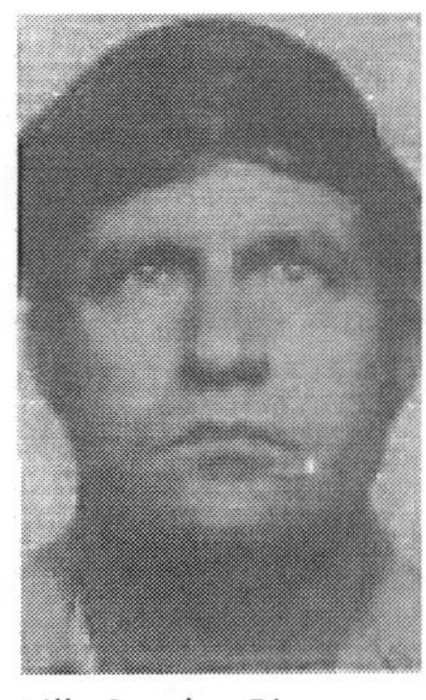
Billy Sunday Birt (Source: The Atlanta Journal-Constitution)

By the late 1960s and into the early 1970s, the Dixie Mafia was full throttle,[2050] and Billy Birt was at the apex of his career. He had become "a multi-faceted criminal," who could burglarize, haul liquor and drugs, con people, and kill.[2051] He took insurance jobs (burning or dynamiting something to collect policy payoffs), and he robbed "big money" establishments (e.g., garment plants, jewelry stores, department stores, liquor stores, banks, armories, and big sporting goods stores where there were large quantities of guns).[2052] He was available and received weekly requests for a variety of contract work.[2053] "From 1968 on, [he] was the undisputed leader of anything he was involved in. No man gave him orders. No man crossed him and got by with it."[2054] The dirt-poor schoolboy once ridiculed for his speech impediment had, in manhood, risen to a place of power and influence. The appetites of the teenaged husband, quarryman, and sometime moonshine runner had been whetted and gratified by the spoils of gambling house heists and burglaries, which soon morphed into an insatiable hunger for higher stakes and higher returns and the need to protect those returns at any cost, even if it necessitated murder. In sharp contrast to the life-giving call of God upon the great evangelist Billy Sunday to see men and women both saved and revived, Sunday's namesake gave no thought to his victims' salvation and made the snuffing out of lives a calling of his own making. While Billy Sunday was a very vocal opponent of the theory of evolution,[2055] even he might have acknowledged that, in Billy Sunday Birt, a killer had evolved.

Although the whiskey business remained a constant means for Birt to keep his crew together and making a living when they weren't doing other things,[2056] "the Dixie Mafia…changed with the times and new opportunities."[2057] When the government began cutting into their business, outlaws had to diversify, and just as in other locales (including Wilkes County, North Carolina), it was a natural progression from "moonshine-running to drug-running" in Northeast Georgia.[2058] Consequently, Birt made monthly trips to Mexico for loads of as many as 200,000 amphetamines[2059] to sell and to use. One trip alone "could bring a profit of hundreds of thousands of dollars, [and] illegal drug-running exploded into a major criminal enterprise."[2060] Known as Biphetamine 20, Black Beauties, and RJSs, these pills "were rampant in the '60s and '70s" and were marketed as diet pills and to help truckers stay awake on long hauls.[2061] Soon, "everybody was eating black pills like they were candy,"[2062] and Birt was thirty-two when he took his first one in the late 1960s.[2063] Consumption of this pharmaceutical "speed" – "the drug of choice for the Dixie Mafia" – could cause paranoia and violence as well as visible and audible hallucinations, but it also enabled its users to stay awake for days, work longer hours, be razor focused, and have a seemingly endless supply of energy.[2064] Birt and his associates seemed invincible, untouchable, and unstoppable. "They feared no one, and for the right price, no one was safe."[2065] But drug use also launched Birt into a downward spiral, causing him to be suspicious of everyone and even to consider eliminating those in his inner circle.[2066] According to Shane Birt, this was when his father's veins turned to ice, and he became accustomed to cruelty. Bob Ingram says this is when the violence, brutality, and out-of-control killing accelerated.[2067]

Between 1967 and 1974, and coinciding with their ever-growing amphetamine use, the activities of Birt, Billy Wayne Davis, and others took a bloody turn. The Dixie Mafia was "running wide open, robbing and killing people" on a monthly if not weekly basis.[2068] "Burglaries turned into armed robberies and murder in Barrow and nearby counties."[2069] As one Georgia state investigator put it, it was "a reign of terror."[2070] The clientele network was also expanding "with contracts for arson and murders for hire and…the money was rolling in." Clients came to Birt and dealt directly and solely with him. Birt was "pulling jobs at an alarming rate – sometimes two or three a night locally."[2071] Described as "well-traveled,"[2072] he would also venture to Florida, North Carolina, South Carolina, Alabama, Tennessee, Texas, or just wherever he was paid to go.[2073]

As law enforcement agencies closed in on illegal alcohol operations,[2074] Birt and his associates, "driven by greed, self-preservation, and ill temper"[2075] began to kill those who could incriminate them. While some of the killings they committed were not moonshine-related, many of them seemed focused on the elimination of witnesses in illegal liquor cases. In 1971, Birt and three others were indicted in a federal liquor conspiracy case, and as witnesses stepped forward and subpoenas were being issued, disappearances and instances of arson and murder became commonplace.[2076] Birt became the solution to the problem of anyone with a loose mouth or a willingness to talk to the law or make damaging statements as a witness. "The witness would never show up to testify…and most of the time would never be heard from or found again."[2077] Soon, however, Birt's victims would not be limited to "rats" or witnesses. According to FBI Agent Ron Webb, "Birt always had a reason to kill. If you were a fellow bootlegger suspected of talking to the ATF or GBI, you were in danger. If you looked at one of Birt's girlfriends, that could be fatal. If you walked in on a robbery in progress, that was bad news. If you kept a large amount of cash around the house…you were also a target. And there were the murders for hire, which he carried out dispassionately."[2078] These posed no dilemma for Birt, nor was he haunted by his actions. "He trained himself to harden his heart when it came to business."[2079]

The criminal activities of northeast Georgia's Dixie Mafia continued to be carried out with regularity except for a dormant period between November 1972 and July 1973 during which Birt served eight and a half months of a two-year term in a federal penitentiary for possession of a firearm following an alleged felony conviction. Within two weeks of his parole, however, Birt was back in business, buying a truck stop between Winder and Statham, Georgia, where plenty of amphetamines were available.[2080] This became the meeting place for Birt and Davis whenever they were planning a job on Birt's side of Georgia.[2081] Davis's turf was west Georgia where he had three high-end used car lots (one of them being Davis Used Cars on Bankhead Highway in Austell where he and Birt rendezvoused to plan jobs on that side of the state), which he used to front the large amount of cash he brought in. Davis's establishments also provided any vehicles needed for crimes committed by him and his associates.[2082]

Before Birt partnered with Davis, Birt was "an in and out contract hit guy," but after they joined forces, "the torture and brutal murders began," including the use of coat hangers and strangulation,[2083] which, alongside shooting, seemed to be the preferred means of death. Most of the murders involved singular victims; on other occasions, two or more were killed. Arson was sometimes employed to burn victims' bodies and destroy crime scenes; other corpses were buried along riverbanks or dumped into wells that were sometimes dynamited.

ATF Agent Jim West

Because of local law enforcement's inability or unwillingness to act during a period of seven or eight years between the late 1960s and early 1970s, partly due to some local officers' fear of Birt and his men, federal authorities decided they must step in. "A rush of state and federal agents" descended upon Barrow County, Georgia "sometimes outnumbering local law enforcement officers of all agencies combined."[2084] In 1970, Tennessee native Jim West, a special agent with the Federal Alcohol, Tobacco, and Firearms (ATF) Bureau, moved near Winder, Georgia to bring down those involved in illegal whiskey manufacturing in Barrow County. For fifteen years, West had earned a reputation "for busting up moonshine operations in North Carolina and Florida."[2085] The target of West and his fellow agent Jack Berry would soon be the Dixie Mafia…and Billy Birt in particular.

CHAPTER 23

IMPLOSION: A HOUSE DIVIDED

"As 1973 drew to a close," Billy Birt and Billy Wayne Davis "were still busy planning and executing bank robberies, home invasions and murders."[2086] By April 1974, law enforcement agents, who had worked in northeast Georgia nearly two years, were searching for clues related to the deaths or disappearances of eight to twelve individuals. Georgia Bureau of Investigation Director Bill Beardsley "said there was a 'similarity in the art' of the murders of at least three bodies found'.... He described each of the unsolved murders...as 'brutal.' To leave a victim dead is one thing. But to leave him dead in a sadistic manner or some other way that attracts attention gets the word around pretty fast. There is a difference between a murder and a brutal murder."[2087] This "similarity in the art" of murder, and brutal murder in particular, provided the behavioral patterns that partially prompted Bob Ingram to compare the Durham and Fleming slayings almost fifty years later.

According to Billy Birt's son Stoney, "Going into 1974, [Birt] cooled it with Davis for a while. Davis had rubbed him wrong on a couple [of] things, and he was just a breath away from getting rid of Davis." Birt recognized "Davis's judgment was faulty," and he came to the realization that, "left to his own devices, he was a screw up" and "had to be told what to do." Birt also recognized "what a cruel streak Davis had in him," something Davis had thought would win Birt's admiration but had actually "had the opposite effect."[2088] Davis's association with Birt had been reduced to bank jobs only. Birt's speech impediment "made his voice easy to recognize,[sssssss] so he liked Davis to go in with him to do the talking, and Davis was good at it. He followed orders...and worked [well] under pressure." While Davis did the talking, Bobby Gaddis drove the getaway car.[2089]

In the spring of 1974, Birt, Gaddis, and Davis robbed the National Bank of Walton County in Loganville, Georgia.[2090] Within days of the robbery, some of the stolen money was linked to Davis when his wife Mary attempted to deposit it. With the money identified, the FBI questioned Mary about it and subsequently "set up a surveillance team" in the Davis home. At the time, Davis, Birt, and others were in Alabama preparing to rob another bank, and when Davis phoned home to check in with his wife, the FBI, being by her side and listening to the conversation, prompted her to ask him to return home but without providing a reason. When he arrived home in Austell, Davis was arrested and held without bail at the Hall County jail in Gainesville, Georgia. He refused to talk for

[sssssss] In order not to be identified, Birt "rarely spoke at a crime scene unless everyone was going to be a victim." If he did speak, it was certainly an indication he planned to leave no witnesses. [Sources: Terrell, Jimmy. E-mail to author. March 21, 2022; Birt, Billy Stonewall. *Rock Solid In His Own Words: The Inside Story of Billy Sunday Birt.* (2017), p. 49.]

three weeks, after which time the FBI, having realized "Mary was Davis's weak spot," arrested her for questioning and made sure Davis was aware of her plight via television and the newspaper. They then told Davis that Mary wanted to see him and asked if he would like to see her, which he did. Mary had been placed in the women's ward, but just prior to Davis's visit with her, they reportedly moved her to "a mop room between two men's dormitories" that were inhabited by inmates who said vile things to her, and they told her she would do the rest of her time there. Having never previously been incarcerated, she "was scared to death." When Davis saw his wife's location and her condition, he assumed she had been there all along, and she begged him to get her out. This broke Davis, and unaware that, due to a 72-hour holding limit, his wife would have been released only two hours later, he confessed his participation in the bank robbery.[2091]

Davis, who, during his seven-year association with Birt, had been periodically picked up, interrogated, and reportedly even beaten by law enforcement officers, had "never come close to cracking." He had remained tight-lipped and had never ratted on those he knew in power, and Birt, who detested a snitch within his inner circle, admired that trait, using it to defend Davis to his [Birt's] associates who did not like or trust Davis. But now, Davis decided to cut a parole deal for himself by agreeing to implicate Birt. Davis asked to speak with ATF Agent Jim West. This appealed to West and certain other law enforcement agents who had wanted to put Birt away for years.[2092]

On April 3, 1974, thirty-six-year-old Billy Birt was arrested; it was his last day as a free man. It was also the end to anyone losing his or her life due to Birt's "job." Bobby Gaddis was arrested the same day. Jailed for the Loganville bank robbery, Birt and Gaddis "faced an eight-count federal indictment." In May 1974, they were tried in the U. S. District Court in Athens, Georgia. Davis turned state's evidence on them, and on the witness stand, [Birt and Gaddis] "denied many of [Davis's] allegations." In June 1974, Birt was convicted of bank robbery and started a twenty-five-year sentence in an Illinois prison. Gaddis also received twenty-five years. Davis pleaded guilty and was sentenced to twenty years, but for his testimony, he was granted A-2 parole status, which meant he could be eligible for parole after ninety days rather than after the customary serving of one-third of his sentence. Birt and Gaddis resolved to serve their time, try to make parole within seven or eight years, and then deal with Davis.[2093] But the wait would not be so long.

In 1975, after Birt's and Gaddis's successful appeals to have their sentences overturned, Davis, who had been reflecting on what he had done to them, realized they would seek revenge. "The die was cast. Davis knew…Birt did not trust him anymore. He knew his former partner would eventually get his pound of flesh…." In fact, Birt had made plans to escape prison to settle his scores with Davis and Jim West, but those plans never came to pass. "Davis started looking for ways to protect himself, one way or another."[2094] According to Birt's son Stoney, Jim West was also afraid of what might happen when Birt was free, and West went to Davis after Birt's sentence was overturned, telling Davis he did not know whose family Birt would kill first – his or Davis's – and Davis had better come up with something fast. Fearful Birt and Gaddis would be released from prison,[2095] and coming under scrutiny for the Fleming murders, Davis, in a smart, self-serving move, decided ratting again would be his way out. He once more went to West, this time offering to testify against Birt, Gaddis, and Charlie Reed in the Fleming Case. West, who was approaching retirement, had spent four years trying to bring Birt down and, frustrated with his inability to do so, he saw this as a final opportunity to accomplish that goal[2096] for the greater public good.[2097]

West allegedly told Davis if he would tell about every murder he had knowledge of that he and Birt had been involved in, and if he would leave nothing out, and if he would be willing to testify to these things, Davis would be cleared of eighteen murders he had committed (some of which he had already been indicted for), and he would be granted immunity.[2098] Davis "had it in writing from Jim West that he could never be charged for anything he told about as long as he testified that Billy Birt was the one who did it."[2099] The deal was indicative of "how badly [lawmen] wanted Birt off the streets for the rest of his life."[2100]

In order to ensure Birt would be put away for good, that Davis would receive immunity for his own murderous confessions, and that Davis's indictments would be dead-docketed or altogether dropped,[2101] Davis implicated Birt and provided West with "a disturbingly detailed account." In "a lengthy statement that sent shock waves throughout law enforcement circles, he rattled off knowledge of a variety of crimes and buried bodies, including fifty-six murders all over the South, and throughout the tale, he pictured Billy Birt as the killer"[2102] while minimizing any role of his own.[2103] (According to Stoney Birt, the report consisted of some cases Davis knew about, some he thought he knew about, and some that were "bullshit" that Davis "add[ed] some truth to in order to make it all sound real."[2104]) Davis claimed that one evening, as Birt sat in a prison cell bed, he [Birt] counted the number of people he had killed, coming up with a tally of fifty-two, twenty of which West claimed he could firmly tie Birt to.[2105] Meanwhile, the eighteen murders Davis admitted to committing were contained in a separate list, which West took care of.[2106]

West, along with fellow ATF Agent Jack Berry and Douglas County Sheriff Earl Lee "were present in the meeting [with Davis] that resulted in" a chronological list of twenty-eight Barrow County, Georgia murders allegedly connected to Billy Birt, and just months before West's retirement, he and Berry compiled this information into a report. Although West never named his informant, it was obviously Davis, who repeatedly and publicly ratted on Birt. This was supported by the fact that "West wrote near the end of his typed report that [Birt] 'went to the informant's car lot in Austell, Georgia,' to talk about killing a man.... Davis owned a car lot in Austell and was one of [Birt's] closest associates." Despite questions about Davis's credibility, "West's report, based on Davis's information, was the most comprehensive account of Georgia murders produced at the time." Because West and Berry "had investigated [Birt] in a number of liquor, firearms, and dynamite cases," in their minds it was simple: "If someone had been murdered, you looked first at Billy Sunday Birt."[2107]

CHAPTER 24

A SNITCH'S COMEUPPANCE

Of those indicted in the Fleming Case, Billy Birt stood trial first and was convicted.[tttttt] In June 1975, he was sentenced to death in the electric chair. At Bobby Gaddis's August 1975 trial for the Fleming murders, Birt testified on his behalf as a witness for the defense, and during his testimony, "his eyes blazed with hatred as he told the jury that he [Birt] and Davis had done more dirt than any two people they had ever seen… He told them that Davis was a good liar and actor, and that Davis was as cold and low down as anyone he ever knew and he was lying to them about the Wrens murders. Then he proceeded to tell them of a number of murders that he and Davis had done together and why, and that Davis had a cruelness in him that was [as] hard and cold as hell."[2108]

Immediately after his sentencing in the Fleming Case, Birt requested to make a phone call to confess to two additional murders – those of Drs. Warren and Rosina Matthews. He phoned attorney Bobby Cook, who had represented some of the men who had already been convicted for the Matthews murders,[2109] and he also stated his confession to the murders in two letters to *The Atlanta Constitution*.[2110] Birt admitted to participating in the Matthews robbery and murders and implicated Davis and associate Willie Hester, Jr. (by this time deceased) as his accomplices. Because Birt's and Davis's bond of friendship had been shattered – Davis twice testifying against Birt – and because Birt had been sentenced to death for the Fleming murders, he "knew it was over with" for himself, and he believed "all the truth should come out." According to Cobb County, Georgia District Attorney Tom Charron, "It was the 'revenge motive' between Birt and Davis that broke the Matthews case. 'In some cases, like this one, it is good to have people trying to get back at somebody.'" Not only did Birt want to take Davis down in return, but according to Birt, no matter how cold-hearted he [Birt] was, he hated to see others in prison for a crime he committed.[2111] Seven other men (aka "The Marietta Seven"[uuuuuuu]) had been convicted of that crime in five separate trials between 1973 and 1975. One of those men – James "Jimmy" Creamer – was sentenced to die in the electric chair, and the other six were sentenced to life. The hesitation to believe Birt's claims was due, in part, to the fact that some of the convicted men had offered payments totaling $20,000 to Birt's wife for his confession and any resulting indictments and convictions. These men were later exonerated when it was determined they had been wrongly convicted based on the testimony of a

---

[tttttt] Birt was acquitted in the burglary of the Jerry Haymon home because Billy Wayne Davis had no details regarding it. [Source: Birt, Billy Stonewall. *Rock Solid: The True Story of Georgia's Dixie Mafia.* (2017), p. 142.]
[uuuuuuu] The inked impressions of six of the men who comprised "The Marietta Seven" – James Creamer, George Emmett, Larry Hacker, James Hoyt Powell, Sr., Charles Benjamin Roberts, and Alton Wayne Ruff – were compared to the finger and palm prints lifted from the home and vehicle in the Durham murder case. [Sources: Watauga County Sheriff's Office investigation file 118-H-1/2/3.]

perjurious witness,[2112] Debbie Kidd, a South Carolina prostitute, who was romantically involved with one of the investigators assigned to the case.[2113] Creamer was a "habitual criminal" who had met Kidd in July 1971, two months after the Matthews murders. Kidd had been part of Creamer's group of thieves until "they cast her off in early 1972 after Creamer was sent to prison for armed robbery." Kidd subsequently manufactured the story of this group's involvement in the Matthews murders.[2114]

In August 1976, Birt also confessed to the murder of Charles "Mac" Sibley, Sr. and, in retaliation for Davis testifying against him in the Fleming Case, he sent word from prison that he would be willing to testify that Davis had hired him to kill Sibley. On December 8, 1971, Sibley, a gambler and package store owner in Lithia Springs, Georgia and an associate of Davis, was shot and killed in his home. Davis owed Sibley around $14,000 in gambling debts, and Birt suggested to Davis that they rob Sibley and pay him back with his own money. Davis took it a step further and decided to rob and kill Sibley and keep his money. Davis and Birt used a key to enter Sibley's house, and when Sibley arrived, they robbed him of several thousand dollars. Birt then put Sibley in a closet and shot him, his body being discovered the next day. Davis paid Birt with cash and a car. Bobby Gaddis and Charlie Reed also testified against Davis, and both Birt and Davis were indicted for Sibley's murder, although Birt's case never went to trial. Birt was the chief witness against Davis, and Sheriff Earl Lee and GBI Agent Bob Ingram brought him from prison in Marion, Illinois to Douglasville, Georgia to testify. At one point during the trial, Birt told the judge "me and that man [Davis] may have killed more people than you can imagine." Law enforcement officers, however, testified Birt was "a chronic liar." Davis's defense attorney stated Birt was "behind bars…not walking the streets and not killing anyone because of Mr. Davis's assistance. Now he's asking you to 'get' Davis to carry out his revenge." The defense attorney also referred to Birt as a "mad dog," but the prosecutor retorted that "mad dogs 'run in packs sometimes.'" Although Davis denied being at Sibley's home or participating in his murder, he was convicted and sentenced to life in prison, only avoiding the death penalty because it "was not in force" at the time of Sibley's murder. Davis unsuccessfully appealed his conviction in 1977 and 1991.[2115]

Davis's actions had caused what seemed to be an irreparable rift between him and Birt. When Davis began pointing his finger at Birt, Birt's impressions of Davis as an extremely smart man who had once been his best friend crumbled. Birt began seeing Davis as a different breed, who had no honor whatsoever. Bad blood endured between them for many years. A furious Birt stated he hated Davis and would kill him if he could,[2116] and when Birt and Davis were both in the same prison for a three-to-four-month period, Birt told Davis he was going to kill him.[2117] Davis, who became cautious of Birt,[2118] also admitted trying to have Birt killed in prison.[2119] Birt would later write, "The more [a snitch] tells, the more he believes the law is going to help him get out. I can say this – the law used the hell out of [Davis]…..[vvvvvvv] He had told Jim West, a federal officer, about 50 or 60 murders I [was] supposed to have committed over the years….. Had him telling murder after murder. He took them up in Barrow County and showed them where a lot of bodies was buried, but he always told them he never was with me when I killed these people. But they used him, and the stupid bastard is still in prison….[2120] When a man starts snitching for the law, there's no stopping him but to kill the

---

[wwwww] According to Stoney Birt, West and others did not do what they did for Davis's sake, but for the conviction of his father. [Source: Birt, Billy Stonewall. *Rock Solid: The True Story of Georgia's Dixie Mafia*. (2017), p. 140.]

bastard."[2121] Birt's hatred allegedly even extended to "used car dealers because that's what Billy Wayne Davis was."[2122][wwwwwww]

Despite Birt's confession to the Matthews slayings, it took authorities until 1979 to give it credence and indict him. That October, he finally had his opportunity to testify before a jury against Davis in the Matthews murder case, and he reportedly did so in a matter-of-fact manner devoid of emotion.[2123] By this time, the two were "bitter enemies,"[2124] and "this was [Birt's] chance to get back at Davis for testifying against him in the Loganville bank robbery" and the Fleming murders, the latter for which Davis had gone scot-free. "It was payback time." On the stand, Birt said, "I am testifying here today because that man there (motioning to Davis) once was my best friend. We robbed banks together, we done everything together, and he testified against me."[2125] During much of Birt's testimony, a seated Davis tapped his fingertips against his lips.[2126]

According to Birt, Davis phoned him the night before the Matthews murders, saying, "I've got pigs ready for sale." "'Pigs' meant robbery or burglary, and 'hogs' meant murder." The two used these code words in case authorities had bugged their phones. It was believed there was $40,000-$50,000 in the Matthews safe. Birt said the robbery was Davis's idea, and Davis was the one who botched it. Birt said he, Davis, and Willie Hester, Jr. (all wearing ski masks) went to rob the home, but things went wrong, and they had to kill the couple. Birt testified they were waiting outside when Warren Matthews opened his garage door to leave for work. Davis drew a gun, and Matthews "went wild" and removed Davis's mask. Birt stated he and Davis had a rule between them – that if any of their victims could identify either of them, the victims must die. Birt then removed his mask because he knew Matthews had already seen Davis's face and had to be killed. "After a brief struggle in the garage, Matthews took off running down his driveway, and [Birt] shot him twice in the back as he ran. After Rosina Matthews appeared in the doorway holding a .38 pistol, [she and Birt] exchanged gunfire in the garage. [Birt] wounded the woman, but it was Davis…who chased her into the backyard patio, held her down with his knee, and shot her in the back of the head with her own pistol, which she had dropped. The three men fled the scene and returned to [Birt's] car, which had been left parked down a side street." At times, during Birt's testimony, "he glared hatefully at Davis," who "was sitting there smiling."[2127]

In August 1975, Davis had provided police with a statement in which he said he was supposed to have driven Birt and Hester to the Matthews home but decided at the last minute not to go. Davis later said that statement was a fabrication and he "had nothing whatsoever to do with that occurrence. I didn't kill either one of those people, and I don't know anything about it. I was in jail with Birt in 1974, and he told me then that if I testified against him in the Jefferson County [i.e., Fleming] case, then he would implicate me in the Matthews murder."[2128] Because Birt declined to answer certain polygraph questions, authorities believed Davis[2129] may have played a lesser accessory role such as that of a "wheel man," driving the getaway car.[2130] At the conclusion of the trial, the jury's "indecision was understandable. [Birt] had admitted in court that he held a grudge against Davis. How would the jurors know if he was telling the truth about Davis's involvement?" While Georgia law enforcement agencies agreed Birt and Davis had a particular criminal style,

[wwwwwww] Years later, Billy Birt would write that he was no longer mad at Davis; he had forgiven him and felt sorry for him, and after all was said and done, he still liked "the ole son-of-a-bitch" and wished Davis could be released from prison. [Sources: Birt, Billy Stonewall. *Rock Solid In His Own Words: The Inside Story of Billy Sunday Birt.* (2017), pp. 100 & 105; Birt, Billy Stonewall. *Rock Solid: The True Story of Georgia's Dixie Mafia.* (2017), p. 3.]

saying, "It's like them to rob a house and kill the folks,"[2131] Davis was acquitted of the Matthews murders on November 3, 1979.[2132]

Shane Birt would later state his father told him Davis was not present at the Matthews home and "he [Billy Birt] had concocted the whole lie to get back at his former friend and partner." Shane said his father told him both Warren and Rosina Matthews came out of their home shooting, but he did not say who ended up shooting the couple. "When [Birt] concocted this scenario in court, he figured there was no reason not to name Willie Hester as one of the would-be robbers. He was dead [Birt claiming Davis killed Hester to silence him[2133]]. But he didn't want to rat on the others.... He left them out of the made-up story. He named Billy Wayne Davis instead." Because Davis testified against him, Birt wanted to turn the tables on Davis. "He would do anything to get back at Davis, even make up a crime he [Davis] didn't commit."[2134]

While prosecutors and lawmen were grateful "that sometimes criminals tell on each other," and while they sought "to exploit the hatred and desire for revenge between Birt and Davis to...solve crimes they never thought could be solved,"[2135] this tit for tat that continued between Davis and Birt amounted to double hearsay from convicted felons.[2136] "Lawmen [said] that with the bitter feud between Davis and Birt, neither's testimony [was] of much value any longer."[2137]

By the late 1970s, Billy Birt, Billy Wayne Davis, Bobby Gaddis, and Charlie Reed were all in prison, having been handed life sentences for murder, and Birt and Gaddis were facing death in the electric chair. The incarcerations of Birt and Davis, in particular, enabled authorities to effectively dismantle the nucleus of that sect of the Dixie Mafia,[2138] and despite all the self-preserving benefits Davis had expected in return for his snitching, he found himself in the very same boat in which he had placed others.

CHAPTER 25

THE END OF AN ERA

After several stays of execution, a state judge overturned Billy Birt's death sentence in 1979[xxxxxxx] (a fulfillment of Birt's belief that the death chamber would not take his life), and Bobby Gaddis's death sentence was overturned in 1980.[2139] Both were the result of the judge in the original hearings having improperly instructed the jury.[2140] New sentencing hearings were granted on the murder convictions,[2141] but because no attempts were made over time to reinstate their death sentences, both men were relocated to Georgia State Prison in Reidsville in 1996.[2142] Birt was later moved to Smith State Prison in Glenville and ultimately to Ware State Prison in Waycross, each about a four-hour drive one-way from his hometown of Winder.[2143] In 1997, Birt was taken off of death row and placed in the general population[2144] while continuing to serve a life sentence without the possibility of parole.[2145]

Charlie Reed escaped from prison twice, on one occasion five years prior to his parole, but he was captured two months later. He was paroled in 1991 after serving sixteen years of a life sentence. According to Billy Birt's son Stoney, Sheriff Earl Lee appeared before Reed's parole board, telling them that, although Reed had been Birt's comrade in crime and one of his most trusted gang members, Birt had done all the killing. Lee had promised Birt he would do this because he knew Reed had not participated in the Fleming murders.[yyyyyyy] Following his release and despite being warned, Reed tried to rekindle a romance with a former, now married girlfriend, which resulted in the woman's husband having Reed killed. According to Stoney Birt, "Charlie tried to visit a path he shouldn't have." In 1996, at the age of forty-nine, he was shot to death in Gainesville, Georgia "by a man who said Reed walked in front of his rifle when he was adjusting the scope." The long-range shot from the 30/30 deer rifle that took off most of Reed's head was ruled accidental.[2146]

In 2007, at the age of sixty-six and after serving thirty-three years, Bobby Gaddis reportedly "died a 'horrible death' in prison from disease"[2147] – possibly the result of diabetes and cancer.[2148] Billy Birt outlived Gaddis by a decade, which afforded him plenty of time to reflect on his life and deeds. In 1992, Birt professed faith in Christ and was baptized by his ordained minister middle son, Billy Montana Birt.[2149] Reconciling the dichotomy of born-again Birt and Birt the hitman may have been

---

[xxxxxxx] By this time, Birt had received another life sentence for the July 1972 murder of Donald Chancey. [Source: "1972 Slaying: Billy Sunday Birt Gets Life for Murder," *The Macon Telegraph*, Macon, GA, February 20, 1980, p. 1B.]

[yyyyyyy] Charlie Reed's attorney maintained Reed had been wrongly implicated, and Billy Wayne Davis was guilty of the Fleming murders. [Source: "Reed Innocent, Attorney Says," The Macon News, Macon, GA, November 19, 1975, p. 5-A.]

troubling for some, but for those who knew Birt best, it was no revelation his character was awash with complexity and contradictions. Birt "was really two people in one…. He could be kind, and he could be a killer." He "was a man who would not swat a bug if it landed on him, but also a man who would kill a fellow human being without blinking an eye." He wanted his children to obey laws, respect others, and do right, "yet he robbed and stole and burned and murdered."[2150] According to Shane Birt, the best thing about his father's post-conversion was being able to pray with him and to take him by the same hands that had formerly done awful things.[2151]

In sharp contrast to Birt's homicidal bent and the fact that he shot his own brother six times following an argument over a woman, burned his in-laws' home to prevent his mother-in-law from testifying against another brother, and burned down his grandfather's house to keep family members from squabbling about what they would take from it, he exhibited tenderness to animals (horses and dogs[zzzzzzz] in particular) and generosity to those who needed a helping hand, whether loaning someone money, helping a friend put up hay before a rainstorm, or buying a doll for a little girl whose father could not afford it. At least some of Birt's children experienced him as a loyal and loving father and defender.[2152] Even Shane, the youngest, who was a small child when his father went to prison for the last time, says, "When daddy was not killing, he was one of the best people you could be around." Birt also provided well for his wife, albeit via criminal means, and his son Stoney recalls him as a good husband aside from his adulterous affairs. Stoney describes his father as an enigma – a man with a personality contradiction who, on one hand was the best man he had ever known, but on the other hand was the most coldhearted man he had ever known.[2153]

According to Shane Birt, "My daddy's biggest struggle was his urge to get even. He never forgot anything, especially any wrong done against him or his folks…. He couldn't let go if he perceived he'd been done wrong. He had to get even." Birt's philosophy may well have been "If you cross me, I will punish you." According to his daughter Ann, "If you crossed him, they didn't come no more cold-hearted."[2154] One Winder native stated, "Well, you never crossed Billy Birt. But other than that, you wouldn't never find anybody any nicer."[2155] In the words of Stoney Birt, "I know for a fact that if you didn't cross him or one of his associates or didn't have the misfortune of being at the wrong place at the wrong time, you had nothing to fear from him. To the contrary, he was more apt to be your champion or benefactor, if you were a poor person in need."[2156]

Birt himself seemed conflicted and confused about his own personality and actions, writing from prison, "I loved animals. Never harmed a child in my life and was always real nice to everyone, and I liked people. But I will tell you this, everything I ever did I did for money. I wasn't mad at nobody. Never killed no one in anger. Just a job with me. Wish I could go back. I would sure change my line of work…."[2157] At one point, Birt stated, "If you take another person's life, you have to live with it the rest of your life. There's no getting around it…. A man can't go back in this life, and God doesn't give you the power to re-do what you have done."[2158] As Stoney Birt said of his father, "Billy Sunday Birt was not a man that can easily be explained or understood. His entire life was a conflict

---

[zzzzzzz] One notable aspect of the Durham Case was the survival of the Durhams' small pet dog. According to the late Douglas County [Georgia] Sheriff Earl Lee, who knew Birt extremely well, Birt was kind to animals and told Lee "he'd heap rather kill a man than a dog." [Source: Bill Winn, "Law Officers Believe Billy Birt Was State's Most Prolific Killer," *The Sunday Ledger-Enquirer*, Columbus, GA, August 23, 1987, p. 1.]

between good and bad.[2159] You would never see the side of him that come to get you in the middle of the night to kill you or to learn you a lesson."[2160]

Some law enforcement officials believed Birt to be "'incorrigible' and 'without consideration for human life.'"[2161] In terms of his cold-bloodedness, he was described as "a barrel of a man who unwinds gruesome details of murders with as little emotion as a north Georgia farmer describing sausage-making in autumn." While "there [was] no evidence that Birt [was] a joy-killer or that he ever murdered without provocation – although he apparently [provoked] very easily – he [was] thought to have eliminated several competitors for the favors of women he was dating, and he [appeared] to have murdered most often to eliminate witnesses, including friends who helped him commit crimes."[2162] Driven by survival, he was also very calculating, "walking a narrow path, weighing every word and action, being careful not to stumble on an obstacle that [would] put him on the road to the electric chair."[2163]

In 1987, Georgia law enforcement officers believed Birt to be the "the number one killer in Georgia history,"[2164] and while it is difficult to accurately enumerate his murder victims, the most popular estimate is "over fifty." His former wife, Ruby Nell, does not know how many people he killed: "I only know what I've been told. My kids know more than I do. So do some law officers.... There's no way to know the names of all the people Bill killed, or how many he killed. He didn't talk [about] everything he did, even with the kids." In the late 1970s, twenty-some killings were estimated. According to Bob Ingram, "Billy Wayne Davis claimed he could link [Birt] to fifty-two slayings....[aaaaaaaa] It's fair to say he killed a lot of people." Ingram states that, although Birt lacked the notoriety of Ted Bundy and Jeffrey Dahmer, he was "without a doubt, one of the most prolific killers in our country"[2165] and responsible for more homicides than they were.[bbbbbbbb] Sheriff Earl Lee said Birt himself gave him the number fifty-six. Jimmy Terrell, former Chief of Police in Winder, Georgia, had heard a range of fifty-five to eighty-five but believes the lower number more likely.[2166] According to Stoney Birt, his father told him he killed more than one-hundred people over a fifteen-year period.[2167] Shane Birt says his father told him during a prison visit "he had exterminated 'either 158 or 168 lives," and adds, "Dad never lied to me." Shane also states his father once told him "they" (presumably Billy Birt and/or his associates) had killed victims in all fifty states. Contrary to claims that Birt never embellished or lied, former GBI Agent Ronnie Angel said Birt "embellished his ill deeds to make himself look better, or worse, depending on who was judging. 'Most [criminals] wouldn't tell the whole truth. Birt was the same. But he was pretty honest with me.'"[2168] Bob Ingram believes that, not only is Birt suspected of committing fifty-two to fifty-six homicides over a ten-year span (at least twenty-eight of which occurred in Barrow County[2169]),

---

[aaaaaaaa] In 2019, Davis told North Carolina law officers that Billy Birt told him he had killed twenty-six people, but Davis believed eight to ten people was more realistic. By 2021, Davis substantially upped Birt's victims to the middle hundreds. [Sources: Davis, Billy Wayne. Interview with Len Hagaman, Carolynn Johnson, & Wade Colvard. September 30, 2019; Davis, Billy Wayne. Interview with Bob Ingram, Len Hagaman & Carolynn Johnson. August 3, 2021.]

[bbbbbbbb] Ted Bundy had 35 proven victims and 36-100+ possible victims. Jeffrey Dahmer had 16 proven victims and a possible 17. The estimated number of Billy Birt's murder victims also exceeds those of John Wayne Gacy and rivals those of Gary Ridgeway (aka "The Green River Killer"). Samuel Little is believed to have been the most prolific American serial killer with 60 proven and 93 possible victims (he initially confessed to 90), and investigations into his crimes are ongoing. Little's crimes spanned 35-52 years, so Birt's record is all the more remarkable considering it only spanned about a decade. [Sources: Wikipedia: "List of serial killers by number of victims," https://en.wikipedia.org/wiki/List_of_serial_killers_by_number_of_victims; Wikipedia: Samuel Little, https://en.wikipedia.org/wiki/Samuel_Little.]

he is actually guilty of them, and thirty-six to thirty-eight of them have been confirmed by evidence with the cases closed, some of them after Birt's death. The majority of these murders, which occurred primarily in Georgia but throughout the southeast, were associated with robberies or retaliatory contracts.[2170] Although Shane Birt recalled his father saying, "I can't remember everything that I've done,"[2171] when Bob Ingram interviewed Billy Birt in prison, he was "amazed at how he could recall the smallest details of his killings." Ingram asked him how he could remember all those little things. Birt leaned over and responded, "Have you ever killed anybody? You don't forget."[2172]

Billy Sunday Birt
(Source: Murderpedia.org)

On April 6, 2017, after serving more than forty years, Birt died at the Ware State Prison infirmary in Waycross, Georgia four months shy of his eightieth birthday. "His worst fear [had been] that he would live a long life in prison away from his children..." and he had discussed suicide – either sticking a sharpened pen into a vein in his arm and bleeding out or strangling himself with a sheet. Having been in the infirmary for about two years, Parkinson's disease limiting his mobility to a wheelchair, he ultimately went through with the latter method. "Lying in bed...[he] grabbed hold of the metal triangle above his head – the trapeze bar infirm prisoners use to move in bed. He had ripped off a strip of his bed sheet, tied one end of the strip around the bar and the other end around his neck. Holding onto the bar, he slowly leaned back," the sheet choking the life out of him – perhaps an irony of ironies considering others he had strangled. "And with that one simple movement...Birt took the life of one [last] human being."[2173]

PART IV:
CASE CLOSED?

CHAPTER 26

A QUESTION OF SEMANTICS

In November 2021, at the North Carolina Sheriff's Association office in Raleigh, Sheriff Len Hagaman and Captain Carolynn Johnson of the Watauga County Sheriff's Office, along with SBI Agent Wade Colvard and former North Carolina Attorney General and Secretary of State Rufus Edmisten, met for about an hour and a half with Ginny Durham Mackie and her husband Steve, as well as Ginny's uncle Bill Durham and his son Steve to inform them of the similarities between the Durham and Fleming murder cases, the pertinence of statements made by Shane Birt and Billy Wayne Davis, and the conclusions authorities had reached concerning the identification of Bryce, Virginia, and Bobby Durham's killers.[2174] The meeting was also intended to bring closure to the Durham Case, and at its conclusion, the law enforcement officers and the family felt that had been achieved.[2175]

Around three months later, on February 8, 2022 – fifty years and five days after the murders – the Watauga County Sheriff's Office announcement that the case had been closed was published in the hometown newspaper:

Local triple homicide case solved after 50 years

"BOONE — A tip from a Georgia sheriff's office has helped the Watauga County Sheriff's Office bring closure to a 50-year-old triple homicide case that occurred in Boone on Feb. 3, 1972, known locally as the Durham Case.

"Bryce Durham, 51, his wife Virginia, 44, and son Bobby, 18, were found brutally murdered in their home during a snowstorm. Troy Hall, the Durham's son-in law, found the family deceased after he and his wife — the Durhams' daughter, Ginny — went to check on the family with the help of a neighbor.

"Billy Wayne Davis, 81, currently a resident of a correctional facility in Augusta, Georgia, is believed to be the only surviving perpetrator in the Durham Case. Other perpetrators have been identified as Billy Sunday Birt, Bobby Gene Gaddis and Charles David Reed, all deceased.

"'In May 2019, we received a phone call from the White County Sheriff's Office in Georgia about information that we recognized could be very important to the Durham case,' said Watauga County Sheriff Len Hagaman in a press release. 'We immediately began to investigate the new leads and conducted in-person interviews with Billy Wayne Davis in September 2019, October

2020 and August 2021. It was these interviews that ultimately helped us determine who was responsible through the corroboration of evidence. We are confident that we now know who committed these crimes.'

"Interviews with two sources corroborated evidence from the Durham Case crime scene, and the circumstances of the crime were similar to a 1973 case in Georgia, known as the Fleming Case, in which Birt, Gaddis, Reed and Davis were all involved. Led by Birt, Davis, Reed and Gaddis were part of a loosely organized network known as the Georgia-based 'Dixie Mafia,' which is thought to have engaged in dozens of violent crimes in Georgia and elsewhere across the Southeast in the 1960s and '70s.

"The 2019 lead first surfaced when Birt's son, Shane Birt, was at the White County Sheriff's Office to participate in research for a book about crimes that had taken place in Georgia, including the Fleming Case. Shane Birt shared that he was very close with his father and recalled a story Birt had told him during a prison visit when he admitted to killing three people in the North Carolina mountains during a heavy snowstorm, remembering that they almost got caught.

"After hearing Shane Birt's account, the White County Sheriff's Office immediately contacted WCSO. Davis was interviewed by WCSO investigators at the Georgia facility where he is serving a life sentence for crimes he committed in Georgia. During those interviews, Davis implicated Birt, Gaddis and Reed as engaging in a hired 'hit' in the North Carolina mountains, one where they almost got caught during a bad snowstorm. Davis claimed to have acted only as their getaway driver, and that it was the other three men that entered the house that night.

"'Had Sheriff Hagaman and his team not taken this tip seriously, this case may never have been solved,' said Chris Laws, special agent in charge for the Northwestern District, North Carolina State Bureau of Investigation. 'Many agencies, law enforcement officials, investigators and agents worked diligently on this case for decades.'

"It remains unclear who solicited the crime against the Durham family. In November 2021, the WCSO held a meeting with Durham family members to inform them of their investigation and conclusions.

"'This is a much-needed turning point for the Durham Case,' Hagaman said. 'We cannot begin to express our thanks to all the professionals and community members who collaborated for so many years to help resolve this case. We sincerely thank you for your commitment.'

"Ginny Durham also shared her gratitude in a statement, saying, 'I would like to thank all of the people who worked for decades on my family's case. I know that they sacrificed many days and weekends in order to work on solving this case since 1972.'

"'I would especially like to thank Len Hagaman, Sheriff of Watauga County, who has been involved from the beginning and was dedicated to a closure for myself and my family; Wade Colvard, SBI Special Agent; Carolynn Johnson, Captain of Investigations for Watauga County Sheriff's Office; and Charles Whitman, SBI Special Agent, who continued to work on the case, even in retirement. I am so grateful for his help and friendship during the difficult years.'

"Hagaman thanked the North Carolina State Bureau of Investigation, Watauga County Sheriff's Office, Boone Police Department, White County Sheriff's Office in Georgia, Georgia Bureau of Investigation, Appalachian State University Police Department and many other professionals, community members and their families for their years of hard work on the case.

"'I'd also like to thank WCSO Captain of Investigations Carolynn Johnson, SBI Special Agent in Charge for the Northwestern District, Chris Laws, and White County Sheriff's Office Chief Deputy Bob Ingram for their recent investigative work on this case since 2019,' Hagaman said. 'I know I also speak for the entire Watauga County community when I say that we will never forget to keep the Durham family in our thoughts and prayers. Please, let's remember their continued wishes for privacy.'

"The Watauga County Sheriff's Office also expressed its appreciation for the many professionals that worked to help resolve the Durham Case since 1972. This case touched the High Country community and beyond, and the sheriff's office stated it is grateful for each of these individuals who played a role in helping to find answers for the Durham family and bring this case to a close."[2176]

Sheriff Hagaman acknowledged the sleepless nights endured by state and local law enforcement officers as they devoted hour upon hour conducting countless interviews, pursuing "a whole host of leads" (many of them dead ends), and exploring "what ifs and speculation." Hagaman and other lawmen spent an enormous amount of time on the roadways between Boone, Wilkes County, Winston-Salem, and Raleigh among other places.[2177] The toll of working on the Durham Case and other homicides, no doubt, had a profound effect on many of these civil servants.[cccccccc]

Hagaman told the press many of the deceased investigators who worked on the Durham Case would have loved to have been able to announce that the killers had been identified.[2178] After he left law enforcement, Jerry Vaughn continued to work on the case as a private investigator because it interested him, and because he desired to see it solved before his own death as well as before the deaths of former Watauga County Sheriff Ward Carroll, former Boone Police Chief Clyde Tester, and others.[2179] Tester was obsessed with the case. While still in office in 1973, he stated "he would be 'willing to give up law enforcement' with a satisfied mind if he could see the case closed."[2180] Even on his death bed, he expressed to his family that one of his greatest regrets was that the case had never been solved.[2181] As former SBI Agent Lewis Young stated, "It's frustrating for police officers who can't get to run the last ten yards of a hundred-yard touchdown."[2182] At retired SBI Agent Charlie Whitman's 2015 funeral, Rufus Edmisten delivered a eulogy in which he requested Whitman to send some tips from heaven that would help solve the Durham murders.[2183] According to Whitman's widow Pat, her husband probably worked the longest and hardest on the Durham Case than any other, and she believes, after entering heaven and first meeting God, her husband found the Durhams and asked who killed them.[2184]

While the Watauga County Sheriff's Office announcement was both unexpected and welcomed, many local citizens took issue with some of the terminology used. The terms "closure," "solved," and "resolved" became sticking points. Although Hagaman felt closure had been achieved,

---

[cccccccc] Retired Boone Police Sergeant Jeff Rucker felt strongly entrenched in the Durham Case, especially after meeting the victims' family members, and he believes that is how all the men and women who spent hours on the case felt. [Source: Rucker, Jeff. Phone interview with author October 4, 2023.]

including some degree of it for surviving Durham family members,[dddddddd] onlookers felt it was not fully clear as to how authorities knew the right men had been identified as the killers, and it remained to be established who had solicited the crime and what the motive had been. Some argued the sheriff's office could not achieve complete closure until the instigator of the murders had been identified. Others leveled personal criticism at Hagaman for the timing of the press release, claiming he had announced the case's resolution during an election year to bolster himself as an incumbent.[eeeeeeee] The timing was also curious, in part, because three years had elapsed between Bob Ingram's initial 2019 call to the sheriff's office and the 2022 press release. Had the sheriff's office purposely delayed its announcement to coincide with the fiftieth anniversary of the Durham murders for dramatic effect? In contrast, many other individuals expressed appreciation for Hagaman and his officers. This was echoed by former SBI Agent John Parker, who had worked briefly on the Durham Case. In his estimation, Hagaman did a good job following up on the new developments, but he likewise echoed those who questioned the case being closed: "They really haven't closed the book on who's responsible for it. The big question is 'Who paid for it?'"[2185] Retired Boone Police Sergeant Jeff Rucker says it is unfortunate the case went this long, and he is thankful there is some resolution, but he does not think it is a closed book either.[2186]

Although the Watauga County Sheriff's Office and Bob Ingram felt confident they had proven who killed the Durhams, Keith Billiot, a retired Drug Enforcement Administration agent who reviewed and assessed the recorded interviews with Billy Wayne Davis, disagrees. According to Billiot, "These interviews didn't prove a thing.... If you can't prove it, don't say you've proved it. Don't say that you've closed it if you can't prove it.... If you couldn't take that case into court and prove it, you shouldn't be standing up in front of the world and saying that you've solved the case." Billiot says you can look into a case with the hope of providing true closure to family members, but there are times that is not possible, and a law enforcement officer has to say, "'Hey, you know what? I looked into it. I did the best I could.' That's the time when you have a quiet conversation with the family, and there is nothing wrong with you saying, 'In my mind, I really believe that so and so was involved in this. I believe so and so did this. I believe that these other people were involved.' There's nothing wrong with that. But there's a big, big problem with declaring you've solved the case.... I don't know what the family thinks of this. I can imagine if...a family member of mine had been murdered, obviously [I'd] want law enforcement to come forth and say, "Hey, this is who did it.' But if it were me...I'd like to know...'How did they do it?' 'Well, we think this, we think that.' No, no, no. Did you prove that they did it? And if you can't prove it, well then, why would you tell the family that?"[2187]

Sheriff Hagaman subsequently clarified that the term "closed" is used by law enforcement regardless of whether a case is actually solved or not. Similarly, Rufus Edmisten stated, "You can

---

[dddddddd] According to podcaster Sean Kipe, "The family and friends left behind still feel a void. Even the closing of the case hasn't given them the closure they had hoped for." [Source: Sean Kipe, Imperative Entertainment, *In The Red Clay,* podcast audio, Season 2, Episode 6: *Beneath the Chestnut Tree,* January 6, 2023, http://intheredclaypodcast.com

[eeeeeeee] This was not the first time a Watauga County Sheriff had been criticized in regard to the Durham Case and reelection. Around 1988, Cecil and Mildred Small expressed similar opinions about Sheriff Red Lyons. The Smalls claimed that, when Lyons initially ran for the office, he promised to make the Durham case his highest priority and to solve it, and in their estimation, he had done nothing about it but had begun to bring it up again as the time for his reelection neared – "time to start 'politicking' again," according to the Smalls. [Source: Cecil & Mildred Small, interview with Caroline Walker (*Watauga Democrat* Staff Writer), February 23, 1989, Watauga County Sheriff's Office investigation file 118-H-1/2/3.]

close a case, and that doesn't mean that you've solved it. I could see why the sheriff said the case is closed. That doesn't mean it's solved totally, because until you have a definitive answer, you didn't solve anything."[2188] Hagaman acknowledged his own doubt the case would ever be fully *solved*, while expressing his personal relief that the case had been *resolved*. And, while these statements seem to be contradictory, the words solved and resolved, although close in meaning, have distinct differences. Whereas solving something generally means finding a correct or complete answer or explanation to a problem, resolving something can mean settling or finishing something…bringing a problem to an end or conclusion…even if the choices made do not please everyone[2189] – much like a judge settling a court case and bringing it to an end, even if the litigants are not satisfied with the final outcome. Just as Hagaman and Edmisten clarified, although the Watauga County Sheriff's Office had not completely answered or explained (i.e., solved) the Durham Case, it had brought the case to an end or conclusion (i.e., resolved it). Unfortunately, these two words had not been delineated in the press release and were used interchangeably as if they were synonymous, and this confused laymen. Hagaman had brought the Durham Case to a conclusion, albeit a conclusion that some citizens found unsatisfactory. Comments from the local citizenry did not escape Hagaman's attention; still, he hoped the same sense of relief he felt would also be true for the community. In the court of public opinion, however, there remained a feeling among some of unfinished business and unadministered justice and a reluctance to understand or accept how an unsolved case could be declared closed.[2190]

Within days of the newspaper press release, Hagaman answered additional questions via a press conference and individual interviews. He reiterated that, based on Billy Wayne Davis's confession and what Hagaman perceived to be accurate information that Davis had provided (including pointing the finger at the rest of his comrades), the Watauga County Sheriff's Office had no doubt about who murdered the Durhams. While Hagaman emphasized that no one is left to interview and there is "no way of totally verifying what actually happened" or to "gain any more information regarding the details of the case due to the fact that the most important people involved are deceased and what they knew went with them to the grave," he expressed – almost in a hopeful reversal of thought – his belief that "somebody [probably] knows something somewhere," although he had no earthly idea how to find them, unless something like the power of social media brought them forward.[2191] In somewhat of a reiteration of this, Hagaman stated about the case, "It's closed, but it's not closed."[2192]

Hagaman also stated, "It's…unfortunate that…time has taken a lot of folks away from us that we would love to interview," and he counted Troy Hall in that number, acknowledging some people, including himself, suspected Troy as "the main guy…from day one" – the person who "set this whole thing in motion" – but that proof had been lost due to the deaths of Troy and Billy Sunday Birt. Hagaman speculated Birt was the one who would have worked with the instigator to arrange the crime, and he [Birt] was not the type of person who would divulge the instigator's identity to his associates. "From what I understand in interviews and from what others have said about [Birt]…he would not share that because he wanted to keep control." Hagaman further speculated the reason Billy Wayne Davis did not respond to questions about who instigated the crime was likely because "Davis and his crew were involved in a whole lot of bad things," and some of the details of those crimes ran together.[2193]

It was surprising to Bob Ingram that the detail about a nephew or son-in-law having solicited the murders was never mentioned in the February 2022 press release or press conference. According to Ingram, when he received a courtesy draft of the press release from the Watauga County Sheriff's

Office, prior to its publication, mention of it was included, but it was later removed.[2194] Rufus Edmisten had advised Hagaman to be careful regarding what he stated in the press release,[2195] albeit not necessarily in regard to that specific point, but had that detail been made public from the start, it might have alleviated some of the community's dissatisfaction with the case being declared closed and its yearning to have additional answers as to who was behind the crime. It might also have been beneficial to have elaborated on how the identification of the killers was achieved and all the steps involved in that process. And it may have behooved the sheriff's office to have merely stated there had been new developments in the case rather than declaring the case closed. Word choice and the absence or oversight of certain critical details resulted in the public not having a fuller picture and therefore feeling somewhat frustrated.

In arguments over semantics, individuals disagree about the definition of a word or a phrase, not about material facts.[2196] But soon enough, the material facts would lead to further disagreements as the statements of Shane Birt and Billy Wayne Davis relative to the murders of Bryce, Virginia, and Bobby Durham became intensely scrutinized and questioned.

CHAPTER 27

THOSE FATHER-SON TALKS

The person who reignited the Durham Case in 2019 was Shane Birt, and the conclusion one reaches about the guilt or innocence of Billy Birt, Billy Wayne Davis, Bobby Gaddis, and Charlie Reed hinges, in part, on whether one believes what Shane Birt has said.

Shane's brother, Stoney Birt, had never heard of the Durhams or their murders until the February 2022 Watauga County Sheriff's Office press release, when he saw a television news bulletin. He was shocked to learn of Shane's meetings with Bob Ingram and of the jail cell confessions of Billy Wayne Davis that implicated Billy Birt, Gaddis, and Reed.[2197] According to Stoney, "It knocked me off my feet.... I mean it was right up there with hearing my father got another death sentence. [That] was how it affected me."[2198]

Almost immediately after hearing the announcement, Stoney received a media request and believed he was "in a pickle" because he was being asked to comment on something he was still trying to process.[2199] The day after the press release, Stoney spoke with a North Carolina television station regarding what his father had told his brother: "He'd just sort of hint every once in a while, and he'd say something. On this particular case, he told my baby brother about one time he was in North Carolina in a snowstorm…on a hit, and that was the clue that connected the dots."[2200] A few weeks later, in a newspaper interview, Stoney stated "that his father maintained he participated in the killings of some people in the Carolinas, but…he [Stoney] didn't know the details or names of the victims [and] the snowstorm was never brought up during those conversations." In that same interview, Stoney stated Billy Wayne Davis may have been the one who was contracted in the killings: "It's a toss-up between him and my father. There were no secrets between [them.]"[2201]

Both of these media interviews gave the impression that Stoney was aware of and assenting to his father's likely participation in the Durham murders, but he says he found himself trapped between a rock and a hard place: "It had me all befuddled." According to Stoney, he felt if he declined to comment or attempted to refute his brother's claims about what their father had told Shane, he would appear to be insensitive or callous. People were jubilant the case had been solved, and no one wanted to hear it was not true. Stoney felt that to deny his father's involvement without proof would be the equivalent of not expressing remorse for what his father may have done. Stoney says he wanted people to know he did care, so he chose not to make an issue out of it at that time by saying something negative. Instead, he says he made an attempt at damage control by simply repeating what Shane had said. According to Stoney, "It was the lesser of two evils; say nothing or just try to show a little compassion."[2202] In actuality, Stoney maintains that everything Shane claims to have been told by their father is not only untrue but never happened.[2203]

It is noteworthy that, in the two and a half week period between Shane's April and May 2019 interviews with Bob Ingram, he went from having vague knowledge of a murder his father committed in the early 1970s during a heavy snow somewhere north of Georgia – without specifics of who the victims were or what happened to them – to suddenly knowing the crime occurred in the mountains of North Carolina in 1972 or 1973, the number of victims and their relationships to one another, the husband's occupation, the victims' surname and more or less how they were killed, the killers' identities, that robbery was the motive, and that a relative of the family had set up the murders. This seeming epiphany rouses curiosity as to what transpired in such a short span of time to enable Shane to have these additional and specific details. Shane said his father had originally shared this information with him as many as twenty-five years earlier and certainly no later than 2017 when his father died, which was two years prior to Shane's initial interviews with Ingram. Why had none of these details become clear to him in all of those ensuing years, yet they did so within a two and a half week timeframe? Did the floodgates of his mind suddenly burst open to release suppressed information? Did someone other than his father provide him with those additional details between his April and May 2019 interviews? Is it possible Shane conducted an internet search using his initially scant remembrances and discovered news articles or websites that further educated him about the Durham Case? If the latter were true, then it seems he would have been able to include the water-filled bathtub in his account to Ingram, and he would have encountered the oft reprinted photograph of Bobby Durham, enabling him to know the gender of the "adult kid" he talked about. Then, by November 2020, Shane seemed to have recalled even additional details, including Billy Birt's mention of "Boone" as the location of the murders, that his father drove the getaway car back to Georgia, that the son-in-law or nephew who instigated the murders was young, and the order in which the Durhams were killed.

In describing his own ability or inability to remember details concerning his father's criminal past, Stoney Birt acknowledges his mind is full of so many memories that, due to human limitations, he cannot pull them up like a computer might, but "when it hits, it hits."[2204] This seems to also describe Shane's self-assessment of his own capacity for recall. According to Shane, details of all his father told him continue to unfold. "Still to this day, I can drive by places and know there's something there, but I still can't put my finger on it." He expects that to be true for the remainder of his life: "After my interviews – after me and Bob started talking – it just seemed like small avalanches, like a floodgate every now and then. After three days of me recounting everything I thought daddy told me…there's still some stuff that I know for a fact [is] gonna eventually come home to haunt me that I've forgotten about."[2205]

Even since those 2019-2020 interviews, Shane says he has recalled additional details concerning the Durham Case. In a 2024 interview, he stated this was a for-hire job that had been set up by someone who lied about what would be found in the house. Not only were his father and his father's accomplices supposed to find money, but pills as well, and they were to receive additional money on the backend from the Durhams' life insurance policies. According to Shane, no safe was found in the house, and the house was staged to look like a robbery. He added that the reason his mother only had half a set of silver was that some of the silver his father took from the Durham home had spilled into the ditch line, presumably out of either the Durham's GMC "Jimmy" after it had been taken from the home or the getaway car. Shane also recalled his father telling him that he had drowned the Durhams,[2206] which was contrary to his 2020 statement that Phil Hudgins provided him with that information rather than his father.

One would think that, since the allegations of the Dixie Mafia's participation in the Durham murders became public in 2022, and since the case has received renewed media attention as well as Phil Hudgins devoting a chapter to the murders in his book, Shane would have been exposed to lots of new details concerning the case. On the contrary, Shane says he has only read about 70% of Hudgins' book and has not seen any televised coverage or details of how the Durham Case transpired, indicating that the only knowledge he has of the case is what he remembers his father telling him, plus some details that Hudgins provided to him.[2207]

Shane Birt and Bob Ingram agree that, from the start, due to the volume of information Shane's father reportedly imparted to him over a period of years, Shane was prone to confusion regarding which details pertained to which cases. For example, Shane was certain his father told him a nephew or a son-in-law set up a crime because he had heard his "daddy cuss about this cat forever and ever." Shane was initially convinced this was in relation to the Fleming Case, but once Ingram informed him that was incorrect, he realized it pertained to the Durham Case.[2208] According to Shane, "That's what I mean by everything just jumbled together, and you'd get bits and pieces because [daddy] would talk about this, and he'd talk about this, and he'd talk about that one."[2209]

According to Ingram, there were missing details in *every* case Shane's father told him about, and people have a hard time understanding why Shane's memories are so fragmented and why he struggles with recalling them all at once or in a linear fashion. Ingram compares it to making a cake with fifty-six ingredients, stirring them together, and then trying to individually distinguish them. Ingram reiterates that the things Shane's father told him were not told from beginning to end, and Shane's difficulty with sifting through this information and figuring it out was compounded by both the large number of crimes Billy Birt committed and his speech impediment, which made deciphering his words difficult. According to Shane, however, "What he did reveal was fairly easy to remember, frankly because of his speech impediment. When he would talk to you, he would pronounce a word and then he would ask, 'Do you understand what I said?' Sometimes, Shane said, he would make his listener say the word back to him. It was like practicing for a spelling bee. The listener remembered."[2210]

In terms of the Durham Case, Ingram says Shane initially mentioned "a job in the mountains of North Carolina where they [were] caught in a blinding snowstorm, and then it became Boone, like Daniel Boone, and [then] it became Durham, like Bull Durham, and it started to unravel in pieces." Ingram says he asked Shane to think about these things and try to improve his memory, and Shane was able to do that over time and several interviews, not only with the Durham Case, but with others as well. Ingram says Shane initiated any follow-up with added details, and whenever he phoned Ingram to say, "Hey, I remembered something else," Ingram asked him to come in so it could be recorded.[2211]

When Bob Ingram was asked about the possibility of Shane Birt obtaining information regarding the Durham Case from sources other than his father, including from Ingram himself, Ingram stated, "Did [Shane] get any details from me? Absolutely, positively not."[2212] According to Ingram, he tries not to lead others or put words in their mouths to make what they say fit his own theories:[2213] "Did some of the additional details come to him? Yes. Where did he acquire them? Not from Bob

Ingram." Ingram says he has no idea how Shane would have come up with this information other than hearing it from his father.[2214]

Shane admits to being diagnosed as a narcissist,[2215] and Stoney Birt claims this to be the reason Shane makes up and tells things – that Shane loves attention and feels a need to be "one of the guys."[2216] On the contrary, by some accounts – which Stoney denounces – Shane seeks no attention nor is motivated by it: "I'm not confessing to murders for my dad for any kind of money or any kind of fame or anything like that." According to Bob Ingram, although Shane wants no awards, he [Shane] is responsible for solving the fifty-year-old Durham Case and feels it is a shame that Shane has never been properly thanked for it.[2217]

While "wanting attention, accolades, and validation are not narcissistic in nature…narcissists are unable to make healthy connections and stand in need of attention and admiration. They will deliberately find or create situations in which they are regularly the center of attention, often as a way to stave off" underlying depression, low self-esteem, a lack of confidence, and a perceived lack of acceptance that is "often a result of early childhood trauma and attachment issues" in which the individual's childhood caregivers failed to properly love him, ignored his emotional needs, and/or emotionally abandoned him, "causing psychological damage that extend[ed] into adulthood." An example of narcissistic supply, which "refers to the constant supply of attention and admiration needed by narcissists," is to be publicly recognized for an achievement or accomplishment.[2218] Narcissists frequently "engage in truth distortion" and sometimes "exaggerate the truth."[2219] They also sometimes "twist reality to suit their needs" and "really believe their own lies."[2220] Is it possible that Shane, feeling abandoned by virtue of his father's life imprisonment, developed a need for a father figure (such as Bob Ingram), whose validation and acceptance he sought? Could this have resulted in Shane exaggerating his visits with his father and the things his father told him? And could this have resulted in him offering Durham Case details that he had run across, perhaps during his own research about murders in the southeast? Could he have deliberately found information about the case and then created a situation that would bring him attention? Granted, no proof exists of Billy Birt's admissions of such details to his son other than Shane's word that the conversations took place,[2221] but there is likewise nothing to prove that Shane has falsified a connection between his father and the Durham murders.

When *The Atlanta Journal-Constitution* published an article regarding the opposing viewpoints that Stoney and Shane have of their father, Shane's interview was conducted in the presence of his therapist and Bob Ingram. Stoney argues that this is a way of shielding Shane from hard questions that he would be unable to answer because everything he has said regarding the Durham and other cases involving their father is untrue. But according to Shane, participating in interviews by himself is upsetting; it is helpful to have Ingram present so that he can vouch for the validity of Shane's statements, and Shane's therapist can limit questions that may harm his mental and emotional health.[2222] Shane states that meeting Ingram proved to be therapeutic, and Ingram states he and Shane became friends.[2223] In fact, Shane says he has never had a friend like Ingram, and the first day they met, he could tell he finally had someone in his life he could relate to as it concerned Billy Birt. According to Shane, he and Ingram have experienced the same sleepless nights, and Ingram not only knows the same stories he does, but also knows them to be true.[2224]

Stoney further claims Shane's motivation in linking their father to the Durham Case is partially money-driven.[2225] Stoney says Shane bragged to him about being offered a $40,000 book advance "if he was able to close the [Durham] case." Stoney, however, does not believe this to be a book advance but reward money.[2226] By early 1992, which was the last time the Durham Case reward fund was reported, it stood at $50,000[2227] and consisted of donations from private individuals, businesses, and civic organizations as well as an offering by the State of North Carolina. Contrary to Stoney's claims, Shane says he has never been paid by anyone for the information he has provided.[2228] According to former North Carolina Attorney General and Secretary of State Rufus Edmisten, the state's portion of the reward fund is overseen by the North Carolina Department of Administration.[ffffffff] Edmisten doubts any reward money has been paid to Shane as a lot of bureaucratic paperwork, including affirmations from the Watauga County Sheriff's Office and the State Bureau of Investigation would be required.[2229] As of May 2023, Sheriff Len Hagaman had no knowledge of reward money being paid to anyone,[2230] and Bob Ingram has no knowledge of Shane receiving any money.[2231]

Meanwhile, Stoney has additional thoughts regarding some of the details Shane has imparted. For example, Stoney believes Shane's recollection of their father being caught in a snowstorm was derived from a previously documented account of Billy Birt being in Montana. According to Stoney, Shane specifically took details from the chapter titled "A Cold Day In Montana," in Stoney's book about their father, and wove them into the Durham murder account, set in North Carolina. During one of his interviews with Bob Ingram, Shane stated another of his brothers, Billy Montana Birt, was so named because their father had been on "a job" in Montana and had gotten shot there. But according to Stoney, their father was in Montana after having hitchhiked there as a young teenager, running away from home alongside a childhood friend. The two boys had left Georgia in warm weather, but by the time they arrived in Montana, they were woefully underdressed and almost froze to death in the midst of a surprise blizzard. And while a snowstorm really did play a role in the Durham Case, Stoney believes Shane used their father's Montana blizzard experience to translate him into the "Durham snowstorm."

Regarding Shane's mention of a son-in-law or nephew of the Durhams being the person who instigated their murders, Stoney believes "nephew" was derived from the fact that Otis Reidling, Jr. *[one of Billy Birt's Dixie Mafia members, who Shane, at one point, claimed assisted in the Durham murders rather than Charlie Reed, as he had earlier stated[gggggggg]]* was married to Billy Birt's niece and was, therefore, like a nephew to him. Stoney believes Shane found mention of "son-in-law" during online searches about the Durham murders between his [Shane's] April and May 2019 interviews with Bob Ingram.[2232] Based on "bits and pieces [he] got throughout [his] life," Shane says he believes the son-in-law (presumably Troy Hall) was related to Willie Hester, Jr. (another member of Billy Birt's inner circle). When pressed for more concrete specifics of such a relationship between Hall and Hester, Shane acknowledges that, although people look for solid answers, he does not have them, but he believes this information had to come from his father.[2233][hhhhhhhh] Stoney

---

[ffffffff] The author subsequently contacted the North Carolina Department of Administration and was told neither they nor the North Carolina State Archives had any records concerning the Durham reward money. [Sources: E-mails to the author from the Communications Office, North Carolina Department of Administration, June 6 & July 3, 2023.]
[gggggggg] Billy Wayne Davis also expressed some hesitancy about Charlie Reed's involvement and, paired with Shane Birt's mention of Reidling rather than Reed being his father's accomplice in the Durham murders, that certainly casts doubt on Reed's guilt. Captain Carolynn Johnson states they attempted to explore this discrepancy with Davis but more or less went with some of Davis's statements that *did* implicate Reed. [Source: Johnson, Carolynn. In-person interview with author. January 16, 2024.]
[hhhhhhhh] Willie Hester, Jr.'s mother was Nishey *Hall* Hester, but in his genealogical research, the author found no familial relationship between her and Troy Hall's family or between any of Willie Hester, Jr.'s and Troy Hall's ancestors.

believes Shane mish-mashed all these relationships into his claim regarding a son-in-law's or nephew's involvement in the Durham murders, and while it is almost universally agreed that Durham son-in-law Troy Hall was involved in the murders, Stoney does not believe Shane was provided that information by their father.

When Shane told officers in November 2020 that Otis Reidling, Jr. assisted his father, Billy Wayne Davis, and Bobby Gaddis with the killings in North Carolina, he further stated the Durham murders drove Reidling crazy, causing him to hug (i.e., cling to) his chimney and to say that the ghost of a North Carolina woman jumped on his car one day. *[In the second part of his April 2019 interview with Bob Ingram, Shane had more accurately stated Reidling's breakdown, including that his being on the top of his house hugging the chimney was related to the first or close to the first murder Reidling was present for. But during that interview, Shane made no association between Reidling's breakdown and the Durham murders as he would more than a year and a half later.]* An episode of the *In The Red Clay* podcast[2234] that dealt with Reidling's breakdown[iiiiiiii] – including the rooftop and chimney details – aired on November 15, 2020, and aligned with Shane's 2019 telling of it, but in Shane's subsequent interview on November 16, 2020 (the day after the podcast episode aired), he deviated from both the podcast account and his own earlier account by tying Reidling to the Durham murders.

When asked about the Charlie Reed/Otis Reidling discrepancy in a 2024 interview, Shane had no recollection of mentioning Reidling in the 2020 interview, but he said he may have used him as an example of something. In that same 2024 interview, Bob Ingram, who facilitated the 2020 interview stated, "Otis Reidling's name never came up in regard to the Boone case. Now, Otis Reidling's name came up as one of Bill Birt's associates who Bill Birt and Bill Davis killed, but it never came up as related to the Boone case." Perhaps Shane's and Ingram's memories regarding this mention of Reidling lapsed in the four-year interim between these two interviews, but the audio recording of the 2020 interview clearly proves Shane stated Reidling committed the Durham murders alongside his father and Billy Wayne Davis, subsequently adding in Bobby Gaddis.[2235] Stoney Birt believes this to be yet one more example of Shane's propensity to conflate accounts regarding their father and his associates,[2236] which could, in turn, cast doubt on the accuracy of other things he has said.

Aside from Shane's claims about what his father told him, what were Billy Birt's known habits in discussing the crimes he committed? Although he wrote letters from prison outlining some of his life experiences, including some of his illegal activities, he was generally tight-lipped and "never talked about his crimes to [anyone who wasn't involved], anyone he didn't know, and seldom to those he knew well."[2237] One of the people Birt trusted was Douglas County (Georgia) Sheriff Earl Lee, who "may have been the only person who knew everything Birt did, every crime he committed during the years-long reign of terror, mostly in Barrow and surrounding counties." Lee "heard the truth from the man himself" in conversations that were "usually held behind closed doors."[2238] In Bob Ingram's experience, Birt was never one to elaborate. "He wasn't going to tell you what you didn't know.... He wasn't going to volunteer anything to you." Ingram says he and Birt never lied to one another. "He didn't tell me much, but when he told me something, it was fact."[2239] Birt also

---

[iiiiiiii] In November 1973, Reidling had been the lookout during a double homicide carried out by Billy Birt and Billy Wayne Davis in Georgia. According to Billy Birt, Reidling had never witnessed such murders, and that, combined with a lack of sleep and being on drugs, caused him to go berserk, "hollering, screaming, and crying." [Source: Birt, Ruby Nell (as told to Phil Hudgins), *Grace and Disgrace: Living with Faith and a Dixie Mafia Hit Man* (YAV Publications, Asheville, NC, 2022), p. 190.]

occasionally corresponded with former Winder, Georgia Chief of Police (and Winder's current mayor) Jimmy Terrell, but he "never mentioned his crimes in any of his letters." According to Terrell, if he asked Birt if he was involved in a crime, Birt would not talk, but if he [Birt] was on the periphery of a crime, he would say he might know something about it.[2240]

For a time, even Birt's family knew very little about his criminal activities, although his religious conversion may have motivated him to be more introspective, forthcoming, and confessional. According to his former wife Ruby Nell, "I didn't know the full extent of his crimes until after he was arrested the last time, in 1974. Even then, I didn't know everything he did.... After Bill was imprisoned for the last time, the children and I began to hear stories of disappearance that turned into stories of murder. Bill was tied in some way to nearly all of them.... Bill didn't tell me what he did, but he did confide in the boys, Stoney, Montana, and Shane.... My husband told our sons about a number of murders....[2241] Shane says he never visited his father with the intention of questioning him or picking his brain for information about his crimes. Birt would not volunteer information, but if Shane already knew something about a case and brought it up to him, he would talk about it. Shane says when he opened up to his father about doing things over in his own life, his father reciprocated by opening up to him and began telling him bits and pieces of his "jobs" when the two of them were alone. Shane states his father never told a whole story or provided point by point details, but Stoney refutes this "bits and pieces" style of storytelling and says, on the rare occasions when his father did tell something, it was told thoroughly and as detailed as a cookie recipe.

Stoney says Shane was not in tune with their father's more serious crimes, and the most their father would have told Shane are stories about hauling whiskey.[2242] While Billy Birt told many things to Stoney, Stoney says his father did not confess to him like a man confessing to a priest,[2243] and he adds, "The thought of my father confessing...to Shane is absolutely laughable....[2244] He would not dare influence my baby brother, who he took on hisself such guilt about having to leave...at age two. The last thing my dad would do is tell his youngest son about a damn murder. He never talked, much less tell my brother and mess up his young mind. I mean, what father is going to tell his young son that he's so eat up with self-guilt about having to leave...something that horrible. If he had told Shane that, it would have been no point but bragging. Impossibility." Stoney adds that his father did not discuss out-of-state murders, with the exception of one in Texas,[2245] and Stoney was shocked when he told about that one because he had never heard him say anything like that before. According to Stoney, his father never confessed a murder to him that he did not also confess to the whole world.[2246]

When Billy Birt was arrested for the last time in April 1974, Shane was only a toddler and "never really knew his dad outside of a prison."[2247] Consequently, they "never developed a close relationship." Still, Shane maintains that subsequent to his initial childhood visitations to his father in prison in Illinois, which began in 1975, he visited his father (mostly alone) in prison hundreds of times over a thirty-year period from the time he was able to drive in 1987 until his father's death in 2017, although during his teenage years, he only visited his father alone on three occasions. Stoney, who reportedly never missed a visit with his father *[the frequency of allowed visits being weekends and state holidays (which were typically on Fridays and Mondays) for six hours per day from 9:00 AM to 3:00 PM[2248]]* says this is false, and that Shane was hardly ever there, did not go see their father for an entire twelve-year period, and may have only visited him three times in the last eighteen to twenty years of their father's life (i.e., between around 1997 and 2017).[jjjjjjjj] Whenever Shane did visit at a time that Stoney was also present, Stoney says Shane would only stay for half an hour. Stoney also says that, because of the bad shape that a drug-addicted Shane was in ("looking like a holocaust victim"), their father was heartbroken, blaming himself for Shane's condition, and only wanting to pour love on him rather than share details of his crimes that would place an extra weight of burden upon him.[2249] *[Shane admits the only time he saw his father with tears in his eyes was when Shane visited him during his (Shane's) years of addiction between 1998 and 2003. His father did not initially recognize him in his (Shane's) emaciated state and subsequently tried to convince him to straighten his life up.[2250]]*

Some, including Stoney, further discredit Shane's claims about what his father told him on the basis of Shane's self-admitted methamphetamine abuse.[kkkkkkkk] According to Stoney, Shane and their uncle, Bobby Birt (who Shane says is the source of some of the information concerning his father's crimes), lived together for an extended period of time in the woods in a one-room shack devoid of electricity and running water. Stoney says Bobby, whose sense of worth and belonging was wrapped up in his brother Billy, went downhill after Billy was incarcerated and unable to help him. Stoney says a "drunk and doped-up" Bobby told Shane fantasy "bedtime stories" of his adventures with [Billy], and…Shane hung onto every word of Bobby's "meth induced altered memories."[2251]

According to Shane, his motivations for sharing the details of his father's deeds are partially grounded in his Christian faith. When Shane and his mother, Ruby Nell, joined with Phil Hudgins for the compilation of *Grace and Disgrace: Living with Faith and a Dixie Mafia Hit Man*, Shane hoped the book would be inspirational to readers, and one of his stated purposes was "to apologize to the families of [his] father's victims," not to "glorify him or what he did." In 2019, Shane made an effort to apologize to Hugh Fleming for Billy Birt's role in the murders of Fleming's parents, and he believes "there are other Billy Birt victims who deserve an apology for whatever it's worth…. If I could apologize to everybody, I would." When Shane read Ginny Durham Mackie's response to the Watauga County Sheriff's Office announcement in February 2022, a "hoped-for result" of the book was "partially fulfilled." Shane stated, "That's one of the reasons we did this book. It brought closure. I'd like to bring closure to more of these cases."[2252] He also says one of his greatest fears is that innocent individuals may have been wrongly convicted of and imprisoned for crimes his father committed.[2253]

Throughout his book, Hudgins provides many examples of things (based on the input of Shane and his mother) that Billy Birt shared with Shane. Hudgins, acknowledging there are differences of opinion within the Birt family, offers a disclaimer: "Of course, memories fail and sometimes differ: What one sibling remembers about his or her father might not match with Shane's recollection. But I have come to trust what Shane says. If Shane was wrong about some fact, the mistake was of the head, not the heart." For the writing of the book, "Shane wanted the story to get told – the true story,

---

[jjjjjjjj] The prison visitor logs for Billy Birt would establish how often Shane Birt visited his father but, according to the Georgia Department of Corrections Open Records Center, an offender's visitation records are exempt from the Open Records Act and therefore inaccessible by the public.

[kkkkkkkk] Shane himself, speaking of the long-term effects of his addiction, admits, "I don't know what the dope has done to me." Research studies have demonstrated that chronic methamphetamine addiction affects memory, significantly decreasing the ability to encode (i.e., receive, store) and recall information. [Sources: Birt, Shane. In-person interview with Bob Ingram. April 30, 2019; "Effects of Crystal Meth on the Brain and Central Nervous System," American Addiction Centers, July 18, 2023 (online), https://americanaddictioncenters.org/meth-treatment/effects-on-the-brain-and-cns; "Encoding (memory), Wikipedia, https://en.wikipedia.org/wiki/Encoding_(memory).]

as best he could remember and document it…[and he] wanted to make one thing clear: 'What I told you came from Daddy,' he said. 'Information about what happened came from him. I didn't make anything up.'" According to Shane, the things he says his father told him are not his personal opinions. "There are other versions [of my father's life], which may be right or wrong. But the stories my father told me came from a clear mind unaffected by drugs." Concerning the Durham Case, Shane says, "If there's any discrepancies, I'm sorry, but…one thing I'm 1000% sure of, it was my dad…." [2254]

Shane shares that "Daddy unloaded a lot of his burdens on me"[2255] and adds that bearing so many of those secrets is a like a curse he wishes had never been put upon him. He says he originally never intended for them to be made public: "I never wanted this to come out. Not ever. It was all supposed to die into history." But he says the pressure of what he held within could not be contained: "It's like glass inside my head a bunch of times. I've heard voices in my head my whole lifetime…and beeping and stuff like that."[2256] Phil Hudgins writes that Shane is scarred and has experienced "sleep deprivation and mental anguish, mostly due…to the tension wrought by months of sordid recollections." A sufferer of post-traumatic stress disorder, Shane takes Zoloft and sees a counselor.[2257] But Stoney discounts the narrative of Shane as "a heavily burdened son, who is haunted by…what his father confessed to him…telling him all the horror stories."[2258]

Shane's self-proclaimed good intentions and his reported ensuing trauma aside, a palpable rift exists in the admittedly dysfunctional Birt family. Shane states that his family is "warped to no end…. I wish we were normal people, but we're not…. All this crap, it has destroyed us."[2259] Tongue in cheek, Stoney offers his assessment: "This ain't a normal family feud. This ain't quite *Honey Boo Boo*. This is somewhere between *Jerry Springer* and *Shawshank Redemption*…. The details of my family…[are] stuff of awe and uninspiration."[2260] Stoney takes particular issue with Shane and their mother, especially after they collaborated with Phil Hudgins to write their book, which Shane says was intended "10,000%" as a rebuttal to Stoney's books about their father and the *In The Red Clay* podcast. According to Shane, any stories written or shared about the Birt family should have been a unanimous family decision; after Stoney went solo, Shane says he could not, with a clear conscience, let what Stoney was "peddling" be the last word. Shane says he did not want people thinking his father "died with the guns in his hands" but to understand that he died a broken man. Shane says, "The last three times I went and seen my dad, the first thing he wanted to do was join hands and pray; before we left, what he wanted to do was join hands and pray."

The two portrayals of Billy Birt (Stoney's versus that of Ruby Nell's and Shane's as written by Hudgins) are aligned on some points but strikingly different in other ways. Believing Hudgins' book stepped on the memory and reputation of his father, Stoney made good on his promise to Shane to put a stop to the book. He filed a cease-and-desist order against Hudgins on the basis of copyright infringement (Hudgins allegedly incorporating excerpts from Stoney's books into his own book without Stoney's permission), therefore bringing most of the book's sales and availability to a halt. *[As of 2024, a second edition, with the problematic passages removed, has since been released and is available.]* Stoney's feelings partially came to light in the final episode of the first season of the podcast, in which Stoney discusses his mother (who he believes has been inaccurately portrayed as a martyr) and his siblings. This episode bothered Shane, and, only days prior to the Watauga County Sheriff's Office announcement about the Dixie Mafia connection to the Durham murders, he shared with Hudgins that he was upset with "all the lies" that had been told on the podcast, and particularly with the last episode "which bashed his mother." "The podcast," Shane feels, "is just making a mockery of all the victims and the victims' families."[2261]

Stoney, however, believes the content of the podcast is accurate. Just as Shane found his interviews with Bob Ingram to be an opportunity to unload a lot of his memories and "get some stuff off [his] chest," Stoney experienced a great degree of catharsis in sharing his story via the podcast. He has likewise benefited from the podcast in other ways; media attention has made him somewhat of a celebrity, and it brought increased business to his former Rock Solid distillery and subsequent lines of whiskey and brandy. But Stoney acknowledges that and owns it: "It's completely true…. I want the money. I enjoy the celebrity. I damn sure love bullshitting and going on with people…." He adds that nothing is wrong with that unless you deny it and try to be two-faced, which he believes is the case with some of his father's accusers and detractors.[2262] Still, just as Stoney has strong opinions about the intentions and motives of certain individuals, some of them likewise question his intentions and motives. Some believe him to be the attention-seeking narcissist rather than Shane and a self-centered, self-serving braggart and blowhard with his own history of criminal woes[llllllll] who aims to live off the legend he has glamorized and sensationalized his father to be. Shane and others believe Stoney's intent in writing two books about their father was to make him into a folk hero, and Shane believes Stoney's opinion about their father is not an opinion Billy Birt had of himself.[2263] Season one of the podcast provides a detailed history of Billy Birt's Dixie Mafia and poignantly explores his dual personality and the complex relationship between him and Stoney. One thing that is clear in the podcast is that Stoney reveres his father. "He was a damn decent father to me and my brothers and sisters," he says.[2264] But he also acknowledges his father's evil deeds: "He's a hero as a daddy, but he is a cold-blooded murderer. He killed for self-preservation, for revenge, money, and for hire. They ain't nothing heroic about that."[2265]

As a kid, Stoney was his father's "constant companion,"[2266] and he was as close to his father as anyone and understood him as well as anyone. Stoney sees himself as the keeper, caretaker, and archivist of his father's story – in part because Billy Birt, in his handwritten will, named Stoney as "the foremost authority on [his] life" and bequeathed to him the sole right to review and approve any portrayals of him. Even Shane acknowledges that Stoney is a "treasure trove" of information about their father and knows "more about daddy than anybody could ever know."[2267] As a result of the confidence placed in him by his father, Stoney would expectedly resent any possibility his father would choose to tell Shane some things that he [Billy] never told him [Stoney], perhaps feeling that would be a betrayal of the deep trust he and his father shared. According to Stoney, who at times has seemed to live vicariously to a degree through his father's exploits, "If my father had told one of his children something, it was going to come from me. I'm the only one that lived and breathed him.[2268] I'm the only living or dead person that knows the truth of what my father did on this earth and what he was capable of. Me. No one else. Me."[2269] A rumored television series and perhaps even a movie about his father and the Dixie Mafia may be poised to provide additional avenues through which Stoney can tell his and his father's stories, and Stoney seems not to want anything

---

[llllllll] Stoney's arrests and incarcerations include a twenty-eight-month prison stint on a twenty-seven-year sentence for burglary when he was a teenager in the 1970s and attempting to emulate his father. [Sources: "Billy 'Stoney' Birt arrested twice in one day," *Barrow News-Journal*, Jefferson, GA, February 16, 2022 (online; updated February 18, 2022), https://www.mainstreetnews.com/barrow/billy-stoney-birt-arrested-twice-in-one-day/article_f2a81f45-e445-53ec-90bd-18b4dcc0461d.html; https://thegeorgiagazette.com/barrow/billy-birt-5/; https://recentlybooked.com/GA/Oconee/BILLY-BIRT~1415_BB61MW813202195000; Bo Emerson, "Killer Billy Sunday Birt was a father who left behind a family divided," *The Atlanta Constitution*, Atlanta, GA, June 21, 2022 (online), https://www.ajc.com/news/crime/killer-billy-sunday-birt-was-a-father-who-left-behind-a-family-divided/KEFGYWN3Q5EMTP2XBG7GXX4U2M/; *Rock Solid, The True Story of Georgia's Dixie Mafia* Facebook post by Stoney Birt, September 2, 2023; Birt, Stoney. Text messages to author. July 6, 2023 & April 18, 2024.]

being told unless he is the one telling it or unless he has the opportunity to review and approve it. As Stoney sees it, this is a fulfillment of his father's expressed wishes.

In Bob Ingram's estimation, the fact that Stoney feels anything concerning his father has to come from him makes him territorial. According to Ingram, Stoney tends to criticize and bash anyone else who comes forward with information from his father, declaring the information to be false, imagined, or embellished. Ingram says Stoney dislikes the fact that Shane has come forward and gotten credit for anything because Stoney seeks the credit and the spotlight. "Stoney wants everyone to think that his dad only talked to Stoney. It's preposterous for Stoney to think and portray himself as the only person that possesses the information about Billy Sunday Birt – the only one that has that key…. Did his father tell him things? Sure, he told him plenty of things, but his father told Shane a lot too. Shane's relationship with his father was different. It was based on, according to Shane, Shane's belief in the Lord and his father's conversion to the Lord, and that he told Shane things to try to clear his conscience. And I think he told Stoney things to build himself up…. I think the motive behind Birt talking to his sons, depending on which son it was, was entirely different."[2270]

By 2019, Shane Birt was seemingly on a quest for personal healing that necessitated a coming to terms with his father's past. Did he, within that process, absorb all the jumbled tidbits he had ever read or been told about his father's life and crimes and conglomerate them in such a way that, while containing scraps of truth, they resulted in distorted and imaginative accounts? Has he been so inundated with details that he has misattributed to his father things told to him by other individuals? Is Shane altruistically motivated to make amends for his father's sins and bring closure to victims' families, or has he otherwise, or perhaps in equal measure, been driven by a need for attention, acceptance, notoriety, and possible monetary gain? Is he a victim of his own delusions? Did his years of drug addiction alter his perception of reality? Could it be that, while perhaps not meaning to maliciously perpetrate falsehoods about his father and others as it relates to the Durham Case, he has, over time and with each new detail either remembered or provided to him, become convinced they are true when, in fact, they are not? Or did Billy Sunday Birt actually confess his participation in the Durham murders to his baby boy?

CHAPTER 28

"WHEN WE GOING HOME?"

If one's opinion about Billy Birt, Billy Wayne Davis, Bobby Gaddis, and Charlie Reed having killed the Durhams hinges on whether one believes what Shane Birt said, then it certainly must also hinge on what Billy Wayne Davis said. Authorities consider Davis's so-called confessions to be a corroboration of Shane's statements and proof of these suspects' guilt, so Davis's four interviews are worthy of synopsis and analysis:

September 2019: In his first documented interview, Davis told Sheriff Len Hagaman, Captain Carolynn Johnson, and SBI Agent Wade Colvard that he knew nothing about the murders, knew of no "job" that Billy Birt carried out in the snow, and did not recognize the name Bryce Durham or the surname Hall. Despite his professed lack of knowledge, he wondered what the officers might do for him. According to Sheriff Hagaman, being released was Davis's primary interest. "All Billy Wayne talked about was he wanted out, he wanted out…and he wanted to work out a deal, but no deal was on the table." Hagaman told Davis he and his officers, being from North Carolina, had no jurisdictional authority in Georgia to offer any deals to him.[2271]

October 2020: Davis was next interviewed more than a year later, this time by Bob Ingram. Before Ingram asked Davis anything about the Durham murders, he [Ingram] briefed him [Davis] about the case, telling him that, on February 3, 1972, three victims (one of them a car dealer) had been attacked by Billy Birt and others in their residence in the mountains of Boone, North Carolina. Ingram shared that the victims had been tied, tortured, and robbed, and their bodies were placed in a bathtub. He said the victims' GMC "Jimmy" was taken, that he knew Davis was the driver of the getaway car, and that the perpetrators almost got trapped in a snowstorm. Ingram also told Davis this case was very similar to the Fleming Case. Until the last five minutes of this hour-long interview, Davis really confessed nothing, and at that point in time, he, in typical self-serving fashion, asked Ingram, "When we going home?" Ingram asked Davis if he would like him to inform the parole board about Davis's cooperation, Davis said yes, and Ingram assured him he would. Once that was settled, and with Davis likely believing his cooperation might lead to his release, he seemed to suddenly fall in line, affirming most of what Ingram had presented to him and adding a few additional details. He said he remembered the mountains and the snowstorm and barely getting out of it. He said he drove a 1970 two-wheel drive Chevrolet with a slanted trunk to North Carolina but indicated he had no prior knowledge of Boone. He stated there were three victims and Birt killed them in the house, although he did not know how the house was entered. When Ingram asked if Bobby Gaddis was with Birt, Davis said yes and also added Charlie Reed. He recalled "a wad" of money being taken from the house and stated Birt was probably the one who received information about the victims. One curious thing was that, almost at the very beginning of the Durham Case conversation (and without Ingram even asking Davis about any particular person), Davis asked, "Wasn't he related to them people?" It was unclear who "he" and "them people" referred to. Ingram may have correctly interpreted this to mean whoever set up the murders was a relative of the victims, but Ingram also had his mind made up that Davis was meaning their son-in-law, Troy Hall, and he never clarified this with Davis or explored the possibility that Davis may have been referring to other individuals. When Ingram showed Davis some photos, he vaguely recalled the Durham house and said he recognized Bryce Durham, but he also seemed at times to be confused, thinking the individuals whose pictures he was viewing were perpetrators of something rather than victims.

November 2020: One month later, a third interview with Davis was conducted – this time with Bob Ingram, Len Hagaman, and Carolynn Johnson. As with the previous interview, Ingram drove the conversation. Davis once more said he remembered the snowstorm, but he vacillated on whether anyone got stuck. He said he did not recall getting stuck himself but later stated, "I recall some vehicles getting stuck." As in the previous interview, he said he drove a two-wheel drive car to North Carolina, but this time he stated it was a "an old model coupe" rather than his previous claim of it being a Chevrolet with a slanted trunk. Davis said Billy Birt, Bobby Gaddis, and Charlie Reed were his passengers, but he added a few new details, saying this occurred at night, that he had been to Boone a few times and knew people there, and that Birt drove the car back to Georgia. Davis stated he knew the purpose of the "job" was robbery, and Birt had said the family that lived there had money. But later he said he did not know if a family lived there, nor did he know how many victims there were, or if they were tied up. During the two previous interviews, investigators had already provided Davis with the names and number of victims and how they were attacked and killed, including being tied up, but Davis apparently had no recall of it and said he did not recognize the names Bryce, Virginia, and Bobby Durham. He said he was sure Birt and Gaddis killed the victims, but he was uncertain whether Reed entered the house. At one point he said Birt bragged about the murders but later stated he did not. Davis said he [Davis] was two to three blocks from the house when the victims were killed, but he could not recall where he parked the getaway car. He stated that, at one point, he drove uptown to visit a friend. He remembered a nearby church or a building that looked like a church. He did not know if any items, including silver, were taken from the house. He initially said he did not know how much money was taken, but he thought his share may have been $1,000. He did not know how Birt received information about the Durhams, but he believed it was arranged by a buddy of Birt's who lived near Winder, Georgia. When Ingram asked if this individual "knew these people" (a reference to the Durhams), Davis said yes, and that the person also knew they had money. Davis said the name Troy Hall did not ring a bell.

August 2021: In his fourth and final interview, Davis again said he did not know how many victims there were, but more than one. Although he had previously said Bryce Durham and the Durham home looked familiar to him, when he was shown the same pictures of Bryce, Virginia, and Bobby Durham and their house that Bob Ingram had shown him in a prior interview, Davis said he did not recognize them, their house, or their names. As in his October 2020 interview, while viewing photos of the Durhams, Davis seemed to think they were perpetrators of some crime rather than victims. Davis said he never had dealings with a man named Troy Hall and recalled nothing about a phone call that was placed to say that the murders had been accomplished. Davis stated that the man who set up the murders was deceased and was named West (perhaps confusing a story that involved ATF Agent Jim West?), and that Billy Birt set it in motion. Later within this same interview, Davis contradicted himself, saying he did not remember who set it up. Davis affirmed it was hard to separate cases, and he stated he did not really want to try to remember or relive anything. Still, he did reconfirm some things he had said in previous interviews – that he had been to Boone several times on car business, that he probably drove a Cadillac (taken from his car lot) to Boone and Birt drove it back, and that he was probably paid a small amount for the use of his car. He also reconfirmed that a church was near the crime scene. Although he was not sure, he believed Birt was the one who dropped their group off, although Davis said he could have. He said he was sure Birt was there, but he did not know who killed the victims other than Birt. Davis was unsure about Bobby Gaddis's presence, but he said Charlie Reed was usually around. He said it was normal for items to be taken from victims' homes. This interview also yielded some new information from Davis. Although he did not say that he was specifically referring to Boone, and although the interviewing officers presumed he meant Boone but asked no clarifying questions, Davis stated that whatever location he was thinking of was dry and had no liquor stores (which was true of Boone in 1972 but also likely true of many more locations throughout the conservative southeast). He said it was typical to scope out a job beforehand, and this was the only case he remembered being involved in where there was a bad snowstorm, and that it was almost impossible to get out. Although he initially said in this interview that no one got stuck, he later said he was sure someone did and that he sent a tow truck. Davis recalled that he parked one to two miles from the scene (which corresponds with the distance between the Durham home and the Union 76 station with the phone booth, and with the distance between the Durham home and the location where the Durhams' GMC "Jimmy" was abandoned). He also said there were times Billy Birt was upset about being ripped off (although neither the question asked nor the answer given specified a particular case or location), and that whoever misled Birt should have been killed years ago.

All the interviews except the first were facilitated by Bob Ingram, and Ingram's interrogation style was pursuant to the oft debated, guilt presumptive Reid Technique of interrogation. Initially developed in the mid-1900s by John Reid, a polygraph expert and former Chicago police officer, it has since been widely utilized by law enforcement officers in the United States. The technique "is designed to develop a bond between the interrogator and the suspect, with the ultimate goal of getting [the suspect] to admit to a crime," and it employs nine steps of interrogation once it has been established that the subject has been involved in the crime's commission.

In terms of the development of a bond within the Davis interviews, Ingram periodically made statements to build rapport with Davis, including discussions of the old days – the people and places they were both familiar with in decades past, the similarity in their ages and commiseration about the toll the years had taken on their minds and physical bodies – even Ingram's loaning of his reading glasses to Davis so that Davis could inspect photographs. Ingram also "bonded" with Davis by encouraging him, telling him he was still sharp and capable of retrieving details from the recesses of his mind that would help with this case. And although Ingram has stated Davis did not respond to stroking, Ingram was, nonetheless, periodically complimentary of him, mentioning Davis's intelligence and good looks as a younger man. Davis, perhaps purposely stroking Ingram in return, reciprocated the compliments, telling Ingram what a sharp lawman he was and how well he had done his homework and research. At certain moments, however, Ingram's manner almost shockingly went beyond positive reinforcement and gentle encouragement of Davis's recall, adamantly telling him that he [Davis] not only knew about this case but participated in it – driving the car and dropping off his accomplices. Ingram also insisted Davis knew who had instigated the murders. Of course, Ingram's insistence was, again, in pursuit of information to corroborate the previous statements of Shane Birt.

As for presumption of guilt, Ingram was already convinced, based on Shane's statements and a comparison of the Durham and Fleming Cases, that Davis was involved in the Durham murders. "In the Reid Technique, interrogation is an accusatory process, in which the investigator tells the suspect that the results of the investigation clearly indicate that they did commit the crime in question. The interrogation is in the form of a monologue presented by the investigator rather than a question and answer format." Although Ingram did, oftentimes, ask Davis questions, which Davis mostly answered, and although Ingram adheres to the belief that listening is a dying art and the number one rule in interviewing is to shut up and listen rather than talk endlessly,[2272] the majority of their interviews consisted of Ingram talking *to* Davis. Even when their conversation specifically focused on the Durham murders, much of it entailed Ingram summarizing the case for Davis, comparing it to the Fleming Case, and telling him he [Davis] had knowledge of the case and could help with it.

Among the Reid Technique's nine steps of interrogation is direct positive confrontation, in which the investigator presents a synopsis of facts to the suspect and tells him he is involved in the crime. This is a step Ingram clearly employed by providing details of the Durham murders. Detractors of the Reid Technique say investigators "often feed evidence to suspects [in order to 'refresh' the subject's memory], which accounts for why false confessors sometimes know details about a crime that they wouldn't otherwise know."[2273] According to Ingram, while no one likes to divulge factual information to prompt someone to talk, it is sometimes necessary to demonstrate to the interviewee that you know what you are talking about and to help refresh the interviewee's memory. Individuals like Davis, Ingram says, who killed without any concern for human life, are very difficult to get to open up. "It's a game of mental chess that they're not willing to play unless they think their opponent is worthy."[2274] Another of the steps of interrogation is getting the suspect's attention, including the use of verbal techniques to command it. This is evident in the number of times Ingram emphatically told Davis to listen to him.[2275]

While it does not appear that Ingram religiously adhered to all of the nine steps of interrogation, another that he utilized is the step of minimization, in which the interrogator tells the suspect he understands why he must have committed the crime and offers sympathy or "face-saving excuses" that will hopefully encourage the suspect to more easily confess. An example of a face-saving excuse is blaming an accomplice, and in his interrogation of Davis, Ingram frequently commented on how terrible a person Billy Birt was and affirmed that Davis made a poor life choice by associating himself with Birt, which consequently led to the awful crimes the two of them committed. While Ingram was by no means declaring Davis innocent and occasionally remarked about the many bad things Davis had done, he somewhat softened Davis's guilt by declaring him the driver (rather than a killer), and Davis affirmed that was his role. In essence, and presumably as part of the Reid Technique, Ingram gave Davis somewhat of an out while simultaneously placing more of the blame on Birt and saying had it not been for Birt, Davis might not have been involved in such things.

Proponents of the Reid Technique say it is in "full compliance with the law and judicial guidelines" as long as investigators follow core principles of the technique, including making no promises of leniency, not threatening the suspect with physical harm or inevitable consequences *[Ingram actually stated to Davis in the October 2020 interview that he was not there to threaten him with anything]*, not conducting interviews for excessively lengthy periods of time *[Ingram generally limited his interviews with Davis to around an hour]*, not denying the suspect's rights, treating the suspect with dignity and respect, and not withholding details of the crime from the suspect.[2276] And

Ingram did, indeed, adhere to each of these, although a more detailed discussion of "promises of leniency" will follow.

While it is true that, during the course of these interviews, Davis mentioned some unsolicited details which could accurately be associated with the Durhams and Boone (e.g., a church being near the Durham house and an alcohol-free town), he seemed not to always understand which victims or crime locations were being discussed. Over the course of his criminal career, Davis had been involved in so many offenses that it is not surprising they tended to meld together and became difficult for him to distinguish. Also, Ingram's persistent comparisons of the Fleming and Durham Cases throughout these interviews seemed to keep Davis's mind on what happened in Wrens, Georgia more than a year after the Durham murders. Ingram continually tried to recenter Davis by telling him to remember and focus on the snowstorm. At moments when officers were specifically referring to Boone, North Carolina, Davis was obviously not understanding. In fact, at a few intervals, when Ingram asked Davis if he was tracking with him, Davis answered, "I guess" and "Maybe." And although Davis provided answers to the questions the investigators were intending to be Durham Case-related, those answers may have actually pertained to any number of other people or locations where he had associations or had committed crimes. In the November 2020 interview, Davis said Ingram was right on the money with everything he said, although this seemed to be an affirmation of the general modus operandi of Billy Birt and his confederates that Ingram had reviewed rather than an affirmation of details specific to the Durham Case. Davis's affirmations immediately followed Ingram's recaps of how "jobs" were carried out based on insider information and how victims were bound, tortured, and eliminated. Davis said he knew a lot about what they did – again a seeming affirmation of generalities.

While critics of the Reid Technique acknowledge it "can be 'effective' in producing confessions," they claim it "too easily produces false confessions" among certain groups, including those with "reduced intellectual capacity."[2277] Although Davis seemed to be generally in command of himself in the audio recordings of his interviews, due to his age and his reported diagnosis of dementia and even the early stages of Alzheimer's, one might argue that he fell into that category. Even John E. Reid & Associates, which promotes and teaches the Reid Technique, warns against investigators suggesting possible answers when interviewing an elderly subject: "A cooperative subject often wants to please the investigator by providing requested information. However, if the subject cannot recall the requested information, he or she may be very willing to agree with an answer suggested by the investigator."[2278] "By asking leading questions that can be answered by the suspect in a few words, the interrogator runs the risk that the confession will reflect more about what the interrogator believes happened than what actually happened."[2279] This would also be true of short answers to closed-ended questions such as "True or false?" "Right or wrong?" "Yes or no?" which Ingram often employed. According to retired Drug Enforcement Administration (DEA) Agent Keith Billiot, "Good investigators…realize that you don't go into any investigation with a theory [and then] try to find facts that will support your theory. That's not the way it's supposed to be done. You find the facts, and then you follow those facts wherever they lead you."[2280]

Did Davis's age and health affect the integrity of his memories and answers? Although no medical records have been publicly shared that would reveal the diagnosis or degree of Davis's mental incapacity or a timeline of his condition's onset and progression, his family reportedly confirmed he was so afflicted.[2281] In the October and November 2020 interviews, despite multiple instances in which Davis mentioned the deterioration of his mind, the audio recordings of those interviews depict him as cooperative and generally attentive and engaged, trying to answer the questions asked of him. Sheriff Len Hagaman says although Davis exhibited some confusion at times – perhaps resulting from a combination of his age and elements of his many crimes running together – he was mentally "with it."[2282] "For an eighty-one-year-old...he [was] in very good shape mentally and physically.... He [was] as sharp as a tack, and he [knew] exactly what [was] going on....[2283] Still, the audio recordings reveal Davis struggled at times to recall information, particularly fifty-year-old memories, and there were moments he was undeniably confused, which the interviewing officers recognized, and which Ingram even acknowledged verbally. In the October 2020 interview, Davis told Ingram he would like to be out of prison so he could spend the rest of his time with his family, including his mother and father. He subsequently said his father had died two or three weeks prior to the interview, but his mother was still alive. In reality, both of Davis's parents were already long deceased at that time. His father had died thirty-one years earlier in 1989,[2284] and his mother had died ten years earlier in 2010.[2285] In this same interview, Davis stated his wife had died four to six years prior (i.e., 2014-2016) of natural causes, but in a previous interview unrelated to the Durham Case, he told law officers his wife had been shot and killed by an unknown assailant in 2018, and that he was suspected by some of being involved in her murder.[2286] Even an issue with Davis's *short-term* memory was evident in the October interview. Early on, Ingram told Davis that Billy Birt had hanged himself in prison. Davis affirmed he already knew that, but thirteen minutes later, he asked Ingram what Birt died of, and Ingram told him again. In each of these instances, was Davis simply confused or unaware? Had some degree of dementia prevented his accurate recollection of these things, or was he somehow attempting to manipulate his interviewers by playing dumb or playing on their sympathies?

Even some of the information Davis shared concerning the Durhams was totally inaccurate, particularly when he stated more than once in his November 2020 interview that they had been shot and he had even heard the shots.[mmmmmmmmm] In his last interview in August 2021, although his mental faculties were reportedly good, Davis again exhibited some confusion. On occasion he gave non-sensical answers that were not even responses to the questions asked. He also stated once more, and incorrectly, that the victims had been shot (at least that is what he said he had been told). Although Ingram had previously informed Davis that Bryce Durham was a car dealer, when Ingram asked what Bryce's occupation was, Davis stated Bryce was a factory worker and a preacher. Based on additional details that Davis provided immediately afterwards, it was unclear if he even knew who he was talking about or what location and crime this was in reference to, and he asked if Bryce had a business in Winder, Georgia. According to John E. Reid & Associates, "If the subject claims to recall this type of information and subsequent checking indicates that their recall was faulty, this finding suggests possible other errors in the subject's recollections."[2287] In other words, since Davis was wrong about details concerning the deaths of his own family members as well as the way the Durhams were killed, that would suggest other information he provided to investigators might well also be faulty. Immediately after telling the officers the Durhams were shot, Davis asked, "Now, what case are we talking about here?" In that same November 2020 interview, when asked if his accomplices got the amount of money they expected from North Carolina, Davis replied, "Hmm. I can't even remember that case." At another point, Davis asked, "And where was that at?" Between the October and November 2020 interviews, Davis gave conflicting answers about the type of car he drove, the amount of money taken, and whether anyone had gotten stuck in the snow, and

[mmmmmmmmm] One might wonder if Davis heard the gunshot that fired a bullet into the paneling of the Durhams' den and then assumed the victims were shot, but according to a Durham neighbor, the wind was blowing so harshly that, "if someone had shot a cannon that night, it would not have been heard."

between his October 2020 and August 2021 interviews, he was confused whether Bobby Gaddis and Charlie Reed had participated. At one point in the November 2020 interview, Davis even asked how he could be expected to say something was true or false when he had no knowledge of the subject matter. In light of all this confusion, it would be fair to say that, despite officers deeming these as Davis's "confessions" to the Durham murders, they were not the slam-dunk that had been hoped for nor should they have been considered or portrayed as the silver bullet for closing the Durham Case. Of course, even if Davis really could not recall the Durham murders – perhaps because it was one of dozens of crimes and fifty years into the past – the failure of his memory does not necessarily prove his innocence. Davis's girlfriend, Deborah Wester told investigating officers she believed Davis to be the type of person who could block out some of the things he had done.[2288]

When asked by podcaster Sean Kipe about the issue of Davis's mental health, Bob Ingram said, "[Davis] did have a touch of dementia. Was he feeble? Somewhat. Physically, he was slowed; mentally, he was slowed. Did he have severe dementia? No. Was he a little confused? Yes. A lot confused? No. Was he aware of what was going on? Absolutely. So, him suffering from severe dementia, that was not the case when I talked to him. I've worked over 500 homicides and done over 5,000 interviews in my career. I understand dementia; I know what it is. I've had family that have had it. Him not knowing what was going on and him being influenced to confess? No. Absolutely not."[2289]

Still, there are other law enforcement officers who have reviewed the audio recordings of Ingram's interviews with Davis and have expressed concern. One, a former GBI agent who actually received interview and interrogation training in the Reid Technique from Ingram in the early 2000s and is now critical of the technique, noted red flags in how Davis's confession was solicited. "If you have no memory or if you have a memory that I can mold, the Reid Technique will take you down whatever road you want to take them down…. If you hammer somebody long enough who's weak," you plant doubt within the subject, who then begins to question if he really did do it, especially in light of his interrogator's confidence that he did. In this former agent's opinion, "If that had been taken to trial, it would have been suppressed…but because they weren't using it for criminal conviction, it never got to the point where a judge could look at it.... This is not an interview that I would base any investigation on, much less closing a high profile murder."[2290]

Similarly, retired DEA Agent Keith Billiot, who says the Reid technique "was the Holy Grail of interrogation tactics for the GBI" in preceding decades, personally stopped using it after obtaining a false confession. Billiot likewise has concerns about how the Davis interviews were conducted. In his estimation, almost all of the information obtained was provided by Bob Ingram: "Every time that [Davis] cannot remember something, Bob Ingram provides him with that something. He provides him with the names; he provides him with the events; he provides him with photos. And even then, Mr. Davis says over and over and over, 'Well, I guess so,' or 'Well, it could have been that way,' or 'Well, that's what we would generally do.'" Billiot, who reduces Davis's alleged confessions to mere acknowledgments of what Ingram was telling him [Davis], says, "If the man [Davis] cannot remember the specific acts that allegedly he took part in for this horrific triple murder, then you can't use his acknowledgments…. You can't use [those] as facts to close out a triple homicide…. Even though this is a cold case, "you still are held to the same legal, lawful standards…. You still have to meet those stringent bars of evidence…. You still have to be able to prove things…. [Proving things is] the only way that we can have a civil society and we can bring true justice. [This] would never go to trial…. I can't see any competent prosecutor accepting these three 'interviews' as evidence. There's not a world in which that would happen in the United States judicial system."[2291]

In the October 2020 interview, Ingram asked Davis if he regretted what happened to the victims in question. This, coupled with Ingram's previous mention within the same interview of seeking to put the case to rest for the sake of the victims' family was a curious tactic in light of Ingram's belief that Davis and those like him have no conscience. "What conscience?" Ingram asks. "They have no conscience. Are you going to ask them to bring closure to the family? Family and closure mean nothing to them. Not words in their vocabulary." Ingram feels it is impossible to appeal to the conscience of evil individuals or to implore them to help bring closure to their victims' families. "They ain't wired like we are," says Ingram. "These are not just run of the mill, typical people who you deal with and encounter in law enforcement. These are professional, criminally sophisticated, cold-blooded, brutal, ruthless, torturous killers."[2292] The regret expressed by Davis concerning the victims also stands in contrast to Captain Carolynn Johnson's summation of her face time with Davis: "He would just be cool as a cucumber describing anything to do with any of the murders he was involved with. He was just cold…no emotion about it…no remorse…no anything."[2293] And in his August 2021 interview, Davis stated that, depending on the circumstances and within limitations, it was not that hard to live with killing someone[2294] – not exactly an affirmation of regret over lives lost.

In interviews following the Fleming murders, Davis's associate, Larry Bethune, gave similar insight into Davis's true character: "When you meet him, you think he's a pretty nice guy…. Then you see a different side of him when you get involved with him…. He would kill anybody for anything…. If I wanted somebody killed, I would approach Billy [Davis] and have it done… Billy knows a lot of people that deal in that kind of stuff… Just about anything you want done, you could have gotten Billy to handle it." Bethune warned authorities they would not be able to break Davis. "He's too cold. I mean it ain't gonna bother him." Bethune said a person had to have a conscience in order to be broken, but he did not believe Davis had one. Bethune told investigators, "You'll find out what kind of guy he is," and added that Davis would shoot everyone – not just Bethune – in their interview room, and that he would blow up an entire house with everyone in it and never be disturbed by it. "He's as bad as I say…. If they ever get him and turn him loose, until he gets a lot of years on him, [that] would be a bad mistake." He also said Davis was not the kind of guy to talk. He trusted no one for anything that might jeopardize his life, and he would typically not provide details regarding a "job" until on site. Bethune stated when Davis heard about the death of someone who had been his own victim, he would act shocked. According to Bethune, "You have to know him to see through him. He can put up a front…. He likes to put on a big show in front of everybody."[2295]

Based on others' descriptions of Davis as a cold, soulless, unremorseful man, one might, while listening to the audio recordings of his interviews, expect to hear the gruff, grunting voice of a hardened and reticent criminal marginally tolerant of his interviewers and reluctant to answer their questions. Instead, Davis was surprisingly respectful, engaging, affable – at times jovial – and strangely even likable. But one must also consider Bob Ingram's frequent characterization of Davis as a criminally oriented "master at manipulation…clever and smart."[2296] Shrewd, prone to clamming up, and skilled at deflection and minimizing his involvement, Davis had historically been a "tough nut to crack," and his real motivation for keeping quiet was his eligibility for parole.[2297] Was Davis actually more in control of these interviews than appeared on the surface, perhaps even escaping the awareness of his interviewers? Was he, like Ingram, employing particular techniques? Was he appearing to be helpful in an attempt to satisfy Ingram's pursuit of information while also attempting to gain something for himself? Was he simply assenting to all the details Ingram offered him about the Durham Case in expectation of being released from prison?

It is very telling that, when Ingram asked Davis in each of these interviews if he had any questions, one that Davis always seemed eager to ask was, "When are you gonna get me out of here?" By this time, Davis had already made several appearances before a parole board and had been repeatedly denied release. In the October and November 2020 interviews, Ingram promised nothing to Davis beyond a letter to his parole board confirming his cooperation and truthfulness. In the October interview, Ingram told Davis, "If you help me, I'll try to help you." He also told Davis he had not come to make him promises or enticements, and he did not know when Davis would be released or if that could happen as it was the parole board's decision. Ingram also stated to Davis, "I hope one day you see freedom," which was insincere on Ingram's part as he had consistently attended Davis's parole hearings to help ensure he was never released.[2298] The statement was also not reflective of Ingram's true feelings about Davis. Although Davis told Ingram he "wasn't as mean as he once was," Ingram believed Davis still could and would pull a trigger and kill in a heartbeat, and he said he still saw evil in Davis's eyes. In the final interview in August 2021, when Davis once more asked when he would get out of prison, Ingram answered, "It'll be a while probably. I told the parole board that you cooperated and helped, so, you know, we'll see what happens." Because Ingram's statement insinuated the possibility of release, Davis could easily have interpreted it as something that was eventually going to happen. Although Ingram did inform the parole board about Davis's cooperation in these interviews, he also told the board that "Davis admitted to being involved in a triple murder in 1972" – something that surely would not weigh in favor of his release. Davis was clear that he believed Ingram had more pull than the average person, and even if Davis's expectations were unrealistic, it seems apparent he believed his incarceration might soon terminate. Although serving a life sentence, Davis was eligible for parole and still had "a glimmer of hope that he could get out."[2299] And why not? Davis was renowned for making deals and, no doubt, had come to expect opportunities for being granted immunity, having his crimes dead-docketed and unprosecuted, having charges against him dropped, and exchanging information in return for freedom. These were commonplace and had been such frequent rewards throughout the years that one actually might not fault him for his expectations. Just as Billy Birt had once been addicted to "truck driver pills," Davis had a habit for snitching and was hooked on quid pro quo. However, Joseph Buckley, president of John E. Reid & Associates says, "If a suspect infers leniency from an interrogator's guise of sympathy, that's the suspect's problem."[2300]

Some critics claim the Reid Technique is a contentious tactic that "seeks to psychologically manipulate suspects into confessing," and that investigators are taught to presume the suspect is guilty, which results in a mindset aimed to get a confession rather than seeking the truth.[2301] Although Ingram proclaimed himself during one of the interviews to be a "truth seeker," Davis's "confession" to Ingram could arguably fall into the category of what is known as a "coerced-compliant false confession," in which a suspect believes there is a benefit to confessing.[2302] In Davis's case, parole would have been the benefit. According to the former GBI agent trained by Ingram, in regard to Ingram's offer to speak to Davis's parole board, "Bob would always say, you can't promise anything specific, and anything you promise, you have to follow up with because, otherwise, it's coercive. That's not true. What the Supreme Court actually said was, if the promise in and of itself could be coercive – doesn't matter whether you follow through with it or not – so if you're telling him, 'Yeah, I'll talk to the parole board,' and he believes that that in some way can help this case, the Supreme Court has said that is automatically coercive."[2303]

Although the audio recordings of Davis's interviews confirm Bob Ingram told Davis he could promise nothing more than to write Davis's parole board, were any other deals struck with Davis? Much like the deals in previous years with Jim West and others for immunity, Stoney Birt believes Davis "cut a deal for his confession" to involvement in the Durham Case. "Somehow they made a deal with Davis to say, 'Okay, I was driving.'" Stoney believes Ingram coaxed Davis's confession by planting information in Davis's head that would tell Davis what he needed to remember.[2304] Ingram vehemently denies this, stating, "I do not provide information to criminals; I collect information to produce facts and evidence."[2305] But here again, Ingram did broach the subject of the Durham Case with Davis by recapping all the pertinent details prior to asking him any questions about it, and some may deem that a form of "planting" that information in Davis's mind so that he could be primed to assent to all those same details.

According to Stoney Birt, Davis was in fear for his safety and his life at Macon State Prison: "In prison, no one likes a snitch." Between his first interview in September 2019 and second interview in October 2020, Davis was moved to Augusta State Medical Prison where Stoney believes a more comfortable bed, better food, and better care were available. Stoney suspects these comforts – as well as Davis not being charged with the Durham murders – was how Davis was rewarded for his confession…"a little gold nugget at the end of a little rainbow," as Stoney calls it. "For him saying he drove the getaway car, but my daddy and Bobby Gaddis and Charlie done the murder, is obvious to anybody with any common sense a good deal for him for what he got."[2306] Despite Stoney's assertion that Davis was relocated to a nicer prison as a reward for admitting involvement in the Durham Case,[2307] according to Ingram, by the time of Davis's first confession in October 2020, he had already been transferred from one prison to another due to his age and possibly his health, not because he was being rewarded for his cooperation in the case.[2308] Ingram says he "never promised [Davis] anything whatsoever," and is not aware of anyone doing that.[2309] Sheriff Len Hagaman acknowledges that, when he interviewed Davis in September 2019 and November 2020, Davis was in two different prisons[nnnnnnnn] – initially one in Macon and subsequently one in Augusta, but he also believes the transfer to the medical prison was legitimately because of Davis's health, and Davis had more or less been sent there to die.[2310]

Stoney Birt also questions why Davis was not given a lie detector test, but because he believes Davis cut a deal and that Ingram promised Davis he would try to help get him out of prison if Davis would confess to driving the car in the Durham Case, Stoney assumes authorities did not want Davis to take one.[2311] Ingram calls Stoney's claims about Davis cutting a deal and being promised release absurd. In his audio recordings of his interviews with Davis, Ingram is never heard telling Davis he will try to get him released if he confesses to being the getaway car driver. And Ingram affirms he advised the parole board that Davis, because of his criminal history, should *not* be released.[2312]

Sean Kipe, whose popular and highly acclaimed *In The Red Clay* podcast has covered all things Billy and Stoney Birt, ponders Davis's confessions: "Davis and Billy Birt had it out for each other from the time they both went to prison, turning on one another and telling of murders that were

---

[nnnnnnnn] Confirmation of Davis's actual transfer date would be helpful, but the Georgia Department of Corrections says it cannot release that information, which does little to assuage suspicions about the reason for his transfer. [Source: Wayne Ford, "Athens-area members of notorious criminal band Dixie Mafia linked to 1972 N. C. murders," *Athens Banner-Herald*, Athens, GA, February 22 (updated February 23), 2022 (online), https://www.onlineathens.com/story/news/local/2022/02/22/1972-triple-murder-n-c-linked-northeast-georgias-dixie-mafia/6784300001/.]

committed for the sole purpose of making sure the other would stay in prison for life. Could this new confession be Davis simply getting the last word in…the final stake in the heart of Billy Sunday Birt? …[Was] it just one last ditch effort to demonize his enemy…to have the last laugh? Can we really take Davis's confession as gospel?"[2313] According to Bob Ingram, who, in addition to eliciting what has been deemed Davis's confession in the Durham Case, had gotten Davis to confess in the Fleming Case many years earlier, "I've never taken a confession from anybody as gospel, and I always make sure it can be independently corroborated." Ingram adds that, in all of his lengthy law enforcement career, "I've never, ever once had a confession dismissed."[2314]

Jim West's list of murders that were attributed to Billy Birt based on information provided by Davis is another thing upon which Stoney Birt bases his father's innocence in the Durham Case. "The Durhams aren't on that list. Why would he [Davis] leave that out, especially [when] he was driving? It'd be the first he'd told. Think about it. His immunity depended on it." Some of what Davis shared with West was "gruesome stuff," an indication Davis had no issue with relaying horrible information, so why not also tell of the brutality of the Durham murders? By the time Davis helped West compile the list, the Durham murders were two to three years in the past. Sean Kipe asks, "Why would Davis not include [the Durham murders] as part of his immunity or tell about [them] to further condemn Billy Birt, when instead, he told of murders that had happened up to ten or more years prior?" Likewise, when Birt later flipped on Davis in retaliation, Kipe again asks, "Why weren't the Durham murders mentioned? If [Birt's] intent was to have Davis locked away for life, would he not think of mentioning a recent triple homicide committed across state lines? Birt knew that Davis made a deal with law enforcement, so if he really wanted to be sure that no further deals could be made between Davis and Jim West, would he not bring a whole new state's law force into the picture – law enforcement that Davis had no ties to?"[2315]

In early 2022, Stoney Birt was of the opinion that Davis probably *did* commit the Durham murders, not with his father, Gaddis, and Reed, but with another crew from west Georgia, or perhaps even with the four men from Asheville, North Carolina who were arrested and released in the 1970s. He says although his father and Davis did do jobs together, this was not one of them. He says Davis was not a member of the Dixie Mafia but was "the Billy Birt" of west Georgia and sometimes did jobs with other gangs – men other than Birt's "home boys" in Winder. By late 2022, however, Stoney stated that, although Davis was the very type who would carry out something like the Durham murders, he "would bet hard earned money ten to one" that even Davis was not present at the Durham home. Still, he finds Davis's involvement more plausible than his father's and admits he has no way to make a determination about Davis playing a role or not. Similarly, former Winder, Georgia Chief of Police Jimmy Terrell disbelieves Billy Birt killed the Durhams and, regarding Davis's alleged involvement says, "I truly believe that, if Billy Wayne Davis was there, he was there with some of his cohorts out of west Cobb County."[2316]

Most of the knowledge Stoney possesses about the Durham Case has come from whatever sources he has accessed or been exposed to since the February 2022 press release, including the Watauga County Sheriff's Office investigation case file. He admits he is "out of [his] arena talking about this Durham thing,"[2317] and although he seems to have no information that could solve the case, he maintains his father's innocence in the Durham murders: "I know for a fact my father had nothing to do with that. It ain't happened like that. Billy Wayne Davis is lying, and I got the damn proof of what I'm talking about."[2318] Stoney bases his claim that his father did not murder the Durhams on his own common sense and on his intimate knowledge of his father and the things he has read about the case.[2319] Still, when pressed in February 2023 whether or not he had any evidentiary proof of his father's innocence, Stoney replied he did not.[2320][oooooooo] One hope Stoney clung to for proving his father's innocence in the Fleming and Durham cases was to pay a visit to Davis in prison, but that hope was dashed when Davis died on December 25, 2022, reportedly due to prostate cancer complications. Stoney had already lined up his visit with Davis for the following week, and Davis was expecting him. During the visit, Stoney had planned to whisper something in Davis's ear – something that only Davis and Billy Birt (and Stoney by extension) had knowledge of. Stoney declines to share what he was going to whisper to Davis, stating it is too personal, but he believes that, as long as Davis's dementia did not stand in the way of his comprehension, it would have caused Davis to come undone. Based on Stoney's belief that Bob Ingram had promised Davis he would try to get him out of prison, Stoney also planned to provide Davis with what he says is proof Ingram had reneged on that promise.[2321]

Even if Davis *was* involved in the Durham murders, some agree that he would not have been the driver. According to Stoney, Davis "damn sure wasn't the driver," and he believes the truth would have come to light from Davis had the prison system made it to his benefit to tell it.[2322] Stoney reiterated this in an interview with the *Athens Banner-Herald*: "Billy Wayne Davis…was never a driver. He was always a top man. He was never a soldier. He was his own entity….. It was to his benefit to say he was the driver" to separate himself from the killings and to protect himself against potential legal action.[2323] Stoney would later add, "Saying that Davis [was] the driver of anything is as ridiculous as saying Billy Birt was the driver…. To say Davis drove a car in any crime, if he was here, it'd piss him off because that would mean he wasn't Jesse James, he was a flunky. Only the dumbasses drove cars, like Bobby Gaddis." As Sean Kipe summarized, "What Stoney is saying is, 'Why would someone of Billy Wayne Davis's intellect be reduced to the role of driver?' Surely his skills would be far better served inside the Durhams' home where every second and every move that was made counted."[2324]

Jimmy Terrell also thinks "Davis [was]…probably not telling the entire truth. I'm sure he…pointed the finger at Birt and Gaddis. Billy Wayne would have never driven the car and waited outside, even if he knew the victim."[2325] Bob Ingram thinks with certainty Davis played a larger role in the Durham Case than just being the getaway car driver.[2326] By early April 2022, an unsurprised Sheriff Len Hagaman stated he was receiving additional information that Davis participated in the Durham Case to a much greater extent than Davis had admitted,[2327] but nothing specific resulted from that information.[2328] Cyndi Silvey Lynch, great niece of murder victims Reid and Lois Fleming, likewise disbelieves Davis's claims that placed him on the periphery of murder as a getaway car driver rather than as one of her loved ones' killers. Like many, she feels Davis knew the truth but chose not to reveal it.[2329] According to Hagaman, Davis would lead authorities to a precipice and leave them there, unwilling to go further.[2330] Still, Ingram says you went with what he gave you.[2331]

[oooooooo] Though Stoney cannot ultimately prove his father did not participate in the Durham triple homicide, as podcaster Sean Kipe has said, "Sometimes we just have to accept what is and move on from it, leaving the wreckage in the past." And in the final episode of the "Durham" season of *In The Red Clay*, Stoney shares that, after devoting two years to the Durham Case, he is moving on, no longer worrying about what anyone but his immediate family knows and thinks about his father. Stoney writes, "For the Durham family, I pray [the] truth comes soon. If I knew what happened that awful night, I would tell you. But I don't. All I know is what did not happen." The accusations against Billy Birt have been a personal burden to him, but in his heart, Stoney persists in his belief that his father is innocent of the Durham murders, and going forward, he intends to focus on the love of his family and all the positive and good things that life has to offer. [Sources: Kipe, Sean, *In The Red Clay*, Season 2, Episode 8, *In Plain Sight*, June 11, 2024; Birt, Stoney, Rock Solid, The True Story of Georgia's Dixie Mafia Facebook page post, June 11, 2024.]

In late 2019 and unrelated to the Durham Case, when investigators asked Davis about the Fleming murders, he initially responded as if he had no knowledge of them. After they walked him through a synopsis of the case, he admitted to generally remembering it but said he had nothing to add that was not already known. When offered immunity if he would take a polygraph specifically concerning Billy Birt's involvement in the Fleming murders, Davis declined and gave up nothing. When asked why he was in prison, Davis stated bank robbery rather than murder. That was initially true as his years of incarceration began after his conviction for robbing the bank in Loganville, Georgia, but what kept him in prison was his subsequent conviction for the murder of Mac Sibley. Even when Davis was "smack dab in the middle" of a crime, he took care to distance himself, not necessarily from peripheral involvement in the crime (e.g., as the driver only), but from the actual commission of the crime.[2332]

Despite Davis's denial, Sheriff Hagaman is convinced Davis entered the Durham home – even if only, perhaps, to tell his associates to hurry up and leave – but he does not believe Davis helped kill the Durhams. Hagaman concedes he has no concrete information to support these gut suspicions,[2333] but he says Davis confirmed details of the Durham Case unknown to the public, which he could not have read in a news article. "[Davis] knew enough data points to give law enforcement confidence that he was truly there…. He knew things that no one would have known unless they had first-hand knowledge…. He knew too much [about] the inside of the house *[which is actually not evident in any of Davis's interviews]*, but he would not put himself in the house. He was that calculated…. He [was] still very manipulative…. He [was] very careful in what he [said] and what he kept from me."[2334]

Despite what Billy Wayne Davis said or did not say in these interviews, one must also consider his track record for truth telling. Back in 1974, when Davis was an informant to law officers concerning cases from that era, the Georgia Bureau of Investigation said, "When he's willing, he's pretty damned reliable."[2335] But some who have known Davis question his honesty. Charlie Reed reportedly said Davis was a habitual liar.[2336] "Today," according to Sean Kipe, "so many years later, there's no one left alive to call Davis a liar other than, of course, Stoney [Birt]."[2337] And Stoney says he will defend his father until his dying day.[2338]

So, what shall we make of Billy Wayne Davis? Torturous killer, habitual liar, confidence man, and clever manipulator? Peripheral accomplice, credible witness, sincere repentant, and confused senior citizen? Or a mix of all the above? And what does this mean for the involvement – or not – of Davis, Billy Birt, Bobby Gaddis, and Charlie Reed in the Durham murders?

CHAPTER 29

"I DIDN'T KILL NO OLD PEOPLE"

One final premise for believing Billy Birt, Billy Wayne Davis, Bobby Gaddis, and Charlie Reed committed the Durham murders is the similarity in how the Durham and Fleming Cases were perpetrated. Some – Bob Ingram in particular – have considered the criminal behaviors exhibited in each to be practically identical, and since these four men were believed to have some tie to the Fleming Case – three of them even being convicted for it – it seemed a reasonable deduction (bolstered by Shane Birt's statements and Davis's "confessions") that the same set of men were involved in the Durham Case. But while Billy Birt openly admitted his involvement in other crimes, he specifically denied involvement in the Fleming Case. Upon hearing his sentence of death for murdering Reid and Lois Fleming, he showed no emotion,[2339] but turning his face to the Flemings' son Hugh, he stated, "I want you to know I didn't kill your mama and daddy."[2340] And to the other courtroom observers he said, "I want this whole town to know that I didn't kill no old people."[2341]

In making a case for his innocence, Birt later recounted that, in 1976, after Davis implicated him, Reed, and Gaddis in the Fleming murders, he and Davis ended up in adjacent cells in Sheriff Earl Lee's jail in Douglas County, Georgia, charged with the murders of Drs. Warren and Rosina Matthews. According to Birt, he and Davis began conversing, and Davis told Birt he had been tricked into testifying in the Fleming Case and he was sorry for testifying against Birt and Reed, but he made no mention of Gaddis. Davis's cell was bugged, and Sheriff Lee heard their conversation. Later, when alone with Birt, Lee asked him why Davis apologized for testifying against him and Reed but said nothing about Gaddis. Birt alluding to his and Reed's innocence and Davis's and Gaddis's guilt, replied, "I don't know sheriff. Why do you think?"[2342] As Birt put it, again with a seemingly purposeful exclusion of Gaddis, "In 1975, Billy Davis took me and Charlie Reed down to Jefferson County, GA, on a murder case."[2343] Although Birt had been seen by a couple of witnesses on the evening of the Fleming murders, and although he ultimately admitted to being in Wrens, Georgia, he said he and Reed were there to rob other homes, and he had no interest in the Flemings because he felt more money, as well as drugs, could be found elsewhere. Birt denied being involved in the couple's torture and deaths and claimed Davis and Gaddis were the killers.[2344]

Former Winder, Georgia Chief of Police Jimmy Terrell first became acquainted with Billy Birt in 1975. Terrell interviewed him on a couple of occasions and helped convict him for another crime. He also maintains Birt's innocence in the Fleming Case. Terrell was present at Birt's trial for the murders, and based on his impression of Birt, he says, "I'll never believe Billy [Birt] was in the house when the Wrens couple was killed."[2345] Although Billy Wayne Davis also denied being in the Fleming house, "[Bobby] Gaddis told Terrell that Davis was…there." But Gaddis said Birt was there too, and Birt's claim about burglarizing houses elsewhere at the time of the murders "never came up during his trial." According to Terrell, "I truly believe that Charlie Reed would do whatever Billy [Birt] told him to do. Billy loved safes; he loved to crack them…I believe he and Charlie did the burglaries, and Bobby Gene and Billy Wayne did the killings…. But [Birt] would not claim he was innocent," Terrell said, "because he was part of the overall plan. 'I believe that if Billy [Birt] were sitting here, he would tell you that he was rightfully convicted.'"[2346]

Birt did claim innocence in the physical murders (i.e., torture and strangling) of the Flemings, but his sons, Stoney and Shane, like Terrell, agree that their father assumed at least some guilt. According to Stoney, "If he was sitting here, he would tell you he was responsible."[2347] Stoney clarifies this by stating that, although his father did not personally kill the Flemings, he felt responsible for their deaths because the money he and Reed took from the robberies of Jerry Haymon's house and the pill houses was pooled with the money Davis and Gaddis took from the Fleming house and split among them, and because he could have prevented Davis and Gaddis from robbing and killing the Flemings and did not.[2348]

In subsequent years, when the death penalty was off the table for Birt, he stated, "They almost put me in the electric chair a couple of times…[I] was innocent of what they would have executed [me] for, but not much else was I innocent [of]."[2349] This was, yet again, Birt's proclamation of innocence in the Fleming murders. Still, he "believed in the death penalty" and "always said he deserved all the punishment he received for his crimes." He stated to his family on more than one occasion he deserved to die for the deaths of the Flemings, and he did not want any of his family members to sign petitions to eliminate the death penalty. Yet "he did nothing to discourage appeals to reduce his death sentence to life imprisonment…[and] even encouraged filing a writ of habeas corpus [an order that would bring him before a court to determine if his imprisonment was lawful]…."[2350] Birt's execution was scheduled for August 24, 1975, although his death sentence generated "an automatic appeal to the Georgia Supreme Court," and Birt and his attorneys would make later appeals as well.[2351] In early 1976, Birt's appeal to the Georgia Supreme Court argued, among other things, "that the trial court erred…in overruling his motion for [a] new trial" because "there was not sufficient evidence to corroborate" Davis's testimony "so as to connect the defendant with the crime." In response, the high court stated, in part, that the testimony of the two men who jumped off Birt's broken down vehicle corroborated Davis's testimony and tended to connect Birt with the crime and infer his guilt. Although Birt, during his own testimony at trial, had offered an alternative explanation for his being in Wrens (i.e., the retrieval of Davis's pistol), the court stated Birt's testimony "merely made a question for the jury to decide," and the jury chose not to believe him. The court further affirmed the death sentences imposed on him.[2352] Birt made five more appeals between 1979 and 1986, all without success.[2353]

Despite Birt's conviction for the Fleming murders, and in light of his persistent claims of not having personally harmed them, was he falsely accused and railroaded? According to Stoney Birt, Jim West "was hell bent on taking Billy Birt down" and "had friends in high places," including a trio of attorneys who spent three years effecting the ultimately wrongful conviction of The Marietta Seven in the murders of Drs. Warren and Rosina Matthews.[2354] The confession letter Billy Birt wrote, admitting his guilt in the Matthews Case, "helped knock down what appeared to be a house of cards" that the presiding judge and attorney "Ben Smith and others built around [the] fake confession of Debbie Kidd."[2355] Smith had granted Kidd immunity for her ultimately perjurious testimony against the seven, and he likewise represented Billy Wayne Davis and negotiated his immunity in exchange for Davis's testimony against Birt in the Fleming Case. Smith's law partner and the Cobb County District Attorney facilitated the dead-docketing of a murder indictment against Davis in exchange for his same testimony.[2356]

Stoney also believes Jim West further stacked the deck against his father when, during Billy Birt's arraignment and trial for the Fleming murders, West ordered an extreme amount of security surrounding him to ensure "that every potential juror [saw him] as the most dangerous man in criminal history." According to Stoney, "the courthouse [was] ringed with twenty-five shotgun-wielding state troopers…[and] a dozen GBI agents, and half [a] dozen Federal Marshals" transported his father from the jail to the courthouse. Sharpshooters were on the courthouse roof, a helicopter flew overhead with a sniper, and all courthouse visitors had to pass through an outside metal detector as part of a thorough search process. Stoney says, "It looked like martial law had been declared." Stoney also states a trooper with a shotgun stood behind his father for the entirety of the trial, aiming at him with his finger on the trigger anytime his father stood for recess or to take the stand.[2357] A state habeas corpus court, however, found "that although 'several weapons were visible in the courtroom…they were held at rest and not aimed or pointed directly at [Birt]…[and] that 'several of the law enforcement personnel present in the courtroom, such as the GBI and Federal Marshalls [sic], were dressed in civilian clothes with their weapons not being visible.'"[2358]

Billy Birt's subsequent appeals argued, in part, that the excessive security "deprived him of his constitutional due process right" to the presumption of innocence until proven guilty. The appeals revealed that law enforcement had information indicating friends or relatives of Birt might attempt to kill certain state witnesses, and that sons of Billy Birt and Bobby Gaddis were planning to get a weapon into the courtroom and help Birt escape. It was also indicated that Birt "was an extremely agile individual who was capable of leaping out of a building to secure his freedom." For these reasons, the courts determined it was not unreasonable to search individuals entering the courtroom or to have tight security precautions, and that these measures, including the number of guards involved, helped avoid having to try Birt in shackles, which would have been "much more drastic and prejudicial." The Supreme Court of Georgia did "not find that the trial judge abused his discretion as to security measures or that the petitioner was deprived of his right to a fair trial."[2359] Still, Stoney Birt maintains that, although the premise for the tight security was a precaution against his father escaping: "All this show was done in such a way that all the townspeople, news people, and all the potential jurors would see it. After seeing all this, they could have put any twelve people in a room," instructed them to vote, "and most would have said guilty. The power of suggestion is a D. A.'s best trick."[2360]

Fast forwarding to the allegations of his father's involvement in the Durham Case, Stoney says, "It don't take a rocket scientist to see through this…. They throwed my father into it once again, just for some notoriety….[2361] And I say again, I'm not out to defend the honor of my father because we all know by now that he [was] perfectly capable of this or any other crime he deemed worthy of his time, effort, money, whatever…. His life pretty much spoke for itself. We all know that he would kill you for a damn nickel; he would kill you if it suited him. I'm simply here putting myself back out there again, wide open for anybody to take a punch at me because it just don't damn taste good the way they done it again." According to Stoney, people in power coerced or talked Davis "into making Billy Birt a dumping ground,"[2362] and Stoney refuses to allow others to put "another horrible murder" (i.e., the Durham murders) on his father in the same manner they tied him to the Fleming murders. While Stoney admits his father was a cold-blooded killer who committed a long list of crimes, he says his father cannot be guilty of everything that others try to pin on him. "They have circumvented grand jury, judge, trial, the whole she-boom, took an exceptionally awful case and allowed Davis to once again, without a polygraph, without anything, say okay, yeah, if that's the deal, I was driving the same three that I said killed the [Flemings]. Now, send me to a better place, and feed me meat, or whatever his deal was…me and you'll never know. It ain't in me to sit back and allow that to become history without a rebuttal."[2363] Although Stoney says his father "was railroaded" in the Fleming Case, "at least…he was not denied due process of the law, regardless of the tactics used by law enforcement of that day to get that conviction…. But what's going on now with the Durham Case defies all due process. And it doesn't do justice to the victims. They, above all deserve for the truth to be revealed." Stoney calls for restoration of the integrity of due process. "The public wants it, and the victims deserve it."[2364]

The things that rile Stoney up more than anything are when individuals milk the character flaws of his family for notoriety or profit, and when someone speaks negatively about his father, especially when that someone is Billy Wayne Davis. Stoney says, "Billy Birt has done enough murders and enough crime and enough awful things that the truth is bad enough; it don't need any help. And that's what [Davis has] been allowed to do."[2365] This is a reiteration of what Billy Birt wrote in his will, only ten days before his death:[2366] "I do not want any person to ever again be hurt by my actions or inactions. I do not want anyone to sensationalize my Name or my Memory to be disgraced by any stories that are not true. The truth is bad enough. It does not need anything made up to go with it."[2367]

Because his father is not alive to defend himself against Davis's accusations concerning the Durham murders, Stoney feels obliged to:[2368] "My sole motive in even talking about this case, knowing that it's going to be out there for that family – Bryce's family, the Hall family, everybody – to dissect every word I say, and they might see it as me sticking my nose into it, but my sole motive is because my father has no one to defend him except me….[2369] I'm not out to belittle law enforcement. I believe in law enforcement 100%. And I believe in justice…. I'm not out to take away from the hard work of any police. The law enforcement involved in closing this case are not evil. They are not diabolical. They don't want to cause anybody any harm. I'm not out to stain the career of Bob Ingram." But then, Stoney takes a hard turn: "Hell, they might even believe their own bullshit, but I don't believe it….[2370]

The accuracy of the list of Georgia murders Jim West compiled based on information supplied by Billy Wayne Davis has been questioned, particularly since Davis targeted Birt, and West badly wanted Birt put away. According to author Phil Hudgins, Davis and Birt "had robbed banks and killed several people together, and [Birt] apparently trusted this car dealer [Davis] at one time. He may have told him about a number of murders, robberies, and other crimes. Davis no doubt was a party to some of them. But whether Davis told West the whole truth is debatable. West himself was criticized, even in his own ranks, for being heavy-handed in his investigations, willing to go to any length to get his suspect…. Reading the report Jim West prepared, one might wonder if he was obsessed with tracking down every tiny detail about the ungodly criminal acts of Billy Sunday Birt. West apparently looked under every suspicious rock and noted everything he heard about [Birt]. And he didn't stop there. He also investigated cases that [Birt] might have been involved in, even if the evidence against him was not strong, or was nonexistent." Hudgins further writes, "West included in his report murders that [Birt] may have committed, but he wasn't sure of his theories…. West sometimes would get a little information about a case and then assume Bill Birt was the perpetrator. He may or may not have been involved. But West was bound and determined to put the man in prison." In the words of Stoney Birt, West pursued the Dixie Mafia like "a law dog from hell" and did what he had to do. Although Jimmy Terrell recognizes West "had a job to do" and in no way wants to disparage him, he states, "At the time I read Jim West's report, I believed every word of it. But I came to realize that West was so gung-ho to get them and make cases." Terrell "became skeptical about some of the agent's information." According to Terrell, "In some cases…Davis probably told investigators what they wanted to hear, and it wasn't always the truth."[2371]

In his *In The Red Clay* podcast, Sean Kipe argues that one indicator of Birt's innocence in the Durham murders is that, around the time the Durhams were killed, Birt was being watched very closely.[2372] But Birt is also credited with consistently eluding law enforcement, so one might ask how closely were they really able to keep tabs on him? According to Bob Ingram, "Birt…had 'enormous survival skills;'" he was not a nut job but was clever and smart and knew how to avoid detection.[2373] Kipe also brings up the fact that, in 1972 – the same year as the Durham murders – Birt chose not to kill Sheriff Earl Lee in front of his wife and children,[2374] and Stoney Birt says one of the reasons his father would turn down a job was that "it went against his moral code to kill a family man in front of his wife and kids."[2375] Presumably, then, this would have included turning down a contract to kill Bryce Durham in front of his wife Virginia and son Bobby. But the Durham murders occurred several months prior to the proposed hit on Lee, so Birt may not have had such a "flash of morality" at the time the Durhams were killed. Or perhaps that "moral code" did not apply if a wife and son were killed first and then the husband/father, which is the order of death in the Durham Case that Shane Birt claims his father told him.

Stoney Birt acknowledges his father murdered others during robberies, or because he was hired to, or to take out a "rat,"[2376] but he maintains his father's innocence in the Fleming Case, which seems to be a particular pain point for him. In reconciling his father's criminal past, he seems to be able to come to terms with his father killing people who snitched on him (i.e., "broke 'code'"), or people who put his father in a defensive position (even if the victims were trying to defend their own lives against him), but he cannot bear the thought of his father sadistically torturing someone, as was done to the Flemings. Stoney says his father would just straight out kill his victims, for example, shooting them three times in the head and being done with it versus prolonging it with torture. "He knew how to do it. He made it short and sweet and to the point…."[2377]

Bob Ingram believes the reason Billy Birt did not just go in, take care of business, and get out quickly might be attributed to his heavy dependence on RJSs (Black Beauties). Ingram thinks the associated psychosis and highs and lows the pills produced, combined with little sleep, played havoc on Birt's brain and caused him to be extremely paranoid and dangerous. Is it possible Birt was so addicted by 1972 that his behavior changed and resulted in him becoming erratic and sloppy or sadistic in his work? According to Stoney, there was no observable behavior change (including meanness) in his father. Though Billy Birt did experience paranoia and the pills contributed to his downfall, "he was still, in many ways, at the top of his game." But according to Shane Birt, by the period of 1971-1973, the pills had caused his father to become more violent, dangerous, and out of control, even to the point that Billy Birt's own brothers were reluctant to accompany him on jobs.[2378]

Stoney Birt says his father did not enjoy killing, whereas Billy Wayne Davis killed without mercy and took pleasure in it.[2379] In contrast, retired FBI Agent Ron Webb, who worked for the GBI in the early 1970s and solved a few murder cases involving Billy Birt, said Birt was the worst he had seen – a sociopath who had no remorse and really liked to kill.[2380] According to Webb, regarding two cases he worked on that involved murdered couples, "[Birt] would torture the females, make the guy tell them where the money was hid, then kill 'em."[2381] Bob Ingram says Birt "was more than just a mean-ass redneck from Winder, Georgia." Out of the hundreds of murderers Ingram interviewed or dealt with during his law enforcement career, he says Birt was the toughest and the most dangerous, brutal, and ruthless. Ingram classifies Birt as evil and "the deadliest man in Georgia," who "was damn good at killing." On a scale of one to ten, Ingram ranks Birt as a ten. "If there was an eleven, he'd be eleven." Ingram also states that at least half a dozen of the murders Billy Birt committed involved torture.[2382][pppppppp]

Despite the testimonials of these lawmen, Jimmy Terrell, a former lawman himself, feels Billy Birt was not someone who wanted to watch others in pain. Terrell rather believes Davis and Gaddis did, and that they were the sadistic ones in the group. Of Davis, Terrell writes, "I believe he delighted in the torture of his victims."[2383] Terrell's assessment aligns with Stoney Birt's thoughts about Davis and his [Stoney's] father. According to Stoney, Billy Wayne Davis was sadistic. "My father was just as criminal but was never sadistic."[2384] Stoney says "however many murders [his father] was guilty of, not one ever involved torture." Stoney says his father "never took a job or did a job that called for torture. Anybody that has ever known him will tell you that. He has never had a sadistic bone in his body."[2385]

But "who did the torturing [of the Flemings] is debatable even within the Birt family." Throughout the Fleming trial, although it did not look good for Billy Birt, his wife Ruby Nell believed in his innocence and thought he might have been framed. Still, she recognized there was a chance her husband – "the man who was two people" – could be "one of the killers of these decent, church-going folks, Reid and Lois Fleming…. Frankly, I don't know what Bill did…. [He] never revealed what he did after he left the house practically every night…so, if he'd ever killed anyone, I didn't know it for sure." Stoney and his sister Ann do not believe their father was a torturer. Ann believes he was present in the Fleming home but did not kill anyone. "Stoney says his father was out burglarizing homes when the Flemings were being tortured and killed [by others]."[2386] According to Stoney, "He did not put his hands around them two old people's neck and kill them for money…. You don't kill a hundred people and torture one time." He adds: "My dad killed all these people…but he did not torture any of them. If you take away…Wrens [i.e., the Flemings], then you see a cold-blooded murderer. You don't see a son-of-a-bitch out there gleefully torturing people. You don't see it."[2387] Shane Birt, however, believes Stoney is in denial about their father being a torturer: "Stoney don't like the Boone case 'cause it's gruesome. Stoney don't like the Wrens case 'cause it's gruesome…. Stoney tries to say [daddy] wasn't there, that he didn't have a part in it…."

[pppppppp] One example that is often referred to in support of Billy Birt being a torturer is that of an elderly Winder, Georgia couple who he reportedly strangled and robbed in June 1972. Afterwards, it is claimed that he poured gasoline in their mouths and set them and their home and store on fire. Although the victims were badly burned, autopsies determined they were dead before the fire started. [Sources: Paul Beeman, "Probe to Open in 15 Mystery Deaths," *The Atlanta Constitution*, Atlanta, GA, August 13, 1972, p. 8-A; Paul Lieberman, "Dixie Mafia," *The Atlanta Constitution*, Atlanta, GA, February 28, 1981, p. 4-A; Birt, Ruby Nell (as told to Phil Hudgins), *Grace and Disgrace: Living with Faith and a Dixie Mafia Hit Man* (YAV Publications, Asheville, NC, 2022), pp. 155 & 240.]

And while Shane would like to believe their father was innocent of these murders, he states [of the Fleming murders], "You'll never hear me say that Daddy was not there, and that he did not strangle the people. I do not know because Daddy never would tell me. What he did say is that he was one hundred percent responsible for the deaths."[2388] In a 2019 interview with Bob Ingram, however, Shane said his father *did* tell him how he killed the Flemings – strangling them with coat hangers and torturing them to give up their money – and that Bobby Gaddis and Charlie Reed were with his father. Shane added that he did not know if Billy Wayne Davis was present or not. According to Shane, "If daddy ever had a case that changed him, it was that case there…daddy regretted that case more than any other.... He said [he regretted it] because those people didn't deserve to die. Daddy said they was just sweet old people."

One of Stoney Birt's driving purposes has been to exonerate his father of the Fleming murders, and he has taken multiple steps toward that end, including appealing to Fleming family survivors, writing and speaking about it, and even imploring Bob Ingram to say it did not happen, to which Ingram responded that Stoney was asking the wrong person for such a thing, as he [Ingram] knew Billy Birt tortured and killed the Flemings. According to Ingram, Billy Birt killed the Durhams and the Flemings and so many others.[2389] When the Durham Case and its alleged link to his father hit his radar, Stoney learned it was being compared to the Fleming Case as another instance of binding, gagging, torture, and cruel death. Believing in his father's innocence in the Fleming Case, Stoney likewise believes his father was not involved in the Durham Case and has spent more recent years trying to prove it.

The Flemings' great-niece, Cyndi Silvey Lynch, based on Billy Birt's conviction for those murders, grew up firmly believing he was responsible for the death of her loved ones. But now, as an adult and after learning more about Birt, particularly through the *In The Red Clay* podcast, she questions those beliefs she once espoused. Based on her newly acquired knowledge of the bad blood between Billy Birt and Billy Wayne Davis and of Birt's willingness to admit his involvement in other cases while adamantly declaring his innocence in the Fleming Case, she questions Bob Ingram's confidence about the case and does not totally agree with his assessment of it. Unconvinced of Billy Birt's guilt, she now leans toward him *not* having killed her family members, but she also doubts it will ever be solidly proven one way or another.[2390]

Is there a chance Billy Birt was not guilty of torturing and murdering the Flemings? If so, does that discredit the template used to compare the Durham and Fleming cases, or does it merely remove Birt from the Fleming Case but still make him guilty in the Durham Case, particularly based on his alleged confession to his son?

Regrettably, perhaps the same doubt that Cyndi Silvey Lynch has about the ultimate resolution of her family members' murders also applies to ever knowing for sure who snuffed out the lives of Bryce, Virginia, and Bobby Durham.

CHAPTER 30

AND THEN THERE'S CHARLIE MARTIN

Charlie Martin's tombstone in the Woodbine Cemetery, Jefferson, Georgia (Image courtesy of Theron Rogers) & Bryce Durham's tombstone in the Pleasant Home Baptist Church Cemetery, Roaring River, North Carolina (photo by author) – both bearing the same death date.

In May 2023, while conducting research for this book and searching the internet for information concerning Charlie Martin, who I had learned was one of Billy Birt's alleged victims, I was astonished when I came across a photograph of Martin's tombstone,[2391] etched with a death date that had likewise been etched into my brain. The death date on Martin's grave marker matched that of the Durhams. I immediately texted this information to Stoney Birt – both to share the discovery of it and to inquire if he knew more details of Martin's death. Although Stoney did know the background of his father murdering Martin, and although Stoney had spoken of Martin's murder as part of the *In The Red Clay* podcast and included in one of his own books some newspaper articles concerning the discovery of Martin's body, he was not aware of Martin's exact death date, a compelling piece of information that suddenly cast reasonable doubt on the involvement of Billy Birt in the Durham murders.

Charlie Martin was from Jackson County, Georgia and a maintenance worker at the University of Georgia in Athens. He disappeared in February 1972. His remains were discovered more than four years later in August 1976 in a dynamited well on a farm in Gwinnett County, Georgia (a mile from the Barrow County line) and identified by dental records and recognition by his family of certain pieces of clothing and personal effects. The night of his disappearance, Martin was reportedly scheduled to meet – as an informant – with Barrow County Sheriff Howard Austin and ATF Agent Jim West in Arcade, Georgia regarding whiskey stills and the burial location of Willie Hester, Jr., one of Billy Birt's inner circle who Birt had allegedly killed. But Martin never showed up.

According to Stoney Birt, that very same night, his father and Martin were inside Reece Spencer's Night Owl Lounge, an Athens nightclub,[qqqqqqqq] when a snitch informed Spencer that Martin knew things and was cooperating with law enforcement. In turn, Spencer told Billy Birt he needed to "take care of" Martin and get rid of him as soon as possible. *[One source states that, at the time of Martin's disappearance, he was slated to testify in a federal liquor conspiracy case in which Birt and three other men had been indicted.[2392]]* Birt immediately approached Martin and asked him to give him a ride to his [Birt's] home a short distance away in Statham, Georgia. After pulling into Birt's back yard, Birt shot and killed Martin inside Martin's car.[rrrrrrrr] Stoney says he knew his father killed Martin after hearing "idle, low talk between him and his boys," and around 1980, Ruby Nell Birt told her husband she had witnessed the shooting from inside their home, although she did not know the victim's identity. This surprised Billy Birt, and in their ensuing conversation, with Stoney present, the details of Martin's murder came out once more.[2393]

The pivotal question concerning Martin's death date is, if he disappeared in 1972 and his remains were not discovered until four years later, how was an exact date of death determined? According to the Barrow County Probate Court, there is no death certificate for Martin in all of Georgia's statewide vital records system.[2394] Martin's widow Linda says February 3, 1972 was chosen for his tombstone because that was the date she last saw him. He left their Athens residence between 9:00 and 10:00 PM to take a friend[ssssssss] home to Gainesville, Georgia, and he never returned. She elaborates: "It was not unusual for him to be gone for days sometimes, but our anniversary was February 27, so by then I knew something was wrong. People kept saying, 'He's here or there or gone to Mexico.' I looked for him, but when he wasn't home by Mother's Day, I was pretty sure he wouldn't be back. He wouldn't have missed seeing his Mama."[2395] With February 3, 1972 being the date Martin disappeared, it was as close as his family could come to knowing when he lost his life, and it is highly probable he was murdered that same night. There seem to be no instances where Billy Birt or his associates ever held victims hostage beyond a few hours, at the most, before killing them, and most were murdered straightaway.[2396]

Despite my telling Stoney about the death date on Martin's tombstone, he did not respond with the enthusiasm I imagined he would; in fact, he seemed curiously non-reactionary to it, but I chalked it up to him perhaps being already so convinced of his father's innocence in the Durham Case that he did not find this potentially supporting evidence necessary. However, it was not until my further communication with Stoney a few months later that I learned the real reason for his subdued response to the information I had shared. Stoney told me, "I'm bad about riding down the road without my reading glasses and just half reading something." As a result, he had not realized from my earlier text messages the significance of the death date on Martin's tombstone. Stoney continued: "I didn't give a damn about the date, but when you just said it – February 3rd of '72! Why

---

[qqqqqqqq] According to Stoney Birt, Reece Spencer's nightclub was open on Wednesday through Saturday nights with customers arriving around 8:00 PM and leaving between 1:00 AM and 3:00 AM. [Sources: Birt, Stoney. Phone interview with author. July 3, 2023; Birt, Stoney. Text to author. July 4, 2023.]

[rrrrrrrr] The examination of Martin's remains revealed "an entry defect characteristic of a gunshot wound of entry located in the posterior aspect of the right temporal region." [Source: State of Georgia, Georgia Bureau of Investigation Crime Laboratory Official Report case #76-17891 concerning victim Charles Martin.] The description of this wound would be consistent with Martin sitting behind the wheel of his car, the right side of his head facing Billy Birt.

[ssssssss] When this friend was interviewed more than two years later, he could only recall that he had last seen Martin in late 1971 or early 1972 and had no further information regarding his disappearance. [Wood, Floyd Nelson. Interview with Georgia Bureau of Investigation Special Agent W. G. Brooks. May 1, 1974. Investigative Summary, case #04-0010-01-75.]

didn't I catch that? This right here is a whole different ballgame.... You done rung a bell.... You just give me a good thing to hang my hat on.... [That's] another... good indication that something's amiss in this...story. [It] all adds up to a damn good alibi for Billy Birt. Better believe I'm gonna research it more...."

The following day, Stoney shared with me two pages from Jim West's report that concerned Martin, and Stoney believes that, because Bob Ingram had a copy of this same report and was reviewing it during his interviews with Shane Birt, Ingram knew Martin died the same night as the Durhams and yet persisted in declaring Billy Birt as one of the Durhams' killers. West's report, however, while chronological in its accounting of murders attributed to Billy Birt, and while sandwiching Martin's disappearance between the November 1971 kidnapping and death of Jim Daws and the February 11-12, 1972 disappearance and murder of Carolyn Baird Cooper, fails to state any specific dates for Martin's disappearance or death. *[According to Martin's widow, a deputy from Jackson County, Georgia wanted to speak with Martin because Martin was reportedly "the last and only person who had seen the man" who accompanied Cooper the night she disappeared and was murdered.*[2397] *If that is true, and if Cooper was murdered on February 11 or 12, that would mean Martin, although missing from home, was still alive at that time and was not killed on February 3.]* Also, Ingram was not aware of the Durhams' death date until after Shane's April and May 2019 interviews had concluded and he [Ingram] subsequently discovered all the details of the Durham Case in a news article. On this basis, I told Stoney it is impossible to say Ingram knew Martin died on the same date as the Durhams. In fact, there seems to be no paper trail whatsoever that documents Martin's death date;[ttttttt] only his tombstone states a specific date. A few weeks later, armed with this new information I had discovered about Martin's death date as indicated on his tombstone, Stoney shared it on his "Rock Solid" Facebook page and boldly declared Martin's death as his father's alibi: "It's a damn shame that my father's alibi for the Durham murders is another murder. But it's the truth...."[2398] And while this very well could be true, concrete proof is lacking.

Outside of Stoney Birt's personal knowledge of his father saying he killed Charlie Martin, and Jim West's report stating Billy Birt was believed to have murdered Martin, and a GBI report stating Billy Birt was the suspect, there is, unfortunately, no evidence to prove it, and Billy Birt was never charged with Martin's death. When Martin's case was closed in 1977, the final investigative summary stated, "Sheriff [John Robert] Austin advised that due to the extenuating circumstances surrounding this case, there would not be an effective prosecution of the perpetrator since he is currently under a death sentence and doing Federal time."[2399] Although that perpetrator was not named, this most certainly was a reference to Billy Birt. Also, the GBI file on Martin states that, based on the condition of Martin's skull and the top of his body, officers believed "that dynamite was placed in the victim's mouth or around his head and then exploded."[2400] Billy Birt had access to dynamite and used it often in his crimes.[2401] One might argue it was one of his "calling cards," and it is not difficult to imagine him as Martin's killer, symbolically placing a stick of dynamite in Martin's mouth to represent his silencing of anyone who snitched.

[ttttttt] The Jackson County (GA) Sheriff's Office, the Barrow County (GA) Sheriff's Office, and the Gwinnett County (GA) Sheriff's Office all responded to the author's Open Records Requests, stating they have no investigative files regarding Charlie Martin's disappearance or death. [Sources: Royal, Aleshia (Barrow County Sheriff's Office). Phone conversation with author. May 2023; Jones, Janie (Barrow County Clerk of Superior Court). Phone conversation with author. May 2023; Mangum, Janis (Jackson County Sheriff). E-mail to author. May 23, 2023; Gwinnett County Open Records Office (following a review by the Gwinnett County Sheriff's Office). E-mail to author. August 16, 2023.]

One of Stoney's next steps was to share details of Martin's disappearance and death and Jim West's report with the Watauga County Sheriff's Office, although by this time, I had already shared it with both Sheriff Len Hagaman and Bob Ingram. Although both found the information interesting, they gave no indication that it dissuaded them from believing Billy Birt was one of the Durhams' killers.[2402] Regarding the possibility of Billy Birt killing Charlie Martin on the same night the Durhams were killed, Ingram would later state, "That is not the case. He [Martin] did not die on that day. He disappeared on that day. *[But how can Ingram know Martin was not killed the same day he disappeared?]* That's the last day that his wife saw him. She was not formally interviewed until his body was found. She said that's the date he disappeared but had no knowledge of the date he died, so that's the reason that that date was on the tombstone. I think Birt killed him. Do I think he killed him on February the 3rd? Probably not. *[By saying "probably not," Ingram acknowledges it is a possibility.]* The wife…said he was notorious for being gone for a few days, and nobody gave it any thought."[2403]

After Stoney reached out to Sheriff Hagaman, Hagaman agreed to return to Georgia and meet with him in July 2023. The day of the scheduled meeting, Captain Carolynn Johnson appeared in Hagaman's stead, explaining Hagaman was unable to travel to Georgia because something important had come up that required his attention. The meeting between Stoney and Johnson proceeded in the presence of podcaster Sean Kipe (who recorded the interchange) and former Barrow County, Georgia Sheriff Joe Robinson. According to Stoney, after listening to his presentation and receiving copies of his materials, Johnson agreed it was very interesting and compelling and needed to be looked into further.[uuuuuuuu] She told Stoney she would pass the information on to Hagaman. Until this time, Stoney had vacillated in his opinion of Hagaman. Prior to the meeting with Johnson, he had concluded Hagaman was "a good man that may have been sold a bill of goods from people with obvious ulterior motives…." Stoney's conscience was troubled by the thought of potentially running down the reputation of a good lawman who may have been duped but, having received no communication from Hagaman after the meeting with Johnson and having seen Hagaman's and Johnson's subsequent participation in an August 2023 newscast that once again recounted how Billy Birt's role in the Durham murders had been determined, Stoney reformed his opinion of the two officers and not in a favorable way.[2404] According to Johnson, however, "For us, there is no picking sides in any of it….we don't have a team or a side or a dog in the fight other than trying to bring closure to what family is left. It is what it is, and what truth we can bring, that's what we'll bring."[2405]

As of October 2023, Stoney had presented the circumstances of Charlie Martin's murder as an alibi for Billy Birt in the Durham murders to Jackson County, Georgia Sheriff Janis Mangum, who knows Martin's family and whose uncle married Martin's mother. Mangum expressed interest in further investigating Martin's disappearance and death, and although she recalled when his remains were discovered, she had no files within her office concerning him. Not knowing "which way to go with it," and seeking clarification and guidance, Mangum reached out to Martin's family as well as to Bob Ingram, who she stated was the GBI agent who "worked on that case." Mangum was subsequently notified that Ingram had obtained a GBI file,[vvvvvvvv] presumably concerning Martin,

---

[uuuuuuuu] Six months later, Johnson told the author she thought the death date on Martin's tombstone (due to the passage of time between his disappearance and discovery) had no bearing on the Durham Case. [Source: Johnson, Carolynn. In-person interview with author. January 16, 2024.]

[vvvvvvvv] In response to the author's Open Records Request for Martin's file (which the author submitted at the suggestion of Bob Ingram), the Georgia Bureau of Investigation stated they could find no such file. Sheriff Janis

and she intended to meet with him. In December 2023, Mangum received the GBI's case file on Martin, but stated there was not much to it – only a confirmation of what was already known – that Martin's widow said the last time she saw him was February 3, 1972. In Mangum's opinion, there is no way to determine Martin's death date, and she sees no reason to pursue the matter further.[2406]

But if Billy Birt really did murder Charlie Martin the night of February 3, 1972 in Statham, Georgia, then he could not have murdered Bryce, Virginia, and Bobby Durham that same night in Boone, North Carolina. And if Billy Birt did not murder the Durhams, it is highly unlikely that two of his "soldiers" – Bobby Gaddis and Charlie Reed – did either.[wwwwwwww]

Mangum later provided the author with the case file number, and the author resubmitted an Open Records Request with that information and ultimately received the file. [Sources: Ingram, Bob. Phone interview with author. May 27, 2023; Garner, Monique (GBI Office of Privacy and Compliance, Open Records Unit). E-mail to author. July 27, 2023; Gwinnett County Open Records Office (following a review by the Gwinnett County Sheriff's Office). E-mail to author. August 16, 2023; Mangum, Janis. E-mail to author. December 27, 2023.]

[wwwwwwww] Stoney Birt fully agrees with the author's assessment of the involvement of Gaddis and Reed, stating, "They didn't do nothing without his [Billy Birt's] direction." [Source: Birt, Stoney. Phone conversation with author. July 3, 2023.]

CONCLUSION

By this time, you can surely agree that the long-drawn-out Durham Case is, indeed, a convoluted one, and you have surely gathered that the deepest and most recent division of opinion about the case concerns the alleged involvement of Georgia's Dixie Mafia. As previously discussed, some are convinced Billy Birt, Billy Wayne Davis, Bobby Gaddis, and Charlie Reed are guilty of the murders of Bryce, Virginia, and Bobby Durham; others are equally convinced of their innocence.

Bob Ingram once said to me, "I don't know how much you realize how unique of a case you're involved in and how unique the individuals who are involved."[2407] At the time of his comment, I had already invested two years into researching and writing about the Durham Case, and I was most definitely aware of the uniqueness of it and its cast of characters. As it concerns Billy Sunday Birt, in particular, one might argue that, if some relatively unknown criminal had been accused of killing the Durhams under the same circumstances that Birt was accused, the news might have garnered less attention and certainly less debate and controversy. But Birt, although he was initially little known in North Carolina, was notorious in Georgia, and his notoriety had, not long prior to the Watauga County Sheriff's Office press release, been expanded to an audience of thousands via the *In The Red Clay* podcast. And because of his close relationship with his son Stoney, and Stoney's reverence for and defense of his father, the accusation made in 2022 became what Captain Carolynn Johnson aptly stated to be "a complicated mess and deal,"[2408] and probably more complicated than authorities anticipated. More than two years after the press release announced Billy Birt's involvement in the Durham triple homicide, it remains a hot topic in certain circles, and Stoney Birt has been determined to prove his father's innocence and to discredit, if not shame, his father's accusers. Podcaster Sean Kipe says no matter what, Stoney will continue to believe his father is innocent of the Durham murders, saying, "Billy Birt was certainly more than capable of this crime but being capable and being guilty are two different things."[2409]

Though there is no hard evidence[2410] (no fingerprints, DNA, etc.) linking Billy Birt and his associates to the crime scene, and although no eyewitnesses have positively identified them, Bob Ingram is resolute: "I don't blow smoke. I don't bullshit. When I tell you something, it's because I know what I'm talking about, and I know it's factual." Ingram says this is not speculative; he doesn't *think* Birt did it (i.e., murdered the Durhams), he *knows* he did.[2411] Ingram says his directness and straightforwardness (which his detractors may deem arrogance) served him well during his lengthy law enforcement career, and he still exhibits those traits when he says, "I think when it looks like a duck, quacks like a duck, and water runs off its back, it's a damn duck…. I'm just telling it like it is…. I am 100% that Birt did both crimes on the Fleming Case and the Durham Case," and the behavioral evidence supports that. "There's no question in my mind – none, zero – that the same people were involved."[2412]

Sheriff Len Hagaman is also convinced (with a 99 and 44/100ths percent certainty) that these men from Georgia committed the Durham murders,[2413] and a totally convinced Rufus Edmisten concurs: "There's one thing for certain. There is no doubt about the crowd that did it. [Sheriff Hagaman] and I have talked about that before. You don't need to have any [more] mystery about that. It was done by the Dixie Mafia."[2414] Retired SBI Agent Larry Wagner also agrees on the basis of these men's behavioral patterns, paired with the statements of Shane Birt and Billy Wayne Davis, including the indication that a nephew or son-in-law of the Durhams set up the job. Without all those elements in place, Wagner says he would not feel as comfortable saying the same men killed the Durhams and the Flemings.[2415] Still, Wagner exercises a degree of caution, saying the case is "inconclusive."[2416] Jerry Vaughn, who worked as a lawman and private investigator for forty-seven years, including many years on the Durham Case, felt the Dixie Mafia theory was plausible and as close as investigators had come in years to piecing the case together.[2417]

While both sides have their reasons for believing what they do, and while they offer valid arguments worth contemplating, not everyone can be right; someone must be wrong. And as much as I dislike being a fence straddler, I cannot unequivocally say at this point who is right and who is wrong or if, perhaps, the truth lies somewhere in between. If there was irrefutable proof one way or another, I would certainly trumpet it as loudly as possible, but sadly, that degree of proof is lacking in my estimation.

I never embarked on a crusade to take sides or to prove a certain theory over another. I have no ulterior motive, no hidden agenda, no bones to pick, no axe to grind, no score to settle. Simply put, I sought the truth as best I could. My aim was to glean people's knowledge of, or at least what they believed to be true about the Durham Case and then to accurately impart the same. To be a good investigative reporter, I was compelled to be transparent about people's opposing opinions – both about the case and about each other, while taking care not to pit them against one another or assassinate their characters. I aspired to fairly present all sides and to give an equal voice to all.

Unfortunately, these aspirations in the absence of proof do not ultimately solve anything. And while I would argue my inability to solve the Durham Case has not diminished my ability to successfully articulate this story, I imagine that, in the eyes of some, I am a disappointment because I have not fully embraced or advocated for their point of view. There have been moments when, if I made it known I had given any credence whatsoever to information supplied by a particular person, another person would insinuate I had been hoodwinked. Some individuals brought into question my ability to discern truth and to be taken seriously as a writer simply because I remained open to hearing and considering what everyone had to say. At other times, I was the appreciative beneficiary of encouraging compliments. Bob Ingram told me, "You'd have made a hell of a good investigator,"[2418] and Stoney Birt likewise said to me, "If you ever lose your job, go into investigation because you're pretty damn good." Stoney further described me as "an epitome of a Mayberry good citizen," telling podcaster Sean Kipe, "I think he's seen about everybody involved…and everybody likes him, and I think everybody that meets him trusts him. He's a man of integrity…able to look objectively without emotion…. I'll forever be in awe of his investigative skills."[2419] I am humbled by these remarks.

As I navigated diametrically opposed camps of opinion regarding the who, how, and why of the Durham murders, I sometimes felt pressured to choose sides. This put me in an uncomfortable position because I have found all the people who have assisted me to be generally likable and credible as well as gracious and respectful toward me, and I feel I am on good terms with all despite having occasionally pushed some people's buttons. I have given everyone the benefit of the doubt, and it is within me to look for and expect the best in others. I like to think that, as I pursued the truth of the Durham Case, no one manipulated me and had only good and helpful intentions toward me, yet I have sense enough to know that is not always how people are or how life works. Still, I hold firm in my belief that the individuals who contributed information for this book are, by and large, honorable and integrous, though neither perfect nor infallible. I believe the same about myself. In creating this work, I have striven to be as credible, balanced, objective, rational, and unbiased as possible. You, the readers, may judge my success in that regard.

At the risk of sacrificing my self-proclaimed objectivity and lack of bias, I, like many other people, from law enforcement officers and investigative reporters to true crime junkies and armchair detectives, have personal opinions about the events that took place in February 1972. I admit I am a layman and not a lawman, so it may seem presumptuous of me to put forth my opinions about this case, but in light of all I have presented in this book, and because I am often asked, I will share those here in a series of "I believe" statements.

Due to his rough upbringing and some degree of poverty, I believe Troy Hall aspired to a higher station in life, and he craved wealth, position, and respect. I believe he was extremely smart and utilized his intelligence to devise schemes to transcend his circumstances. By the time he met Ginny Durham and realized her father owned a car dealership, he was already involved in unsavory activities, and I believe he envisioned himself becoming an accepted member of their family and one day running the family business, perhaps even with the thought of using it as a front for illegal purposes such as the trafficking of drugs and stolen goods. I believe he lied about his background in hopes of gaining his in-laws' confidence.

When it became clear Bryce and Virginia Durham intensely disliked Troy, wanted him out of their family and their business, encouraged their daughter to leave him, changed the locks to their dealership and home, cut off his access to vehicles, began investigating his family background and suspicious dealings, and intended to change their wills, I believe Troy bemoaned his plight to others, and by mid-January 1972, together they masterminded a plan that would eliminate his problem and still enable him to achieve his goals. I believe Troy not only desired to rid his life of his in-laws' scrutiny, interference, and rejection but also desired to gain control of their estates. I believe these were his motives for murder, especially considering Ginny would be her family's sole heir and beneficiary.

I believe there is something very telling about Ginny's statement, "Let's suppose…that night, Daddy was the payoff man, and Troy tricked him, and Daddy didn't know what it was all about, so they murdered him." Troy was a known liar and deceiver, and I believe it likely that he, unbeknownst to Bryce, used Bryce's identity and business reputation to advance himself within some of his [Troy's] criminal dealings, and that this placed Bryce in a very precarious situation that may have blindsided him. Troy and his accomplices may have put word out (true or not) that the Durhams kept a large amount of money in their home, or that Bryce was going to be the "payoff man" for some debt Troy owed. And while this may have resulted in the killers taking that bait, invading the Durham home, and killing the Durhams in anger when the money was not found, I believe the extermination of the Durhams was the primary intent all along. Reoccurring themes of car and drug deals and shady business transactions and payoffs – hypothetical or otherwise – are woven throughout this saga, and while the murders may have been associated, I believe the slaying of the Durhams was not merely the fallout of any of these things but was ultimately the result of Troy Hall wanting the Durhams dead. I believe it is also possible that the killers (which I believe did not include Troy) were hired via a yet-to-be identified intermediary, who was most likely based in North Carolina, and that they were paid with cash in advance of their work rather than payment being promised in the form of money they would find inside the house, although any money found may have been an added incentive or bonus. I further believe those who helped Troy plan the murders and provided logistical support were compensated in some, if not all, cases after the murders with "gifts-in-kind" utilizing proceeds from his in-laws' estates, the control of which Troy wrangled from his subdued and subjugated wife.

I believe Troy was aided in the planning and execution of the murder plot by a small contingent of individuals utilizing various vehicles, and that the corner of Highway 105 and the 105 Bypass as well as the phone booth near the Union 76 station were predesignated spots for observation and communication. I believe the killers were in Boone sometime prior to the day of the murders to scout out the Durham home and the surrounding vicinity. I believe they explored the dead-end road (present-day Fox Hill Road) as a possible avenue from which to access the house and also Poplar Grove Road as a location to abandon the Durhams' vehicle. I believe Troy and his accomplices checked out these locations in the week or two prior to the murders and relayed their findings and recommendations to the killers.[xxxxxxxx]

I believe Troy used his alleged study time at the university library as an alibi, and that he did not spend several hours there but left at some point to participate in unknown ways in the events of that night. I believe he may have traveled the short distance (approximately one mile) along King Street in Boone from the library to his in-laws' car dealership, monitored their movements, and contacted the killers who may have been waiting for his call at a predetermined phone booth. I believe Troy (in a white Ford) followed his in-laws from King Street, onto the 105 Extension, Highway 105, and the 105 Bypass, somehow flagging them down (perhaps with flashing headlights) at Westview Baptist Church for some feigned purpose while, in reality, using the opportunity to verify that all three family members – Bryce, Virginia, and Bobby – were inside the vehicle and heading home.

I believe, as the Durhams proceeded up Clyde Townsend Road and then their driveway, Troy (in the white Ford) pulled to the side of the 105 Bypass, witnessed their arrival home and subsequently relayed that information to the killers and the getaway car driver before going to his own home. I believe the getaway car (a black vehicle) was then driven onto the dead-end road around 9:30 PM, long enough to drop off the killers, who came up the hill behind the Durham house between 9:30 and 9:45 PM and gained entry through an unlocked door. Taking into consideration the coroner's ruling that the Durhams died between 9:00 and 11:00 PM and neighbors seeing their vehicle arrive home around 9:00 PM, if the intruders entered the house by 9:45 PM, that would have allowed forty-five minutes for the Durhams to settle in, prepare food, and begin to relax in front of the television while consuming the food. I believe the killers departed the Durham home by 10:20 PM which caused the neighbors' dogs to bark. By 10:50 PM, Troy Hall had reported finding the

[xxxxxxxx] Retired lawmen Jerry Vaughn and Jeff Rucker likewise believe(d) there were others involved. Vaughn did not feel Troy Hall was smart enough to carry out the murders alone, and Rucker believes some of the accomplices are probably still living. According to Rucker, "They had a lot of help...it required a lot of logistical support." Rucker believes that, when the white vehicle and the Durhams' "Jimmy" were seen pulling out from Westside Baptist Church near the Durham home on the night of the murders (as witnessed by Lester Johnson), that was a significant part of the events that subsequently unfolded. [Sources: Rucker, Jeff. Phone interview with author. October 4, 2023; Vaughn, Jerry. In-person interview with author. October 13, 2023.]

Durhams' bodies to the Boone Police Department, and the "Jimmy" had already been abandoned on Poplar Grove Road, which I believe was purposely done rather than being accidentally wrecked and left behind.

With all this in mind, I believe the most likely timeframe for the Durhams to have been broken in upon and killed and for the house to have been ransacked was between 9:45 and 10:15 PM. While this was a very narrow thirty-minute window of time, I believe it was sufficient for the killers to overpower and subdue their victims, variously striking and binding/gagging them, and inflicting some degree of torture upon them before ultimately strangling them and placing them headfirst into the bathtub of water. I believe once the Durhams had been subdued, one or two individuals may have killed them one by one while others carried out the ransacking. I believe the ransacking was a secondary activity to search for "bonus" money and/or other valuables and/or certain documents, and that the attack and torture of the victims was leveraged to help locate such items, but the overarching objective was to snuff out the lives of Bryce, Virginia, and Bobby Durham and to not leave the house until that mission was completed.

I believe Virginia Durham never placed a phone call to anyone from her home that night concerning an attack or any other subject. I believe she was already dead between 10:00 and 10:15 PM, which is the time Troy Hall allegedly received a call. I believe the phone did ring and one of the killers or an accomplice was calling to let Troy know the murders had been accomplished.

While it is possible the battery in Troy's car died immediately after his arrival home from the library, I believe it is more likely he tampered with the car so it would not start and so he would have reason to involve Cecil Small in the discovery of the bodies.

I believe Troy's to-do list that day and night included the following:

- ✓ Go to the university library to establish an alibi
- ✓ Leave the library sometime during the five-hour "study period" and logistically assist the killers
- ✓ Arrive home and tamper with the car so it would not start
- ✓ Receive a call from a killer/accomplice verifying the Durhams were dead
- ✓ Pretend that call was from his mother-in-law and lie to Ginny about what was said
- ✓ Recruit Cecil Small and go to the Durham home with him as a witness
- ✓ Feign surprise upon discovery of the bodies

I believe when Troy left Ginny inside Small's car on Clyde Townsend Road, he already knew her family was dead. I believe when Troy and Small began to enter the den of the Durham house, Troy already knew the murders had been accomplished and the killers had vacated the premises because they had already told him so via the phone call, and the absence of the "Jimmy" from the Durham home confirmed it. I believe Troy took hold of the doorknob and then hesitated about entering because he was feigning fear and anxiety about what awaited them and/or doing a final mental check about having covered all his bases before letting Small inside the house. I believe after Troy and Small entered the house, instead of Troy following Small (which would have made sense since Small had a gun), Troy split from Small and went in the opposite direction inside the house because he wanted Small to find the bodies.

I believe due to the unpredictability of the weather and of people and of circumstances, anything could have gone wrong at any time with the planning and commission of this crime, but even if some originally calculated aspect did go askew, I believe there were likely contingencies in place to put things back on course. In the end, with perhaps the exception of the killers barely getting away undiscovered while abandoning the "Jimmy" on Poplar Grove Road, everything seemingly came together, and I believe Troy (and others) got away with murder.

Although Billy Birt, Billy Wayne Davis, Bobby Gaddis, and Charlie Reed have been declared the killers, I believe the allegations against them, as they relate to the Durham murders, have been overconfidently stated, and if these men were living and were charged with and tried for the murders, the proof needed to convict them would be lacking, much as it was lacking when the four Asheville men were accused shortly after the murders. Although I do recognize similarities between the Fleming and Durham cases, I believe other criminal groups besides the Dixie Mafia exhibited similar behaviors and that, in the absence of physical evidence and eyewitnesses, a behavioral pattern would not carry enough evidentiary weight in a court of law to remove all reasonable doubt in the minds of jurors regarding these men's guilt.

I believe the inconsistencies in some of Shane Birt's recollections cast doubt on the accuracy of the information he has attributed to his father.

I believe that, based on Billy Wayne Davis's history of snitching, self-preservation, and the degree of confusion he exhibited in his interviews, his word is not reliable enough to say with certainty that the accused Georgia men killed the Durhams. I also believe Davis would have said anything if he thought it would benefit him in some way, and I believe his assent to details of the Durham Case that were presented to him during his interviews and his indictment of Birt, Gaddis, and Reed are highly suspect and must be questioned if not outright discounted.

I believe the possibility (perhaps probability) that Billy Birt killed Charlie Martin in Georgia on the same night as the Durham murders casts serious doubt about Birt's (and Gaddis's and Reed's) involvement in the latter and potentially exonerates them.

I believe some of the other accounts that have been put forth throughout the decades of investigation regarding how the murders were conducted – ones outlined in this book – have as much feasibility as law enforcement's most recent conclusion that the Durhams were killed by the Dixie Mafia. I believe accounts pointing to North Carolina suspects from Wilkes, Caldwell, and Buncombe counties are worth reconsideration. Although I believe it is feasible the murders were arranged via a network of criminal connections across various locations – perhaps even including Georgia and the Dixie Mafia – I believe it is more likely the murders were arranged and carried out by those from North Carolina rather than recruiting out of state killers.

I believe some will disagree with the beliefs I have expressed, and if additional revelatory information about the case surfaces, I will reevaluate my present beliefs.

Despite the passage of time and those connected to the case, I believe it is possible more information could still come forth, and I believe there are at least a few people left who know the full truth of that awful night. To reiterate what local citizen Joy Elvey Lamm wrote to the *Watauga Democrat* in 1972, "...we need somehow to reach the conscience of anyone who knows the facts, who knows truths he fears to tell, concerning the Durham murders. We need to speak to those involved about the horror of their atrocity; for it will be locked up in their bodies and their souls, hounding their days and sleepless nights for the rest of their lives until they confess what it is they know."[2420]

In the words of William Shakespeare, "Truth will come to sight; murder cannot be hid long."[2421] While the Durham murders were not hidden long, the victims' bodies being discovered almost immediately after the crime, the coming to sight of the truth behind the murders has been tedious and prolonged and continues to be incomplete. Whether any of us are ever fully made privy to all the truths of the Durham Case, I believe that an all-seeing, all-knowing God will ultimately administer justice and mercy according to His divine wisdom:

"For there is nothing hidden which will not be revealed, nor has anything been kept secret but that it should come to light." (Mark 4:22)

Is this case closed? It has been officially declared so, but should it be since there are unanswered questions? According to former Watauga County Sheriff Red Lyons, "You never close the door on an unsolved murder."[2422] In fairness to the Watauga County Sheriff's Office, which has, to some extent, received the ire of an unsatisfied public, current Sheriff Len Hagaman and his staff are in no wise saying they refuse to spend one more minute on the Durham Case. Certainly, if and when additional information or leads come to their attention, they will pursue them,[2423] and hopefully quickly as these windows of opportunity can often be time sensitive and prone to extinguish like a flame in the wind. And while this case has been of particular interest to the community (and, obviously, to this author), one must keep in mind that our present officers are committed to safeguarding the here and now wellbeing of that same community. Current crimes and threats necessarily take precedence over cases that are more than a half century old, and small town budgets can only be stretched so far.

Although hard to concede, there are things about this case that will likely never be known during any lifetime. Some of those things were either unattainable or lost from the start. The passage of time has dimmed the memories of some and silenced the mouths of others. These recent revelations have left Sheriff Hagaman acknowledging the mystique of the Durham Case and "wondering what did everybody know that we'll never find out?"[2424]

Is this case closed? It took more than fifty years to get to this point. What will happen next and when? In the words of the late Sheriff Ward Carroll stating the obvious, "Well, you just can't tell on these things. Something might come up at any time and then again it might be a long time."[2425]

Is this case closed? You be the judge.

Appendix 1

Twenty Questions

When asked if the Durham murder case could be classified as one of the most unusual cases he ever worked on, retired SBI Agent Larry Wagner responded, "Oh sure, definitely...you keep on getting all these weird twists and turns."[2426] To say the least, this case is complex. Conflicting testimonies, incompatible observations, opposing theories, lack of evidence, and the passage of time have made it so, and the pursuit of truth has been arduous, both for law officers and the sleuthing public. For the latter group, of which I am a member, limited access to certain investigative materials that might shed critical light on the case exacerbates the challenge.

Considering the various law enforcement agencies that have been involved in the Durham Case, the sum total of the information they have assembled regarding the murders is presumably substantial. The Watauga County Sheriff's Office has several boxes of materials and numerous binders containing interviews, crime scene photos, and newspaper articles. Sheriff Len Hagaman has generously shared them with particular researchers, including myself, and although he considers these materials to be latent and benign,[2427] they have nonetheless been very informative and helpful. The Boone Police Department has confirmed that any records they may have had concerning the case are now in the possession of the Watauga County Sheriff's Office or the SBI.[2428][yyyyyyyy] In 1977, North Carolina Attorney General Rufus Edmisten stated the Durham Case had "the largest file of any the SBI [was] working on."[2429] In 1989, SBI supervisor Joe Momier said, "The [case] file takes up more than a drawer in the filing cabinet."[2430] In 2022, retired agent Steve Wilson, who served with the SBI between 1986 and 2010 acknowledged the existence of multiple shelves of three-ring binders containing information about the case.[2431] According to Larry Wagner, the SBI's documentation associated with the Durham Case is "huge," and he states there are "numerous, numerous, numerous" files. The bulk of these are maintained by the agency's Northwestern District office in Hickory, North Carolina with duplicates in Raleigh.[2432] Due to the constraints of North Carolina General Statute 132-1.4, which pertains to both open and closed criminal cases (as no distinction between those is stated within the statute), the public is not privy to most information pertaining to criminal investigation files.[zzzzzzzz] This includes the majority of materials amassed over the decades by the SBI pertaining to the Durham Case, even though the Watauga County Sheriff's Office maintains jurisdiction over the case.

[yyyyyyyy] Upon his 2007 retirement from the Boone Police Department, Sergeant Jeff Rucker (who joined the department in 1984) returned to clean out his locker and filing cabinet and found that his items, including his Durham Case notes, containing names, dates, and times associated with the interviews he had conducted, had disappeared, perhaps being randomly tossed to make room for the new sergeant. Rucker says that some of the individuals he interviewed had previously provided law enforcement officers with information but had not been interviewed a second time. Sheriff Len Hagaman likewise says he does not know what happened to his [Hagaman's] Durham Case notes from his previous tenure as a Boone policeman. [Sources: Rucker, Jeff. Phone interview with author. October 4, 2023; Hagaman, Len. In-person interview with author. January 16, 2024.]

[zzzzzzzz] NCGS 132-1.4(c) does designate certain information collected by law enforcement agencies as public information, including the time, date, location, and nature of a violation; the name, sex, age, address, employment, and alleged violation of law of a person arrested, charged, or indicted; the circumstances surrounding an arrest; certain contents of "911" and other emergency calls received; content of communications between or among employees of public law enforcement agencies that are broadcast over the public airways; and the name, sex, age, and address of a complaining witness.

Another challenge is discerning fact from fiction. Not everything reported in the media, or published in magazines and books, or posted on the internet, or even stated by individuals (including within the sheriff's office investigative file) is true. Sometimes errors have been made, and even if not intentionally or maliciously so, they still tend to confound serious students of this case and leave them wondering what is accurate. Likewise, as I spoke with individuals, many of those conversations shed great light and helped my understanding, while others left me scratching my head. But confusion surrounding this case is not new; it began immediately after the murders. A person who posted in an online forum accurately wrote, "In those days rumors were flying around Boone like grains of sand caught up in a windstorm. Everyone had a theory or opinion. The only problem with rumors, you never know if they are really true or just a rumor."[2433]

In the process of researching this case, among the resources I availed myself of were web sites where amateur detectives, hobbyists, or otherwise interested parties engaged in discussion threads. Some of these sites were little more than local gossip parties generating fodder for the rumor mill; others were bent on solving mysteries, particularly cold case crimes, the Durham Case being one of many. Some of these sites contained dozens upon dozens of pages and posts ad nauseum. Still, I read them all. Most were laden with speculations, and some comments and theories were utterly ridiculous, but every now and again I ran across interesting nuggets in the forms of legitimate hypotheses and good investigatory questions.

For the bulk of this book, I have reported information drawn from multiple sources, including the news media, interviews, published works, videos, and podcasts. This chapter consists of some frequently asked questions generated by the heretofore presented information, and we will consider them from various points of view. Unfortunately, many of these questions foster additional questions, and they come with no promise of answers. Some may ask, if they know who killed the Durhams and the case has been declared closed, why keep questioning the details? The answer to that partially hinges on whether one believes the killers[aaaaaaaaa] have accurately been identified and on the fact that who arranged the murders and why has never been definitively and satisfactorily explained. Once that is achieved, then many of the questions raised here may also be answered or will not matter anymore. Until then, an examination of them may prove helpful and are therefore worth time and consideration.

How did the weather conditions of February 3, 1972 affect movement and evidence?

While the *Watauga Democrat* reported "blizzard-like weather in the Boone area, which slowed down traffic and caused hazardous traveling conditions,"[2434] some sources took it further, reporting that an actual blizzard occurred and that, by the afternoon, Boone was paralyzed, most roads were impassable,[2435] the temperature was nearly zero, and Watauga County was buried in snow.[2436] In reality, the entire county was not "buried in snow," nor were most roads "impassable." It seems that everyone involved in the case who was on the roadways on the night of the murders, with the exceptions of Cecil Small and Durham neighbors Bruce Faw and Paul Allen – all of whom were unable to fully ascend Clyde Townsend Road – reached their destinations without issue.

[aaaaaaaaa] When reference is made to whoever committed the murders, it is in the plural – killers, murderers, etc. – under the assumption that more than one person attacked the Durhams.

In late January 1972, local temperatures on some days reached the 50s but sharply dropped on subsequent days within the same week. A January 22 Boy Scout snow event was postponed due to unseasonably warm weather.[2437] The weekend of January 29-30 was dominated by warm sunshine until the afternoon of the 30th when a cold front moved through.[2438] On January 31, the *Watauga Democrat* stated the weather continued to be warm and rainy, absent of "snow and chill."[2439] On Ground Hog Day, February 2 – the day prior to the murders – "warmer than normal temperatures" prevailed.[2440] Highs in the mountains reached the mid- to upper 40s, and increasing cloudiness and rain, with highs in the upper 40s were predicted for February 3.[2441] But Boone weather is notoriously fickle and can turn on a dime as it apparently did on February 3.

For certain, there was snow, and Cecil Small reported four inches during his drive to the Durham home between 10:30 and 10:45 PM. Reed Trivette, who traversed that night with his cousin along the 105 Bypass reported a foot of snow, but that was surely a gross miscalculation on his part unless he was referring to occasional drifts caused by the wind. When dispatcher Johnny Tester, after the conclusion of his shift, reached Clyde Townsend Road sometime after 11:00 PM, he noted that the lower part of the road was clear while the upper part was snow-covered.[2442] Pictures taken of the GMC "Jimmy" the night of the murders and of the exterior of the Durham home the day after reveal a very minimal amount of snow on the ground, seemingly not even deep enough to cover an average pair of shoes.[2443] Although the snow was coming down heavily, the wind would easily have caused drifts in some places and very scant accumulations in others.

Eyewitnesses from the day and night of the murders made the following observations:

- Jeff Rucker, who was a senior at Watauga High School and would, in later years, work on the Durham Case as a Boone policeman, recalls that the weather was not so bad during the day. Although there was snow on the ground, there was not much of an accumulation. The wind, combined with the blowing snow cut down on visibility.[2444]

- Durham neighbor Evelyn Greer, who arrived home from work around 5:30 PM that evening with her husband Larry, recalls it was snowing so badly you could hardly see the road.[2445]

- Cecil Small recalled "the drive over to the Durham house was a rough one" and he remembered "the terrible snowstorm that night and the high winds which caused a lot of drifting and limited visibility."[2446] He stated when he and Troy Hall arrived at the Durham home, he saw no tire tracks or footprints because of the drifting snow. He also said the conditions were blizzard-like to the point that neither he nor Troy could see – even the Durham house ahead of them – until it let up.[2447]

- SBI Agent Charlie Whitman described the weather as "Boone winter. It started snowing about three o'clock that afternoon, and it got worse, and it got worse, and it got worse. At nine o'clock that night there was a good three inches of snow on the ground. It was still coming down fiercely. The winds were blowing and howling. I doubt seriously the next-door neighbor could have heard anything going on. The wind was really howling. Had there been any shoe tracks or car tracks, they would have been covered up."[2448]

- When Jerry Harrison was driving from his home in Boone to his job near Foscoe around 10:30 PM, he stated it was snowing as hard as he had ever seen it, and the wind was blowing.[2449]

- John Paul Brown, who was residing at the Daniel Boone Hotel in downtown Boone stated, "There was a blizzard going on outside…one of the worst blizzards I think we've had here in the mountains…."[2450]

- When asked if it was snowing when he arrived at the Durham home, Dr. Clayton Dean, who served as the medical examiner that night, said, "Yeah boy. Snowing and frozen and cold. It was below freezing. It was cold and windy. I had on leather bottom shoes. I couldn't walk up the driveway…. I hadn't planned on being in the snow." Dr. Dean (much like Cecil Small and Troy Hall before him) had to move from the icy driveway into a ditch to make it on foot to the house.[2451]

- A neighbor of the Durhams said, "It was a howlin' and a blowin.'"[2452] A neighbor (perhaps the same one) stated, "It was so cold that night, and the wind was blowing so hard if there were screams, no one could [have] heard them."[2453] According to neighbor Paul Allen, if someone had shot a cannon that night, it would not have been heard because of the wind.[2454]

The weather and road conditions were bad enough to warrant Bryce Durham's use of the GMC "Jimmy" from the late afternoon onward, and eyewitness testimony verifies that. Fellow Rotarian Phil Vance appreciated how the "Jimmy" plowed the way for his own following vehicle. The "everyday" cars driven by Earl Petrey, Bryce and Virginia Durham, and Bobby Durham were deemed inadequate, or at least not preferable, for navigating the condition of the roads. When Troy and Ginny Hall and Cecil Small traveled the four miles from their trailer park to the Durham home, the journey took them about twenty minutes – around double the normal time required. Perhaps the roads were less treacherous than Small's caution as a driver, so he may have driven slower than conditions demanded. Upon reaching Clyde Townsend Road, Small's car was unable to reach the Durham home. Perhaps this was because halfway up the road, they encountered snow as Johnny Tester described. Other contributing factors to the difficulty may have been the general capability of Small's car or the type and condition of his tires, which he stated to be "fair," but not new.[2455]

Although Sheriff Ward Carroll reportedly took castings of tire tracks following the murders, Sheriff Len Hagaman does not believe tire tracks could have been reasonably or accurately analyzed, especially those on Clyde Townsend Road, and particularly in light of the heavy volume of traffic up and down the road on the night of the murders.[2456] This included the Durhams' vehicle, potentially the killers' vehicle, Cecil Small's vehicle, all the vehicles driven by various law enforcement officers and emergency personnel, and the vehicles of any neighbors who entered and exited. SBI Agent Charlie Whitman would later recall they were able to "account for every vehicle that went up [Clyde Townsend Road] that night during this critical period of time,"[2457] although the basis of and method used for this accounting were not elaborated upon. If true, this would indicate the vehicle driven by the killers did not travel on Clyde Townsend Road but was used elsewhere to drop off the persons who entered the house and to later pick up whoever took and abandoned the "Jimmy." Although crime scene photographs include some of tire tracks, Hagaman says you cannot determine much from them.[2458]

While there was enough snow on the ground for tire tracks to be seen and for some imprints to be taken, in terms of footprints around the exterior of the Durham home, officers were at a disadvantage due to windblown snow having quickly covered them. Perhaps tire tracks left a deeper impression than footprints which resulted in their endurance and discovery. Assuming the Durhams did not pull the "Jimmy" into the garage, at least half of which, as seen in crime scene photographs, was primarily used for storage, both they and their killers would have walked around the exterior of the house at whatever point of entry they used that night. Investigators noted Virginia's and Bobby's shoes had been removed and left by the front door. The soles of their shoes were still wet, however, which indicates they most likely walked in the snow from the "Jimmy" to the front door, which entered the foyer, versus exiting the vehicle directly onto the dry garage floor. The fact that tins of MRE foodstuffs from Bryce's Rotary meeting were found inside the front door supports the family's front door entrance. By the time authorities arrived, Troy Hall and Cecil Small had, by their own account, walked the perimeter of the house, checking doors and peering into windows, so their footprints likely overlayed and perhaps obliterated any previously existing ones left by the Durhams and/or their killers. Then, as multiple law officers, investigators, examiners, and photographers arrived in rapid succession, more footprints accumulated.

The same held true of tracks inside the house. Shoes that had stepped in snow would have tracked snow inside, and the melting snow would have resulted in water. Virginia and Bobby would not have tracked snow into the house if they removed their shoes immediately by the door versus walking inside first and then returning to the door to take them off. When his body was discovered, Bryce's oxfords were on his feet, but his rubber over boots were found in his upstairs bedroom. Assuming he was wearing the boots when he arrived home, he could have removed them at the door and carried them upstairs, or he may have wiped them dry on an entrance mat, or he could have worn them up the staircase and removed them in the bedroom, the latter scenario possibly resulting in tracks.

In terms of the interior tracks of the killers, it is difficult to say with certainty what the order of events was. Some have wondered if one or more of them could have entered the house earlier in the day or that evening and been lying in wait for the Durhams. If true, they would conceivably have had time to wipe their feet or their tracks, or even to remove their shoes (which seems improbable), or the tracks may have had time to dry. If they entered the house after the Durhams, they would likely have tracked in snow. If they were surprising their victims, it seems very doubtful they would have wiped their feet, removed their shoes, or mopped up snow or water after the murders. Still, there seems to be no mention of inside tracks being discovered or investigated, and this might again be attributed to the fact that Troy and Cecil and a whole fleet of successors entered the house in the one to two hours after the murders, and this high level of foot traffic likely disrupted the discovery of possible evidence. Even if there had been detectible footprints, they would have to have been matched against shoes worn by any number of individuals,[2459] and to have employed such a process to help identify the killers would have been a tremendously daunting task. Without knowledge of the killers' connection to a particular type of footwear, it was impossible.

Did the killers enter the home prior to or after the Durhams' arrival?

There were no signs of forced entry.[2460] If a spring on one of the garage doors truly was in disrepair and allowed the door to be partially open, or if the Durhams purposely left it partially open to provide a cat access to the garage, perhaps the intruders entered that way (just as Troy Hall and Cecil Small did) and either assumed or had been told there was an entrance into the main house located inside the garage. Even so, they may not have had assurance that door would be unlocked unless that was the typical practice of the Durhams or had been prearranged by an insider. When Troy and Cecil entered the house, that door was unlocked. Of course, that was after the murders had occurred, and one of the killers could have unlocked the door from the inside and exited it, or it may have never been locked to begin with. It was not unusual for homes during that era to be unlocked. As Clyde Townsend, who built the Durham home and lived less than 100 yards away at the time of the murders, said, "It's the quietest neighborhood in the county. You don't care if you leave your doors unlocked."[2461] In fact, prior to the murders, many local residents had never locked their doors.[2462] When Troy and Cecil arrived at the house, the front door was reportedly locked. Was it locked by the Durhams after returning home? Did they leave the doors unlocked during the day and lock them at night? At one point, Bryce and Virginia reportedly had the locks changed on the house and told Ginny her key would no longer work. If the goal of changing the locks was to keep individuals out of the house whenever Bryce, Virginia, and Bobby were away, then it would be unreasonable for them to leave their doors unlocked.

In May 1971, when Billy Birt and others killed Drs. Warren and Rosina Matthews in Marietta, Georgia, "police theorized that the attack was planned by two or more men who waited near a greenhouse and tool shed for the doctor to open his garage door from the inside. 'According to all the stomping around, they [the killers] had to be out there a good while. And they had to know he went to work early.'"[2463] In December 1971, when Birt shot and killed Mac Sibley in Austell, Georgia at Billy Wayne Davis's request, Davis had a key to Sibley's house, and they entered and awaited Sibley's arrival.[2464] These cases prove nothing for the Durham Case; they merely demonstrate that, on at least two occasions, these particular killers were waiting for their victims on or inside the victims' properties. And this may have been a modus operandi of any number of killers, not just the Dixie Mafia. Immediately after the Durham murders, Sheriff Ward Carroll theorized the killers had entered the den door from the garage[2465] and perhaps had even been hiding in the garage.[2466] At some point prior to July 1973, Carroll thought the Durhams' killers had hidden in the basement.[2467][bbbbbbbbb]

The morning of the murders, probably around 11:00 AM, Durham next-door-neighbor Clara Wilson allegedly heard someone inside her house say, "We're in the wrong house."[2468] If true, could this have been two or more of the killers and/or their accomplices exploring the neighborhood and looking for the Durham house in anticipation of that night's brutal activities? Were they intending to be in the house that early to await the Durhams' return, perhaps not knowing their arrival home would occur much later than usual due to Bryce's Rotary meeting and bad weather delays? If the killers found and entered the Durham house shortly after 11:00 AM, would they have remained there for ten hours until the Durhams arrived at 9:00 PM? That seems unlikely, but not impossible. It is difficult to say how much the killers knew about the Durhams' plans and activities for that evening or if an insider passed those details to them, but perhaps an "advance team" of sorts went to the house early in the day and got some things logistically lined up for the killers who would come later, maybe even to unlock the door between the den and the garage. If the den door was locked, then the other entry doors were also likely locked, which begs the question how these

[bbbbbbbbb] Frank Jolley, whose grandfather, E. J. Durham, Sr., helped bring the clairvoyant M. B. Dykshoorn to Boone following the murders, seems to recall that Dykshoorn believed the killers parked at a nearby laundromat, walked to the Durham home, entered the basement and came up the basement stairs. This is problematic in that there was no nearby laundromat (not even in Clyde Townsend's apartment complex), and there is no outside entry to the fully underground basement, as verified by the current homeowner, Karen Coffey, as well as by plumber Keith Norris. Norris and his brother Van were called to the Durham home immediately after the murders to reattach the sink in the bathroom where the bodies were found as it had been somewhat loosened from the wall. According to Norris, there was no outside entrance to the basement, but there was a crawl space accessed from inside the basement that would allow stand-up access to pipes, etc. [Sources: Jolley, Frank. Phone interview with author. December 8, 2023; Townsend, Mike. Text to author. January 20, 2024; Norris, Keith. Phone conversation with author. February 2, 2024.]

individuals got inside the house. If whoever was in the Wilson house was actually in search of the Durham house, that means they had no familiarity with the Durham house and had either not received directions, had received inaccurate directions, or had gotten mixed up about those directions.

A 1989 newspaper article stated, "Detectives said Durham, the owner of the Modern Buick dealership in Boone, had returned from a Rotary meeting and was snacking and watching television with his family that night. They said several men apparently entered the house through a garage, surprised the Durhams and killed them."[2469] Of course, this report doesn't specifically say the intruders arrived at the premises *after* the Durhams. Prior knowledge or surveillance of the Durham home and habits may have revealed that the Durhams did not park their vehicles inside the garage, and perhaps this would have given the intruders assurance the garage would be a safe place to hide and wait. *[And regarding this 1989 article, it seems very presumptuous for detectives to have said "several men apparently entered the house" when there was no way for them to know the number or gender of the attackers.]*

Unless the killers cleaned up their snow tracks and hid themselves well and quietly, it seems unlikely they would have already been in the house when the Durhams arrived. At one point, Shane Birt told authorities his father said he and his accomplices were in the house waiting on them, that they arrived before the snowstorm started, and that the Durhams arrived home later than anticipated. More than three years later, Shane said he did not recall that his father was already in the house awaiting the Durhams. When Durham employee and neighbor Dean Combs arrived home around 5:30 PM, he noticed lights were on inside the Durham home prior to the Durhams' subsequent arrival. He wondered if they had mistakenly left the lights on when they left home earlier that day. Could this have indicated the intruders were in the house at that time? If the lights were still on when the Durhams arrived home, there is no way to know if that concerned them or if they merely wondered, like Combs, if they had failed to turn the lights off.

Shortly after 10:00 PM, the only light that neighbor Priscilla Faw observed at the Durham home was an outside light that was on. When Cecil Small and Troy and Ginny Hall neared the house around 10:45 PM, several lights were reportedly on inside the house. Assuming lights were on during the murders and the ransacking, then off when Mrs. Faw observed the house, and then on again by 10:45 PM, could that mean the intruders turned off all the lights at some point and then on again prior to their departure? And if so, why? A contradictory account passed around later within the Faw family said that, while Priscilla Faw waited in the car, her husband Bruce went to the Durham house to request assistance due to their car being stuck, and he saw lights on inside the house as well as heard voices and saw movement within.

If the killers were already in the house when the Durhams arrived home, their attack was not immediate as the Durhams had time to remove their coats and shoes and settle in front of the television with some food. This is supported by their autopsies, which revealed the contents of their stomachs, some of which aligned with the food found at the crime scene, and some of the chicken from one of the plates was strewn on the floor, probably as a result of the attack or the subsequent ransacking.

Where was Troy Hall during certain windows of time on the night of the murders?

According to Ginny, Troy was very smart, had a photographic memory, seldom attended his university classes and never worked at his assignments yet still managed to get good grades.[2470] This was reiterated by Troy's friend and fellow student at Appalachian State University, "Babes" Lowe, who said Troy rarely studied.[2471] These statements make it highly unlikely Troy would have wanted or needed a five-hour study session.

Troy allegedly left home around 5:00 or 5:30 PM, had dinner with one of his brothers *(none of whom lived in Boone, which causes one to wonder why one of them would have been there that late on such a bad weather evening)*, and then went to the university library. Several eyewitnesses reportedly placed him there, although no times of those sightings were stated, unless that is within the SBI's investigative files.[2472] Troy spoke to a friend outside the library around 8:00 PM, but no one could verify when he left the library for the final time that night.[2473] He reportedly told the library service desk attendant he was going out for just a minute,[2474] left at 9:30 PM and returned home around 10:00 PM. But does anyone know with certainty that Troy was at the library between his arrival and his 8:00 PM conversation with a friend? And does anyone know if he remained at the library for the full period of time between 8:00 and 9:30 PM? Did he go to the library and make sure he was seen there at some point for the purpose of establishing an alibi in the event he should he need one? This information is not in the investigation files of the Watauga County Sheriff's Office; according to Sheriff Len Hagaman, these types of notes would likely be in SBI files.[2475] Although law officers were suspicious of Troy's whereabouts,[2476] Rufus Edmisten has no recollection of Troy's alibi ever being verified.[2477] According to forensic psychologist Richard Walter, Troy attempted to get one of his friends to lie concerning his whereabouts, but the friend refused.[2478] This friend was likely Roger Dick, who was supposed to be Troy's alibi in conjunction with Troy studying at the library and checking out a book. Dick said he only saw Troy for about ten minutes, and Troy appeared to be very nervous.[2479]

Could Troy have utilized one of these windows of time to have gone to the Durham home to unlock doors or put certain things in order at the scene to facilitate the crime that was imminent? Since the timeframe of his study session corresponded with increasingly bad weather, that would seem risky considering he might not be able to ascend the Durhams' driveway, and considering his car had a busted muffler that tended to draw attention. Since the dealership was only about a mile from the library, could Troy have conducted some reconnaissance in terms of observing and reporting his in-laws' movements? Could he have been handling some logistical details in advance of the attack? Could he have used that time to meet the killers at an agreed upon location and led them to his in-laws' home? Could he have been the person in the white Ford who Lester Johnson observed interacting with the passengers of what was likely the Durhams' "Jimmy" at Westview Baptist Church just prior to the Durhams arriving home? Could that interaction have entailed flagging down the Durhams under some pretense (such as wanting to be sure they were safely navigating the bad weather home) in order to verify that Bryce, Virginia, and Bobby were all three inside the vehicle and heading home together versus Bobby having gone to attend some social activity and arriving home separately and at a later time? Could Troy have facilitated entrance into the home based on foreknowledge of his in-laws' activities that night? Did he ring the bell or knock on the door, perhaps even in the company of one or more of the killers? Despite their badly strained relationship, did his in-laws invite him and his acquaintance(s) into the house not realizing what was about to happen? Might this align with the parapsychologist M. B. Dykshoorn's belief that Virginia was familiar with whoever approached her door and gave them entrance?

Did Troy and Ginny Hall really receive a phone call at their home the night of the murders?

In 1982, Attorney General Rufus Edmisten stated, "We have never had anything more than hearsay evidence that the phone call was ever made. There is no more evidence that it was made than it wasn't made." He added that "'every angle of that phone call has been checked' and that nothing ever checked out. But he made it clear that in questioning the accuracy of the statements about the phone call, he was not making any accusations."[2480]

Watauga County Sheriff Ward Carroll said he did not believe Virginia ever phoned her son-in-law the night of the murders. "In my opinion, Mrs. Durham never made that phone call. When some people come into your house to kill you, they are not going to let you make a phone call." Carroll also said "he [did] not know why the Halls would have said they got a phone call if no call was made."[2481]

SBI Agent Charlie Whitman disagreed with Sheriff Carroll about the call. Whitman found Ginny, who described the call and what she and Troy were doing that evening, to be a reliable and cooperative witness. At one point he even took her to be placed under hypnosis, and during that session, "she alluded to the phone call."[2482]

Cecil and Mildred Small believed the killers forced Virginia to call Troy and Ginny so they would come to the Durham house and the killers could murder them as well.[2483] Although the Smalls said in 1989 they heard the phone ring on the extension they had inside their home to Troy's and Ginny's phone, the Smalls contradicted this when they told Boone Policemen Zane Tester and Jeff Rucker that the phone never rang. In both 1973 and 1989, Cecil stated it was Ginny, not Troy who answered the phone.[2484] That confusion may have stemmed from Troy telling Cecil that "Babe [Ginny] received a phone call from her mother," even though Troy was the one who answered the phone. Ginny also shared with the Smalls what her mother had said, and while she was merely relaying what Troy had told her was said, the Smalls may have misinterpreted Ginny's statement to mean she had spoken directly to her mother. Later, Cecil supposedly stated there was no phone call. That may not mean that the phone didn't ring, but that Cecil believed no one was calling.[2485][ccccccccc]

Bob Ingram, on the premise that Billy Birt, Billy Wayne Davis, Bobby Gaddis, and Charlie Reed killed the Durhams, believes Troy's claim that Virginia called is both nonsense and ridiculous. "If you believe the phone call, you need to go see somebody; your medication needs to be switched. The phone call is preposterous. Knowing these people [the alleged Dixie Mafia killers], and letting a victim get to the phone, there's no way in hell. None. Zero. When they come into that house, you are under their complete control, total control, and they're going to bind you immediately."[2486] According to Ingram, when these guys came into a house, no one was going to make a phone call unless it was one of them.[2487] Ingram does not discount that Troy may have received a call, but if he did, it was not from his mother-in-law. Someone may have called him to say the deed was done, or "I'll be back to visit you because we didn't get the money promised," and Troy then had to come up with an explanation for the call for Ginny's benefit. Ingram believes Troy would have been better

---

[ccccccccc] According to a phone message left by Gayle Durham Mauldin with the Watauga County Sheriff's Office, "Cecil Small told Mr. Moore that there was never a phone call." Mr. Moore's first name is not mentioned, but the phone number provided within the message is a Rockford, IL number that appears to belong to a Herbert Moore (aged 80+ years as of 2023). The author attempted unsuccessfully to call the number. [Sources: Phone message from Gayle Durham Mauldin, September 23, 1990, Watauga County Sheriff's Office investigation file 118-H-1/2/3; https://unmask.com/phone/803-534-3147/.]

off to have said nothing at all and feels it was equally preposterous for Troy to have gone with Ginny and Cecil Small to the Durham home where family members were being attacked and then leave Ginny alone in the car. "Every single part of it is not only unacceptable and unbelievable, but it's preposterous; it's bullshit, to use the technical term." Ingram believes Troy, for whatever reason, may have felt he needed to "discover" the bodies. Perhaps Troy had been inside the house earlier in the day and, fearing that some trace evidence of his presence might be detected, he needed to return again later with Cecil as an explanation for that evidence. Ingram attributes Troy's odd actions to the fact that he was not an experienced criminal, and when you lack criminal experience, you do stupid things.[2488]

At the time Troy said the call came, music was reportedly playing, and Ginny was said to have been preparing for bed – perhaps changing clothes, washing her face, brushing her teeth, or whatever her nighttime rituals were. At the funeral home, Ginny told her aunt, Gayle Mauldin, that she was taking a bath when the phone rang.[2489] In 1976, Ginny told Boone police officers her and Troy's phone had been out of order all day on February 3, 1972, which she said was not unusual in bad weather.[ddddddddd] She added that she normally answered the phone in their home, but on this occasion, Troy got to it first.[2490] In 1991, she told SBI Agent Richard Lester that, on the day of the murders, Troy had been working on the telephone. That night, only a few minutes or less before the phone rang, an alarm clock went off. Troy turned off the alarm, and when the phone rang, he leapt over Ginny (meaning she was not in the bathroom at the time), almost throwing her in the floor, and answered it after only one ring.[2491] This may indicate Troy wired the alarm clock to the rotary phone to make the phone ring, meaning that, although the phone rang, there was no caller, and Troy manufactured the call to fake a conversation with Virginia. It could alternatively indicate Troy had set an alarm clock for the time that had been agreed upon for one of the killers or accomplices to phone him, and he wanted that heads up to be sure he got to the phone first. Regardless of how the phone call came and where Ginny was at the time, she did not participate in the conversation, and if she heard any part of it, it was one-sided, only hearing what Troy was saying. Based on reports, Troy told her about the call afterwards. In other words, all she knew was what Troy told her.

If Virginia made the call and then the line went dead as claimed by Troy, that would mean the intruders either temporarily took their eyes off of her or she was perhaps in another part of the house undiscovered by them until she was in the midst of the call. Sheriff Carroll and Agent Whitman believed if Virginia was calling from the kitchen wall phone, which was near the back door, she would have had the opportunity to go out that door and run to a neighbor's for assistance,[2492] although that door reportedly stuck in the wintertime.[2493] There was more than one phone in the Durham residence (including one in the upstairs master bedroom and perhaps another downstairs besides the one in the kitchen), and it is unclear if or how the various phones were disabled. Because the kitchen wall phone was at least partially disabled, the assumption has been that, if Virginia did make a call, it was from the kitchen phone, and the intruders caught her using it. Based on Bobby Durham's fellow Boy Scout, Sam Round, calling the Durham house every fifteen minutes between 8:00 and 9:30 PM and getting a busy signal each time, it is possible the phone had been disabled as

[ddddddddd] The local newspaper noted about a month prior to the murders that residents weren't always satisfied with their phone service, but Southern Bell was attempting to bring "better service to our fast-growing town," and had established new quarters in Boone. Its new equipment was to be activated and tentatively completed in August 1972, promising better service as a result. [Source: "Telephones Essential," *Watauga Democrat*, Boone, NC, December 20, 1971, p. 1.]

early as 8:00 PM, an hour before the Durhams arrived, and this would mean Virginia (or anyone) could not have placed a call from within the house after that time.

Virginia's autopsy revealed she was dead prior to being placed in the bathtub. If she did make the phone call and was caught, how did the intruders know she had not called the police department or a next-door neighbor who might show up in a matter of minutes? And with that being a possibility, why would they take additional time to move her corpse to the bathtub unless they were not convinced she had expired and wanted her head underwater to ensure it? Not knowing who she called would presumably have caused the killers to speed up their activities and wrap things up perhaps sooner than they had planned.

Troy's and Ginny's phone number was reportedly written on a wall beside a phone within the Durham home.[2494] If true, was the number written there – perhaps by Troy – for the benefit of the killers who were supposed to call him after the murders? It is also possible someone involved in the murders could have placed a call to Troy from the phone booth at the Union 76 station near the corner of Highway 105 and the 105 Bypass. There was certainly more than one eyewitness that night who reported activity at that phone booth. Eyewitness Jerry Harrison stated he witnessed a woman at the phone booth around 10:30 PM, which was within the thirty-minute period following the alleged phone call from Virginia. Could this woman have placed the call to Troy to inform him the murders were done?

Perhaps the call was part of the pre-arrangements and served as Troy's cue to set into motion whatever steps were to follow, including going to the Durham house to "discover" the bodies. But if the call never happened, why go to the trouble of making it up and going to the house rather than just staying home and letting someone else discover the bodies after Bryce, Virginia, and Bobby failed to report to work and school the next day? *[It was actually oddly and erroneously reported by one news outlet that <u>authorities</u> went to the Durham home and discovered the bodies when Bryce and Virginia failed to show up for work the morning after the murders. Bryce's sister, Gayle Mauldin, recalled a similar report in a Morristown, Tennessee newspaper that stated <u>workers</u> had found the bodies the following morning.[2495]]*

If the call did happen and Virginia was the caller, that does not preclude Troy from being involved, and it would mean that, if by some slim chance Virginia actually did elude the intruders long enough to make a call, it is possible she unwittingly phoned a co-conspirator (i.e., Troy).

What about the "three black men"?

The plausibility of this claim is contingent upon several factors. If Virginia did make the phone call, did she actually say three (or any number) of black men or "niggers" were in her house? Was use of that racial slur in keeping with her character and normal conversation? If Virginia did call and mention "black men," when Troy communicated the call to others, perhaps he was the one who chose to use the slur in the retelling of the conversation. Perhaps that was his own manner of communicating information regarding blacks and not Virginia's word at all. On the other hand, maybe Virginia was known to use the word, and when Troy used it to relay what she said, no one thought anything of it. Perhaps it even contributed to others believing she had really made the call. Troy said the call was muffled and frantic, so maybe he misunderstood. A private investigator who looked into the case in 2012 and decided a next-door neighbor was the murderer, theorizes Virginia quietly said, "the neighbor," which Troy misinterpreted as "three niggers."

As the recipient of the alleged phone call, only Troy could have claimed Virginia said these things, although he later said he could not recall the specifics of the conversation, particularly regarding the race and number of the attackers. But he obviously stated these things at one point and early on as media outlets included it in their news reports as soon as the day following the murders. Did Troy bring race into the conversation in an attempt to divert law enforcement officers from the trail of the real killers? Sheriff Ward Carroll, obviously not wanting to dismiss any possible lead, gave enough credence to the claim that he stated investigators were pursuing the possibility of black killers.

Watauga County's black population has always been small, and since the county's founding in 1849, the occurrence of black on white crime was practically unheard of.[2496] Roberta Hagler Jackson, a lifelong resident of Boone's historic black Junaluska community, remembers the claim that black men may have attacked and killed the Durhams, and she recalls the local black community being upset and angered by it: "Black men from our community? No way!" According to Jackson, whose father, brothers, and cousins were among the black men fingerprinted, "We knew that wasn't true." Jackson, remembering lots of snow from the night of the murders, adds, "Nobody black is gonna be out in this kind of weather, at least not from here."[2497]

Of course, no one publicly stated the killers were from the local black community (although some were investigated), and it was possible black men from outside of Watauga County had killed the Durhams. According to convicted murderer Paul Bare, in his 1989 interview with Watauga County Sheriff Red Lyons, Jerry Cassada (white) and two black men from Wilkes County (one being Jimmy Redding) were the killers. If this was true, then the claim attributed to Virginia Durham that black men were in her house attacking Bryce and Bobby could be accurate. And if that statement was accurate, then could Virginia have actually made the phone call to Troy and Ginny? Or could the detail about black men have been added by Troy because he had arranged for them to be there? That would then beg the question as to why Troy would share any details, even if true? Why would he share any firsthand knowledge that might incriminate himself? Could his mention of black men have been a slip up on his part?

Would there have been any reason for Virginia to have misidentified white intruders as being black? Members of the Dixie Mafia sometimes wore ski masks (perhaps black ones), but typically only during daytime crimes – as in bank robberies and the attack on Drs. Warren and Rosina Matthews – where they risked being seen by witnesses. It seems quite a stretch Virginia would mistake black ski masks for black skin even while consumed with terror. One account states two Spaniards helped kill the Durhams, and that Virginia perhaps mistook them as being black.

As the investigation progressed, no ultimate credence seems to have been given to blacks being involved at all, and the Watauga County Sheriff's Office has since stated the killers, all white men, have confidently been identified. If this is accurate, then Virginia probably never made comments about black men being in her house, and if she did not make those comments, she likely never even made a phone call.

Why wasn't law enforcement called earlier?

Although perhaps unrealized by younger generations who have never experienced otherwise, the 911 system was first implemented in 1968, but only fifty percent of Americans had it in 1987, and the system was not being utilized in Boone in 1972.[2498] In order to connect with law enforcement, the options in Watauga County at that time were to either call the operator and asked to be connected, or, using a seven-digit number,[eeeeeeeee] 264-8851 (Amherst4-8851[2499]), to directly dial the Boone Police Department, which served as the dispatcher for rescue personnel and law enforcement alike, including both their own department and the sheriff's department.[2500] About four months prior to the murders, the *Watauga Democrat* contained a Southern Bell ad stating, "In an emergency, the first thing you reach for is a telephone."[2501] If that was an accurate assessment of human behavior, would the parties involved in this case not have availed themselves of these options? Assuming Virginia really did have the opportunity to place a call, why would she not have called the operator or the police department versus phoning Troy and Ginny? And why would Troy or Ginny not have done the same from their home? *[At least a couple of newspapers – and likely others via a UPI dispatch – erroneously reported that Troy immediately phoned police[2502] before proceeding to his in-laws' residence.[2503]]* Likewise, why would Cecil or Mildred Small not call from their home after knowing there was trouble at the Durham residence? And why would Cecil or Troy not have attempted to call for help before starting to leave the Durham home or neighborhood?[fffffffff] Granted, Troy ultimately did so, but seemingly only because Cecil's car got stuck leaving the scene.

Boone Police Chief Clyde Tester was always baffled by Troy's and Cecil's intentions and why, after discovering the bodies, they "didn't immediately go to a telephone…and call the police before they started to leave." Tester said they were "within fifty feet of a dozen telephones," referring to the homes of the Durhams' neighbors. When Tester asked Troy that question, Troy bizarrely replied, "I was brought up in a family in Wilkes County and taught never to call the police for anything."[2504] However, this was not in alignment with what Troy testified to at the probable cause hearing of the four Asheville men. There, he stated that, after he and Cecil had discovered the bodies, Cecil told him they needed to alert authorities, and after they left the house and returned to Cecil's car, he [Troy] told Ginny they needed to quickly make a phone call.[2505]

It is difficult to second guess the mindsets of others or to consider what we may have done had we been in their shoes and in the midst of such terrifying circumstances. All we can do is surmise. In the cases of the Halls and the Smalls, perhaps a sense of urgency and or panic precluded the presence of mind to call for help, although one would think that, before approaching and entering a house where a family was reportedly being beaten, the summoning of law enforcement would have been a priority. When asked in 1976 why they didn't call the police when they first became aware something was wrong, Ginny simply stated she did not know.[2506]

When considering human nature, it is not unreasonable that someone such as Virginia, in the midst of a home invasion, if afforded the opportunity to place an emergency call, might reach out to a nearby family member whose phone number was perhaps committed to memory. This would have been easier and quicker than looking up the police department's or an unremembered neighbor's number in the phone book, although dialing "0" for the operator would have been even more expedient. The phones in the Durham home were rotary dial phones, which meant every digit of a phone number had to be dialed with a finger or instrument such as a pencil, moving the dial to the right and waiting for its return to its original position before the next digit could be dialed. This took extra seconds, and when under attack, those seconds would have been critical and excruciating on

---

[eeeeeeeee] Within the Boone and Blowing Rock telephones systems, it only became necessary to dial all seven digits of a telephone number in August 1971. [Source: Southern Bell public service announcement, *Watauga Democrat*, Boone, NC, August 5, 1971, p. 13B.]
[fffffffff] One source states Cecil and Troy went to call police from within the house, only to find the phone had been ripped from the wall. [Source: "3 Major Updates to Cases Previously Featured on Criminally Listed Part 7," "The Durhams," beginning at 21:48, https://youtube.com/watch?v=ojpVA30b3n0.]

ones nerves, although again, dialing "0" for the operator would have only required one turn of the dial. Perhaps the mind defaulted to a number that was frequently dialed, and if Troy's and Ginny's phone number really was written on the wall, perhaps the Durhams had put it there for ease of access. But since Virginia was at least somewhat estranged from Ginny and disliked Troy, would she have phoned *them*? Maybe and maybe not. Would such dire circumstances have been reason enough for a truce? In 2015, a woman whose grandmother [Elsie Veach Taylor of Mocksville, North Carolina[2507]] was a half-sister to Bryce Durham's mother, Collie Durham, reported to the Watauga County Sheriff's Office her grandmother had been aware of the family feud involving Troy and Ginny, and Collie had said Virginia would have called the devil before she would have called her son-in-law.[2508] Virginia's niece, Jerri Bumgarner Waddell, echoed this in her belief that, due to their strained relationship, Virginia would have never called Troy and Ginny.[2509]

It is easy to judge the actions of others, and hindsight is always 20/20, but the consideration of these individuals' actions in terms of calling or not calling authorities may once again be shaped by whether one believes Virginia actually made a call or if there even was a call. Another factor is whether one believes Troy Hall was involved in the murders, and if so, how would his deliberate failure to call the police prior to going to the Durham home play into that scenario?

What is revealed by the manner in which the Durhams were killed?

Forensic psychologist Richard Walter is "renowned for describing the personality subtypes of murderers in a scientific fashion,"[2510] and the following four major and distinct psychological subtypes have proven to be "a useful tool for investigators."[2511]

1) Power-Assertive, which is purposeful and organized and does not count unless the perpetrator tells someone about it; the murder is not over when the victim dies, but when the perpetrator ceases to derive satisfaction from the murder.

2) Power-Reassurance, which involves the power to control what is happening in the perpetrator's life and his victim's life; the perpetrator sometimes employees fantasy, and this subtype is often sexual in nature.

3) Anger-Retaliatory, in which the perpetrator murders out of intense anger in response to a real or imagined threat from the victim. If the perpetrator personally knows the victim, he finds satisfaction in the process of killing and the percussion of death (e.g., hitting or strangling the victim). The perpetrator may attack any part of the victim's body, but primarily prefers to attack the head. And even when the perpetrator knows the victim is dead, and though the perpetrator is very alert and not fantasy-driven or delusional, he refuses to leave the victim looking outward at him as he exits and will, for example, roll the victim over or cover the victim's face or eyes, almost as if not allowing the victim the last look or the last "word." The perpetrator does not feel guilt for his crime and often exudes charm and feels relief as if he's had "fifty pounds of emotional baggage" lifted from his shoulders. The perpetrator typically has a sense of relief for about forty-five minutes to an hour and a half, after which he resumes plotting his next steps to avoid being caught.

4) Anger-Excitation, which involves sadism, which could be either sexual or non-sexual.[2512]

Walter categorizes the "relatively vicious" Durham homicides as examples of the Power-Assertive subtype, and says the murders were "all about power and control." According to Walter, "One can discern from this crime scene that for this kind of personality, it's the satisfaction of a mission accomplished, a job well done. Oftentimes, the uninitiated fail to grasp how much pleasure is involved for the killer."[2513] Assuming for a moment that the Dixie Mafia was involved, Walter believes Troy Hall had a desire to be an outlaw and that, if Billy Birt, Billy Wayne Davis, Bobby Gaddis, and Charlie Reed were at the Durham home, it was because Troy may have been fascinated by them and aspired to be like them, and he invited them to watch as he solely killed his in-laws to prove how tough he was. Walter agrees cold-blooded Dixie Mafia hitmen would not fit these subtypes because they have no particular feelings for or conscience about their victims and see the killings as "all in a day's work." This was certainly true of Birt. According to his wife, if he had a conscience, "his trigger finger didn't know it." Birt's son Shane said his father told him he lost his conscience after shooting his brother. Although Birt had regrets later in life, he certainly did not at first. According to Shane, Birt "didn't see anything wrong with what he did." To him, it was just a job. "Retired GBI Agent Ronnie Angel said [Birt] had 'a weird sense of justification about him.' Unlike some other murderers, he didn't kill people because he enjoyed killing people. He killed them for a reason: to rob them and leave no witnesses behind, [etc.]. In his twisted thinking, he could justify every killing." Bob Ingram theorizes Birt was able to live with himself because he compartmentalized his wicked actions.[2514]

For that lack of feeling and conscience, and because he believes the Durham murders clearly point to a Power-Assertive killer, Walter concludes it could only have been Troy who killed them, and the roles of Birt, Davis, Gaddis, and Reed (if present at all) would be reduced to observers only.[2515] Understanding these four men and their criminal histories, however, makes it extremely unlikely (perhaps borderline impossible) they would have only been witnesses to Troy killing his in-laws or that they would have allowed an inexperienced person and one outside of their inner circle such as Troy to be present while they carried out the murders. To suggest four members of the Dixie Mafia would drive from Georgia to Boone, North Carolina, even if paid for their time, to only observe Troy Hall killing his in-laws seems farfetched.

To account for the details Birt allegedly provided to his son Shane, Walter says he [Billy Birt] could have obtained those from newspapers, and that his motivation for claiming involvement could have been braggadocio or to achieve "street cred" (i.e., credibility/acceptance/respect) with his son.[2516] Based on a deeper understanding of Birt, however, this reasoning does not seem likely. While there is a difference in opinion whether Birt was a braggart or embellisher, in light of the 50+ murders he is believed to have committed, he certainly would not have needed to falsely associate himself with the Durham murders to bolster his credibility or criminal reputation.

As I spoke with Walter about these psychological subtypes, I could understand his rationale for placing Troy Hall in the Power-Assertive category, but my sense is, if Troy was the killer, he better fits the Anger-Retaliatory subtype. I asked Walter if it is possible for a killer to transition between two subcategories, and he agreed it is. Walter says Troy, as the hypothetical killer, could have started out in a Power-Assertive mode, then became angry, transitioning into the Anger-Retaliatory mode, and then cooled off, returning to the Power-Assertive mode. This transition to the Anger-Retaliatory mode would account for the Durhams being primarily attacked about their heads (including bruises on their faces, broken eyeglasses, bloody noses, and strangulation), and their bodies not left looking outward but turned over with their heads placed downward into water. If Troy actually killed them or assisted with killing them, he would be capable of taking out his anger for the grief he probably felt his father- and mother-in-law gave him concerning his relationship with Ginny as well as banishing him from the car dealership and reportedly cutting Ginny (ergo him) out of their wills, and he could subsequently feel no guilt for their deaths and could, in fact, be outwardly charming, and then resume planning his next steps.[2517]

Walter further explains that these cases, in addition to the crime scene itself, consist of pre-crime and post-crime behaviors. In terms of Troy's pre-crime behavior, Walter believes he had a plan to murder his in-laws, to remain with his wife (i.e., "his meal ticket") until she came into her inheritance, to cheat her out of that money, to divorce her, and to ultimately make all his dreams reality. Walter believes Troy derived post-crime behavioral satisfaction from the murders because his pre-crime behavioral plans had come to fruition.[2518] These plans are supported by the assessment of Troy's one-time friend, "Babes" Lowe, who stated Troy was a manipulator and a very shady character who, if he murdered the Durhams, did so because he wanted the money from his in-laws' estates. Lowe said Troy did not marry Ginny because he loved her, but because he wanted her family's money.[2519] A friend of Bobby Durham's recalls meeting Troy and thinking of him as a "weaselly" kind of fellow who thought more highly of himself than he should have and who wanted to be upwardly mobile. Incapable of accomplishing that without assistance, he married up.[2520]

According to the Power-Assertive subtype, the killer is not satisfied unless he tells someone about it. On the surface, this seems not to fit Troy as he was always secretive[2521] and remained tight-lipped throughout the decades, refusing to answer many law officers' questions. It is possible, though, he could have privately confessed his involvement in the murders to trusted individuals. Walter says Troy attended one of his lectures on these psychological subtypes, and he believes this occurred in 1991 at Guilford College in Greensboro, North Carolina. He recalls Troy introducing himself, using his new name of Justin, and asking follow-up questions, which Walter became suspicious of. Walter was unaware of Troy's identity until he was informed by someone afterwards. Walter considers Troy's presence and subsequent questions to be an example of subtly bragging about his involvement in the murders and not having been caught. Walter also considers Troy's 1974 statement to Ted Brown about needing to stay three or four moves ahead of the SBI to be both an admission and a form of bragging, believing himself to be smarter. Walter believes that, in order for him [Walter] to have caught Troy, Troy would have had to be interviewed in a particular manner, which would have initially involved making him angry at his in-laws all over again by reviewing all the "unjust" things they had done to him (e.g., banishing him, disliking him, rejecting him, etc.). Ideally, Troy would then have blown his top and said he killed them, to which Walter, as the interviewer, would have expressed disbelief of that confession. Finally, in order to overcome the interviewer's disbelief and prove he had committed the crime (which would ultimately fulfill his need to tell someone and brag about it as well as prove how tough and smart he was), he would have gone into detail about how he carried out the murders.[2522]

During an "analysis of the nature of the offense and the manner in which it was committed,"[2523] one of the aspects considered is the distinction between organized and disorganized offenders. "Organized offenders plan and execute their crimes in organized ways because they are scheming, deliberate, and methodical individuals. The organized offender is a self-absorbed psychopath lacking empathy and remorse. Most organized offenders are well-spoken, outgoing, and pleasant. Because of this, they appear non-threatening at first. Organized offenders target their victims...bring their own weapons and take them from the crime scene. Organized offenders are careful; they often take time to clean up or remove evidence...[and] often...will move or conceal the body. In contrast, disorganized offenders are loners with poor social skills [who] often feel inadequate and have difficulty maintaining friendships and loving relationships. Their crimes are usually committed impulsively, sparked by a mental disorder, drugs, alcohol, youth, or inexperience. The disorganized offender tends to attack people they know, such as family, friends, neighbors, or acquaintances. Their victims are incapacitated quickly without much warning and usually left badly mutilated. They often kill their victims with items at the crime scene and make no effort to hide the weapons or the bodies afterwards. This type of offender leaves a chaotic mess." According to Stephen G. Michaud and Roy Hazelwood in *The Evil Men Do*, "The organized offender is a crafty wolf, while the disorganized offender is more like a wild dog." It is possible for a killer to be a "combination offender" – someone who demonstrates "an equal number of characteristics from both offender categories," and "some crime scenes demonstrate elements of both criminal sophistication and chaos."[2524]

If Richard Walter is correct about Troy being the mastermind and/or killer, it seems Troy exhibited a combination of both organization and disorganization. What was perpetrated on the Durhams was certainly deliberate and methodical with at least some degree of planning involved, and although the ransacking of the house appeared chaotic (some have said unprofessional and amateurish), Bob Ingram states ransacking should not be mistaken for disorganization. Ingram believes the ransacking was a normal occurrence and was part of everything being very well organized, planned, and carried out.[2525] Troy's personality better fits that of an organized offender, but because he was not a professional criminal and was only twenty at the time of the murders and thus youthful and inexperienced, he also partially fits the description of a disorganized offender.

Aside from this more formal discussion of forensic psychology, let us take a look at some of the other details of how the Durhams were attacked and murdered. Although none of the victims were shot, the intruders are believed to have had at least one gun among them, which likely fired the shot into the paneling of the Durhams' den.[ggggggggg] It is possible each of the intruders had a gun and used them to control the Durhams. Still, why were no guns or knives used on the victims? Guns make noise, and these types of weapons would also certainly have resulted in substantial blood loss. Perhaps the killers didn't want to be bloodied while carrying out their gruesome tasks or risk leaving law enforcement additional forensic evidence, despite forensic analysis capabilities being limited in 1972. For certain, strangulation was a method of killing sometimes employed by the Dixie Mafia (albeit by other, non-Dixie Mafia criminals as well), and both strangulation and drowning are very up close and personal methods of murder that can be indicative of organized, professional criminals or killers who are associated with their victims.

All three of the Durhams had rope burns on their necks,[2526] and all three were strangled. Only Virginia died solely from strangulation, while Bryce and likely Bobby drowned in the bathtub either during or following strangulation. Was the rope left around Bryce's neck the one that was used to strangle him as well as Virginia and Bobby, or were individual ropes used on Virginia and Bobby,

---

[ggggggggg] Some have wondered if the bullet hole in the paneling might have been created during the tenancy of previous residents of the Durham home, having nothing whatsoever to do with the attack on the Durhams. Only two families lived there prior to the Durhams – the Clyde and Snow Townsend family and the "Butch" and Sarah Wilcox family. According to Mike Townsend and Sarah Wilcox, the bullet hole was not there when their families lived in the house. In fact, Wilcox says law enforcement contacted her after the murders with that very question. Another possibility is that Bryce or Virginia Durham, both of whom were known to carry guns, could have accidentally fired into the wall, even sometime prior to the night they were murdered, and that the bullet hole had nothing to do with the attack. [Sources: Townsend, Mike. Text to author. February 2, 2024; Wilcox, Sarah. Phone interview with author. February 15, 2024.]

and had those been taken by the killers? An autopsy summary stated, "No other ropes or ties were present…or elsewhere in the house." If individual ropes were used, did the killers simply fail to take the one used on Bryce, or was it left on purpose, and if so, why? Perhaps the leaving behind of the rope meant nothing from the killers' perspective, although it certainly provided some degree of evidence for investigators.[2527] If the same rope was used on all three of the Durhams, and if it was used on each person, one by one and then ultimately left around Bryce's neck, perhaps each person was tied up, strangled, and then unbound, and perhaps the killers used the rope on Bryce last. If the rope (whether one or multiple pieces) was pre-measured/pre-cut and brought by the killers, that would be evidence of premeditation and organized planning. It is also possible that the one (and perhaps only) rope discovered was obtained inside the house by the killers and was the same rope Bobby Durham used to practice knot tying as part of his scouting activities.

One source states Bryce's and Bobby's hands were bound behind their backs.[2528] Both Bryce's and Bobby's autopsy reports mention their wrists – one of Bryce's and both of Bobby's – and crime scene photos depict these marks.[2529] Sheriff Ward Carroll stated "rope burns were on [the victims'] necks *and their hands*."[2530] Some sources refer to the Durhams as having been hogtied,[2531] which typically would mean the hands and feet were tied and strung together. The rope around Bryce's neck was about five feet in length, which would have been long enough to have accomplished hogtying, although none of the three autopsy reports mention feet being involved. Of course, that does not mean all three victims' wrists or ankles were not tied, simply that one of Bryce's wrists and both of Bobby's wrists were all that exhibited limb-tying marks; perhaps their socks prevented rope burns around their ankles. Had each victim's hands first been bound with one end of the rope with the other end then extended to loop around the neck for strangulation? If the Durhams were being tortured, the rope could be extended and placed around the neck. Is it possible these things were only true of Bryce and Bobby, and Virginia was never bound but only strangled?

Another source states that, when Cecil Small and Troy Hall discovered the bodies, the victims' "hands were bound behind their backs,"[2532] but this seems to be an error. None of the crime scene photos of the Durhams' bodies depict them with ropes around their wrists or ankles. The photos depicting them in the bathtub show their bodies from behind and face down. Bobby's right arm and hand and Bryce's left arm and hand appear to be somewhat pulled back behind them. This may indicate their hands had been bound when they were placed in the bathtub and the rope(s) were removed afterwards, presumably by the killers. It was also hypothesized that, rather than hands being tied, they could have been handcuffed to the shower door track along the edge of the tub.[2533] This hypothesis may have stemmed from a call to the Boone Police Department from an anonymous Atlanta, Georgia woman. She stated she and her husband, a deputy, had participated in a card game during which a discussion ensued that caused her to believe the Durhams had been handcuffed and then placed in the bathtub, and that law enforcement knew more than they were letting on.[hhhhhhhhh]

Bobby's autopsy revealed (and crime scene photos substantiate) he had rope burns on each side of his mouth, which probably caused the laceration inside his gum. This may indicate he was gagged at some interval of time (as was concluded by Medical Examiner Dr. Clayton Dean), and it would

---

[hhhhhhhhh] Sergeant Jeff Rucker took this call and believed it may have been a diversion generated by those involved in the Durham murders. Rucker believes those involved were aware of the publicity that Crimestoppers was generating about the murders, and realizing the investigation was not over, any time they felt the heat, they attempted to divert. According to Rucker, an unsuccessful attempt was made to trace this phone call. [Source: Rucker, Jeff. Phone interview with author. October 4, 2023.]

be pointless to gag a victim without also restraining his hands to prevent him from pulling at or removing the gag. The rope burns around Bobby's mouth might also indicate the killers used the rope to torture him and keep his mouth open or, as they were slipping the rope over his head to place it around his neck, Bobby bent his head forward, resulting in the rope temporarily going around his mouth. Neither Bryce nor Virginia seem to have been gagged – only Bobby.

In light of the Durham Case being compared to the Fleming Case, and in the absence of ropes – other than the one found around Bryce's neck – is it possible the Durhams could have been bound and strangled with coat hangers or electrical cords? The assumption is that forensics, even in the early 1970s, would have been able to distinguish marks left by ropes versus other "instruments," and the medical examiner's narrative summary does state, "There were *rope* burns around all three victims' neck[s]."[2534] But was that statement based on the rope around Bryce's neck and an assumption that rope was the "murder weapon" in all three deaths, or were marks on all the victims' necks specifically matched with or compared to a rope?

In Georgia, coat hangers were used in the Dixie Mafia's kidnapping and death of Jim Daws in 1971 and in the murders of the Flemings in 1973,[iiiiiiii] so if the same killers also murdered the Durhams, it seems slightly unusual the Durhams were strangled with rope rather than coat hangers, especially since their murders were "bookended" by the Daws and Fleming murders. Nonetheless, the similarity of wounds between the Flemings and the Durhams is noteworthy. All were strangled and had ligature marks around their necks. Mr. Fleming had abrasions on his right ear and cheek, multiple contusions around his eyes, and other head injuries "possibly caused by multiple impacts of [his] head against the floor." Bryce had an abrasion on the side of his nose and a contusion on his forehead, either indicating he had been struck or his head hit against something. Virginia had a bloodied nose, which may indicate she was struck in the face or that her face was smashed into something such as a wall or floor. Blood and fluid were found in Mrs. Fleming's nose and mouth. Bryce also had blood in his nose and mouth, and froth was in Bobby's nose. Both Virginia's and Mrs. Flemings' tongues were pushed forward.[2535] At least some of these physiological traits, however, seem consequential to any strangulation and have no way of indicating the same killers were involved.

The Flemings were believed to have died between 10:00 and 11:00 PM after a prolonged torture session. Mr. Fleming had two lines on his throat "caused by repeated applications of a ligature," and injuries to the structure of his throat and "signs of oxygen deprivation, indicated that there were several episodes of asphyxia" due to the "bonds" around his neck being "tightened, and loosened, only to be tightened again." It was concluded the Flemings did not die instantly but after "prolonged episodes of abuse."[2536] Although the timeline for the Durhams was much tighter and may not have allowed for as prolonged a period of torture, they were also killed at night, probably between 9:45

[iiiiiiii] In the Daws Case, the local sheriff said the use of coat hangers was Billy Birt's modus operandi and that he used them "for every damn thing." In the Fleming Case, Dr. Larry Howard, Director of the Georgia State Crime Laboratory stated, "from his general knowledge...coat hangers were a common practice in tieing [sic] someone up or in strangling a victim." In a least one instance, Birt admitted to using a rope to strangle an unidentified female victim in Georgia in 1973. In separate interviews, both Stoney and Shane Birt brought up the fact that their father utilized coat hangers on some of his victims. [Sources: Birt, Billy Sunday. Interview with Hall County, Georgia Sheriff Earl Lee & Chief Deputy Ron Attaway, SBI Agent Stanley Thompson, and other. April 13, 1978; Sean Kipe, Imperative Entertainment, *In The Red Clay*, podcast audio, Chapter 4: *A Cold Wind From The West*, September 1, 2020, http://intheredclaypodcast.com; Investigative Summary, Fleming Murder Case #70-0302-01-73.]

and 10:15 PM. If the Durhams' killers had not been under such a time constraint due to the hindering weather, it is possible torture would have been more of a factor.

Were Bryce and Bobby pulled into the bathroom to remove them from other rooms in the house (i.e., the den, living room, kitchen, bedrooms) that needed to be ransacked or staged? If Virginia did call Troy and Ginny, and if she was understood as saying Bryce and Bobby were being beaten in "the back room" (perhaps indicating the den, which was at the back of the house), as has been alleged, could she have instead said "the bathroom?" The kitchen wall phone that Virginia was believed to have called from was within at least partial view of the den, so if that was the "back room" being referred to, it would be another indicator that Virginia did not place a call – at least from that phone – because the killers could have easily observed her from at least a portion of the den. On the other hand, the kitchen wall phone had a very long cord that could have been stretched, perhaps even into the dining area, out of view from the den. If Virginia did not call, did Troy Hall say "back room" in his retelling of her alleged call because he knew that was the room where his in-laws would be attacked?

Did the killers intentionally only strangle Bryce and Bobby unconscious (or nearly so) and then put them into the tub to drown? Were they trying to strangle them slowly (either simultaneously or individually as another victim was made to watch) in a tortuous attempt to cajole information from them about the location of money or whatever was being searched for? In the Fleming Case, Mr. Fleming was reportedly slowly strangled in a torturous fashion in front of Mrs. Fleming to make her tell the attackers where their money was hidden. Similarly, Bob Ingram believes one of the Durhams was being dunked into the bathtub of water while two others were forced to watch in an attempt to elicit information about money.[2537] Although Shane Birt stated his father told him that Virginia died first, followed by Bobby, and Bryce last, it is not difficult to imagine Bobby as the first victim, and that Bryce and/or Virginia were forced to watch him being brutalized. Few things could be as heart-wrenching as watching one's child being strangled and drowned, and the killers may have purposely done this, knowing the effect it would have on the parents and that the two of them, likely more so than Bobby, would know the location of any items stashed in the house. If Bobby was the first victim, that may explain why he was discovered as being first in the tub and how the bodies were overlapped – Bobby first, followed by Bryce, then by Virginia. Although Virginia's body appears to have been the last one placed in the bathtub, former SBI Agent Larry Wagner, surmises she may have put up a strong fight and was the first to be killed.[2538] Based on interviews with various people, investigators learned Virginia was not a passive person but a pretty tough lady who could take care of herself, and it was theorized that, because she did not have water in her lungs, she may have resisted being taken toward the tub and perhaps put up such a struggle that she had to be killed straightaway.[2539] Perhaps the killers were not certain Virginia was dead and added her to the tub to ensure it, or maybe even knowing she was dead, turning her downward into the tub as Bobby and Bryce had been placed was indicative of the Anger-Retaliatory killer personality subtype. *[Although bathtubs were not ordinarily employed in assaults waged by the accused Dixie Mafia members, it did happen on at least one previous occasion. Billy Birt and Billy Wayne Davis were indicted for the December 23, 1970 robbery of Jack and Elaine Williams in Douglasville, Georgia. The couple was tied up and robbed of more than $5,000 in cash and jewelry, and the assailants placed Mr. Williams in the bathtub and threatened to electrocute him with an extension cord.[2540]]*

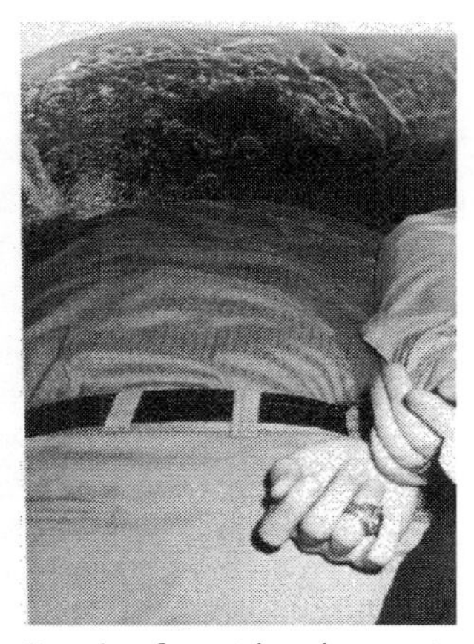

Running faucet barely seen to the left of Bobby Durham's body (Image courtesy of Watauga County Sheriff's Office)

There are conflicting reports regarding the bathtub and the water. Some indicate that, when the bodies were discovered, the faucet was still running, the tub was overflowing, and water had flooded a portion of the house.[2541] Crime scene photographer George Flowers reportedly said the faucet was running (and at least one photo of the bodies in the tub with the faucet running confirms this), but an overflow drain in the tub prevented water from spilling onto the floor. *[When I examined the bathtub, which has existed in the Durham home ever since the murders, I confirmed the presence of an overflow drain.]* Cecil Small and Troy Hall were reportedly "almost too stunned to turn off the tap," and Small would later state, "The water was still running, but I didn't cut it off."[2542] When medical examiner Dr. Clayton Dean arrived, the water was still running, and he turned it off.[2543] Although the water level in the tub would have risen each time a body was added,[2544] SBI Agent Charlie Whitman recalled the bathroom floor was completely dry,[2545] and this is confirmed by crime scene photos.[2546] According to Whitman, "I have found this to be significant. There was not one drop of water on the floor outside the tub, which means none of them floundered around or resisted a great deal after they went in the tub."[2547] As a result of being placed in the water, the Durhams' clothing, particularly on their upper bodies, would have become increasingly saturated over time, and crime scene photos do reflect that the shirts worn by Bobby and Bryce had begun to absorb water.[2548] The assumption might be that water would eventually drip from the clothing onto the floor underneath them, but the fact that the absorption was minimal and the bathroom floor was dry would align with the bodies not having been in the tub that long before they were discovered. Had any water been on the floor, it is doubtful the killers would have mopped it up, especially considering the seemingly tight timeline they were working within.[jjjjjjjjj]

Were the Durhams' bodies unnecessarily moved?

According to Cecil Small, upon discovering the Durhams headfirst in the tub, Troy Hall headed toward for the bodies, but Small told him not to touch them. Perhaps Small was drawing upon his experience as a private investigator and realized a crime scene should not be disturbed. On the other hand, how did they know for certain the Durhams were dead and why would they not have pulled them from the water to see if they were alive or attempt resuscitation? Small, in particular, seemed very frightened by the discovery and was eager to flee the scene. And even if Troy was involved in

[jjjjjjjjj] A very similar murder to that of the Durhams occurred almost exactly two months prior, in December 1971, in Randolph County, North Carolina (two hours east of Boone) when 76-year-old widow Ethel Stout Leach, who lived alone, was asphyxiated by strangulation (per her death certificate, although a newspaper account said she was both strangled and drowned). She was placed fully clothed in her water-filled bathtub. The tub had overflowed, and the water was still running. It was initially thought she had suffered a stroke and fallen into the tub, but by the time foul play was determined and the SBI summoned to the scene, "there was virtually no physical evidence to be found." The water had been drained from the tub, most of the discovered fingerprints belonged to rescue workers, and any footprints that might have been in the snow around the house had been melted by the sun. Robbery was not believed to be a motive. The case remains unsolved. [Sources:; North Carolina, U. S., Death Certificates, 1909-1976 for Ethel Leach, Ancestry.com; "Unsolved killings are sources of frustration, mystery," *The News and Observer*, Raleigh, NC, January 25, 1981, p. 28; Leach, Dale Trenton (Ethel Leach's grandson). Facebook messages to author. July 29, 2024.]

planning the murders, he may not have known exactly how the Durhams would be killed, and this might have resulted in some level of surprise for him as well.

On the night of the murders, after Small gave his statement to Sheriff Ward Carroll and reentered the Durham house, Bev Ballard, according to Small, was photographing the bodies, and he ran out of film. Ballard asked Small to retrieve a case from his [Ballard's] car. Small complied and returned, and Ballard reloaded his camera and returned to the bathroom.[2549] Upon seeing the photographs at some later point in time, Small claimed Virginia's legs had been repositioned. According to Small, when he discovered the bodies, Virginia's legs had been overlapping Bryce's at floor level, and in these photos, they were now resting higher – one on the toilet seat and the other on the toilet tank. According to Small, he accused Ballard of moving her legs, and Ballard denied it, saying, "No, I didn't touch a thing." "The hell you didn't," Small replied. "She couldn't move them. How did they get moved?" "Well, I don't know," Ballard answered.[2550]

If Virginia's legs *were* actually moved, that would have occurred prior to the entrance into the bathroom of Watauga Rescue Squad responder Cecil Harmon, who, when he first encountered the victims, saw her legs and feet atop the toilet seat and tank. He also recalled medical examiner Dr. Clayton Dean had to force at least one of Virginia's legs down because it had gotten cold and stiff[2551] – an indicator of rigor mortis having set in. Dean, however, firmly states he never touched any of the bodies nor examined them. He merely saw them in the bathtub, declared them dead, and ordered the autopsies. He left the premises prior to the bodies being removed from the bathtub.[2552]

When interviewed in 1989, seventeen years after the murders, Harmon had some difficulty recalling how he saw the bodies. He was pretty sure the rope had been around Bobby's neck and that Bryce's hands had been tied – things not supported by the crime scene photographs – although he vacillated whether the reverse was true. He also stated Virginia's head was almost on the water spigot when photos clearly show her on the other end of the tub. Because Harmon remembered Virginia's legs and feet on the toilet, which was on the opposing wall from the spigot end of the tub, then he was confused; otherwise, it would mean Virginia's body had been moved from one end of the tub to the other, but Harmon believed his recollections of the positioning of her head, legs, and feet to be simultaneously true, and that is not possible.[2553]

Because of the way the bodies were "stacked" or overlapped, investigators believed Bobby was put in the tub first, followed by Bryce, and then by Virginia, but Harmon believed the order was Virginia, Bryce, and Bobby, although his statements once more revealed a confusion as to which end of the tub was which. Although photographs clearly show Bryce's left arm and shoulder resting on top of Bobby's body, Harmon remembered Bobby's shoulder overlapping his father's body. He also believed Bryce's legs may have been repositioned on the bathroom floor to overlap Bobby's as seen in photographs. Although Harmon's meaning and who he was referring to is unclear, he stated to Sheriff Red Lyons, "That's one of the things they've forgot to do. Somebody's trying to fool you here…."[2554]

Whether the positions of the Durhams' bodies were altered or tampered with is debatable. Even if they were, it would not seem to have impacted the case in a major way. Of course, the order that the bodies were placed into the bathtub tells a story, but it seems implausible anyone could or would have reordered them in the tub during the post-crime scene phase. It would be more plausible limbs were moved, but again, even if that were true, it likely would have been done for dramatic, yet unethical, photographic effect, as in the suggested repositioning of Virginia's legs, rather than for the sinister purpose of misleading investigators. If there was any unnecessary movement of bodies or limbs, it should not have occurred, but again, if it did happen, it seems relatively inconsequential in the grand scheme of the investigation.

Were there post-mortem photographs of the victims other than official crime scene and autopsy photographs?

Mildred Small made remarks to a reporter about Virginia Durham having rope burns all over her body – around her neck, waist, arms, and hands. She stated someone had shown her and her husband Cecil pictures of the bodies "laid out on a slab."[2555] Only pictures of a completely disrobed Virginia, if in existence and only likely taken during her autopsy, would have revealed rope burns around her waist, which Mildred claimed existed, and no such rope burns were mentioned in Virginia's autopsy report.

Reportedly, Cecil Small had in his personal possession, at his home, color Polaroid[kkkkkkkkk] photographs of each of the three victims. In the photograph of Virginia Durham, a man's hand was reportedly positioned on her forehead with his fingers pulling back her eyelids, while another hand was under her chin. This photograph allegedly revealed that the man's hand belonged to an individual wearing a red shirt and dark gray coat. *[Among the autopsy photos is a black and white photo of a gloved hand pulling Virgnia's right eyelid open.]* In the photographs of Bryce and Bobby Durham that Small allegedly possessed, one hand was pulling back their noses, while another hand pressed down on their chins, as if to open their mouths. The manner in which the Durhams' heads were being positioned in these photographs is indicative of one person handling them and another person operating the camera. An individual to whom Small showed these pictures[lllllllll] tends to recall Virginia's hair was wet, which would indicate the photographs were taken after the bodies were removed from the bathtub. The wet or dry condition of the Durhams' hair and upper torsos in these Polaroid photos is critical. If dry, that would mean the photos were taken before the bodies were placed in the bathtub and would mean that whoever took the photos and whoever handled their heads in the photos would likely have been present for their murders.

The identities of the photographer and the "handler" of the Durhams' bodies in these photographs are unknown. Although George Flowers and Bev Ballard, two of the crime scene photographers, both owned Polaroid cameras at the time, they were not known to carry them. Flowers always took his 35-millimeter camera with black and white film to such assignments.[2556] Perhaps these were additional photos taken as part of the autopsy process, but even if so, why would they be in Small's possession unless someone who knew of Small's role and interest in the case gave them to him? Could Small have requested or obtained them out of morbid curiosity?

What were the motives for the murders?

Because the murders were likely, although not necessarily, a two-partied crime – one party being whoever wanted the Durhams dead and the other party being whoever killed them – two or more motives could be at play. We will begin with who killed the Durhams.

[kkkkkkkkk] Polaroid cameras were introduced in 1947, and the introduction of the Polacolor pack in 1963 made instant color photographs possible. [Source: https://srbijafoto.rs; https://en.wikipedia.org/wiki/Polaroid_SX-70.]

[lllllllll] The source for this information was personally shown these photographs by Cecil Small at Small's home, and Small warned the source to never reveal what had been seen. The present whereabouts of these photographs is unknown. [Source: Anonymous source via Facebook message to author. November 5, 2022.]

Based on the "confessions" of Billy Wayne Davis, he, Billy Birt, Bobby Gaddis, and Charlie Reed were all involved. If this is true, what was these men's motive? According to Sheriff Len Hagaman, these members of the Dixie Mafia committed homicides "for robbery, money, cash, whatever they could find…," and he speculates this was true of the Durham Case.[2557] Used car dealers commonly conduct cash transactions, and they may be particular targets for robbery, their assailants presuming they have large amounts of money in their possession and on premises.

Rufus Edmisten echoes this opinion: "They came with the thought that they would find money in the house from the proceeds of the dealership. They made the trip on that premise – that there was money in the house. The Dixie Mafia [was] too smart and too vicious to have done any sort of thing like this…without some prospect of great reward. They had too many places at home [in Georgia] or nearby to [target]." But Edmisten does not believe Bryce Durham's car dealership generated the kind of money the killers hoped for, and although no one knows for sure if the Durhams kept money at their home, he does not believe there was any substantial amount there.[2558] The bank deposit bag left at the scene may not have contained a great sum of money. There seems to be no record of how much the bag contained or what forms of payment it held unless that information is in the SBI's case file. Aside from some silver pieces being taken from the home and the male Durhams' wallets being rifled, no one knows for sure what or how much the killers found of monetary value, but it may have been very little.

An early newspaper account stated there was "evidence that the killers knew the victims had money in the house" and "Police are not revealing their theories on why the murders were so brutal since the probable motive for the intrusion was robbery. Possibly the killer became angered when [Bryce] Durham…wouldn't tell them where he had money in the house."[2559] Could it be Bryce had a large amount of cash in his home, and an insider – perhaps a family member – relayed that information to the killers, telling them the cash would be their payoff for the murders? This is what former SBI Agent Larry Wagner thought possible based on interviews he conducted (including one with dealership sales manager Ike Eller): "There was reason to believe that Bryce kept a large sum of money in the house, either from the sale of contraband or to avoid taxes. Troy [Hall] knew about this and fingered him. The killers were briefed about the money. That was their payment. The house was ransacked to find the money."[2560] And then there was the scenario Ginny Durham once proposed to authorities: "Let's suppose…that night, Daddy was the payoff man, and Troy tricked him, and Daddy didn't know what it was all about, so they murdered him."

It has been speculated Bryce could have had as much as $30,000-$35,000 in the home.[2561] Perhaps this particular amount is mentioned because Billy Birt's going rate for contract killings outside of the Dixie Mafia's network was $10,000 per hit, and $30,000-$35,000 would have sufficiently covered the murders of three people. Despite the money hypothetically being in the Durham house for the killers to retrieve upon arrival, it would seem they were taking a risk on the information they had been provided, particularly considering the distance Birt, Davis, Gaddis, and Reed would have traveled to North Carolina. After all, what if they had driven all the way from Georgia only to discover the promised money was not there? And this may have been what happened since Birt was reportedly furious and said he was going to return to North Carolina and "kill that SOB" (referring to the nephew or son-in-law who had initiated the crime) who had ripped him off. Birt was also reportedly upset they had almost gotten caught, and despite his expressed desire to return to Boone and deal with the person who had misled him, it was "too hot."[2562]

One source stated hundreds of thousands of dollars were reportedly sewn into a chair utilized in the home by Bryce; another source claimed the killers were paid with $160,000 in dope money inside the Durham home in a location known by Troy Hall. Could Troy have placed the money inside the house without the Durhams' knowledge in anticipation of it being the payoff money? If so, where would Troy have gotten that kind of cash – via drug trafficking, stolen goods, and other illegal means? Another possibility is that Troy may have been in debt to drug dealers and arranged the crime, promising the killers cash/valuables in the house if they would forgive that debt, making the saving of his own skin a motive.

Firm in his belief that Birt, Davis, Gaddis, and Reed killed the Durhams, Rufus Edmisten dismisses any thought of the Dixie Mafia traveling from Georgia to North Carolina and committing the crime on the basis of a grudge that any one of them may have personally harbored. Rather, he says, everything they did related to stealing something, or cheating someone out of money, or killing for money. Edmisten also does not believe the Durhams were targeted at random – that someone driving along the 105 Bypass would just happen to spot their home on the hill and impulsively decide to rob it. Edmisten believes insider information had to be exchanged in order for the killers to know how and where to go and how many people to involve.[2563] Bob Ingram agrees: "There's no way on God's green earth that Billy Birt and that group would know about a Durham family in Boone, North Carolina. No way. Who would believe that? No way, unless somebody said, 'Hey…this family has money.' They didn't just drive to the Durham house…by accident. I'm sure they did some preliminary work prior to the day of the crime…and then everything during the crime and after the crime…."[2564] Ingram adds, "This was all planned – the planning, commission, and concealment of a crime. These were all clever, smart, and experienced criminals that have committed a lot of crimes. When you think about, behaviorally, how much experience was demonstrated in that crime…."[2565] When asked if the Durham murders were a result of a hired hit, Sheriff Len Hagaman stated, "They wouldn't have done it without being hired; they only did it for money. Killing for money is what they did, and they did it quite well."[2566] But killing because you are paid to do so (i.e., hired) is not the same as killing for whatever loot is thought will be found in a victim's residence.

At this point, it is worth a brief discussion of what is meant by the terms "hit" or "hired hit." The only use of either term in the February 8, 2022 Watauga County Sheriff's Office press release was: "Davis implicated Birt, Gaddis and Reed as engaging in a hired 'hit'." In the sheriff's office's subsequent February 11 press conference, usage of these or related terms also occurred. Sheriff Hagaman referred to "the hit" and "a lot of their hits," and in three separate questions, reporters asked Hagaman, who hired the hit. Culturally and societally speaking, most people understand "hit," in a criminal sense, to be a murder, and a "hired hit" means a murder that was paid for or contracted by someone wanting the victim dead. Of course, depending on the criminal, for example one who primarily cases and robs homes, he may refer to robbing a home as having "hit" that home, regardless of whether murder was involved. When Billy Birt took a contract for a job, that job wasn't always for a murder. Contract work, for example, could also be for hauling whiskey, robbery, or arson. Still, a "hit" most commonly denotes murder. According to Merriam-Webster, a hit, from a criminal viewpoint, is "a premeditated murder committed especially by a member of a crime syndicate." Oxford Languages defines it as "a murder, typically one planned and carried out by a criminal organization." Certainly, some members of the Dixie Mafia, and Birt in particular, were known hitmen, who could be contracted/hired/paid to murder individuals, so when these terms were used regarding the Dixie Mafia's involvement in the deaths of the Durhams, the implication is that

Birt, Davis, Gaddis, and Reed were specifically hired to murder the Durhams. When the terms "hit" and "hired hit" were communicated by the Watauga County Sheriff's Office, this is what the public understood.

One individual, who had the occasion to be around numerous contract killers while serving decades in prison, argues that the thought of the Durham murders being contracted killings is both ridiculous and a fiasco and says the main focus of a contract killing is to get in and out as fast as possible, not to ransack a house looking for something or spend time putting victims in a bathtub in an attempt to get them to give up information. "Any investigator worth a nickel, when he walks into a crime scene knows if it's a robbery, or if information was being extracted, or if it was a contract killing."[2567]

According to Stoney Birt, this was not a "burglary gone bad," and [Billy Birt, Davis, Gaddis, and Reed] would not have traveled to Boone to steal money or jewelry. "They did not take stuff like that. You go there for what you were hired to do."[2568] This implies the focus of the crime was contracted murder versus a motive of robbery. Even if the Durham Case was not a robbery/murder scenario like the Fleming Case, but a murder for hire scenario, money would still have been involved in the form of a payoff.

Rufus Edmisten, however, deviates from the idea that the murders were contracted killings (as does Bob Ingram).[2569] Edmisten believes Birt, Davis, Gaddis, and Reed were there for money, but he will not go so far as to say they were hired to kill the Durhams. Edmisten's theory, which he dubs "the Rufus Theory," is that the perpetrators were promised money, and when they didn't find it in the house, particularly considering the long trip they had made in bad weather, they were so furious that they went on a rampage, ransacking the house and taking out their vengeance by murdering the Durhams. One might argue the money that was supposed to be awaiting the killers inside the house equates payment for a hired hit, but according to Edmisten, had these been contracted killings, the hitmen would have expected at least half the promised payment upfront, and in his experience, he has never known of a contract killer willing to wait for full payment after a murder or to be paid in installments. Although there is no proof one way or another concerning any money that may have been exchanged for such a "hired hit," Edmisten's "old Watauga County boy" sense, as he calls it, is that these Dixie Mafia members came into the home for the express purpose of finding a large amount of money, tied the Durhams up and interrogated them about its location, searched the house, and not finding what they came for, chose to murder them.[2570] Edmisten also assumes Troy Hall "thought there would be a pile of money there, and he would get his share.... He thought, in my opinion, that there was going to be a sack of money there that would be worth their [the Dixie Mafia's] trip up there to the mountains, and he would get his share. And, of course, I can just imagine how pissed off they were at him for sending them on this wild goose chase where they had to kill three people in the meantime."[2571]

Bob Ingram also believes the killers were looking for money,[2572] and in his estimation, even had the killers found the money they hoped to find, the Durhams would still have been murdered as eliminated witnesses. By this way of thinking, the motive of the killers was not that they were specifically being paid to murder the Durhams (i.e., hired as hitmen to kill them), but they were at the Durhams' home for the primary purpose of robbery – of finding and taking a large sum of money – and that the murders were incidental or secondary.[2573]

As for the motive(s) of those who wanted the Durhams dead, and in addition to the possible motives of Troy Hall that have already been discussed, it is common for surviving family members of murder victims to be considered suspects, and particularly if those survivors are the beneficiaries of estates, insurance policies, etc., but these circumstances do not mean they are guilty. One source reported Bryce Durham to be "a wealthy Boone automobile dealer."[2574] Another stated "the family's prosperous auto dealership brought them a lavish home;"[2575] yet another referred to their house as a "sprawling" residence.[2576] Others stated they lived in a $50,000 home in a fashionable neighborhood.[2577] Their house, while perhaps larger than some homes, was not lavish nor necessarily sprawling, but neither was it necessarily "quaint" as stated by yet another source.[2578] And, although a few sources described the family as well-to-do,[2579] wealthy, and/or affluent,[2580] both Ginny Durham and her uncle, Bill Durham, have stated Bryce did not have a lot of money in his checking account. Ginny also reportedly stated to Cecil and Mildred Small that her parents were not wealthy, but they did have money.

Stoney Birt agrees money had to be involved in the Durham murders – "This had to be done on the promise of pay and what they got out of the house" – but, as already much discussed, he disagrees about who actually did the killing. Based on what he read in the Watauga County Sheriff's Office case file, Stoney says he is a rocket scientist compared to the people who carried out this crime. According to podcaster Sean Kipe, "By 1972, Billy Sunday Birt was a killing machine – cold, calculated, methodical. He was a professional hitman with one hell of a resume. He was extremely good at his job." According to Stoney, his father did "not spend the time to drown three people when he'd just kill 'em." Stoney believes it is obvious that whoever committed the murders were a group of "unprofessional young punks compared to the hardened, seasoned Dixie Mafia." Stoney further believes that, if the Dixie Mafia had been involved, they would have taken charge, called the shots, and carried it out more professionally. "Instead," Stoney says, "everything was done on Troy Hall's timeline. Everything. Nobody could've done that except Troy Hall.... [Troy was] bent out of shape with frustration and anger.... How in the hell are you gonna call up Billy Davis or Billy Birt in Dixie Mafia Land, Georgia in that timeframe and set this up and have them come there and do that from the time the shit hit the fan? The shit hit the fan within forty-eight hours of them dying.... I cannot see why people are trying to import any type of professional into this.... That has all the signs of a local-yocal.... They's nothing about it professional. Naw, they Forrest Gumpped through this. It don't none of it make sense. Here's what makes sense – Troy Hall was desperate. He wanted to find that will if they was one."[2581]

Dissenting from Stoney in terms of who killed the Durhams, Bob Ingram states, "I am 100% on the Fleming Case, and I'm 100% on the Durham Case." But one thing Ingram and Stoney agree on, along with most others who have looked into the Durham Case, is Troy Hall. According to Ingram, "I'm also 100% on Troy Hall setting that whole thing up."[2582] And that leads us to our next question – the million dollar question.

How were the murders facilitated?

One of the men from the Asheville-based burglary ring who was arrested in March 1972 was charged with possessing marijuana with the possible intent to resell it.[2583] Many who were acquainted with Troy either knew or suspected he was dealing in dope and had perhaps even gone to Mexico for drugs. Could Troy have been associated with one or more of these men and purchased drugs from or sold drugs to them? And could the drug connections among the Asheville men have included members of the Dixie Mafia, who were peddling biphetamines from Mexico?

Another intriguing consideration is that dealing in automobiles seems to be a recurring theme. Both Bryce and Virginia had experience in that field of work, even prior to purchasing the dealership in Boone. Troy Hall's brother Ray reportedly dabbled in cars.[2584] Dean Chandler, one of the accused from Asheville, was convicted of transporting stolen cars across the North Carolina and Tennessee state line. A few of Billy Birt's associates/acquaintances – Harold Chancey and Kenneth Royster – were likewise involved in the illegal interstate transportation of stolen cars from South Carolina to Winder, Georgia. The 1973 North Carolina "Mummy Murders" *(see pp. 466-467)* involved car dealership employees reportedly being murdered by members of the Dixie Mafia. Reid Fleming, one of the strangling victims of the Dixie Mafia, was a semi-retired used car dealer. Billy Wayne Davis fronted his illegal activities out of used car lots in Georgia and "had used car connections all over the place" through business, the underworld, and poker/gambling.[2585] Davis told investigators he had previously been to Boone several times on car deals.[2586]

When Bob Ingram first determined the identities of the men he believes robbed and murdered the Durhams, he wondered how individuals from Winder and Metro Atlanta, Georgia became connected to victims in Watauga County, North Carolina. He knew for sure that finding the Durhams and their residence did not happen by chance, and someone had to set it up and provide information. He believes Troy Hall and the used car business are the common denominators. Could Billy Wayne Davis have been to Bryce Durham's dealership, and if so, could he have met Troy there? It is certainly possible, although Davis never mentioned either and said he was not familiar with the name Troy Hall. That does not mean Troy was not involved; it may simply mean Davis never saw him or had any direct dealings with him. If Davis was being truthful about not knowing Troy, and if Troy was the one who initiated the crime against his in-laws, it may have been another member of the Dixie Mafia or an intermediary from another crime ring or criminal element who entered the deal with Troy. Or perhaps an agent of Troy and not Troy himself dealt with Davis or whoever carried out the murders. According to Stoney Birt, his father and Billy Wayne Davis had North Carolina connections (whose identities, Stoney says, are unknown to him),[2587] however, his father would refuse a job if too many people knew about the plan or if it would create too much heat.[2588]

In Rufus Edmisten's estimation, "Troy was very resourceful. He had a bad background when he was brought up in Wilkes County…. It wouldn't have been hard for Troy to do that (i.e., make the connections to arrange the murders) because his mind seemed to work that way of finding people of ill repute to associate with." Edmisten continues: "And without Troy ever being touched by any law enforcement – they never had enough to arrest him on, quite obviously, which is how smart he was – …it's just sort of by chance that this came up – the information out of Georgia, some fifty years later. In every aspect, how can a man go on, become a lawyer, become an assistant prosecutor…unless you are smart enough to be two steps in front of law enforcement all the time, and Troy did it. He pulled it off."[2589]

In the estimation of former Boone Police Department Sergeant Jeff Rucker, there were people in Wilkes County and other places who would have been glad to accommodate Troy Hall in his orchestration of the murders.[2590] According to an anonymous source, a particular man in Wilkes County, who was a friend of the Halls and was well-connected and renown for keeping his mouth shut, was approached to see if he knew anyone who could take on the murder for hire of the Durhams. The source has no indication of who approached this man, or if the man subsequently facilitated the request, but if so, that may have been how the murders were precipitated.

It is even possible entire networks of people or criminal enterprises were utilized to arrange and carry out the Durham murders – "knowing a guy who knows some guys." For example, perhaps within Troy's sphere of associates in Wilkes County were individuals connected to the criminal element in the Asheville area who knew the Dixie Mafia in Barrow County, Georgia. Sheriff Len Hagaman and former SBI Agent John Parker agree that such a network of connections is likely.[2591] Bob Ingram, however, believes the communication between Troy and Davis was more direct and less weblike. Ingram is a proponent of Occam's Razor, a principle which says, when attempting to explain something, no more assumptions should be made than necessary, and that simpler theories are preferable to more complex ones. In Ingram's mind, Troy had to be the link between his in-laws and their killers, and he is firm in his belief Troy was the one who communicated with the Dixie Mafia. He bases this certainty on the fact that Shane Birt says his father told him it was arranged by a nephew or son-in-law of the Durhams.[2592] Granted, between Bryce and Virginia Durham, they had at least thirteen nephews who would have been aged eighteen or older in 1972,[2593] but none have ever, at any time, to this writer's knowledge, been suspected of involvement in the case. None had the motives Troy had, and Troy was certainly the Durhams' only son-in-law.

Previous chapters have outlined other tales of how the murders may have been instigated, including ones without any mention of the Dixie Mafia, and more than a few claiming Troy Hall was the initiator. Among those accounts is an individual (and convicted murderer) who says, like Ingram, he adheres to Occam's Razor, but he believes the "Asheville boys" killed the Durhams and that that is a simpler, more likely, and more direct scenario than four men coming from Georgia to commit the murders. He dismisses the idea the Dixie Mafia was involved or even had knowledge of the Durham family.[2594] At least one witness said she saw a money transaction between Troy and the men from Asheville; another person said Troy paid big money to a different man from Asheville to arrange the murders. And at one point, Ginny Durham believed individuals in Lenoir, North Carolina may have been involved.

If the Dixie Mafia committed the murders, exactly how the communication between Troy and them would have transpired, and exactly what was communicated remains a mystery. As Bob Ingram wryly says, hitmen are not listed in the phone book. Did Troy talk openly about his in-laws keeping a large sum of money in their home, and did he merely suggest robbery, which happened to result in them also getting killed? In the Fleming Case, when Carswell Tapley told George Leisher about the Flemings' money, he was not asking Leisher to have them killed, but it happened just the same. Ingram says a similar scenario is possible in the Durham Case, but regardless of what was said, it would not take the initiator long to know these men were dangerous and capable of doing serious harm to others. If Birt, Davis, Gaddis, and Reed became involved, death was a certainty, even if the original intention of the informant had only been robbery. According to Ingram, once information about big money reached these men, the next thing you heard about was dead bodies. He knows of no one Birt robbed (during a home invasion in which the residents were present) that he also did not kill. Ingram is positive the Durhams were targeted for robbery, but Troy may have additionally been intentional about their murders and knew these men would carry the crime through to that end.[2595]

Among those who question whether the Durhams' killers have been accurately identified is Richard Walter, the forensic psychologist and crime scene analyst who reviewed the Durham Case in the early 1990s. Walter is not convinced Birt, Davis, Gaddis, and Reed are the killers. He says he figured out who murdered the Durhams and why more than thirty years ago, and that Troy Hall is the guilty party, not only for masterminding the crime, but for actually killing his in-laws. He believes Troy had ample time during his library study alibi to go to the Durham home, subdue Bryce, Virginia, and Bobby with a weapon, have them help tie one another, and then kill them one by one. Although Walter concedes Troy may have had an accomplice in the murders, he believes the conclusions reached about Dixie Mafia involvement are incorrect. Walter takes particular issue with the Georgia Bureau of Investigation and says he cannot think of a more incompetent agency. Based on his years of experience, he claims the GBI loves to grandstand and be heroic, which is well and fine if they are right.[2596] As recently as July 2022, Walter stated he hoped Sheriff Len Hagaman would be attending the upcoming North Carolina Homicide Investigators Conference. Walter, one of the conference's keynote speakers, planned to carry his Durham file and attempt to dissuade Hagaman and others from what Walter believes to be a misidentification of the killers.[2597]

Former lawman and private investigator Jerry Vaughn's big question was where would the money have come from to pay the Dixie Mafia?[2598] Retired SBI Agent Larry Wagner struggles with a similar question: If Troy was the person who instigated his in-laws' murders by the Dixie Mafia and subsequently shortchanged them, how did he stay alive considering these men from Georgia were brutal killers who would think nothing about taking him out?[2599] One possibility may be that, if an acquaintance of Troy was the intermediary with the Dixie Mafia, perhaps that person was eliminated as a result of the monetary shortchange, thereby satisfying the desire for payback. If so, that was never part of what Shane Birt says his father told him. In fact, Shane says his father cussed the person who shortchanged him until his dying day, which would indicate satisfaction had never been achieved.

Was Troy Hall the SOB who Billy Birt allegedly wanted to return to North Carolina to kill for shortchanging him? It seems doubtful that Troy, as a twenty-year-old married college student from a poor family and living in a trailer park, would have the means to pay a group of criminals out-of-pocket unless he had access to cash through his illegal dealings or network of acquaintances, or unless he truly believed there was sufficient cash stashed in the Durham home to compensate the killers for their work. If he did shortchange the killers, could this explain why he eventually relocated to Georgia and practiced law in Lawrenceville, only a thirty-minute drive from Billy Birt's base in Winder? Could attorney and judge Gene Reeves, who shared family connections with both Troy and Birt, have smoothed things out between them? Did Troy move there to save his own life by paying off a debt he owed? Sheriff Len Hagaman wonders the same thing: "Maybe Troy made himself whole with Billy [Birt] and company?"[2600] But according to Stoney Birt, that's not how the Dixie Mafia worked. Despite Troy's intelligence, Stoney believes Troy was not very street smart because he exhibited desperate behavior in his ranting and raving and his search of the dealership the morning following the murders. Stoney believes if his father had been involved in the Durham murders, he would have seen Troy as a liability that needed to be dealt with. "My father would have killed him within a week.... He'd never lived. They's no way in hell that Troy would've lived if my father had've done it."[2601] If Troy knew where these Dixie Mafia members were from, and if he did shortchange them and did not plan to make it up to them, why would he have moved near them? Of course, by the time he relocated to Georgia, Birt, Davis, Gaddis, and Reed were already in prison, so perhaps – if he really did have an association with them – he felt confident he was outside of their reach, particularly since he changed his name and became an attorney.

In the weeks following the February 2022 press release, Sheriff Hagaman received information "that a direct connection," potentially identifying Troy as "the one who set up the homicide," might be forthcoming, that Stoney Birt might have that information, and that the Watauga County Sheriff's Office was considering an additional trip to Winder, Georgia to interview him about it.[2602] As of

April 2022, the sheriff's office had not interviewed Stoney about this new information and Hagaman told me to feel free to ask Stoney about it during my upcoming trip to Georgia.[2603] I first visited Stoney in Winder on April 18, 2022 and asked him if he knew anything about Troy Hall. He said he did not, and if he had, he would have already shared that with the authorities.[2604] In late June 2022, I shared pictures of Troy Hall with Stoney, asking if he had ever seen this man, but without stating who the man was. Stoney replied, "No. I have never seen him."[2605] Stoney says it is impossible that young Troy Hall could have called up Billy Birt and, with no money to offer in exchange, had him run up to North Carolina to kill Troy's in-laws, and he does not believe Troy would have even known anyone who could reach out to the Dixie Mafia.[2606] Stoney says it is ludicrous to think Troy could have messed with a man like Billy Birt and "not get killed his damn self."[2607]

Was there a reason the murders happened when they did?

Some have questioned why the murders were carried out that particular night, especially considering the bad weather. What made the crime so urgent it could not wait for better conditions? Was something about to transpire that required the immediate elimination of the Durhams?

This crime seemingly required forethought and planning, and arrangements had almost certainly been set into motion before that night. There is a good chance the crime had been prearranged for that date without any expectation or consideration of bad weather moving in. And again, "warmer than normal temperatures" were experienced the day before the murders.[2608]

If the killers were from out of town – from Georgia or elsewhere – which decades of investigation have pointed to, they likely would have been en route before the snow began and perhaps were already in Boone a day or days before the murders, casing the town as well as the Durhams' dealership, neighborhood, and house and taking into consideration driving routes, drop-off points, and timing. Rather than leave and come back another time, they may have wanted to follow through with their activities while they were in the area.

Also, if Bryce and Virginia were on Troy's trail (as was stated to family members) by continuing to look into his background and dealings, perhaps they were on the brink of discovering things Troy did not want them to know. And perhaps their claims of having recently changed their wills was a motivator to kill them quickly. It could be that they had not yet officially had the revised wills notarized or made entirely legal (which might be supported by the fact that hundreds of attorneys had no knowledge of the wills), and the goal was to eliminate Bryce and Virginia and their newly designated sole heir, Bobby, before that could be accomplished.

Were the ransacking of the Durham home and the abandonment of their vehicle staged?

Although we have previously discussed motive, ransacking is tied to it. If the motive was robbery, then ransacking – the searching for money and/or other valuables or documents – would not have been staged. How easily or not the intruders found what they came for would determine the necessity and extent of the ransacking to accomplish their objective. Or were the ransacking of the home and the taking of a few items meant to merely portray a robbery and to deter law enforcement from detecting a different motive?

Within days after the murders, SBI agents stated "it would not have been necessary for the slayers to 'tear the place apart' unless they were looking for something on the order of a strongbox or a wall-type safe."[2609] When asked if robbery was a motive for the Durham murders, Richard Walter expressed a differing opinion, saying, "No. On the contrary, it was rather clumsily staged to look like a robbery."[2610] Bob Ingram, however, believes the ransacking was not staged but real, and the intruders were specifically looking for something. According to Ingram, in both the Durham and Fleming cases, that "something" was money, and the crime scene photos of the houses from both cases look similar in terms of the ransacking.[2611]

In Sheriff Len Hagaman's estimation, the ransacking of homes was normal for the Dixie Mafia, which wanted to make the homes appear as if they had been searching for things.[2612] This seems to be supported in the instance of the murder of elderly Samuel Thompson in Mableton, Georgia in November 1971 (only three months before the Durham murders), when Billy Birt stated in court in 1976, "My job was to ransack so it would look like a burglary. I tore up the whole house."[2613] Perhaps the focus of the ransacking of the Durham home was not money but something else, such as Bryce's and Virginia's alleged new wills. And since those were never found by investigators, perhaps the killers were successful in locating them. Perhaps the Durhams were abused to the point of giving them up. The following morning, as Troy was searching the dealership, one account alleges he said, "I know there's *a copy* of that damn thing here somewhere." If Troy was referring to the will, perhaps this is an indication he already possessed the original and wanted to confiscate any copies.

Regarding the Durhams' GMC "Jimmy," did the killers intend to steal it but end up accidentally wrecking it, or was it purposely abandoned, along with the pillowcase containing stolen silver, to give the impression of a failed robbery attempt? If the killers really intended to steal the vehicle, it seems like a precarious move to risk being potentially seen or caught driving a vehicle belonging to their victims. And if they were attempting to depart Boone in it, why would they turn onto a side road like Poplar Grove Road, particularly in bad weather, versus staying on a quicker, primary route? Because Poplar Grove Road was not a road that county outsiders would normally travel, it was suggested the killers were familiar with the area, especially since many rural roads in the mountains dead end, although this one did not.[2614] If the driver of the getaway car actually did park at a convenience store that was part of the Union 76 station on Highway 105, and if the killers intended to abandon the "Jimmy," then perhaps when they passed the getaway car, they simply turned onto the next available side road, which would have been Poplar Grove Road, and left it there in a ditch (purposely or not), with the getaway car following close behind to pick them up.

Carroll Garland and his daughter Sonya recall that, for ten to fourteen days prior to the murders, a white, circa 1963 Ford Thunderbird turned several times in their driveway at 1315 Poplar Grove Road. Carroll Garland's wife also witnessed this and reported it to him, but he initially assigned little significance to it. Later, deciding to drive around Boone to see if they could spot the car, they located it in front of Troy and Ginny Hall's mobile home.[2615] Was Troy Hall scoping out Poplar Grove Road days in advance to determine the best and nearest side road for the killers to leave the Durhams' vehicle? The Garlands also distinctly recall the "Jimmy" being abandoned adjacent to their driveway (2.4 miles from the Durham home), which they say is the reason the SBI searched their house, basement, and camper and utilized their home as a temporary headquarters. Brad Poe, who was with his father and brother when they encountered the "Jimmy" on the night of the murders, also recalls it being near this location. However, Johnny Tester, who served as the dispatcher for the Boone Police Department and took Troy Hall's call reporting the murders, went to the vehicle later that night and distinctly remembers it being abandoned twenty feet beyond where Coffey Knob Road intersects with Poplar Grove Road (approximately 2.2 miles from the Durham home). Garry Henson, whose parents lived on Poplar Grove Road just below the Garland home, concurs with Tester that it was abandoned near the intersection of Coffey Knob Road.[2616][mmmmmmmmmm] On the one hand, the Garlands' recollections regarding both Troy Hall's actions before the murders, and the SBI's actions after the murders, seem to perfectly align with the vehicle being found near their home. But Tester's recollection also makes sense from the perspective that there were no homes near where he says the vehicle was abandoned. Why would the killers choose to abandon the vehicle near a home where they might be spotted? This again begs the question: Did the killers purposely ditch the vehicle (in which case they would surely have chosen a spot where they would not likely be seen), or did they actually wreck the vehicle (in which case they may have simply gone into the ditch line near the Garland home, not of their own volition)? And did Troy Hall, if he really was looking for a spot for the vehicle to be abandoned, drive north along Poplar Grove Road, select the non-inhabited stretch of the road just past Coffey Knob Road as the dumping site, and continue until he encountered the next visible houses along the road (i.e. the Henson and Garland homes in immediate succession), at which point he turned in the Garlands' driveway and backtracked to take another look?

Contrary to at least one source that said the vehicle had skidded into the ditch,[2617] there was no evidence of that,[2618] bringing into question whether it "had been purposely positioned to draw attention." Because the passenger side of the "Jimmy" was so close to the bank beside the road, its passenger(s) could only have exited from the driver's side.[2619] Based on tire track analysis, the "Jimmy" was driven into the ditch on Poplar Grove Road as opposed to sliding into it due to the road being slick. The fact it was driven into the ditch, however, does not speak to the intent of the driver. It does not necessarily mean the driver purposely put the "Jimmy" into the ditch with the intention of abandoning it for a staged purpose; he or she could have accidentally driven into the ditch. Sheriff Len Hagaman believes the killers, if they truly were members of Georgia's Dixie Mafia, had an accident because, based on where they traditionally committed their crimes, they were not used to a lot of snow and ice.[2620] The vehicle being in a ditch, however, whether on purpose or accidentally, does not preclude the possibility that the occupants intended to abandon the vehicle all along.

On the night of the murders, at some point after the killers left Poplar Grove Road, they reportedly encountered snow-related vehicle difficulties, which required the services of a tow truck from Wilkes County...services that had allegedly been pre-arranged and on standby because of the inclement weather.[2621] The alleged tow truck driver was a close friend of the Halls, and a former employer of Ray Hall, but it is unknown whether the driver knew the identities of the passengers inside the car he pulled or if he was aware of the murders they had just committed. The alleged recollection of Billy Birt saying he and his accomplices almost got trapped in a snowstorm may be a reference to this, or perhaps he and his accomplices (or an entirely different set of killers) either saw SBI Agent Wally Hardwick, Jr. and his friend Gary Morgan approaching the "Jimmy" on Poplar Grove Road (even if only their headlights) or read about it later in a newspaper, which caused them [the killers] to realize how close they had come to being caught. In his August 2021 interview, Billy

[mmmmmmmmmm] In no wise diminishing their recollections, it should be noted that Sonya Garland and Brad Poe were five and six years old, respectively, at the time of the murders, although their memories were, no doubt, bolstered by the recollections of their adult parents.

Wayne Davis stated he was sure someone got stuck and that he sent a tow truck to get a vehicle out. Could he have been referring to this tow truck from Wilkes County?

If the Durhams' killers really were the accused members of the Dixie Mafia, then it is helpful to recall details of the 1971 Matthews and 1973 Fleming murder cases. In the Matthews Case, Warren Matthews' bloodstained Mercedes convertible was found on a street less than a mile from their home.[2622] In the Fleming Case, "police officers testified that the Flemings' home had been completely ransacked…and that the Flemings' Ford automobile was found about 2 miles from their home." The Durhams' home was also completely ransacked, and their vehicle was abandoned approximately 2.3 miles from their home. Regarding the Flemings' car, Davis, who claimed not to be at the Fleming home (similar to how he claimed not to have entered the Durham home), testified that, after Birt, Gaddis, and Reed arrived, they bound the Flemings, and while Gaddis stood watch, Birt and Reed drove their own car as well as the Flemings' car down a side road away from the home and then returned to the home in the Flemings' car. Presumably, this would have been so that no neighbors or passersby would have recognized anything odd, only seeing the Flemings' car at their home and no strange car in the driveway. After the murders, the killers then drove the Flemings' car back to the location of their own car and abandoned the Flemings' car.[2623] The similarities between these cases demonstrate a trend and indicate the killers never intended to steal their victims' vehicles, but to use them to escape the crime scene and then abandon them. It is likely, however, that any number of criminal gangs – not just the Dixie Mafia – handled their victims' vehicles in similar fashion.

What is indicated by items taken from the Durham home or left behind?

It seems highly unlikely robbers and/or contracted killers would collect their pay solely in the form of cash rifled from their victims' wallets or the stolen silver pieces found in the pillowcase inside the abandoned "Jimmy," unless, as has been suggested, the large sum of money they were promised could not be found, even after a thorough ransacking of the home, and they took whatever they could. The value of what was taken is unknown in terms of cash and other items. By taking the silver pieces, the killers may have been attempting to convey the message – whether accurately or misleadingly – that robbery was their primary objective with the killing of the Durhams being secondary.

Regarding the silver, if the killers meant to remove it from the "Jimmy" and take it with them, perhaps they were on the verge of being discovered, and with time running short, they quickly jumped out of the "Jimmy" and fled in the getaway car, leaving their loot behind. This sense of urgency may also be supported by the "Jimmy" being left running with headlights and wipers on. Both Shane Birt and Bob Ingram believe some of the silver in Ruby Nell Birt's possession, given to her by her husband in the early 1970s, was taken from the Durham home. Shane states his father was only able to bring a portion of what was taken because some of it fell into a ditch. If this comment pertains to silver falling out of the "Jimmy" when the killers abandoned it on Poplar Grove Road, that scenario is unlikely. The passenger doors opposite the driver's side of the "Jimmy" were so close to the bank that they could not be opened, and this is the same side the ditch line was on, meaning nothing could have fallen out into the ditch. There are also no official reports of any silver being discovered in a ditch either at that location or elsewhere.

Although an inventory of the silver items is housed within the Watauga County Sheriff's Office investigative file, the items themselves are missing, and there are no known photographs of them. According to Sheriff Len Hagaman, everyone had assumed through the years the silver was with the SBI in Raleigh, and although SBI Agent Wade Colvard asked for it several times, including making a trip to the state laboratory, the SBI told him it was not in their possession. The Watauga County Sheriff's Office cannot locate any documentation, including a chain of custody, pertaining to what was done with the silver.[2624] According to Captain Carolynn Johnson, things were done differently in past years, and she says, "Because so many agencies were involved, it is unclear where the silver went once it left the 'Jimmy.'"[2625]

Unfortunately, Ginny Durham Mackie did not recognize the pieces of silver that officers brought from Ruby Nell Birt, and they did not match any of the other family silver in Ginny's possession, although it is possible the items in Ruby Nell's possession comprised a single serving set that would not match other pieces. Ginny stated other automobile dealerships and manufacturers frequently gifted items to her father, including certificates for redemption, and silver pieces were sometimes awarded him during contests connected to his car business. Perhaps the pieces submitted by Ruby Nell were pieces Bryce had acquired in that fashion and were unknown to Ginny.[2626] Bob Ingram had also hoped to compare Ruby Nell's pieces to the silver that had been found inside the pillowcase, but in the absence of those pieces or photographs of them, that was impossible.[2627] In March 1972, Ginny's index, middle, and little fingers on her right hand matched latent prints lifted in the Durham case, including one on the stolen silver found in the "Jimmy," although she stated she had helped her mother polish and put it away several months prior to the murders.[2628]

Cecil Small told Boone policemen that Virginia Durham had taken those silver pieces to the dealership to utilize for refreshments at an event intended to attract customers to the business. According to Small, Virginia had placed the pieces in a pillowcase to transport them back home. It is unclear how or why Small would have had this knowledge, but if true, then perhaps the silver was already in the GMC "Jimmy" when the Durhams went home on the night of the murders and were not pieces taken by the killers after all.[2629] However, the fact that the pillowcase also contained a silver brush and mirror set[2630] would not seem supportive of Small's statement, unless Virginia also took those to the dealership for personal use.

Some have asked why the killers would have left the bank deposit bag of money in the Durhams' house. There is always a chance it was simply overlooked or inadvertently left behind or that it partially contained personal checks the killers did not want to mess with or be linked to if they cashed them. After Billy Birt, in company with Billy Wayne Davis, killed Mac Sibley in December 1971, two months prior to the Durham murders, police "found a bag containing a considerable amount of money" that had either been overlooked, forgotten, or purposely left behind by the intruders.[2631] The fact that the bank deposit bag was left behind in the Durham home does not prove robbery was not the motive, nor does it prove the Dixie Mafia was or was not involved. And the fact that Birt and Davis left behind a bag of money at Sibley's home does not mean they are guilty of the Durham murders.

Because of the way the house was ransacked, with cash left behind and silver taken, Stoney Birt is led to "double down on his belief that this was not done by a professional like his father.... To put Billy Birt's name on it is a joke," he says. "Everything I heard pointed to a hit by somebody, and the dummies that done it got silverware and left the damn money. That wasn't Billy Birt. That wasn't the way Billy Birt worked. He didn't mess with silverware. He wouldn't even take jewelry off a person. No, no…. He don't steal silverware…."[2632]

The bottom line is no one knows for sure what or how much was taken from the Durham home.

What, exactly, is the Dixie Mafia, and was it ever previously on the radar of those investigating the Durham Case?

Although Billy Birt, Billy Wayne Davis, Bobby Gaddis, and Charlie Reed were based in Georgia, the Dixie Mafia was actually a much broader network of predominantly white criminals, who were active in a ten-state area throughout the South, from Florida to North Carolina and as far west as Texas. Some were professional crooks while others were more "rag-tag…thugs and ne'er do wells," but each had their "illicit niches." Acquainted with one another in locally based pockets, they were in constant motion and prone to band together in various combinations, doing anything for a buck from drugs, prostitution, gambling, and extortion to robbery, arson, and murder. Unlike the traditional Mafia, the Dixie Mafia (sometimes referred to as the "Cornbread Cosa Nostra") was informal, and loosely configured. While exhibiting some degree of coordination and sophistication, it did not equal the syndicate-type operations or financial backing of its historically northern-based counterpart. The Dixie Mafia had no system of lieutenants and no Godfather types. It was not "in the shape of an octopus reaching out from a 'family head.'"[2633]

The origination of the term "Dixie Mafia" is uncertain, although it seems to have come into usage between 1968 and 1970. Some believe it first surfaced during a regional law enforcement conference in Atlanta, Georgia. Others believe it was coined in Texas, either by a Houston newspaperman or a Dallas policeman. Still others thought it first appeared in an interview with an Alcohol, Tobacco, and Firearms agent.[2634] While some discounted the existence of such a network, stating the term to be "pure bull" and believing it to be "loaded with erroneous and misleading implications," many in law enforcement adopted it "because it [created] a lot of cooperation between [their] agencies nationwide." It is believed those who comprised the Dixie Mafia resented it and may have feared being misunderstood as a rival of "the real Mafia" and consequently being "knocked off."[2635] In Georgia, Billy Birt claimed he never heard the term "Dixie Mafia" until 1971 when a newspaper named him as the group's hitman,[2636] and Billy Wayne Davis was reportedly "a little hacked" about the moniker and said he and his associates did not go by that name.[2637] Still, the term stuck and was stretched to include "almost every professional thug who ever traveled from one Southern state to another, teamed up with other thugs, and committed a crime."[2638]

In North Carolina, two Gastonia department store safe robberies were attributed to the group in 1969,[2639] and by 1971, SBI Director Charles Dunn stated the Dixie Mafia posed a major problem in the state and was just as ruthless as the northern Mafia. He added that the group had "specialists" in explosives, arson, and safecracking, and had carried out several gangland executions in the state. Dunn said the Dixie Mafia's "core may number between 125 to 150 persons, many of them with long criminal records, and may involve hundreds of others from time to time." Dunn told the state's Senate Judiciary Committee it was time for North Carolinians to "recognize that there is organized crime in our state."[2640] In July 1971, North Carolina Governor Bob Scott established a council "to determine the size and scope of organized crime in this state and develop ways to suppress it."[2641]

It was generally believed the Dixie Mafia had a headquarters centered around the Gulf Coast casinos in Mississippi, and it was blamed for "assassination-style murders around Biloxi," but some authorities tended to feel the group's presence in North Carolina was less lethal. Former Assistant Attorney General Howard Satisky stated, "I think this concept of the Dixie Mafia was, to law enforcement, always more of a flash in the pan. It just sort of glamorized a bunch of thugs that had the sense to work together."[2642] But others believed that, by the fall of 1972, "the criminal activity of The Dixie Mafia had increased in North Carolina," and "violence had become very much a part of their culture."[2643]

Johnny Tester, the dispatcher who had taken Troy Hall's call to the Boone Police Department, recalls his father, the late Boone Police Chief Clyde Tester, saying one of the snitches in the Buncombe County, North Carolina jail said rumor had it the Dixie Mafia was involved in the Durham murders.[2644] For whatever reasons, this lead seems not to have been pursued. Perhaps it was because no one believed the Deep South-based network would reach as far as northwestern North Carolina, or perhaps officers felt confident they had correctly identified the four Asheville prisoners as the killers.

In 1982, Paul Bare made a sworn statement to investigators regarding the Durham Case. By that time, Bare had been convicted of the Lonnie Gamboa murder in neighboring Ashe County, and in association with that case, Bare made mention of the Dixie Mafia, claiming certain members of it had wanted him "to drive and deliver some 'hot cars' for them," but he refused, and they had tried to kill him. He stated he had previously "made runs for them as a decoy car, but [had] never carried any of the stuff." Bare further stated the Dixie Mafia was run by a motorcycle gang, and the circumstances surrounding the Gamboa murder were complex. Bare stated to authorities, "You boys just don't realize how much is going on. I need to talk to an FBI Agent. There are a lot of Big People involved, and the Dixie Mafia."[2645]

Whether realized at the time of the Durham murders or not, of those individuals who had criminal records or associations and whose inked prints were compared in the 1970s to latent prints in the Durham Case, more than fifty percent were allegedly linked to the Dixie Mafia.[nnnnnnnnn] Granted, the period between the late 1960s and mid-1970s was the heyday of the Dixie Mafia, and because it lacked organization and was unclearly defined, practically any criminal from the South might be claimed, accurately or not, to have ties to it.

Among the individuals whose prints were compared to those from the Durham crime scene[2646] and who were alleged to be Dixie Mafia-affiliated were bootleggers, drug runners, cocaine smugglers, burglars, thieves, robbers, safecrackers, and murderers (including contract killers). Their bases of operation and targets stretched across the South – Texas, Alabama, Mississippi, Georgia, Florida, South Carolina, Tennessee, Virginia, and North Carolina.[ooooooooo] Some of their victims had suffered

---

[nnnnnnnnn] The author individually researched approximately 400 names on the fingerprint list within the Watauga County Sheriff's Office Durham Case file.

[ooooooooo] Among the individuals whose prints were compared to those in the Durham Case were Dawson family members from Muscle Shoals, Alabama and the Greenville, South Carolina-based "Dawson Gang." Those associated with the latter group included used car dealers Luke Cannon and Arlo "Sonny" Barger; Larry Hacker and Alton Wayne Ruff (two of the "Marietta Seven," who were convicted of the murders of Drs. Warren and Rosina Matthews in Marietta, GA but later exonerated, in part, based on the confession of Billy Birt to the murders); Theo Donald "Smooth" McDaniel (who later resided in Winder, Georgia, which was the base of operations for Billy Birt's sect of the Dixie Mafia); and Forest McGuire and "Fast Eddie" Williamson, who took part in an October 1, 1971 Hickory, NC home invasion/robbery during which a man and his wife and son were attacked while watching television around 10:15 PM. [A daughter entered the home later that evening and was likewise attacked.] The victims' hands and feet were bound with wire, and they were beaten and tortured in an effort to have them reveal where money was

fates similar to the Durhams – their homes invaded and being tortured and bound and sometimes gagged. At least one Alabama victim was submerged in his bathtub and threatened with death to force disclosure of his money's location.[2647] But no one's prints matched those in the Durham Case. Of course, any of these suspects could still have been guilty and merely worn gloves during the commission of the murders.

All these pieces of information seem to have been overlooked or inadequately investigated or forgotten with the passage of time because, when the Dixie Mafia's name resurfaced in 2022 in conjunction with the Durham Case, Watauga County Sheriff Len Hagaman stated it as being out of left field with no previous mention or suspicion of them.[2648] According to Frank Guy, who served as a Boone policeman from 1973 to 1999 and worked on the Durham Case for a period of time, the Dixie Mafia had never been mentioned, and the possibility of the Durhams' killers coming from Georgia had never crossed investigators' minds.[2649] Likewise, Captain Dee Dee Rominger, who investigated the case on behalf of the Watauga County Sheriff's Office in the 2000s, stated the Dixie Mafia had never been on her radar, and she was totally shocked by this news and found it unbelievable.[2650] Pat Whitman, widow of SBI Agent Charlie Whitman, who worked the Durham Case for years, recalls nothing about Georgia or anyone going to Georgia.[2651]

Although identification of the Durhams' murderers was announced in February 2022, and although revelation of the Dixie Mafia's activity in northwestern North Carolina seemed to be previously unheard of,[2652] this was not the first time a Dixie Mafia group had been linked to a brutal triple homicide in North Carolina. Another one, known as the "Mummy Murders," occurred on January 15, 1973, eleven months after the Durham murders. Fifty-seven-year-old Grover "Shep" Broadwell, thirty-three-year-old Michael "Mike" Collins, and nineteen-year-old Della Murray were found dead in Broadwell's Raleigh apartment and were believed to have been killed four days earlier.[2653] Their arms were extended above their bodies, and their wrists, hands, knees, and ankles were tightly bound with heavy silver duct tape, electrical cords, neckties, and scarves.[2654] Their heads and faces were completely wrapped, "mummy-style," with the same duct tape. "Collins was tied by his neck with [appliance[2655]] cords extending to a bed on one side and a door on the other."[2656] No weapons or blood were found at the crime scene.[2657] Broadwell's and Collins's causes of death were ruled as asphyxia due to being gagged and having their mouths and noses bound; Murray's cause of death was ruled as strangulation.[2658] Although the apartment had been completely ransacked, it was

hidden. This incident took place about forty-five miles southeast of Boone and only four months prior to the Durham murders. Another individual whose prints were compared to those in the Durham Case was Doyle Ray Henderson, a criminal associate of Billy Wayne Davis, who claimed to have information regarding the roles Davis and Billy Birt played in the Matthews murders. [Sources: Watauga County Sheriff's Office investigation file 118-H-1/2/3; "One-time crime 'kingpin' Dewitt Dawson dead at 58," The Anniston Star, Anniston, AL, September 9, 1997, p. 6A; "No Pleasure but Meanness: The Untold History of the Kingpin of Organized Crime in Alabama," January 6, 2018, https://snakeandtree.com/2018/01/06/no-pleasure-but-meanness-the-untold-history-of-the-kingpin-of-organized-crime-in-alabama/; Brad Willis, *Murder, etc.*, podcast audio, Episode 10: *Good Ol' Boys*. https://murderetcpodcast.com/episode-10-good-ol-boys/; North Carolina Reports, Volume 297, Supreme Court of North Carolina, Spring Term 1979, Raleigh, NC, 1979, State of North Carolina v. Forest Denzil McGuire, Alton Wayne Ruff, and Ronald Hal Wellman, No. 57, filed April 20, 1979, pp. 70-73; David Morrison & Joyce, Fay S., "Ex-DA Reports 'Confession' in Matthews Case," The Atlanta Constitution, Atlanta, GA, August 5, 1975, p. 12-A; Don Hicks, "Matthews Robbery Suspect Henderson Plans To Surrender," The Atlanta Constitution, Atlanta, GA, July 3, 1979, p. 2-C; Don Hicks, "Matthews Robbery Charge Dismissed," The Atlanta Constitution, Atlanta, GA, August 22, 1979, p. 4-C; David Morrison, "Debbie Spends 2 ½ Hours Before Cobb Grand Jury," The Atlanta Constitution, Atlanta, GA, January 23, 1976, p. 23-A.]

unclear if robbery was a motive.[2659] Broadwell wore a diamond ring that was not taken.[2660] All three victims were employees of Auto Bargains, Inc., a used car lot belonging to Murray's uncle.[2661]

Although seemingly unrelated cases, it is interesting to note some similarities between the Durham murders and the "Mummy Murders." Both were triple homicides that took place in North Carolina within a year's time. Victims in both cases consisted of two males and one female, and victims in both cases were employed in the used car business. The female victim in each case died strictly from strangulation. The Durham males had been strangled but ultimately died from the asphyxiation of drowning. The males in the Raleigh case died from the asphyxiation of having their mouths and noses wrapped in duct tape. Bryce Durham's body was found with a rope around his neck; Mike Collins's body was found with appliance cords around his neck. A diamond ring was not taken in the Raleigh case, and watches, rings, and a bank deposit bag containing money were not taken in the Durham Case. The residences in both cases were ransacked. A partial pair of glasses was found in the kitchen sink in the Raleigh case, and Bryce Durham's broken glasses were found in a hallway of his home. And, of course, finally, both cases were attributed to the Dixie Mafia, but consisting of different gang members.

Within a week of the Raleigh murders, newspaper headlines announced the Dixie Mafia was being blamed and investigated.[2662] North Carolina Attorney General Robert Morgan (who later was to head the SBI) told the press, "Everything I have seen indicates to me it is the work of the loosely knit organization we know as the Dixie Mafia," and stated, "he believed the killings might have resulted from a professional effort to kill Collins."[2663] Within months, this was reiterated by police, who said it "apparently was a Dixie Mafia contract killing."[2664] A dubious Raleigh detective said, "I wish someone would tell me what the Dixie Mafia is,"[2665] and an unidentified top official within Governor Jim Holshouser's administration said the press had been "played like a violin" by Morgan, stating, "If there's organized crime to the extent Morgan says there is, we've seen no evidence of it."[2666] Still, Morgan maintained that organized crime in the state was "fact, not fiction."[2667]

One Wilkes County, North Carolina native recalls "Dixie Mafia" being a familiar term in the county at the time of the Durham murders, although he believes it referred to criminals in Georgia and Alabama rather than North Carolina. He also recalls a notorious Wilkes County bootlegger approaching a Wilkesboro service station owner, seeking to have the Dixie Mafia murder someone for him.[2668] Some believe the Dixie Mafia had a historical existence inside of Wilkes County and that elements of it remain active there; at the very least, "a lot of bad dudes" are said to have run around there for years. As one native states, "They're a bunch of bad asses. They don't play games. They take people out. I believe that Wilkes Countians played a much larger role [in the Durham murders] than Georgians. I'm pretty sure of it. Very sure of it."[2669]

Could illegal liquor or drugs have played a role in the murders, particularly stemming from Wilkes County, North Carolina?

No place is completely devoid of crime, including the scenic Blue Ridge Mountains encompassing Watauga County, North Carolina. Although rare, Watauga has witnessed its share of brutal murders through the years, and eerily, some of its neighboring counties even have landmarks proven to be disposal sites for bodies, including "The Jumping Off Place," a 200-foot cliff near the Ashe and Wilkes county line, and the Ore Knob Mine shaft in Ashe County. But Wilkes County seems to have had its inordinate share of criminal activity, with some natives going so far as to deem it the most crooked county in the state.[2670] This home to both the Durham and Hall families has "an odd duality" and is the "juncture of criminality and civic pride," where both "flourish side by side, [and] where good and evil sometimes seem to walk hand-in-hand."[2671] This appears to stem, in part, from the interwoven relationships between individuals running the gamut from moonshiners, drug dealers, money launderers, and killers to civic and community leaders, church-goers, businessmen, political officeholders, and law enforcement officers. This is further complicated by a great deal of intermarriage between families – a common occurrence in the South – resulting in multiple blood-kin relationships, and it has likely been perpetuated and exacerbated by such phenomena as the transformation of formerly criminal moonshine runners into NASCAR legends and legal distillery tycoons who are celebrated as folk heroes. Over time, certain individuals with criminal pasts became community movers and shakers, whose charitable and developmental contributions to the county were lauded and also afforded them a particular insulation and "good ole boy" favor that looked the other way.

In earlier days, because of the widespread presence of stills and the large network of interrelated people who oversaw the distribution of illicit liquor up and down the eastern United States, Wilkes County was known as "the moonshine capital of the world."[ppppppppp] But by the 1980s, it had become a center for growing and smuggling marijuana, so much so that the street value of marijuana plants found in the county at one time surpassed "the combined value of three of the county's...top crops of apples, tobacco, and forest products."[2672] In 1980, the Wilkes County Sheriff's Department destroyed more than 200,000 marijuana plants, which were estimated to be only ten percent of the crop. As one newspaper noted, "The revenuers have left Wilkes County and the drug runners have taken their place."[2673] During this same era, several persons disappeared under mysterious circumstances, and Wilkes County's "reputation of harboring various kinds of lawbreaking" (e.g., white liquor, prostitution, and pills like Black Beauties and Yellow Jackets) led to "a federal task force" probing "possible public corruption...and widespread illegal activity involving public officials...including allegations of large-scale drug trafficking...."[2674]

Because at least some Wilkes County moonshiners migrated into drug trafficking, retired SBI Agent Larry Wagner, during his 1970s investigation of the Durham murders, believed (and continues to believe – as does retired Boone Police Sergeant Jeff Rucker) that whoever instigated the murders may have utilized a liquor or drug connection to set things in motion, and that there was participation in the murders from within Wilkes County. Decades later, when Bob Ingram acknowledged to Wagner that folks in north Georgia also manufactured liquor, Wagner thought perhaps Wilkes County, North Carolina liquor and north Georgia liquor was the connection – somebody from one locale knowing someone from the other. In fact, moonshiners from Alabama, Georgia, Tennessee,

---

[ppppppppp] Even relatives of Virginia Durham were known to have engaged in such activities, including her brother-in-law, George Bumgarner, who ran moonshine, and her sister, Sally, who is said to have bootlegged at one time or another. Virginia's cousin, Rom Church, was an early purveyor of illicit liquor in Wilkes County. In 1905, Church, "who [had] the reputation of being one of the 'slickest' vendors of moonshine whiskey in Western Carolina," traveled to Boone "with a load of blockade and was having a big frolic with about 75 people present when the sheriff took charge of him." Church was jailed in Boone and was also wanted in several cases in Wilkes County. He apparently continued in liquor trafficking for many years; in 1922 he was arrested for transporting thirteen gallons of whiskey. That same year he was caught with a load of liquor in Jefferson, NC and was simultaneously wanted in Wilkes County for violating the national prohibition act. [Sources: Edwards, Diana (Virginia Durham's great-niece). Phone interview with author. October 14, 2023; Genealogical research by author; *The Chronicle*, Wilkesboro, NC, 5/24/1905, p. 1; *The Union Republic*, Winston-Salem, NC, via the *Wilkesboro Chronicle*, 6/1/1905, p. 7; *Watauga Democrat*, Boone, NC, 5/25/1905, p. 3 & 8/10/1905, p. 3; "Unlucky Day For Church," *The Charlotte News*, Charlotte, NC, 1/28/1922, p. 10; *Carter's Weekly*, North Wilkesboro, NC, 2/16/1922, p. 2 & 4/13/1922, p. 5.]

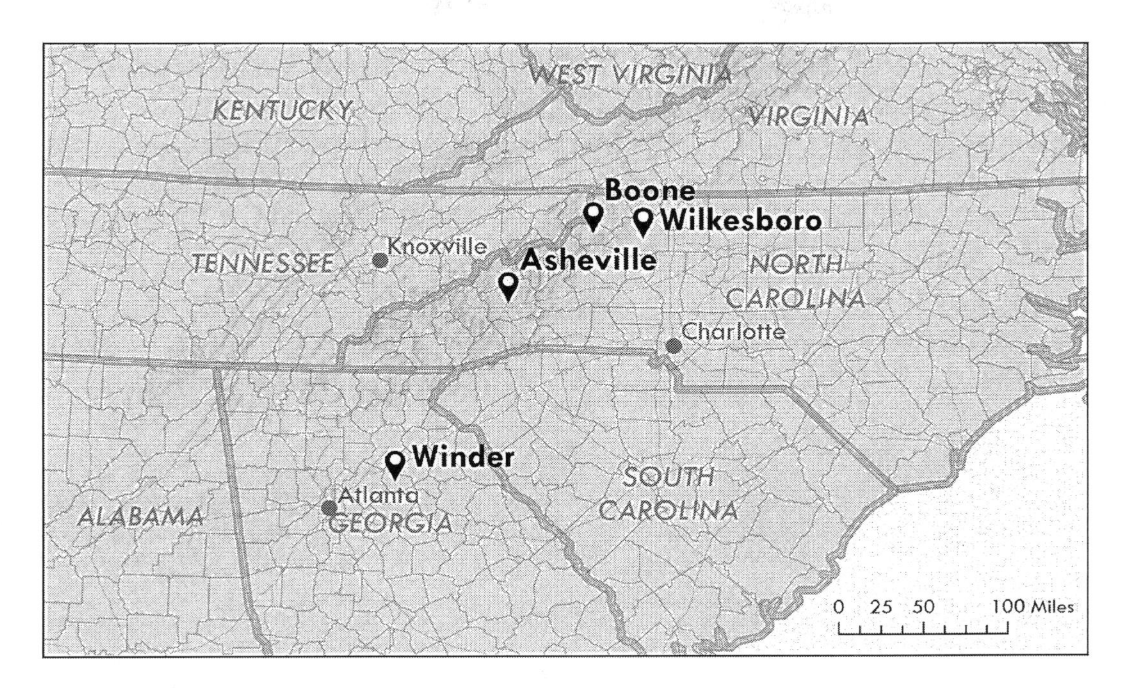

and North Carolina all peddled their wares throughout the Appalachian Mountains, overlapping and competing with one another in the same distribution locales. It makes sense to Wagner, but he concedes, "I can't answer that question and exactly what the connection was. We will never know."[2675]

Is there any physical evidence that substantiates the killers' identities?

With the exception of blood that was traced to Virginia Durham, there were no other bodily fluids found at the crime scene. Aside from latent finger and palm prints that could, perhaps, someday produce results, one of the few pieces (perhaps only piece) of physical evidence is the rope found around Bryce Durham's neck. The SBI was in possession of the rope for many years. In August 1981, the lead SBI agent, Steve Cabe, turned the rope over to SBI supervisor Charlie Whitman, who had seen the rope firsthand at the crime scene in 1972. Whitman had exclusive control of the rope until he gave it to SBI Assistant District Supervisor Dave Keller in November 1985. At some later date (perhaps December 18, 1996 – a date written on the evidence bag containing the rope), the SBI gave the rope to the Watauga County Sheriff's Office, and Sheriff Red Lyons passed it to Sheriff-elect Mark Shook on November 27, 2002. Although there was no signed transference or chain of custody documentation between Shook and present Sheriff Len Hagaman, the rope continues to be housed at the sheriff's office.[2676]

There may possibly be viable DNA on the rope. At one point in time, the SBI had informed the Watauga County Sheriff's Office that, if the rope had been submerged in water (which it had), the DNA would not be viable,[2677] but later on, former Guilford County, North Carolina Sheriff B. J. Barnes shared that his office had its own lab and a spectrometer that could process submerged DNA. Barnes was the Guilford County Sheriff for decades, and when he was not reelected in 2018, pursuit of the topic ceased.[2678] In March 2022, I presented Sheriff Hagaman with information regarding Parabon Nanolabs in Reston, Virginia as a possible resource for this analysis, particularly in light of their very successful employment of familial DNA and forensic genetic genealogy.[2679][qqqqqqqqq] This process consists of comparing an unknown suspect's DNA with the DNA of any possible relatives who may have uploaded their results to public genealogy DNA databases. While the existence of viable DNA after a fifty-year period may be a longshot, it would still be worth pursuing to know for sure. In July 2022, Hagaman attended the North Carolina Sheriff's Association Education Group in Asheville, North Carolina, where he planned to see SBI Director Bob Schurmeier and North Carolina State Crime Laboratory Director John Byrd, and to speak with Guilford County Sheriff Danny Rogers (Barnes's successor) about the capability of his crime lab to test the rope and if it would be a viable option.[2680] Rogers recommended Hagaman speak with Rogers' lab manager, and Hagaman traveled to Guilford County in August 2022 to once more explore the possibility of recovering submerged DNA.[2681] A special agent with the SBI subsequently directed Hagaman to High Point, North Carolina, but as of October 2022, no further progress had been made.[2682]

I previously shared with Sheriff Hagaman various DNA news articles, including one containing information regarding the preferability of recovering and testing the DNA "under the specific format required to do forensic genealogy research," including testing for as many markers as possible and expanding the pool of potential matches beyond just CODIS (the FBI's Combined DNA Index System) and into genealogy databases.[2683] As a member of the Investigative Genetic Genealogy (DNA Detectives) Facebook group, I posed the question to other members about the viability of fifty-year-old DNA that had been submerged in a bathtub of water for five to six hours and received the recommendation that the DNA be retrieved using the M-VAC system (a wet vacuum sampling device), which expands the potential of collecting DNA from porous and rough objects and surfaces, including rope and including items submerged in water. I subsequently shared this with Hagaman.[2684]

When I interviewed retired SBI Agent Sam Pennica (who had worked on fingerprint comparisons in the Durham Case and is now Director at the Raleigh/Wake City-County Bureau of Identification), he stated most North Carolina city/county/sheriff's office crime labs, with the exception of the Charlotte/Mecklenburg lab, do not have the capability of testing the rope to the necessary professional degree, and he recommended the rope be taken to the state crime lab in Raleigh.[2685] I shared this with Hagaman,[2686] and he said he would be glad to hand deliver the rope there the week of February 20, 2023.[2687] When I followed up with the sheriff in May 2023 to inquire if this had occurred, he stated that he was told the rope would likely have to be tested by an independent lab, something budgetarily prohibitive for the sheriff's office. When I inquired about the possibility of me personally paying for the test or raising the necessary funds, Hagaman stated he would first want to confirm if DNA could actually be extracted.[2688] Former SBI Agent Wade Colvard, who worked many cold cases during his career, says the state crime lab's willingness to test the rope may be influenced by the fact that the Durham Case has been declared closed and/or by its workload and current policies.[2689] Captain Carolynn Johnson echoes this, stating it is difficult to get the lab excited about a fifty-year-old case and that, even with active cases, lab results can take six to eight months.[2690]

[qqqqqqqqq] The author himself has nearly fifty years of genealogical experience, including having helped individuals identify their birth parents utilizing DNA in the very same fashion that forensic genealogists have used it to help solve cold cases.

During my January 2024 meeting with them, Hagaman and Johnson shared that the state crime lab has continued giving the Watauga County Sheriff's Office conflicting responses whether DNA could be extracted from evidence that has been submerged. Johnson says, "Until we have a clear cut [response that] the SBI can and will process it, then we don't think there's any point in sending it in…." While it seems no one from the sheriff's office is actively seeking that clarification from the lab, Johnson says it is difficult to get an answer from them, and that the sheriff's office is busy with other cases, which affects their ability to follow up, with lots of time lapses between attempts.[2691] *[Almost a year earlier, however, in March 2023, Hagaman stated in an e-mail to another individual, "Made inquiry with state lab about potential (got mixed response) of testing DNA from submerged ligature around Bryce Durham's neck. Lab finally agrees they* ***cannot*** *perform such a test."]*[2692]

Sam Pennica asked me if there were other items from the Durham Case that might be DNA tested. I told him about the missing silver, and I wondered aloud about the pillowcase that contained the silver – if it had been retained or was also missing – as well as the clothing the Durhams were wearing when murdered. Pennica stated that, if these items could be located, they could be tested for touch DNA.[2693] In 2009, Dana Way, a forensic chemist/medical investigator specializing in DNA contacted Captain Dee Dee Rominger with the Watauga County Sheriff's Office to inquire about the possibility of checking for DNA on the shirts of the deceased Durhams and to offer her assistance if any clothing could be located in evidence. According to retired SBI Agent Larry Wagner, in some instances, clothing might have been held for a period of time, but long-term storage, particularly of bloody clothing (which was minimal to none in the Durham Case), posed a problem due to biohazards (e.g., mold, etc.). The ability to test for touch DNA did not exist at the time of the Durham murders, and the most common processing in that era would have been the typing of blood.[2694]

When I asked Sheriff Hagaman about these items of evidence, he stated, "It's a shame that very little processing of evidence was done over the years." He again shared that the silver was still missing, and he did not have any knowledge of the Durhams' clothing but suggested I contact Special Agent in Charge Chris Laws in the SBI's Hickory, North Carolina district office.[2695] North Carolina General Statute 132-1.4 prohibits the SBI from discussing with the public a criminal investigation, whether active or inactive, open or closed, but Laws was able to explain to me the agency's processing of evidence. According to Laws, if a homicide occurred today and the SBI collected evidence in the case, it would turn that evidence over to the local agency with jurisdiction in the case probably that same day or week, or within a month or two at the most. Although Laws was not with the SBI in 1972 and cannot speak specifically as to what was practiced at that time, he said rapid turnover of evidence has been the guideline for many years. He added that the SBI does not hold evidence in homicide cases forever – even for three or four years – and the local agency with jurisdiction would have information whether all evidence had been transferred to them from the SBI. Concerning the Durham Case in particular, Laws stated, "We do not have any evidence regarding that case. That would have been transferred back to the sheriff's office at that time." However, Laws subsequently stated, "Something that's been since 1972, there is a high probability that the SBI possesses no evidence in something this old." Although Laws said he was speaking hypothetically and not specifically about the Durham Case, his statement of "high probability" seems to leave open at least some degree of possibility that evidence in the Durham Case could still be in the SBI's possession. When asked about the Durham silver, Laws stated, "I can tell you that all the evidence that we have, every item is tracked and accounted for many, many, many times over. Every piece or item we handle is tracked by a chain of custody document."[2696]

Former SBI Agent Wade Colvard states that, while the bureau's evidence policy has changed a lot through the years, its current record-keeping processes are "unbelievable." Like Laws, he thinks whatever evidence the SBI had regarding the Durham Case should have been returned to the Watauga County Sheriff's Office by this time. Colvard adds that evidence is sometimes inadvertently shifted around at the county level in between sheriffs' administrations,[2697] and in 2023, Sheriff Hagaman said there was a possibility a previous sheriff may have received the Durham silver from the SBI and disposed of it or returned it to someone. Hagaman also conceded at that time that the silver might still be locally located within a separate storage building on the sheriff's office campus, which would require another look,[2698] but in 2024, he said, "We know it ain't here."[2699]

I also contacted SBI Public Information Director Angie Grube to inquire about any pieces of physical evidence the SBI might be holding relative to the Durham Case, and I specifically mentioned the silver, the pillowcase, and the clothing.[2700] She responded saying, "We've checked and we do not have any items of evidence related to that investigation."[2701]

Was this destined to be a cold case?

Obviously, no one intended this to become a cold case, but there were several strikes against it from the beginning. The initial investigation of the triple homicide was, in part, a fatality of the era in which it transpired. Trained personnel, resources, and technology were lacking, and these shortfalls contributed to the challenges faced by succeeding generations of investigators. General investigative practices and overall education of law enforcement officers were not as developed at that time, and since then, there have been great advancements in forensic technology.

As of 1972, and still to a great extent today, crimes of this type and magnitude were unheard of in Watauga County and foreign to local law enforcement agencies, including both the Watauga County Sheriff's Office and the Boone Police Department. Officers were likely at a loss as to how best approach and secure the scene and collect evidence. According to Sheriff Len Hagaman, "It was sensational in Watauga County to have not one but three murders at the same time and as a family. I just think a lot of it was just over folks' heads."[2702] In Bob Ingram's assessment, "[While] there were clearly good people who investigated the Durham Case…there were others who were flying by the seat of their pants."[2703]

Regrettably, no one kept a log to record visitors to the crime scene. It was later determined more than one-hundred individuals (one source says two-hundred and another three-hundred, although those figures seem high) passed through the Durham home that night.[2704] According to Hagaman, "a lot of people…went through the scene,"[2705] and he recalls a random encounter with a gentleman in another county who said he had been in the house at some point (although perhaps not the night of the murders), because "he had nothing better to do."[2706] An online forum poster recalled in 2002 that their father and grandfather, friends of the Durhams, went to the scene that night and did not return until the following morning. Although they did not state these men had entered the house or that they spent the entire time away from home at the scene, the fact that they said it was a scene they would not soon forget implies they may have entered the house and seen the bodies,[2707] as did many people that night. Even the girlfriend of a responding SBI agent called to the murder scene stated she accompanied him and entered the house that night.[2708][rrrrrrrr]

Without a doubt, the crime scene was insufficiently secured to preserve and maximize the integrity of evidence, and excessive foot traffic, as well as indiscriminate handling and touching of items and the alleged moving around of the victims' limbs and/or bodies may have undermined those efforts. Many years after the murders, "state investigators...remarked that the number of officers present could have altered the crime scene."[2709]

When SBI Agent John Parker arrived a day or two after the murders, his initial impression was that the crime scene had not been preserved at all, and the fact that dozens of people had tramped in and out of the house made it difficult to gather evidence.[2710] According to Sheriff Hagaman, "The crime scene was a total disaster as 80+ fingerprints had to be eliminated; the then Sheriff [Ward Carroll] had gobs of people going through the house. It was a CIS [sic; CSI] nightmare."[2711]

Ginny Durham complained officers had done a really sloppy job handling the crime scene, with spectators running in and out like it was a museum.[2712] Durham neighbor Dean Combs stated he had never seen so much traffic in and out of a place: "Everybody and his brother in the community went in there."[2713] Rufus Edmisten stated, "Several people were in that house.... They messed up the evidence. They were going through that house like it was an exhibit hall. It was just a terrible crime scene to try to work with, and I'm not blaming that on anybody except there were too many people in that house."[2714] Edmisten would reiterate this decades later: "The crime scene was like something out of Lum and Abner or The Three Stooges with how that got messed up.... Back in those days it was sort of wild west in law enforcement; it was just a bungled crime scene. They moved things around; they tromped all over the place. If you went about it with all today's stuff, you would have preserved a lot more evidence. From what I've been told, it was just a mammoth screw-up at the crime scene. Everybody was just tromping around...."[2715]

SBI Agent Larry Wagner echoed this: "The reason that the case is unsolved is that the original crime scene was totally destroyed.... Too many people [were allowed] to go into the house. There were numerous fingerprints we couldn't identify. Some of them may have been from the murderers; some were from people who had no business there. No effort to preserve evidence.... The crime scene was a mess. I am convinced that critical evidence was destroyed."[2716] Sheriff Hagaman is of the same opinion: "It was probably one of the worst handled crime scenes that's ever existed.... It's frustrating to know it could have been handled differently, but it is what it is. It was just so screwed up. It was a different time.... A lot of doors got closed."[2717]

"By their own admission, law enforcement did not do the best job preserving forensic evidence since a number of people went through the crime scene that night."[2718] The scene was disastrously processed with such a high rate of contamination, it was a wonder any useful evidence was obtained. According to former Watauga County Chief Deputy Paula May, it was a classic example of how not to work a crime scene.[2719] Former Sheriff Ward Carroll admitted in later years he would have handled things differently. "Too many people were trying to solve the case. It was the worst case in

---

[rrrrrrrr] This girlfriend, who later became this agent's wife, contradictorily stated in an earlier interview that she only learned of the Durham murders when someone at work told her the following day. [Source: Whitman, Pat. Interview with Carolynn Johnson & Wade Colvard. July 17, 2019. Handwritten notes of Watauga County Sheriff's Office Capt. Carolynn Johnson.]

the history of Watauga County, perhaps all of North Carolina. We wanted to solve it. We tried too hard. Today, I would restrict the people working on the case."[2720]

It was not uncommon for crime scenes in that era to be poorly contained, and, although the SBI's first training academy was conducted in 1969, it was not until 1972 (the year of the murders) that the State of North Carolina mandated a law enforcement officer to have a minimum amount of basic training, which consisted of one-hundred and sixty hours.[2721]

Ten months before the murders, it had been noted more Boone policemen were needed, the current force was overworked and underpaid, and the annual turnover was 100%.[2722] Six months before the murders, the Boone Police Department was staffed by its chief, five officers, one meter maid, two radio dispatchers, and two radio-equipped cars.[2723] Only two weeks before the murders, the Northwest Planning Council for Crime Deterrence announced the sheriffs' offices throughout the Northwest Planning Region, including Watauga County, were "understaffed, underpaid, undertrained, and underequipped." The problem areas identified by the council were "the shortage of financial allocations; the absence of record keeping; the shortage of manpower; the antiquity of communication equipment; [and] the lack of proper training." The council stated, "There exists a very inadequate, ineffective, and inefficient level of law enforcement within the northwest region." Among those on the Regional Policy Board at that time were Boone Police Chief Clyde Tester and Watauga County Sheriff Ward Carroll.[2724]

Jerry Vaughn was hired as a Boone policeman two months following the Durham murders, and the Boone Police Department was still sorely lacking in resources and manpower. Vaughn recalled their small office space in downtown Boone, the chief's desk being positioned in a hallway, and a toilet at the end of the corridor serving as their interrogation room, officers resting their feet on the toilet bowl as they took notes, utilizing the toilet tank as a makeshift desk. He also remembered there being only one file cabinet in the department. Two drawers held relic gas masks, one held a box of empty file folders, and another held about eight active case files. Telecommunications were rudimentary, and Vaughn, with the assistance of locally based SBI Agent Wally Hardwick, Jr., was able to implement better radio protocols. Vaughn, who had prior training from the police department in Winston-Salem, North Carolina, also helped establish a better filing system.[2725]

Although perhaps hard to imagine, Vaughn recalled the Watauga County Sheriff's Department was in even more dire straits.[2726] While running for sheriff, one of Ward Carroll's campaign promises had been "to upgrade and improve the Sheriff's Department." In 1970-1971, the sheriff had two full-time deputies, one car, and despite Carroll's claim that "he and his men [were] 'properly trained' for the job," his department actually had little or no training, poor communications and a 'very bad' problem of crimes of breaking and entering." The department served "all areas outside the corporate limits of Boone and Blowing Rock with protection services, and in so doing [had] an enormous area of service as compared to the personnel available to render this service." By May 1972, the department had "six full-time officers," Carroll had "received some 300 hours of police science training and all his deputies [had] received training." The department was "a part of a half-a-million-dollar communication system," and Carroll was planning for additional upgrades.[2727]

In addition to the lack of resources and manpower, there unfortunately seems to be many instances in which evidence for this unsolved triple homicide was either not retained or is unaccounted for, including the alleged disappearance of case files between the administrations of sheriffs Ward Carroll and Red Lyons, the missing silver, the Durhams' clothing (if ever retained), and the absence of certain photographs, such as ones of the silver (if they even existed). One must concede, however, that, just because there appears to be gaps or absent information or a lack of follow-up on particular leads within the Watauga County Sheriff's Office Durham Case file, it does not mean those elements do not exist at all. In fact, the much more extensive SBI files likely contain a lot of what is undiscovered within the sheriff's office. For example, the Watauga County file contains no interviews with crime scene photographer George Flowers, but retired SBI Agent Larry Wagner confirms the SBI spoke with Flowers a few times, and the SBI files contain one of the interviews with Flowers that Wagner personally wrote up.[2728]

Was Troy Hall a psychopath?

From the time he was a boy, Troy seems to have exhibited a dichotomous personality. While, on occasion, he could be outgoing, good-humored, and charming, he could, at other times, seem cold with eyes that looked soulless. A Greenway Trailer Park neighbor said Troy was "not quite right,"[2729] and Rufus Edmisten described him as "a strange bird."[2730] Ted Brown, who grew up in the Fairplains community of Wilkes County and attended Fairplains Elementary School with Troy, looked up to Troy because he was mature, bright, and different. One Saturday morning, when Brown was around six years old, he went to play with Troy. When he entered the Halls' basement home, which was located beneath an old country store, he saw Troy sitting affixed to a chair, steadily staring straight ahead, never speaking, never making eye contact, and never acknowledging Brown's presence. Meanwhile, Troy's mother lurked in the background, down a dark hallway, peering at them. Feeling uncomfortable and unwelcomed, Brown cut his visit short.[2731] In Brown's opinion, Troy's brain processed things inordinately, and he believes there to be only "a hair's difference" between him and Ted Bundy (a renowned psychopath).[2732] Ginny Durham told the SBI and forensic psychologist Richard Walter that Troy fit the profile of someone with a psychopathic personality.[2733]

Following are traits associated with psychopathy,[2734] each of which Troy seems to have exhibited:

- Superficial Charm – Psychopaths are often likable on the surface. They are good conversationalists, share stories that make them look good, and may be funny and charismatic. *[Troy was known to have shared false information about himself that cast himself in a favorable light.]*

- Need for Stimulation – Psychopaths love excitement and having constant action in their lives, and they frequently want to live in the "fast lane." Quite often, they break rules and may enjoy the thrill of getting away with something or the fact that they might get caught at any moment. *[Troy was known to have researched and commented on getting away with the perfect crime and staying ahead of the SBI.]*

- Pathological Lying – Psychopaths tell lies to look good or to get out of trouble and will tell lies to cover up previous lies. They have difficulty keeping their stories straight as they sometimes forget what they have said. If challenged, they simply change their story or rework the facts to fit the situation. *[When Troy first met Ginny Durham's extended family, he lied about having a wealthy father and attending military school. Troy's friend "Babes" Lowe actually did have a wealthy father and actually had attended military school prior to entering Appalachian State University at Troy's invitation. While at ASU, Lowe claimed to have supported Troy monetarily and paid some of his tuition, although Troy reportedly had a college foundation loan. In fact, Lowe had paid Troy to take the SAT on his behalf.*[2735]

According to Lowe, Troy was very jealous of him because Lowe had money and Troy did not but wanted to.[2736] *It appears Troy may have partially assumed Lowe's persona as his own when presenting himself to Ginny's family. After the murders, when investigators asked him questions regarding subjects he had been previously interrogated about, Troy told them he would have to check his notes to see what he had previously stated. As a former Boone policeman stated, Troy was a pretty sharp boy but also pretty slick. "You couldn't believe anything he told you, really."*[2737]*]*

- Grandiose Sense of Self-Worth – Psychopaths have an inflated view of themselves and see themselves as important and entitled. They often feel justified to live according to their own rules, and they think that laws don't apply to them. *[Troy became angry when his father-in-law would not give him and Ginny a car, and he told Bryce he owed it to them...that it was due them. Following the murders, Troy immediately saw himself as the beneficiary to his in-laws' estates and as the new leader of the family's automobile dealership.]*

- Manipulative – Psychopaths are really good at getting other people to do what they want. They may play on a person's guilt while lying to get someone else to do their work for them. *[Troy's sister-in-law at the time, Kay Hall, said if Troy planned the murders, he "would let someone else do his dirty work." Troy also exhibited dishonesty by asking others to lie on his behalf in legal proceedings.*[2738]*]*

- Lack of Remorse and Empathy– Psychopaths do not care how their behavior affects other people, and they ultimately don't experience any guilt for causing people pain. In fact, they often rationalize their behavior and blame other people. They are completely indifferent to people who are suffering, even when it is a close friend or family member. *[The morning following the murders, Troy's behavior at the car dealership, rifling through files, breaking into Virginia's desk, and kicking her high-heeled shoes across the showroom certainly do not align with the expected demeanor of someone whose in-laws had been brutally murdered only hours before, regardless of personal difficulties with them.]*

- Shallow Affect – Psychopaths do not show many emotions – at least not genuine ones. They may appear cold and unemotional much of the time, but when it serves them well, they might exhibit a dramatic display of feelings. These are usually short-lived and quite shallow. *[This may explain Troy's demeanor and flat affect during Ted Brown's childhood visit.]*

- Parasitic Lifestyle – Psychopaths take advantage of the kindness of others by depending on them financially. They use people to get whatever they can with no regard for how a person may feel. *[Troy reportedly relied at times on his friend "Babes" Lowe to pay his college tuition, and Troy certainly sponged off of his in-laws when given the opportunity. At least some, and perhaps many, of his relationships were based on what was in it for him.]*

- Poor Behavioral Controls – Psychopaths struggle to follow rules, laws, and policies much of the time. *[Troy certainly did not like restrictions placed upon him by his in-laws and would lash out both behaviorally and verbally. In Georgia, as "Justin" Hall, he continually pushed boundaries governing the DUI and defensive driving school industry.]*

- Promiscuous Sexual Behavior – Since they do not care about the people around them, psychopaths are likely to cheat on their partners. They may engage in unprotected sex with strangers, or they may use sex as a way to get what they want. Sex is not an emotional or loving act. *[Troy was consistently unfaithful to his wives, participated in and promoted the use of pornography, was rough – perhaps even abusive – in at least one of his extramarital sexual relationships, and allegedly had multiple sexual encounters.]*

- Irresponsibility – Promises don't mean anything to psychopaths, and they are not trustworthy. They also don't accept responsibility for the problems in their lives. They see their issues as always being someone else's fault. *[During Troy's extremely litigious divorce from his last wife, he was suspected of hiding or transferring assets out of his name to avoid court-ordered alimony and child support, and he offered multiple excuses for his inability to pay.]*

- Many Marital Relationships – Psychopaths may get married because it serves them well (e.g., they may want to spend their partner's income). But their behavior often leads to frequent divorces. *[Troy was married and divorced at least three times. One motivation behind his first marriage may have been to gain control of and spend Ginny's inheritance. Money and other assets were points of contention in each of his three known divorce proceedings.]*

- Criminal Versatility – Psychopaths tend to view rules as suggestions, and they usually view laws as restrictions that hold them back. Their criminal behaviors can be quite varied and can include acts of violence. Some may operate under shady businesses or engage in unethical practices that do not lead to an arrest. *[Although seemingly never arrested, Troy reportedly dealt in drugs and stolen goods and participated in arson-related insurance fraud and sexually related blackmailing.]*

Is it possible Troy Hall is still alive?

This is a question asked by some and a theory adhered to by others. One man even asked me to look him in the eyes, giving him my full attention, as he soberly expressed his belief that Troy Hall is living.[2739] Although mass surveillance and technological advancements like facial recognition tools are making faked deaths increasingly difficult, they are not impossible. Known as a staged death or pseudocide, faking one's death (which is statistically more common among males) is not necessarily illegal unless activities like insurance fraud or evading the law are involved.[2740]

Steven Rambam is a renowned private investigator who heads up Pallorium, Inc., based in Brooklyn, New York with worldwide offices and affiliates. According to Rambam, who specializes in locating missing people and has solved approximately 800 suspected fake death cases over the course of his 40+ year career,[2741] "A lot of people believe that people who faked their deaths are dummies. And that's just not true. Faking your death is a full-time job. If you fake your own death, you have to maintain your [new] identity and lifestyle perfectly. You cannot make one mistake." He adds that "people who plan thoroughly from the very beginning are the best at it."[2742] If Troy really did, during any of his divorces, fraudulently transfer his marital and separate individual assets to other persons for the purpose of avoiding equitable division of property and alimony expenses, and if he really was reduced to an income consisting only of Social Security disability payments, perhaps that eliminated the need for a will or an estate settlement, the absence of which could be indicative of a faked death. If he did not die and the multimillion-dollar life insurance policies he maintained for the support of his son paid out as planned, that would constitute insurance fraud.

Troy Hall was no dummy. Many who have known him speak of his high degree of intelligence. He was also remembered for always looking for the best way to get something done, which is indicative of his being a planner. If he was involved in his in-laws' murders and was the intermediary who provided information and helped lay out the plans for the crime, then he was certainly cunning enough to fake his own death. If he truly did get away with murder for the past 50+ years, perhaps he is continuing to do so under the guise of an alternate identity.

It is curious the Watauga County Sheriff's Office received information from Georgia about the involvement of a nephew or son-in-law in May 2019, and Troy died around six months later. Could Troy have learned there was new information that might link him to the case? Was he aware investigators desired to question him again? Did he then set a plan in motion to disappear and fake his death before they could reach him?

Troy's death certificate, which names him as "Troy Justin Hall," social security #240-88-9666, indicates he suffered a heart attack on Thursday morning, December 19, 2019 and within hours was dead on arrival at 9:00 AM at Gwinnett Medical Center in Duluth, Georgia where he was pronounced dead by Dr. Donald Chapman, an Emergency Medicine physician who was likely on call in the emergency room. Troy's personal and biographical information on the death certificate was provided by his brother Ray, and Troy's obituary reads as follows:

On December 19, 2019, Justin T. Hall, loving father of Grant Tristin Hall, passed away at the age of 68.

Justin was born on November 8, 1951, in North Wilkesboro, North Carolina to Robert and Carrie Waddell Hall. He received his law degree and practiced law for over 30 years. His life revolved around his young son Grant. Justin was an avid lover of history and was known for his quick wit and unparalleled business sense. Justin was loyal to those he loved and had an infectious smile and spirit that will be remembered by all who were fortunate enough to know him.

Justin was preceded in death by his parents, his brothers, Roy and Claude and his sister, Lois Hall Sebastian.

He is survived by the light of his life, his son, Grant Tristin Hall; sister, Dorothy Hall Jones and her husband Morris; brothers, John Hall, Ray and his wife Josey Hall; many nieces and nephews.

A viewing will be held Sunday, December 29th, beginning at 1:00 pm, with a service to follow at 3:00 pm, at Bill Head Funeral Home, Duluth Chapel, 3088 Highway 120, Duluth, Georgia 30096.

In lieu of flowers, donations can be made in the honor of Justin's son, Grant Hall, to his school, Notre Dame Academy, 4635 River Green Parkway, Duluth, GA 30096.

Arrangements by Bill Head Funeral Homes and Crematory, Duluth Chapel, (770) 476-2535.[2743]

The online "tribute wall" associated with the obituary contains an entry from a couple who remembered "Justin" as "truly an extraordinary and generous person much loved…."[2744] This was in sharp contrast to the reaction of former North Carolina Attorney General and Secretary of State

Rufus Edmisten: "When I read his obituary, I almost gagged at what a kind and gentle man he was. Oh yeah, absolutely, I almost vomited."[2745]

It is interesting to note the viewing was held ten days after Troy's death, which seems to be an atypically long period of time. The day after his funeral, he was cremated by Stephen M. Wimmer at Bill Head Funeral Home and Crematory on Lawrenceville Highway in Lilburn, Georgia. On January 2, 2020, Troy's death was certified by Dr. Randy B. Cronic, a family physician in Duluth. Curiously, Troy's photograph accompanying his obituary was either added or revised on February 5, 2020, more than a month after his funeral.[2746]

Although the most popular method of "fake dying" is drowning and being "washed out to sea," which makes the absence of a body plausible,[2747] Troy's hypothetical choice to fake his sudden death via heart attack would still be preferable to a lengthy illness that might have required hospitalization or extended care or medical attention. *[Certainly, however, Troy's divorce records indicate a whole slew of ailments he suffered from over an extended period of time as well as the medications he was taking to treat them.]* Under the circumstances portrayed by Troy's death certificate, a body was seen and pronounced dead. But was it actually his body? "Securing a body to stand in for one's own seems like an impossible burden to law-abiding citizens," but according to Steven Rambam, "It's ridiculously easy to get a dead body in a lot of places."[2748] He has "worked many cases where people have bought bodies from a crooked morgue or even had someone killed to make their pseudocide more convincing. In one, the body of a supposedly dead woman was checked and signed off on after an autopsy by both a coroner and a police officer…but it turned out the body they'd placed in the coffin for the funeral – which was attended by 200 mourners – didn't match her features or bodily proportions at all. In another, Rambam's target had a homeless man shot in the face five times to obscure his features. Then, he had his wallet placed in the man's pocket to make it seem it was him who had been shot, and even paid a coroner to fingerprint him and say the prints belonged to the man he'd killed. [Although] a body can easily be identified by fingerprints or dental records…the only way to obscure the identity of a body [and to prevent its exhumation] is to cremate it," but that won't work in a situation involving insurance fraud where the actual body of the insured had to be produced rather than ashes.[2749]

Could it be that someone else's body was delivered to the hospital under Troy's name and seen by a hospital staff and attending ER physician who had no prior knowledge of him or what he looked like? Was a photo ID required to match the body with an identity? If so, could a fake ID have been generated using Troy's name and a picture matching or approximating the appearance of the body brought to the hospital? Was the body subsequently transported to a funeral home where Troy was also unknown to the staff?

The fact that Troy's obituary states "a viewing" was held, which typically implies the body of the deceased is in an open casket and on display for viewing by mourners and those paying their respects, might thwart a faked death theory unless the casket was closed. If the casket was indeed closed, it could have contained the body of an unknown person or no body at all. Was Dr. Randy Cronic Troy's personal physician? If so, he obviously would have been able to recognize Troy, but since he medically certified the death three days after the body was cremated, does that mean he never saw the body?

Short of a scenario in which Troy's body was unseen by those who would have recognized him, and a stranger's substitutionary body was seen by those who did not know Troy, the only other possibility for a successful pseudocide would likely require payoffs of unscrupulous medical and funeral home personnel to fake his death certificate and cremation. Despite his denial of assets during his last divorce proceeding, Troy likely had the financial resources needed for such payoffs, but there is nothing to indicate any of the individuals or facilities named in connection to Troy's death and his funeral and cremation arrangements were less than above board.

According to Steven Rambam, there may be red flags in Troy's history that point to his involvement in the Durham murders, but on the surface, the details provided on his death certificate do not lean heavily toward a faked death. Still, in the absence of an actual investigation, Rambam says anything is possible, and that is what keeps him involved in such cases.[2750]

Could Troy Hall still be alive, possibly living under a new name, even in another country such as Micronesia where he reportedly spent time in days past? Perhaps a search of passport records might yield information, but according to the Watauga County Sheriff's Office, no such investigation has ever been launched to their knowledge.[2751]

Playing on the words of the coroner in *The Wizard of Oz*, Troy may not only be merely dead, but really most sincerely dead. At a DUI driving school industry conference, one of Troy's former employees informed another that Troy was sick and dying.[2752] According to Sheriff Len Hagaman, when Wilkes County Sheriff Chris Shew[sssssssss] spotted Troy at his [Troy's] sister Lois's 2012 funeral, Shew thought "he looked like death warmed over."[2753] But considering the man in question, until time transcends a reasonable, or perhaps even an extraordinary life expectancy for someone born in 1951, there may remain a sliver of doubt.

[sssssssss] Shew's wife, Janet Hall Shew, is Troy Hall's niece, the daughter of Troy's brother Claude Hall.

Appendix 2

The House on the Hill

The Durham family's former home still stands on the outskirts of Boone, North Carolina atop the hill that is the apex of Clyde Townsend Road. I have passed by it well over 10,000 times[tttttttt] throughout my life, and while there are moments I give it little thought, more often than not, my eyes are drawn to it, and I wonder about the horror that took place within its walls – the murders of Bryce and Virginia Durham and their son Bobby, which resulted in the permanent labeling of their house so that it evokes their family name no matter who has succeeded them as its inhabitants. Those of us living in the county in February 1972 have since known this residence as "the Durham house" with its weighty shroud of mystery and unanswered questions.[uuuuuuuuu]

Construction of this four-bedroom house began in August 1967. It was designed by builder Clyde Townsend, who was the eventual namesake for the road on which the house stands. The split-level architecture reflects the era in which it was built, and the exterior is a mix of brick and siding. Townsend salvaged 30,000 bricks from Watauga County's third courthouse, which was erected in 1904 and razed in 1967.[2754] The Durham family began its brief residency in the house in late 1970.[2755] In light of the brutal slayings that followed just over a year later, there is irony in the realization that the house is partially clad in remnants from a hall of justice, yet justice has never been meted out for the transgressions wrought against its most notorious occupants.

1967 construction of what would become the Durham home. (As published in the Watauga Democrat)

The Durhams resided in their Boone home prior to the days of house numbers. Before circa 1997, the road leading to the house never had a name but was merely part of a rural mail delivery route. At the time of the murders, the house was simply located at Route 3, Boone.[2756] Years would pass before the emergency 911 system would necessitate more specific identification. Eventually the house was numbered as 187 Clyde Townsend Road. Eerily, "187" is the number denoting the crime of murder in California's penal code and has been used as a slang term for murder by gangs and those within the hip-hop and rap communities in other parts of the United States and the world.[2757]

On October 3, 1972, exactly eight months to the day after the Durhams were killed, Troy and Ginny Durham Hall sold the house to Donald Joseph Kidder and his wife, Geraldine T. Kidder, for

---

[tttttttt] This is not hyperbole but based on actual calculations.

[uuuuuuuuu] Ironically, Johnny Tester, the Boone Police Department dispatcher who received the call about the murders from Troy Hall on the night of February 3, 1972, now lives in a house directly behind the former Durham home.

The house circa 1970 when occupied by Butch & Sarah Wilcox, not long before it was sold to the Durham family. (Courtesy of Sarah Wilcox)

$27,000. At the time the Kidders purchased the house, the county assessor valued it at more than $40,000, but the events that had occurred there affected the sales price.[2758] Understandably, buyers had qualms about purchasing a "murder house," and one neighbor expressed doubt it would ever be sold.[2759]

The Kidders and their four children moved into the house, and Mr. Kidder, a construction supervisor and expert carpenter, refinished the basement. On occasion, when her children were outside of the house, Mrs. Kidder would show visitors the bathroom where the Durhams' bodies were discovered; she had removed a leftover blood stain from the bathtub using oven cleaner. Mrs. Kidder recalled that, during her first night in the home, she had a nightmare and thought she heard Bobby Durham calling, but after that incident, she had no similar experiences.[2760]

The Kidders owned the home until late 1974, when it was foreclosed on by a mortgage company, which auctioned it to another.[2761] On the day of the Kidders' departure, a fire occurred on the first floor of the house, but Clyde Townsend noticed and reported it, and the fire department was able to extinguish it before it resulted in much more than smoke damage.[2762] The fire appeared to have been deliberately set in the center of the floor of the den – the same room in which the Durhams are believed to have been attacked on the night of their murders, and the room in which blood had been found on the carpet and a bullet hole in the wall. There were no electrical wires at that spot and no apparent reason for a fire to have started there other than arson, and there was talk of insurance fraud. Plumber Billy Harmon and his brother Tommy were hired to replace plastic pipes that had melted, and Kent Adams, who owned a local building supply, was brought in to replace the cabinets in the laundry area between the den and the kitchen, the cabinets' finish having been marred by the heat of the fire.[2763]

After the damaged areas had been remodeled, the house was sold to Robert M. Rogers and his wife, Clarice Lillian Rogers, in 1976.[2764] They, in turn, sold the house in 1978 to Gary and Donna Townsend Cook[2765] (son-in-law and daughter of the home's original builder and occupant Clyde Townsend), and the Cooks sold it in 2002 to Christopher and Karen Coffey Wood,[2766] who had been leasing it with an option to purchase since 1997. The house had been on the market for a long time, and the Woods got a good deal on it because of the continuing stigma of it being the scene of not just one, but three homicides. The first night the Woods spent in the house was an anniversary of the murders.[2767] But as Karen's father, Harold Coffey,[vvvvvvvvvv] encouragingly reminded her when she bought the property, "the house didn't kill anybody."

A Boone native, Karen Coffey (having resumed her maiden name) has lived there ever since, and although she has made changes to the house, the original downstairs bathroom where the deceased

[vvvvvvvvvv] The Durhams frequently patronized the Hilltop Drive-In, a locally popular eating establishment not quite a mile from their home, and Harold Coffey was the proprietor.

Durhams were discovered remains mostly untouched. While the toilet and sink have been replaced, the same lavender tile is on the walls, and the same bathtub in which the Durhams were placed by their killers is still in use. While some might find living in the house unimaginable considering what transpired there, Karen does not mind, although she and her children have had what might be described as paranormal experiences within the house. She believes the house is inhabited by the ghosts of the Durhams, but in a non-threatening way.[2768]

For its age, the house naturally has some creaks, but Karen says while sitting in the den, she has heard footsteps in the master bedroom above or running up and down the staircase. She has also felt a presence of sorts in her bedroom and sometimes lying next to her. At various times, her dog barked at the bathroom, picture frames fell, and a television and stereo turned on and changed channels and volume by themselves. During their childhoods, her son and daughter saw apparitions – sometimes in the form of a man standing downstairs in what was formerly Bobby Durham's bedroom across from the bathroom or in the form of a woman with an undiscernible face, dressed in white, sitting on the living room couch looking at the clock and fireplace.[2769] Karen saw the same woman's form standing by her bedside early one morning.[2770] On one occasion, her son "said that a boot was hurled down the stairs…when he was home alone." Although Karen admits some of these goings on are creepy, she would affirm and reassure her children by telling them the ghosts meant no harm. "I'm not afraid of them. I don't feel like it's a scary presence. I do feel something. I believe there are spirits that are lost."[2771]

Accustomed to these spectral occurrences, Karen is equally accustomed to inquiries about her home.[2772] Curiosity about the house began within days of the murders when traffic on the 105 Bypass increased due to "gawkers" driving by to see it.[2773] Approximately two months later, on one particular Sunday alone, a neighbor reported that the occupants of about twenty-five cars had stopped to look at the uninhabited and curtained house.[2774] The fascination continues today, although in much more occasional and isolated instances. According to Karen, "It happens sometimes; people are so intrigued over this place."[2775] Among the curious have been journalists and authors and even college students who were compiling a paper on the murders and requested to walk through the house step by step in hopes of somehow solving the case.[2776]

The house is relatively unchanged in outward appearance, and though it is more veiled in summertime by trees and other thick foliage that has grown up in the past half century, it is still visible from the 105 Bypass. And while the dwelling remains, Bryce, Virginia, and Bobby Durham are gone, and perhaps those who killed them are dead as well. If so, the house is the last surviving witness to the events of that horrible night.

If walls could talk indeed.

"The Durham House" – Spring 2022
(Photos by author)

(Photos by author – December 2023)

Then & Now – 1972 (above) & 2023 (below)
(Top photo courtesy of Watauga County Sheriff's Office; bottom photo by author)

ENDNOTES

[1] Greer, Justin. Text to author. February 8, 2022; "Local triple homicide case solved after 50 years," *Watauga Democrat*, Boone, NC, February 8, 2022. https://www.wataugademocrat.com/news/local/local-triple-homicide-case-solved-after-50-years/article_d9e9302b-b771-5bf3-bf30-11b161257c89.html.
[2] Maps created with Esri's ArcGIS Pro software; Layer credits: Esri, OpenStreetMap, NC OneMap (CGIA), USGS.
[3] Tester, Johnny. In-person conversation with author. March 6, 2022.
[4] Tester, Johnny. Phone conversation with author. October 16, 2022.
[5] "Jailed After Body of Boone Woman Found In Coal Bin," *Watauga Democrat*, Boone, NC, December 4, 1969, p. 1; North Carolina death certificates, 1969, No. 40779.
[6] Ron Alridge, "Boone Baffled: Murder Victims 'Marvelous People,'" *The Charlotte Observer*, Charlotte, NC, February 6, 1972, p. B1.
[7] Gary Greene, "No Motive Found In Boone Deaths," *Bristol Herald Courier*, Bristol, VA-TN, February 6, 1972, p. 1.
[8] "Bodies of family found in tub," *The Sun-Herald*, Sydney, Australia, February 6, 1972, p. 19.
[9] Bev Ballard, "3 Murder Suspects Jailed," *Watauga Democrat*, Boone, NC, April 27, 1972, p. 14A.
[10] "Neighborhood uneasy: Search continues for three suspects in Boone murders," *The Sunday Star-News*, Wilmington, NC, February 6, 1972, p. 1.
[11] Robert B. Cullen, "Boone Stranglings Still A Mystery To SBI, Sheriffs," *Durham Morning Herald*, Durham, NC, July 2, 1973, p. 1B.
[12] "Who killed the Durham family? Here's my story," gowilkes.com, August 11, 2010, posted by "asku." gowilkes.com/voice/who-killed-the-durham-family-heres-my-story/77993/?startview=200&h=094028.
[13] Jay Ettman, "Wildest Day in Daniel Boone Country," *Front Page Detective Magazine*, October 1972, p. 48.
[14] "Who killed the Durham family? Here's my story," gowilkes.com, August 11, 2010, posted by "Maco4." gowilkes.com/voice/who-killed-the-durham-family-heres-my-story/77993/?startview=200&h=094028.
[15] Oliver, Lottie (niece of Lois Thomas). Facebook message to author. May 22, 2023.
[16] Edmisten, Rufus. The Weather Channel's *Storm of Suspicion*, Season 4, Episode 19: "Triple Torment," May 30, 2023.
[17] Rucker, Jeff. Phone interview with author. October 4, 2023.
[18] Bev Ballard, "In Durham Family Slaying: 3 Murder Suspects Jailed," *Watauga Democrat*, Boone, NC, April 27, 1972, p. 1A; "June 4 In Boone: Triple-Murder Suspect's Trial Set," *The Charlotte Observer*, Charlotte, NC, May 18, 1973, p. 1B.
[19] "Murder Investigations Take Time: Break-Ins Wane In County, Sheriff Says; Bev Ballard, Many Gun Permits Issued," *Watauga Democrat*, Boone, NC, March 2, 1972, p. 1A; "Sheriff Has Busy Time During March," *Watauga Democrat*, Boone, NC, April 3, 1972, p. 1A; Ballard, "In Durham Family Slaying," pp. 1A & 14A; "$50,000 Bond Is Set In Boone Murder Case," *Asheville Citizen-Times*, Asheville, NC, July 20, 1972, p. 21.
[20] Gary Greene, "No Motive Found," p. 1.
[21] Facebook comment by Doris Weaver Greer, February 12, 2022.
[22] Facebook post; unretrievable link.
[23] Dowell, Tim. In-person conversation with author. March 18, 2023.
[24] Winston Jones, "Triple Murders Left Indelible Etch On Town: Two Months Later, Boone Begins To Forget...," *Bristol Herald Courier*, Bristol, VA-NC, April 13, 1972, p. 1.
[25] Ibid.
[26] Edmisten, Rufus. The Weather Channel's *Storm of Suspicion*, Season 4, Episode 19: "Triple Torment," May 30, 2023.
[27] North Carolina, U. S., Birth Indexes, 1800-2000, https://ancestry.com/imageviewer/collections/8783/images/NCVR_B_C104_66001-0188?pId=6534212.
[28] https://ancestry.com/family-tree/person/tree/170690419/person/252358548575/facts.
[29] 1920, 1930, 1940 United States Federal Census; Coy Durham obituary, *Winston-Salem Journal*, Winston-Salem, NC, June 8, 1983, p. 16; Collie Durham obituary, *Winston-Salem Journal*, Winston-Salem, NC, June 4, 1992, p. 16; Bullard, Tim, *The Durham Murders*, Kindle Edition, 2012, p. 773.
[30] Durham, Bill. The Weather Channel's *Storm of Suspicion*, Season 4, Episode 19: "Triple Torment," May 30, 2023.
[31] "Ronda Seniors Entertained," *The Journal-Patriot"*, North Wilkesboro, NC, January 27, 1938, p. 4; "Church-Durham Betrothal Announced," *The Journal-Patriot*, North Wilkesboro, NC, February 25, 1946, p. 6.
[32] Pitts, Grace (Appalachian State University Registrar's Office). E-mail to author. March 23, 2022
[33] Durham, Bill. The Weather Channel's *Storm of Suspicion*, Season 4, Episode 19: "Triple Torment," May 30, 2023.
[34] "10 Wilkes Lads To Take NYA Defense Course," *Twin City Sentinel*, Winston-Salem, NC, January 1, 1942, p. 3.

[35] "NYA Youth Most Valuable to War Production Chosen," *The Durham Sun*, Durham, NC, February 16, 1942, p. 9; "Bryce Durham Receives Most Deserving Award," *The Herald-Sun*, Durham, NC, February 17, 1942, p. 13.
[36] U. S., World War II Draft Cards Young Men, 1940-1947 for Baxter Bryce Durham, https://ancestry.com/imageviewer/collections/2238/images/32892_1020705388_0052_00764?pld+1025642.
[37] Lemke-Santangelo, Gretchen and Charles Wollenberg, "A Day's Work: Hunters Point Shipyard Workers, 1945-1945" (online), https://www.foundsf.org/index.php?title=A_Day%27s_Work:_Hunters_Point_Shipyard_Workers,_1940-1945; Honolulu, Hawaii, U. S., Arriving and Departing Passenger and Crew Lists, 1900-1959, https://ancestry.com/imageviewer/collections/1502/images/31073_169441-00374?pld=644587.
[38] Durham, Bill. The Weather Channel's *Storm of Suspicion*, Season 4, Episode 19: "Triple Torment," May 30, 2023.
[39] "Church-Durham Betrothal Announced," *The Journal-Patriot*, North Wilkesboro, NC, February 25, 1946, p. 6; North Carolina, U. S., Discharge and Statement of Service Records, 1940-1948, https://ancestry.com/imageviewer/collections/61952/images/FS_007387079_01234?pld=106039.
[40] "Buick Agency Purchased By Bryce Durham," *Watauga Democrat*, Boone, NC, November 27, 1969, p. 1; Henderson, Leonard, "Rub-Out, Rub-Out, Rub-Out: Three Bodies in a Tub," *Startling Detective*, September 1972, p. 62.
[41] Durham, Bill. The Weather Channel's *Storm of Suspicion*, Season 4, Episode 19: "Triple Torment," May 30, 2023.
[42] North Carolina, U. S., Birth Indexes, 1800-2000, https://ancestry.com/imageviewer/collections/8783/images/NCVR_B_C104_66001-0131?pld=6529738.
[43] https://ancestry.com/family-tree/person/tree/170690419/person/252216026020/facts.
[44] North Carolina, U. S., Deaths, 1906-1930 for Calvin Church; https://ancestry.com/discoveryui-content/view/898316:60090.
[45] 1920 United States Federal Census.
[46] North Carolina, U. S., Deaths, 1906-1930 for Calvin Church; https://ancestry.com/discoveryui-content/view/898316:60090.
[47] https://ancestry.com/family-tree/person/tree/170690419/person/252216142671/facts.
[48] U. S., Find a Grave Index, 1600s-Current; https://ancestry.com/discoveryui-content/view/97477969:60525?ssrc=pt&tid=170690419&pid=252358546176.
[49] North Carolina, U. S., Deaths, 1906-1930 for Docia Victora Church; https://ancestry.com/imageviewer/collections/60090/images/004218111_03188?pld=1768881.
[50] Mackie, Ginny Durham. Interview with Carolynn Johnson & Wade Colvard. December 7, 2020.
[51] Edwards, Diana. Phone interview with author. October 14, 2023.
[52] 1930 United States Federal Census.
[53] Edwards, Diana (daughter of Jerri Bumgarner Waddell). Phone interview with author. October 14, 2023.
[54] 1940 United States Federal Census.
[55] "Church-Durham Betrothal Announced," p. 6.
[56] Henderson, Leonard, "Rub-Out," p. 62; Bullard, Tim, *The Durham Murders*, pp. 610 & 782.
[57] "Church-Durham," *The Charlotte Observer*, Charlotte, NC, February 24, 1946, p. 36.
[58] "Miss Virginia Church Bride of Mr. Durham," *The Journal-Patriot*, North Wilkesboro, NC, March 16, 1946, p. 6; "Virginia Dare Church Is Wed To B. B. Durham," *The Charlotte Observer*, Charlotte, NC, March 24, 1946, p. 36; https://ellerfamilyassociation.co,/chronicles/feb95/feb95p8.html; https://findagrave.com/memorial/91328107/betty-jo-eller
[59] "Miss Virginia Church," p. 6; "Buick Agency Purchased," p. 1; Henderson, Leonard, "Rub-Out," p. 62.
[60] Durham, Bill. The Weather Channel's *Storm of Suspicion*, Season 4, Episode 19: "Triple Torment," May 30, 2023.
[61] Durham, Bill & Steve Durham. Interview with Len Hagaman, Kelly Redmon, Carolynn Johnson, & Wade Colvard, retired SBI Agent Larry Wagner, and Rufus Edmisten. August 6, 2019.
[62] Raleigh, NC City Directories, 1949, https://www.ancestry.com/imageviewer/collections/2469/images/11210283?pId=596992628 & https://www.ancestry.com/imageviewer/collections/2469/images/11282470?pId=605582312.
[63] "At Banquet Tonight: Home Finance Notes Best Year," *The Charlotte News*, Charlotte, NC, October 24, 1953, p. 24.
[64] Mauldin, Charles & Gayle. Interview with Red Lyons, February 21, 1989, Watauga County Sheriff's Office investigation file 118-H-1/2/3.
[65] North Carolina Birth Indexes, Wilkes Co., NC, Vol. 39a, p. 274 & Vol. 40a, p. 214; "Birth Is Announced," *Winston-Salem Journal*, Winston-Salem, NC, June 3, 1952, p. 4.
[66] "Galax Kiwanians Elect New Head," *The Roanoke Times*, Roanoke, VA, November 8, 1953, p. 26; "Bryce Durham Elected Head of UCT at Galax," *The Roanoke Times*, Roanoke, VA, April 1, 1953, p. 3; "Galax Council, UTC, Elects New Officers," *The Roanoke Times*; Roanoke, VA, March 11, 1951, p. 17; "Galax Kiwanis Club Votes Book Donation," *Winston-Salem Journal*, Winston-Salem, NC, October 9, 1955, p. 12B; "Kiwanis Club Officers Installed at Lexington,"

Winston-Salem Journal, Winston-Salem, NC, January 3, 1960, p. 3; "Mrs. Frazier Named Head Of Junior Woman's Club," *The Roanoke Times*, Roanoke, VA, April 3, 1959, p. 20.

[67] Home Finance Co. Grand Opening ad, *Florence Morning News*, Florence, SC, July 12, 1961, p. 3.

[68] "Rotarians See Parley Slides," *Florence Morning News*, Florence, SC, September 12, 1961, p. 2.

[69] "Buick Agency Purchased," p. 1; "Florentines Who Knew N. C. Murder Victims 'Shocked,'" *Florence Morning News*, Florence, SC, February 8, 1972, p. 2.

[70] Moss Brennan, "Hagaman considers case of Durham family murders 'closed' in his mind," *Watauga Democrat*, Boone, NC, February 17, 2022 (online), https://www.wataugademocrat.com/blowingrocket/news/hagaman-considers-case-of-durham-family-murders-closed-in-his-mind/article_1d314335-a1a3-5d91-85b0-a027c9094bb6.html.

[71] Jesse Poindexter, "Boone Area Men Sought for Murder," *Winston-Salem Journal*, Winston-Salem, NC, February 5, 1972, p. 8.

[72] "New Auto Loans" (photo caption), *The Mount Airy News*, Mount Airy, NC, November 8, 1963, p. 8A.

[73] Mackie, Ginny Durham. E-mail to Dee Dee Rominger. March 26, 2013 & Mackie, Ginny Durham. Interview with Dee Dee Rominger. March 26, 2013, Watauga County Sheriff's Office investigation file 118-H-1/2/3.

[74] "New Auto Loans" (photo caption), *The Mount Airy News*, Mount Airy, NC, November 8, 1963, p. 8A; "Buick Agency Purchased," p. 1; "Prominent Boone Family Is Found Dead," *The News and Observer*, Raleigh, NC, February 5, 1972, p. 3.

[75] Poindexter, "Boone Area Men Sought," p. 8.

[76] "Police Search For Killers Of Boone Couple, Teen Son," *The Charlotte Observer*, Charlotte, NC, February 5, 1972, p. 2A.

[77] Poindexter, "Boone Area Men Sought," p. 8.

[78] Paul Dillon, "Durham Murders Remain Big Mystery," *The Mount Airy News*, Mount Airy, NC, August 13, 1989, pp. 1A & 3A.

[79] Bullard, *The Durham Murders*, pp. 764, 773, & 782; Mauldin, Jeff. The Weather Channel's *Storm of Suspicion*, Season 4, Episode 19: "Triple Torment," May 30, 2023.

[80] Michael Capuzzo, *The Murder Room* (New York: Gotham Book, Penguin Group, Inc., 2010), 83-84. https://www.kingauthor.net/books/Michael%20Capuzzo/The%20Murder%20Room/The%20Murder%20Room%20-%20Michael%20Capuzzo.pdf.

[81] "Durham Family Slayings: Boone Murders Remain Unsolved After Months," *Bristol Herald Courier*, Bristol, VA-NC, July 4, 1973, p. 24.

[82] Mount Airy High School yearbook, 1969, pp. 95 & 103.

[83] Ibid., p. 102.

[84] Facebook posts, February 2022; unretrievable links.

[85] Mount Airy High School yearbook, 1969, p. 135.

[86] "Buick Agency Purchased," p. 1.

[87] Facebook posts, February 2022; unretrievable links.

[88] Mackie, Ginny Durham. Interview with Carolynn Johnson & Wade Colvard.

[89] "Watauga's Galloping Growth Is Reviewed," *Watauga Democrat*, Boone, NC, April 1, 1971, p. 1

[90] Ibid.; "Economy Dominant Theme In Old Year," *Watauga Democrat*, Boone, NC, January 3, 1972, p. 2A.

[91] "Tally Gives County Gain Of 33%; Boone Up 137%," *Watauga Democrat*, Boone, NC, January 7, 1971, p. 1; "Boone Leads Watauga Growth In Population, Study Report Says," *Watauga Democrat*, Boone, NC, December 2, 1971, p. 2C.

[92] "More Expansion In Sight," *Watauga Democrat*, Boone, NC, January 30, 1969, p. 2.

[93] "Boone...Show Place 'Go' Place Of The 70's," *Watauga Democrat*, Boone, NC, January 1, 1970, p. 8.

[94] https://en.wikipedia.org/wiki/Lost_Provinces; "Thanks To Blowing Rock," *Watauga Democrat*, Boone, NC, October 16, 1969, p. 2.

[95] "Burley Tobacco Is Important To Welfare Watauga Farmers," *Watauga Democrat*, Boone, NC, September 18, 1969, p. 1.

[96] Digital Watauga, Description of Eric Plaag Collection, https://digitalwatauga.org/collections/show54.

[97] "Electronics Factory Is Assured," *Watauga Democrat*, Boone, NC, July 9, 1953, p. 1.

[98] "New Lingerie Plant Slated For Watauga," *Watauga Democrat*, Boone, NC, April 18, 1957, p. 1.

[99] "New Shoe Factory Begins Operations," *Watauga Democrat*, Boone, NC, October 31, 1963, p. 1.

[100] "Enormous Business Boom Witnessed In Watauga," *Watauga Democrat*, Boone, NC, August 21, 1969, p. 1.

[101] "Thanks To Blowing Rock," *Watauga Democrat*, Boone, NC, October 16, 1969, p. 2; "Boone Thoroughfare Yet On Unfinished Basis; Hazardous," *Watauga Democrat*, Boone, NC, August 14, 1969, p. 1.

[102] "Boone Shopping Center Will Cost $1.5 Million," *Watauga Democrat*, Boone, NC, June 19, 1969, p. 1; "Owners Of Land To Build Boone Shopping Center," *Watauga Democrat*, Boone, NC, August 28, 1969, p. 1; "Coming Soon" (photo caption), *Watauga Democrat*, Boone, NC, September 16, 1969, p. 15B; "Review Of Happenings That Made

News In 1970," *Watauga Democrat*, Boone, NC, January 7, 1970, p. 3A; "Work To Start At Once On New Shopping Center," *Watauga Democrat*, Boone, NC, April 2, 1970, p. 1; "Watauga Village Takes Shape," *Watauga Democrat*, Boone, NC, June 18, 1970, p. 1; "Progress At The Shopping Center" (photo caption), *Watauga Democrat*, Boone, NC, December 24, 1970, p. 15C; Photo caption, *Watauga Democrat*, Boone, NC, September 16, 1971; Roses advertisement, *Watauga Democrat*, Boone, NC, January 13, 1972, p. 10A.
[103] "Thanks To Blowing Rock," p. 2; https://www.hcpress.com/front-page/richard-sparks.html.
[104] Photo caption, *Watauga Democrat*, Boone, NC, April 23, 1970, p. 6.
[105] "Four ASU Residence Halls to Be Dedicated," *Watauga Democrat*, Boone, NC, May 15, 1969, p. 1; "$1.8 Library Facility To Be Dedicated At ASU," *Watauga Democrat*, Boone, NC, May 29, 1969, p. 1; "Nears Completion" (photo caption), *Watauga Democrat*, Boone, NC, December 25, 1969, p. 9; "Inaugural '70!" *Watauga Democrat*, Boone, NC, April 23, 1970, p. B7.
[106] "Rotary Programs Cover Sidelights On Economy," *Watauga Democrat*, Boone, NC, December 13, 1971, p. 7A.
[107] "6,800 Enter To Triple Number Ten Years Ago," *Watauga Democrat*, Boone, NC, October 23, 1969, p. 1.
[108] "ASU Ends Fall Term With 7668," *Watauga Democrat*, Boone, NC, October 11, 1971, p. 1.
[109] "Long-Range Campus Plan Is Approved By University Board," *Watauga Democrat*, Boone, NC, November 11, 1971, p. 1.
[110] "Thanks To Blowing Rock,"p. 2.
[111] "Robbins Says Caribbean To Promote Whole Area," *Watauga Democrat*, Boone, NC, January 21, 1971, p. 6B.
[112] "New Ski Resort Ready At Foscoe For Season," *Watauga Democrat*, Boone, NC, December 16, 1971, p. 8C.
[113] "Beginning of Robbins Bros. Empire Related Nationally," *Watauga Democrat*, Boone, NC, October 9, 1969, p. 8; "Ski Resorts Change Economic Outlook," *Watauga County*, Boone, NC, December 27, 1971, p. 7A.
[114] "Busy Weekend," *Watauga Democrat*, Boone, NC, June 26, 1970, p. 2.
[115] "Watauga's Galloping Growth Is Reviewed," *Watauga Democrat*, Boone, NC, April 1, 1971, p. 1.
[116] "'Good Life In Watauga May Be Short-Lived," *Watauga Democrat*, Boone, NC, January 13, 1972, p. 1B.
[117] Bullard, *The Durham Murders*, p. 170.
[118] Storie, Gail. Phone interview with author. September 18, 2022.
[119] Mauldin, Charles & Gayle. Interview with Red Lyons, February 21, 1989.
[120] "Buick Agency Purchased," pp. 1-2.
[121] Hagaman, David. Phone interview with author. November 5, 2022.
[122] Henderson, "Rub-Out," p. 62.
[123] Ron Alridge, "Unlikely Victims: Killings of 'Friendly' Boone Family Baffle Town," *The Charlotte Observer*, Charlotte, NC, February 6, 1972, p. 1C. "Killers Almost Spotted In Boone Triple Murder," *The Robesonian*, Lumberton, NC, February 6, 1972, p. 2A; "Durham Family Slayings," p. 24; Wagner, Larry. Phone interview with author. December 22, 2022; Edwards, Diana (great-niece of Virginia Durham). Phone interview with author. October 14, 2023.
[124] Hagaman, David. Phone interview with author. November 5, 2022.
[125] Mauldin, Charles & Gayle. Interview with Red Lyons, April 17, 1989.
[126] Modern Buick-Pontiac Co. advertisement, *Watauga Democrat*, Boone, NC, January 22, 1970, p. 5.
[127] "At Modern Buick-Pontiac" (photo caption), *Watauga Democrat*, Boone, NC, August 6, 1970, p. B8; Modern Buick-Pontiac Co. "Grand Opening" advertisement, *Watauga Democrat*, Boone, NC, August 6, 1970, p. B16; "Business Byliners," *Watauga Democrat*, Boone, NC, August 13, 1970, p. 13.
[128] Reece, Lester. Phone interview with author. September 12, 2022.
[129] Hagaman, David. Phone interview with author. November 5, 2022.
[130] Storie, Gail. Phone interview with author. September 18, 2022.
[131] Ginn, Phil. Zoom interview with author. March 12, 2022.
[132] Jolley, Frank. Phone interview with author. December 8, 2023.
[133] Edwards, Diana. Phone interview with author. October 14, 2023.
[134] Mackie, Ginny Durham. Interview with Carolynn Johnson & Wade Colvard..
[135] Hagaman, David. Phone interview with author. November 5, 2022.
[136] Webb, J. B. Webb. Interview with Arlie Isaacs, September 18, 1974, Watauga County Sheriff's Office investigation file 118-H-1/2/3.
[137] Alridge, "Unlikely Victims," p. 1C.
[138] Poindexter, "Boone Area Men Sought," p. 8.
[139] Hagaman, David. Phone interview with author. November 5, 2022.
[140] Mackie, Ginny Durham. Interview with Carolynn Johnson & Wade Colvard..
[141] Hagaman, David. Phone interview with author. November 5, 2022.
[142] Garland, Carroll. In-person interview with the author. April 5, 2022.
[143] Ibid.
[144] Hagaman, David. Phone interview with author. November 5, 2022.
[145] Ibid. & December 8, 2022.

[146] Durham, Bill. Interview with Len Hagaman, Kelly Redmon, Carolynn Johnson, Wade Colvard, Larry Wagner, & Rufus Edmisten. August 6, 2019.
[147] Pitts, Grace (Appalachian State University Registrar's Office). E-mail to author. March 23, 2022.
[148] Rick Jackson, *North Carolina Murder & Mayhem* (Charleston, SC: History Press, 2019), https://books.google.com/books?id=PHytDwAAQBAJ&pg=PT28&lpg=PT28&dq=north+carolina+murder+and+mayhem+rick+jackson+bryce+durham&source=bl&ots=J5nMJ1qwdR&sig=ACfU3U0KeyZht7edYL2BrUYA3b4EAamqfg&hl=en&sa=X&ved=2ahUKEwiwzPmKz4r3AhVTkGoFHal9AwQQ6AF6BAgVEAM#v=onepage&q=north%20carolina%20murder%20and%20mayhem%20rick%20jackson%20bryce%20durham&f=false.
[149] Watauga County Sheriff's Office investigation file 118-H-1/2/3.
[150] Ibid.
[151] Watauga County Register of Deeds, Deed Book 107, p. 479 & Deed Book 115, p. 886; "Deaths and Funerals In North Carolina," *The Charlotte Observer*, Charlotte, NC, February 1, 1977, p. 8A.
[152] Watauga County Register of Deeds Office, Deed of Trust Book 129, p. 443.
[153] Wilcox, Sarah. Phone interview with author. February 15, 2024.
[154] Henderson, "Rub-Out," p. 62. Harmon, Jerry. Phone interview with author. March 24, 2022
[155] "95 Gridders Begin Hi School Practice" & "Watauga High Football Team" (photo caption, *Watauga Democrat*, Boone, NC, August 27, 1970, p. B2; 1971 Musket Vol. 6 (Watauga High School yearbook), pp. 72 & 74; Edmisten, Gary. Phone conversation with author. June 18, 2022.
[156] Alridge, "Unlikely Victims," p. 1C.
[157] Harmon, Jerry. Phone interview with author. March 24, 2022.
[158] "Scout Merit Badge Recipients" (photo caption), *Watauga Democrat*, Boone, NC, November 18, 1971, p. 7A; "Memorial Fund Is Established," *Watauga Democrat*, Boone, NC, March 23, 1972, p. 13B; Watauga County Sheriff's Office investigation file 118-H-1/2/3.
[159] Sale, Arvil. Phone interview with author. January 25, 2023.
[160] Ginn, Phil. Zoom interview with author. March 12, 2022.
[161] Sean Kipe, Imperative Entertainment, *In The Red Clay*, podcast audio, Season 2, Episode 6: *Beneath the Chestnut Tree*, January 6, 2023, http://intheredclaypodcast.com.
[162] Cornell, Tommy. Personal conversation with author. March 2022.
[163] Edmisten, Gary. Conversations with author. June 2022 & May 20, 2023.
[164] Reece, Lester. Phone interview with author. September 12, 2022.
[165] "Killers Almost Spotted," p. 2A. Ginn, Phil. Zoom interview with author. March 12, 2022.
[166] Alridge, "Unlikely Victims," p. 1C.
[167] Ginn, Phil. Zoom interview with author. March 12, 2022.
[168] "WHS Students To Don Caps, Gowns," *Watauga Democrat*, Boone, NC, May 27, 1971, p. 1; "260 High School Seniors Will Receive Diplomas," *Watauga Democrat*, Boone, NC, June 3, 1971, p. 1.
[169] "Prominent Boone Family," p. 3. Pitts, Grace (Appalachian State University Registrar's Office). E-mail to author. March 23, 2022.
[170] Ginn, Phil. Zoom interview with author. March 12, 2022.
[171] Alridge, "Unlikely Victims," p. 1C. Henderson, "Rub-Out," p. 62.
[172] "WHS Honor Roll," *Watauga Democrat*, Boone, NC, June 24, 1971, p. 12A.
[173] "Prominent Boone Family," p. 3.
[174] Mackie, Ginny Durham. Interview with Carolynn Johnson & Wade Colvard; Ginn, Phil. Zoom interview with author. March 12, 2022. Harmon, Jerry. Phone interview with author. March 24, 2022.
[175] Vines, Jackie. Phone interview with author. March 10, 2022; Vines, Jacquelyn. Facebook post, September 6, 2023.
[176] Ginn, Phil. Zoom interview with author. March 12, 2022; Mackie, Ginny Durham. Interview with Carolynn Johnson & Wade Colvard. December 7, 2020.
[177] Alridge, "Unlikely Victims," p. 1C.
[178] "Prominent Boone Family," p. 3; "Family strangled, stuffed into tub," *Independent Press-Telegram*, Long Beach, CA, February 5, 1972, p. A-10; Mackie, Ginny Durham. Interview with Carolynn Johnson & Wade Colvard. December 7, 2020; Ginn, Phil. Zoom interview with author. March 12, 2022.
[179] Ginn, Phil, Jerry Harmon, & Jackie Vines. Interviews with author. March 2022; Steele, Brad Barron. Comment on Facebook post by Jackie Vines. September 7, 2023; Rucker, Jeff. Phone interview with author. October 4, 2023.
[180] Alridge, "Unlikely Victims," p. 1C.
[181] Ginn, Phil, Jerry Harmon, & Jackie Vines. Interviews with author. March 2022; Vines, Jacquelyn. Facebook post. September 6, 2023.
[182] Hagaman, David. Phone interview with author. November 5, 2022.
[183] "Investigation of Durham family's slaying continues," *Watauga Democrat*, Boone, NC, January 31, 2015 (online), https://www.wataugademocrat.com/news/investigation-of-durham-family-s-slaying-continues/article_e16a2616-a983-11e4-9e07-bbfdbdd91c44.html.

[184] Ginn, Phil. Zoom interview with author. March 12, 2022.
[185] Modern Buick-Pontiac Co. advertisement, *Watauga Democrat*, Boone, NC, October 28, 1971, p. 11A; Eller, Ike. Interview with Arlie Isaacs. September 27, 1974, Watauga County Sheriff's Office investigation file 118-H-1/2/3.
[186] Combs, Dean. Interview with Red Lyons. July 5, 1989, Watauga County Sheriff's Office investigation file 118-H-1/2/3.
[187] Eldreth, Anita Combs (daughter of Dean Combs). Phone interview with author. March 20, 2023.
[188] Combs, Dean. Interview with Red Lyons.
[189] Eller, Ike. Interview with Arlie Isaacs; York, Debbie. "Cold Weather-Cold Hearts," 2012, unpublished. (Per Jerry Combs, brother of Dean Combs.); Investigative notes, March 26, 2013 & February 13, 2015 (interviews with Ginny Durham Mackie), Watauga County Sheriff's Office investigation file 118-H-1/2/3.
[190] Alridge, "Unlikely Victims," p. 1C.
[191] Eller, Tom (son of Ike Eller). Phone interview with author. July 14, 2022.
[192] Eldreth, Anita Combs (daughter of Dean Combs). Phone interview with author. March 20, 2023.
[193] Combs, Dean. Interview with Red Lyons..
[194] Shealy, Sheila (former wife of Bobby Ashley). Phone interview with author. December 5, 2022; Greer, Evelyn. Phone interview with author. April 3, 2023.
[195] Townsend, Mike. In-person conversation with author. January 15, 2023; Townsend, Mike. Text to author. October 11, 2023.
[196] Real estate, deed, and genealogical research by author.
[197] Cornell, Tommy (son of Jerry Cornell). In-person conversation with author. April 2, 2023.
[198] Townsend, Mike (son of Clyde Townsend). Text to author. March 24, 2022.
[199] Allen, Jane. Phone interview with author. January 31, 2023.
[200] Shealy, Sheila (former wife of Bobby Ashley). Phone interview with author. December 5, 2022.
[201] Roberson, Darlene Benge Norris (widow of Bill Norris, Jr.). Phone interview with author. December 8, 2022.
[202] Wilson, Pat (daughter of Clinard & Clara Wilson). Phone interview with author. March 30, 2022.
[203] Greer, Evelyn. Phone interview with author. April 3, 2023.
[204] Eldreth, Anita Combs (daughter of Opal Combs). Phone interview with author. March 20, 2023.
[205] Cornell, Tommy (son of Jerry Cornell). In-person conversation with author. April 2, 2023.
[206] Shealy, Sheila (formerly Ashley). Phone interview with author. December 5, 2022. Marcotte, Allison Faw (daughter of Bruce & Priscilla Faw). Facebook message to author. December 5, 2022.
[207] Allen, Jane. Phone interview with author. January 31, 2023.
[208] "Tally Gives County Gain Of 33%; Boone Up 137%," *Watauga Democrat*, Boone, NC, January 7, 1971, p. 1.
[209] "Who Said Everybody Likes Boone," *Watauga Democrat*, Boone, NC, November 25, 1971, p. 2.
[210] "Investigation of Durham family's slaying continues."
[211] Mackie, Ginny Durham. Interview with Carolynn Johnson & Wade Colvard.
[212] Alridge, "Unlikely Victims," p. 1C.
[213] "Andrews Chevrolet Is Bought By Lee Barnett," *Watauga Democrat*, Boone, NC, February 4, 1971, p. 1.
[214] "Quiet Neighborhood Shocked By Murders," *The Times*, San Mateo, CA, February 5, 1972, p. 10.
[215] Jesse Poindexter, "Daughter Inherits All: Boone Couple's Wills Filed," *Winston-Salem Journal*, Winston-Salem, NC, February 11, 1972, p. 18.
[216] Storie, Gail. Phone interview with author. September 18, 2022.
[217] "Quiet Neighborhood Shocked," p. 10.
[218] "Police Lacking Clues In Family Murder," *Fort Lauderdale News*, Fort Lauderdale, FL, February 7, 1972, p. 8A.
[219] "3 Slayers Hunted After Family Strangled In N. Carolina Home," *The Napa Register*, Napa, VA, February 5, 1972, p. 4-A.
[220] Roberson, Darlene Benge Norris. Phone interview with author. December 8, 2022.
[221] Eldreth, Anita Combs. Phone interview with author. March 20, 2023.
[222] Shealy, Sheila Ashley. Phone interview with author. December 5, 2022.
[223] Faw, Priscilla. Interview with Arlie Isaacs. September 12, 1974, Watauga County Sheriff's Office investigation file 118-H-1/2/3.
[224] Allen, Jane. Phone interview with author. January 31, 2023.
[225] Facebook post by Allyson Lyons, February 8, 2022.
[226] Edmisten, Gary. Phone conversation with author. June 18, 2022.
[227] Alridge, "Unlikely Victims," p. 1C.
[228] "Police Lacking Clues," p. 8A.
[229] Alridge, "Boone Baffled,'" p. B1.
[230] Alridge, "Unlikely Victims," p. 1C.
[231] Ibid.; Henderson, "Rub-Out," p. 62.
[232] "Services Held for Murdered Family," *The News and Observer*, Raleigh, NC, February 7, 1972, p. 7.

[233] Henderson, "Rub-Out," p. 62.
[234] "No New Telephone Number Available Here; 25 Wait," *Watauga Democrat*, Boone, NC, January 23, 1969, p. 1.
[235] "'Good Life In Watauga," p. 1B.
[236] "The Trend Of Violence," *Watauga Democrat*, Boone, NC, May 1, 1969, p. 2.
[237] Mackie, Ginny Durham. Interview with Carolynn Johnson & Wade Colvard.
[238] "Tragedy Hits Home," *Watauga Democrat*, Boone, NC, September 10, 1970, p. 2.
[239] Dickens, Charles. "A Tale Of Two Cities," 1859.
[240] Pitts, Grace (Appalachian State University Registrar's Office). E-mail to author. March 23, 2022.
[241] "Enormous Business Boom Witnessed In Watauga," *Watauga Democrat*, Boone, NC, August 21, 1969, p. 1; Small, Cecil & Mildred. Interview with Caroline Walker (Watauga Democrat Staff Writer), ca. 1988, Watauga County Sheriff's Office investigation file 118-H-1/2/3; Troy Houser, "Two Suspects Bound In Durham Case, Two Released In Triple-Murder Hearing," *Watauga Democrat*, Boone, NC, June 19, 1972, p. 2; Cecil Small obituary, *The Charlotte Observer* (*The Gaston Observer* edition), Charlotte, NC, May 21, 1991, p. 6; York, "Cold Weather;" Hagaman, Len. The Weather Channel's *Storm of Suspicion*, Season 4, Episode 19: "Triple Torment," May 30, 2023.
[242] Overcash, Charlie. Phone interview with author. March 19, 2022.
[243] Small, Cecil. Interview with Arlie Isaacs. September 5 & 6, 1974, Watauga County Sheriff's Office investigation file 118-H-1/2/3.
[244] Notes compiled by Gayle Durham Mauldin, Watauga County Sheriff's Office investigation file 118-H-1/2/3; Mauldin, Charles & Gayle. Interview with Red Lyons. February 21, 1989, Watauga County Sheriff's Office investigation file 118-H-1/2/3; Russ Pearson, "Youthful Recollections Of Old Wilkesboro – Part III," https://rpears1310.typepad.com/blog/.
[245] "Daughter Inherits Durhams' Property," *Twin City Sentinel*, Winston-Salem, NC, February 11, 1972, p. 5; Notes compiled by Gayle Durham Mauldin; Mauldin, Charles & Gayle. Interview with Sheriff Red Lyons. February 21, 1989.
[246] Durham, Bill. Interview with Len Hagaman, Kelly Redmon, Carolynn Johnson, Wade Colvard, Larry Wagner, & Rufus Edmisten.
[247] Mackie, Ginny Durham. Interview with Carolynn Johnson & Wade Colvard.
[248] Notes compiled by Gayle Durham Mauldin.
[249] Durham, Bill. Interview with Len Hagaman, Kelly Redmon, Carolynn Johnson, Wade Colvard, Larry Wagner, & Rufus Edmisten.
[250] Mackie, Ginny Durham. Interview with Carolynn Johnson & Wade Colvard.
[251] Notes compiled by Gayle Durham Mauldin.
[252] Ibid.
[253] Small, Cecil. Interview with Arlie Isaacs. September 5, 1974, Watauga County Sheriff's Office investigation file 118-H-1/2/3.
[254] Mackie, Ginny Durham. Interview with Carolynn Johnson & Wade Colvard.
[255] Notes compiled by Gayle Durham Mauldin; Mauldin, Charles & Gayle. Interview with Red Lyons. February 21, 1989.
[256] Cullen, "Boone Stranglings," p. 1B; Durham, Bill. Interview with Len Hagaman, Kelly Redmon, Carolynn Johnson, Wade Colvard, Larry Wagner, & Rufus Edmisten.
[257] "Daughter Inherits Durhams' Property," p. 5.
[258] Cullen, "Boone Stranglings," p. 1B.
[259] Alridge, "Unlikely Victims," p. 1C.
[260] Notes compiled by Gayle Durham Mauldin; Divorce decree, The General Court of Justice, Yadkin Co., NC, District Court Division File & Docket No. 76 CVD 185; Confession of Judgment, The General Court of Justice, Superior Court Division, Wilkes County, NC, Ginny Durham Hall (Plaintiff) vs. Troy Hall, Individually, Carolina Construction Company of North Wilkesboro, Inc., Troy Hall, Incorporator (Defendants), February 27, 1976; Mackie, Ginny Durham. Interview with Carolynn Johnson & Wade Colvard.
[261] Small, Cecil. Interview with Arlie Isaacs. September 5 & 6, 1974; Reece, Lester. Phone interview with author. January 25, 2023.
[262] Small, Cecil. Interview with Arlie Isaacs. September 5 & 6, 1974.
[263] Small, Cecil & Mildred Small. Interview with Caroline Walker.
[264] Suburban Propane advertisement, *Watauga Democrat*, Boone, NC, April 23, 1970, p. 3; Small, Cecil. Interview with Arlie Isaacs. September 5, 1974; Dollar, John H. Interview with Arlie Isaacs. September 10, 1974, Watauga County Sheriff's Office investigation file 118-H-1/2/3; Shuford, Joe & Phil Spann, interviews with Arlie Isaacs. September 11, 1974, Watauga County Sheriff's Office investigation file 118-H-1/2/3; Brown, Gerald. Interview with Arlie Isaacs. February 6, 1975, Watauga County Sheriff's Office investigation file 118-H-1/2/3.
[265] Small, Cecil. Interview with Arlie Isaacs. September 5, 1974, p. 2.
[266] York, "Cold Weather."
[267] Brown, Gerald. Interview with Arlie Isaacs.

[268] Watauga County Sheriff's Office investigation file 118-H-1/2/3.
[269] Mackie, Ginny Durham. Interview with Carolynn Johnson & Wade Colvard.
[270] Low, Harry and Tom Leyden, "The rise and fall of Quaaludes." BBC News, July 9, 2015 (online), https://www.bbc.com/news/magazine-33428487.
[271] Watauga County Sheriff's Office investigation file 118-H-1/2/3; Mauldin, Charles & Gayle. Interview with Red Lyons, February 21, 1989.
[272] York, "Cold Weather."
[273] Anonymous informant.
[274] Bullard, *The Durham Murders*, p. 727.
[275] Eller, Ike. Interview with Arlie Isaacs. September 27, 1974, Watauga County Sheriff's Office investigation file 118-H-1/2/3; *Special Edition of WBTV News*, March 1978.
[276] Nelson, Minnie. Interview with Arlie Isaacs. October 8, 1974, Watauga County Sheriff's Office investigation file 118-H-1/2/3.
[277] Webb, J. B. Webb, Arlie Isaacs. September 18, 1974, Watauga County Sheriff's Office investigation file 118-H-1/2/3.
[278] Eller, Ike. Interview with Red Lyons & Fred Myers. September 7, 1989, Watauga County Sheriff's Office investigation file 118-H-1/2/3
[279] Mauldin, Charles & Gayle. Interview with Red Lyons. February 21, 1989; Durham, Bill. Interview with Len Hagaman, Kelly Redmon, Carolynn Johnson, Wade Colvard, Larry Wagner, & Rufus Edmisten.
[280] Durham, Bill. Interview with Len Hagaman, Kelly Redmon, Carolynn Johnson, Wade Colvard, Larry Wagner, & Rufus Edmisten.
[281] Combs, Dean. Interview with Red Lyons, July 5, 1989. Watauga County Sheriff's Office investigation file 118-H-1/2/3.
[282] Small, Cecil. Interview with Arlie Isaacs.
[283] Small, Cecil & Mildred Small. Interview with Caroline Walker; Eller, Ike. Interview with Arlie Isaacs. January 16, 1975, Watauga County Sheriff's Office investigation file 118-H-1/2/3; Durham, Bill. Interview with Len HagamanKelly Redmon, Carolynn Johnson, Wade Colvard Larry Wagner, & Rufus Edmisten..
[284] Notes compiled by Gayle Durham Mauldin; Mauldin, Charles & Gayle. Interview with Red Lyons, February 21, 1989.
[285] Watauga County Sheriff's Office investigation file 118-H-1/2/3; Combs, Dean. Interview with Red Lyons.
[286] Walter, Richard. Phone conversation with author. May 10, 2022.
[287] Reece, Lester. Phone interview with author. September 12, 2022.
[288] Combs, Jerry (brother of Dean Combs). Phone interview with author. March 15, 2023.
[289] Edwards, Diana (Virginia Durham's great-niece). Phone interview with author. October 14, 2023.
[290] Combs, Dean. Interview with Red Lyons..
[291] Notes compiled by Gayle Durham Mauldin.
[292] Eller, Ike. Interview with Arlie Isaacs. September 27, 1974, Watauga County Sheriff's Office investigation file 118-H-1/2/3.
[293] Auston, John. Interview with Clyde Tester & Arlie Isaacs. April 3, 1976, Watauga County Sheriff's Office investigation file 118-H-1/2/3.
[294] Watauga County Sheriff's Office investigation file 118-H-1/2/3.
[295] Notes compiled by Gayle Durham Mauldin.
[296] Mackie, Ginny Durham. Interview with Carolynn Johnson & Wade Colvard.
[297] Durham, Bill. Interview with Len Hagaman, Kelly Redmon, Carolynn Johnson, Wade Colvard, Larry Wagner, & Rufus Edmisten.
[298] Small, Cecil. Interview with Arlie Isaacs. September 5, 1974; Small, Cecil. Interview with Charles Heatherly. December 12, 1987.
[299] Wagner, Larry. Interview with Charles Heatherly. December 18, 1987; Carroll, Ward. Interview with Charles Heatherly. September 1988.
[300] Eller, Ike. Interview with Arlie Isaacs. September 27, 1974.
[301] Eller, Ike. Interview with Arlie Isaacs. January 16, 1975.
[302] Hall, Kay. Interview with Clyde Tester & Arlie Isaacs. February 15, 1975, Watauga County Sheriff's Office investigation file 118-H-1/2/3.
[303] York, "Cold Weather."
[304] Durham, Bill. Interview with Len Hagaman, Kelly Redmon, Carolynn Johnson, Wade Colvard, Larry Wagner, & Rufus Edmisten.
[305] Notes compiled by Gayle Durham Mauldin.
[306] Webb, J. B. Interview with Arlie Isaacs.

[307] Notes compiled by Gayle Durham Mauldin; Mackie, Ginny Durham. Interview with Carolynn Johnson & Wade Colvard.
[308] Lowe, William Asa. Interview with James C. Lyons. June 27, 1994, Watauga County Sheriff's Office investigation file 118-H-1/2/3.
[309] Notes compiled by Gayle Durham Mauldin.
[310] Ibid.
[311] Wilson, Clara. As stated in notes compiled by Gayle Durham Mauldin; Mauldin, Charles & Gayle. Interview with Sheriff Red Lyons. February 21, 1989.
[312] Notes compiled by Gayle Durham Mauldin.
[313] Auston, John. Interview with Clyde Tester & Arlie Isaacs; Rominger, Dee Dee. Phone interview with author. July 31, 2023.
[314] Notes compiled by Gayle Durham Mauldin.
[315] Vines, Jackie. Phone interview with author. March 10, 2022; Report by Boone Police Department Captain Arlie Isaacs, September 5, 1974, p. 2, Watauga County Sheriff's Office investigation file 118-H-1/2/3.
[316] Ginn, Phil. Zoom interview with author. March 12, 2022.
[317] Notes compiled by Gayle Durham Mauldin.
[318] North Carolina State Board of Health, Bureau of Vital Statistics, Certificate of Live Birth for Troy Hall, Wilkes County, NC, Vol. 38A, p. 361; North Carolina State Board of Health, Bureau of Vital Statistics, Certificate of Live Birth for Roy Hall, Wilkes County, NC, Vol. 38A, p. 362; https://www.findagrave.com/memorial/100722104/robert-gilbreath-hall; https://www.findagrave.com/memorial/133281387/carrie-mae-hall.
[319] https://www.ancestry.com/family-tree/person/tree/170690419/person/252358587399/facts.
[320] North Carolina State Board of Health, Bureau of Vital Statistics, Certificate of Live Birth for Troy Hall, Wilkes County, NC, Vol. 38A, p. 361.
[321] Brown, Ted. Phone interview with author. April 4, 2022.
[322] "R. G. Hall Rites Held At Mulberry Tabernacle 28th," *The Journal-Patriot*, North Wilkesboro, NC, January 29, 1976, p. A12.
[323] Lipsig, David, M.D. Letter to Patrick Meriwether, Esq., October 15, 2012, p. 5, containing Troy's self-reported personal history, Gwinnet County, Georgia Superior Court, Civil Action File #12-A-06853-10, Melanie Hall, Plaintiff v. Justin Hall, Defendant, February 4, 2013.
[324] Brown, Ted (via an anonymous source). Text to author. January 31, 2023.
[325] Lipsig, David, M.D. Letter to Patrick Meriwether, Esq., October 15, 2012, p. 5
[326] Brown, Ted. Phone interview with author. April 4, 2022.
[327] "Who killed the Durham family? Here's my story," gowilkes.com, August 21, 2010, posted by "Pepper22." gowilkes.com/voice/who-killed-the-durham-family-heres-my-story/77993/?startview=80&h=090021.
[328] Lipsig, David, M.D. Letter to Patrick Meriwether, Esq., October 15, 2012, p. 6.
[329] Lowe, William Asa. Interview with James C. Lyons; Durham, Steve. Interview with Len Hagaman, Carolynn Johnson, Wade Colvard, Larry Wagner, & Rufus Edmisten. August 6, 2019.
[330] Lowe, William Asa. Interview with James C. Lyons; Kipe, Sean, Imperative Entertainment, *In The Red Clay*, podcast audio, Season 2, Episode 4: *The Company of Wolves*, December 12, 2022, http://intheredclaypodcast.com; https://www.tributearchive.com/obituaries/2167099/John-T-Frazier
[331] Wilkes Central High School "Green and Gold" yearbooks, 1958, 1959, & 1961.
[332] Eller, Tom. Phone interview with author. July 14, 2022.
[333] https://en.wikipedia.org/wiki/Oliver_(singer).
[334] https://en.wikipedia.org/wiki/W._Kerr_Scott_Dam_and_Reservoir.
[335] Frazier, John. Interview with Clyde Tester & Arlie Isaacs. September 20, 1974, Watauga County Sheriff's Office investigation file 118-H-1/2/3.
[336] Eller, Tom. Phone interview with author. July 14, 2022.
[337] Notes compiled by Gayle Durham Mauldin.
[338] "Making A Will Is Good New Year's Resolution," *Watauga Democrat*, Boone, NC, January 13, 1972, p. 12A.
[339] Eller, Ike. Interview with Arlie Isaacs. September 27, 1974.
[340] Notes compiled by Gayle Durham Mauldin; Durham, Bill. Interview with Len Hagaman, Kelly Redmon, Carolynn Johnson, Wade Colvard, Larry Wagner, & Rufus Edmisten.
[341] Notes compiled by Gayle Durham Mauldin; Mauldin, Charles & Gayle. Interview with Red Lyons. February 21, 1989.
[342] Small, Cecil. Interview with Arlie Isaacs. September 6, 1974.
[343] Small, Cecil. Interview with Arlie Isaacs. September 8, 1974.
[344] Small, Cecil. Interview with Arlie Isaacs. September 6, 1974.
[345] Townsend, Barbara & Judy Carroll Johnson. Interviews with Arlie Isaacs. September 23, 1974, Watauga County Sheriff's Office investigation file 118-H-1/2/3.

[346] Hall, Ginny Durham. Interview with Ward Carroll, Clyde Tester, Arlie Isaacs, Larry Wagner. February 8, 1975, Watauga County Sheriff's Office investigation file 118-H-1/2/3.
[347] Notes compiled by Gayle Durham Mauldin.
[348] Small, Cecil. Interview with Arlie Isaacs, September 5, 1974; Small, Cecil & Mildred. Interview with Caroline Walker.
[349] Notes compiled by Gayle Durham Mauldin.
[350] Ibid.
[351] Rick Jackson, *North Carolina Murder & Mayhem* (Charleston, SC: History Press, 2019), https://books.google.com/books?id=PHytDwAAQBAJ&pg=PT28&lpg=PT28&dq=north+carolina+murder+and+mayhem+rick+jackson+bryce+durham&source=bl&ots=J5nMJ1qwdR&sig=ACfU3U0KeyZht7edYL2BrUYA3b4EAamqfg&hl=en&sa=X&ved=2ahUKEwiwzPmKz4r3AhVTkGoFHal9AwQQ6AF6BAgVEAM#v=onepage&q=north%20carolina%20murder%20and%20mayhem%20rick%20jackson%20bryce%20durham&f=false.
[352] Eller, Ike. As stated in notes compiled by Gayle Durham Mauldin; Houser, "Two Suspects Bound," p. 2.
[353] Ettman. "Wildest Day," p. 19.
[354] Notes compiled by Gayle Durham Mauldin.
[355] Townsend, Barbara. Interview with Arlie Isaacs..
[356] Rucker, Jeff. Phone interview with author. October 4, 2023.
[357] Nelson, Chester & Minnie Nelson. Interviews with Arlie Isaacs. October 8, 1974, Watauga County Sheriff's Office investigation file 118-H-1/2/3.
[358] Eller, Ike. As stated in notes compiled by Gayle Durham Mauldin.
[359] Modern Buick-Pontiac Co. advertisement "Meet Jimmy," *Watauga Democrat*, Boone, NC, February 4, 1971, p. 2A; Bullard, *The Durham Murders*, p. 233; Combs, Dean. Interview with Red Lyons.
[360] Small, Cecil & Mildred. Interview with Caroline Walker.
[361] Monte Mitchell, "Slayings mystery grips Boone 40 years later," *Winston-Salem Journal*, Winston-Salem, NC, February 5, 2012, p. A16; Edmisten, Rufus. The Weather Channel's *Storm of Suspicion*, Season 4, Episode 19: "Triple Torment," May 30, 2023.
[362] Bev Ballard, "Triple Slaying Stuns Boone Area," *Watauga Democrat*, Boone, NC, February 7, 1972, p. 1.
[363] Henderson, "Rub-Out," p. 62.
[364] Small, Cecil & Mildred. Interview with Caroline Walker.
[365] https://www.ancestry.com/family-tree/person/tree/170690419/person/252216103171/facts.
[366] Small, Cecil & Mildred. Interview with Caroline Walker.
[367] Mitchell, "Slayings mystery," p. A19.
[368] Small, Cecil & Mildred. Interview with Caroline Walker.
[369] Ginn, Phil. Zoom interview with author. March 12, 2022.
[370] "Killers Almost Spotted," p. 2A.
[371] Ettman, "Wildest Day," pp. 19-20.
[372] "Police Work Doggedly To Piece Together Parts Of Bizarre Triple-Slaying Puzzle," *The Bee*, Danville, VA, February 7, 1972, p. 2-B; Mitchell, "Slayings mystery," p. A16.
[373] Ettman, "Wildest Day," pp. 19-20; "Killers Almost Spotted," p. 2A; Petrey, Dustin (grandson of Earl Petrey). Facebook message to author. November 8, 2022.
[374] Henderson, "Rub-Out," p. 34.
[375] Combs, Dean. Interview with Red Lyons.
[376] "Killers Almost Spotted," p. 2A.
[377] Ibid.; Vance, Glenda (wife of Phil Vance). Phone conversation with author. January 28, 2023.
[378] Ettman, "Wildest Day," pp. 19-20.
[379] "Green Berets To Train At French-Swiss Facility," *Watauga Democrat*, Boone, NC, December 16, 1971, p. 1; "Advance Green Berets Look Over Ski Area," *Watauga Democrat*, Boone, NC, December 20, 1971, p. 7A; "First Green Berets Arrive For Training," *Watauga Democrat*, Boone, NC, January 17, 1972, pp. 1A & 2A; "Salute To Green Berets," *Watauga Democrat*, Boone, NC, February 14, 1972, p. 4A.
[380] Mitchell, "Slayings mystery," p. A16.
[381] Bullard, *The Durham Murders*, pp. 207 & 216.
[382] "Killers Almost Spotted," p. 2A.
[383] Bullard, *The Durham Murders*, p. 233.
[384] Ginn, Phil. Zoom interview with author. March 12, 2022.
[385] Ibid.
[386] Bullard, *The Durham Murders*, pp. 241 & 249.
[387] Watauga County Sheriff's Office investigation file 118-H-1/2/3 (per Mildred Small).
[388] Mitchell, "Slayings mystery," p. A19.
[389] Hall, Kay Hall. Interviews with Clyde Tester & Arlie Isaacs. February 15, 1975 & April 7, 1975.

[390] Bullard, *The Durham Murders*, p. 216.
[391] Ibid., p. 224.
[392] "Killers Almost Spotted," p. 2A.
[393] Ettman, "Wildest Day," p. 20.
[394] Johnson, Lester. Interview with Arlie Isaacs. September 10, 1974, Watauga County Sheriff's Office investigation file 118-H-1/2/3.
[395] Ibid.
[396] York, "Cold Weather."
[397] Combs, Jerry (brother of Dean Combs). Phone interview with author. March 15, 2023; Eldreth, Anita Combs (daughter of Dean Combs). Phone interview with author. March 20, 2023; Combs, Dean. Interview with Red Lyons.
[398] Mitchell, "Slayings mystery," p. A16.
[399] "3 Slayers Hunted," p. 4-A.
[400] Jones, "Triple Murders Left Indelible Etch," p. 2A.
[401] Whitman, Charlie. Interview with Charles Heatherly. December 22, 1987.
[402] Townsend, Mike. In-person conversation with author. January 15, 2023.
[403] Jackson, *North Carolina Murder & Mayhem*.
[404] Brown, John Paul Brown. Interview with Del Williams. February 21, 1989, Watauga County Sheriff's Office investigation file 118-H-1/2/3.
[405] Wilson, Pat (daughter of Clinard & Clara Wilson). Phone interview with author. March 30, 2022; "Services Held," p. 7; Rucker, Jeff. Phone interview with author. October 4, 2023; https://www.ultimate70s.com/seventies_history/19720203/television.
[406] Oakwood Mobile Homes advertisement (stating the business location as Highway 105 & 421 Bypass), *Watauga Democrat*, Boone, NC, August 10, 1972, p. 3A; Mobile Home Brokers, Inc. advertisement (stating the same location), *Watauga Democrat*, Boone, NC, September 14, 1972, p. 12B.
[407] Trivette, Reed. Interview with Del Williams & Chuck Henson. Circa 1989, Watauga County Sheriff's Office investigation file 118-H-1/2/3; Trivette, Reed. Phone call to Boone Area Crimestoppers. February 5, 1992, Watauga County Sheriff's Office investigation file 118-H-1/2/3; Trivette, Reed. Interview with Paula May. February 1, 2000, Watauga County Sheriff's Office investigation file 118-H-1/2/3; May, Paula. Phone interview with author. March 27, 2022. May, Paula. Facebook message to author. April 14, 2022.
[408] Wagner, Larry. Interview with Charles Heatherly.
[409] Faw, Priscilla. Interview with Arlie Isaacs; Combs, Dean. Interview with Red Lyons.
[410] Combs, Dean. Interview with Red Lyons.
[411] Kipe, *In The Red Clay*, Season 2, Episode 3: *Nothing As It Seems*, December 5, 2022; Marcotte, Allison Faw. Facebook message to author. December 9, 2022.
[412] Aldridge, Richard. In-person conversation with author. June 26, 2022.
[413] Norris, Jack (nephew of the subject Jack Norris). Phone interview with author. October 9, 2023.
[414] Cullen, "Boone Stranglings," p. 1B.
[415] Mitchell, "Slayings mystery," p. A19.
[416] "Killers Almost Spotted," p. 1; Bullard, *The Durham Murders*, p. 258; https://www.ultimate70s.com/seventies_history/19720203/television
[417] Mitchell, "Slayings mystery," p. A19.
[418] Durham, Ginny. Interview with Clyde Tester, Arlie Isaacs, L. D. Hagaman, Jr. December 1, 1976, Watauga County Sheriff's Office investigation file 118-H-1/2/3; Mackie, Ginny Durham. Interview with Carolynn Johnson & Wade Colvard; Walter, Richard. Phone conversation with author. May 10, 2022; Watauga County Sheriff's Office investigation file 118-H-1/2/3.
[419] "In Triple Murder – Officers Still After Clues," *Rocky Mount Telegram*, Rocky Mount, NC, February 7, 1972, p. 1; Watauga County Sheriff's Office investigation file 118-H-1/2/3.
[420] Alridge, "Unlikely Victims," p. 1.
[421] Ettman, "Wildest Day," p. 20.
[422] Mitchell, "Slayings mystery," p. A19.
[423] "Three Men Charged In Boone Slayings," *Statesville Record and Landmark*, Statesville, NC, April 25, 1972, p. 1; "Murders At Boone Probed," *Rocky Mount Telegram*, Rocky Mount, NC, February 5, 1972, p. 1; "Three in Boone Family Found Slain at Home," *The News and Observer*, Raleigh, NC, February 5, 1972, p. 1; Ettman, "Wildest Day," p. 20; Diane Suchetka, "New Twists Could Clinch Mysterious Boone-Area Murders," *The Charlotte Observer*, Charlotte, NC, July 3, 1989, p. 2B; "Murder Reward Increased," *Asheville Citizen-Times*, Asheville, NC, February 12, 1972, p. 11; "State Suspends Prosecution Of Suspect In Triple Slaying," *The Charlotte Observer*, Charlotte, NC, June 5, 1973, p. 2C; "Doors now locked: Murder shatters the 'quiet,'" *Tucson Daily Citizen*, Tucson, AZ, February 5, 1972, p. 1; Alridge, "Unlikely Victims," p. 1C; "Clairvoyant Consulted In Killings," *The Charlotte Observer*, Charlotte, NC,

April 26, 1972, p. 2A; Bullard, *The Durham Murders*, pp. 592 & 659; "Neighbors shaken by murder of 3," *The Bryan Times*, Bryan, OH, February 5, 1972, p. 3.
[424] "Clairvoyant Consulted," p. 2A.
[425] Alridge, "Unlikely Victims," p. 1C; "Police try to assemble clues in triple murder," *The Gastonia Gazette*, Gastonia, NC, February 7, 1972, p. 1.
[426] "Two Men Will Be Tried In Murders Of Boone Auto Dealer, Wife And Son," *The Charlotte Observer*, Charlotte, NC, June 16, 1972, p. 2C.
[427] Mitchell, "Slayings mystery," p. A19; Houser, "Two Suspects Bound," p. 2.
[428] Mackie, Ginny Durham. Interview with Carolynn Johnson & Wade Colvard..
[429] Bullard, *The Durham Murders*, p. 295.
[430] Ettman, "Wildest Day," p. 21.
[431] Nelson, Chester & Minnie. Interviews with Arlie Isaacs.
[432] Bullard, *The Durham Murders*, pp. 295 & 304.
[433] Small, Cecil & Mildred. Interview with Caroline Walker.
[434] https://en.wikipedia.org/wiki/Chevrolet_big-block_engine#:~:text=A%20409%20cu%20in%20(6.7,or%202X4%2Dbarrel%20Rochester%20carburetors; https://www.motortrend.com/vehicle-genres/chevy-409-v-8-engine-history/.
[435] Ettman, "Wildest Day," pp. 20-21.
[436] Small, Cecil & Mildred. Interview with Caroline Walker; https://www.ultimate70s.com/seventies_history/19720203/television.
[437] Small, Cecil. Interview with Charles Heatherly.
[438] Small, Cecil & Mildred. Interview with Caroline Walker.
[439] Henderson, "Rub-Out," p. 35.
[440] Small, Cecil. Interview with Charles Heatherly.
[441] Henderson, "Rub-Out," p. 35.
[442] Ibid., p. 61.
[443] Small, Cecil & Mildred. Interview with Caroline Walker.
[444] Henderson, "Rub-Out," p. 35.
[445] Small, Cecil. Interview with Charles Heatherly.
[446] Henderson, "Rub-Out," p. 35.
[447] Small, Cecil & Mildred. Interview with Caroline Walker.
[448] Henderson, "Rub-Out," p. 35.
[449] Small, Cecil & Mildred. Interview with Caroline Walker.
[450] Henderson, "Rub-Out," p. 35.
[451] Ibid., p. 61.
[452] *Special Edition of WBTV News*.
[453] Small, Cecil & Mildred. Interview with Caroline Walker; Henderson, "Rub-Out," p. 35.
[454] Harrison, Jerry. Interviews with Arlie Isaacs. March 7, 1989 & Red Lyons. March 8 & 15, 1989, Watauga County Sheriff's Office investigation file 118-H-1/2/3; Mauldin, Charles & Gayle. Interview with Red Lyons, August 7, 1989. Watauga County Sheriff's Office investigation file 118-H-1/2/3.
[455] Hagaman, David. Phone interview with author. November 5, 2022.
[456] Small, Cecil. Interview with Charles Heatherly.
[457] Small, Cecil & Mildred. Interview with Caroline Walker.
[458] Small, Cecil. Interview with Arlie Isaacs. September 5, 1974.
[459] "Killers Almost Spotted," p. 1.
[460] Small, Cecil & Mildred. Interview with Caroline Walker.
[461] Ettman, "Wildest Day," p. 21.
[462] Faw, Priscilla. Interview with Arlie Isaacs.
[463] Tester, Johnny. Phone conversation with author. February 26, 2022.
[464] Henderson, "Rub-Out," p. 61.
[465] Small, Cecil & Mildred. Interview with Caroline Walker.
[466] Henderson, "Rub-Out," p. 61.
[467] Small, Cecil & Mildred. Interview with Caroline Walker.
[468] Henderson, "Rub-Out," p. 61.
[469] Townsend, Mike. In-person conversation with author. January 15, 2023.
[470] Henderson, "Rub-Out," p. 61.
[471] Small, Cecil & Mildred. Interview with Caroline Walker.
[472] Henderson, "Rub-Out," p. 61.

[473] Small, Cecil & Mildred. Interview with Caroline Walker; Ettman, "Wildest Day," pp. 20-21; Henderson, "Rub-Out," p. 61.
[474] Jackson, *North Carolina Murder & Mayhem.*
[475] Small, Cecil & Mildred. Interview with Caroline Walker; Henderson, "Rub-Out," p. 61.
[476] Henderson, "Rub-Out," p. 61.
[477] Houser, "Two Suspects Bound," p. 2.
[478] Henderson, "Rub-Out," p. 61.
[479] Small, Cecil. Interview with Charles Heatherly.
[480] Houser, "Two Suspects Bound," p. 2; Ettman, "Wildest Day," p. 21.
[481] Small, Cecil & Mildred. Interview with Caroline Walker.
[482] Bullard, *The Durham Murders*, p. 313.
[483] Henderson, "Rub-Out," p. 61.
[484] Jackson, *North Carolina Murder & Mayhem.*
[485] Bullard, *The Durham Murders*, p. 313.
[486] Small, Cecil. Interview with Arlie Isaacs. September 5, 1974; *Special Edition of WBTV News*; "Durham murders remembered," *Watauga Democrat*, Boone, NC, February 27, 1989, p. 5.
[487] Crime scene photo. Watauga County Sheriff's Office. Personal observance of author. March 14, 2022.
[488] Bullard, *The Durham Murders*, p. 313.
[489] Personal observance of author while visiting home, March 28, 2022.
[490] Cook, Donna. Phone interview with author. April 2, 2024; Crime scene photos, Watauga County Sheriff's Office.
[491] Ettman, "Wildest Day," p. 22.
[492] Small, Cecil & Mildred. Interview with Caroline Walker.
[493] J. A. C Dunn, "Watauga Murders Unsolved," *Winston-Salem Journal*, Winston-Salem, NC, June 5, 1973, p. 2; Small, Cecil. Interview with Arlie Isaacs, September 5, 1974; Bullard, *The Durham Murders*, p. 322.
[494] Henderson, "Rub-Out," p. 61; Small, Cecil & Mildred. Interview with Caroline Walker.
[495] Ettman, "Wildest Day," p. 22.
[496] *Special Edition of WBTV News*.
[497] Small, Cecil & Mildred. Interview with Caroline Walker.
[498] *Special Edition of WBTV News*.
[499] Small, Cecil. Interview with Charles Heatherly.
[500] Small, Cecil & Mildred. Interview with Caroline Walker.
[501] "Durham murders remembered," p. 5; Small, Cecil. Interview with Boone Police Department Arlie Isaacs. September 5, 1974, p. 1.
[502] *Special Edition of WBTV News*; Henderson, "Rub-Out," p. 61; Small, Cecil. Interview with Charles Heatherly.
[503] Houser, "Two Suspects Bound," p. 2.
[504] "Killers Almost Spotted," p. 2A; Henderson, "Rub-Out," p. 61.
[505] Small, Cecil & Mildred. Interview with Caroline Walker.
[506] "Killers Almost Spotted," p. 2A. Henderson, "Rub-Out," p. 61.
[507] Small, Cecil & Mildred. Interview with Caroline Walker.
[508] *Special Edition of WBTV News*; Small, Cecil & Mildred. Interview with Caroline Walker; "Durham murders remembered," p. 5.
[509] Houser, "Two Suspects Bound," p. 2.; Small, Cecil. Interview with Arlie Isaacs. September 5, 1974; Small, Cecil & Mildred. Interview with Caroline Walker.
[510] Townsend, Mike. Phone conversation with author. March 10, 2022.
[511] *Special Edition of WBTV News*.
[512] Bullard, *The Durham Murders*, p. 322.
[513] *Special Edition of WBTV News*.
[514] Small, Cecil & Mildred. Interview with Caroline Walker.
[515] Henderson, "Rub-Out," p. 61; Small, Cecil. Interview with Arlie Isaacs. September 5, 1974, p. 1.
[516] Houser, "Two Suspects Bound," p. 2.
[517] "Durham murders remembered," p. 5.
[518] Small, Cecil & Mildred. Interview with Caroline Walker.
[519] Alridge, "Unlikely Victims," p. 1C; https://www.findagrave.com/memorial/33393326/edward_clay-lowrance.
[520] Townsend, Mike. Phone conversation with author. March 10, 2022.
[521] Small, Cecil & Mildred. Interview with Caroline Walker.
[522] Townsend, Mike. In-person conversation with author. January 15, 2023.
[523] Ettman, "Wildest Day," p. 22; Tester, Johnny. Communication with author. 2022.
[524] "Boone Couple, Son Slain," *The Charlotte News*, Charlotte, NC, February 4, 1972, p. 1. Bullard, *The Durham Murders*, p. 557.

[525] Cullen, "Boone Stranglings," p. 1B.
[526] "3 Killed In Boone; Murderers Sought," *Asheville-Citizen Times*, Asheville, NC, February 5, 1972, p. 1.
[527] Capuzzo, *The Murder Room*, p. 84.
[528] "Slayings in Boone Revealed," p. 1.
[529] Small, Cecil & Mildred. Interview with Caroline Walker.
[530] Henderson, "Rub-Out," p. 61; Cullen, "Boone Stranglings," p. 1B.
[531] *Special Edition of WBTV News*.
[532] Ettman, "Wildest Day," p. 22.
[533] Ibid.
[534] Tester, Johnny. Phone conversation with author. February 26, 2022.
[535] Tester, Johnny. Facebook message to author. February 25, 2022.
[536] Hagaman, Len. Watauga County Sheriff's Office press conference, February 11, 2022.
[537] Tester, Johnny. Facebook message to author. February 25, 2022. Tester, Johnny. Phone conversation with author. October 16, 2022.
[538] "Ward G. Carroll For Sheriff," *Watauga Democrat*, Boone, NC, May 7, 1970, p. 3; "Re-Elect Ward Carroll Sheriff," *Watauga Democrat*, Boone, NC, October 15, 1970, p. 3B; "GOP Wins Board, Clerk; Democrats Keep Sheriff," *Watauga Democrat*, Boone, NC, November 5, 1970, p. 1; Guy, Frank. Phone interview with author. September 17, 2022.
[539] Ballard, "In Durham Family Slaying," p. 1A.
[540] Tester, Johnny. Facebook message to author. February 25, 2022; Tester, Johnny. Phone conversation with author. October 16, 2022.
[541] Ballard, "In Durham Family Slaying," p. 1A; Henderson, "Rub-Out," p. 62.
[542] Tester, Johnny. Phone conversation with author. February 26, 2022.
[543] Townsend, Mike. Text communication with author. March 24, 2022; Small, Cecil & Mildred. Interview with Caroline Walker; Allen, Jane. Phone interview with author. January 31, 2023.
[544] Tester, Johnny. Facebook message to author. February 25, 2022.
[545] Small, Cecil & Mildred. Interview with Caroline Walker.
[546] Mackie, Ginny Durham. Interview with Dee Dee Rominger. March 26, 2013, Watauga County Sheriff's Office investigation file 118-H-1/2/3.
[547] "Durham murders remembered," p. 5.
[548] Alridge, "Unlikely Victims," p. 1C.
[549] Small, Cecil & Mildred. Interview with Caroline Walker.
[550] "Durham murders remembered," p. 5.
[551] Small, Cecil & Mildred. Interview with Caroline Walker.
[552] Danner, George C. III (brother of Deryl Danner). Phone interview with author. September 8, 2023.
[553] Coffey, Karen. Den photos sent to author via Facebook Messenger. March 8, 2023.
[554] Harmon, Cecil Harmon. Interview with Red Lyons. March 23, 1989, Watauga County Sheriff's Office investigation file 118-H-1/2/3.
[555] Ibid.
[556] Jackson, Mozella. Phone conversation with author. January 25, 2023.
[557] Small, Cecil & Mildred. Interview with Caroline Walker.
[558] Henderson, "Rub-Out," p. 62.
[559] Durham, Ginny. Interview with Clyde Tester, Arlie Isaacs, & L. D. Hagaman, Jr.
[560] Small, Cecil & Mildred. Interview with Caroline Walker.
[561] Ibid.
[562] Hall, Kay Hall. Interview with Clyde Tester & Arlie Isaacs, February 15, 1975, Watauga County Sheriff's Office investigation file 118-H-1/2/3.
[563] Watauga County Sheriff's Office investigation file 118-H-1/2/3; Durham, Bill. Via e-mail communication from Stephanie Durham McClain to the author. August 9, 2022.
[564] Mauldin, Charles & Gayle. Interview with Red Lyons. April 1, 1989, Watauga County Sheriff's Office investigation file 118-H-1/2/3.
[565] Ettman, "Wildest Day," p. 22.
[566] Henderson, "Rub-Out," p. 62.
[567] Reports of Investigation by Medical Examiner, February 17, 1972, Watauga County Sheriff's Office investigation file 118-H-1/2/3. Dean, Dr. Clayton. Phone interview with author. November 16, 2022. Bullard, *The Durham Murders*, p. 677.
[568] "Business, Civic Leaders in United Fund," *Watauga Democrat*, Boone, NC, September 23, 1971, p. 3A.
[569] Flowers, Art (son of George Flowers). Phone interview with author. January 26, 2023; "Obituary of George A. Flowers" (online), https://austinandbarnesfuneralhome.com/tribute/details/1738/George-Flowers/obituary.html.

[570] York, "Cold Weather."
[571] Personal observance of author while visiting home. March 28, 2022.
[572] Crime scene photos, Watauga County Sheriff's Office investigation file 118-H-1/2/3.
[573] Bullard, *The Durham Murders*, p. 161; Crime scene photos, Watauga County Sheriff's Office investigation file 118-H-1/2/3.
[574] Bullard, *The Durham Murders*, pp. 188, 277, & 659.
[575] Henderson, "Rub-Out," p. 62.
[576] Jesse Poindexter, "Boone Slayings: Probe Yields No Arrests," *Winston-Salem Journal*, Winston-Salem, NC, April 23, 1972, p. 1.
[577] Henderson, "Rub-Out," p. 62.
[578] Poindexter, "Daughter Inherits All," p. 1.
[579] Henderson, "Rub-Out," p. 62.
[580] Young, Lewis. Phone interview with author. February 1, 2023.
[581] Caroline D. Walker, "Former SBI agent still baffled," *Watauga Democrat*, Boone, NC, 1989, p. 1; Bullard, *The Durham Murders*, p. 118.
[582] Parker, John. Phone interview with author. November 7, 2022.
[583] Tester, Johnny. Phone conversations with author. February 26, 2022 & May 19, 2022; Tester, Johnny. Facebook message to author. February 25, 2022; Tester, Johnny. Phone conversation with author. October 16, 2022. "Boone Policeman Selected For Police Science Degree," *Watauga Democrat*, Boone, NC, September 25, 1972, p. 1.
[584] Harmon, Cecil. Interview with Red Lyons.
[585] Ballard, "Triple Slaying," p. 1.
[586] Ettman, "Wildest Day," p. 22.
[587] Alridge, "Unlikely Victims," p. 1C.
[588] "Boone Murder Reward $17,050," *The Daily News*, Kingsport, TN, March 3, 1972, p. 1, https://news.google.com/newspapers?nid=P-MJmu9ZMwQC&dat=19720303&printsec=frontpage&hl=en.
[589] Ballard, "In Durham Family Slaying," p. 1A.
[590] Whitman, Charlie. Interview with Charles Heatherly. December 22, 1987.
[591] Ibid.
[592] Bullard, *The Durham Murders*, pp. 152 & 161; Hudgins, Phil & Ruby Nell Birt, *Grace and Disgrace: Living with Faith and a Dixie Mafia Hit Man* (YAV Publications, Asheville, NC, 2022), p. 258.
[593] "Killers Almost Spotted," p. 2A.
[594] Ettman, "Wildest Day," p. 22; Crime scene photograph; Whitman, Charlie. Interview with Charles Heatherly.
[595] Crime scene photograph; Whitman, Charlie. Interview with Charles Heatherly.
[596] Henderson, "Rub-Out," p. 61; Crime scene photographs.
[597] Ettman, "Wildest Day," p. 22.
[598] "Killers Almost Spotted," p. 2A.
[599] "Killers Almost Spotted," p. 2A.; Poindexter, "Boone Area Men Sought," p. 8; Ettman, "Wildest Day," p. 22; Whitman, Charlie. Interview with Charles Heatherly; Crime scene photographs.
[600] "Killers Almost Spotted," p. 2A; Bullard, Tim, *The Durham Murders*, Kindle Edition, 2012, p. 710.
[601] "Killers Almost Spotted," p. 2A; Henderson, Leonard. *Rub-Out, Rub-Out, Rub-Out: Three Bodies in a Tub*. Startling Detective, September 1972, p. 62.
[602] Henderson, "Rub-Out," p. 62; Crime scene photographs, Watauga County Sheriff's Office investigation file 118-H-1/2/3.
[603] "Family strangled, stuffed into tub," p. A-10; Bullard, *The Durham Murders*, p. 331.
[604] Whitman, Charlie. Interview with Charles Heatherly.
[605] Ettman, "Wildest Day," p. 23.
[606] Whitman, Charlie. Interview with Charles Heatherly.
[607] Ettman, "Wildest Day," p. 22.
[608] Henderson, "Rub-Out," p. 62; Crime scene photographs, Watauga County Sheriff's Office investigation file 118-H-1/2/3.
[609] Crime scene photographs, Watauga County Sheriff's Office investigation file 118-H-1/2/3; Whitman, Charlie. Interview with Charles Heatherly.
[610] "Family strangled, stuffed into tub," p. A-10; "Boone Murder Reward $17,050," p. 1, https://news.google.com/newspapers?nid=P-MJmu9ZMwQC&dat=19720303&printsec=frontpage&hl=en; Crime scene photographs.
[611] Bullard, *The Durham Murders*, p. 384.
[612] "Killers Almost Spotted," p. 2A.

[613] Horror History.net – "Unsolved: family of three killed in home, their heads submerged in their bathtub," February 3, 2020, https://horrorhistory.net/2020/02/03/unsolved-family-of-three-killed-in-home-their-heads-submerged-in-their-bathtub/
[614] Bullard, *The Durham Murders*, pp. 540, 618, & 642.
[615] Ettman, "Wildest Day," p. 22; Bullard, *The Durham Murders*, p. 179.
[616] Bullard, *The Durham Murders*, pp. 313 & 322.
[617] Whitman, Charlie. Interview with Charles Heatherly.
[618] Henderson, "Rub-Out," p. 61.
[619] Hagaman, Len. In-person interview with author. March 14, 2022.
[620] "Investigation of Durham family's slaying continues.".
[621] "Family strangled, stuffed into tub," p. A-10.
[622] Ettman, "Wildest Day," p. 22.
[623] Crime scene photo. Watauga County Sheriff's Office investigation file 118H-1/2/3.
[624] "Prominent Boone Family," p. 3.
[625] Ettman, "Wildest Day," p. 22.
[626] "Prominent Boone Family," p. 3.
[627] Hagaman, Len. In-person interviews with author. March 14, 2022 & May 24, 2022.
[628] Ettman, "Wildest Day," p. 22; Henderson, "Rub-Out," p. 62; Bullard, *The Durham Murders*, p. 601.
[629] Small, Cecil & Mildred. Interview with Caroline Walker.
[630] York, "Cold Weather."
[631] Ettman, "Wildest Day," p. 50.
[632] Edwards, Diana (daughter of Jerri Bumgarner Waddell). Phone interview with author. October 14, 2023.
[633] Ettman, "Wildest Day," p. 23.
[634] "Killers Almost Spotted," p. 2A.
[635] Ettman, "Wildest Day," p. 23.
[636] Whitman, Charlie. Interview with Charles Heatherly.
[637] *Special Edition of WBTV News*; Hagaman, Len. In-person interview with author. May 24, 2022; "Gary Morgan Heads ASU Security Unit," *Watauga Democrat*, Boone, NC, July 10, 1969, p. B1.
[638] Whitman, Charlie. Interview with Charles Heatherly.
[639] *Special Edition of WBTV News*.
[640] "Killers Almost Spotted," p. 1.
[641] "Poe Named To New Post," *Watauga Democrat*, Boone, NC, January 10, 1972, p. 10A.
[642] Bullard, *The Durham Murders*, p. 340.
[643] "3 Killed In Boone," p. 2. "Murders At Boone Probed," p. 1.
[644] "Killers Almost Spotted," p. 2A.
[645] Ibid.
[646] Ettman, "Wildest Day," p. 23; Henderson, "Rub-Out," p. 62; Poe, Brad. Phone interview with author. March 26, 2022.
[647] Small, Cecil & Mildred. Interview with Caroline Walker.
[648] Hall, Kay. Interviews with Clyde Tester & Arlie Isaacs. February 15, 1975, March 22, 1975, & April 7, 1975.
[649] Tester, Johnny. Facebook message to author February 25, 2022 and in-person conversation with author March 6, 2022.
[650] Tester, Johnny. Phone conversation with author. May 19, 2022.
[651] Ettman, "Wildest Day," p. 23.
[652] SBI Request For Examination Of Physical Evidence, submitted by Watauga County Sheriff Ward Carroll, Watauga County Sheriff's Office investigation file 118-H-1/2/3.
[653] "Slayings In Boone Revealed," p. 1; Ettman, "Wildest Day," p. 23.
[654] Whitman, Charlie. Interview with Charles Heatherly.
[655] "Murders At Boone Probed," p. 5.
[656] "Killers Almost Spotted," p. 2A. Ettman, "Wildest Day," p. 48.
[657] Ettman, "Wildest Day," pp. 23 & 48.
[658] Ibid., p. 48.
[659] Watauga County Sheriff's Office investigation file 118-H-1/2/3.
[660] Henderson, "Rub-Out," p. 63.
[661] Ibid.
[662] Watauga County Sheriff's Office investigation file 118-H-1/2/3.
[663] Roark, Lisa. Facebook messages to author. March 11 & 14, 2022.
[664] Henderson, "Rub-Out," p. 63.
[665] Roark, Lisa. Facebook messages to author. March 11 & 14, 2022.

[666] Watauga County Sheriff's Office investigation file 118-H-1/2/3.
[667] Jackson, T. J. Phone conversation with author. October 14, 2023.
[668] Ettman, "Wildest Day," p. 48.
[669] Whitman, Charlie. Interview with Charles Heatherly.
[670] "Investigation of Durham family's slaying continues.".
[671] Whitman, Charlie. Interview with Charles Heatherly.
[672] Rucker, Jeff. Phone interview with author. October 4, 2023.
[673] Whitman, Charlie. Interview with Charles Heatherly.
[674] Bullard, *The Durham Murders*, p. 331.
[675] Whitman, Charlie. Interview with Charles Heatherly.
[676] Bullard, Tim, *The Durham Murders*, Kindle Edition, 2012, p. 331.
[677] Watauga County Sheriff's Office investigation file 118-H-1/2/3.
[678] Harrison, Luther (Mrs. Wilson's grandson). In-person conversation with author. May 26, 2022.
[679] Wilson, Pat (daughter of Clinard & Clara Wilson). Phone interviews with the author. March 30 & April 4, 2022.
[680] Kipe, *In The Red Clay*, Season 2, Episode 3: *Nothing As It Seems*; Marcotte, Allison Faw. Facebook message to author. December 9, 2022.
[681] Shealy, Sheila. Phone interview with author. December 5, 2022; Marcotte, Allison Faw (daughter of Bruce and Priscilla Faw). Facebook message to author. December 5, 2022; Kipe, *In The Red Clay*, Season 2, Episode 3: *Nothing As It Seems*; Priscilla Alice Corliss obituary, *The Laconia Daily Sun*, May 1, 2019, https://www.laconiadailysun.com/community/obituaries/priscilla-alice-corliss-76/article_60fb7bd6-6c27-11e9-b970-fb6118b041a3.html.
[682] Roberson, Darlene Benge Norris. Phone interview with author. December 8, 2022
[683] Notes compiled by Gayle Durham Mauldin; Eller, Ike. Interview with Red Lyons & Fred Myers.
[684] Eller, Tom. Phone interview with author. July 14, 2022.
[685] Combs, Dean. Interview with Red Lyons. Eller, Ike. Interview with Red Lyons & Fred Myers.
[686] Notes compiled by Gayle Durham Mauldin; Kipe, *In The Red Clay*, Season 2, Episode 6: *Beneath the Chestnut Tree*.
[687] Harmon, Cecil. Interview with Red Lyons.
[688] Crime scene photograph. Watauga County Sheriff's Office, Boone, NC.
[689] Dean, Dr. Clayton. Phone interview with author. November 16, 2022.
[690] Harmon, Cecil. Interview with Red Lyons.
[691] Ibid.
[692] Report of Autopsy, Office of the Chief Medical Officer, Chapel Hill, NC, February 4, 1972, ME-72-39 (Robert [sic] Durham); Crime scene photographs. Watauga County Sheriff's Office, Boone, NC.
[693] Ibid.
[694] "Killers Almost Spotted," p. 2A; Crime scene photographs, Watauga County Sheriff's Office investigation file 118-H-1/2/3; Whitman, Charlie. Interview with Charles Heatherly.
[695] Bullard, *The Durham Murders*, pp. 268 & 531; Physical evidence bag containing rope, Watauga County Sheriff's Office investigation file 118-H-1/2/3.
[696] Reports of Autopsy, Office of the Chief Medical Officer, Chapel Hill, NC, February 4, 1972.
[697] Crime scene photographs, Watauga County Sheriff's Office investigation file 118-H-1/2/3.
[698] Henderson, "Rub-Out," p. 62; "Mute Witness," *Watauga Democrat*, Boone, NC, February 7, 1972, p. 4A; Crime scene photos, Watauga County Sheriff's Office investigation file 118-H-1/2/3; Whitman, Pat. Interview with Carolynn Johnson & Wade Colvard. July 17, 2019.
[699] Small, Cecil & Mildred. Interview with Caroline Walker.
[700] Harmon, Cecil. Interview with Red Lyons.
[701] Ettman, "Wildest Day," p. 23; Bullard, *The Durham Murders*, p. 566.
[702] Henderson, "Rub-Out," p. 62.
[703] Poindexter, "Boone Slayings," p. 1.
[704] Crime scene photograph. Watauga County Sheriff's Office, Boone, NC.
[705] Pearce, Bill. Phone interviews with author. March 28, 2023.
[706] Hall, John. Interview with Arlie Isaacs & Larry Wagner. January 27, 1975, Watauga County Sheriff's Office investigation file 118-H-1/2/3.
[707] Small, Cecil & Mildred. Interview with Caroline Walker.
[708] Hall, John. Interview with Arlie Isaacs & Larry Wagner.
[709] Small, Cecil & Mildred. Interview with Caroline Walker.
[710] York, "Cold Weather."
[711] Combs, Dean. Interview with Red Lyons.
[712] York, "Cold Weather."

[713] Combs, Dean. Interview with Red Lyons.
[714] Eldreth, Anita Combs (daughter of Dean Combs). Phone interview with author. March 20, 2023.
[715] York, "Cold Weather."
[716] Combs, Dean. Interview with Red Lyons.
[717] Notes compiled by Gayle Durham Mauldin; Eller, Frances. Interview with Arlie Isaacs, January 16, 1975, Watauga County Sheriff's Office investigation file 118-H-1/2/3.
[718] Eller, Ike. Interview with Arlie Isaacs.
[719] Hall, John. Interview with Arlie Isaacs & Larry Wagner.
[720] Eller, Tom. Phone interview with author. July 14, 2022.
[721] Notes compiled by Gayle Durham Mauldin.
[722] Eller, Ike. Interview with Arlie Isaacs.
[723] Notes compiled by Gayle Durham Mauldin.
[724] Ibid.
[725] Eller, Ike. Interview with Red Lyons & Fred Myers.
[726] Eller, Tom. Phone interview with author. July 14, 2022.
[727] Notes compiled by Gayle Durham Mauldin.
[728] Eller, Ike. Interview with Red Lyons & Fred Myers.
[729] Hall, John. Interview with Arlie Isaacs & Larry Wagner.
[730] Small, Cecil & Mildred. Interview with Caroline Walker.
[731] Durham, Bill. Via e-mail communication from Stephanie Durham McClain to the author. August 9, 2022; Durham, Bill. The Weather Channel's *Storm of Suspicion*, Season 4, Episode 19: "Triple Torment," May 30, 2023.
[732] "Killers Almost Spotted," p. 1.
[733] Henderson, "Rub-Out," p. 61.
[734] https://sunrise.maplogs.com/boone_nc_nc_usa.214222.html?year=1972.
[735] Notes compiled by Gayle Durham Mauldin; Mauldin, Charles & Gayle Durham. Interview with Red Lyons. April 1, 1989; Poindexter, "Daughter Inherits All," p. 18.
[736] Hall, Kay. Interview with Clyde Tester & Arlie Isaacs. April 7, 1975.
[737] Ginn, Phil. Zoom interview with author. March 12, 2022.
[738] "Investigation of Durham family's slaying continues."
[739] Edmisten, Gary. Phone conversation with author. June 18, 2022.
[740] Henson, Jack. Personal communication with author. March 23-24, 2002.
[741] Allen, Jane. Phone interview with author. January 31, 2023.
[742] Edwards, Diana. Phone interview with author. October 14, 2023.
[743] *Special Edition of WBTV News*.
[744] Wilson, Mike. In-person conversation with author. August 6, 2023.
[745] Poindexter, "Boone Area Men Sought for Murder," p. 8.
[746] Smith, Louise. Interview with Arlie Isaacs. November 26, 1974, Watauga County Sheriff's Office investigation file 118-H-1/2/3; Harold [sic; Harrold], Harriett. Interview with Arlie Isaacs & Larry Wagner. December 12, 1974, Watauga County Sheriff's Office investigation file 118-H-1/2/3; separate handwritten note concerning Mrs. Harrold's call to Mrs. Collie Durham, Watauga County Sheriff's Office investigation file 118-H-1/2/3.
[747] Anonymous source. In-person conversation with author. August 14, 2023.
[748] Mauldin, Charles & Gayle. Interview with Red Lyons. February 21, 1989.
[749] https://www.findagrave.com/memorial/93505090/disa-pauline-newman.
[750] Genealogical research by author; http://padurham.com/gen/durham_calvin_j.html.
[751] Ibid.
[752] https://www.legacy.com/obituaries/name/jimmie-haynes-obituary?pid=178961039.
[753] Mauldin, Charles & Gayle. Interview with Red Lyons. February 21, 1989.
[754] "4-Year Sentence," *The Charlotte Observer*, Charlotte, NC, May 2, 1980, p. 2C.
[755] Mauldin, Charles & Gayle. Interview with Red Lyons. February 21, 1989.
[756] Watauga County Sheriff's Office investigation file 118-H-1/2/3.
[757] Combs, Dean. Interview with Red Lyons.
[758] Durham, Steve. Interview with Len Hagaman, Kelly Redmon, Carolynn Johnson, Wade Colvard, Larry Wagner, & Rufus Edmisten.
[759] Combs, Dean. Interview with Red Lyons.
[760] Report by Boone Police Department Captain Arlie Isaacs, September 5, 1974, Watauga County Sheriff's Office investigation file 118-h-1/2/3; Small, Cecil. Interview with Arlie Isaacs, September 8, 1974.
[761] York, "Cold Weather"; Reports of Autopsy, Office of the Chief Medical Officer, Chapel Hill, NC, February 4, 1972.
[762] Report of Autopsy, Office of the Chief Medical Officer, Chapel Hill, NC, February 4, 1972, ME-72-37 (Virginia Durham).

[763] Ibid., ME-72-38 (Bryce Durham).
[764] Ibid., ME-72-39 (Robert [sic] Durham).
[765] "Three in Boone Family," p. 1. Henderson, "Rub-Out," p. 62.
[766] Reports of Investigation by Medical Examiner, February 17, 1972, Watauga County Sheriff's Office investigation file 118-H-1/2/3.
[767] Report of Autopsy, Office of the Chief Medical Officer, Chapel Hill, NC, February 4, 1972, ME-72-38 (Bryce Durham); Bullard, *The Durham Murders*, p. 710; The Trail Went Cold, podcast Episode 234 – The Durham Family Murders, July 14, 2021, http://trailwentcold.com/2021/07/14/the-trail-went-cold-episode-234-the-durham-family-murders/; Crime scene photographs, Watauga County Sheriff's Office investigation file 118-H-1/2/3.
[768] Report of Autopsy, Office of the Chief Medical Officer, Chapel Hill, NC, February 4, 1972, ME-72-37 (Virginia Durham); "Boone Couple, Son Slain," p. 1; Bullard, *The Durham Murders*, pp. 179 & 667; Crime scene photographs, Watauga County Sheriff's Office investigation file 118-H-1/2/3.
[769] https://pathologyoutlines.com/topic/forensicsbluntforce.html.
[770] Report of Autopsy, Office of the Chief Medical Officer, Chapel Hill, NC, February 4, 1972, ME-72-39 (Robert [sic] Durham); Crime scene photographs, Watauga County Sheriff's Office investigation file 118-H-1/2/3.
[771] Henderson, "Rub-Out," p. 63.
[772] "Commencement Speakers" (photo caption), *Watauga Democrat*, Boone, NC, June 3, 1971, p. 4B.
[773] https://en.wikipedia.org/wiki/Turn!_Turn!_Turn!
[774] "The Community Mourns," *Watauga Democrat*, Boone, NC, February 7, 1972, p. 4A.
[775] "Rotary Memorial Held For Deceased Member," *Watauga Democrat*, Boone, NC, February 17, 1972, p. 6A.
[776] "Memorial Fund Is Established," *Watauga Democrat*, Boone, NC, March 23, 1972, p. 13B.
[777] Richardson, David Wayne (friend and co-counselor). Facebook comment. February 11, 2022.
[778] "Modern New Mortuary To Be Dedicated On Weekend," *Watauga Democrat*, Boone, NC, May 22, 1969, p. 7; Hampton, Barney. Phone interview with author. February 2, 2023; Anonymous source. Phone conversation with author. March 23, 2023; Death certificates for Bryce, Virginia, and Bobby Durham, Watauga County Register of Deeds Office.
[779] Notes compiled by Gayle Durham Mauldin.
[780] Wilson, Clinard. As stated in notes compiled by Gayle Durham Mauldin.
[781] Hampton, Barney. Phone interview with author; Anonymous source. Phone conversation with author. March 23, 2023.
[782] "Who killed the Durham family? Here's my story," gowilkes.com, August 21, 2010, posted by "countryguy."
[783] "Deaths And Funerals," *The Charlotte Observer*, Charlotte, NC, February 5, 1972, p. 27. Ballard, "Triple Slaying Stuns Boone Area," p. 2.
[784] "New Baptist Minister Is A Man Of Varied Interests," *Watauga Democrat*, Boone, NC, January 20, 1972, p. 8A.
[785] "Services Held," p. 7; Hampton, Barney. Phone interview with author.
[786] "Boone Murder Victims Buried; No New Developments Reported," *Asheville Citizen-Times*, Asheville, NC, February 7, 1972, p. 1 & 6. "Services Held," p. 7; Edmisten, Gary. Phone conversation with author. June 18, 2022.
[787] Small, Cecil & Mildred. Interview with Caroline Walker.
[788] "Services Held," p. 7; Hampton, Barney. Phone interview with author.
[789] "Boone Murder Victims Buried," p. 6.
[790] Bullard, *The Durham Murders*, p. 727.
[791] "Who killed the Durham family? Here's my story," gowilkes.com, August 21, 2010, posted by "countryguy."
[792] Edmisten, Gary. Phone conversation with author. June 18, 2022.
[793] "Deaths And Funerals," p. 27; Google Maps.
[794] John C. W. Gardner, Sr. obituary, *Winston-Salem Journal*, Winston-Salem, NC, December 27, 2012 (online), https://www.legacy.com/us/obituaries/winstonsalem/name/john-gardner-obituary?id=20918209; Poindexter, "Daughter Inherits All," p. 1; "Durham Estate Is $107,585," *The News and Observer*, Raleigh, NC, February 13, 1972, p. 5; Jesse Poindexter, "SBI Widens Its Probe Of 3 Boone Slayings," *Winston-Salem Journal*, Winston-Salem, NC, February 17, 1972, p. 12; Henderson, "Rub-Out," p. 63.
[795] Watauga County Clerk of Court, Estate File 72, Docket Numbers E-12, E-13, & E-16.
[796] "Daughter Inherits Durhams' Property," p. 5.; Poindexter, "Daughter Inherits All," p. 18.
[797] Durham, Bill. Interview with Len Hagaman, Kelly Redmon, Carolynn Johnson, Wade Colvard, Larry Wagner, & Rufus Edmisten.
[798] *Special Edition of WBTV News*; Wagner, Larry. Phone interview with author. December 22, 2022.
[799] "Durham Estate Is $107,585," p. 5; Henderson, "Rub-Out," p. 63.
[800] Watauga County Clerk of Court, Estate File 72, Docket Numbers E-12, E-13, & E-16.
[801] Ibid.
[802] Poindexter, "SBI Widens Its Probe," p. 12.
[803] "Local Buick Dealership Purchased By Mack Brown," *Watauga Democrat*, Boone, NC, March 2, 1972, p. 12.

[804] Combs, Dean. Interview with Red Lyons.
[805] Poindexter, "Daughter Inherits All," p. 18.
[806] Nelson, Minnie. Interview with Arlie Isaacs.
[807] "Who killed the Durham family? Here's my story," gowilkes.com, August 21, 2010, posted by "countryguy."
[808] Eller, Ike & Frances. Interview with Arlie Isaacs & Clyde Tester, January 18, 1975, Watauga County Sheriff's Office investigation file 118-H-1/2/3.
[809] Notes compiled by Gayle Durham Mauldin; Eller, Ike & Frances. Interview with Arlie Isaacs & Clyde Tester.
[810] Hall, Kay. Interview with Clyde Tester & Arlie Isaacs. March 22, 1975.
[811] Eller, Tom. Phone interview with author. July 14, 2022.
[812] Jesse Poindexter, "Lawyer Retained In Boone Case," *Winston-Salem Journal*, Winston-Salem, NC, February 29, 1972, p. 8.
[813] Poindexter, "Daughter Inherits All," p. 18.
[814] Watauga County Clerk of Court, Estate File 72, Docket Numbers E-12, E-13, & E-16; Brown, Jerry (son of Mack Brown, Sr.). Phone interview with author. March 15, 2022.
[815] Anonymous informant. Phone interview with author. March 15, 2022.
[816] "Local Buick Dealership Purchased," p. 12.
[817] Advertisement, *Watauga Democrat*, Boone, NC, May 11, 1972, p. 2B.
[818] Watauga County Clerk of Court, Estate File 72, Docket Numbers E-12, E-13, & E-16.
[819] Ibid.; "Daughter Inherits Durhams' Property," p. 5.
[820] Deed Book 133, p. 478, Watauga County Register of Deeds Office, Boone, NC, executed October 3, 1972, registered October 10, 1972; Watauga County Clerk of Court, Estate File 72, Docket Numbers E-12, E-13, & E-16.
[821] Mauldin, Charles & Gayle. Interview with Red Lyons, August 7, 1989.
[822] Deed Book 163, page 198, Office of the Clerk of Court, Grayson, Co., VA, notarized December 28, 1976, recorded December 29, 1976.
[823] Watauga County Clerk of Court, Estate File 72, Docket Numbers E-12, E-13, & E-16.
[824] Mauldin, Charles & Gayle. Interview with Red Lyons, February 21, 1989.
[825] "Durham Family Slayings," p. 24.
[826] Wake Bridges, "Trio Charged In Watauga Murders," *Hickory Daily Record*, Hickory, NC, April 25, 1972, p. 15; Billy Pritchard, "Four Asheville Men Charged With Boone Triple Murder," *Asheville Citizen-Times*, Asheville, NC, April 26, 1972, p. 2; Henderson, "Rub-Out," p. 63; Jesse Poindexter, "Slain Durhams' Daughter Divorced," *Winston-Salem Journal*, Winston-Salem, NC, September 29, 1976, p. 21.
[827] The Trail Went Cold.
[828] Watauga County Clerk of Court, Estate File 72, Docket Number E-13.
[829] Ibid.
[830] "Letters Protest Murders," *Watauga Democrat*, Boone, NC, February 17, 1972, p. 4A.
[831] "Letters To The Editor," *Watauga Democrat*, Boone, NC, February 24, 1972, p. 2B.
[832] "Says Keep The Death Penalty," *Watauga Democrat*, Boone, NC (via the *Newton-Observer News-Enterprise*), February 14, 1972, p. 4A.
[833] "Murder Investigation Takes Time: Break-Ins Wane In County, Says Sheriff; Ballard, Many Gun Permits Issued," p. 1A; "Sheriff Has Busy Time During March," *Watauga Democrat*, Boone, NC, April 3, 1972, p. 1A.
[834] "Investigation of Durham family's slaying continues."
[835] Reward Up To $14,000," *Watauga Democrat*, Boone, NC, March 27, 1972, p. 2A.
[836] "Identity Of Informant In Murder May Be Secret," *Watauga Democrat*, Boone, NC, March 6, 1972, p. 1B.
[837] Ballard, "In Durham Family Slaying," p. 1A.
[838] "4th Durham Suspect Brought To Carolina," *Watauga Democrat*, Boone, NC, May 1, 1972, p. 1.
[839] "Probe of Slayings Yields No Arrests," p. A15.
[840] Pritchard, "Four Asheville Men Charged," p. 2.
[841] https://www.dignitymemorial.com/obituaries/raleigh-nc/haywood-starling-8940006.
[842] Henderson, "Rub-Out," p. 63.
[843] Cullen, "Boone Stranglings," p. 1B.
[844] "Probe of Slayings Yields No Arrests," p. A15.
[845] Ettman, "Wildest Day," p. 48.
[846] Gary Greene, "No Motive Found," p. 1; Parker, John. Phone interview with author. November 7, 2022.
[847] Ballard, "Triple Slaying Stuns Boone Area," p. 2.
[848] Ettman, "Wildest Day," p. 23.
[849] Henderson, "Rub-Out," p. 63.
[850] Jim Maxwell, "Watauga Sheriff Defends Charges," *The Charlotte News*, Charlotte, NC, July 2, 1973, p. 3B; Handwritten notes and North Carolina Department of Justice, Bureau of Investigation, Latent Evidence Section, April 3, 1975, Watauga County Sheriff's Office investigation file 118-H-1/2/3.

[851] Watauga County Sheriff's Office investigation file 118-H-1/2/3.
[852] Houser, "Two Suspects Bound," p. 2; Small, Cecil & Mildred. Interview with Caroline Walker.
[853] Watauga County Sheriff's Office investigation file 118-H-1/2/3.
[854] Pennica, Sam. Phone interview with author. January 28, 2023.
[855] Parker, John. Phone interview with author. November 7, 2022.
[856] SBI evidence cards with rope samples dated April 7, 1972, Watauga County Sheriff's Office investigation file 118-H-1/2/3.
[857] Ettman, "Wildest Day," p. 48.
[858] Mast, Doug. Facebook comment. February 3, 2021.
[859] Combs, Dean. Interview with Red Lyons.
[860] Vines, Jackie. Phone interview with author. March 10, 2022; Vines, Jacquelyn. Facebook post. September 6, 2023; Vines, Jacquelyn. Facebook message to author. September 8, 2023; George C. Danner III (brother of Bobby Durham's friend Deryl Danner). Phone interview with author. September 8, 2023.
[861] "Slayings in Boone Revealed," p. 1.
[862] "Police Lacking Clues," p. 8A; Capuzzo, *The Murder Room*, p. 84.
[863] "Killers Almost Spotted," p. 2A; Mackie, Ginny Durham. Interview with Carolynn Johnson & Wade Colvard.
[864] Whitman, Charlie. Interview with Charles Heatherly.
[865] Allen, Jane. Phone interview with author. January 31, 2023.
[866] Ballard, "Triple Slaying Stuns Boone Area," p. 2.
[867] Alridge, "Unlikely Victims," p. 1C.
[868] Tester, Johnny. Facebook message to author. February 25, 2022.
[869] Alridge, "Unlikely Victims," p. 1C.
[870] Henderson, "Rub-Out," p. 62; Whitman, Charlie. Interview with Charles Heatherly.
[871] Ettman, "Wildest Day," p. 22; Henderson, "Rub-Out," p. 62.
[872] Facebook comment by Doris Weaver Greer, April 17, 2022.
[873] Whitman, Charlie. Interview with Charles Heatherly.; Bullard, *Durham Murders*, p. 241.
[874] Whitman, Charlie. Interview with Charles Heatherly.
[875] Ibid.
[876] "Prominent Boone Family," p. 3. Henderson, "Rub-Out," p. 62.
[877] "Boone Couple, Son Slain," p. 1.
[878] "Services Held," p. 7.
[879] "3 Killed In Boone," p. 2.
[880] "Killers Almost Spotted," p. 1; Henderson, "Rub-Out," p. 62.
[881] Ettman, "Wildest Day," p. 48.
[882] "Triple Murder Former Wilkes Residents Remains Unsolved," *The Journal-Patriot*, North Wilkesboro, NC, February 7, 1972, p. 1.
[883] Ettman, "Wildest Day," p. 48.
[884] Poindexter, "Boone Area Men Sought," p. 8; "More Agents Join Search For Family's Killers," *Winston-Salem-Journal*, Winston-Salem, NC, February 6, 1972, p. A14; Henderson, "Rub-Out," p. 62; Unidentified newspaper copy shared by Debbie York.
[885] "Probe of Slayings Yields No Arrests," p. A15.
[886] Edwards, Diana (Virginia Durham's great-niece). Phone interview with author. October 14, 2023.
[887] Ettman, "Wildest Day," p. 48.
[888] "Garland Is Named Key Banker," *Watauga Democrat*, Boone, NC, December 13, 1971, p. 7A; "Triple Murder: Woman Sought Help Minutes Before Three Died In Boone," *The Daily Times-News, Burlington*, NC, February 5, 1972, p. 2-A; Garland, Sonya. Facebook message to author. April 4, 2022; Garland, Carroll. Personal interview with author. April 5 & 7, 2022.
[889] "Where Day's News Was," *Leader-Times*, Kittanning-Ford City-New Bethlehem, PA, February 5, 1972, p. 1.
[890] "'Good Clues' Are Found," *Winston-Salem Journal*, Winston-Salem, NC, February 6, 1972, p. A1; Capuzzo, *The Murder Room*, p. 84.
[891] Wake Bridges, "Hunt For Slayers Pushed," *Hickory Daily Record*, February 5, 1972, p. 1.
[892] Jesse Poindexter, "Search for Killers Begins at Boone," *Winston-Salem Journal*, Winston-Salem, NC, February 5, 1972, p. 1.
[893] "Neighborhood uneasy," p. 1.
[894] Bridges, "Hunt For Slayers Pushed," p. 1.
[895] "'Good Clues' Are Found," *Winston-Salem Journal*, Winston-Salem, NC, February 6, 1972, p. A1.
[896] "$8000 reward offered in Boone triple slaying," *Johnson City Press-Chronicle*, Johnson City, TN, February 12, 1972, p. 1.

[897] "Boone Deputies At Dead End In Investigation Of 3 Deaths," *The Daily News*, Kingsport, TN, February 8, 1972, p. 1.
[898] Poindexter, "Daughter Inherits All," p. 1.
[899] Poindexter, "SBI Widens Its Probe," pp. 1 & 12.
[900] "Probe of Slayings Yields No Arrests," p. A15.
[901] Poindexter, "SBI Widens Its Probe," pp. 1 & 12.
[902] Small, Cecil & Mildred. Interview with Caroline Walker.
[903] Durham, Ginny. Interview with Clyde Tester, Arlie Isaacs, & L. D. Hagaman, Jr.
[904] "$13,750 reward posted in deaths of Boone family," *Wilmington Morning Star*, Wilmington, NC, March 6, 1972, p. 8.
[905] *Special Edition of WBTV News*.
[906] Whitman, Charlie. Interview with Charles Heatherly.
[907] Carroll, Ward. Interview with Charles Heatherly.
[908] "Identity Of Informant," p. 2B.
[909] "Probe of Slayings Yields No Arrests," *Winston-Salem Journal*, Winston-Salem, NC, April 23, 1972, p. A15.
[910] Small, Cecil & Mildred. Interview with Caroline Walker.
[911] Poindexter, "Dead Man's Automobile Firm Sold," p. 25; "$13,750 reward posted in deaths of Boone family," p. 8.
[912] "Identity Of Informant," p. 2B; *Special Edition of WBTV News*.
[913] "4th Durham Suspect," p. 2.
[914] "Identity Of Informant," p. 2B.
[915] Small, Cecil & Mildred. Interview with Caroline Walker.
[916] Combs, Dean. Interview with Red Lyons.
[917] Anonymous. Facebook message to author. November 5, 2022.
[918] Unexplained-Mysteries.com: Unsolved Triple Murder, North Carolina, 1972, comment by "mbrn30000," https://www.unexplained-mysteries.com/forum/topic/262185-unsolved-triple-murder-north-carolina-1972/page/35/#comments.
[919] Source misplaced.
[920] Small, Cecil & Mildred. Interview with Caroline Walker.
[921] "Probe of Slayings Yields No Arrests," p. A15.
[922] Rucker, Jeff. Phone interview with author. October 4, 2023.
[923] Small, Cecil, Interview with Charles Heatherly.
[924] https://austinandbarnesfuneralhome.com/tribute/details/488/Mildred-Small/obituary.html.
[925] "Durham murders remembered," p. 5.
[926] Small, Cecil & Mildred. Interview with Caroline Walker; Small, Cecil. Interview with Arlie Isaacs, September 8, 1974.
[927] Ibid.
[928] Ibid.
[929] Notes compiled by Gayle Durham Mauldin.
[930] Ibid.
[931] Ibid.
[932] Eller, Ike. Interview with Red Lyons & Fred Myers.
[933] Notes compiled by Gayle Durham Mauldin.
[934] Hall, Kay. Interviews with Clyde Tester & Arlie Isaacs, March 22, 1975 & April 7, 1975.
[935] Durham, Ginny. Interview with Clyde Tester, Arlie Isaacs, & L. D. Hagaman, Jr.
[936] Notes compiled by Gayle Durham Mauldin.
[937] Watauga County Sheriff's Office investigation file 118-H-1/2/3.
[938] Notes compiled by Gayle Durham Mauldin.
[939] Mauldin, Charles & Gayle. Interview with Red Lyons, August 7, 1989..
[940] Eller, Tom. Phone interview with author. July 14, 2022.
[941] Jesse Poindexter, "Boone Couple's Estate Is Valued at $107,585," *Winston-Salem Journal*, Winston-Salem, NC, February 12, 1972, pp. 1 & 10.
[942] Reward of $4,000," *Watauga Democrat*, Boone, NC, February 7, 1972, p. 1A; "Optimists Add To Reward Fund," *Watauga Democrat*, Boone, NC, February 10, 1972, p. 10A; "Reward For Killers Continues To Grow," *Watauga Democrat*, Boone, NC, February 10, 1972, p. 1A; "Reward in Boone Killings Now $5,000," *Winston-Salem Journal*, Winston-Salem, NC, February 10, 1972, p. 22; "Durham Case Reward Upped; $5,000 Offered For Information," *The Journal-Patriot*, North Wilkesboro, NC, February 10, 1972, p. 1; "Reward For Slayers Mounts To $10,600," *Watauga Democrat*, Boone, NC, February 14, 1972, p. 1A; "Reward Growing In Murder Case," *Watauga Democrat*, Boone, NC, February 21, 1972, p. 2A; "Reward Fund Now $14,500," *Asheville Citizen-Times*, Asheville, NC, February 28, 1972, p. 7; "Reward For Slayers Reaches $17,050," *Watauga Democrat*, Boone, NC, February 28, 1972, p. 1A; "Boone Murder

Reward $17,050," p. 1, https://news.google.com/newspapers?nid=P-MJmu9ZMwQC&dat=19720303&printsec=frontpage&hl=en; "Identity Of Informant," p. 1B; "Murder of Durhams Remains Unsolved; Reward Is $13,750," *The Journal-Patriot*, North Wilkesboro, NC, March 9, 1972, Section 2, p. 1; "Reward Increased In Killings," *The Charlotte Observer*, Charlotte, NC, March 24, 1972, p. 4A; "Reward Up To $14,000," p. 2A; Ballard, "In Durham Family Slaying," pp. 1A & 14; Watauga County Clerk of Court Criminal File #72-CR-1072, State vs. Jerry Ray Cassada [The checks/copies of checks are in an envelope attached to this file.].

[943] "Reward Growing In Murder Case," p. 2A.

[944] "Identity Of Informant," pp. 1B & 2B; "Murder of Durhams Remains Unsolved," Section 2, p. 1.

[945] "Reward Up To $14,000," p. 2A.

[946] Bullard, *The Durham Murders*, p. 793.

[947] Genealogical research by author.

[948] Bullard, *The Durham Murders*, p. 755.

[949] "Reward Growing In Murder Case," p. 2A; Watauga County Clerk of Court Criminal File #72-CR-1072, State vs. Jerry Ray Cassada [The checks/copies of checks are in an envelope attached to this file.]; Jolley, Frank (grandson of E. J. Durham). E-mail to Tim Bullard. January 14, 2011, Watauga County Sheriff's Office investigation file 118-H-1/2/3; Jolley, Frank. Phone interview with author. December 8, 2023; Bullard, *The Durham Murders*, p. 745.

[950] Ettman, "Wildest Day," p. 49.

[951] Dot Jackson, "Psychic Says He's Willing To Aid In MacDonald Case," The Charlotte Observer, Charlotte, NC, January 1, 1971, p. 1B; Prudy Taylor, "Dutch Psychic Reveals Past, Future," News-Press, Fort Myers, FL, November 13, 1972, p. 1-D; Maureen Bashaw. "Solves Murders: Clairvoyant Sees Via Divining Rod," News-Press, Fort Myers, FL, July 18, 1974, p. 1D.

[952] Jesse Poindexter, "Psychic Consulted In Boone Slayings," *Winston-Salem Journal*, Winston-Salem, NC, March 28, 1972, p. 2.

[953] "Clairvoyant Consulted," p. 2A.

[954] Poindexter, "Psychic Consulted," p. 2.

[955] Dot Jackson, "Marinus Bernardus Dykshoorn – His Job Is Solving Mysteries," The Charlotte Observer, Charlotte, NC, August 2, 1970, p. 1C; June Kronholz, "This Clairvoyant Does It With Wires," The Miami Herald, Miami, FL, August 23, 1971, p. 1B; Warren Barnard, "He's A Professional Clairvoyant," The Charlotte News, Charlotte, NC, March 23, 1972, p. 1B; David Mannweiler, "Dutch Seer Finds Money," The News, Indianapolis, IN, April 21, 1978, p. November 13, 1972, p. 2; Bashaw. "Solves Murders," p. 5D; "Clairvoyant Will Speak At Beach Club," Naples Daily News, Naples, FL, August 25, 1974, p. 7B; Bob Wisehart, "Under Occupation It Reads Clairvoyant," The Charlotte News, Charlotte, NC, October 22, 1975, p. 14A.

[956] Jackson, "Psychic Says He's Willing To Aid," p. 1B; Kronholz, "This Clairvoyant Does It With Wires," p. 1B; Barnard, "He's A Professional Clairvoyant," p. 1B; Taylor, "Dutch Psychic Reveals Past, Future," p. 1-D; Bashaw. "Solves Murders," p. 1D.

[957] Jackson, "Marinus Bernardus Dykshoorn," p. 2C; Jackson, "Psychic Says He's Willing To Aid,"p. 1B; Kronholz, "This Clairvoyant Does It With Wires," p. 1B; Barnard, "He's A Professional Clairvoyant," pp. 1B & 20B; Bashaw. "Solves Murders," p. 5D; Wisehart, "Under Occupation It Reads Clairvoyant," p. 14A.

[958] Poindexter, "Lawyer Retained In Boone Case," p. 1.

[959] "Clairvoyant Consulted," p. 2A.

[960] "Clairvoyant Is Hired In Murder Case," *The Charlotte Observer*, Charlotte, NC, March 25, 1972, p. 2C.

[961] Barnard, "He's A Professional Clairvoyant," p. 1B.

[962] "Clairvoyant Is Hired In Murder Case," *The Charlotte Observer*, Charlotte, NC, March 25, 1972, p. 2C; Wisehart, "Under Occupation It Reads Clairvoyant," p. 12A.

[963] "Clairvoyant Joins In Hunt For Murderers," *Watauga Democrat*, Boone, NC, March 30, 1972, p. 1A.

[964] Jones, "Triple Murders Left Indelible Etch," p. 1.

[965] Ettman, "Wildest Day," p. 49.

[966] Tommy Denton, "Officers, Others Disagree – Did Dykshoorn Solve Case?" *The Charlotte News*, Charlotte, NC, April 26, 1972, p. 4A.

[967] "Three Men Held In Boone Deaths," *The Charlotte News*, April 25, 1972, p. 8A.

[968] Denton, "Officers, Others Disagree," p. 4A.

[969] "Clairvoyant Is Hired In Murder Case," p. 2C.

[970] Ettman, "Wildest Day," p. 49.

[971] Kronholz, "This Clairvoyant Does It With Wires," p. 1B; Wisehart, "Under Occupation It Reads Clairvoyant," pp. 12A & 14A.

[972] Ettman, "Wildest Day," p. 49.

[973] Auston, John. Interview with Clyde Tester & Arlie Isaacs.

[974] Kipe, *In The Red Clay*, Season 2, Episode 4: *The Company of Wolves*.

[975] Jones, "Triple Murders Left Indelible Etch," p. 2A.

[976] "Jeffery MacDonald & 1972 Durham triple murders same killers theory," July 20, 2015, posted by "redpill," text from Journal Now and Yes Weekly. https://jbrwdi.forumotion.com/t715-jeffrey-macdonald-1972-durham-triple-murders-same-killers-theory.
[977] Hagaman, David. Phone interview with author. November 5, 2022.
[978] Bullard, *The Durham Murders*, p. 391; "Investigation of Durham family's slaying continues."
[979] Henderson, "Rub-Out," p. 62.
[980] Letter to Sheriff James C. Lyons, February 21, 1989, Watauga County Sheriff's Office investigation file 118-H-1/2/3.
[981] Edmisten, Rufus L., *That's Rufus: A Memoir of Tar Heel Politics, Watergate and Public Life* (Jefferson, NC: McFarland & Company, Inc., 2019), pp. 121-122.
[982] Edmisten, Rufus. Zoom interview with author. March 31, 2022.
[983] Wagner, Larry. Phone interview with author. December 22, 2022; Carroll Gardner obituary, *Winston-Salem Journal*, Winston-Salem, NC, January 7, 2004 (online), https://www.legacy.com/us/obituaries/winstonsalem/name/carroll-gardner-obituary?id=28987220.
[984] Odometer Fraud/Signs of Car Odometer Rollback Fraud, https://www.everlance.com/blog/odometer-fraud-detection#:~:text=Odometer%20fraud%2C%20also%20know%20as,the%20value%20of%20a%20car; Office of the Law Revision Counsel, United States Code, Chapter 46: Motor Vehicle Information and Cost Savings, Subchapter IV – Odometer Requirements, http://uscode.house.gov/view.xhtml?path=/prelim@title15/chapter46&edition=prelim; The United States Department of Justice: The Federal Odometer Tampering Statutes, https://www.justice.gov/civil/case/federal-odometer-tampering-statutes; "New Law Effective On Motor Vehicle Mileage," *Watauga Democrat*, Boone, NC, December 7, 1972, p. 1.
[985] Wagner, Larry. Interview with Charles Heatherly; Anonymous informant. Phone conversation with author.
[986] Reece, Lester. Phone interview with author. September 12, 2022.
[987] Durham, Ginny. Interview with Clyde Tester, Arlie Isaacs, & L. D. Hagaman, Jr.
[988] Anonymous informant.
[989] Durham, Ginny. Interview with Clyde Tester, Arlie Isaacs, & L. D. Hagaman, Jr.
[990] Cook, Dan (son of John Cook, part owner of the Johnson-Cook Ford dealership in Boone, NC). Comment on Facebook Post by Jackie Vines. September 6, 2023.
[991] "In the winter of 1972, Troy Hall received a frantic call...," March 20, 2022, posted by "Pop-Massive," https://reddit.com/r/UnresolvedMysteries/comments/4zsb03/in_the_winter_of_1972_troy_hall_received_a/.
[992] Wagner, Larry. Interview with Charles Heatherly.
[993] Jackson, *North Carolina Murder & Mayhem*.
[994] Wagner, Larry. Interview with Charles Heatherly.
[995] The Trail Went Cold.
[996] Bullard, *The Durham Murders*, p. 350.
[997] Jackson, *North Carolina Murder & Mayhem*.
[998] Inside Carolina, posted by "NOVAHEEL13," July 4, 2017. https://247sports.com/college/north-carolina/Board/102717/Contents/my-annual-summer-is-boring-unsolved-NC-murder-thread-73380860/?page=1.
[999] Watauga County Sheriff's Office investigation file 118-H-1/2/3.
[1000] Ibid.
[1001] Durham, Ginny. Interview with Clyde Tester, Arlie Isaacs, & L. D. Hagaman, Jr.
[1002] Vaughn, Jerry. In-person interview with author. October 13, 2023.
[1003] Edwards, Diana (Virginia Durham's great-niece). Phone interview with author. October 14, 2023.
[1004] Bullard, *The Durham Murders*, p. 350.
[1005] Jolley, Frank. Phone interview with author. December 8, 2023.
[1006] "Under Bond On Drug Charge," *Watauga Democrat*, Boone, NC, March 6, 1969, p. 1; "Drug Problem Exists at WHS, Dr. Miller Tells Board," *Watauga Democrat*, Boone, NC, December 4, 1969, p. 1; "Law Enforcing Dilemma," *Watauga Democrat*, Boone, NC, September 30, 1971, p. 2; "Drug Problem The Way It Is," *Watauga Democrat*, October 7, 1971, p. 2; "Alarming Drug Situation In State Cited by Dunn," *Watauga Democrat*, Boone, NC, October 7, 1971, p. 6A.
[1007] "Boone Police Finish Course," *Watauga Democrat*, Boone, NC, January 1, 1970, p. 2.
[1008] "21 Drug Arrests Made In Watauga County In Year," *Watauga Democrat*, Boone, NC, December 16, 1971, p. 1B.
[1009] Ginn, Phil. Zoom interview with author. March 12, 2022.
[1010] Vines, Jackie. Phone interview with author. March 10, 2022.
[1011] Henderson, "Rub-Out," p. 62.
[1012] Bullard, *The Durham Murders*, p. 350.
[1013] Ibid., pp. 198 & 207.
[1014] "Investigation of Durham family's slaying continues."
[1015] Ibid.
[1016] Edmisten, *That's Rufus*, p. 121; Wagner, Larry. Interview with Charles Heatherly.

[1017] Bullard, *The Durham Murders*, p. 268.
[1018] "Advance Green Berets Look Over Ski Area," *Watauga Democrat*, Boone, NC, December 20, 1971, p. 7A.
[1019] Watauga County Sheriff's Office investigation file 118-H-1/2/3.
[1020] Jackson, *North Carolina Murder & Mayhem*.
[1021] John Downey, "Investigators Say Murders Will Be Solved," *Winston-Salem Journal*, Winston-Salem, NC, January 31, 1982, p. B6.
[1022] "Investigation of Durham family's slaying continues."
[1023] Henderson, "Rub-Out," p. 62.
[1024] Bullard, *The Durham Murders*, pp. 90 & 101.
[1025] "Who killed the Durham family? Here's my story," gowilkes.com, August 23, 2010, posted by "SofaKingCrazy." gowilkes.com/voice/who-killed-the-durham-family-heres-my-story/77993/?startview=40&h=084614. "Jeffery MacDonald & 1972 Durham triple murders same killers theory."
[1026] Parker, John. Phone interview with author. November 7, 2022.
[1027] "Jeffery MacDonald & 1972 Durham triple murders same killers theory."
[1028] Ingram, Bob. In-person interview with author. April 19, 2022.
[1029] "Who killed the Durham family? Here's my story," gowilkes.com, August 20, 2010, posted by "richardcastle." gowilkes.com/voice/who-killed-the-durham-family-heres-my-story/77993/?startview=100&h=091330.
[1030] "Student Says That PSTA Provides Chance To Turn Unrest To Action," *Watauga Democrat*, Boone, NC, November 13, 1969, p. 1; "Boone, North Carolina, February 1972: The Bizarre and Unexplained Murder of Bryce Durham, Virginia Durham, and Their Son Bobby Joe," January 17, 2021, posted by "Basic_Bichette." https://reddit.com/r/UnresolvedMysteries/comments/kz1bcp/boone_north_carolina_february_1972_the_bizarre/.
[1031] Small, Cecil. Interview with Charles Heatherly; Small, Cecil & Mildred Small. Interview with Caroline Walker.
[1032] Small, Cecil & Mildred Small. Interview with Caroline Walker.
[1033] Ibid.
[1034] Ibid.; Brown, Ted. Phone conversation with author. June 25, 2022.
[1035] Small, Small, Cecil & Mildred. Interview with Caroline Walker.
[1036] Ibid.
[1037] Ettman, "Wildest Day," p. 48; "Four Men Arrested In Break-Ins," *Asheville Citizen-Times*, Asheville, NC, February 9, 1972, p. 16; Billy Pritchard, "Eight Men Arrested In Raid By Deputies," *Asheville Citizen-Times*, Asheville, NC, March 2, 1972, p. 25.
[1038] Ettman, "Wildest Day," p. 48.
[1039] Ballard, "In Durham Family Slaying," p. 1A.
[1040] Ettman, "Wildest Day," p. 48.
[1041] Pritchard, "Four Asheville Men Charged," p. 2.
[1042] Pritchard, "Eight Men Arrested," p. 25; Ettman, "Wildest Day," p. 49.
[1043] Anonymous source. E-mail to author. January 25, 2023.
[1044] Ibid; Ettman, "Wildest Day," p. 48.
[1045] Ettman, "Wildest Day," p. 49.
[1046] Jones, "Triple Murders Left Indelible Etch," p. 1.
[1047] Ettman, "Wildest Day," p. 49.
[1048] Ettman, "Wildest Day," p. 49.
[1049] Pritchard, "Four Asheville Men Charged," p. 2; "Fourth Suspect In Boone Triple Murder Surrenders To Police," *Asheville Citizen-Times*, Asheville, NC, April 27, 1972, p. 8; "Triple-Murder Defendant Gets 5 Years For Car Theft," *Asheville Citizen-Times*, Asheville, NC, July 11, 1972, p. 13.
[1050] "Fourth Suspect In Boone Triple Murder," p. 8; Billy Pritchard, "Hearing On Boone Murders Reportedly Set For June 15," *Asheville Citizen-Times*, Asheville, NC, June 6, 1972, p. 13.
[1051] "Couple Held On Charges Of Theft, Forgery," *The Asheville Citizen*, Asheville, NC, April 19, 1972, p. 10; "Attorney Pleads Guilty To Charge Of Embezzlement," *Asheville Citizen-Times*, Asheville, NC, November 14, 1972, p. 13.
[1052] Ettman, "Wildest Day," p. 49.
[1053] Ibid.
[1054] Chandler, Dean & Anne. Interviews with Charlie Whitman. April 22, 1972, Watauga County Sheriff's Office investigation file 118-8-1/2/3; Ettman, "Wildest Day," p. 50.
[1055] Chandler, Dean & Anne. Interviews with Charlie Whitman.
[1056] Ibid.
[1057] https://en.wikipedia.org/wiki/North_Carolina_Highway_105.
[1058] Chandler, Dean & Anne. Interviews with Charlie Whitman.
[1059] Ibid.
[1060] Ibid.
[1061] Ibid.

[1062] Ibid.
[1063] Ettman, "Wildest Day," pp. 49-50.
[1064] Chandler, Dean & Anne. Interviews with Charlie Whitman.
[1065] Henderson, Leonard. *Rub-Out, Rub-Out, Rub-Out: Three Bodies in a Tub*. Startling Detective, September 1972, p. 63.
[1066] Chandler, Dean & Anne. Interviews with Charlie Whitman.
[1067] Ibid.
[1068] Ibid.
[1069] Ibid.
[1070] Ibid.
[1071] Ibid.
[1072] Ibid.
[1073] Notes compiled by Gayle Durham Mauldin.
[1074] Bev Ballard, "200 Quizzed In Murder," *Watauga Democrat*, Boone, NC, April 24, 1972, p. 1; Henderson, "Rub-Out," p. 63.
[1075] "200 Questioned In Murder," *Watauga Democrat*, Boone, NC, April 24, 1972, p. 2.
[1076] Watauga County, NC Clerk of Court's Office, Criminal Files #72-CR-1072, -1073, -1074, State vs. Jerry Ray Cassada, Warrants For Murder, April 24, 1972.
[1077] Ibid.; Watauga County, NC Clerk of Court's Office, Criminal Files #72-CR-1078, -1079, -1080, State vs. Dean Chandler, Warrant For Accessory Before the Fact, Murder, April 24, 1972; "Hearing In Murders May Be Postponed," Asheville Citizen-Times, Asheville, NC, May 12, 1972, p. 15.
[1078] Cullen, "Boone Stranglings," p. 1B.
[1079] Bridges, "Trio Charged In Watauga Murders," pp. 1 & 15.
[1080] Pritchard, "Four Asheville Men Charged," p. 2; "Fourth Suspect In Boone Triple Murder," p. 8; "Triple-Murder Defendant Gets 5 Years For Car Theft," *Asheville Citizen-Times*, Asheville, NC, July 11, 1972, p. 13.
[1081] "Boone Slaying Suspects Whisked To Watauga Jail," *The Charlotte News*, Charlotte, NC, April 25, 1972, p. 1.
[1082] Ballard, "In Durham Family Slaying" (photo caption), p. 1A.
[1083] Ibid.
[1084] Arlene Edwards, "Man Sought in Boone Deaths Gives Up," *Winston-Salem Journal*, Winston-Salem, NC, April 27, 1972, p. 1.
[1085] "4th Durham Suspect," p. 2.
[1086] Hall, Kay. Interview with Clyde Tester & Arlie Isaacs.
[1087] "Boone Slaying Suspects Whisked," p. 1.
[1088] Pritchard, "Four Asheville Men Charged," p. 2.
[1089] Arlidge, "Clairvoyant Consulted," p. 1; "Clairvoyant Consulted," p. 2A.
[1090] Pritchard, "Hearing On Boone Murders," p. 13; "Asheville Man Sought In Slayings; Surrenders To Maryland Police," *The Charlotte Observer*, Charlotte, NC, April 27, 1972, p. 16C.
[1091] Jesse Poindexter, "Men Charged In Boone Ask For Lawyers," *Winston-Salem-Journal*, Winston-Salem, NC, May 11, 1972, p. 1.
[1092] "Clairvoyant Consulted," p. 2A
[1093] Bullard, *The Durham Murders*, p. 810.
[1094] Ibid. Ettman, "Wildest Day," p. 50.
[1095] Watauga County Sheriff's Office investigation file 118-H-1/2/3.
[1096] Wisehart, "Under Occupation It Reads Clairvoyant," p. 12A.
[1097] Taylor, "Dutch Psychic Reveals Past, Future," p. 1D.
[1098] "Clairvoyant Consulted," p. 2A; Denton, "Officers, Others Disagree," p. 4A.
[1099] Denton, "Officers, Others Disagree," p. 4A.
[1100] Pritchard, "Four Asheville Men Charged," p. 2.
[1101] "Clairvoyant Consulted," p. 2A.
[1102] Wisehart, "Under Occupation It Reads Clairvoyant," pp. 12A & 14A.
[1103] Tommy Denton, "Did Dykshoorn Solve Boone Murder?" *The Charlotte News*, April 26, 1972, pp. 1 & 4A.
[1104] "Clairvoyant Consulted," p. 2A.
[1105] Billy Pritchard, "Fourth Slaying Suspect Surrenders To Police," *The Asheville Citizen*, Asheville, NC, April 27, 1972, p. 1; "Fourth Slaying Suspect Surrenders In Maryland," *The News and Observer*, Raleigh, NC, April 27, 1972, p. 5.
[1106] "4th Man Hunted," *The Charlotte News*, April 26, 1972, p. 4.
[1107] "Fourth Suspect In Boone Triple Murder," p. 8.
[1108] "Asheville Man Sought," p. 16C.
[1109] "Coffey Brought To Boone," *Asheville Citizen-Times*, Asheville, NC, April 29, 1972, p. 9.

[1110] "Wanted Man Returned," *Winston-Salem Journal*, Winston-Salem, NC, April 28, 1972, p. 1; Tester, Johnny. Facebook message to author, February 25, 2022.
[1111] "Wanted Man Returned," p. 1; Ettman, Jay. *Wildest Day in Daniel Boone Country*. Front Page Detective Magazine, October 1972, p. 50.
[1112] "Police Question 4 Charged in Slayings," *Winston-Salem Journal*, Winston-Salem, NC, April 29, 1972, p. 3; "4th Durham Suspect," p. 1; Ettman, "Wildest Day," p. 50.
[1113] Nelson, Chester. Interview with Arlie Isaacs.
[1114] Watauga County Sheriff's Office investigation file 118-H-1/2/3.
[1115] Ibid.
[1116] "Murder Suspects Seek Aid," *The Charlotte Observer*, Charlotte, NC, May 12, 1972, p. 11A.
[1117] "Murder Trial Attorneys Appointed," *Asheville Citizen-Times*, Asheville, NC, May 16, 1972, p. 13.
[1118] "Reports List Men's Assets and Debts," *Winston-Salem Journal*, Winston-Salem, NC, May 11, 1972, p. 2.
[1119] "Counsel Appointed For Durham Murder Suspects," *Watauga Democrat*, Boone, NC, May 18, 1972, p. 1A.
[1120] Watauga County, NC Clerk of Court's Office, Criminal Files #72-CR-1072, -1073, -1074, State vs. Jerry Ray Cassada, Order Of Assignment Of Counsel, May 15, 1972; Watauga County, NC Clerk of Court's Office, Criminal Files #72-CR-1078, -1079, -1080, State vs. Dean Chandler, Order Of Assignment Of Counsel, May 15, 1972; "Murder Trial Attorneys Appointed," p. 13; "To Open Law Office Here," *Watauga Democrat*, Boone, NC, July 22, 1971, p. 1.
[1121] "Counsel Appointed," p. 1A.
[1122] Ibid.
[1123] Ibid.
[1124] "Murder Trial Attorneys Appointed," p. 13.
[1125] Ettman, "Wildest Day," p. 50.
[1126] "Council For Suspects Set During This Court Term," *Watauga Democrat*, Boone, NC, May 15, 1972, p. 2A.
[1127] "Hearing In Murders May Be Postponed," p. 15; Pritchard, "Hearing On Boone Murders," p. 13.
[1128] Notes compiled by Gayle Durham Mauldin.
[1129] Jesse Poindexter, "Two Freed in Boone Slayings," *Winston-Salem Journal*, Winston-Salem, NC, June 16, 1972, pp. 1-2; Houser, "Two Suspects Bound," p. 1.
[1130] Watauga County, NC Clerk of Court's Office, Criminal Files #72-CR-1072, -1073, -1074, State vs. Jerry Ray Cassada & Files -1078, -1079, State vs. Dean Chandler, Writ of Habeas Corpus Ad Testificandum, June 5, 1972.
[1131] "Four Are Held In Madison Break-In Probe," *The Asheville Times*, Asheville, NC, February 9, 1972, p. 15.
[1132] Watauga County, NC Clerk of Court's Office, Criminal Files #72-CR-1072, -1073, -1074, State vs. Jerry Ray Cassada & & Files -1078, -1079, -1080, State vs. Dean Chandler, Subpoena, June 6, 1972, served in person by Madison County Deputy Sheriff John (Hamby?), June 8, 1972.
[1133] Ibid., served in person by Buncombe County Deputy Sheriff E. M. Foster, June 8, 1972.
[1134] Ibid., served by telephone/mail by Wake County Deputy M. T. Munn, June 8, 1972.
[1135] Ibid., served in person by Watauga County Deputy Sheriff Jerry Farmer, June 8, 1972.
[1136] Ibid., served in person by Buncombe County Deputy Sheriff E. M. Foster, June 8, 1972; "Chief Deputy Sorrells Quits Post," *The Asheville Citizen*, Asheville, NC, April 26, 1972, p. 13.
[1137] Watauga County, NC Clerk of Court's Office, Criminal Files #72-CR-1072, -1073, -1074, State vs. Jerry Ray Cassada & Files -1078, -1079, -1080, State vs. Dean Chandler, Subpoena, June 6, 1972, served in person by Buncombe County Deputy Sheriff E. M. Foster, June 8, 1972; "Chief Deputy Sorrells Quits Post," p. 13.
[1138] Watauga County, NC Clerk of Court's Office, Criminal Files #72-CR-1072, -1073, -1074, State vs. Jerry Ray Cassada & Files -1078, -1079, -1080, State vs. Dean Chandler, Subpoena, June 6, 1972, served in person by Buncombe County Deputy Sheriff E. M. Foster, June 8, 1972.
[1139] Ibid., served in person by Donald McCaleb, June 8, 1972.
[1140] Ibid., served in person by Buncombe County Deputy Sheriff E. M. Foster, June 9, 1972.
[1141] Ibid.
[1142] Ibid.
[1143] Ibid.
[1144] Ibid., served in person by Buncombe County Deputy Sheriff Gray A. Burleson, June 13, 1972.
[1145] Ibid., served in person by Watauga County Sheriff Ward Carroll, June 14, 1972.
[1146] Ibid.
[1147] Ibid., served in person by Buncombe County Deputy Sheriff J. V. Staggs, June 14, 1972.
[1148] Ibid., served in person by Jerry Shockley, June 14, 1972.
[1149] Chandler, Dean & Anne. Interviews with Charlie Whitman.
[1150] Ibid.; Houser, "Two Suspects Bound," p. 2.
[1151] Jesse Poindexter, "Boone Murder Case Takes New Direction," *Winston-Salem Journal*, Winston-Salem, NC, June 23, 1973, p. 13; Watauga County, NC Clerk of Court's Office, Criminal Files #72-CR-1072, -1073, -1074, State vs. Jerry Ray Cassada, Statement of time and expenses from attorney Charles C. Lamm, Jr., January 23, 1974.

[1152] Ibid.; Ettman, "Wildest Day," p. 50; Houser, "Two Suspects Bound," p. 2.
[1153] Houser, "Two Suspects Bound," p. 1.
[1154] "2 Held, 2 Released In Boone Slayings," *Asheville Citizen-Times*, Asheville, NC, June 16, 1972, p. 1.
[1155] Pritchard, "Hearing On Boone Murders," p. 13.
[1156] "2 Held, 2 Released In Boone Slayings," p. 1; Ron Alridge, "2 Of 4 Suspects Face Trial In Boone Killings," *The Charlotte Observer*, Charlotte, NC, June 16, 1972, p. 3C.
[1157] "2 Held, 2 Released In Boone Slayings," p. 1.
[1158] Houser, "Two Suspects Bound," p. 1.
[1159] Ballard, "In Durham Family Slaying," p. 1A.
[1160] "Sheriff Ward Carroll Named Lawman Of Year," *Watauga Democrat*, Boone, NC, May 4, 1972, p. 1A.
[1161] Poindexter, "Two Freed in Boone Slayings," pp. 1-2.
[1162] Ibid.
[1163] Cullen, "Boone Stranglings," p. 1B.
[1164] Houser, "Two Suspects Bound," p. 2.
[1165] Poindexter, "Two Freed in Boone Slayings," pp. 1-2; Houser, "Two Suspects Bound In," p. 2.
[1166] "Two Men Will Be Tried," p. 2C.
[1167] Edwards, Diana (daughter of Jerri Bumgarner Waddell). Phone interview with author. October 14, 2023.
[1168] Poindexter, "Two Freed in Boone Slayings," pp. 1-2.
[1169] Watauga County Sheriff's Office investigation file 118-H-1/2/3; North Carolina, U. S. Birth Indexes, 1800-2000 for Frances Marie Ballard, Buncombe, 1946-1956, https://ancestry.com/discoveryui-content/view/304977:8783; North Carolina, U. S., Death Certificate, 1909-1976 for Dewey Lee Cassada (infant son of Jerry Ray Cassada & Frances Marie Ballard), Buncombe, August 1971.
[1170] Mauldin, Charles & Gayle. Interview with Red Lyons. April 17, 1989.
[1171] Watauga County Sheriff's Office investigation file 118-H-1/2/3.
[1172] Watauga County, NC Clerk of Court's Office, Criminal Files #72-CR-1072, -1073, -1074, State vs. Jerry Ray Cassada, Order, July 18, 1972; "$50,000 Bond Is Set In Boone Murder Case," *Asheville Citizen-Times*, Asheville, NC, July 20, 1972, p. 21; "Boone Case Defendant's Bail Is Set," *Winston-Salem Journal*, Winston-Salem, NC, July 21, 1972, p. 16; "Placed Under $50,000 Bail," *Watauga Democrat*, Boone, NC, July 24, 1972, p. 1.
[1173] "Triple-Murder Defendant Gets 5," p. 13; "Fourth Suspect In Boone Triple Murder," p. 8.
[1174] "Boone Case Defendant's Bail Is Set," p. 16.
[1175] "Murder Case Figure Facing Other Charges," *Asheville Citizen-Times*, Asheville, NC, August 3, 1972, p. 38.
[1176] "Asheville Man Given 8-10 Year Jail Term," *Asheville Citizen-Times*, Asheville, NC, August 4, 1972, p. 13.
[1177] https://grocefuneralhome.com/obits/gray-a-burleson.
[1178] Watauga County Sheriff Office investigation file 118-H-1/2/3.
[1179] Ibid.
[1180] Ibid.
[1181] Ibid.
[1182] Ibid.
[1183] Ibid.
[1184] Ibid.; Mauldin, Charles & Gayle. Interview with Red Lyons. February 21, 1989.
[1185] Blankenship, Opal. Interview with Arlie Isaacs & Larry Wagner. December 12, 1974, Watauga County Sheriff's Office investigation file 118-H-1/2/3; Mauldin, Charles & Gayle. Interview with Red Lyons. February 21, 1989.
[1186] "Bawdyhouse Raided By City Policemen," *Statesville Landmark and Record*, Statesville, NC, December 15, 1971, p. 12-A.
[1187] "Charges Dismissed After Court Hearing," *Statesville Landmark and Record*, Statesville, NC, December 22, 1971, p. 2-A.
[1188] Watauga County Sheriff Office investigation file 118-H-1/2/3.
[1189] Notes compiled by Gayle Durham Mauldin; Anonymous source. Phone interview with author. October 15, 2022.
[1190] Ibid.; Anonymous source. E-mail to author. December 2, 2022.
[1191] Plemmons, Ellen. Interview with John Parker, May 2, 1972, Watauga County Sheriff's Office investigation file 118-H-1/2/3; Notes compiled by Gayle Durham Mauldin; Anonymous source. E-mails to author. September 11 & 27, 2022; Anonymous source. Phone conversation with author. October 15, 2022.
[1192] Notes compiled by Gayle Durham Mauldin.
[1193] Lewis, SBI Special Agent M. L. Letter to the SBI Director. February 29, 1972, Watauga County Sheriff's Office investigation file 118-H-1/2/3.
[1194] Notes compiled by Gayle Durham Mauldin.
[1195] Watauga County, NC Clerk of Court's Office, Criminal File #72-CR-1072, State vs. Jerry Ray Cassada & File #72-CR-1078, State vs. Dean Chandler, Subpoena, September 14, 1972, served in person by Watauga County Clerk Jacqueline Dunn, September 22, 1972.

[1196] Ibid.
[1197] Watauga County, NC Clerk of Court's Office, Criminal File #72-CR-1072, State vs. Jerry Ray Cassada, Subpoena, September 14, 1972, "Too Late for Service," September 18, 1972.
[1198] "Suspects May Face Indictment," *Watauga Democrat*, Boone, NC, September 14, 1972, p. 1; "Two Indicted In Murder," *Watauga Democrat*, Boone, NC, September 21, 1972, p. 2A.
[1199] Edmisten, Harold. Phone interview with author. January 21, 2023; Reese, Sherry. Phone interview with author. February 2, 2023.
[1200] Watauga County, NC Clerk of Court's Office, Criminal Files #72-CR-1072, -1073, -1074, State vs. Jerry Ray Cassada & Files #72-CR-1078, -1079, -1080, State vs. Dean Chandler, Indictment - Murder, September 18 & 19, 1972; Connie Blackwell, "Cassada, Chandler Indicted In Watauga County Murders," *Asheville Citizen-Times*, Asheville, NC, September 20, 1972, p. 1.
[1201] Watauga County, NC Clerk of Court's Office, Criminal Files #72-CR-1072, -1073, -1074, State vs. Jerry Ray Cassada & Files #72-CR-1078, -1079, -1080, State vs. Dean Chandler, Indictment - Murder, September 18 & 19, 1972.
[1202] Blackwell, "Cassada, Chandler Indicted," p. 1; "2 Indicted In Durham Murder," *Watauga Democrat*, Boone, NC, September 21, 1972, p. 1.
[1203] "Two Men Indicted," *Statesville Record and Landmark*, Statesville, NC, September 21, 1972, p. 7-B.
[1204] "Chandler Again Given Jail Term," *Asheville Citizen-Times*, Asheville, NC, October 2, 1972, p. 9.
[1205] Watauga County, NC Clerk of Court's Office, Criminal File #72-CR-1072, State vs. Jerry Ray Cassada, Appearance Bond, October 9, 1972.
[1206] Watauga County, NC Clerk of Court's Office, Criminal File #72-CR-1078, State vs. Dean Chandler, Certificate Of Inmate Status, May 7, 1973.
[1207] Notes compiled by Gayle Durham Mauldin.
[1208] Ibid.
[1209] Ibid.
[1210] "Investigation Continues Into Durham Murders," *Watauga Democrat*, Boone, NC, February 5, 1973, pp. 1A & 2A.
[1211] Watauga County, NC Clerk of Court's Office, Criminal File #72-CR-1078, State vs. Dean Chandler, Certificate Of Inmate Status, May 7, 1973; Arlene Edwards, "Trial Date Is Set In Boone Murders," *Winston-Salem Journal*, Winston-Salem, NC, May 11, 1973, p. 25; "June 4 In Boone," p. 1B.
[1212] "Trial Set In Boone Slayings," *Winston-Salem Journal*, Winston-Salem, NC, January 17, 1974, p. 18.
[1213] Watauga County, NC Clerk of Court's Office, Criminal Files #72-CR-1078, -1079, -1080, State vs. Dean Chandler, Motion, February 20, 1973; Maxwell, "Watauga Sheriff Defends Charges," p. 3B.
[1214] "State Suspends Prosecution," p. 2C.
[1215] Watauga County, NC Clerk of Court's Office, Criminal File #72-CR-1078, State vs. Dean Chandler, Inmate's Notice of Place Of Imprisonment And Request For Disposition Of Indictments, Informations Or Complaints & Offer To Deliver Temporary Custody, May 7, 1973.
[1216] Carroll, Johnny. Phone interview with author. June 29, 2022.
[1217] Watauga County, NC Clerk of Court's Office, Criminal Files #72-CR-1078,-1079, -1080, State vs. Dean Chandler, Subpoena, May 17, 1973.
[1218] Ibid.
[1219] Ibid.
[1220] Ibid.
[1221] Ibid., served by telephone by Buncombe County Sheriff Tom Morrissey & Deputy Sheriff Ron Harwood, May 31, 1973.
[1222] Anonymous source. Phone interview with author. September 17, 2022.
[1223] Handwritten note from Madison County Sheriff E. Y. Ponder, Watauga County, NC Clerk of Court's Office, Criminal Files #72-CR-1078, State vs. Dean Chandler, Subpoena, May 17, 1973.
[1224] Watauga County, NC Clerk of Court's Office, Criminal Files #72-CR-1078, -1079, -1080, State vs. Dean Chandler, Order, June 4, 1973; J. A. C Dunn, "Watauga Murders Still Not Solved," *Winston-Salem Journal*, Winston-Salem, NC, June 5, 1975, p. 1.
[1225] Watauga County, NC Clerk of Court's Office, Criminal Files #72-CR-1078, -1079, -1080, State vs. Dean Chandler, Order, June 4, 1973; "State Suspends Prosecution," p. 2C.
[1226] Watauga County, NC Clerk of Court's Office, Criminal Files #72-CR-1078, -1079, -1080, State vs. Dean Chandler, Order, June 4, 1973 & File #72-CR-1078, letter from Dean Chandler to the Watauga County Clerk of Superior Court, August 15, 1973.
[1227] Maxwell, "Watauga Sheriff Defends Charges," p. 3B.
[1228] Poindexter, "Boone Murder Case Takes New Direction," p. 13.
[1229] Dunn, "Watauga Murders Unsolved," p. 2.
[1230] Poindexter, "Boone Murder Case Takes New Direction," p. 13.

[1231] Small, Cecil & Mildred. Interview with Caroline Walker.
[1232] Maxwell, "Watauga Sheriff Defends Charges," p. 3B.
[1233] Cullen, "Boone Stranglings," p. 1B.
[1234] Vaughn, Jerry. In-person interview with author. October 13, 2023.
[1235] Poindexter, "Boone Murder Case Takes New Direction," p. 13.
[1236] Cullen, "Boone Stranglings," p. 1B.
[1237] Edwards, Diana (daughter of Jerri Bumgarner Waddell). Phone interview with author. October 14, 2023.
[1238] Watauga County Sheriff's Office investigation file 118-H-1/2/3.
[1239] Jesse Poindexter, "Charges Dropped in Triple Slaying Case," *Winston-Salem Journal*, Winston-Salem, NC, January 24, 1974, p. 27.
[1240] Watauga County, NC Clerk of Court's Office, Criminal Files #72-CR-1072, -1073, -1074, State vs. Jerry Ray Cassada, Order, January 23, 1974; "4th Suspect In 3 Deaths Is Released," *The Charlotte Observer*, Charlotte, NC, January 24, 1974, p. 1B.
[1241] Watauga County, NC Clerk of Court's Office, Criminal Files #72-CR-1072, -1073, -1074, State vs. Jerry Ray Cassada, Motion For Speedy Trial, September 21, 1973; "Fourth Defendant In Boone Slayings Released By State," *Asheville Citizen-Times*, Asheville, NC, January 25, 1974, p. 26.
[1242] "Trial Opens Today In Boone Killings," *Winston-Salem Journal*, Winston-Salem, NC, June 4, 1973, p. 13; Poindexter, "Boone Murder Case Takes New Direction," p. 13.
[1243] "Fourth Defendant In Boone Slayings," p. 26.
[1244] Carroll, Ward. Interview with Charles Heatherly.
[1245] Cassada, Jerry & Eugene Garren. Interviews with Clyde Tester & Arlie Isaacs, September 17, 1974, Watauga County Sheriff's Office investigation file 118-H-1/2/3.
[1246] Chandler, Dean. Interview with Arlie Isaacs, October 2, 1974, Watauga County Sheriff's Office investigation file 118-H-1/2/3.
[1247] Chandler, Dean. Interview with Arlie Isaacs, February 26, 1975, Watauga County Sheriff's Office investigation file 118-H-1/2/3.
[1248] Lacey, Robert H. Interview with Southern Oral History Project, Notable North Carolinians, University of North Carolina Law School, C0095_Audio_3. February 27, 1992, https://dc.lib.unc.edu/cdm/ref/collection/sohp/id/10177 (transcription: pp. 41, 42, & 65.)
[1249] "7 Men Nabbed Here In Wave Of Narcotics Arrests," *The Asheville Citizen*, Asheville, NC, August 20, 1976, p. 15.
[1250] "Licensed To Wed," *Asheville Citizen-Times*, Asheville, NC, December 29, 1977, p. 19.
[1251] Edmisten, Rufus. The Weather Channel's *Storm of Suspicion*, Season 4, Episode 19: "Triple Torment," May 30, 2023.
[1252] *Special Edition of WBTV News*.
[1253] Capuzzo, *The Murder Room*, p. 170.
[1254] https://tributearchive.com/obituaries/2166128/Baxter-Bryce-Prevette.
[1255] "2 More Face Drug Charges," *Durham Morning Herald*, Durham, NC, April 8, 1982, p. 18A.
[1256] Charles & Gayle Durham Mauldin, interview with Red Lyons, April 17, 1989; Genealogical research by author.
[1257] "Wilkes man charged in slaying," *The Durham Sun*, Durham, NC, November 24, 1980, p. 7-A; "North Carolina Deaths," *The Charlotte Observer*, Charlotte, NC, November 22, 1980; p. 3A.
[1258] Mauldin, Charles & Gayle. Interview with Red Lyons, April 17, 1989.
[1259] Brown, John Paul Brown. Interview with Del Williams.
[1260] Ibid.
[1261] Notes compiled by Gayle Durham Mauldin.
[1262] "Wilkes Man Dies In Boone Of Sword Wound," *Watauga Democrat*, Boone, NC, November 13, 1972, p. 2A; North Carolina, U. S., Death Certificates, 1909-1976, Ancestry.com, https://www.ancestry.com/imageviewer/collections/1121/images/S123_649-0274?treeid=170690419&personid=252216082607&hintid=&queryId=e70b2a7f900762b4262c7d055c613aca&usePUB=true&_phsrc=rKl31306&_phstart=successSource&usePUBJs=true&_gl=1*ln25fs*_ga*MTM2NjgyNjU0Mi4xNTM2NTQ0NDQ4*_ga_4QT8FMEX30*MTY1Mzc1OTg3OC40Mi4xLjE2NTM3NTk5MTMuMA..&_ga=2.145958452.1601180215.1653709235-1366826542.1536544448&pId=1948426.
[1263] Watauga County Sheriff's Office investigation file 118-H-1/2/3.
[1264] Notes compiled by Gayle Durham Mauldin.
[1265] "Wilkes Man Dies In Boone Of Sword Wound," p. 2A.
[1266] Watauga County Sheriff's Office investigation file 118-H-1/2/3.
[1267] Cornell, Roy Dale. Interview with Red Lyons, June 8, 1989, Watauga County Sheriff's Office investigation file 118-H-1/2/3.
[1268] Watauga County Sheriff's Office investigation file 118-H-1/2/3.

[1269] "Assault Puts One In Hospital, One In Jail," *The Newberry Observer*, Newberry, SC, May 24, 1979, p. 12; Jerry Ray Cassada obituary, *The Newberry Observer*, Newberry, SC, December 3, 2003, p. 8.
[1270] Eugene "Little Gene" Garren obituary, *Asheville Citizen-Times*, Asheville, NC, March 5, 2006, p. B5.
[1271] Dean Chandler obituary, *News-Record & Sentinel*, Mars Hill-Marshall-Hot Springs-Weaverville, NC, February 6, 2008, p. 20.
[1272] Henry Dewey Coffey obituary, Groce Funeral Home & Cremation Service, https://www.grocefuneralhome.com/obits/henry-dewey-coffey/.
[1273] Edmisten, *That's Rufus*, p. 121.
[1274] Edmisten, Rufus. Zoom interview with the author. March 31, 2022.
[1275] Mitchell, "Slayings mystery," p. A19.
[1276] Poindexter, "Boone Murder Case Takes New Direction," p. 13.
[1277] Poindexter, "Boone Murder Case Takes New Direction," p. 13.
[1278] Notes made by Captain Arlie Isaacs, September 5, 1974, Watauga County Sheriff's Office investigation file 118-H-1/2/3.
[1279] Wagner, Larry. Phone interview with author. December 22, 2022; Hagaman, Len. In-person interview with author. May 19, 2023.
[1280] "Boone Policeman Selected For Police Science Degree," *Watauga Democrat*, Boone, NC, September 25, 1972, p. 1.
[1281] Small, Cecil & Mildred. Interview with Caroline Walker.
[1282] Hagaman, Len. In-person interview with author. May 24, 2022; Hudgins and Birt, *Grace and* Disgrace, pp. 257 & 262; Wagner, Larry. Phone interview with author. December 22, 2022; Jones, Teresa Isaacs (daughter of Arlie Isaacs). Facebook message to author. June 18, 2022.
[1283] Poindexter, "Lawyer Retained In Boone Case," p. 1.
[1284] "Probe of Slayings Yields No Arrests," p. A15; Poindexter, "Boone Murder Case Takes New Direction," p. 13.
[1285] Poindexter, "Lawyer Retained In Boone Case," pp. 1 & 8; Cullen, "Boone Stranglings," p. 1B; Gryder, Bob. Interview with Clyde Tester & Arlie Isaacs. September 19, 1974, Watauga County Sheriff's Office investigation file 118-H-1/2/3; Small, Cecil & Mildred. Interview with Caroline Walker; Mackie, Ginny Durham. Interview with Carolynn Johnson & Wade Colvard.
[1286] Small, Cecil & Mildred. Interview with Caroline Walker.
[1287] Gryder, Bob. Interview with Clyde Tester & Arlie Isaacs.
[1288] Mackie, Ginny Durham. Interview with Carolynn Johnson & Wade Colvard.
[1289] Walter, Richard. Phone conversation with author. May 10, 2022.
[1290] Confession of Judgment, Wilkes County, NC Superior Court, Ginny Durham Hall (Plaintiff) vs. Troy Hall, Individually, Carolina Construction Company of North Wilkesboro, Inc., Troy Hall, Incorporator (Defendants), February 27, 1976.
[1291] Cullen, "Boone Stranglings," p. 1B.
[1292] Brown, Ted. Phone interview with author. April 4, 2022.
[1293] "Who killed the Durham family? Here's my story," gowilkes.com, August 12, 2010, posted by "countryguy"; Mackie, Ginny Durham. Interview with Carolynn Johnson & Wade Colvard.
[1294] Mackie, Ginny Durham. Interview with Carolynn Johnson & Wade Colvard.
[1295] Mauldin, Charles & Gayle. Interview with Red Lyons, August 7, 1989.
[1296] "Who killed the Durham family? Here's my story," gowilkes.com, August 12, 2010, posted by "countryguy."
[1297] Mauldin, Charles & Gayle. Interview with Red Lyons, August 7, 1989.
[1298] Mackie, Ginny Durham. Interview with Carolynn Johnson & Wade Colvard.
[1299] Ibid.; Hudgins and Birt, *Grace and* Disgrace, p. 271.
[1300] Mackie, Ginny Durham. Interview with Carolynn Johnson & Wade Colvard.
[1301] Frazier, John. Interview with Clyde Tester & Arlie Isaacs; Small, Cecil & Mildred. Interview with Caroline Walker.
[1302] Small, Cecil & Mildred. Interview with Caroline Walker.
[1303] Mackie, Ginny Durham. Interview with Carolynn Johnson & Wade Colvard; Hudgins and Birt, *Grace and* Disgrace, p. 271.
[1304] Brown, Ted. Interview with Len Hagaman & Carolynn Johnson; Brown, Ted. Phone interview with author, April 4, 2022; Kipe, *In The Red Clay*, Season 2, Episode 4: *The Company of Wolves*.
[1305] Denny, Billy Lee. Interview with Arlie Isaacs, January 30, 1975, Watauga County Sheriff's Office investigation file 118-H-1/2/3.
[1306] Anonymous source.
[1307] Ibid.
[1308] Walter, Richard. Phone conversation with author. May 10, 2022.
[1309] Brown, Ted. Phone interviews with author. April 4 & 5, 2022 and March 6, 2023.
[1310] Lowe, William Asa. Interview with James C. Lyons.

[1311] Garris, Jerry. Interview with Arlie Isaacs, September 19, 1974, Watauga County Sheriff's Office investigation file 118-H-1/2/3.
[1312] Walter, Richard. Phone conversation with author. May 10, 2022.
[1313] Investigative notes, August 24, 2015, Watauga County Sheriff's Office investigation file 118-H-1/2/3.
[1314] Frazier, John. Interview with Clyde Tester & Arlie Isaacs.
[1315] Anonymous source.
[1316] Kipe, *In The Red Clay*, Season 2, Episode 4: *The Company of Wolves*.
[1317] Report by Boone Police Department Captain Arlie Isaacs, September 6, 1974, Watauga County Sheriff's Office investigation file 118-H-1/2/3.
[1318] Anonymous source.
[1319] Mackie, Ginny Durham. Interview with Carolynn Johnson & Wade Colvard; Lipsig, David, M.D. Letter to Patrick Meriwether, Esq., October 15, 2012, p. 5.
[1320] Modern Buick-Pontiac Co. advertisement, *Watauga Democrat*, Boone, NC, January 8, 1970, p. 2
[1321] Hall, Troy & Ginny Hall. Interview with Clyde Tester & Arlie Isaacs. September 13, 1974, Watauga County Sheriff's Office investigation file 118-H-1/2/3.
[1322] Ibid.
[1323] Ibid.
[1324] Hall, Ginny Durham. Interview with Clyde Tester & Arlie Isaacs. September 20, 1974, Watauga County Sheriff's Office investigation file 118-H-1/2/3.
[1325] Hall, Troy. Phone conversation with Arlie Isaacs., September 23, 1974, Watauga County Sheriff's Office investigation file 118-H-1/2/3.
[1326] Edmisten, Rufus. Zoom interview with author. March 31, 2022.
[1327] "Investigation of Durham family's slaying continues."
[1328] Wikipedia: Rufus L. Edmisten, https://en.wikipedia.org/wiki/Rufus_L._Edmisten; "Investigation of Durham family's slaying continues."
[1329] "SBI to Reopen Case," *Winston-Salem Journal*, Winston-Salem, NC, January 28, 1975, p. 11.
[1330] Edmisten, *That's Rufus*, p. 121.
[1331] Guy, Frank. Phone interview with author. September 17, 2022.
[1332] Edmisten, *That's Rufus*, p. 121.
[1333] Mitchell, "Slayings mystery," p. A19.
[1334] "N. C. sheriff dusting cobwebs off old murder case," *The Durham Sun*, Durham, NC, February 20, 1989, p. 5-A.
[1335] "Murders Are Still Unsolved After 10 Years," *Watauga Democrat*, Boone, NC, February 1, 1982, p. 2.
[1336] Hall, Troy & Ginny. Interview with Ward Carroll, Clyde Tester, Arlie Isaacs, & Larry Wagner. February 8, 1975, Watauga County Sheriff's Office investigation file 118-H-1/2/3.
[1337] Jesse Poindexter, "SBI to Intensify Probe Into Boone Murders," *Winston-Salem Journal*, Winston-Salem, NC, March 12, 1975, p. 9; "Edmisten Is Hopeful Of Slaying Solution," *Asheville Citizen-Times*, Asheville, NC, March 20, 1975, p. 19.
[1338] "New Probe Of Killings Scheduled," March 12, 1975 (clipping from Watauga County Sheriff's Office investigation file 118-H-1/2/3, newspaper name and page number unidentified).
[1339] Poindexter, "SBI to Intensify Probe," p. 9.
[1340] "New Probe Of Killings Scheduled."
[1341] Bullard, *The Durham Murders*, pp. 433 & 442.
[1342] Poindexter, "SBI to Intensify Probe," p. 9.
[1343] "State Ups Reward In Boone Slayings," *The News and Observer*, Raleigh, NC, June 3, 1975, p 20; Poindexter, "SBI to Intensify Probe," p. 9; "Edmisten Is Hopeful Of Slaying Solution," p. 19.
[1344] "Edmisten Is Hopeful Of Slaying Solution," p. 19.
[1345] "State Ups Reward In Boone Slayings," p 20; "Reward Money Increased," *Winston-Salem Journal*, Winston-Salem, NC, June 3, 1975, p. 11.
[1346] Hall, Kay. Interview with Clyde Tester & Arlie Isaacs. March 22, 1975.
[1347] Ibid.
[1348] Mauldin, Charles & Gayle. Interview with Red Lyons, August 7, 1989.
[1349] Hall, Ray. Interview with Clyde Tester & Arlie Isaacs, March 22, 1975, Watauga County Sheriff's Office investigation file 118-H-1/2/3.
[1350] "Arrests In Deaths Expected," *Winston-Salem Journal*, Winston-Salem, NC, May 5, 1975, p. 10.
[1351] "State Ups Reward In Boone Slayings," p. 20; "Reward Money Increased," p. 11.
[1352] Mackie, Ginny Durham. Interview with Carolynn Johnson & Wade Colvard.
[1353] Order, File No. 76 CVS 46, Wilkes County, NC Superior Court, Ginny Durham Hall (Plaintiff) vs. Troy Hall (Defendant), February 27, 1976, filed March 2, 1976; Order, File No. 76 CVS 47, Wilkes County, NC Superior Court, Ginny Durham Hall (Plaintiff) vs. Troy Hall, Individually, Carolina Construction Company of North Wilkesboro, Inc.,

Troy Hall, Incorporator, Carrie Mae Waddell Hall (Defendants), February 27, 1976, filed March 2, 1976; Poindexter, "Slain Durhams' Daughter Divorced" & "Daughter of Family Slain In Boone Divorces Husband," pp. 21 & 23.

[1354] Confession of Judgment, Wilkes County, NC Superior Court, Ginny Durham Hall (Plaintiff) vs. Troy Hall, Individually, Carolina Construction Company of North Wilkesboro, Inc., Troy Hall, Incorporator (Defendants), February 27, 1976.

[1355] Divorce decree, The General Court of Justice, Yadkin Co., NC, District Court Division File & Docket No. 76 CVD 185

[1356] "Durham Family Survivor Divorces Her Husband," September 29, 1976 (clipping from Watauga County Sheriff's Office investigation file 118-H-1/2/3, newspaper name and page number unidentified).

[1357] Poindexter, "Slain Durhams' Daughter Divorced" & "Daughter of Family Slain In Boone Divorces Husband," pp. 21 & 23.

[1358] Mackie, Ginny Durham. Interview with Carolynn Johnson & Wade Colvard; Walter, Richard. Phone conversation with author. May 10, 2022.

[1359] Small, Cecil & Mildred. Interview with Caroline Walker.

[1360] Divorce decree, The General Court of Justice, Yadkin Co., NC, District Court Division File & Docket No. 76 CVD 185

[1361] Edwards, Diana (Ginny's first cousin once removed). Phone interview with author. October 14, 2023.

[1362] "Officers Puzzled by 2 Murders," *Winston-Salem Journal*, Winston-Salem, NC, February 28, 1977, p. 19.

[1363] https://www.millerfuneralservice.com/obituaries/Charles-Reginald-Reggie-Colvard-Sr?obId=24091874.

[1364] Anonymous source

[1365] Dennis Whittington, "2 Murders A Puzzle To Officers," *Winston-Salem Journal*, Winston-Salem, NC, February 28, 1977, p. 17.

[1366] Wagner, Larry. Phone interview with author. December 22, 2022.

[1367] Roberson, Darlene Benge Norris. Phone interview with author. December 8, 2022; "Benge-Norris Wedding Set For Aug. 17," *The Asheville Citizen*, Asheville, NC, June 17, 1975, p. 7; Whitman, Pat. Interview with Carolynn Johnson & Wade Colvard.

[1368] Poindexter, "Slain Durhams' Daughter Divorced," p. 21.

[1369] Application for Non-Testimonial Identification Order, November 15, 1976, Watauga County Sheriff's Office investigation file 118-H-1/2/3.

[1370] Watauga County Sheriff's Office investigation file 118-H-1/2/3; Mauldin, Charles & Gayle. Interview with Red Lyons, February 21, 1989; Wagner, Larry. Phone interview with author. September 19, 2023.

[1371] Durham, Ginny. Interview with Clyde Tester, Arlie Isaacs & L. D. Hagaman, Jr.

[1372] Young, Lewis. Phone interview with author. February 1, 2023.

[1373] Ibid.

[1374] Ibid.

[1375] Watauga County Sheriff's Office investigation file 118-H-1/2/3.

[1376] https://en.wikipedia.org/wiki/Peter_Hurkos; https://www.tsemrinpoche.com/tsem-tulku-rinpoche/film-tv-music/the-mysterious-monsters-narrated-by-peter-graves.html.

[1377] Watauga County Sheriff's Office investigation file 118-H-1/2/3.

[1378] "Daughter of Family Slain In Boone Divorces Husband," p. 23; Lowder, Randy. Facebook comment. February 8, 2022.

[1379] 1950 United States Federal Census for Steven R. Mackie, https://www.ancestry.com/imageviewer/collections/62308/images/43290879-North_Carolina-154240-0039?pId=148836420.

[1380] Watauga County Sheriff's Office investigation file 118-H-1/2/3.

[1381] *Special Edition of WBTV News*; Bowers, Bruce. Phone interview with author. December 29, 2022.

[1382] Dennis Whittington, "Greene Brothers' Deaths, Aborted Drug Deal Linked," *Winston-Salem Journal*, Winston-Salem, NC, June 9, 1977, p. 1.

[1383] Dennis Whittington, "Edmisten Gives Vow To Find Murderers," *Winston-Salem Journal*, Winston-Salem, NC, June 19, 1977, pp. 1 & 2.

[1384] "Who Killed Brenda? SBI Reexamines Case," *The Charlotte Observer*, Charlotte, NC, November 14, 1977, p. 4A.

[1385] *Special Edition of WBTV News*.

[1386] Ibid.

[1387] Dennis Whittington, "Arrests Expected In 1976 Murders," *Winston-Salem Journal*, Winston-Salem, NC, November 5, 1977, pp. 13 & 14; Downey, "Investigators Say Murders Will Be Solved," p. B6.

[1388] Frank Byrd. "SBI Will Reopen Triple Murder Probe," *The Times-News*, Hendersonville, NC, December 14, 1977, p. 22.

[1389] Whittington, "Arrests Expected In 1976 Murders," pp. 13 & 14.

[1390] Whittington, "Arrests Expected In 1976 Murders," p. 14.

[1391] Ron Alridge, "TV News Magazine's Debut Encouraging, But Uneven," *The Charlotte Observer*, Charlotte, NC, March 7, 1978, p. 13A.
[1392] Reeve, Brent. E-mail to Tim Bullard. August 11, 2010, Watauga County Sheriff's Office investigation file 118-H-1/2/3.
[1393] "Crimestoppers to air Durham murder case," *Watauga Democrat*, Boone, NC, June 2, 1989, p. 1; Bowers, Bruce. Phone interview with author. December 29, 2022.
[1394] *Special Edition of WBTV News*.
[1395] Ibid.
[1396] "Investigation of Durham family's slaying continues."
[1397] Edmisten, *That's Rufus*, p. 121; Hudgins and Birt, *Grace and Disgrace*, p. 273.
[1398] "Investigation of Durham family's slaying continues."
[1399] Edmisten, Rufus. Zoom interview with author. March 31, 2022.
[1400] Edmisten, *That's Rufus*, p. 121.
[1401] *Special Edition of WBTV News*.
[1402] Watauga County Sheriff's Office investigation file 118-H-1/2/3; Hagaman, Len. E-mail communication with author. July 20, 2022; Guy, Frank. Phone interview with author. September 17, 2022.
[1403] Hagaman, Len. In-person interview with author. May 19, 2023.
[1404] Campaign ad, *Watauga Democrat*, Boone, NC, April 17, 1978, p. 2A.
[1405] "The Sheriff's Office And The Durham Murders," 1978 (publication name, month, day, and page number unidentified).
[1406] "Arlie Isaacs Speaks To The People Of Watauga County," *Watauga Democrat*, Boone, NC, April 27, 1978, p. 11A.
[1407] "Investigator Files For Watauga Sheriff," *Winston-Salem Journal*, Winston-Salem, NC, January 31, 1978, p. 13; Campaign ad, Watauga Democrat, April 27, 1978, p. 2B.
[1408] Carroll, Johnny. Phone interview with author. June 29, 2022.
[1409] Watauga County Sheriff's Office investigation file 118-H-1/2/3.
[1410] Dennis Whittington, "Murder Squad In SBI Ended; High Costs Cited," *Winston-Salem Journal*, Winston-Salem, NC, October 28, 1979, p. B-1.
[1411] John Downey, "Investigators Say Boone Murders Will Be Solved," *Winston-Salem Journal*, Winston-Salem, NC, January 31, 1982, p. B1.
[1412] "Murders Are Still Unsolved After 10 Years," pp. 1 & 2.
[1413] Whitman, Charlie. Interview with Charles Heatherly.
[1414] "Murders Are Still Unsolved After 10 Years," pp. 1 & 2; Whitman, Charlie. Interview with Charles Heatherly.
[1415] Downey, "Investigators Say Boone Murders Will Be Solved," p. B1.
[1416] Downey, "Investigators Say Murders Will Be Solved," p. B6.
[1417] Downey, "Investigators Say Boone Murders Will Be Solved," pp. B1 & B6.
[1418] Downey, "Investigators Say Boone Murders Will Be Solved," p. B6.
[1419] Ibid.
[1420] Ibid.
[1421] Downey, "Investigators Say Boone Murders Will Be Solved," p. B1.
[1422] Mauldin, Charles & Gayle. Interview with Red Lyons, February 21, 1989.
[1423] Mauldin, Charles & Gayle. Interviews with Red Lyons, February, 21, April 17 & August 7, 1989.
[1424] Mackie, Ginny D. Letter to Gayle Mauldin. 1982. Watauga County Sheriff's Office investigation file 118-H-1/2/3.
[1425] Hall, Kay. Interview with Clyde Tester & Arlie Isaacs, April 7, 1975.
[1426] Luck, Bill. Interview with Arlie Isaacs, February 14, 1975, Watauga County Sheriff's Office investigation file 118-H-1/2/3.
[1427] Ibid.
[1428] Hall, Kay. Interview with Clyde Tester & Arlie Isaacs, April 7, 1975.
[1429] "Man Charged With Murder," *Winston-Salem Journal*, Winston-Salem, NC, June 22, 1972, p. 11; "Thomasville Man Charged in Deaths," *Winston-Salem Journal*, Winston-Salem, NC, November 2, 1973, p. 9; "Man Sentenced in Killings," *Winston-Salem Journal*, Winston-Salem, NC, March 20, 1975, p. 39.
[1430] Watauga County Sheriff's Office investigation file 118-H-1/2/3.
[1431] Bullard, *The Durham Murders*, p. 362; Bullard, Tim. E-mail to Dee Dee Rominger. September 3, 2007, Watauga County Sheriff's Office investigation file 118-H-1/2/3; additional source misplaced.
[1432] Mackie, Ginny D. Letter to Gayle Mauldin. 1982. Watauga County Sheriff's Office investigation file 118-H-1/2/3.
[1433] Mauldin, Charles & Gayle. Interview with Red Lyons, August 7, 1989.
[1434] Mackie, Ginny Durham. Interview with Carolynn Johnson & Wade Colvard.
[1435] Bullard, *The Durham Murders*, p. 755.
[1436] Durham, Steve. Interview with Len Hagaman, Kelly Redmon, Carolynn Johnson, Wade Colvard, Larry Wagner, & Rufus Edmisten.

[1437] Mauldin, Charles & Gayle. Interview with Red Lyons, April 17, 1989.
[1438] Durham, Bill & Steve Durham. Interview with Len Hagaman, Kelly Redmon, Carolynn Johnson, Wade Colvard, Larry Wagner, & Rufus Edmisten; Mackie, Ginny Durham. Interview with Carolynn Johnson & Wade Colvard.
[1439] Edmisten, Rufus. Zoom interview with author. March 31, 2022; Kipe, *In The Red Clay*, Season 2, Episode 4: *The Company of Wolves*.
[1440] Durham, Bill. Interview with Len Hagaman, Kelly Redmon, Carolynn Johnson, Wade Colvard, Larry Wagner, & Rufus Edmisten; Edwards, Diana (great-niece of Virginia Durham). Phone interview with author. October 14, 2023.
[1441] Notes compiled by Gayle Durham Mauldin.
[1442] Cullen, "Boone Stranglings," p. 1B.
[1443] Hagaman, Len. The Weather Channel's *Storm of Suspicion*, Season 4, Episode 19: "Triple Torment," May 30, 2023.
[1444] Carroll, Ward. Interview with Charles Heatherly.
[1445] Mackie, Ginny Durham. Interview with Carolynn Johnson & Wade Colvard.
[1446] "Durham Murder Case: New Details Revealed During February 15th Interview with Watauga County Sheriff Len Hagaman," *High Country Press*, Boone, NC, February 18, 2022 (online), https://www.hcpress.com/front-page/durham-murder-case-new-details-revealed-during-interview-with-watauga-county-sheriff-len-hagaman.html; Hudgins and Birt, *Grace and Disgrace*, p. 271; Kipe, *In The Red Clay*, Season 2, Episode 4: *The Company of Wolves*; Hagaman, Len. In-person interview with author. May 19, 2023.
[1447] Hagaman, Len. In-person interview with author. May 24, 2022.
[1448] Kipe, *In The Red Clay*, Season 2, Episode 4: *The Company of Wolves*.
[1449] Caroline D. Walker, "Murder case attracting new interest," *Watauga Democrat*, Boone, NC, February 17, 1989, p. 10.
[1450] Anonymous informant.
[1451] Vaughn, Jerry. In-person interview with author. October 13, 2023.
[1452] Bullard, *The Durham Murders*, pp. 286 & 295.
[1453] Ibid., p. 350.
[1454] Coy Durham obituary, *Winston-Salem Journal*, Winston-Salem, NC, June 8, 1983, p. 16.
[1455] Diane Suchetka, "New Twists Could Solve Boone-Area '72 Murders," *The Charlotte Observer*, Charlotte, NC, July 3, 1989, p. 1B.
[1456] "Unsolved Murders Fill Police Files," *Winston-Salem Journal*, Winston-Salem, NC, November 11, 1984, p. B10.
[1457] Dillon, "Durham Murders Remain Big Mystery," p. 3A.
[1458] Walker, "Murder case attracting new interest," pp. 1 & 10.
[1459] Bullard, *The Durham Murders*, p. 188.
[1460] Caroline D. Walker, "Durhams aid investigation," *Watauga Democrat*, Boone, NC, March 22, 1989, p. 3A.
[1461] Walker, "Former SBI agent still baffled," p. 2.
[1462] Dillon, "Durham Murders Remain Big Mystery," p. 3A.
[1463] Watauga County Sheriff's Office investigation file 118-H-1/2/3.
[1464] "Watauga County Officials Hope Reward May Solve Old Murders," March 7, 1989 (clipping from Watauga County Sheriff's Office investigation file 118-H-1/2/3; newspaper name and page number unidentified); "17 Years After 3 Killings, Investigators Keep Pressing," *The Charlotte Observer*, Charlotte, NC, February 17, 1989, p. 1B.
[1465] Lyons, Sheriff James C. "Red." Letter to Governor James G. Martin. March 6, 1989, Watauga County Sheriff's Office investigation file 118-H-1/2/3.
[1466] "Reward For Info Raised," *Asheville Citizen-Times*, Asheville, NC, April 12, 1989, p. 1B.
[1467] Martin, Governor James G. Martin. Proclamation. April 7, 1989, Watauga County Sheriff's Office investigation file 118-H-1/2/3.
[1468] "Reward For Info Raised," p. 1B.
[1469] "Reward increased for 1972 murder case," *Watauga Democrat*, Boone, NC, April 12, 1989, p. 1.
[1470] Walker, "Murder case attracting new interest," p. 1.
[1471] Walker, "Murder case attracting new interest," p. 1.; Charlie Peek, "Watauga: Motive Missing in Family's Slaying," *Winston-Salem Journal*, Winston-Salem, NC, October 8, 1989, p. A10.
[1472] Watauga County Sheriff's Office investigation file 118-H-1/2/3.
[1473] Walker, "Murder case attracting new interest," p. 1.
[1474] Walker, "Murder case attracting new interest," p. 1.
[1475] Rucker, Jeff. Phone interview with author. October 4, 2023.
[1476] "Watauga County Officials Hope Reward May Solve Old Murders."
[1477] Watauga County Sheriff's Office investigation file 118-H-1/2/3.
[1478] Rucker, Jeff. Phone interview with author. October 4, 2023.
[1479] Peek, "Watauga: Motive Missing in Family's Slaying," p. A10.
[1480] "Reward increased for 1972 murder case," pp. 1 & 2.

[1481] May, Paula. Phone interview with author. March 27, 2022.
[1482] "Crimestoppers to air Durham murder case," pp. 1 & 12; Rucker, Jeff. Phone interview with author. October 4, 2023.
[1483] "Watauga County Officials Hope Reward May Solve Old Murders."
[1484] Caroline D. Walker, "Durhams aid investigation," p. 3A.
[1485] Kipe, *In The Red Clay*, Season 2, Episode 6: *Beneath the Chestnut Tree*.
[1486] Suchetka, "New Twists," July 3, 1989, p. B1.
[1487] Caroline D. Walker, "Durhams aid investigation," p. 3A.
[1488] Walker, "Murder case attracting new interest," p. 10.
[1489] Suchetka, "New Twists Could Clinch," p. 2B.
[1490] Walker, "Murder case attracting new interest," p. 10.
[1491] Walker, "Murder case attracting new interest," p. 1.
[1492] Suchetka, "New Twists," July 3, 1989, p. B1.
[1493] Walker, "Murder case attracting new interest," p. 1.
[1494] Diane Suchetka, "New Twists In 1972 Murders: More Evidence, Reward Could Help Clinch Case," *The Charlotte Observer*, Charlotte, NC, July 3, 1989, p. 3B.
[1495] Dillon, "Durham Murders Remain Big Mystery," p. 3A.
[1496] Rucker, Jeff. Phone conversation with author. April 3, 2023.
[1497]Watauga County Sheriff's Office investigation file 118-H-1/2/3.
[1498] "N. C. sheriff dusting cobwebs off," p. 5-A.
[1499] Suchetka, "New Twists," July 3, 1989, p. 2B.
[1500] Rucker, Jeff. Phone interview with author. October 4, 2023.
[1501] Harrison, Jerry. Interview with Arlie Isaacs, March 7, 1989.
[1502] Mauldin, Charles & Gayle. Interviews with Red Lyons, February 21 & April 17, 1989.
[1503] Anonymous phone call to Boone Area Crimestoppers, July 3, 1989, Watauga County Sheriff's Office investigation file 118-H-1/2/3.
[1504] Triplett, Coaker. Interview with Red Lyons. April 20, 1989, Watauga County Sheriff's Office investigation file 118-H-1/2/3.
[1505] Lukens, Sue. Phone calls with Red Lyons, April 21 & 24, 1989, Watauga County Sheriff's Office investigation file 118-H-1/2/3.
[1506] Watauga County Sheriff's Office investigation file 118-H-1/2/3.
[1507] "Paul Bare Convicted of Kidnaping, Murder," *The Charlotte Observer*, Charlotte, NC, June 11, 1982, p. 2C.
[1508] Haynes, Rose M. *The Ore Knob Mine Murders: The Crimes, the Investigation and the Trials* (McFarland & Company, Inc., Publishers, Jefferson, NC, 2013), p. 9.
[1509] Bare, Paul. Letter to Watauga County Sheriff's Office, July 3, 1989, Watauga County Sheriff's Office investigation file 118-H-1/2/3.
[1510] Bare, Paul. Interview with Red Lyons. September 23, 1989, Watauga County Sheriff's Office investigation file 118-H-1/2/3.
[1511] "Police Make Arrests In Tire Cuttings," *The Asheville Citizen*, Asheville, NC, June 22, 1955, p. 14; "Tire Cutters Get 5-Year Sentences," *The Asheville Citizen*, Asheville, NC, June 23, 1955, p. 39; "News Of Public Record; Police Court," *Asheville Citizen-Times*, Asheville, NC, June 2, 1957, p. 4; "5 Nabbed In Robbery," *Durham Morning Herald*, Durham, NC, June 27, 1957, p. C-3; "News Of Public Record," *The Asheville Citizen*, Asheville, NC, July 17, 1957, p. 2; "News Of Public Record; Superior Court Action," *The Asheville Citizen*, Asheville, NC, April 26, 1960, p. 3; "News Of Public Record; Superior Court Action," *The Asheville Citizen*, Asheville, NC, April 29, 1960, p. 12.
[1512] Bare, Paul. Interview with Red Lyons.
[1513] "2 Felons Flee Mitchell Camp," *The Asheville Citizen*, Asheville, NC, June 12, 1962, p. 3.
[1514] "2 Convicts Escape," *The Asheville Citizen*, Asheville, NC, September 28, 1962, p. 17.
[1515] "1 Escapee Caught, Another At Large," *Asheville Citizen-Times*, Asheville, NC, August 30, 1962, p. 3.
[1516] "Sentence Given For Assault," *The Asheville Citizen*, Asheville, NC, March 18, 1969, p. 11.
[1517] "Youth Pleads Guilty To Manslaughter," *The Asheville Citizen*, Asheville, NC, March 19, 1969, p. 14.
[1518] "19 Felons Escape At Marion Prison; Eight Recaptured," *The Asheville Citizen*, Asheville, NC, July 17, 1969, p. 23; "Two Convicts Captured Near Polkville, Cleveland County" (photo caption) & "Posse Nabs Escapee On Catawba," *The Charlotte Observer*, Charlotte, NC, July 17, 1969, p. 1; "Ten Escapees Have Charlotte Connections," *The Charlotte Observer*, Charlotte, NC, July 17, 1969, p. 2; "Escapee's Hiding Place Is Discovered," *The Asheville Citizen*, Asheville, NC, November 20, 1971, p. 6.
[1519] Bare, Paul. Interview with Red Lyons.
[1520] "Man Is Charged After Incident In Wilkes County," *Winston-Salem Journal*, Winston-Salem, NC, October 26, 1971, p. 6.
[1521] Bare, Paul. Interview with Red Lyons; "Paul Bare Convicted," p. 2C.

[1522] https://fiindagrave.com/memorial/180661246/james-george-redding; James George Redding in the U. S. Index to Public Records, 1994-2019, https://ancestry.com/discoveryui-content/view/69252540:62209.]
[1523] Bare, Paul. Interview with Red Lyons.
[1524] https://tributearchive.com/obituaries/2162759/Haggie-William-Faw.
[1525] Bare, Paul. Interview with Red Lyons.
[1526] Durham, Ginny. Interview with Clyde Tester, Arlie Isaacs & L. D. Hagaman, Jr.
[1527] "6 Plead Guilty To Operation of Sussex Still: Charged With Maintaining 22 Illegal Devices To Make Untaxed Liquors," *Journal-Every Evening*, Wilmington, DE, October 6, 1941, p. 6.
[1528] Bare, Paul. Interview with Red Lyons.
[1529] Ibid.; "Widow Says Real Story May Never Surface," *The Times-News*, Hendersonville, NC, February 1, 1982, p. 9. "Paul Bare Indicted in Death; Abandoned Mine Slayings Case," *Asheville Citizen-Times*, Asheville, NC, March 23, 1982, Section Two, p. 11.
[1530] Anonymous source. Phone interview with author. September 20, 2022.
[1531] State of North Carolina v. Gary Hansford Miller and Alan Ray Hattaway, Supreme Court of North Carolina, April 2, 1986, https://law.justia.com/cases/north-carolina/supreme-court/1986/317a85-0.html; "Reputed Outlaws Indicted in Sex, Kidnapping Case," *Asheville Citizen-Times*, Asheville, NC, May 29, 1982, Section Three, p. 19.
[1532] "Ore Knob Mine saga; Wilkes author's book recalls murders, related events," *The Journal-Patriot*, North Wilkesboro, NC, October 9, 2013 (online), https://www.journalpatriot.com/news/ore-knob-mine-saga-wilkes-author-s-book-recalls-murders-related-events/article_3b324cc6-310a-11e3-b55b-001a4bcf6878.html.
[1533] "Paul Bare Convicted," p. 1C; Haynes, *The Ore Knob Mine Murders*, p. 134.
[1534] Haynes, *The Ore Knob Mine Murders*, pp. 186-187.
[1535] Haynes, *The Ore Knob Mine Murders*, pp. 10, 58-59, 178-179, & 210-211; "Buncombe Bust Nets Drugs, Guns," *Asheville Citizen-Times*, Asheville, NC, November 8, 1981, p. 1; "Reputed Outlaws Indicted," p. 19.
[1536] Watauga County Sheriff's Office investigation file 118-H-1/2/3; Anonymous source. Phone interview with author. September 20, 2022.
[1537] Haynes, *The Ore Knob Mine Murders*, p. 188.
[1538] Anonymous source. Phone interview with author. September 20, 2022.
[1539] Ibid.
[1540] https://www.carolana.com/NC/Transportation/aviation/nc_airports_airfields_by_county.html.
[1541] Bare, Paul. Interview with Red Lyons.
[1542] Anonymous source. Phone interview with author. September 20, 2022.
[1543] Ibid.
[1544] Ibid.
[1545] Haynes, *The Ore Knob Mine Murders*, p. 78.
[1546] Anonymous source. Phone interview with author. September 20, 2022.
[1547] "Alexander County Prison Inmate Dies Of Heart Attack," *The Charlotte Observer*, Charlotte, NC, October 25, 1989, p. 2B.
[1548] Walter, Richard. Phone conversation with author. April 28, 2022.
[1549] Ibid. May 10, 2022.
[1550] https://moodlehub.ca/mod/book/tool/print/index.php?id=5293.
[1551] https://www.albionpleiad.com/2013/04/qa-with-richard-walter-criminal-profiler-and-psychologist/.
[1552] Whitman, Pat. Phone interview with author. March 10, 2022.
[1553] Walter, Richard. Phone conversation with author. May 10, 2022.
[1554] Capuzzo, *The Murder Room*, pp. 83-85 & 167-168..
[1555] Edmisten, Rufus. Zoom interview with author. March 31, 2022.
[1556] Carroll, Ward. Interview with Charles Heatherly; Bullard, Tim. E-mail to Watauga County Sheriff Len Hagaman, July 25, 2011, Watauga County Sheriff's Office investigation file 118-H-1/2/3; Josh Green e-mail to Tim Bullard, July 30, 2011, Watauga County Sheriff's Office investigation file 118-H-1/2/3; Bullard, Tim. E-mail to Gwinnett Daily Post Staff Writer Josh Green of Lawrenceville, GA, August 3, 2011, Watauga County Sheriff's Office investigation file 118-H-1/2/3; Edmisten, Rufus. The Weather Channel's *Storm of Suspicion*, Season 4, Episode 19: "Triple Torment," May 30, 2023.
[1557] Vaughn, Jerry. In-person interview with author. October 13, 2023.
[1558] Wagner, Larry. Interview with Charles Heatherly; Wagner, Larry. Phone interview with author. December 22, 2022.
[1559] Wagner, Larry. Interview with Charles Heatherly; Pitts, Grace (Appalachian State University Registrar's Office). E-mail to author, July 7, 2022; Wagner, Larry. Phone interview with author. December 22, 2022.
[1560] Watauga County Sheriff's Office investigation file 118-H-1/2/3.
[1561] Hagaman, Len. In-person interview with author. March 14, 2022; Hudgins and Birt, *Grace and Disgrace*, p. 270.
[1562] Gryder, Bob. Interview with Clyde Tester & Arlie Isaacs.
[1563] Hall, Kay. Interviews with Clyde Tester & Arlie Isaacs, February 15, 1975 & March 22, 1975.

[1564] Eller, Ike. Interview with Red Lyons & Fred Myers.
[1565] Notes compiled by Gayle Durham Mauldin.
[1566] Eller, Tom. Phone interview with author. July 14, 2022.
[1567] Wagner, Larry. Interview with Charles Heatherly
[1568] Hagaman, Len. In-person interviews with author. March 14 & May 24, 2022.
[1569] Wagner, Larry. Interview with Charles Heatherly
[1570] Bullard, *The Durham Murders*, p. 745.
[1571] Hagaman, Len. In-person interview with author. March 14, 2022.
[1572] "Durham Murder Case: New Details Revealed."
[1573] Rucker, Jeff. Phone interview with author. October 4, 2023.
[1574] Ingram, Bob. In-person interview with author. April 19, 2022; Kipe, *In The Red Clay*, Season 2, Episode 6: *Beneath the Chestnut Tree*.
[1575] Small, Cecil & Mildred. Interview with Caroline Walker.
[1576] Hall, John Hall. Interview with Arlie Isaacs & Larry Wagner.
[1577] Cardamone, Lindsay (Troy Hall's great-niece), February 1, 2018. https://www.amazon.com/Durham-Murders-Tim-Bullard-ebook/dp/B007PKNY5Q?language=en_US; Cardamone, Lindsay. Facebook message to author. June 22, 2022.
[1578] Frazier, John. Interview with Clyde Tester & Arlie Isaacs.
[1579] Lowe, William Asa. Interview with James C. Lyons.
[1580] Brown, Ted. Phone and text conversations with author. Eller, Tom. Phone interview with author. July 14, 2022.
[1581] Brown, Ted. Phone and text conversations with author.
[1582] Eller, Tom. Phone interview with author. July 14, 2022.
[1583] Brown, Ted. Phone and text conversations with author.
[1584] Durham, Steve (Bryce Durham's nephew). Interview with Len Hagaman, Kelly Redmon, Carolynn Johnson, Wade Colvard, Larry Wagner, & Rufus Edmisten; Edwards, Diana (Virginia Durham's great-niece). Phone interview with author. October 14, 2023; Jolley, Frank (E. J. Durham, Sr.'s grandson). Phone interview with author. December 8, 2023.
[1585] "Unsolved murders reach 20th year; reward reaches $50,000," *Watauga Democrat*, Boone, NC, February 5, 1992, p. 1.
[1586] Watauga County Sheriff's Office investigation file 118-H-1/2/3, July 9, 1990.
[1587] Collie Durham obituary, *Winston-Salem Journal*, Winston-Salem, NC, June 4, 1992, p. 16.
[1588] Mitchell, "Slayings mystery," p. A19.
[1589] Hudgins and Birt, *Grace and Disgrace*, p. 273.
[1590] Watauga County Sheriff's Office investigation file 118-H-1/2/3; Rucker, Jeff. Phone interview with author. October 4, 2023; https://www.noreenrenier.com/; https://noreenrenier.com/media/tv/listofappearances.htm; https://noreenrenier.com/testimonials.htm; https://www.amazon.com/Mind-Murder-Real-Life-Psychic-Investigator/dp/1571745734.
[1591] Watauga County Sheriff's Office investigation file 118-H-1/2/3.
[1592] Watauga County Sheriff's Office investigation file 118-H-1/2/3.
[1593] Hagaman, Len. In-person interviews with author. March 14, 2022 & May 24, 2022; "Young Man Is Fatally Hurt, Girl Injured In Auto Crash," *The Journal-Patriot*, North Wilkesboro, NC, March 16, 1978, p. 16; Vincent Morris, "'Worry': Exhumation request upsets family," *Winston-Salem Journal*, Winston-Salem, NC, June 20, 1994, p. 4; "Who killed the Durham family? Here's my story," gowilkes.com, August 12, 2010, posted by "magnumpi." gowilkes.com/voice/who-killed-the-durham-family-heres-my-story/77993/?startview=180&h=093827; York, "Cold Weather."
[1594] https://www.findagrave.com/memorial/71775270/phillip-edward-fausnet.
[1595] Watauga County Sheriff's Office investigation file 118-H-1/2/3, January 5, 2004.
[1596] "2 Plead Guilty to $250,000 Extortion Plot," *The Los Angeles Times*, Los Angeles, CA, November 28, 1978, Part II, p. 12; Phillip Edward Fausnet, Petitioner vs. The Superior Court for the State of California, for the County of Los Angeles,
https://books.google.com/books?id=Cgxg9o3J31cC&pg=PP85&lpg=PP85&dq=phillip+edward+fausnet&source=bl&ots=8hcYCHCAYH&sig=ACfU3U2pZ41Cy-_H1QxVGdLoLn3BBuKElw&hl=en&sa=X&ved=2ahUKEwjF_-311qH4AhUHeN8KHSAQDtQQ6AF6BAgREAM#v=onepage&q=phillip%20edward%20fausnet&f=false.
[1597] Phillip Edward Fausnet, Petitioner vs. The Superior Court for the State of California, for the County of Los Angeles.
[1598] May, Paula. Phone interview with author. March 27, 2022; Watauga County Sheriff's Office investigation file 118-H-1/2/3, January 5, 2004.
[1599] "Arrested Man Has 'Pen Pistol'," *Watauga Democrat*, Boone, NC, September 17, 1970, p. 1.
[1600] May, Paula. Phone interview with author. March 27, 2022; Watauga County Sheriff's Office investigation file 118-H-1/2/3.

[1601] "Young Man Is Fatally Hurt," pp. 1 & 16; Vincent Morris, "'Worry': Exhumation request," p. 4; "Who killed the Durham family? Here's my story," gowilkes.com, August 12, 2010, posted by "magnumpi"; York, "Cold Weather"; "Who killed the Durham family? Here's my story," go.wilkes.com, August 31, 2010, posted by "Biteyourtongue," https://www.gowilkes.com/voice/who-killed-the-durham-family-heres-my-story/77993/?startview=0&h=190441; Watauga County Sheriff's Office investigation file 118-H-1/2/3; North Carolina Department of Human Resources, Division of Health Services – Vital Records Branch, Medical Examiner's Certificate of Death, Vol. 65, p. 254.
[1602] Watauga County Sheriff's Office investigation file 118-H-1/2/3.
[1603] Vincent Morris, "Staley," *Winston-Salem Journal*, Winston-Salem, NC, June 23, 1994, p. 17.
[1604] Jule Hubbard, "Body's Exhumation Sought For Prints: Related To Unsolved Watauga Case," *The Journal-Patriot*, North Wilkesboro, NC, June 13, 1994, p. 1; Vincent Morris, "DA wants to exhume body after 16 years," *Winston-Salem Journal*, Winston-Salem, NC, June 14, 1994, p. 15; "Body could help solve '72 killings," *The Charlotte Observer*, Charlotte, NC, June 15, 1994, p. 4C.
[1605] Hubbard, "Body's Exhumation Sought For Prints," p. 1.
[1606] Morris, "'Worry': Exhumation request upsets family," p. 1.
[1607] "Body could help solve '72 killings," p. 4C.
[1608] "Hearing is delayed on exhuming body," *Winston-Salem Journal*, Winston-Salem, NC, June 22, 1994, p. 14.
[1609] Watauga County Sheriff's Office investigation file 118-H-1/2/3.
[1610] Vincent Morris, "Chances to get prints unclear," *Winston-Salem Journal*, Winston-Salem, NC, June 15, 1994, p. 13; "Investigators Want To Exhume Body Of Wreck Victim," *The Mount Airy News*, Mount Airy, NC, June 21, 1994, p. 1.
[1611] Watauga County Sheriff's Office investigation file 118-H-1/2/3; Vincent Morris, "Officials will not exhume corpse," *Winston-Salem Journal*, Winston-Salem, NC, June 23, 1994, p. 15; Watauga County Sheriff's Office investigation file 118-H-1/2/3.
[1612] Vincent Morris, "Staley," p. 17.
[1613] Confidential informant, interviews with Captain Paula Townsend, July 13, 14, 23 & 2001, September 26, 2002, & October 1, 2002, Watauga County Sheriff's Office investigation file 118-H-1/2/3; Caldwell County Sheriff's Office Captain Barlowe. Interview with Captain Paula Townsend. July 24, 2001, Watauga County Sheriff's Office investigation file 118-H-1/2/3; Wake Bridges, "Women, Juveniles Arrested in Caldwell," *Hickory Daily Record*, Hickory, NC, May 3, 1984, p. 7A; Joseph Galarneau, "Prosecutor: Stray Bullet Killed Innocent Man," *The Charlotte Observer*, Charlotte, NC, December 8, 1989, p. 4B; Sarah Helton, "Judge Gives Killer 20 Years in Prison," *Hickory Daily Record*, Hickory, NC, December 15, 1989, pp. 1A & 8A; Minton, Michelle (daughter of Elaine Chapman Edmisten). Facebook messages. April 12, 2024.
[1614] Shook, Mark. Phone interview with author. March 24, 2022.
[1615] Hagaman, Len. In-person interview with author. May 19, 2023.
[1616] Rominger, Dee Dee. Phone interview with author. April 4, 2023.
[1617] Shook, Mark. Phone interview with author. March 24, 2022.
[1618] Anonymous source.
[1619] Watauga County Sheriff's Office investigation file 118-H-1/2/3; "Police Probing Stabbing Deaths of 2 N. C. Men," *The Charlotte Observer*, Charlotte, NC, December 3, 1983, p. C1; https://findagrave.com/memorial/49937317/gary-keith-huffman; https://findagrave.com/memorial/98721021/carl-stuart-cockerham; North Carolina Department of Human Resources, Division of Health Services – Vital Records Bureau, Medical Examiner's Certificates of Death, Vol. 70, pp. 90 & 185.
[1620] Watauga County Sheriff's Office investigation file 118-H-1/2/3.
[1621] Bullard, *The Durham Murders*, p. 433.
[1622] "Investigation of Durham family's slaying continues"; Hagaman, Len. In-person interview with author. May 19, 2023.
[1623] Bullard, *The Durham Murders*, p. 423.
[1624] Bill Durham & Len Hagaman, email correspondence, August 17, 2009, Watauga County Sheriff's Office investigation file 118-H-1/2/3.
[1625] Hagaman, Len. E-mails to Tim Bullard. November 5 & December 16, 2011, Watauga County Sheriff's Office investigation file 118-H-1/2/3.
[1626] Hagaman, Len. In-person interview with author. March 14, 2022; May, Paula. Phone interview with author. March 27, 2022; Watauga County Sheriff's Office investigation file 118-H-1/2/3.
[1627] "Unsolved: Hogtied In High Country," *The News and Observer*, Raleigh, NC, July 29, 2018, p. 7A.
[1628] Hagaman, Len. Watauga County Sheriff's Office press conference. February 11, 2022.
[1629] Ibid.
[1630] Rominger, Jaska "Dee Dee." E-mail to Len Hagaman. December 19, 2011, Watauga County Sheriff's Office investigation file 118-H-1/2/3; Rominger, Dee Dee. Phone interview with author. April 3, 2023.

[1631] "Star Scouts" (photo caption), *Watauga Democrat*, Boone, NC, November 18, 1971, p. 2A; Watauga County Sheriff's Office investigation file 118-H-1/2/3.
[1632] Bullard, *The Durham Murders*, p. 73.
[1633] Mitchell, "Slayings mystery," p. A19.
[1634] Bullard, *The Durham Murders*, pp. 90 & 101.
[1635] Mitchell, "Slayings mystery," p. A19.
[1636] Ibid.
[1637] Hagaman, Len. In-person interview with author. March 14, 2022.
[1638] Investigative notes, August 24, 2015 (interview with Ginny Durham Mackie), Watauga County Sheriff's Office investigation file 118-H-1/2/3.
[1639] Edwards, Diana (Ginny's first cousin once removed). Phone interview with author. October 14, 2023.
[1640] Mitchell, "Slayings mystery," p. A19; Bullard, *The Durham Murders*, p. 687.
[1641] "Jeffery MacDonald & 1972 Durham triple murders same killers theory."
[1642] Edmisten, Rufus. Zoom interview with author. March 31, 2022.
[1643] Bullard, *The Durham Murders*, p. 188.
[1644] Ibid., pp. 382 & 391.
[1645] Ballard, "200 Quizzed In Murder," p. 1; "N. C. sheriff dusting cobwebs off," p. 5-A.
[1646] Mitchell, "Slayings mystery," p. A19.
[1647] Email to Len Hagaman & Tim Bullard. February 11, 2012, Watauga County Sheriff's Office investigation file 118-H-1/2/3; Phone call to the Watauga County Sheriff's Office. February 6, 2012, Watauga County Sheriff's Office investigation file 118-H-1/2/3.
[1648] Lankford, Edward. In-person conversation with author. February 11, 2023.
[1649] Ibid.; Rominger, Dee Dee. Phone interviews with author. April 3 & July 31, 2023; Mackie, Ginny Durham. Interview with Carolynn Johnson & Wade Colvard.
[1650] Rominger, Jaska "Dee Dee." E-mail to Len Hagaman. December 19, 2011; Rominger, Dee Dee. Phone interviews with author. April 3 & July 31, 2023.
[1651] Mackie, Ginny Durham. E-mail to Dee Dee Rominger. March 26, 2013, Watauga County Sheriff's Office investigation file 118-H-1/2/3.
[1652] Ibid.; Mackie, Ginny Durham. Interview with Dee Dee Rominger. March 26, 2013, Watauga County Sheriff's Office investigation file 118-H-1/2/3.
[1653] Mackie, Ginny Durham. Interview with Carolynn Johnson & Wade Colvard.
[1654] Mackie, Ginny Durham. Interview with Dee Dee Rominger. March 26, 2013.
[1655] "Investigation of Durham family's slaying continues."
[1656] Posts by usernames "asheonce" and "Regi," https://unexplained-mysteries.com/forum/topic/262185-unsolved-triple-murder-north-carolina-1972/page/37/#comments, October 4, 2015. Poster "asheonce" stated this information to be from an article published in Discovery ID magazine, possibly in July-September quarterly. The author contacted Discovery ID magazine, but they could not locate the issue.
[1657] Investigative notes, January 14, 2015, Watauga County Sheriff's Office investigation file 118-H-1/2/3; Mackie, Ginny Durham. Interview with Carolynn Johnson & Wade Colvard.
[1658] Investigative notes, February 13, 2015, Watauga County Sheriff's Office investigation file 118-H-1/2/3.
[1659] Chandler, Sean (son of Dean and Darlene Chandler). Phone interview with author. March 4, 2024; Genealogical research by author; "Man pleads guilty to voluntary manslaughter," *Asheville Citizen-Times*, Asheville, NC, January 11, 1997, p. B2.
[1660] Investigative notes, August 24, 2015, Watauga County Sheriff's Office investigation file 118-H-1/2/3.
[1661] Posts by usernames "asheonce" and "Regi."
[1662] Hagaman, Len. In-person interviews with author. March 14, 2022 & May 24, 2022; "Linda Garwood dies at her home; service Saturday" (obituary of Linda Combs Garwood, mother of informant), *Wilkes-Journal Patriot*, North Wilkesboro, NC, January 18, 2013 (online), https://www.journalpatriot.com/obituaries/linda-garwood-dies-at-her-home-service-saturday/article_001dcec0-619f-11e2-9ff5-001a4bcf6878.html; Hayes, Patrick (Benny Staley's great-nephew). Facebook message to author. November 23, 2023.
[1663] Hagaman, Len. In-person interview with author. March 14, 2022
[1664] Watauga County Sheriff's Office investigation file 118-H-1/2/3; Mauldin, Charles & Gayle. Interview with Red Lyons. February 21, 1989.
[1665] York, "Cold Weather"; Combs, Jerry. Phone interview with author. March 15, 2023.
[1666] Watauga County Sheriff's Office investigation file 118-H-1/2/3.
[1667] Rominger, Dee Dee. Phone interview with author. July 31, 2023.
[1668] Investigative notes, July 27, 2016, Watauga County Sheriff's Office investigation file 118-H-1/2/3.
[1669] Rominger, Dee Dee. Phone interview with author. July 31, 2023.

[1670] Hagaman, Len. The Weather Channel's *Storm of Suspicion*, Season 4, Episode 19: "Triple Torment," May 30, 2023.
[1671] *Special Edition of WBTV News*.
[1672] Bullard, *The Durham Murders*, p. 402.
[1673] Jack Warner, "End Of An Era: GBI's class of '72 retiring, led by acclaimed agent," *The Atlanta Journal-Constitution*, Atlanta, GA, July 30, 2000, p. F3; Ingram, Bob. Phone conversation with author. May 12, 2022; Birt, Shane. Interview with Bob Ingram, May 17, 2019; Hudgins and Birt, *Grace and Disgrace*, p. 82.
[1674] Ingram, Bob. In-person interview with author. April 19, 2022; Ingram, Bob. Phone interview with author. December 21, 2022; Hudgins and Birt, *Grace and Disgrace*, p. 404.
[1675] Ingram, Bob. In-person interview with author. April 19, 2022; Hudgins and Birt, *Grace and Disgrace*, p. 82.
[1676] "Former WCSO Chief Deputy Provides Link to Help Close 50-Year-Old Triple Homicide," *White County News*, Cleveland, GA, February 17, 2022, p. 9A (online), https://www.whitecountynews.net/local-newsletter/former-wcso-chief-deputy-provides-link-help-close-50-year-old-triple-homicide.
[1677] "A Gainesville author, a 1972 triple murder in NC and a mystery finally solved," *The Times*, Gainesville, GA, February 23 (updated February 24), 2022 (online), https://www.gainesvilletimes.com/news/history/gainesville-author-1972-triple-murder-nc-and-mystery-finally-solved/.
[1678] Ingram, Bob. In-person interview with author. April 19, 2022.
[1679] Ibid.; Hudgins and Birt, *Grace and Disgrace*, p. 82.
[1680] Hudgins, Phil. Zoom lecture: "Living with Faith and Dixie Mafia Hitman," sponsored by Brenau University Learning & Leisure Institute, February 23, 2023.
[1681] Birt, Shane. Interview with Bob Ingram, Len Hagaman & Carolynn Johnson. November 16, 2020.
[1682] Ingram, Bob. In-person interview with author. April 19, 2022.
[1683] "Former WCSO Chief Deputy Provides Link," p. 9A.
[1684] Ingram, Bob. In-person interview with author. April 19, 2022.
[1685] Ibid.; Kipe, *In The Red Clay*, Season 2, Episode 6: *Beneath the Chestnut Tree*.
[1686] Birt, Shane. Interview with Bob Ingram. April 30, 2019.
[1687] Hudgins and Birt, *Grace and Disgrace*, pp. 183-184, & 221.
[1688] Birt, Shane. Interviews with Bob Ingram. April 30 & May 17, 2019.
[1689] Birt, Shane. Interview with Bob Ingram. April 30, 2019.
[1690] Ingram, Bob. In-person interview with author. April 19, 2022; Hudgins and Birt, *Grace and Disgrace*, p. 184.
[1691] Ingram, Bob. In-person interview with author. April 19, 2022.
[1692] Hudgins and Birt, *Grace and Disgrace*, p. 221.
[1693] Birt, Shane. Interview with Bob Ingram. April 30, 2019.
[1694] Ibid.
[1695] Ibid.
[1696] Birt, Shane. Interview with Bob Ingram. May 17, 2019; Handwritten notes of Watauga County Sheriff's Office Capt. Carolynn Johnson.
[1697] Birt, Shane. In-person interview with author. March 6, 2024.
[1698] Ingram, Bob. Phone conversation with author. May 12, 2022; Ingram, Bob. Phone interview with author. December 21, 2022; Autopsy of Reid Oliver Fleming (Case #73-23816), Georgia Crime Laboratory Division of Investigations, December 23, 1973.
[1699] "A Gainesville author, a 1972 triple murder in NC and a mystery finally solved"; Ingram, Bob. In-person interview with author. April 19, 2022; Hudgins and Birt, *Grace and Disgrace*, p. 255.
[1700] Hudgins and Birt, *Grace and Disgrace*, p. 256; Hudgins, Phil. E-mail to author. December 20, 2022; Hudgins, Phil. Phone interview with author. December 22, 2022.
[1701] Hudgins and Birt, *Grace and Disgrace*, p. 257.
[1702] Birt, Shane. Interviews with Bob Ingram. April 30, 2019.
[1703] Hagaman, Len. In-person interview with author. March 14, 2022; Ingram, Bob. In-person interview with author. April 19, 2022; Hudgins and Birt, *Grace and Disgrace*, p. 268.
[1704] Hudgins and Birt, *Grace and Disgrace*, pp. 255-256; Hudgins, Phil. Phone interview with author. December 22, 2022; Davis, Billy Wayne. Interview with Bob Ingram, Len Hagaman & Carolynn Johnson. November 17, 2020; O'Driscoll, C. A., Facebook post, December 6, 2023, https://www.facebook.com/officialcaodriscoll; O'Driscoll, C. A., "Interview with Billy Wayne Davis," YouTube, December 6, 2023, https://www.youtube.com/watch?v=0l4kEJUnYDg.
[1705] "A Gainesville author, a 1972 triple murder in NC and a mystery finally solved."
[1706] Ingram, Bob. In-person interview with author. April 19, 2022.
[1707] Ibid.

[1708] "A Gainesville author, a 1972 triple murder in NC and a mystery finally solved"; Hudgins and Birt, *Grace and Disgrace*, p. 256; Kipe, *In The Red Clay*, Season 2, Episode 6: *Beneath the Chestnut Tree*; Ingram, Bob. Phone interview with author. May 27, 2023; Ingram, Bob. In-person interview with author. March 6, 2024.
[1709] "Former WCSO Chief Deputy Provides Link," p. 9A.
[1710] Ibid.; Ingram, Bob. Phone interview with author. May 27, 2023.
[1711] https://www.jamesfhwrens.com/obituaries/ReidRO-FlemingJr; Ingram, Bob. In-person interview with author. April 19, 2022; Murderpedia: Billy Sunday Birt, https://murderpedia.org/male.B/b/birt-billy-sunday.htm#:~:text=Billy%20Sunday%20Birt%20was%20born,in%20North%20Georgia%20in%201938.&text=Even %20with%20Birt's%20reputation%20as,Fleming%2C%20in%20Wren%2C%20Georgia; Autopsies of Reid Oliver Fleming (Case #73-23816) and Lois Robinson Fleming (Case #73-23815), Georgia Crime Laboratory Division of Investigations, December 23, 1973.
[1712] CSI Atlanta, "The deadliest man in Georgia," January 20, 2020, https://podcast.app/the-deadliest-man-in-georgia-e84039463/.
[1713] Ingram, Bob. In-person interview with author. April 19, 2022.
[1714] Fleming crime scene photo. Personal observance of author.
[1715] "Couple Found Bound, Strangled," *The High Point Enterprise*, High Point, NC, December 24, 1973, p. 2A.
[1716] Ingram, Bob. In-person interview with author. April 19, 2022
[1717] Ibid.; Murderpedia: Billy Sunday Birt.
[1718] Ingram, Bob. In-person interviews with author. April 19 & December 21, 2022; Kipe, *In The Red Clay*, Season 2, Episode 5: *Black Sheep*, December 19, 2022; Hudgins and Birt, *Grace and Disgrace*, p. 86.
[1719] Bethune, Elvis Larry. Interviews with various law enforcement officers. February 19 & 27, July 30, & August 2, 1974. Investigative Summary, 70-0302-01-73, Mr. And Mrs. R. O. Fleming.
[1720] Ibid.; Davis, Billy Wayne. Interviews with Zollie Compton & R. F. Ingram, January 17, 1975. Investigative Summary, 70-0302-01-73, Mr. And Mrs. R. O. Fleming.
[1721] Ibid.
[1722] Ingram, Bob. In-person interview with author. April 19, 2022; Hudgins and Birt, *Grace and Disgrace*, pp. 85-86; Tapley, Carswell. Interviews with various law enforcement officers. December 27 & 29, 1973, February 26, September 25, & October 25, 1974, & January 31, 1975. Investigative Summary, 70-0302-01-73, Mr. And Mrs. R. O. Fleming; Leisher, George. Interviews with various law enforcement officers. March 25 & September 10, 1974. Investigative Summary, 70-0302-01-73, Mr. And Mrs. R. O. Fleming.
[1723] Tapley, Carswell. Interviews with various law enforcement officers.; Leisher, George. Interviews with various law enforcement officers.
[1724] Ibid.; Davis, Billy Wayne. Interview with Zollie Compton & R. F. Ingram. January 17, 1975.
[1725] Ibid.
[1726] Bethune, Elvis Larry. Interviews with various law enforcement officers.
[1727] Ibid.
[1728] Murderpedia: Billy Sunday Birt; Tapley, Carswell. Interviews with various law enforcement officers.
[1729] Ingram, Bob. In-person interview with author. April 19, 2022.
[1730] Warner, "End Of An Era," p. F3; Hudgins and Birt, *Grace and Disgrace*, p. 86.
[1731] Tom Crawford, "Charron Accuses Darden of Bungling," *The Atlanta Journal*, October 1, 1976, p. 2-A.
[1732] Ingram, R. F. Conversations with Richard Still. August 27 & September 10, 1974.
[1733] Davis, Billy Wayne. Conversation with Zollie Compton & R. F. Ingram. October 28, 1974.
[1734] Hudgins and Birt, *Grace and Disgrace*, p. 87.
[1735] Davis, Billy Wayne. Interview with Zollie Compton & R. F. Ingram. January 17, 1975..
[1736] Hudgins and Birt, *Grace and Disgrace*, p. 88; Mr. And Mrs. R. O. Fleming Case Summary, Case #70-0302-01-73, March 11, 1975, pp. 4-5.
[1737] "Wrens Slaying Charge Dropped," *The Saturday Enquirer and Ledger*, Columbus, GA, December 13, 1973, p. A-5.
[1738] Otwell, William Eugene. Interview with Reginald Thompson, Zollie Compton, & R. F. Ingram. January 31, 1975. Investigative Summary, 70-0302-01-73, Mr. And Mrs. R. O. Fleming; Davis, Billy Wayne. Interview with Zollie Compton & R. F. Ingram. January 17, 1975.
[1739] Reed, Charles David. Interview with R. F. Ingram & Zollie Compton, February 26, 1975. Investigative Summary, 70-0302-01-73, Mr. And Mrs. R. O. Fleming.
[1740] Unidentified newspaper clipping, Birt, Billy Stonewall. *Rock Solid: The True Story of Georgia's Dixie Mafia*. (2017), p. 145; Birt, Hudgins and Birt, *Grace and Disgrace*, p. 94.
[1741] Davis, Billy Wayne. Interview with Zollie Compton & R. F. Ingram. January 17, 1975.
[1742] Ibid.
[1743] Ibid.

[1744] Murderpedia: Billy Sunday Birt; Witness List, Mr. And Mrs. R. O. Fleming Case #70-0302-01-73, March 11, 1975, p. 3.
[1745] Kipe, *In The Red Clay*, Chapter 8: *Unlucky Number 7*, September 29, 2020; Hudgins and Birt, *Grace and Disgrace*, pp. 83 & 86; "Gaddis Witness Tells of Laughter," *The Macon News*, Macon, GA, August 14, 1975, p. 7A; "Witness Says Killing Suspect Joked," *The Atlanta Constitution*, Atlanta, GA, August 14, 1975, p. 3-G; Murderpedia: Billy Sunday Birt.
[1746] Davis, Billy Wayne. Interview with Zollie Compton & R. F. Ingram. January 17, 1975.
[1747] Murderpedia: Billy Sunday Birt.
[1748] Davis, Billy Wayne. Interview with Zollie Compton & R. F. Ingram. January 17, 1975; Rhonda Cook, "5 moved off death row after years spent in limbo," *The Atlanta Constitution*, Atlanta, GA, March 5, 1997, p. B4; Murderpedia: Billy Sunday Birt.
[1749] Davis, Billy Wayne. Interview with Zollie Compton & R. F. Ingram. January 17, 1975..
[1750] Tom Harrison, "Birt denies part in double murders," (newspaper name, date, and page number not indicated in clipping), Birt, Billy Stonewall. *Rock Solid: The True Story*, p. 166; CSI Atlanta, "The deadliest man in Georgia," January 20, 2020.
[1751] Murderpedia: Billy Sunday Birt.
[1752] Birt, Stoney. In-person interview with author. February 17, 2023.
[1753] Birt, Shane. Interview with Bob Ingram, Len Hagaman & Carolynn Johnson. November 16, 2020; Birt, Shane. In-person interview with author. March 6, 2024.
[1754] Murderpedia: Billy Sunday Birt; Hudgins and Birt, *Grace and Disgrace*, p. 96.
[1755] Birt, Stoney. In-person interview with author. February 17, 2023.
[1756] Ibid.; Birt, Stoney. Text to author. June 27, 2023.
[1757] Ingram, Bob. In-person interview with author. April 19, 2022; Hudgins and Birt, *Grace and Disgrace*, p. 97; Ingram, Bob. Phone interview with author. May 27, 2023.
[1758] Ingram, Bob. Phone interview with author. December 21, 2022.
[1759] CSI Atlanta, "The deadliest man in Georgia," January 20, 2020.
[1760] Birt, Stoney. In-person interview with author. February 17, 2023.
[1761] Hudgins and Birt, *Grace and Disgrace*, pp. 92 & 96; "Murder Trial Under Way," *The Columbus Ledger*, Columbus, GA, June 24, 1975, p. A-5.
[1762] Disposition forms for Case #70-0302-01-73; "News Of The State: Louisville," *The Atlanta Constitution*, Atlanta, GA, October 18, 1975, p. 5-A.
[1763] Ingram, Bob. Phone interview with author. December 21, 2022.
[1764] Ingram, Bob. In-person interview with author. April 19, 2022.
[1765] Ibid.; Hudgins and Birt, *Grace and Disgrace*, pp. 265-266.
[1766] Handwritten notes of Watauga County Sheriff's Office Capt. Carolynn Johnson.
[1767] Ingram, Bob. In-person interview with author. April 19, 2022.
[1768] Handwritten notes of Watauga County Sheriff's Office Capt. Carolynn Johnson.
[1769] "Local triple homicide case solved after 50 years."
[1770] Maureen Wurtz, "Blue Ridge Runs Red: Growing up with the deadliest man in the Southeast," *Queen City News*, Charlotte, NC, August 18, 2023 (on air), https://www.qcnews.com/news/investigations/airing-tonight-unraveling-the-truth-about-billy-sunday-birt-a-killer-who-hunted-in-the-south-and-in-the-carolinas/.
[1771] Ingram, Bob. In-person interview with author. April 19, 2022; Hudgins and Birt, *Grace and Disgrace*, pp. 257 & 263; Wayne Ford, "Dogged pursuit: Interview leads veteran cop to link unsolved triple murder to Dixie Mafia," *Athens Banner-Herald*, Athens, GA, March 6, 2023 (online), https://onlineathens.com/story/news/crime/2023/03/06/a-cops-interview-uncovers-dixie-mafia-leads-that-solve-50-year-old-triple-murder-case/69969405007/.
[1772] "Local triple homicide case solved after 50 years"; Handwritten notes of Watauga County Sheriff's Office Capt. Carolynn Johnson.
[1773] Wagner, Larry. Phone interview with author. December 22, 2022.
[1774] Ingram, Bob. In-person interview with author. April 19, 2022; "Former WCSO Chief Deputy Provides Link," p. 9A.
[1775] Ingram, Bob. In-person interview with author. April 19, 2022; Ingram, Bob. Phone interview with author. December 21, 2022.
[1776] Ibid.
[1777] Wagner, Larry. Phone interview with author. September 19, 2023.
[1778] Ingram, Bob. In-person interview with author. April 19, 2022; Ingram, Bob. Phone interview with author. December 21, 2022; Ford, "Dogged pursuit."
[1779] Handwritten notes of Watauga County Sheriff's Office Capt. Carolynn Johnson.
[1780] Wagner, Larry. Phone interview with author. September 19, 2023; Handwritten notes of Watauga County Sheriff's Office Capt. Carolynn Johnson.
[1781] Vaughn, Jerry. In-person interview with author. October 13, 2023.
[1782] Handwritten notes of Watauga County Sheriff's Office Capt. Carolynn Johnson.

[1783] North Carolina State Crime Laboratory Report to Watauga County Sheriff's Office, October 6, 2020, Watauga County Sheriff's Office investigation file 118-H-1/2/3; North Carolina State Crime Laboratory Evidence Transfer to Watauga County Sheriff's Office, February 24, 2021, Watauga County Sheriff's Office investigation file 118-H-1/2/3.
[1784] Durham, Bill & Steve Durham. Interview with Len Hagaman, Kelly Redmon, Carolynn Johnson, Wade Colvard, Larry Wagner, & Rufus Edmisten.
[1785] Handwritten notes of Watauga County Sheriff's Office Capt. Carolynn Johnson.
[1786] Wayne Ford, "Athens-area members of notorious criminal band Dixie Mafia linked to 1972 N. C. murders," *Athens Banner-Herald*, Athens, GA, February 22 (updated February 23), 2022 (online), https://www.onlineathens.com/story/news/local/2022/02/22/1972-triple-murder-n-c-linked-northeast-georgias-dixie-mafia/6784300001/.; Hagaman, Len. In-person interview with author. May 24, 2022; Hudgins and Birt, *Grace and Disgrace*, p. 263.
[1787] Kipe, *In The Red Clay*, Season 2, Episode 3: *Nothing As It Seems*.
[1788] Davis, Billy Wayne. Interview with Len Hagaman, Carolynn Johnson, & Wade Colvard. September 30, 2019; Johnson, Carolynn. In-person interview with author. January 16, 2024.
[1789] Kipe, Sean. Phone conversation with author. May 16, 2022; Kipe, *In The Red Clay*, Season 2, Chapter 1: *Brutal, Savage, Senseless*, November 21, 2022 & Season 2, Chapter 7: *Bonus Episode,* October 24, 2023.
[1790] Birt, Stoney. In-person interview with author. February 17, 2023.
[1791] Hagaman, Len. In-person interview with author. May 24, 2022; Hudgins and Birt, *Grace and Disgrace*, pp. 263-264; Kipe, *In The Red Clay*, Season 2, Chapter 1: *Brutal, Savage, Senseless*; Birt, Stoney. Interview with Len Hagaman, Carolynn Johnson, Wade Colvard, & Nic Johnson. October 1, 2019.
[1792] Davis, Billy Wayne. Interview with Len Hagaman, Carolynn Johnson & Wade Colvard. September 30, 2019; Johnson, Carolynn. In-person interview with author. January 16, 2024.
[1793] Wester, Deborah. Interview with Len Hagaman, Carolynn Johnson, & Wade Colvard. October 1, 2019.
[1794] Ingram, Bob. In-person interview with author. April 19, 2022; Ingram, Bob. Phone interview with author. December 21, 2022; Kipe, *In The Red Clay*, Season 2, Episode 3: *Nothing As It Seems*.
[1795] Ingram, Bob. In-person interview with author. April 19, 2022; Ingram, Bob. Phone interviews with author. December 21, 2022 & May 27, 2023; Kipe, *In The Red Clay*, Season 2, Episode 6: *Beneath the Chestnut Tree*; Ford, "Dogged pursuit."; Ingram, Bob. Phone conversation with Len Hagaman & Carolynn Johnson. November 26, 2019.
[1796] "Former WCSO Chief Deputy Provides Link.".
[1797] Ingram, Bob. In-person interview with author. April 19, 2022; Ingram, Bob. Phone interview with author. December 21, 2022.
[1798] Davis, Billy Wayne. Interview with Bob Ingram. October 21, 2020; Ingram, Bob. In-person interview with author. April 19, 2022; Ingram, Bob. Phone interview with author. December 21, 2022; Hudgins and Birt, *Grace and Disgrace*, p. 265; Kipe, *In The Red Clay*, Season 2, Episode 6: *Beneath the Chestnut Tree*.
[1799] Davis, Billy Wayne. Interview with Bob Ingram. October 21, 2020.
[1800] Ibid.; Hudgins and Birt, *Grace and Disgrace*, p. 265.
[1801] Davis, Billy Wayne. Interview with Bob Ingram. October 21, 2020.
[1802] Ibid.
[1803] Ibid.
[1804] Ingram, Bob. In-person interview with author. April 19, 2022; Ingram, Bob. Phone interview with author. December 21, 2022; Hudgins and Birt, *Grace and Disgrace*, p. 265; Kipe, *In The Red Clay*, Season 2, Episode 6: *Beneath the Chestnut Tree*.
[1805] Ingram, Bob. In-person interview with author. April 19, 2022; Ingram, Bob. Phone interview with author. December 21, 2022; Hudgins and Birt, *Grace and Disgrace*, pp. 267 & 272.
[1806] Ingram, Bob. Phone conversation with Watauga County Sheriff's Office. September 1, 2020.
[1807] Birt, Shane & Bob Ingram. In-person interview with author. March 6, 2024.
[1808] Birt, Billy Stonewall. *Rock Solid: The True Story*, pp. 102 & 103.
[1809] Birt, Shane. In-person interview with author. March 6, 2024.
[1810] Ibid.
[1811] Birt, Shane. Interview with Bob Ingram, Len Hagaman & Carolynn Johnson. November 16, 2020.
[1812] Ingram, Bob. In-person interview with author. April 19, 2022.
[1813] Davis, Billy Wayne. Interview with Bob Ingram, Len Hagaman & Carolynn Johnson. November 17, 2020; O'Driscoll, C. A., Facebook post, December 6, 2023, https://www.facebook.com/officialcaodriscoll; O'Driscoll, C. A., "Interview with Billy Wayne Davis," YouTube, December 6, 2023, https://www.youtube.com/watch?v=0l4kEJUnYDg.
[1814] Notes compiled by Carolynn Johnson, May 2023.
[1815] Mackie, Ginny Durham. Interview with Carolynn Johnson & Wade Colvard; Johnson, Carolynn. In-person interview with author. January 16, 2024.
[1816] Ingram, Bob. In-person interview with author. April 19, 2022; Ingram, Bob. Phone interview with author. December 21, 2022.

[1817] Hagaman, Len. In-person interview with author. January 16, 2024.
[1818] Kipe, *In The Red Clay*, Season 2, Episode 3: *Nothing As It Seems*.
[1819] Handwritten notes of Watauga County Sheriff's Office Capt. Carolynn Johnson.
[1820] Ingram, Bob. Phone conversation with author. May 12, 2022; Hudgins and Birt, *Grace and Disgrace*, p. 272.
[1821] "Former WCSO Chief Deputy Provides Link," p. 1A.
[1822] "Opinion: Bob Ingram deserves the credit for solving triple murder," *The Times*, Gainesville, GA, March 3, 2022 (online), https://www.gainesvilletimes.com/opinion/letter-editor/opinion-bob-ingram-deserves-credit-solving-triple-murder/.
[1823] Ingram, Bob. Phone interview with author. December 21, 2022.
[1824] Hagaman, Len. In-person interview with author. May 24, 2022.
[1825] Hudgins and Birt, *Grace and Disgrace*, p. 275; "Five dead including two deputies after April 28 standoff," *Watauga Democrat*, Boone, NC, April 29, 2021 (online), https://www.wataugademocrat.com/news/five-dead-including-two-deputies-after-april-28-standoff/article_9fd68304-d7c9-594e-89c0-bbfbcd59062b.html.
[1826] https://clustrmaps.com/person/Carrington-at8li3.
[1827] Anonymous source. Phone interview with author. May 11, 2023.
[1828] Eller, Tom. Phone interview with author. July 14, 2022.
[1829] "3 in Family Killed, Left In Bathtub," *Detroit Free Press*, Detroit Michigan, February 5, 1972, p. 7-B & "3 Slayers Hunted," p. 4-A (as two examples of a UPI report).
[1830] "Large Crowd Hears Rites For Durhams," *Winston-Salem Journal*, Winston-Salem, NC, February 7, 1972, p. 2.
[1831] Anonymous source.
[1832] Anonymous source. Phone interview with author. May 11, 2023.
[1833] Church, Monica. Watauga Online Facebook post. February 10, 2022; York, "Cold Weather."
[1834] "Accidents Kill Four in State," *The Atlanta Constitution*, Atlanta, GA, January 7, 1979, p. 10-A; "8 Die In Accidents," *The Macon News*, Macon, GA, January 8, 1979, p. 11A; "Nine People Are Killed In Weekend Accidents," *The Atlanta Constitution*, Atlanta, GA, January 8, 1979, p. 2-C; York, "Cold Weather."
[1835] "Who killed the Durham family? Here's my story," gowilkes.com, August 12, 2010, posted by "Mr. Ed." gowilkes.com/voice/who-killed-the-durham-family-heres-my-story/77993/?startview=180&h=093827.
[1836] Mauldin, Charles & Gayle. Interview with Red Lyons, August 7, 1989.
[1837] Wagner, Larry. Interview with Charles Heatherly; Wagner, Larry. Phone interview with author. December 22, 2022.
[1838] Mauldin, Charles & Gayle. Interview with Red Lyons, August 7, 1989.
[1839] Anonymous source (step-niece of Debbie Foster). Facebook messages with author. June 18, 2022 & June 25, 2024.
[1840] John Marshall Law School Registrar's Office, Atlanta, GA. Phone conversation with author. March or April 2022.
[1841] Exhibit A, Plaintiff's Motion to Request that the Elected Judge Hear Cases, Civil Action File No. 17A03026-10/Consolidated Case: 17-A-04192-10, Gwinnett County, GA Superior Court, Justin Hall (Plaintiff) v. Melanie Hall (Defendant), filed June 29, 2017, https://www.gabar.org/MemberSearchDetail.cfm?ID=MzE5MzM3.
[1842] Hagaman, Len. In-person interview with author. March 14, 2022.
[1843] Lipsig, David, M.D. Letter to Patrick Meriwether, Esq.
[1844] Smith, Judge R. Rucker. E-mail communication with author. August 22, 2022; Anonymous source.
[1845] https://en.wikipedia.org/wiki/Palau.
[1846] https://en.wikipedia.org/wiki/First_inauguration_of_Ronald_Reagan.
[1847] Bowers, Bruce. Phone interview with author. December 29, 2022.
[1848] Mackie, Ginny Durham. Interview with Carolynn Johnson & Wade Colvard; Investigative notes. August 24, 2015, Watauga County Sheriff's Office investigation file 118-H-1/2/3; Rominger, Dee Dee. Phone interview with author. July 31, 2023; Hagaman, Len. In-person interviews with author. March 14 & May 24, 2022.
[1849] Lipsig, David, M.D. Letter to Patrick Meriwether, Esq.; https://casetext.com/case/knighton-v-state-14; "Rape trial begins," *The Macon News*, Macon, GA, May 25, 1982, p. 1B; "Judge declares mistrial in rape case," *The Macon News*, Macon, GA, May 26, 1982, p. 6B; Smith, Judge R. Rucker. E-mail communication with author. August 22, 2022.
[1850] Smith, Judge R. Rucker. E-mail communication with author. August 22, 2022; "District Attorney Hires Americus Attorney," *The Columbus Enquirer*, Columbus, GA, July 21, 1981, p. B-6.
[1851] Smith, Judge R. Rucker. E-mail communication with author. August 22, 2022.
[1852] Carroll, Ward. Interview with Charles Heatherly, September, 1988; Sheriff Red Lyons, September 7, 1989, Watauga County Sheriff's Office investigation file 118-H-1/2/3; Aldridge, Richard. In-person conversation with author. June 26, 2022; Carroll, Johnny. Phone interview with author. June 29, 2022; Hudgins and Birt, *Grace and Disgrace*, p. 271; Rucker, Jeff. Phone interview with author. October 4, 2023.
[1853] Smith, Judge R. Rucker. E-mail communication with author. August 22, 2022.

[1854] O'Quinn, Miles (Investigator & Operations Manager, District Attorney's Office, Southwestern Judicial Circuit of Georgia). Phone conversation with Jack Henson (summarized in an e-mail from Henson to author). O'Quinn was relaying to Henson the recollections of Judge R. Rucker Smith. July 18, 2022.
[1855] Bowers, Bruce. Phone interview with author. December 29, 2022.
[1856] https://lawyers.justia.com/lawyer/justin-troy-hall-336108
[1857] Help Wanted advertisement, *The Atlanta Constitution*, Atlanta, GA, February 2, 1986, p. 143.
[1858] "Civil Suits: Injunctive Relief," *The Atlanta Constitution*, Atlanta, GA, November 22, 1991, p. J3.
[1859] "DeKalb public defender Richard Loftis under attack," *The Atlanta Constitution*, Atlanta, GA, June 23, 1983, p. 4C; "Loftis leaving defender's office to begin private practice career," *The Atlanta Constitution*, Atlanta, GA, June 28, 1984, p. 1B.
[1860] Wikipedia, "James Walraven," https://en.wikipedia.org/wiki/James_Walraven; "Man Convicted, Condemned In Decatur Bathtub Slaying," *The Valdosta Daily Times*, Valdosta, GA, November 17, 1981, p. 6; "Walraven Loses Bid For New Trial On 'Bathtub Murders'," *The Atlanta Constitution*, Atlanta, GA, March 11, 1982, p. 22-A; "Walraven conviction tossed out," *The Atlanta Constitution*, Atlanta, GA, November 24, 1982, p. 1.
[1861] "Who killed the Durham family? Here's my story," gowilkes.com, August 22, 2010, posted by "Pepper22."
[1862] https://rpears1310.typepad.com/blog/2007/03/my-sister-annette.html; Special Proceeding Notice, Benny James Wyatt, Petitioner for the adoption of Ray Anthony Wyatt and Glenn Pearson Wyatt, Plaintiff vs. Ray Hall, Defendant, *Winston-Salem Journal*, Winston-Salem, NC, September 16, 1968, p. 16; https://www.findagrave.com/memorial/125491434/margaret_annette_hall_wyatt_bray.
[1863] Final Judgment And Decree Of Divorce, Civil Action File No. 91-A01696-1, Gwinnett County, GA Superior Court, Justin T. Hall (Plaintiff) v. Carmen Wells-Hall (Defendant), August 24, 1992.
[1864] Anonymous source. Text to author. July 8, 2023.
[1865] https://www.wagesfuneralhome.com/obituaries/Carmen-Shackelford/#!/Obituary; Anonymous source. Phone interview. May 11, 2023.
[1866] "DeKalb Couple Found Slain," *The Atlanta Constitution*, Atlanta, GA, December 28, 1967, p. 17.
[1867] Genealogical research by author. https://ancestry.com/family-tree/person/tree/170690419/person/252358585871/facts; Defenses, Answer And Countercomplaint Of Defendant, Civil Action File No. 91A-01696-1, Gwinnett County, GA Superior Court, Justin T. Hall (Plaintiff) v. Carmen Wells-Hall (Defendant), May 15, 1991.
[1868] Mackie, Ginny Durham. Interview with Carolynn Johnson & Wade Colvard; Hagaman, Len. In-person interview with author. March 14, 2022.
[1869] Jim Stewart, "Gene Reeves: Innocent Victim Who Was 'Just In The Way," *The Atlanta Constitution*, Atlanta, GA, March 8, 1978, p. 8-A.
[1870] Justia US Law – Billy Sunday Birt v. Charles N. Montgomery, Warden, Georgia State Prison, https://law.justia.com/cases/federal/appellate-courts/F2/725/587/58035/; Stewart, "Gene Reeves: Innocent Victim" p. 8-A; Birt, Ruby Nell (as told to Phil Hudgins), Grace and Disgrace: Living with Faith and a Dixie Mafia Hit Man (YAV Publications, Asheville, NC, 2022), pp. 93 & 96; Genealogical research by author.
[1871] Anonymous source. Phone interview. May 11, 2023.
[1872] Ibid
[1873] Ibid.
[1874] Ibid.
[1875] Anonymous source; Motion for Protective Order & Affidavit Of James D. Nichols, Jr., Civil Action File No. 91-A01696-1, Gwinnett County, GA Superior Court, Justin T. Hall (Plaintiff) v. Carmen Wells-Hall (Defendant), February 19, 1992.
[1876] Anonymous source. Phone interview. May 11, 2023; Anonymous source.
[1877] Anonymous sources.
[1878] Anonymous source. Phone interview with author. May 11, 2023.
[1879] Defenses, Answer And Countercomplaint Of Defendant, Civil Action File No. 91A-01696-1, Gwinnett County, GA Superior Court, Justin T. Hall (Plaintiff) v. Carmen Wells-Hall (Defendant), May 15, 1991.
[1880] Response To Defendant's Motion To Reopen And Compel Discovery, Civil Action File No. 91-A01696-1, Gwinnett County, GA Superior Court, Justin T. Hall (Plaintiff) v. Carmen Wells-Hall (Defendant), March 18, 1992; "Divorce Filings," *The Atlanta Constitution*, Atlanta, GA, April 25, 1991, p. J16.
[1881] Anonymous source.
[1882] Anonymous source. Phone interview with author. May 11, 2023.
[1883] Rucker, Jeff. Phone interview with author. October 4, 2023.
[1884] Defenses, Answer And Countercomplaint Of Defendant & Notice To Produce And Request For Production Of Documents & Domestic Relations Financial Affidavit, Civil Action File No. 91A-01696-1, Gwinnett County, GA Superior Court, Justin T. Hall (Plaintiff) v. Carmen Wells-Hall (Defendant), May 15, 1991; Josh Green, email to Tim Bullard, August 5, 2011, Watauga County Sheriff's Office investigation file 118-H-1/2/3.

[1885] Motion For Emergency Temporary Relief, Civil Action File No. 91-A01696-1, Gwinnett County, GA Superior Court, Justin T. Hall (Plaintiff) v. Carmen Wells-Hall (Defendant), February 4, 1992.
[1886] Defendant's Motion To Reopen And Compel Discovery & & Brief In Support Of Defendant's Motion To Reopen And Compel Discovery, Civil Action File No. 91-A01696-1, Gwinnett County, GA Superior Court, Justin T. Hall (Plaintiff) v. Carmen Wells-Hall (Defendant), March 13, 1992.
[1887] Motion In Limine (x2), Civil Action File No. 91-A01696-1, Gwinnett County, GA Superior Court, Justin T. Hall (Plaintiff) v. Carmen Wells-Hall (Defendant), March 24, 1992; Green, Josh. E-mail to Tim Bullard, August 5, 2011, Watauga County Sheriff's Office investigation file 118-H-1/2/3.
[1888] Anonymous source. Phone interview with author. May 11, 2023.
[1889] Final Judgment And Decree Of Divorce & List Of Assets And Debts, Civil Action File No. 91-A01696-1, Gwinnett County, GA Superior Court, Justin T. Hall (Plaintiff) v. Carmen Wells-Hall (Defendant), August 24, 1992
[1890] https://www.legacy.com/us/obituaries/greenvilleonline/name/terry-wright-obituary?id=21730358.
[1891] Anonymous source. Phone interview with author. May 11, 2023; Anonymous source. Text to author. July 8, 2023.
[1892] https://www.wagesfuneralhome.com/obituaries/Carmen-Shackelford/#!/Obituary.
[1893] Defendant's Answer And Counterclaim For Divorce, Civil Action File No. 12-A-06853-10, Gwinnett County, GA Superior Court, Melanie Hall (Plaintiff) v. Justin Hall (Defendant), September 14, 2012.
[1894] https://www.ancestry.com/discoveryui-content/view/309400980:62209?ssrc=pt&tid=170690419&pid=252384524755.
[1895] https://www.linkedin.com/in/melanie-hall-a552b177/; Expedited Motion For Independent Medical Examination And Production Of All Medical, Pharmacy, And Psychological Records, Civil Action File No. 12-A-06853-10, Gwinnett County, GA Superior Court, Melanie Hall (Plaintiff) v. Justin Hall (Defendant), February 4, 2013.
[1896] intelius.com/dashboard/reports/79ec5aff-2dc8-4080-ac4c-8e3508943911; intelius.com/dashboard/reports/a9a3a005-ab9e-4e3d-befa-dcf51fc4c93e; Anonymous source. Phone interview with author. May 11, 2023; Anonymous source. Text to author. November 9, 2023; "White-Reynolds" (marriage announcement), *The Macon Telegraph*, Macon, GA, May 21, 1985, p. 4B; Genealogical research by author.
[1897] https://www.legacy.com/us/obituaries/macon/name/ed-roberts-obituary?id=21042679; https://www.tributearchive.com/obituaries/10881160/Justin-T-Hall; Domestic Relations Financial Affidavit, Civil Action File No. 17A03026-10, Gwinnett County, GA Superior Court, Justin Hall (Plaintiff) v. Melanie Hall (Defendant), filed August 7, 2017; https://www.whitepages.com/name/Melanie-Hall/Alpharetta-GA/PK3dkvB7Nqy.
[1898] Expedited Motion For Independent Medical Examination And Production Of All Medical, Pharmacy, And Psychological Records, Civil Action File No. 12-A06853-10, Gwinnett County, GA Superior Court, Melanie Hall (Plaintiff) v. Justin Hall (Defendant), February 4, 2013, Exhibit 1, Affidavit of David S. Lipsig, M.D., October 16, 2012; Defendant's Answer And Counterclaim For Divorce, Civil Action File No. 12-A-06853-10, Gwinnett County, GA Superior Court, Melanie Hall (Plaintiff) v. Justin Hall (Defendant), September 14. 2012; intelius.com/dashboard/reports/ga:suwanee:30024:4226bavertondr.
[1899] Georgia Government Transparency And Campaign Finance Commission, https://media.ethics.ga.gov/search/Campaign/Campaign_ByContributionsearchresults.aspx?Contributor=hall&Zip=&City=duluth&ContTypeID=0&PAC=&Employer=&Occupation=&From=&To=&Cash=&InK=&Filer=&Candidate=&Committee; Watauga County Sheriff's Office investigation file 118-H-1/2/3.
[1900] "Traffic violators: Block bill for online courses," The Atlanta Constitution, Atlanta, GA, February 22, 2007, p. A18.
[1901] Georgia Government Transparency And Campaign Finance Commission, https://media.ethics.ga.gov/search/Lobbyist/Lobbyist_Name.aspx?&FilerID=L20080227.
[1902] https://ecorp.sos.ga.gov/BusinessSearch/BusinessInformation?businessId=721693&businessType=Domestic%20Profit%20Corporation&fromSearch=True.
[1903] https://ecorp.sos.ga.gov/BusinessSearch/BusinessFilings, Troy Hall Construction, Inc. Control Number J706383, Annual Registration (2015) - Filing Number 12053782, February 2, 2015; https://opencorporates.com/companies/us_ga/J706383.
[1904] https://georgiacompanyregistry.com/companies/homes-by-try-hall-inc/.
[1905] https://opengovus.com/georgia-business/723046.
[1906] Checkpeople.com Background Report on Justin Hall (Deceased).
[1907] Ibid.
[1908] https://ecorp.sos.ga.gov/BusinessSearch/BusinessFilings (Annual Registration (2015) - Filing Number 0982275, February 2, 2015; https://opengovus.com/georgia-business/762307.
[1909] https://ecorp.sos.ga.gov/BusinessSearch/BusinessInformation?businessId=193126&businessType=Domestic%20Profit%20Corporation&fromSearch=True.

[1910] https://ecorp.sos.ga.gov/BusinessSearch/BusinessInformation?businessId=892456&businessType=Domestic%20Profit%20Corporation&fromSearch=True.

[1911] https://georgiacompanyregistry.com/companies/chamblee-dui-defensive-driving-school-inc/.

[1912] https://georgiacompanyregistry.com/companies/secret-witness-detective-agency-inc/.

[1913]https://georgiacompanyregistry.com/companies/creative-insurance-agency-inc-2/.

[1914] https://ecorp.sos.ga.gov/BusinessSearch/BusinessFilings, North Wilkesboro Services, Inc. Control Number 11044322, Annual Registration (2014) - Filing Number 12035297, February 17, 2014 & Annual Registration (2015) – Filing Number 11110581, February 2, 2015; https://opengovus.com/georgia-business/1631939.

[1915] Checkpeople.com Background Report on Justin Hall (Deceased).

[1916] https://lawyers.findlaw.com/profile/view/2539521_1.

[1917] https://www.yelp.com/biz/drive-now-lawrenceville.

[1918] https://www.facebook.com/josey.hall.98; https://en.wikipedia.org/wiki/Kosrae.

[1919] https://clustrmaps.com/d/GA/Duluth/Sweet-Bottom-Drive; intelius.com/dashboard/reports/ga:duluth:30096:3788sweetbottomdr.

[1920] Gwinnett Tax Assessor's Office, https://gwinnettassessor.manatron.com, Property ID R6321 011; https://zillow.com/homes/3788-Sweet-Bottom-Dr-Duluth-GA-30096_rb/14796621_zpid/.

[1921] Expedited Motion For Independent Medical Examination And Production Of All Medical, Pharmacy, And Psychological Records, Civil Action File No. 12-A06853-10, Gwinnett County, GA Superior Court, Melanie Hall (Plaintiff) v. Justin Hall (Defendant), February 4, 2013, Exhibit 1, Affidavit of David S. Lipsig, M.D., October 16, 2012; Defendant's Answer And Counterclaim For Divorce, Civil Action File No. 12-A-06853-10, Gwinnett County, GA Superior Court, Melanie Hall (Plaintiff) v. Justin Hall (Defendant), September 14. 2012; Anonymous source. Phone interview with author. May 11, 2023.

[1922] Domestic Relations Financial Affidavit, Civil Action File No. 17A03026-10, Gwinnett County, GA Superior Court, Justin Hall (Plaintiff) v. Melanie Hall (Defendant), filed August 7, 2017.

[1923] Final Judgment & Decree, Civil Action File No. 12-A-06853, Gwinnett County, GA Superior Court, Melanie Hill (Plaintiff) v. Justin Hall (Defendant), September 17, 2012.

[1924] Defendant's Answer And Counterclaim For Divorce, Civil Action File No. 12-A-06853-10, Gwinnett County, GA Superior Court, Melanie Hall (Plaintiff) v. Justin Hall (Defendant), September 14, 2012.

[1925] Expedited Motion For Independent Medical Examination And Production Of All Medical, Pharmacy, And Psychological Records, Civil Action File No. 12-A06853-10, Gwinnett County, GA Superior Court, Melanie Hall (Plaintiff) v. Justin Hall (Defendant), February 4, 2013, Exhibit 1, Affidavit of David S. Lipsig, M.D., October 16, 2012

[1926] Settlement Agreement, Civil Action No. 12-A-06853-10, Gwinnett County, GA Superior Court, Melanie Hall (Plaintiff) v. Justin Hall (Defendant), September 16, 2012.

[1927] Ibid.

[1928] Motion To Set Aside Settlement Agreement And Final Judgment And Decree, Civil Action File No. 12-A06853-10, Gwinnett County, GA Superior Court, October 17, 2012.

[1929] Expedited Motion For Independent Medical Examination And Production Of All Medical, Pharmacy, And Psychological Records, Civil Action File No. 12-A06853-10, Gwinnett County, GA Superior Court, Melanie Hall (Plaintiff) v. Justin Hall (Defendant), February 4, 2013, Exhibit 1, Affidavit of David S. Lipsig, M.D., October 16, 2012.

[1930] Ibid.

[1931] Ibid.; Defendant's Answer And Counterclaim For Divorce, Civil Action File No. 12-A-06853-10, Gwinnett County, GA Superior Court, Melanie Hall (Plaintiff) v. Justin Hall (Defendant), September 14. 2012.

[1932] Anonymous source.

[1933] Expedited Motion For Independent Medical Examination And Production Of All Medical, Pharmacy, And Psychological Records, Civil Action File No. 12-A06853-10, Gwinnett County, GA Superior Court, Melanie Hall (Plaintiff) v. Justin Hall (Defendant), February 4, 2013, Exhibit 1, Affidavit of David S. Lipsig, M.D., October 16, 2012.

[1934] Ibid.

[1935] Ibid.

[1936] https://en.wikipedia.org/wiki/Mini-Mental_State_Examination.

[1937] Expedited Motion For Independent Medical Examination And Production Of All Medical, Pharmacy, And Psychological Records, Civil Action File No. 12-A06853-10, Gwinnett County, GA Superior Court, Melanie Hall (Plaintiff) v. Justin Hall (Defendant), February 4, 2013, Exhibit 1, Affidavit of David S. Lipsig, M.D., October 16, 2012.

[1938] Ibid.

[1939] Ibid.

[1940] Motion for Contempt, Civil Action File No. 12-A-06853-10, Gwinnett County, GA Superior Court, Melanie Hall (Plaintiff) v. Justin Hall (Defendant), November 7, 2012; Response To Defendant's Motion To Set Aside Settlement Agreement And Final Judgment And Decree, Civil Action File No. 12-A-06853-10, Gwinnett County, GA Superior Court, Melanie Hall (Plaintiff) v. Justin Hall (Defendant), November 13, 2012.

[1941] Defendant's Response To Plaintiff's Motion For Contempt, Civil Action File No. 12-A-06853-10, Gwinnett County, GA Superior Court, Melanie Hall (Plaintiff) v. Justin Hall (Defendant), December 11, 2012.
[1942] Motion For Contempt Of Child Support, Civil Action File No. 12-A-06853-10, Gwinnett County, GA Superior Court, Melanie Hall (Plaintiff) v. Justin Hall (Defendant), December 26, 2012
[1943] Motion For Attorney's Fees, Civil Action File No. 12-A-06853-10, Gwinnett County, GA Superior Court, Melanie Hall (Plaintiff) v. Justin Hall (Defendant), January 18, 2013.
[1944] Notice To Produce And Request For Production Of Documents, Civil Action File No. 12-A-06853-10, Gwinnett County, GA Superior Court, Melanie Hall (Plaintiff) v. Justin Hall (Defendant), January 24, 2013.
[1945] Defendant's Responses To Plaintiff's First Interrogatories To Defendant, Civil Action File No. 12-A-06853-10, Gwinnett County, GA Superior Court, Melanie Hall (Plaintiff) v. Justin Hall (Defendant), January 22, 2013.
[1946] https://silo.tips/download/jeanmonod-daniel-date-of-birth-march-13-maturite-b-gymnase-cantonal-lausanne; https://loop.frontiersin.org/people/670473/bio.
[1947] Notice of Deposition, Civil Action File No. 12-A-06853-10, Gwinnett County, GA Superior Court, Melanie Hall (Plaintiff) v. Justin Hall (Defendant), January 24, 2013; Expedited Motion For Independent Medical Examination And Production Of All Medical, Pharmacy, And Psychological Records, Civil Action File No. 12-A-06853-10, Gwinnett County, GA Superior Court, Melanie Hall (Plaintiff) v. Justin Hall (Defendant), February 4, 2013.
[1948] Expedited Motion For Independent Medical Examination And Production Of All Medical, Pharmacy, And Psychological Records, Civil Action File No. 12-A-06853-10, Gwinnett County, GA Superior Court, Melanie Hall (Plaintiff) v. Justin Hall (Defendant), February 4, 2013.
[1949] Ibid.
[1950] Ibid.
[1951] Ibid.
[1952] Ibid.
[1953] Ibid.
[1954] Ibid.
[1955] Defendant's Response To Plaintiff's Motion For Attorney's Fees, Civil Action File No. 12-A-06853-10, Gwinnett County, GA Superior Court, Melanie Hall (Plaintiff) v. Justin Hall (Defendant), February 20, 2013.
[1956] Order For Psychiatric And Psychological Evaluation, Civil Action File No. 12-A-06853-10, Gwinnett County, GA Superior Court, Melanie Hall (Plaintiff) v. Justin Hall (Defendant), February 13, 2013.
[1957] Timothy Jones Trial Day 13 Dr. Julie Rand Dorney Part 1, https://www.youtube.com/watch?v=qqbG8glH01w.
[1958] GA v. Neuman (2012), https://www.courttv.com/title/32-ga-v-neuman-dr-adriana-flores/.
[1959] Order For Psychiatric And Psychological Evaluation, Civil Action File No. 12-A-06853-10, Gwinnett County, GA Superior Court, Melanie Hall (Plaintiff) v. Justin Hall (Defendant), February 13, 2013.
[1960] Order Rescinding Telephone Conferences In Lieu Of Formal Hearings, Civil Action File No. 12-A-06853-10, Gwinnett County, GA Superior Court, Melanie Hall (Plaintiff) v. Justin Hall (Defendant), February 22, 2013.
[1961] Plaintiff's Motion to Request that the Elected Judge Hear Cases, Civil Action File No. 17A03026-10/Consolidated Case: 17-A-04192-10, Gwinnett County, GA Superior Court, Justin Hall (Plaintiff) v. MelanieHall (Defendant), filed June 29, 2017.
[1962] Final Consent Order On Modification Action & Final Consent Order On All Pending Issues, Civil Action File No. 12-A-06853-10, Gwinnett County, GA Superior Court, Melanie Hall (Plaintiff) v. Justin Hall (Defendant), March 11, 2013.
[1963] Petition for Modification of Child Support, Civil Action File No. 17A03026-10, Gwinnett County, GA Superior Court, Justin Hall (Petitioner) v. Melanie Hall (Respondent), filed March 28, 2017.
[1964] Ibid.; Plaintiff's Motion to Request that the Elected Judge Hear Cases, Civil Action File No. 17A03026-10/Consolidated Case: 17-A-04192-10, Gwinnett County, GA Superior Court, Justin Hall (Plaintiff) v. Melanie Hall (Defendant), filed June 29, 2017.
[1965] Consent Order on Modification Action, Civil Action File No. 13-A02120-10, Gwinnett County, GA Superior Court, Justin Hall (Plaintiff) v. Melanie Hall (Defendant), filed March 11, 2013.
[1966] Motion for Contempt, Civil Action File No. 17-A04192-10, Gwinnett County, GA Superior Court, Melanie Hall (Plaintiff) v. Justin Hall (Defendant), filed May 1, 2017; Answers and Defenses, Civil Action File No. 17-A04192-10, Gwinnett County, GA Superior Court, Justin Hall (Plaintiff) v. Melanie Hall (Defendant), filed May 1, 2017
[1967] Joint Motion To Open and Inspect Probate Files in Gwinnett County Modification Action, Civil Action File No. 17-A04192-10, Gwinnett County, GA Superior Court, Justin Hall (Plaintiff) v. Melanie Hall (Defendant), filed June 26, 2017.
[1968] Plaintiff's Motion to Request that the Elected Judge Hear Cases, Civil Action File No. 17A03026-10/Consolidated Case: 17-A-04192-10, Gwinnett County, GA Superior Court, Justin Hall (Plaintiff) v. Melanie Hall (Defendant), filed June 29, 2017; Order Denying Motion to Request that the Elected Judge Hear Cases, Civil Action File No. 17A03026-10, Gwinnett County, GA Superior Court, Justin Hall (Plaintiff) v. Melanie Hall (Defendant), filed July 10, 2017

[1969] Domestic Relations Financial Affidavit, Civil Action File No. 17-A-03026-10, Gwinnett County, GA Superior Court, Justin Hall (Plaintiff) v. Melanie Hall (Defendant), filed August 7, 2017; Form SSA-1099-Social Security Benefit Statement for Troy Hall, 2016.
[1970] Georgia Child Support Worksheet, Civil Action File No. 17-A-03026-10, Gwinnett County, GA Superior Court, Melanie Hall (Plaintiff) v. Justin Hall (Defendant), filed February 26, 2018.
[1971] intelius.com/dashboard/reports/79ec5aff-2dc8-4080-ac4c-8e3508943911.
[1972] https://www.linkedin.com/in/melanie-hall-a552b177/; https://theorg.com/org/clearcare/org-chart/melanie-hall.
[1973] Child Support Addendum, Civil Action File No. 17-A-03026-10 & Consolidated Case No. 17-A-04192-10, Gwinnett County, GA Superior Court, Melanie Hall (Plaintiff) v. Justin Hall (Defendant), filed March 13, 2018.
[1974] Joint Final Consent Order, Civil Action File No. 17-A-03026-10 & Consolidated Case No. 17-A-04192-10, Gwinnett County, GA Superior Court, Melanie Hall (Plaintiff) v. Justin Hall (Defendant), filed March 13, 2018.
[1975] https://en.wikipedia.org/wiki/Notre_Dame_Academy_(Georgia).
[1976] Joint Final Consent Order, Civil Action File No. 17-A-03026-10 & Consolidated Case No. 17-A-04192-10, Gwinnett County, GA Superior Court, Melanie Hall (Plaintiff) v. Justin Hall (Defendant), filed March 13, 2018.
[1977] Ibid.
[1978] Hagaman, Len. In-person interview with author. May 24, 2022.
[1979] Georgia Death Certificate, State File Number 2019GA000081051 for Troy Justin Hall.
[1980] Hudgins and Birt, *Grace and Disgrace*, p. 274.
[1981] Notes compiled by Carolynn Johnson, May 2023.
[1982] Georgia Death Certificate, State File Number 2019GA000081051 for Troy Justin Hall.
[1983] Hagaman, Len. In-person interviews with author. March 14, 2022 & May 19, 2023.
[1984] WSOC-TV, February 9, 2022, *https://wsoctv.com/news/local/murder-suspects-son-recalls-clues-father-that-cracked-1972-boone-cold-case/2D4P4MYBYFD2VJUR6POGW2BTZE/.*
[1985] Kipe, *In The Red Clay*, Chapter 1: *From Humble Beginnings*, July 18, 2020.
[1986] Hudgins and Birt, *Grace and Disgrace*, p. 235.
[1987] Kipe, *In The Red Clay*, Chapter 1: *From Humble Beginnings*.
[1988] Kipe, *In The Red Clay*, Chapter 10: *The Hand of God*, October 13, 2020.
[1989] Herbert Emory, "Sheriff Blames Birt's Record On Poor Schooling, Drugs," *The Atlanta Constitution*, Atlanta, GA, July 2, 1979, p. 2-C; David Morrison, "Birt Describes Doctors' Deaths," *The Atlanta Constitution*, Atlanta, GA, October 26, 1979, p. 1-C.
[1990] Kipe, *In The Red Clay*, Chapter 1: *From Humble Beginnings*.
[1991] Hudgins and Birt, *Grace and Disgrace*, p. 9; Genealogical research by author.
[1992] Kipe, *In The Red Clay*, Chapter 1: *From Humble Beginnings* & Chapter 3: *The Kid*, August 25, 2020.
[1993] Birt, Billy Stonewall. *Rock Solid In His Own Words: The Inside Story of Billy Sunday Birt.* (2017), pp. 33-36 & 39.
[1994] Birt, Stoney, CSI Atlanta, "Georgia's Dixie Mafia," January 10, 2020.
[1995] Kipe, *In The Red Clay*, Chapter 1: *From Humble Beginnings*, Chapter 2: *Of Monsters And Men*, August 25, 2020, & Chapter 3: *The Kid*.
[1996] Birt, Billy Stonewall. *Rock Solid In His Own Words*, pp. 49 & 53.
[1997] Birt, Stoney. In-person interview with author. February 17, 2023.
[1998] David Morrison, "Birt," *The Atlanta Constitution*, Atlanta, GA, November 26, 1979, p. 24-C; Warner, "End Of An Era," p. F3.
[1999] Kipe, *In The Red Clay*, Chapter 2: *Of Monsters And Men*.
[2000] Birt, Billy Stonewall. *Rock Solid In His Own Words,* pp. 49 & 53.
[2001] Kipe, *In The Red Clay*, Chapter 2: *Of Monsters And Men*.
[2002] Kipe, *In The Red Clay*, Chapter 1: *From Humble Beginnings*.
[2003] Hudgins and Birt, *Grace and Disgrace*, p. vii; Stoney Birt, CSI Atlanta, "Georgia's Dixie Mafia," January 10, 2020; Kipe, *In The Red Clay*, Chapter 3: The Kid.
[2004] Mr. and Mrs. R. O. Fleming case file #70-0302-01-73.
[2005] "2 Arrested in Robbery," *The Macon Telegraph*, Macon, GA, February 14, 1966, p. 5.
[2006] Ford, "Athens-area members of notorious criminal."
[2007] Kipe, *In The Red Clay*, Season 2, Episode 5: *Black Sheep*; Terrell, Jimmy. Personal communication with author. March 26, 2022.
[2008] Kipe, *In The Red Clay*, Chapter 8: *Unlucky Number 7* & Season 2, Episode 5, *Black Sheep*; Birt, Stoney. E-mail to author. April 10, 2023.
[2009] Birt, Stoney. Phone conversation with author. July 3, 2023; Ford, "Athens-area members of notorious criminal band."
[2010] Kipe, *In The Red Clay*, Season 2, Episode 5, *Black Sheep*.
[2011] Mr. and Mrs. R. O. Fleming case file #70-0302-01-73; Kipe, *In The Red Clay*, Season 2, Episode 5, *Black Sheep*.

2012 Kipe, *In The Red Clay*, Chapter 3: *The Kid*.
2013 Birt, Billy Stonewall. *Rock Solid: The True Story,* p. 202.
2014 Hudgins and Birt, *Grace and Disgrace*, p. 85.
2015 Kipe, *In The Red Clay*, Season 2, Episode 5, *Black Sheep*.
2016 "3 More Held In Seizure Of Fake Bills," *The Atlanta Constitution*, Atlanta GA, November 10, 1966, p. 18.
2017 "$2 Million In Counterfeit Bills Seized," *The Columbus Ledger*, Columbus, GA, November 10, 1966, pp. 1 & 2.
2018 "Suspect Charged In Holdup," *The Atlanta Constitution*, Atlanta, GA, March 21, 1974, p. 12-A.
2019 Kipe, *In The Red Clay*, Season 2, Episode 2: *The Informer*, November 28, 2022.
2020 Kipe, *In The Red Clay*, Chapter 4: *A Cold Wind From The West*, September 1, 2020.
2021 Kipe, *In The Red Clay*, Season 2, Episode 5, *Black Sheep*.
2022 Kipe, *In The Red Clay*, Chapter 4: *A Cold Wind From The West*.
2023 Kipe, *In The Red Clay*, Season 2, Episode 5, *Black Sheep*.
2024 Kipe, *In The Red Clay*, Season 2, Episode 2: *The Informer*.
2025 Emory, "Sheriff Blames Birt's Record On Poor Schooling, Drugs," p. 2-C.
2026 Birt, Billy Stonewall. *Rock Solid: The True Story*, p. 203.
2027 Birt, Billy Stonewall. *Rock Solid In His Own Words*, p. 103
2028 Kipe, *In The Red Clay*, Season 2, Episode 5, *Black Sheep*.
2029 Birt, Stoney. In-person interview with author. February 17, 2023.
2030 Ingram, Bob. In-person interview with Shane Birt. April 30, 2019.
2031 Birt, Billy Stonewall. *Rock Solid In His Own Words*, p. 103.
2032 *Rock Solid, The True Story of Georgia's Dixie Mafia* Facebook post by Stoney Birt, June 12, 2020.
2033 Kipe, *In The Red Clay*, Chapter 4: *A Cold Wind From The West*.
2034 Birt, Billy Stonewall. *Rock Solid: The True Story*, p. 203.
2035 Source misplaced.
2036 Hudgins and Birt, *Grace and Disgrace*, p. 382.
2037 Ingram, Bob. In-person interview with author. April 19, 2022; Ingram, Bob. Phone interview with author. May 27, 2023.
2038 Birt, Billy Stonewall. *Rock Solid In His Own Words*, p. 103; Emory, "Sheriff Blames Birt's Record On Poor Schooling, Drugs," p. 2-C; Birt, Billy Stonewall. *Rock Solid: The True Story*, p. 203.
2039 "Skeleton May Give Clues To Unsolved Murders," *Macon Telegraph and News*, Macon, GA, October 22, 1978, p. 1C.
2040 Kipe, *In The Red Clay*, Season 2, Episode 5, *Black Sheep*.
2041 In The Red Clay Blog, September 1, 2020, https://www.intheredclaypodcast.com/post/a-cold-wind-from-the-west-chapter-4.
2042 Kipe, *In The Red Clay*, Season 2, Episode 5, *Black Sheep*.
2043 "2 Georgia Outlaws Suspected In 50 to 55 Killings, DA Says," *The Macon Telegraph*, Macon, GA, June 29, 1979, p. 2B.
2044 Kipe, *In The Red Clay*, Chapter 12: *A Child No More*, October 28, 2020, http://intheredclaypodcast.com.
2045 Birt, Billy Stonewall. *Rock Solid: The True Story*, p. 100.
2046 Kipe, *In The Red Clay*, Season 2, Episode 5, *Black Sheep*.
2047 Kipe, *In The Red Clay*, Chapter 4: *A Cold Wind From The West* & Chapter 6: *On The Banks Of The Mulberry*, September 15, 2020; Birt, Shane. Interview with Bob Ingram. April 30, 2019.
2048 Birt, Billy Stonewall. *Rock Solid In His Own Words*, p. 103.
2049 Kipe, *In The Red Clay*, Season 2, Episode 5, *Black Sheep*.
2050 Kipe, *In The Red Clay*, Chapter 3: *The Kid*.
2051 Hudgins and Birt, *Grace and Disgrace*, p. 160.
2052 Birt, Billy Stonewall. *Rock Solid: The True Story*, p. 49.
2053 Kipe, *In The Red Clay*, Chapter 1: *From Humble Beginnings*.
2054 Birt, Billy Stonewall. *Rock Solid In His Own Words*, p. 49.
2055 https://en.wikipedia.org/wiki/Billy_Sunday.
2056 Birt, Billy Stonewall. *Rock Solid In His Own Words*, p. 71.
2057 Hudgins and Birt, *Grace and Disgrace*, p. 238.
2058 "Opinion: The Dixie Mafia and the enduring tales of murder," *The Atlanta Constitution*, Atlanta, Georgia, June 24, 2022 (online), https://www.ajc.com/opinion/columnists/opinion-the-dixie-mafia-and-the-enduring-tales-of-murder/Q4IMHPOLBNHUJDXEIOZXIU2GSU/; Hudgins and Birt, *Grace and Disgrace*, p. 238.
2059 Birt, Billy Stonewall. *Rock Solid In His Own Words*, p. 56.
2060 Hudgins and Birt, *Grace and Disgrace*, p. 238.
2061 "'Black Beauties' capsules in the 1970's – What drug was that?," https://www.drugs.com/medical-answers/remember-taking-black-capsule-1970s-called-black-2367873/; Martin Waldron, "U. S. Crackdown on

Amphetamines Driving Up Prices," *The New York Times*, New York, NY, January 22, 1972 (online), https://www.nytimes.com/1972/01/22/archives/u-s-crackdown-on-amphetamines-driving-up-prices.html; https://urresearch.rochester.edu/institutionalPublicationPublicView.action?institutionalItemId=27719; Kipe, *In The Red Clay*, Season 2, Episode 4: *The Company of Wolves*.
[2062] Birt, Billy Stonewall. *Rock Solid: The True Story*, p. 123.
[2063] Hudgins and Birt, *Grace and Disgrace*, p. 283.
[2064] Kipe, *In The Red Clay*, Chapter 3: *The Kid*; Warner, "End Of An Era," p. F3.
[2065] Kipe, *In The Red Clay*, Chapter 3: *The Kid* & Chapter 4: *A Cold Wind From The West*.
[2066] Birt, Shane. Interview with Bob Ingram. May 17, 2019; Shane. Interview with Bob Ingram, Len Hagaman & Carolynn Johnson. November 16, 2020.
[2067] Birt, Shane and Bob Ingram. In-person interview with author. March 6, 2024.
[2068] Ford, "Dogged pursuit."
[2069] Hudgins and Birt, *Grace and Disgrace*, p. 238.
[2070] Susan Wells, "Silence Was Golden During Murder Years," *The Atlanta Journal-Constitution*, Atlanta, GA, October 28, 1979, p. 24-A.
[2071] Birt, Billy Stonewall. *Rock Solid: The True Story*, p. 99; Kipe, *In The Red Clay*, Chapter 3: *The Kid*.
[2072] Stewart, "Gene Reeves: Innocent Victim,'" p. 8-A.
[2073] Kipe, *In The Red Clay*, Chapter 3: *The Kid*.
[2074] Paul Lieberman, "Dixie Mafia," *The Atlanta Constitution*, Atlanta, GA, February 28, 1981, p. 4-A.
[2075] Warner, "End Of An Era," p. F3.
[2076] Source misplaced.
[2077] Birt, Billy Stonewall. *Rock Solid In His Own Words*, p. 48.
[2078] Bo Emerson, "Killer Billy Sunday Birt was a father who left behind a family divided," *The Atlanta Constitution*, Atlanta, GA, June 21, 2022 (online), https://www.ajc.com/news/crime/killer-billy-sunday-birt-was-a-father-who-left-behind-a-family-divided/KEFGYWN3Q5EMTP2XBG7GXX4U2M/.
[2079] Birt, Billy Stonewall. *Rock Solid In His Own Words*, p. 47.
[2080] Birt, Billy Stonewall. *Rock Solid: The True Story*, pp. 108, 110, & 117; Hudgins and Birt, *Grace and Disgrace*, p. 150; Birt, Stoney. Text to author. June 28, 2023.
[2081] Birt, Billy Stonewall. *Rock Solid: The True Story*, p. 118.
[2082] "Suspect Charged In Holdup," p. 12-A; Davis, Billy Wayne. Interview with Bob Ingram, Len Hagaman & Carolynn Johnson. August 3, 2021; Kipe, *In The Red Clay*, Chapter 4: *A Cold Wind From The West* & Season 2, Episode 5: *Black Sheep*; Ingram, Bob. In-person interview with author. April 19, 2022.
[2083] Terrell, Jimmy. Phone conversation with author. March 22, 2022.
[2084] Birt, Shane. Interview with Bob Ingram. April 30, 2019; Ingram, Bob. In-person interview with author. April 19, 2022; Ingram, Bob. Phone interview with author. May 27, 2022; Hudgins and Birt, *Grace and Disgrace*, p. 238.
[2085] Birt, Billy Stonewall. *Rock Solid: The True Story*, p. 77.
[2086] In The Red Clay Blog, September 22, 2020, https://www.intheredclaypodcast.com/post/billy-and-billy-chapter-7.
[2087] Keeler McCartney & Jim Stewart, "Winder Man Shot: Body is Found In Hall Hunt," *The Atlanta Constitution*, Atlanta, GA, April 10, 1974, pp. 1-A & 20-A.
[2088] Birt, Billy Stonewall. *Rock Solid: The True Story*, pp. 122-123.
[2089] Birt, Billy Stonewall. *Rock Solid: The True Story*, pp. 123-124.
[2090] "Two Men Sentenced," *Waycross Journal-Herald*, Waycross, GA, May 16, 1974, p. P-2.
[2091] Birt, Billy Stonewall. *Rock Solid In His Own Words*, p. 99-105.
[2092] Birt, Billy Stonewall. *Rock Solid: The True Story*, pp. 110, 137, 203, & 208.
[2093] Ibid., p. 136; Hudgins and Birt, *Grace and Disgrace*, pp. 55, 56, & 62.
[2094] Birt, Billy Stonewall. *Rock Solid In His Own Words*, pp. 109-110; Birt, Stoney. *Rock Solid, The True Story of Georgia's Dixie Mafia* Facebook post. November 16, 2018; Hudgins and Birt, *Grace and Disgrace*, p. 89.
[2095] Kipe, *In The Red Clay*, Season 2, Episode 2: *The Informer*.
[2096] Birt, Billy Stonewall. *Rock Solid: The True Story*, pp. 137, 140, 172, & 225.
[2097] Birt, Stoney. Texts & e-mail to author. June 27 & 28, 2023.
[2098] Kipe, *In The Red Clay*, Season 2, Episode 2: *The Informer*; Birt, Stoney. Text to author, containing images of eight pages of West's report. July 4, 2023.
[2099] Birt, Billy Stonewall. *Rock Solid: The True Story*, p. 208.
[2100] Kipe, *In The Red Clay*, Season 2, Episode 5: *Black Sheep*.
[2101] Birt, Billy Stonewall. *Rock Solid: The True Story*, pp. 207-208.
[2102] Lieberman, "Dixie Mafia," p. 4-A; Kipe, *In The Red Clay*, Season 2, Episode 2: *The Informer*.
[2103] David Morrison, "Birt's Story: 'We Had to Kill Them Both'," *The Atlanta Constitution*, Atlanta, GA, January 19, 1976, p. 12-A.

[2104] Birt, Stoney. Text to author. June 28, 2023. Birt, Stoney. Phone conversation with author. July 3, 2023.
[2105] Lieberman, "Dixie Mafia," p. 4-A.
[2106] Kipe, *In The Red Clay*, Season 2, Episode 2: *The Informer*.
[2107] Hudgins and Birt, *Grace and Disgrace*, pp. 187, 193, & 194; Terrell, Jimmy. Phone conversation with author. May 9, 2023; Kipe, *In The Red Clay*, Season 2, Episode 2: *The Informer*.
[2108] Birt, Billy Stonewall. *Rock Solid: The True Story*, p. 152.
[2109] Ibid., pp. 150-151; "News Of The State: Louisville," *The Atlanta Constitution*, Atlanta, GA, October 18, 1975, p. 5-A.
[2110] David Morrison, "'We Had to Kill Them': Billy Sunday Birt's Version of the Matthews Murders," *The Atlanta Constitution*, Atlanta, GA, January 19, 1976, p. 1; Hudgins and Birt, *Grace and Disgrace*, p. 114.
[2111] Birt, Billy Stonewall. *Rock Solid In His Own Words*, p. 111; Beau Cutts & Don Hicks, "Matthews," *The Atlanta Constitution*, June 29, 1979, p. 5-C; David Morrison, "Matthews," *The Atlanta Constitution*, Atlanta, GA, October 26, 1979, p. 2-C; Hudgins and Birt, *Grace and Disgrace*, pp. 114, & 116-117; "Cobb," *The Atlanta Constitution*, Atlanta, GA, July 1, 1979, p. 7-B; Don Hicks, "Matthews Robbery Suspect Henderson Plans To Surrender," *The Atlanta Constitution*, Atlanta, GA, July 3, 1979, p. 2-C; "Actual Factual Georgia," *The Atlanta Journal- Constitution*, Atlanta GA, November 19, 2012 (online), https://www.ajc.com/news/actual-factual-georgia/1fLhwelEGhNrs2TvcXwdlM/.
[2112] Morrison, "'We Had to Kill Them'," p. 1; David Morrison, "Matthews," *The Atlanta Constitution*, Atlanta, GA, October 26, 1979, p. 2-C.
[2113] Wikipedia – "Marietta Seven," https://en.wikipedia.org/wiki/Marietta_Seven; Ingram, Bob. In-person interview with author. April 19, 2022.
[2114] Gregory Jaynes, "The Matthews Case, Postmortem," *The Atlanta Constitution*, Atlanta, GA, July 31, 1975, p. 18-A & August 1, 1975, p. 22-A.
[2115] Ingram, Bob. In-person interview with author. April 19, 2022; Herbert Emory, "Davis Is Given Life In '71 Douglas Slaying," *The Atlanta Constitution*, Atlanta, GA, August 7, 1976, p. 3-A; Hudgins and Birt, *Grace and Disgrace*, pp. 122 & 300; Davis v. State, https://casetext.com/case/davis-v-state-2480; Davis v. Thomas, https://www.leagle.com/decision/1991520410se2d1101506; Ingram, Bob. Phone interview with author. May 27, 2023; "Witness Said To Be Liar," *The Macon News*, Macon, GA, August 6, 1976, p. 6B.
[2116] Wells, "Silence Was Golden," p. 24-A; Birt, Shane. Interview with Bob Ingram. April 30, 2019; Ingram, Bob. Phone interview with author. May 27, 2023.
[2117] Davis, Billy Wayne. Interview with Len Hagaman, Carolynn Johnson, & Wade Colvard.
[2118] Davis, Billy Wayne. Interview with Bob Ingram, Len Hagaman & Carolynn Johnson. August 3, 2021.
[2119] Wester, Deborah. Interview with Len Hagaman, Carolynn Johnson, & Wade Colvard..
[2120] Birt, Billy Stonewall. *Rock Solid In His Own Words*, p. 110.
[2121] Ibid.
[2122] Hudgins and Birt, *Grace and Disgrace*, p. 328; Birt, Shane. Interview with Bob Ingram. April 30, 2019.
[2123] Morrison, "Birt Describes Doctors' Deaths," p. 1-C.
[2124] "Arraignment set in Matthews deaths," *Rome News-Tribune*, Rome, GA, September 10, 1979, p. 3.
[2125] Hudgins and Birt, *Grace and Disgrace*, pp. 114-116.
[2126] Morrison, "Matthews," p. 2-C.
[2127] Hudgins and Birt, *Grace and Disgrace*, pp. 116-117; Morrison, "Birt Describes Doctors' Deaths," p. 1-C.
[2128] Hudgins and Birt, *Grace and Disgrace*, p. 118.
[2129] David Morrison, "Birt Caught In Tangled Web Of Crime," *The Atlanta Constitution*, Atlanta, GA, November 26, 1979, p. 1-C.
[2130] Morrison, "Birt Describes Doctors' Deaths," p. 1-C; Morrison, "Birt's Story," p. 12-A.
[2131] David Morrison, "Matthews Clue? Cobb Police Fail to Find Body in Sanderville," *The Atlanta Constitution*, Atlanta Georgia, November 14, 1975, p. 6-A.
[2132] Hudgins and Birt, *Grace and Disgrace*, p. 119.
[2133] Morrison, "Birt's Story," p. 12-A.
[2134] Hudgins and Birt, *Grace and Disgrace*, pp. 119-120, & 221.
[2135] Morrison, "Birt," p. 24-C.
[2136] "Chancey," *The Atlanta Constitution*, Atlanta, GA, June 28, 1982, p. 10-A.
[2137] Lieberman, "Dixie Mafia," p. 4-A.
[2138] Ingram, Bob. In-person interview with author. April 19, 2022.
[2139] Cook, "5 moved off death row," p. B4; Birt, Shane. Interview with Bob Ingram. April 30, 2019; Murderpedia: Billy Sunday Birt.
[2140] Warner, "End Of An Era," p. F3.
[2141] "Farmer Wants Sentence Overturned," *The Atlanta Constitution*, Atlanta, GA, August 7, 1979, p. 2-C; "New hearing ordered for prisoner," *The Macon News*, Macon, GA, June 25, 1981, p. 2B; Fran Hesser, "Execution Verdict Overturned," *The Atlanta Constitution*, Atlanta, GA, June 25, 1981, p. 4-C.

[2142] Cook, "5 moved off death row," p. B4; Hudgins and Birt, *Grace and Disgrace*, p. 318; Birt, Stoney. E-mail to author. April 10, 2023.
[2143] Birt, Stoney. In-person interview with author. February 17, 2023.
[2144] Cook, "5 moved off death row," p. B4; Birt, Stoney. E-mail to author. April 10, 2023.
[2145] CSI Atlanta, "The deadliest man in Georgia," January 20, 2020.
[2146] Ford, "Athens-area members of notorious criminal band"; Kipe, *In The Red Clay*, Season 2, Episode 5: *Black Sheep*; Birt, Shane. Interview with Bob Ingram. April 30, 2019; https://www.findagrave.com/memorial/173640603/charles-d-reed; Ford, "Dogged pursuit"; Birt, Stoney. Texts to author. June 27 & 28, 2023; Birt, Stoney. Phone conversation with author. July 3, 2023.
[2147] Ford, "Athens-area members of notorious criminal band,"; Kipe, *In The Red Clay*, Season 2, Episode 5: *Black Sheep*; Birt, Shane. Interview with Bob Ingram. April 30, 2019; https://www.findagrave.com/memorial/173640603/charles-d-reed; https://www.findagrave.com/memorial/172081380/bobby-gene-gaddis; Ford, "Dogged pursuit"; Birt, Stoney. Texts to author. June 27 & 28, 2023; Birt, Stoney. Phone conversation with author. July 3, 2023.
[2148] Terrell, Jimmy. Phone conversation with author. March 22, 2022.
[2149] Kipe, *In The Red Clay*, Chapter 10: *The Hand Of God*.
[2150] Hudgins and Birt, *Grace and Disgrace*, pp. vii, 38, 135, 146, & 327.
[2151] Birt, Shane. Interview with Bob Ingram. May 17, 2019.
[2152] Birt, Stoney. *Rock Solid, The True Story of Georgia's Dixie Mafia* Facebook posts, May 31 & June 19, 2019 and March 31, 2020; Sheryl McCollum, "Raised in Clay: The deadliest man in Georgia History," November 17, 2019, https://www.crimeonline.com/2019/11/17/raised-in-clay-the-deadliest-man-in-georgia-history/; Hudgins and Birt, *Grace and Disgrace*, p. 20, 157, & 158.
[2153] Birt, Stoney. *Rock Solid, The True Story of Georgia's Dixie Mafia* Facebook post. May 16, 2020; Birt, Shane. Interview with Bob Ingram. April 30, 2019.
[2154] Hudgins and Birt, *Grace and Disgrace*, pp. 219, 364, & 375.
[2155] Wells, "Silence Was Golden," p. 24-A.
[2156] Birt, Stoney. *Rock Solid, The True Story of Georgia's Dixie Mafia* Facebook post. May 16, 2020.
[2157] Birt, Billy Stonewall. *Rock Solid In His Own Words*, p. 80.
[2158] Birt, Stoney. *Rock Solid, The True Story of Georgia's Dixie Mafia* Facebook post. March 4, 2019.
[2159] Birt, Billy Stonewall. *Rock Solid In His Own Words*, p. 5.
[2160] Kipe, *In The Red Clay*, Chapter 12: *A Child No More*.
[2161] "Birt Plea Rejected By Court," *The Atlanta Constitution*, Atlanta, GA, December 14, 1976, p. 3.
[2162] Bill Winn, "Law Officers Believe Billy Birt Was State's Most Prolific Killer," *The Sunday Ledger-Enquirer*, Columbus, GA, August 23, 1987, p. A-8.
[2163] Morrison, "Birt," p. 24-C.
[2164] Bill Winn, "Georgia's Multiple Murders: It's a Terrifying – But Not New – Menace," *The Sunday Ledger-Enquirer*, Columbus, GA, August 16, 1987, p. A-4.
[2165] Kipe, *In The Red Clay*, Chapter 8: *Unlucky Number 7*.
[2166] Hudgins and Birt, *Grace and Disgrace*, pp. 149, 164, 173, 284, 300, & 365.
[2167] Kipe, *In The Red Clay*, Season 2, Episode 2: *The Informer*; Birt, Stoney. Text to author. June 28, 2023.
[2168] Birt, Shane. Interview with Bob Ingram. May 17, 2019; Hudgins and Birt, *Grace and Disgrace*, p. 150.
[2169] Emerson, "Killer Billy Sunday Birt."
[2170] Ingram, Bob. In-person interview with author. April 19, 2022; Ingram, Bob. Phone interview with author. December 21, 2022.
[2171] Birt, Shane. Interview with Bob Ingram. May 17, 2019.
[2172] Warner, "End Of An Era," p. F3.
[2173] Birt, Shane. Interview with Bob Ingram. April 30, 2019; Hudgins and Birt, *Grace and Disgrace*, p. 335; Kipe, *In The Red Clay*, Chapter 12: *A Child No More*.
[2174] Hagaman, Len. In-person interview with author. March 14, 2022; "Local triple homicide case solved after 50 years."
[2175] Typewritten case details by Watauga County Sheriff's Office Capt. Carolynn Johnson; Johnson, Carolynn. In-person interview with author. January 16, 2024.
[2176] "Local triple homicide case solved after 50 years."
[2177] Hagaman, Len. Watauga County Sheriff's Office press conference, Boone, NC, February 11, 2022.
[2178] Hagaman, Len. Watauga County Sheriff's Office press conference, February 11, 2022.
[2179] Vaughn, Jerry. In-person interview with author. October 13, 2023.
[2180] Dunn, Watauga Murders Unsolved," p. 2.
[2181] Tester, Johnny. Personal interview with author. March 6, 2022.
[2182] Young, Lewis. Phone interview with author. February 1, 2023.

[2183] Edmisten, Rufus. Zoom interview with author. March 31, 2022.
[2184] Whitman, Pat. Phone interview with author. March 10, 2022.
[2185] Parker, John. Phone interview with author. November 7, 2022.
[2186] Rucker, Jeff. Phone interview with author. October 4, 2023.
[2187] Billiot, Keith. Interview with Sean Kipe.
[2188] Kipe, *In The Red Clay*, Season 2, Episode 5: *Black Sheep*.
[2189] https://preply.com/en/question/what-is-the-difference-between-solve-and-resolve-78351; Williams, Phil, "What's the difference between 'solve' and resolve'"? English Lessons Brighton, April 23, 2015 (online), https://englishlessonsbrighton.co.uk/whats-the-difference-between-solve-and-resolve/.
[2190] Kipe, *In The Red Clay*, Season 2, Episode 3: *Nothing As It Seems*.
[2191] Ibid.
[2192] Hagaman, Len. In-person interview with author. January 16, 2024.
[2193] Hagaman, Len. Watauga County Sheriff's Office press conference, Boone, NC, February 11, 2022; "Durham Murder Case: New Details Revealed.".
[2194] Ingram, Bob. In-person interview with the author. April 19, 2022.
[2195] Hagaman, Len. In-person interview with the author. May 24, 2022.
[2196] Connon, Tara. "Let's not argue over semantics!" LinkedIn, January 20, 2019 (online), https://www.linkedin.com/pulse/lets-argue-over-semantics-tara-connon/.
[2197] Kipe, *In The Red Clay*, Season 2, Chapter 1: *Brutal, Savage, Senseless*; Birt, Stoney. In-person interview with author. February 17, 2023.
[2198] Kipe, *In The Red Clay*, Season 2, Chapter 7: *Bonus Episode*.
[2199] Birt, Stoney. In-person interview with author. February 17, 2023.
[2200] "Murder suspect's son recalls clues from father than cracked 1972 Boone cold case," WSOC-TV, February 9, 2022, *https://wsoctv.com/news/local/murder-suspects-son-recalls-clues-father-that-cracked-1972-boone-cold-case/2D4P4MYBYFD2VJUR6POGW2BTZE/;* Birt, Stoney, *Rock Solid, The True Story of Georgia's Dixie Mafia* Facebook page post, February 9, 2022.
[2201] Ford, "Athens-area members of notorious criminal band."
[2202] Birt, Stoney. In-person interview with author. February 17, 2023.
[2203] Birt, Stoney. In-person interviews with author. April 18, 2022 & February 17, 2023.
[2204] Kipe, *In The Red Clay*, Season 2, Chapter 7: *Bonus Episode*.
[2205] Birt, Shane. In-person interview with author. March 6, 2024.
[2206] Ibid.
[2207] Ibid.
[2208] Birt, Shane. Interview with Bob Ingram, Len Hagaman & Carolynn Johnson. November 16, 2020.
[2209] Birt, Shane. In-person interview with author. March 6, 2024.
[2210] Hudgins and Birt, *Grace and Disgrace*, pp. 171-173; Ingram, Bob. In-person interview with author. April 19, 2022; Ingram, Bob. Phone interview with author. December 21, 2022; Birt, Stoney. In-person interview with author. February 17, 2023; Birt, Shane. In-person interviews with Bob Ingram. April 30 & May 17, 2019; Birt, Shane. Interview with Bob Ingram, Len Hagaman, & Carolynn Johnson. November 16, 2020; Ingram, Bob. In-person interview with author. March 6, 2024.
[2211] Ingram, Bob. Phone interviews with author. December 21, 2022 & May 27, 2023; Ingram, Bob. In-person interview with author. March 6, 2024.
[2212] Ingram, Bob. E-mail to author. May 26, 2023; Ingram, Bob. Phone interview with author. May 27, 2023.
[2213] Ingram, Bob. Phone interview with author. December 21, 2022.
[2214] Ibid. & May 27, 2023.
[2215] Hudgins and Birt, *Grace and Disgrace*, p. 394.
[2216] Birt, Stoney. In-person interview with author. February 23, 2023.
[2217] Ingram, Bob. In-person interview with author. March 6, 2024.
[2218] Nakpangi Thomas, Ph.D., "What Is Narcissistic Supply?" Choosing Therapy, May 24, 2023, https://choosingtherapy.com/narcissistic-supply/
[2219] https://drgeorgesimon.com/narcissistic-truth-distortion-is-just-manipulation/#:~:text=Narcissists%20engage%20in%20truth%20distortion,the%20seriousness%20of%20their%20missteps.
[2220] https://thehealthyjournal.com/faq/how-dows-a-narcissist-view-reality.
[2221] Anonymous source. Phone interview with author. September 20, 2022.
[2222] Birt, Shane. In-person interview with author. March 6, 2024.
[2223] Emerson, "Killer Billy Sunday Birt"; Birt, Stoney. Phone conversation with author. July 3, 2023.
[2224] Birt, Shane. In-person interview with author. March 6, 2024.
[2225] Birt, Stoney. Text to author. March 2, 2023.

[2226] Ibid.
[2227] "Unsolved murders reach 20th year," p. 1.
[2228] Birt, Shane. In-person interview with author. March 6, 2024.
[2229] Edmisten, Rufus. E-mail to author. May 16, 2023.
[2230] Hagaman, Len. In-person interview with author. May 19, 2023.
[2231] Ingram, Bob. Phone interview with author. May 27, 2023.
[2232] Birt, Stoney. Text to author. December 15, 2023.
[2233] Hudgins, Phil. E-mails to author. December 14, 2023; Birt, Shane. In-person interview with author. March 6, 2024.
[2234] Kipe, *In The Red Clay*, Season 1, Chapter 6: *On The Banks Of The Mulberry*.
[2235] Birt, Shane & Bob Ingram. In-person interview. March 6, 2024.
[2236] Birt, Stoney. Texts to author. December 10 & 15, 2023.
[2237] Hudgins and Birt, *Grace and Disgrace*, pp. 151, 312, 313, & 341.
[2238] Terrell, Jimmy. Phone conversation with author. May 9, 2023; Hudgins and Birt, *Grace and Disgrace*, p. 300.
[2239] Birt, Shane. Interview with Bob Ingram. April 30, 2019
[2240] Terrell, Jimmy. Phone conversation with author. May 5, 2022.
[2241] Hudgins and Birt, *Grace and Disgrace*, pp. 66-67, 110, 150-151, 172-173, 300, 313, & 329-330.
[2242] Birt, Stoney. In-person interview with author. February 23, 2023.
[2243] Birt, Stoney. Interview with Len Hagaman, Carolynn Johnson, Wade Colvard & Nic Johnson.
[2244] Birt, Stoney. Text to author. December 15, 2023.
[2245] Kipe, *In The Red Clay*, Season 2, Episode 2: *The Informer*, Episode 5: *Black Sheep*, & Episode 6: *Beneath the Chestnut Tree*.
[2246] Birt, Stoney. In-person interview with author. February 23, 2023.
[2247] Hudgins and Birt, *Grace and Disgrace*, pp. 33 & 65.
[2248] Birt, Stoney. Text to author. April 18, 2024.
[2249] Birt, Shane. Interviews with Bob Ingram. April 30 & May 17, 2019; Ingram, Bob. In-person interview with author. April 19, 2022; Hudgins and Birt, *Grace and Disgrace*, p. 37; Kipe, *In The Red Clay*, Season 2, Episode 2: *The Informer* & Episode 5: *Black Sheep*; Birt, Stoney. Texts to author. July 3 & December 15, 2023 & February 12, 2024.
[2250] Birt, Shane. Interview with Bob Ingram. April 30, 2019; Kipe, *In The Red Clay*, Season 2, Episode 5: *Black Sheep*,.
[2251] Hudgins and Birt, *Grace and Disgrace*, pp. 34-37; Birt, Stoney. Texts to author. June 27 & July 3, 2023 & March 3, 2024.
[2252] Hudgins and Birt, *Grace and Disgrace*, pp. viii, 34-37, 361-363, 397, & 406; Birt, Shane. In-person interview with Bob Ingram. April 30, 2019.
[2253] Birt, Shane. Interview with Bob Ingram, Len Hagaman & Carolynn Johnson. November 16, 2020; Birt, Shane. In-person interview with author. March 6, 2024.
[2254] Hudgins and Birt, *Grace and Disgrace*, p. ix, & 367-368; Birt, Shane. In-person interview with author. March 6, 2024.
[2255] Birt, Shane. Interview with Bob Ingram, Len Hagaman & Carolynn Johnson. November 16, 2020.
[2256] Ibid.; Birt, Shane. In-person interview with author. March 6, 2024.
[2257] Birt, Shane. Interview with Bob Ingram. April 30, 2019; Hudgins and Birt, *Grace and Disgrace*, pp. 393 & 395.
[2258] Birt, Stoney. Text to author. December 21, 2023.
[2259] Birt, Shane. Interview with Bob Ingram, Len Hagaman & Carolynn Johnson. November 16, 2020.
[2260] Birt, Stoney. In-person interview with author. February 17, 2023. Birt, Stoney. Phone conversation with author. July 3, 2023.
[2261] Hudgins and Birt, *Grace and Disgrace*, p. 396; Birt, Stoney. Text to author. April 6, 2022. (This text message contains a March 30, 2022 cease and desist letter to Phil Hudgins from Gregory Scott Smith, Esq., of the Smith/Tempel law firm of Atlanta, GA.); Kipe, *In The Red Clay*, Season 2, Chapter 7: *Bonus Episode*.
[2262] Birt, Shane. Interview with Bob Ingram. May 17, 2019; Birt, Shane. Interview with Bob Ingram, Len Hagaman & Carolynn Johnson. November 16, 2020; Birt, Stoney. In-person interview with author. February 17, 2023.
[2263] Birt, Shane. Interviews with Bob Ingram. April 30 & May 17, 2019.
[2264] Birt, Stoney. In-person interview with author. February 17, 2023.
[2265] CSI Atlanta, "Georgia's Dixie Mafia," January 10, 2020.
[2266] Hudgins and Birt, *Grace and Disgrace*, p. 103.
[2267] Birt, Shane. Interviews with Bob Ingram. April 30 & May 17, 2019.
[2268] Kipe, *In The Red Clay*, Season 2, Episode 5: *Black Sheep*.
[2269] Birt, Stoney. Text to author. June 28, 2023.
[2270] Ingram, Bob. Phone interview with author. May 27, 2023.
[2271] Hudgins and Birt, *Grace and Disgrace*, p. 263.
[2272] Ingram, Bob. In-person interview with author. April 19, 2022; Ingram, Bob. Phone interview with author. December 21, 2022.

[2273] Gretchen Gavett, "A Rare Look at the Police Tactics That Can Lead to False Confessions," Frontline, December 9, 2011, https://www.pbs.org/wgbh/frontline/article/a-rare-look-at-the-police-tactics-that-can-lead-to-false-confessions/.
[2274] Ingram, Bob. In-person interview with author. April 19, 2022; Hudgins and Birt, *Grace and Disgrace*, p. 265; Kipe, *In The Red Clay*, Season 2, Episode 6: *Beneath the Chestnut Tree*; Ingram, Bob. Phone interview with author. May 27, 2023; Wurtz, "Blue Ridge Runs Red."
[2275] "The Reid 9 Steps of Interrogation, In Brief," https://uapdi.com/my/docs/reidinterrogation.pdf.
[2276] Louis C. Senese, "Setting the record straight on the Reid Technique: The Reid Technique of interviewing and interrogation is supported by the courts," Police1, August 22, 2023, https://www.police1.com/investigations/articles/setting-the-record-straight-on-the-reid-technique-8wlPwHfQTlk8PhBe/.
[2277] "Reid Technique," Wikipedia, https://en.wikipedia.org/wiki/Reid_technique#:~:text=The%20Reid%20technique%20user's%20goal,as%20justification%20for%20their%20behavior; Saul M. Kassin, "The Psychology of Confession Evidence," *American Psychologist*, March 1997, p. 223, https://web.williams.edu/Psychology/Faculty/Kassin/files/Kassin1997.pdf; "Is the Reid Technique on the Way Out? Law Offices of Walter M. Reaves, Jr., PC, https://www.reaveslegal.com/blog/is-the-reid-technique-on-the-way-out-.cfm.
[2278] "How to interview elderly subjects," John E. Reid & Associates, Inc., Police1, April 23, 2008, https://www.police1.com/police-products/investigation/articles/how-to-interview-elderly-subjects-aRYFnTlcscWiJdN8/.
[2279] Aldert Vrij, "Interrogation and Interviewing: 6.2 Concerns with the Reid Technique," *Encyclopedia of Applied Psychology*, 2004, https://www.sciencedirect.com/topics/psychology/reid-technique.
[2280] Billiot, Keith. Interview with Sean Kipe.
[2281] Kipe, Sean, *In The Red Clay*, Season 2, Episode 8: *In Plain Sight*, June 11, 2024.
[2282] Hagaman, Len. In-person interview with author. May 24, 2022.
[2283] "Durham Murder Case: New Details."
[2284] Obituary for Clyde A. Davis, *The Atlanta Journal-Constitution*, Atlanta, GA, July 21, 1989, p. D-10.
[2285] Obituary for Ann Bearden Davis, Northside Chapel Funeral Directors and Crematory, northsidechapel.com/obituaries/Ann-Davis-1434/#!/Obituary.
[2286] Davis, Billy Wayne. Interview with Walton County (GA) Sheriff Joe Chapman & retired Barrow County (GA) Sheriff Joe Robinson, October 2019.
[2287] "How to interview elderly subjects," John E. Reid & Associates, Inc., Police1, April 23, 2008, https://www.police1.com/police-products/investigation/articles/how-to-interview-elderly-subjects-aRYFnTlcscWiJdN8/.
[2288] Wester, Deborah. Interview with Len Hagaman, Carolynn Johnson, & Wade Colvard.
[2289] Kipe, *In The Red Clay*, Season 2, Episode 8: *In Plain Sight*.
[2290] Ibid.
[2291] Ibid.; Billiot, Keith. Text message to Sean Kipe.
[2292] Ingram, Bob. In-person interview with author. April 19, 2022; Ford, "Dogged pursuit."
[2293] Wurtz, "Blue Ridge Runs Red."
[2294] Davis, Billy Wayne. Interview with Bob Ingram, Len Hagaman & Carolynn Johnson. August 3, 2021.
[2295] Bethune, Elvis Larry. Interviews with various law enforcement officers.
[2296] Kipe, *In The Red Clay*, Chapter 12: *A Child No More*.
[2297] Ibid.; Ingram, Bob. In-person interview with author. April 22, 2019; Birt, Stoney. In-person interview with author. February 17, 2023.
[2298] Kipe, *In The Red Clay*, Season 2, Episode 6: *Beneath the Chestnut Tree*.
[2299] Hagaman, Len. Watauga County Sheriff's Office press conference, Boone, NC, February 11, 2022. Hagaman, Len. In-person interview with author. May 24, 2022.
[2300] Douglas Starr, "The Interview," *The New Yorker*, December 1, 2013, https://www.newyorker.com/magazine/2013/12/09/the-interview-7.
[2301] Utkarsh Shukla, "Reid Technique: An Interrogation Technique," tutorialspoint, October 27, 2023, https://www.tutorialspoint.com/reid-technique-an-interrogation-technique.
[2302] Saul M. Kassin, "The Psychology of Confession Evidence," *American Psychologist*, March 1997, p. 225, https://web.williams.edu/Psychology/Faculty/Kassin/files/Kassin1997.pdf.
[2303] Kipe, *In The Red Clay*, Season 2, Episode 8: *In Plain Sight*.
[2304] Kipe, *In The Red Clay*, Season 2, Episode 2: *The Informer*; Birt, Stoney. In-person interview with author. February 17, 2023.
[2305] Ingram, Bob. E-mail to author. May 26, 2023.

[2306] Kipe, *In The Red Clay*, Season 2, Episode 2: *The Informer*; Birt, Stoney. In-person interview with author. February 17, 2023.
[2307] Birt, Stoney. Personal interview with author. April 18, 2022.
[2308] Ingram, Bob. In-person interview with author. April 19, 2022.
[2309] Kipe, *In The Red Clay*, Season 2, Episode 6: *Beneath the Chestnut Tree*.
[2310] Hagaman, Len. In-person interview with author. May 24, 2022.
[2311] Kipe, *In The Red Clay*, Season 2, Episode 6: *Beneath the Chestnut Tree*.
[2312] Ingram, Bob. Phone interview with author. May 27, 2023.
[2313] Kipe, *In The Red Clay*, Season 2, Episode 2: *The Informer* & Episode 5: *Black Sheep*.
[2314] Ingram, Bob. Phone interview with author. May 27, 2023.
[2315] Kipe, *In The Red Clay*, Season 2, Episode 2: *The Informer* & Episode 5: *Black Sheep*.
[2316] Birt, Stoney. In-person interviews with author. April 18, 2022 & February 17, 2023; Terrell, Jimmy. Phone interview with author. May 9, 2023.
[2317] Kipe, *In The Red Clay* Facebook page post, November 17, 2022.
[2318] Kipe, *In The Red Clay*, Season 2, Episode 1: *Brutal, Savage, Senseless*.
[2319] Kipe, *In The Red Clay*, Season 2, Episode 2: *The Informer* & Season 2, Chapter 7: *Bonus Episode*.
[2320] Birt, Stoney. In-person interview with author. February 17, 2023.
[2321] Ford, "Dogged pursuit"; Birt, Stoney. In-person interview with author. February 17, 2023.
[2322] Birt, Stoney. "Rock Solid, The True Story of Georgia's Dixie Mafia" Facebook page comment, February 20, 2022.
[2323] Ford, "Athens-area members of notorious criminal band."
[2324] Kipe, *In The Red Clay*, Season 2, Episode 2: *The Informer*.
[2325] Terrell, Jimmy. Facebook comment on Rock Solid, The True Story of Georgia's Dixie Mafia Facebook page post. February 10, 2022; Terrell, Jimmy. E-mail to author. March 22, 2022
[2326] Ingram, Bob. In-person interview with author. April 19, 2022.
[2327] Hagaman, Len. E-mail to author. April 6, 2022.
[2328] Hagaman, Len. In-person interview with author. May 24, 2022.
[2329] Lynch, Cyndi Silvey. Phone interview with author. September 25, 2022.
[2330] Hagaman, Len. In-person interview with author. March 14, 2022.
[2331] Ingram, Bob. In-person interview with author. April 19, 2022.
[2332] Kipe, *In The Red Clay*, Chapter 12: *A Child No More*; Ingram, Bob. In-person interview with author. April 22, 2019; Birt, Stoney. In-person interview with author. February 17, 2023.
[2333] Hagaman, Len. In-person interviews with author. March 14, 2022 & January 16, 2024.
[2334] "Durham Murder Case: New Details"; Hagaman, Len. In-person interview with author. May 24, 2022.
[2335] "Bodies," *The Atlanta Constitution*, Atlanta, GA, April 10, 1974, p. 20-A.
[2336] @tracyshoemake9686 (who knew Charlie Reed). Comment on YouTube. https://www.youtube.com/watch?v=0l4kEJUnYDg&lc=UgzPye29CnB9g3DyChV4AaABAg.
[2337] Kipe, *In The Red Clay*, Season 2, Episode 2: *The Informer*.
[2338] Kipe, *In The Red Clay*, Season 2, Episode 8: *In Plain Sight*.
[2339] Hudgins and Birt, *Grace and Disgrace*, p. 97.
[2340] Birt, Stoney. In-person interview with author. February 17, 2023.
[2341] Hudgins and Birt, *Grace and Disgrace*, p. 95.
[2342] Birt, Billy Stonewall, *Rock Solid In His Own Words*, pp. 111-112; Birt, Stoney. E-mail to author. April 10, 2023.
[2343] Birt, Stoney. *Rock Solid, The True Story of Georgia's Dixie Mafia* Facebook post. February 1, 2021.
[2344] Kipe, *In The Red Clay*, Chapter 8: *Unlucky Number 7*.
[2345] Terrell, Jimmy. E-mail to author. March 21, 2022; Terrell, Jimmy. Phone conversation with author. May 5, 2022.
[2346] Hudgins and Birt, *Grace and Disgrace*, pp. 240-241.
[2347] CSI Atlanta, "The deadliest man in Georgia," January 20, 2020.
[2348] Birt, Stoney. In-person interview with author. February 17, 2023. Birt, Stoney. Phone conversation with author. July 3, 2023.
[2349] Birt, Billy Stonewall. *Rock Solid In His Own Words*, p. 80.
[2350] Hudgins and Birt, *Grace and Disgrace*, p. 245.
[2351] Hudgins and Birt, *Grace and Disgrace*, p. 97.
[2352] Murderpedia: Billy Sunday Birt.
[2353] Ibid.; https://casetext.com/case/birt-v-hopper; https://cite.case.law/ga/256/483/1210452/; https://case-law.vlex.com/vid/birt-v-montgomery-no-887337477; https://case-law.vlex.com/vid/birt-v-montgomery-no-893692576.
[2354] Birt, Billy Stonewall, *Rock Solid: The True Story*, pp. 138-139; "The Eyewitness Who Wasn't, The Matthews Murder Trials; No. 1; Part 2, American Archive of Public Broadcasting (a collaboration of the Library of Congress and GBH), https://americanarchive.org/catalog/cpb-aacip-4b48e14edc1; Emmett v. Ricketts, 397 F. Supp. 1025 (N.D. Ga.

1975), Justia US Law, https://law.justia.com/cases/federal/district-courts/FSupp/397/1025/1674341/; "Unsolved Murder Case Revived," *The Atlanta Constitution*, Atlanta, GA, October 1, 1976, p. 12-A.
[2355] Hudgins and Birt, *Grace and Disgrace*, p. 114.
[2356] Birt, Billy Stonewall, *Rock Solid: The True Story*, pp. 138-139; "The Eyewitness Who Wasn't"; Emmett v. Ricketts.
[2357] Birt, Billy Stonewall, *Rock Solid: The True Story*, pp. 140-141; Hudgins and Birt, *Grace and Disgrace*, pp. 91-92.
[2358] https://casetext.com/case/birt-v-montgomery-2
[2359] Ibid.; https://casetext.com/case/birt-v-hopper.
[2360] Birt, Billy Stonewall, *Rock Solid: The True Story*, p. 141.
[2361] Kipe, *In The Red Clay*, Season 2, Episode 2: *The Informer* & Episode 6: *Beneath the Chestnut Tree*; Birt, Stoney. *Rock Solid, The True Story of Georgia's Dixie Mafia* Facebook post. January 10, 2023; Birt, Stoney. E-mail to author. June 28, 2023.
[2362] Kipe, *In The Red Clay*, Season 2, Episode 2: *The Informer*.
[2363] Ibid. & Season 2, Chapter 7: *Bonus Episode*.
[2364] Birt, Stoney. *Rock Solid, The True Story of Georgia's Dixie Mafia* Facebook post. January 10, 2023.
[2365] Kipe, *In The Red Clay*, Season 2, Episode 2: *The Informer*; Birt, Stoney. Phone conversation with author. July 3, 2023.
[2366] CSI Atlanta, "The deadliest man in Georgia," January 20, 2020.
[2367] Birt, Billy Stonewall, *Rock Solid: The True Story*, p. 238.
[2368] Kipe, *In The Red Clay* Facebook page post, November 17, 2022.
[2369] Kipe, *In The Red Clay*, Season 2, Episode 2: *The Informer*.
[2370] Kipe, *In The Red Clay*, Season 2, Episode 6: *Beneath the Chestnut Tree*; Warner, "End Of An Era," p. F3.
[2371] Hudgins and Birt, *Grace and Disgrace*, pp. 227, 233, & 240; Birt, Stoney. In-person interview with author. February 17, 2023.
[2372] Kipe, *In The Red Clay*, Season 2, Episode 2: *The Informer* & Episode 6: *Beneath the Chestnut Tree*.
[2373] Ingram, Bob. Interviewing Shane Birt. May 17, 2019; Wurtz, "Blue Ridge Runs Red."
[2374] Kipe, *In The Red Clay*, Season 2, Episode 2: *The Informer* & Episode 6: *Beneath the Chestnut Tree*.
[2375] Birt, Billy Stonewall, *Rock Solid: The True Story*, p. 195.
[2376] Birt, Stoney. In-person interview with author. April 18, 2022.
[2377] Kipe, *In The Red Clay*, Season 2, Episode 2: *The Informer*.
[2378] Birt, Shane. In-person interview with Bob Ingram. May 17, 2019; Ingram, Bob. Phone interview with author. May 27, 2023.
[2379] Birt, Stoney. Interview with Len Hagaman, Carolynn Johnson, Wade Colvard & Nic Johnson..
[2380] "Opinion: The Dixie Mafia and the enduring tales of murder."
[2381] Emerson, "Killer Billy Sunday Birt.".
[2382] Hudgins and Birt, *Grace and Disgrace*, p. 167; Maureen Wurtz, "Blue Ridge Runs Red"; Ingram, Bob. Phone interview with author. May 27, 2023; Kipe, *In The Red Clay*, Chapter 8: *Unlucky Number 7*; Warner, "End Of An Era," p. F3; Ford, "Dogged pursuit."
[2383] Terrell, Jimmy. *Rock Solid, The True Story of Georgia's Dixie Mafia* Facebook page comment, February 20, 2022; Terrell, Jimmy. E-mail to author. March 26, 2022; Terrell, Jimmy. Phone conversation with author. May 5, 2022.
[2384] Birt, Stoney. *Rock Solid, The True Story of Georgia's Dixie Mafia* Facebook page comment, February 20, 2022.
[2385] Birt, Billy Stonewall, *Rock Solid: The True Story*, pp. 140 & 171.
[2386] Hudgins and Birt, *Grace and Disgrace*, pp. 83, 88, 91, & 94.
[2387] Kipe, *In The Red Clay*, Season 2, Chapter 7: *Bonus Episode*.
[2388] Birt, Shane. Interview with Bob Ingram. May 17, 2019; Hudgins and Birt, *Grace and Disgrace*, pp. 88 & 94; CSI Atlanta, "The deadliest man in Georgia," January 20, 2020; Birt, Shane. In-person interview with author. March 6, 2024.
[2389] Ingram, Bob. In-person interview with author. April 19, 2022.
[2390] Lynch, Cyndi Silvey. Phone interview with author. September 25, 2022.
[2391] https://www.findagrave.com/memorial/132294598/charles-e-martin.
[2392] Wells, "Silence Was Golden During Murder Years," p. 24-A.
[2393] Birt, Stoney. Text messages to author. May 8 & 29 and July 4, 2023; Birt, Stoney. Phone conversation with author. July 3, 2023; Kipe, *In The Red Clay*, Season 2, Chapter 7: *Bonus Episode*.
[2394] Barrow County Probate Court. Phone conversation with author. May 10, 2023.
[2395] Martin, Zoobie (son of Charlie Martin). Texts to author. June 21, September 8, & September 16, 2023; Georgia Bureau of Investigation case file #80-0079-01-77 regarding Charlie Martin.
[2396] Birt, Stoney. Phone conversation with author. July 3, 2023; Kipe, *In The Red Clay*, Season 2, Chapter 7: *Bonus Episode*.
[2397] Georgia Bureau of Investigation case file #80-0079-01-77 regarding Charlie Martin.

[2398] Birt, Stoney. Text messages to author. May 7 & July 3-4, 2023; Birt, Stoney. Phone conversation with author. July 3, 2023; Birt, Stoney. *Rock Solid, The True Story of Georgia's Dixie Mafia* Facebook posts. July 18-19, 2023; Kipe, *In The Red Clay*, Season 2, Chapter 7: *Bonus Episode*.
[2399] Final Investigative Summary by Special Agent J. L. Massey, June 27, 1977, Georgia Bureau of Investigation case file #80-0079-01-77 regarding Charlie Martin.
[2400] Report by Special Agent J. L. Massey, August 17, 1976, Georgia Bureau of Investigation case file #80-0079-01-77 regarding Charlie Martin.
[2401] Kipe, *In The Red Clay*, Season 2, Episode 8: *In Plain Sight*.
[2402] Hagaman, Len. In-person interview with author. May 19, 2023; Ingram, Bob. Phone interview with author. May 27, 2023.
[2403] Kipe, *In The Red Clay*, Season 2, Episode 8: *In Plain Sight*.
[2404] Kipe, *In The Red Clay*, Season 2, Episode 2: *The Informer* & Episode 6: *Beneath the Chestnut Tree* & Chapter 7: *Bonus Episode*; Birt, Stoney. *Rock Solid, The True Story of Georgia's Dixie Mafia* Facebook post. January 10, 2023; Birt, Stoney. E-mail to author. June 28, 2023; Birt, Stoney. Text messages to author. July 12, 2023; Wurtz, "Blue Ridge Runs Red."
[2405] Johnson, Carolynn. In-person interview with author. January 16, 2024.
[2406] Kipe, *In The Red Clay*, Season 2, Chapter 7: *Bonus Episode*; Mangum, Janis. E-mails to author. December 27, 2023.
[2407] Ingram, Bob. In-person interview with author. March 6, 2024.
[2408] Johnson, Carolynn. In-person interview with author. January 16, 2024.
[2409] Kipe, *In The Red Clay*, Season 2, Episode 6: *Beneath the Chestnut Tree*.
[2410] Johnson, Carolynn. In-person interview with author. January 16, 2024.
[2411] Ingram, Bob. In-person interview with author. April 19, 2022; Kipe, *In The Red Clay*, Season 2, Episode 5: *Black Sheep*.
[2412] Ingram, Bob. Phone interviews with author. December 21, 2022 & May 27, 2023.
[2413] Hagaman, Len. In-person interview with author. January 16, 2024.
[2414] Edmisten, Rufus. Zoom interview with author. March 31, 2022; Kipe, *In The Red Clay*, Season 2, Episode 4: *The Company of Wolves*.
[2415] Wagner, Larry. Phone interview with author. December 22, 2022.
[2416] Wagner, Larry. Phone interview with author. September 19, 2023.
[2417] Vaughn, Jerry. In-person interview with author. October 13, 2023.
[2418] Ingram Bob. Phone interview with author. December 21, 2022.
[2419] Kipe, *In The Red Clay*, Season 2, Chapter 7: *Bonus Episode*.
[2420] "Letters To The Editor," *Watauga Democrat*, Boone, NC, February 24, 1972, p. 2B.
[2421] Shakespeare, William. "The Merchant of Venice," Act 2, Scene 2.
[2422] "Reward increased for 1972 murder case," pp. 1 & 2.
[2423] Hagaman, Len & Carolynn Johnson. In-person interview with author. January 16, 2024.
[2424] Hagaman, Len. In-person interview with author. May 24, 2022.
[2425] "Boone murders probe continues," *The Sunday Star-News*, Wilmington, NC, February 8, 1972, p. 2.
[2426] Wagner, Larry. Phone interview with author. December 22, 2022.
[2427] Hagaman, Len. In-person interview with author. March 14, 2022.
[2428] Main, Stephanie (Records Unit, Boone Police Department, Boone, NC). Phone conversation with author. October 17, 2022.
[2429] Dennis Whittington, "Arrests Expected In 1976 Murders," p. 13.
[2430] "17 Years After 3 Killings," p. 2B.
[2431] Wilson, Steve. Phone conversation with author. February 22, 2022.
[2432] Wagner, Larry. Phone interview with author. September 19, 2023.
[2433] "Who killed the Durham family? Here's my story," gowilkes.com, August 20, 2010, posted by "Pepper22."
[2434] Ballard, "Triple Slaying," p. 1.
[2435] Ettman, *Wildest Day*, p. 19; Maxwell, "Watauga Sheriff Defends Charges," p. 3B.
[2436] Ettman, *Wildest Day*, p. 19
[2437] "Klondike Derby Is Postponed," *Watauga Democrat*, Boone, NC, January 27, 1972, p. 1.
[2438] "Ski Country's Ups and Downs," *The Charlotte Observer*, Charlotte, NC, February 1, 1972, p. B1.
[2439] "We'd Cherish Some Snow," *Watauga Democrat*, Boone, NC, January 31, 1971, p. 4A.
[2440] "Ground Hog Weather," *Watauga Democrat*, Boone, NC, February 7, 1972, p. 4A.
[2441] "Weather: The Mountains," *Twin City Sentinel*, Winston-Salem, NC, February 2, 1972, p. 32.
[2442] Tester, Johnny. Phone conversation with author. February 26, 2022.
[2443] Crime scene photos, Watauga County Sheriff's Office investigation file 118-H-1/2/3.
[2444] Rucker, Jeff. Phone interview with author. October 4, 2023.

[2445] Greer, Evelyn. Phone interview with author. April 3. 2023.
[2446] "Durham murders remembered," p. 5.
[2447] Small, Cecil & Mildred. Interview with Caroline Walker.
[2448] Bullard, *The Durham Murders*, pp. 128 & 136; Walker, "Former SBI agent still baffled," p. 1.
[2449] Harrison, Jerry. Interview with Red Lyons.
[2450] Brown, John Paul. Interview with Del Williams.
[2451] Bullard, *The Durham Murders*, p. 667; Dean, Dr. Clayton. Phone interview with author. November 16, 2022.
[2452] Cullen, "Boone Stranglings," p. 1B.
[2453] Source misplaced.
[2454] Allen, Jane. Phone interview with author. January 31, 2023.
[2455] "Durham murders remembered," p. 5.
[2456] Ibid.
[2457] Bullard, *The Durham Murders*, p. 340.
[2458] Ibid.
[2459] Ibid.
[2460] "Slayings in Boone Revealed," p. 1.
[2461] "Neighbors shaken by murder of 3," p. 3.
[2462] Phillips, Anna Boyce. In-person conversation with author. September 6, 2023; Lewis, Evie. Comment on Facebook post by Jackie Vines. September 6, 2023.
[2463] "Revenge Hinted in Matthews Hunt," *The Atlanta Constitution*, Atlanta, GA, August 3, 1975, p. 20.
[2464] Davis v. State, https://casetext.com/case/davis-v-state-2480
[2465] "Triple Murder Former Wilkes Residents," p. 7.
[2466] *Special Edition of WBTV News*.
[2467] Cullen, "Boone Stranglings," p. 1B.
[2468] Wilson, Pat. Phone interview with the author. April 4, 2022.
[2469] "17 Years After 3 Killings," p. 2B.
[2470] Walter, Richard. Phone conversation with author. May 10, 2022.
[2471] Lowe, William Asa. Interview with James C. Lyons.
[2472] The Trail Went Cold.
[2473] Ibid.
[2474] Rucker, Jeff. Phone interview with author. October 4, 2023.
[2475] Hagaman, Len. In-person interview with author. March 14, 2022.
[2476] Ford, "Athens-area members of notorious criminal band."
[2477] Edmisten, Rufus. Zoom interview with author. March 31, 2022.
[2478] Walter, Richard. Phone conversation with author. May 10, 2022.
[2479] Wagner, Larry. Interview with Charles Heatherly; Wagner, Larry. Phone interview with author. December 22, 2022.
[2480] Downey, "Investigators Say Boone Murders Will Be Solved," p. B1.
[2481] Ibid.
[2482] Mitchell, "Slayings," p. A19.
[2483] Small, Cecil & Mildred. Interview with Caroline Walker.
[2484] Dunn, "Watauga Murders Still Not Solved," p. 1; "Durham murders remembered," p. 5; Small, Cecil & Mildred. Interview with Caroline Walker; Rucker, Jeff. Phone interview with author. October 4, 2023.
[2485] Phone message from Gayle Durham Mauldin, September 23, 1990, Watauga County Sheriff's Office investigation file 118-H-1/2/3.
[2486] Ingram, Bob. Personal interview with author. April 19, 2022.
[2487] Ingram Bob. Phone interview with author. December 21, 2022.
[2488] Ingram, Bob. In-person interview with author. April 19, 2022; Ingram Bob. Phone interview with author. December 21, 2022; Kipe, *In The Red Clay*, Season 2, Episode 6: *Beneath the Chestnut Tree*.
[2489] Watauga County Sheriff's Office investigation file 118-H-1/2/3.
[2490] Durham, Ginny. Interview with Clyde Tester, Arlie Isaacs & L. D. Hagaman, Jr.
[2491] Mackie, Ginny Durham. Interview with Carolynn Johnson & Wade Colvard; Walter, Richard. Phone conversation with author. May 10, 2022; Watauga County Sheriff's Office investigation file 118-H-1/2/3.
[2492] Carroll, ,Ward. Interview with Charles Heatherly; Whitman, Charlie Whitman. Interview with Charles Heatherly.
[2493] Small, Cecil & Mildred. Interview with Caroline Walker.
[2494] (Carroll, Ward?), interview with Charles Heatherly.
[2495] "Police Lacking Clues," p. 8A; Mauldin, Charles & Gayle. Interview with Red Lyons, April 17, 1989.
[2496] Author's extensive research into the history of crime in Watauga County, NC.
[2497] Jackson, Roberta. Phone interview with author. December 9, 2022.

[2498] https://en.wikipedia.org/wiki/9-1-1; Hagaman, Len. Watauga County Sheriff's Office press conference, February 11, 2022.
[2499] Kipe, *In The Red Clay*, Season 2, Episode 3: *Nothing As It Seems*.
[2500] Hagaman, Len. Watauga County Sheriff's Office press conference. February 11, 2022.
[2501] "Someone Called For Help" (advertisement), *Watauga Democrat*, Boone, NC, September 27, 1971, p. 6A.
[2502] "Three in Boone Family" & "Prominent Boone Family," *The News and Observer*, Raleigh, NC, February 5, 1972, pp. 1 & 3.
[2503] "Family strangled, stuffed into tub," p. A-10.
[2504] *Special Edition of WBTV News*.
[2505] Houser, "Two Suspects Bound," p. 2.
[2506] Durham, Ginny. Interview with Clyde Tester, Arlie Isaacs & L. D. Hagaman, Jr.
[2507] Genealogical research by author
[2508] Watauga County Sheriff's Office investigation file 118-H-1/2/3.
[2509] Edwards, Diana (daughter of Jerri Bumgarner Waddell). Phone interview with author. October 14, 2023.
[2510] https://www.mulhollandbooks.com/books/heating-up-the-cold-case-files/.
[2511] https://the-line-up.com/trio-helped-catch-ted-bundy.
[2512] Walter, Richard. Phone conversations with author. April 28 & May 10, 2022; Capuzzo, Michael, *The Murder Room: Breaking the Coldest Cases*, RSA Conference 2011 Keynote, YouTube; https://www.wbur.org/npr/129032377/story.php; https://publicsafety.fandom.com/wiki/Offender_profiling.
[2513] Walter, Richard. Phone conversations with author. April 28 & May 10, 2022; Capuzzo, *The Murder Room*, pp. 167-168.
[2514] Hudgins and Birt, *Grace and Disgrace*, pp. 65, 144, 169, 219, & 252; Birt, Shane. In-person interview with Bob Ingram. April 30, 2019.
[2515] Walter, Richard. Phone conversation with author. May 10, 2022.
[2516] Walter, Richard. Phone conversation with author. April 28, 2022.
[2517] Walter, Richard. Phone conversations with author. April 28 & May 10, 2022; Capuzzo, *The Murder Room*, p. 84..
[2518] Walter, Richard. Phone conversation with author. April 28, 2022.
[2519] Lowe, William Asa. Interview with James C. Lyons.
[2520] Ginn, Phil. Zoom interview with author. March 12, 2022.
[2521] Walter, Richard. Phone conversation with author. May 10, 2022.
[2522] Walter, Richard. Phone conversations with author. April 28 & May 10, 2022.
[2523] https://publicsafety.fandom.com/wiki/Offender_profiling.
[2524] https://moodlehub.ca/mod/book/tool/print/index.php?id=5293.
[2525] Ingram, Bob. Phone interview with author. May 27, 2023.
[2526] Bullard, *The Durham Murders*, p. 659; Crime scene photos, Watauga County Sheriff's Office investigation file 118-H-1/2/3; Personal observance of author. March 7, 2022.
[2527] Bullard, *The Durham Murders*, p. 566. "Slayings in Boone Revealed," p. 1.
[2528] Henderson, *Rub-Out*, p. 62.
[2529] Crime scene photo, Watauga County Sheriff's Office investigation file 118-H-1/2/3; Personal observance of author. March 7, 2022.
[2530] "Police Looking For Killers In Brutal Family Slaying," *Florence Morning News*, Florence, SC, February 5, 1972, p. 16.
[2531] "Unsolved: Hogtied In High Country," p. 7A.
[2532] Jackson, *North Carolina Murder & Mayhem*.
[2533] Hagaman, Len. In-person interview with author. May 24, 2022.
[2534] Dean, Clayton, Report Of Investigation By Medical Examiner, North Carolina State Board of Health, Office of the Chief Medical Examiner, Chapel Hill, NC, February 17, 1972, Watauga County Sheriff's Office investigation file 118-H-1/2/3.
[2535] Murderpedia: Billy Sunday Birt.
[2536] Birt v. State, Supreme Court of Georgia, 1976, https://law.justia.com/cases/georgia/supreme-court/1976/30638-1.html.
[2537] Ingram, Bob. In-person interview with author. April 19, 2022.
[2538] Wagner, Larry. Interview with Charles Heatherly.
[2539] Wagner, Larry. Phone interview with author. December 22, 2022; Rucker, Jeff. Phone interview with author. October 4, 2023.
[2540] Crawford, Tom, "Birt May Testify Against Defendant," *The Atlanta Journal*, Atlanta, GA, June 23, 1976, p. 2.
[2541] "Boone Couple, Son Slain," p. 1; "Slayings in Boone Revealed," p. 1.
[2542] "Durham murders remembered," p. 5.
[2543] Dean, Dr. Clayton. Phone interview with author. November 16, 2022.

[2544] Whitman, Charlie, Interview with Charles Heatherly.
[2545] Mitchell, "Slayings," p. A19.
[2546] Crime scene photos, Watauga County Sheriff's Office investigation file 118-H-1/2/3; Personal observance of author.
[2547] Bullard, *The Durham Murders*, p. 391.
[2548] Crime scene photos, Watauga County Sheriff's Office investigation file 118-H-1/2/3; Personal observance of author.
[2549] Small, Cecil & Mildred. Interview with Caroline Walker.
[2550] Ibid.
[2551] Harmon, Cecil. Interview with Red Lyons.
[2552] Dean, Dr. Clayton. Phone interview with author. November 16, 2022.
[2553] Harmon, Cecil. Interview with Red Lyons.
[2554] Ibid.
[2555] Small, Cecil & Mildred. Interview with Caroline Walker.
[2556] Flowers, Art (son of George Flowers). Phone interview with author. January 26, 2023; Ballard, Loy (son of Bev Ballard). Phone interview with author. April 22, 2023.
[2557] Hagaman, Len. Watauga County Sheriff's Office press conference. February 11, 2022.
[2558] Edmisten, Rufus. Zoom interview with author. March 31, 2022.
[2559] "Police try to assemble clues," p. 1.
[2560] Wagner, Larry Wagner. Interview with Charles Heatherly; Wagner, Larry. Phone interview with author. December 22, 2022.
[2561] "Durham Murder Case: New Details;" Hagaman, Len. The Weather Channel's *Storm of Suspicion*, Season 4, Episode 19: "Triple Torment," May 30, 2023.
[2562] Edmisten, Rufus. Zoom interview with author. March 31, 2022.
[2563] Ibid.
[2564] Ingram, Bob. Phone interview with author. December 21, 2022; Kipe, *In The Red Clay*, Season 2, Episode 5: *Black Sheep* & Episode 6: *Beneath the Chestnut Tree*.
[2565] Ingram, Bob. In-person interview with author. April 19, 2022.
[2566] "Durham Murder Case: New Details."
[2567] Anonymous source. Phone interview with author. September 20, 2022.
[2568] Ford, "Athens-area members of notorious criminal band.".
[2569] Ingram, Bob. Personal interview with author. April 10, 2022.
[2570] Edmisten, Rufus. Zoom interview with author. March 31, 2022; Edmisten, Rufus. The Weather Channel's *Storm of Suspicion*, Season 4, Episode 19: "Triple Torment," May 30, 2023.
[2571] Kipe, *In The Red Clay*, Season 2, Episode 4: *The Company of Wolves*.
[2572] Hudgins and Birt, *Grace and Disgrace*, p. 262.
[2573] Ingram, Bob. In-person interview with author. April 19, 2022.
[2574] Bridges, "Trio Charged In Watauga Murders," p. 1.
[2575] Ettman, *Wildest Day*, p. 20.
[2576] Source misplaced.
[2577] "Neighbors shaken by murder of 3," p. 3; "Where Day's News Was," *Leader-Times*, Kittanning-Ford City-New Bethlehem, PA, February 5, 1972, p. 1.
[2578] Dillon, "Durham Murders Remain Big Mystery," p. 1A.
[2579] Poindexter, "Search for Killers Begins," p. 1.
[2580] "Police Seek Clues In Boone Slayings," *The Charlotte News*, Charlotte, NC, February 7, 1972, p. 8A; Capuzzo, *The Murder Room*, p. 83.
[2581] Kipe, *In The Red Clay*, Season 2, Episode 2: *The Informer* & Episode 4: *The Company of Wolves*.
[2582] Ingram, Bob. Phone interview with author. December 21, 2022.
[2583] Pritchard, "Eight Men Arrested In Raid By Deputies," p. 25.
[2584] Hagaman, Len. In-person interview with author. March 14, 2022.
[2585] Terrell, Jimmy. Personal communication with author. March 26, 2022.
[2586] Hagaman, Len. In-person interviews with author. March 14 & May 24, 2022.
[2587] Birt, Stoney. In-person interview with author. February 17, 2023.
[2588] Birt, Billy Stonewall, *Rock Solid: The True Story*, p. 194.
[2589] Kipe, *In The Red Clay*, Season 2, Episode 4: *The Company of Wolves*.
[2590] Rucker, Jeff. Phone interview with author. October 4, 2023.
[2591] Hagaman, Len. In-person interview with author. May 24, 2022; Parker, John. Phone interview with author. November 7, 2022.

[2592] Ingram, Bob. In-person interview with author. April 19, 2022; Kipe, *In The Red Clay*, Season 2, Episode 4: *The Company of Wolves*.
[2593] Genealogical research by author.
[2594] Anonymous source. Phone interview with author. September 20, 2022.
[2595] Ingram, Bob. In-person interview with author. April 19, 2022.
[2596] Walter, Richard. Phone conversation with author. April 28, 2022.
[2597] Walter, Richard. Phone conversation with author. July 17, 2022.
[2598] Vaughn, Jerry. In-person interview with author. October 13, 2023.
[2599] Wagner, Larry. Phone interview with author. December 22, 2022.
[2600] Hagaman, Len. In-person interview with author. May 19, 2023.
[2601] Birt, Stoney. In-person interview with author. February 17, 2023.
[2602] Hagaman, Len. E-mail communication with author. February 24 & April 6, 2022; Hagaman, Len. In-person interview with author. March 14, 2022.
[2603] Hagaman, Len. E-mail communication with author, April 6, 2022.
[2604] Birt, Stoney. In-person conversation with author. April 18, 2022.
[2605] Birt, Stoney. Text message communication with author. June 26, 2022.
[2606] Birt, Stoney. In-person interview with author. February 17, 2023.
[2607] Kipe, *In The Red Clay*, Season 2, Chapter 7: *Bonus Episode*.
[2608] "Ground Hog Weather," p. 4A.
[2609] Poindexter, "Search for Killers Begins," p. 1.
[2610] Capuzzo, *The Murder Room*, p. 84.
[2611] Ingram, Bob. Personal interview with author. April 19, 2019.
[2612] Hagaman, Len. In-person interview with author. March 14, 2022.
[2613] Keeler McCartney, "Of Package Store Owner: Birt Says Davis Paid Him to Do the Killing," *The Atlanta Constitution*, Atlanta, GA, August 5, 1976, p. 8-C.
[2614] "Slaying," *Rocky Mount Telegram*, Rocky Mount, NC, February 7, 1972, p. 2.
[2615] Garland, Sonya. Facebook comment. February 8, 2022; Garland, Sonya. Phone interview with author. April 20, 2022; Garland, Sonya. Facebook message to author. October 6, 2023.
[2616] Garland, Sonya. Facebook message to & phone conversation with author. October 11, 2023; Tester, Johnny. Facebook message to author. October 11, 2023; Henson, Garry. Phone conversation with author. October 11, 2023; Poe, Brad. Phone conversation with author. October 12, 2023.
[2617] Ettman, "Wildest Day," p. 23.
[2618] Bullard, *The Durham Murders*, p. 340.
[2619] Tester, Johnny. Phone conversation with author. February 26, 2022; Crime scene photos.
[2620] Hagaman, Len. In-person interview with author. March 14, 2022.
[2621] Anonymous source.
[2622] "Murder Weapons Search Fruitless So Far in Cobb," and "Revenge Hinted in Matthews Hunt," *The Atlanta Constitution*, Atlanta, GA, August 3, 1975, pp. 1 & 20.
[2623] Murderpedia: Billy Sunday Birt.
[2624] Notes compiled by Carolynn Johnson, May 2023; Hagaman, Len. In-person interview with author. May 19, 2023.
[2625] Johnson, Carolynn Johnson. In-person interview with author. January 16, 2024.
[2626] Hagaman, Len. In-person interview with author. March 14, 2022; Hudgins and Birt, *Grace and Disgrace*, p. 269.
[2627] Ingram, Bob. Personal interview with author. April 19, 2019.
[2628] Watauga County Sheriff's Office investigation file 118-H-1/2/3; Wagner, Larry. Interview with Charles Heatherly; North Carolina State Crime Laboratory Report to Watauga County Sheriff's Office, October 6, 2020, Watauga County Sheriff's Office investigation file 118-H-1/2/3.
[2629] Rucker, Jeff. Phone interview with author. October 4, 2023.
[2630] SBI Request For Examination Of Physical Evidence, submitted by Watauga County Sheriff Ward Carroll, Watauga County Sheriff's Office investigation file 118-H-1/2/3.
[2631] "Davis, Sibley Companions State Contends," *The Atlanta Constitution*, Atlanta, GA, August 4, 1976, p. 2-A.
[2632] Kipe, *In The Red Clay*, Season 2, Episode 2: *The Informer* & Episode 4: *The Company of Wolves*.
[2633] "Local Man In Dixie Crime Ring," *The Charlotte Observer*, Charlotte, NC, July 14, 1969, p. 9C; "Opinion: The Dixie Mafia and the enduring tales of murder"; "2 Men Found Guilty In Louisburg Trial," *The News and Observer*, Raleigh, NC, May 5, 1973, p. 21; Ishak, Natasha. *The Little-Known Story of the Dixie Mafia, the 'Cornbread Cosa Nostra' of the South, March 2, 2021. https://allthatsinteresting.com/dixie-mafia;* Dallas Lee, "Lawmen Scoff At Term 'Dixie Mafia,'" *The Charlotte Observer*, Charlotte, NC, December 25, 1973, p. 6B; "'Dixie Mafia' Controls Much Of N. C. Crime, Dunn Warns," *The Charlotte Observer*, Charlotte, NC, May 21, 1971, p. 9A.
[2634] Lee, "Lawmen Scoff,'" p. 6B; Pat Smith, "'Dixie Mafia' Phrase A Loosely Used Label," *The News and Observer*, Raleigh, NC, January 30, 1973, p. 34; Kipe, *In The Red Clay*, Chapter 1: *From Humble Beginnings*.

[2635] Smith, "'Dixie Mafia' Phrase," p. 34.
[2636] Birt, Billy Stonewall, *Rock Solid In His Own Words*, p. 121.
[2637] Hagaman, Len. In-person interview with author. May 24, 2022.
[2638] Smith, "'Dixie Mafia' Phrase," p. 34; Lee, "Lawmen Scoff,'" p. 6B.
[2639] Gary Martin, "'Dixie Mafia' Safecrackers Rob Grant Department Store," *The Gastonia Gazette*, Gastonia, NC, November 24, 1969, p. B1.
[2640] "'Dixie Mafia' Controls Much Of N. C. Crime, Dunn Warns," *The Charlotte Observer*, Charlotte, NC, May 21, 1971, p. 9A.
[2641] "'The Dixie Mafia,'" *The Charlotte News*, Charlotte, NC, July 16, 1971, p. 18A.
[2642] "Shaffer," *The News and Observer*, Raleigh, NC, August 13, 2012, p. 7A.
[2643] The North Carolina State Bar vs. Johnny S. Gaskins, Wake County, NC, August 21, 2017; https://www.ncbar.gov/handlers/FileHandler.ashx?id=1081
[2644] Tester, Johnny. In-person conversation with author. March 6, 2022.
[2645] Haynes, *The Ore Knob Mine Murders*, pp. 163 & 164.
[2646] Watauga County Sheriff's Office investigation file 118-H-1/2/3.
[2647] "Two Former Hobbsans on FBI's List," *Hobbs News-Sun*, November 16, 1967, p. 16.
[2648] Hagaman, Len. Watauga County Sheriff's Office press conference, February 11, 2022.
[2649] Guy, Frank. Phone interview with author. September 17, 2022.
[2650] Rominger, Dee Dee. Phone interviews with author. April 3 & July 31, 2023.
[2651] Whitman, Pat. Interview with Carolynn Johnson & Wade Colvard.
[2652] Hagaman, Len. Watauga County Sheriff's Office press conference, Boone, NC, February 11, 2022.
[2653] "Witness says man bragged of killing," *The News and Observer*, Raleigh, NC, March 11, 1982, p. 3C.
[2654] "Murder Method Probed," *The News and Observer*, Raleigh, NC, January 17, 1973, p. 1; "No prints of defendant uncovered, experts say," *The News and Observer*, Raleigh, NC, March 10, 1982, p. 4C.
[2655] Volume 307, Supreme Court of North Carolina, November 3, 1982, March 8, 1983, Raleigh, NC 1983; State v. Mills, p. 505.
[2656] "No prints of defendant uncovered, experts say," *The News and Observer*, Raleigh, NC, March 10, 1982, p. 4C.
[2657] "Police Check Break-In, Surprised By Corpses," *The Charlotte Observer*, Charlotte, NC, January 16, 1973, p. 2C.
[2658] North Carolina Death Certificates, Wake Co., NC, 1973.
[2659] "Murder Method Probed," p. 1
[2660] "Shaffer," *The News and Observer*, Raleigh, NC, August 13, 2012, p. 7A.
[2661] "No prints of defendant found at slaying scene, experts say," *The News and Observer*, Raleigh, NC, March 10, 1982, pp. 1C & 4C; "Police Check Break-In, Surprised By Corpses," *The Charlotte Observer*, Charlotte, NC, January 16, 1973, p. 2C; North Carolina Death Certificates, Wake Co., NC, 1973.
[2662] "Dixie Mafia Gets Blame," *The Charlotte News*, Charlotte, NC, January 23, 1973, p. 16B & *The Daily Times-News*, Burlington, NC, January 22, 1973, p. 5.
[2663] "Dixie Mafia Gets Blame," p. 16B.
[2664] "Dixie Mafia linked to witnesses' deaths," *The Gastonia Gazette*, Gastonia, NC, April 18, 1973, p. 6C.
[2665] "Triple Slaying Believed Work of Organized Crime," *The News and Observer*, Raleigh, NC, January 23, 1973, p. 30.
[2666] "N. C. Organized Crime – Fact Or Fiction?" *The Charlotte Observer*, Charlotte, NC, February 25, 1973, p. 1.
[2667] "Crime, Officials May Have Ties, Morgan Implies," *The Charlotte Observer*, Charlotte, NC, March 9, 1973, p. 1C.
[2668] Anonymous source. In-person conversation with author. August 14, 2023.
[2669] Anonymous source
[2670] Anonymous sources.
[2671] John Monk, "An Odd Duality: Wilkes County Is Juncture Of Criminality, Civic Pride," *The Charlotte Observer*, Charlotte, NC, January 2, 1983, p. 1A.
[2672] Monk, "An Odd Duality," p. 1A.
[2673] "Wilkes County Replaces Whiskey With Pot," *The Chapel Hill Newspaper*, Chapel Hill, NC, September 3, 1981, p. 4A; "Chicken Coops, Pot Plants Replace Stills In Hills," *The Charlotte Observer*, Charlotte, NC, September 28, 1979, p. C1.
[2674] Monk, "An Odd Duality," p. 1A.; Kipe, *In The Red Clay*, Season 2, Episode 4: *The Company of Wolves*.
[2675] Anonymous source; Wagner, Larry. Phone interviews with author. December 22, 2022 & September 19, 2023; Rucker, Jeff. Phone interview with author. October 4, 2023.
[2676] Physical evidence, Watauga County Sheriff's Office investigation file 118-H-1/2/3.
[2677] Rominger, Jaska "Dee Dee," Criminal Investigations Unit, Watauga County Sheriff's Office. E-mail to Len Hagaman. December 19, 2011. Watauga County Sheriff's Office investigation file 118-H-1/2/3.
[2678] Hagaman, Len. In-person interview with author. March 14, 2022; http://triadtoday.com/knights-of-the-round-table/about-bj-barnes/.
[2679] Author's e-mail communication to Len Hagaman. March 16, 2022.

[2680] Hagaman, Len. E-mail communication with author. July 22, 2022.
[2681] Hagaman, Len. E-mail communication with author. August 4 & 6, 2022.
[2682] Sources misplaced.
[2683] Michael Ruiz, "JonBenet Ramsey cold case: DNA expert explains how mystery might be solved in short order," Fox News, July 26, 2022, https://www.foxnews.com/us/jonbenet-ramsey-cold-case-dna-expert-explains-how-mystery-might-be-solved-short-order; "The breakthrough new DNA evidence that could find JonBenet Ramsey's killer," 60 Minutes Australia, https://www.youtube.com/watch?v=93UdoApio5s; Arunava Chakrabarty, "JonBenet Ramsey murder: Cops urged to use advanced tech to re-test DNA on 3 key pieces of evidence," Meaww.com/News/Crime & Justice, updated December 17, 2022, https://meaww.com/jon-benet-ramsey-murder-re-test-dna-key-evidence-cindy-smit-marra-john-anderson-boulder-police?fs=e&s=cl#l6i6a055ve8zt7isu9b.
[2684] Author's e-mail communication to Len Hagaman. August 6, 2022; Author's post to the Investigative Genetic Genealogy (DNA Detectives) Facebook group page, August 6, 2022; https://www.m-vac.com/; https://www.m-vac.com/why-mvac/where-it-works;
[2685] Pennica, Sam. Phone interview with author. January 28, 2023.
[2686] Author's e-mail to Len Hagaman. January 31, 2023.
[2687] Hagaman, Len. E-mail to author. January 31, 2023.
[2688] Hagaman, Len. In-person interviews with author. May 19, 2023 & January 16, 2024.
[2689] Colvard, Wade. Phone conversation with author. August 1, 2023.
[2690] Johnson, Carolynn. In-person interview with author. January 16, 2024.
[2691] Hagaman, Len & Carolynn Johnson. In-person interview with author. January 16, 2024.
[2692] Hagaman, Len. E-mail to Carrie-Anne Eagen. March 20, 2023.
[2693] Pennica, Sam. Phone interview with author. January 28, 2023.
[2694] Wagner, Larry. Phone interview with author. September 19, 2023.
[2695] Hagaman, Len. E-mail to author. January 31, 2023.
[2696] Laws, Chris. Phone interview with author. May 1, 2023.
[2697] Colvard, Wade. Phone conversation with author. August 1, 2023.
[2698] Hagaman, Len. In-person interview with author. May 19, 2023.
[2699] Hagaman, Len. In-person interview with author. January 16, 2024.
[2700] Author's e-mail to Angie Grube. January 31, 2023.
[2701] Grube, Angie. E-mail to author. February 13, 2023.
[2702] Hagaman, Len. In-person interview with author. May 19, 2023.
[2703] Ingram, Bob. In-person interview with author. April 19, 2022.
[2704] May, Paula. Phone interview with author. March 27, 2022; Hudgins and Birt, *Grace and Disgrace*, p. 261; Kipe, *In The Red Clay*, Season 2, Episode 3: *Nothing As It Seems*.
[2705] Mitchell, "Slayings," p. A16.
[2706] Hagaman, Len. In-person interview with author. March 14, 2022.
[2707] "Who killed the Durham family? Here's my story," gowilkes.com, August 11, 2010, posted by "countyline." gowilkes.com/voice/who-killed-the-durham-family-heres-my-story/77993/?startview=200&h=094028.
[2708] Whitman, Pat. Phone interview with author. March 10, 2022.
[2709] "Investigation of Durham family's slaying continues."
[2710] Parker, John. Phone interview with author. November 7, 2022.
[2711] E-mail from Len Hagaman, October 9, 2005, Watauga County Sheriff's Office investigation file 118-H-1/2/3.
[2712] Durham, Ginny. Interview with Clyde Tester, Arlie Isaacs & Officer L. D. Hagaman, Jr.
[2713] Combs, Dean. Interview with Red Lyons.
[2714] *Special Edition of WBTV News*.
[2715] Kipe, *In The Red Clay*, Season 2, Episode 4: *The Company of Wolves*.
[2716] Wagner, Larry. Interview with Charles Heatherly; Wagner, Larry. Phone interview with author. December 22, 2022.
[2717] Hagaman, Len. In-person interview with author. May 19, 2023.
[2718] The Trail Went Cold.
[2719] May, Paula. Phone interview with author. March 27, 2022.
[2720] Carroll, Ward. Interview with Charles Heatherly.
[2721] Pennica, Sam. Phone interview with author. January 28, 2023.
[2722] "Cites Boone's Need For More Officers," *Watauga Democrat*, Boone, NC, April 22, 1971, pp. 1A & 2A.
[2723] "Watauga Study Notes Strength In Emergency Service," *Watauga Democrat*, Boone, NC, August 5, 1971, p. 14B.
[2724] "'The Revolving Door' Opens Law Enforcement," *Watauga Democrat*, Boone, NC, January 20, 1972, p. 1B.
[2725] Vaughn, Jerry. In-person interview with author. October 13, 2023.
[2726] Ibid.

[2727] "Men For Clerk, Sheriff," *Watauga Democrat*, Boone, NC, October 29, 1970, p. 10A; "Watauga Study Notes Strength In Emergency Service," *Watauga Democrat*, Boone, NC, August 5, 1971, p. 14B; "Sheriff Carroll," *Watauga Democrat*, Boone, NC, May 4, 1972, p. 2A.
[2728] Wagner, Larry. Phone interview with author. September 19, 2023.
[2729] Notes of Boone Police Department Captain Arlie Isaacs, September 5, 1974, Watauga County Sheriff's Office investigation file 118-H-1/2/3.
[2730] Kipe, *In The Red Clay*, Season 2, Episode 4: *The Company of Wolves*.
[2731] Brown, Ted. Interview with Len Hagaman & Carolynn Johnson. May 21, 2019; Brown, Ted. Phone interview with author, April 4, 2022; Kipe, *In The Red Clay*, Season 2, Episode 4: *The Company of Wolves*.
[2732] Brown, Ted. Interview with Len Hagaman & Carolynn Johnson; Brown, Ted. Personal phone interview with author. April 4, 2022.
[2733] Walter, Richard. Phone conversation with author. May 10, 2022.
[2734] Amy Morin, "What Is a psychopath?" verywellmind, updated November 7, 2022, https://www.verywellmind.com/what-is-a-psychopath-5025217
[2735] Mackie, Ginny Durham. Interview with Carolynn Johnson & Wade Colvard..
[2736] Lowe, William Asa. Interview with James C. Lyons; "Daughter Inherits Durhams' Property," p. 5.
[2737] Guy, Frank. Phone interview with author. September 17, 2022.
[2738] Anonymous source.
[2739] Anonymous sources.
[2740] Wikipedia, "Faked death," https://en.wikipedia.org/wiki/Faked_death.
[2741] Tom Gillespie, "You only live twice: The man who catches people who fake their own deaths," Sky News, February 19, 2019, news.sky.com/story/you-only-live-twice-the-man-who-catches-people-who-fake-their-own-deaths-11637341; Adam Janos, "Why People Fake Their Own Death," A&E True Crime Blog: Stories & News, February 9, 2021 (updated November 10, 2021), https://aetv.com/real-crime/why-people-fake-their-death.
[2742] Janos, "Why People Fake Their Own Death."
[2743] https://www.tributearchive.com/10881160/justin-t.-hall
[2744] Tribute Archive, January 1, 2020. https://www.tributearchive.com/obituaries/10881160/Justin-T-Hall/wall
[2745] Kipe, *In The Red Clay*, Season 2, Episode 4: *The Company of Wolves*.
[2746] https://www.tributearchive.com/obituaries/10881160/Justin-T-Hall/wall
[2747] Wikipedia, "Faked death."
[2748] Janos, "Why People Fake Their Own Death."
[2749] "Inside the World of Investigators Who Know You've Faked Your Death," *MEL Magazine*, August 26, 2019, https://melmagazine.com/en-us/story/inside-the-world-of-investigators-who-know-youve-faked-your-death
[2750] Rambam, Steven. Phone conversation with author. May 9, 2022.
[2751] Hagaman, Len & Carolynn Johnson. In-person interview with author. January 16, 2024.
[2752] Anonymous source. Phone conversation with author. May 11, 2023.
[2753] Hagaman, Len. In-person interview with author. May 24, 2022.
[2754] "The Second Time Around," *Watauga Democrat*, Boone, NC, October 12, 1967, p. B-1.
[2755] Watauga County Register of Deeds, Deed Book 107, p. 479 & Deed Book 115, p. 886
[2756] Reports of Investigation by Medical Examiner, February 17, 1972, Watauga County Sheriff's Office investigation file 118-H-1/2/3.
[2757] Wikipedia, "187 (slang)," https://en.wikipedia.org/wiki/187_(slang)#.
[2758] Watauga County Register of Deeds, Deed Book 133, p. 478; Cullen, "Boone Stranglings," p. 1B.
[2759] Jones, "Triple Murders Left Indelible Etch," p. 2A.
[2760] Cullen, "Boone Stranglings," p. 1B.
[2761] Watauga County Register of Deeds, Deed of Trust Book 148, p. 634; Deed Book 153, p. 122.
[2762] Cook, Donna. Phone interview with author. April 2, 2024.
[2763] Townsend, Mike. Phone and text communication with the author. March 2022; Harmon, Billy. In-person conversation with author. August 13, 2022; Allen, Jane. Phone interview with author. January 31, 2023.
[2764] Watauga County Register of Deeds, Deed Book 162, p. 671.
[2765] Watauga County Register of Deeds, Deed Book 186, p. 327.
[2766] Watauga County Register of Deeds, Deed Book 710, p. 2.
[2767] Kipe, *In The Red Clay*, Season 2, Episode 4: *The Company of Wolves*; Coffey, Karen. Facebook message to author. January 6, 2023.
[2768] Bullard, Tim, *Haunted Watauga County, North Carolina* (Charleston, SC: Haunted America, a division of The History Press, 2011), pp. 41-42; Kipe, *In The Red Clay*, Season 2, Episode 4: *The Company of Wolves*.
[2769] Bullard, *The Durham Murders*, pp. 471, 480, & 489; Kipe, *In The Red Clay*, Season 2, Episode 4: *The Company of Wolves*.
[2770] Coffey, Karen. In-person conversation with author. March 28, 2022.

[2771] Bullard, *The Durham Murders*, pp. 471, 480, 489, & 872; Bullard, *Haunted Watauga*, p. 65; Kipe, *In The Red Clay*, Season 2, Episode 4: *The Company of Wolves*.
[2772] Coffey, Karen. Personal communication with author. March 8, 2022.
[2773] York, "Cold Weather."
[2774] Jones, "Triple Murders Left Indelible Etch," pp. 1 & 2A.
[2775] Coffey, Karen. Personal communication with author. March 8, 2022.
[2776] Bullard, *The Durham Murders*, p. 471.

INDEX

[wwwwwwwww] The terms "the Durhams," "the Durhams'," and "the Durham family" most often refer collectively to Bryce, Virginia, and Bobby Durham, but due to the frequent occurrence of those terms, they have not been individually indexed.